The Cult of the Black Moon

For detailed information about the Caelverse, please check out the

separately published: *The Caelverse Compendium*

Teloston University

Book One

The Cult of the Black Moon

A Caelverse: Realm of Cycles Novel

CALEB STEELE

ASTRAL
WELLSPRING
PRESS

First (edition) published in 2018 (Copyright © 2018 Caleb Steele) by Astral Wellspring Press, Australia

This edition (the 2nd and greatly-enhanced and revised edition) first published in 2024 by Astral Wellspring Press, Australia

Copyright © 2024 Caleb Steele

Cover artwork by (and updated by) Darko Tomic – Paganus
Cover artwork Copyright © Caleb Steele
Additional images created by Caleb Steele

No part of this book was written by artificial intelligence.
No artwork was done by artificial intelligence.

National Library of Australia
Cataloguing-in-Publication (CIP) data:

Caleb Steele
Teloston University: The Cult of the Black Moon

(Paperback version – this version): ISBN: 978-0-6483786-2-4
(e-book version): ISBN: 978-0-6483786-3-1
(Hardback version): ISBN: 978-0-6483786-4-8

ASTRAL WELLSPRING PRESS

As of the date of publication (2024), the following link to the author website may be accessed (which contains further links to various social media):
www.calebsteele.com

I dedicate this book to my fellow mages; and since there are some pretty cool non-mages as well, I guess I dedicate this book to you guys, too.

Acknowledgements

I wish to thank the handful of people who read my original book. I also wish to thank some of my family members and a few other people for their support, as this allowed me the time and energy to work on revising the book into the glorious work of art it is today. For reasons of privacy, I will not list their names.

Unfortunately, a few people passed away during the writing of this book (both for the first edition and the second). I would like to acknowledge:

My Grandpa, John Ambrose Kelly. You were a great storyteller. Your delivery was always entertaining. Although you may not have approved of my book in every aspect, I hope you are some place nice now.

Wayne Henderson: You were a very charismatic person. I am so sorry you didn't get to read my book. May your spirit be thriving and forever learning.

Matthew Tonkin (Tonks): You took me in when I needed help, yet you struggled with your own issues. Thank you, and may your spirit be at peace.

My Grandma, Elizabeth Kelly. We always had interesting conversations about the world. I always learned something interesting. I hope now that your spirit is enjoying many creative pursuits.

CONTENTS

Author's Note

I first published this novel back in November 2018. I had written a few unpublished books before that, but I was never truly happy with them. *The Cult of the Black Moon* was different. I *did* publish it, and I felt a great amount of joy at such an achievement... But then I learned that marketing my book was another story. I met many authors who were in the same boat as me; we couldn't reach enough readers. So, while I was working out how to best market the book, I decided to add some nice, small touches to my book, as I wanted the best possible edition to be read. This, however, led me to think about completely rewriting the book from the ground up. I managed to keep most of what I had for my new plans, and I thought I would be able to quickly republish the book, but I kept coming up with more and more ideas; and of those ideas, I kept refining them again and again and again...

The previous edition (henceforth, *N1*) had a compendium at the back, consisting of 18,660 words. While rewriting N1, the compendium ballooned out, and I realized that I had to separate it into another book. Finally published, *The Caelverse Compendium* now has 231,952 words (with this figure including the contents page, dictionary, and abbreviation list – while the e-book version has 70 words less than this due to the different contents page formatting). I had to revise the magic system of N1, and it was this issue that took most of my time to finish. I thought I would be finished at one deadline after another, but I knew I couldn't release something that I wasn't fully happy with, so I bit the bullet and kept pressing on. It was quite the lonely process, too.

Some of the changes finalized in The Caelverse Compendium have actually changed the outcome for the Teloston University series. Many of these changes will be subtle, and some won't even be noticed, but they do exist, and they are important changes. The story itself now has many new *noticeable* changes as well. These include: a new magic system;

new and properly-developed lore; new and/or improved scenes and dialogue; then some people may notice new architecture, technology, and cultures. Finally, of course, there are grammar, punctuation, and spelling fixes. Oh, and I learned about many interesting things since N1, such as eggcorns, so I fixed issues like that as well. Since there are critical alterations to the updated version, I now consider N1 not to be part of canon (but the work is still copyrighted). Still… this is at least as far as possible timelines are considered… So, who knows? Maybe N1 is part of a separate timeline…

The original *story* had 134,847 words, whereas the updated story now has an *extra* 20,955 words – and that's a *net* difference, so that's not a *mere* 20,955 words added. Thus, the story itself (including chapter titles) is now 155,802 words long. This also is not including the extra details I have provided at the back of the book, which includes some of the cosmology of the Caelverse, followed by one of the schools of magic I have invented, and then a dictionary has been added to help readers with some of the more obscure words found in the text. Still, the dictionary doesn't contain some of the obscure, old words found in the 'journal' you will come to read, as that's *meant* to be hard to read!

I have continued to use mixed – yet consistent – spelling. That is, the book uses mostly Oxford spelling, but there are some Australian and even American conventions present. For example, *civilization* is spelled with a 'z', not an 's'; meanwhile, I spell *colour* with a 'u'.

The story also covers political topics. While reading the book, consider that if the text seems to suggest one idea, this may not actually be the case, and nuance also has to be taken into consideration.

And lastly, if, for any reason, something doesn't make sense, well… um… a ~~wizard~~ mage did it…

Chapter One

The Temple's Test

A black mist drifted in from the end of the long corridor, blanketing the cracked floor teeming with thorny weeds. Various bugs hastily crawled away through the holes copiously lining the walls, with dirt and crumbs of stone trickling down after them. Despite the mist's eeriness, it didn't grab the attention of the young man, who marched with a face exuding determination and fortitude. He was too focused on his destination. His task. His fate.

Marching beside him was a longstanding mentor, whose face seemingly changed expressions as the light from the modern fire torches periodically flashed across his deep wrinkles. Both men were draped in ceremonial robes, their loose hems fluttering against leather boots overpowering every minor sound with each step.

The mentor suddenly halted. "Korin," he said, staring critically into his student's striking green eyes, "your dedication to our faith has been incredible over the last few months." He held Korin's shoulders firmly. "Of course, even the greatest of our faith are put to the most challenging of tests."

"I'm ready for what you have," Korin replied earnestly, his white skin glowing burnt orange in the dim light.

"Mm." The elder's eyes squinted, face turned slightly. "As we have covered many times before, even prophets in the past questioned Draghar's will; still, they eventually understood what was required of them, and so should all followers of our most glorious God."

"I understand. But can you finally tell me what I'll face, Elder Visten?" Korin brushed an insect off his head, the coarse stubble a week old.

"Soon. I must reaffirm what you've been taught. Remember, it is through sacrifice that we grow," Visten said passionately, clenching his fist. "Without it, we stagnate and eventually degenerate into the depths of depravity. Although sacrifice may be easy on the microcosmic level -- we do it all the time -- on the macrocosmic level, however, it is no walk in the park. It is brutal. It is painful. And it is the hardest of all tasks. Ultimate sacrifice means complete and utter devotion and submission to Draghar's will." He paused to let the message set in as Korin remained quiet. "I want you to remember the parable of Percei the Great. Through the prophet of that time, Draghar asked Percei to sacrifice his entire family in order to prove his faith and devotion. It was a great achievement. Yes?"

Korin looked away for a moment, slightly disturbed by the extreme example. His religion, Sacrenderism, espoused many types of sacrifices, but he was always uneasy about *that* story of literal life and death – brutal death, to be accurate. "Uh… yeah," Korin answered with unease, scratching his neck.

"Good. Percei was indeed a great man, Korin, but it can be easy for any of us to slip and lose our faith. In the end, the Temple completely provided for Percei, and he became a saint."

Korin nodded slowly, trying to conjure thoughts on what to say.

"Worry not, Korin. All will be well in time." He patted Korin's strong back. "Consider this test an honour. Most who even get this opportunity are generally late into their lives. You, however, are only seventeen years old."

Korin's desire to prove himself was as strong as ever as he breathed heavily while broadening his shoulders and chest. Nevertheless, his nerves tingled haphazardly as his stomach silently churned.

Visten grinned. "I can tell you're eager. Good. I think it's time. Let's carry on."

Both men continued down the corridor, with Korin's eyes now unfocused. Mostly concealed under his dark green robes, Korin's movements stiffened the closer he approached his challenge. Visten's presence that night didn't convey protection, but rather, assessment. From his experiences in the past, Korin believed the elder would want him to complete his task without any help, anyway.

"You've learned much, Korin," Visten said. "We were doubtful of your ability to hold faith when you were young; your questioning nature needed… adjusting. But… it's good that you've come to see matters as we see them."

Visten's comments caused Korin's curiosity to spike, but he restrained from opening up sceptical dialogue. Before long, Korin asked, "Will the prophet be there?"

"Although this *is* certainly a special night, you have to bear in mind that the prophet is a very important person, who constantly has grand matters to attend to. He hasn't even visited our planet in a few months. But I'm sure he would've chosen to attend if he had the opportunity. We do have Juntas's arch-priest conducting the ceremony, though."

Multiple scenarios of success and failure crossed Korin's mind. The mist's darkness grew as it began whisking up around Korin's knees, and he finally noticed it. A shoddy wooden door came into view, opening into a lobby with massive stone doors on the other side, where a deep hum of om-chanting seeped through, making Korin shiver slightly.

"We're about to enter," Visten said. "When we do, you will take direction from the arch-priest. Obey his commands, and the process will be swift. Don't be alarmed by anything you see. It is all necessary in order to spiritually grow. Do you understand?"

Korin glanced at the doors, realizing his life was about to radically change – for the better or worse. "I…" Korin looked down, sighing out his nerves. "Yes, I'm not going to cower away. Let's do this."

Without any further comment, Visten continued forth, leading Korin through the doors, slowly having to push them open with a heave. Once inside, Visten took a minute to bar the entrance, sealing away Korin's old reality…

Red light emitted from the centre of the room, vanishing into the mist on the outskirts swarming up the walls. Six standalone archways encircled the vicinity, each with blood dribbling from their horned tips, pooling through the undulating and perforated carpet of fog before reaching the floor. Each stone archway encased black energized liquid that appeared alive whilst reacting positively to the chanting. At a steady rate, particles of the oscillating, vertical liquid leached out as the mist.

The focal point was a damaged concrete altar containing tiny shards of steel wedged in its grooves and chips. At each tip were attached statuettes of demonic monsters symbolically ready to consume whatever fodder or fare that was offered. Red candles massed around the altar's base like fiery beings breaking through the shadowy veil of the most frightening spiritual abyss, drooling their craggily-plopped wax away as if salivating at the sensation of foreboding death all around.

Six priests were meditatively-positioned on their knees – one behind each archway – chanting heavily without collective respite. Just outside the circle was also a spiked, looming throne that gave the impression it would normally feature impaled people; and, sitting imposingly with his head held high while wearing a crimson robe that extended well onto the ground, the arch-priest lorded the atmosphere. He was the only person masked in the room, sporting goatish outgrowths of formidable magnitude above a facial structure that glared with malevolence. Two men on each of the arch-priest's sides stood patiently; their dark robes, too, were luxuriously thick and multilayered in design.

All but one priest was recognizable.

Korin froze with fear at the sight before him, feeling a sensation of extreme evil from every facet of the room. Even though Korin imagined the test would involve facing an evil force, such as a blood-thirsty creature, the current scene was disturbingly different. The very fact that such a presence radiated from his leaders started to shock Korin's system in a way he had never experienced before. Prickly sensations formed on his outer being as the evil wrapped around him. It then dug in and headed towards the centre of his anatomy, clutching his very core and causing his body to partially cave as if being stabbed in the heart.

He kept himself from collapsing on the floor, eyes now staring away from the priests and into the murky depths of the environment. Before he could contemplate the fundamentals of his actual religion itself and all that he had been taught over the years, the danger of the evil seized such thoughts, triggering his survival instincts to the fore of his mind.

Visten approached Korin's side, gesturing for him to move to the centre of the chamber. However, Korin didn't budge, only peripherally glimpsing his teacher instead. The arch-priest stood up and thrust his ceremonial staff high into the air as if signalling his men to charge for war. Korin instantly flinched. The arch-priest then began advancing toward the altar while the four priests to his sides took a few steps forward, arcing between the archways.

"Step forward, my child," the arch-priest boomed.

Korin remained still, finally looking at Visten, who nodded for Korin to make his move. Registering that he was locked inside, Korin decided to play along until an escape plan struck his mind. Hesitantly, Korin took a step forward, and then another step… and then another step. He inhaled sharply before looking the arch-priest right in the now partly-visible eyes, knowing he had to keep to his word that he wouldn't cowardly back out of anything dangerous. Korin *had* to face his challenge, even though it was now for his own honour and not for the priests.

Unsure why he couldn't detect such evil in the priests' souls before, Korin theorized that they were able to somehow mask their true nature until now. But a significant amount of the evil actually pulsated from the archways. Korin promptly recognized this, questioning his own perceptions. He subsequently thought perhaps the *source* of the evil came from the archways, *irradiating* the priests. Then he thought the test's goal was to possibly overcome something that would spawn from them.

But why the dark chanting? Korin thought. *Why are the priests… no… something… they're evil. They're evil.*

Conflicting thoughts menaced Korin as the arch-priest slowly curled his finger for the young man to approach. Korin carefully complied, steadily making his way toward the altar. Once in front, the arch-priest raised his arms, chanting two sentences in another language before looking at Korin again.

"The time has come, Korin," the arch-priest declared in a creepy, raspy voice. "It is of Draghar's divine will that you must join him this very glorious night. Do not hesitate or question his will. Your faith will be put to the ultimate test. Now, lay down on the altar, and we will begin."

"What are you going to do? Korin asked shakily, understanding that he was to be literally sacrificed.

"We will give you the experience of Draghar's Burden. Only your physical body will die, but your spirit will live on, eternally by Draghar's side in his sacred garden of light."

Khorshit, Korin thought, delaying a response. "I… I take it I have no choice?"

"Oh, we intended on giving you a choice once you laid down. Where would we be without freewill?" He chuckled as the surrounding priests smirked. "It's obvious you do not wish to proceed. That is understandable."

Korin glared at the horned leader, disliking the prospect of his alternative 'choice'. The arch-priest raised a hand and double-clicked his fingers, prompting two priests to fetch a stretcher; on top was a tied-up and gagged teenage girl clothed in a lengthy, lacy, and exquisite white dress. The priests transferred the young woman to the altar as she hopelessly tried to kick them and spit her gag out. Her long brown hair was scattered across her milky-white, very pretty face; with effort, she managed to clear her vision, revealing desperation in her dilated, green eyes.

"Evelyn was also given a choice," the arch-priest said. "She didn't wish to perform her duties, so this is now her fate." He smoothly waved his hand. "Your choice is to either be sacrificed or to perform a sacrifice. We wish you to gut Evelyn and rip her entrails out all over her body. You are then to feast upon her flesh, drink her blood, and then perform an *extra-special* ritual with her mutilated remains."

Korin's. Jaw. Dropped.

Holy shit, these priests really are evil, Korin thought, just managing to keep the words from falling out of his agape mouth. *Shit! What do I… shit… What do I do?*

"Well, what say you?" the arch-priest asked, rocking his staff back and forth.

"I… I need a moment to think," Korin replied, staring down, focusing on a plan.

"Fine. You have one minute to decide. If you have no answer, that is a decision itself. You have been warned."

Barely a cogent thought sprung forth in Korin's hurried panic. He clenched his eyes closed, shaking his head, wishing he could reverse time and escape into a sunny meadow. His entire religious upbringing began ramming to the fore of his mind, even though he knew he had to think of the present. Still, he was insatiably curious. "Wait!" Korin opened his eyes. "I have questions."

"Now isn't the time for questions," the masked one responded. "You will be enlightened when you pass over or after you finish your task. But… we… may indulge you with a quick question or two."

"Good." Korin took a couple of seconds to gather his thoughts. "Why exactly are you doing this, and what are those black pools of energy?"

"I already told you; this is the greatest test you can pass."

Korin was infuriated with both the answer and his ill-thought-out question. He realized that the priests could've sacrificed anyone, so Korin wondered why they had chosen him.

"As for the spirit frames, they help Draghar witness the offering," the arch-priest added.

Korin noticed that the word 'Draghar' gave validation to the black liquid as it rippled with excitement. *Draghar?* he thought. *He's watching me now?* He frowned, one eyebrow trying to shoot up. "Can I talk to him?"

"He cannot see or hear us in the sense you may be thinking. While he can already see our etheric auras, the spirit frames refine the energies and refocus certain aspects to give him a clearer picture. Now, Korin, your time is up. Choose," the arch-priest said commandingly.

On the verge of breaking down, Korin suppressed his unearthing emotions, thinking hard in the few seconds he had. "I'll… I'll do it," he answered slowly. "I'll kill her."

Evelyn squirmed with rage, glaring at Korin with hatred.

"Ah, splendid," the arch-priest said. "Bring out the equipment," he ordered two priests.

In the minute the priests were gathering the killing tools, Korin scanned the chamber for alternative exits. A heavy bar sealed the doors behind him, and while the doors *were* an option, he knew it would take too long to unbar them in time. Korin then spotted a lighted corridor on the opposite side of the room, acknowledging it as the only option.

The priests approached with a tray of torture equipment, setting it on the countertop to the side. Korin had no idea what some of the equipment was exactly used for, only noticing that most were sharp and serrated. In the centre was a dagger.

As Korin picked the central weapon up, Evelyn was still shaking about, unable to loosen any of her ropes. Korin glanced around the room, noting where each priest stood and any obstacles in the way of his escape. The unrecognizable priest, however, gave Korin a different look – one of odd curiosity. Korin dismissed the expression, focusing back on the task at hand. The blade was deadly sharp, and the young man held it in front of Evelyn's scrunched face as she thumped against the altar, muttering unclear curses at him. Reaching over Evelyn's body, Korin partially covered her as she screamed; and, with her body under his top half, he was able to slice the ropes without the priests seeing. The last of the ropes, however, were manifest, and the priests glanced at one another. Evelyn was freed.

"Run!" Korin told Evelyn, grabbing her arm so she felt her freedom.

As Evelyn fell off the altar, Korin turned to the arch-priest and threw the dagger with all the force he could muster, sending the steel right into his chest. Korin was too nerve-racked to concern himself a second more over the arch-priest, snagging whatever sharp instrument he could from the tray before grabbing a staggered Evelyn off the floor. Half the priests turned to their leader, attending to his wound as he collapsed, just as the other half promptly stopped chanting and jumped up to handle the escapees. Visten, meanwhile, was too stupefied to even move.

As soon as Korin approached one of the spirit frames, the black liquid violently twisted and turned, its oppressive darkness causing Korin to shudder. Evelyn resultingly stumbled, and Korin had to quickly pick her up again. Two priests blocked the way just past the archways, drawing daggers. Comprehending the limited time he had, Korin chose not to attack, carefully running past his enemies instead. The two dagger-wielding priests closely followed, and when Korin reached the exit, he turned around and kicked one priest in the gut, knocking him over into the second priest. Having secured extra time, Korin managed to close the doors and lock the clergymen inside.

Korin then turned to Evelyn, saying, "I don't think it'll hold them off for too long. Are you alright to run?"

"Yes." Evelyn nodded, gathering her breath. "Thank you for saving me." She glanced around the massive lobby. "Where do we go?"

"I… have no idea."

The door banged. On the other side of the lobby was an arced wall with eight archways and corresponding corridors.

"I hope none of these are dead ends," Korin muttered. "Uh… this way." He grabbed a fire torch, leading the way.

Panting heavily at the end of the curved corridor, they encountered a locked door, fortunate enough to spot the key hanging on a hook beside it. After a few annoyingly-fiddly moments, Korin opened the door just as he heard a much louder bang, guessing the priests broke through the first doors. Quietly, Korin closed the door and pressed on, trying to ensure his footsteps made little noise.

Browned, crusty dribbles ran down sharp utensils on the walls, acting now as a form of garnishment. The disturbingly-decorated hallway branched off in various directions, all oozing a foul presence. Knowing he had not even a minute to explore, Korin wondered what secrets were stored in the rooms he passed.

There was another locked door once they reached the end of a heavily-furnished room. "I can't see any keys," Korin said, scanning the area frantically, placing the steel-handled torch into a holding on the wall so both his hands were free.

"Should we backtrack?" Evelyn asked, eyes wide.

"No, keep searching. There's bound to be something nearby."

Time, though, slid by as both rummaged through various draws and containers, finding nothing. Eventually, footsteps neared, alarming the teenagers into a sudden state of stiff suspension.

"Hide," Korin mimed to Evelyn before drawing his weapon.

The young woman faltered prior to crouching behind a cabinet, and Korin opted to hide as well, unsure how many would approach. Even if it was just one, he theorized, any confrontation could create enough sound to alert the others. His torch was still active, but since there was another nearby, it didn't induce suspicion. Sure enough, one of the men entered the room, scouring every detail while meditatively tuning into the area's energies.

"I know you're in here, Korin," the man claimed confidently. "There's no point hiding. I will find you." He momentarily closed his eyes. "You're behind the blue steel box."

Korin knew he was compromised, so he slowly stood up with his weapon ready, seeing the unrecognizable priest who gave him the unusual countenance. "Who are you?" Korin asked, deciding to inquire before throwing his utensil.

The suave man chuckled. "Whatever I need to be."

Korin winced in confusion, briefly discerning that he probably wasn't confronting an actual priest. With so many questions rampaging through Korin's mind, he hated having to end their meeting so abruptly. He raised the piece of metal and threw it at the so-called priest, but a flash of blue, luminescent energy radiated from a small gravitational singularity in front of the man; in turn, the weapon stopped mid-air before it pathetically dropped to the ground.

Magic? Korin thought. *What's a mage doing —*

"A pity. Your death will be such a waste," the mysterious man said. "Your energy signature is unlike the rest. We could have raised you to become one of us. Alas, I can sense your moral conviction would be too hard to break now." His eyes sharpened. "Hmm, seeing how you know my little secret, I will have to deal with you myself before you can inform those silly priests."

The man raised his hand, and the singularity returned, telekinetically lifting a suspended Korin off the ground. Korin tried breaking free as he was drawn closer to the mage, but he could only marginally move. Just as the phoney priest was about to do something with his other hand, Evelyn emerged with a metal pipe and whacked him over the head. Immediately, both guys fell to the ground, but only Korin managed to stand up.

"Wow, that was close," Korin uttered with immense relief. "I guess we're even now."

Evelyn nodded and smiled before quickly changing her appearance back to one of unease. "I think he's dead," she expressed with shock as blood pooled around the battered head.

"That's… I can't believe you easily killed a mage like that!"

"I know." She held her heart, face riddled with guilt.

"Hey, he was evil, so it's okay. Anyway, we need to focus on getting out of here. I wonder if he has a key." Korin searched the man's body, touching the unbreathing chest.

The body then twitched, and all of a sudden, a bright yellow auric light encased Korin and the body before a windowed ring portal appeared above. Swiftly, the portal fell to the ground, teleporting both guys away before quickly vanishing when they arrived.

Although Korin was unsure where he had been taken, he was positive it was a different place, very far away. Monumental black stone walls encircled them, reaching so high up, Korin couldn't even see the ceiling. Despite the atrium's simplicity, its grand size and spaciousness undeniably induced a sense of loftiness, suiting for very powerful and 'important' beings. There was, however, a massive flag on the wall featuring a vertically-slit eye inside an inverted eleven-pointed star possessing the geometry of connected pairs of points every four steps. A black, round cloud surrounded the eye, spawning deathly tree branches and roots on each vertical side respectively. A web lay in the background, its form as creepy as the rest of the symbol. The same symbol was also engraved on the floor, but its massive size eluded Korin from its presence.

A particular light then caught Korin's eye.

About a hundred metres away in another massive chamber, a crystal sparking with energy floated between two archways like the spirit frames; though, these ones weren't active. Before investigating the ringed, multi-tetrahedron-shaped crystal, Korin checked the body, finding that he was indeed dead. There wasn't much else Korin could do in his situation, so he stood up and slowly walked towards the crystal, which began hypnotically captivating him. The closer Korin approached, the more the static electricity played with his hair. At last, Korin stood in front of it, correctly sensing that much of the energy – its full power – actually wasn't even 'there', as such. The energy, in fact, was seeping in from somewhere else – entering, and connecting with, the broader reality around him. Simply amazed, he refrained from touching it. But then, the archways roared, and energized liquid emerged from small holes, its blackness ever so chilling.

Korin could feel he was being watched. "Oh, no," he muttered, taking a defensive stance.

The energy in the archways boiled and built up, almost as if giant fists of liquid were about to explode out of them. Korin was about to flee, but since his entire life had already taken a radical turn, he thought he might as well try his luck – or embrace his potential fate – at grabbing the crystal. His hand almost didn't reach it as the power intensified, causing him to tremble. As soon as he managed to touch it, the crystal exploded, throwing Korin right into the air and into the previous room. Closing his eyes, Korin missed witnessing the bizarre energies erratically releasing from the fragmented crystal and zapping into the very fabric of reality. Just as he was about to open his eyes, another portal emerged – but this one lacked a yellow aura; it then haphazardly bounded around the room before teleporting Korin back to where he was before – this time, without the dead body.

"You're alive!" Evelyn shouted. "Are you okay?"

"Ugh…" Korin responded, blinking rapidly and unevenly. "I'm… not sure." His hands still shook, both lucky to be without wounds.

"What happened to you?"

"I… have no clue… except that I probably destroyed… something big." He panted for a moment, soon recollecting his dire situation. "Quick, we still have to leave this place before the rest find us. Here, hand me that pipe." Grabbing the pipe, Korin rushed to the door and quickly bashed the handle off, revealing a room unfortunately leading to a dead end. *Oh, great. All that effort*, he thought. About to hit the wall in anger, Korin heard running water, soon spotting a crack in the mossy wall. "Hey, help me move this." He started pushing a large crate.

Evelyn helped, and once they moved the crate, she and Korin managed to slip through the tight crack, entering a rocky tunnel with deepening puddles. Assorted bugs crawled and slithered around their feet, and a few even weaved through their clothes. Evelyn naturally squealed.

"Quiet! You'll give away our position!" Korin whispered loudly at an unmoving Evelyn. "Ugh, fine, get on my back." He motioned impatiently.

As she hopped on, Korin felt something small biting his leg, but he didn't let it bother him. He pressed on, gritting his teeth.

"I'm so sorry about this," she said, crying slightly.

"It's fine," he replied after a moment, trying hard to hold on to her and the torch while brushing past the bothersome vines at the same time.

The vines soon thickened, correspondingly matching the entangled and confused thoughts in Korin's mind, blocking any sense of freedom and clarity. His suppressed thoughts regarding his religion surfaced, and due to his mind feeling quite off-centre, semi-lucid flashbacks to his past were induced.

"And may Draghar watch over you," a priest said to a younger Korin after a sermon.

Just as Korin exited the temple, he turned around and scrutinized the lobby's exquisite furniture and decorations. "If sacrifice is so important, why does the Temple have so much?"

"We not only preach sacrifice in and of itself, Korin," the priest answered, "but you must also consider that sacrifice is part of a greater picture, and that greater picture is ultimately Draghar's will. And his will is that everyone submits to his divinity."

"But how does all the stuff here help?" He scratched his head.

"Well, with more wealth, we have more opportunities to grow. Surely you wouldn't want to see others not be informed of our teachings?"

"Well, I guess." Korin stopped to think. "But shouldn't the message be enough?"

"Korin, Korin." The priest patted the boy's shoulder. "I know you like to ask a lot of questions, and that's good! But you need to ask the right *type* of questions. Our practices make perfect sense! You just need to ask for more information on how to better yourself through sacrifice. Do you see?"

After thinking it over, Korin shook his head. "No. I don't."

"Look, Korin, it's easy to get carried away with all these questions, but… you…" He sighed. "We're going to enrol you in a special program to help you understand these matters more. You'll come through as a different and better person."

Korin brought himself back to the present moment, faintly convulsing. *I can't believe they manipulated me this whole time,* he thought. *Those evil bastards.*

His stomach riled with revulsion and turmoil, while his hatred filled the space in the tunnel ahead. A small tear emerged from the corner of one eye, but his building fury clogged the rising waterworks. His face eventually twitched, crammed with too many emotions to carry out their respective expressions. Before erupting with rage, he focused hard on his footing, having nearly slipped over multiple times. Evelyn stayed quiet most of the time; she, too, had much on her mind.

A while later after trudging through the cave tunnel, they arrived at a large opening, where rapid water flowed roughly ten metres below. Crashing intensely up against the jagged rocks, splashes of water managed to flick across their faces.

"There's no other way," Korin muttered. "We'll have to jump in." He took one last, fleeting look behind him, seeing no-one. "You'll have to take that dress off."

"I can't just *take* this dress off," Evelyn responded snappily.

"Okay." Korin chuckled lightly, brushing off her anger. "I hope you can make it." He removed his robes, revealing ripped abdominals.

Evelyn glanced at Korin with frustration before looking at her dress and sighing. "Fine," she finally grumbled. "Unlace my back."

Rocks suddenly rolled in a tunnel nearby, the echoes alerting Korin instantly. Unsure if the priests caused it, he wasn't going to stay around to see. "There's no time," he whispered. "Just hold on."

Evelyn wasn't exactly ready, but she nevertheless grabbed the excess of her dress and ran forth with Korin for the jump. Hitting the water hard after they leapt in, the underwater current sounded deeper and more ferocious than before. It was a task in itself just to keep their heads above the water as they attempted to swim to the other side while flailing around. The fear of the priests washed away as quickly as the rapid flow of the water; still, Korin worried more about the safety of Evelyn, who was struggling the most. With every tug to keep Evelyn above water, Korin balanced the effect out, sinking under. They couldn't immediately reach the other side, being swept downstream quite a distance before managing to grasp onto a rocky surface. Korin pulled himself up first, having to heave Evelyn out, as her attire continually dragged her back into the water. At last, the water released its hold on Evelyn, and Korin flew back, with the former landing on top. Both shivered as they took a minute to catch their breaths.

Evelyn stared at Korin, shortly giving him a small kiss on the cheek, saying, "Thank you," before rolling off.

Korin was too exhausted to reply. A couple of minutes later, he lifted himself up and surveyed the area.

"So, are you going to tell me what happened back there?" Evelyn asked, still lying down.

"I teleported somewhere. Not sure where, but there was a symbol with an eleven-pointed star. Probably belonged to the mage."

"I still don't understand why a mage was here. Are the mages infiltrating Sacrenderism?"

"Perhaps. But even when I was there, I think I ran into Draghar's energy. I touched some crystal, and it exploded. And now I'm back here. I still feel a bit tingly." Korin paused for a minute in befuddled thought. "Um, look, we can think more of this later. Are you ready to continue?"

Evelyn sat up, groaning. "I think I need a moment."

"Alright. I'll scout ahead and return shortly."

Korin had ditched his torch before diving in, yet he wasn't aware as to why the cave was lit up. Within a short distance, Korin spotted the cave's opening, triggering him to jump for joy. Formed with chunky shards, the fractalized surface of the waxing-crescent crystal moon was relatively strong that night, tinting the forest with its silvery aqua. Further away were some of the twelve elemental moons, their gibbous forms beaming down as if bright lollies or marbles; a large number were fire moons, except most were presently on the opposite side of the planet. The geometrically-connected constellations stamped across the sky in a line induced the feeling of being under a momentous yet homey firmament, one that also meaningfully embraced and integrated Korin's home world, Juntas, with at least a part of the Caelverse. And then, encompassing the constellations were fantastic nebulae, with the one directly above providing a pink and emerald touch to the night sky.

Making his way through a bunch of heavy roots, Korin tripped on one, which happened to be connected to a mesh of other roots. He badly scratched his leg on the rocks, and when Korin picked himself up, he started limping. The roots, nevertheless, disturbed a set of unstable rocks nearby, so Korin jumped out of the way in the nick of time before they came crashing down, fully blocking the entrance.

Needing a moment to gather himself after shielding himself from small rocks and dust, he waved his hand to clear his sight. "Shit," Korin murmured quietly, staring at the rocks. "Damn it!" He banged the rocks with his fist. *We were so close!* He almost shouted aloud. "There has to be a…"

Korin searched around for any gaps, finding none. He tried lifting a few of the huge rocks, but they were mostly piled on top of one another. Stopping, he thought hard, only to soon continue thumping the rocks even harder in his frustration, bruising himself before his unremitting actions caused blood to drip down his hands. He hammered indefatigably as tears ran wildly down his cheeks… But then he heard howling.

Wolves.

"Oh, shit." He muttered, turning around without delay.

The wolves weren't actually ordinary wolves; they were semi-sapient wolves known as *khastwolves*; and, they happened to be *mutants* with specific monstrous mutations; such mutations were also a phenomenon that occurred with greater frequency for such beings. The pack was standing at the top of a ridge, their springy, muscular legs ready to take off. Korin easily saw them – it was the gold, glowing eyes that really gave their position away, piercing the cold atmosphere with their vitality. The large, forward-arching pincers on their backs quivered when they spotted Korin, and each chest – rippled with spikes – puffed out. Although he didn't want to leave Evelyn behind, Korin, with his sore leg and tired body, commenced running for his life downhill. Evergreens and an assortment of other sizeable trees teemed the seemingly endless forest, leaving few spaces for the small, twig-thin trees that filled the gaps. On the way down, he tripped, and a sharp tree branch ripped through his unharmed leg.

Blood relentlessly poured from the wound.

He noticed that the branch possessed purple spikes, and then he looked at his skin, seeing a purple pattern growing… festering. Unable to properly run, he fell and rolled continuously, gaining momentum, despite hitting several small trees in the process. He soon stopped rolling after encountering a large tree, bludgeoning his headache. Trying to wipe the dirt out of his eyes, he only exacerbated the problem with the soil and blood already on his hands. The khastwolves sounded close, and Korin realized it was pointless climbing a tree, as the beasts could stand on two legs and jump fairly high. Barely seeing through his grime-coated eyes, Korin cried in pain as he continued forth.

Saliva whisked past the creatures' muzzles in their frenzy, almost evaporating in the heated, whipped air behind them. Korin saw a small opening in a bulky log, nimbly squeezing in just as one of the khast-wolves reached him and began bashing the fallen tree with its fists. The rest of the khastwolves started using their pincers to break through the log as Korin traversed a network of tight, interconnected pathways to avoid the attacks, all the while scraping his body against thorns and spikes. Due to the dark, Korin had to feel his way through, bumping his head several times. The khastwolves' thumping even created clouds of dirt to permeate the air; and with every thump, Korin imagined his head being squashed in. He almost suffocated. Their attacks were closing in on him, and with no more pathways left, Korin neared the log's exit. Suddenly, there was a loud roar, and the bashing immediately ceased…

Yelping noises ensued.

It was clear another creature had joined the action with the roars, so Korin quietly and rapidly exited the log, dashing away without looking back. Korin was unsure what had stopped the khastwolves, but such a fight, he believed, wouldn't last long. At this point, Korin was delirious, almost collapsing a couple of times.

"So, what do you enjoy in your free time?" a priest asked Korin while outdoors in the sun.

"I like playing sports," an early-teens Korin replied, smiling. "Especially vergeball."

"Oh, that's nice. Although, I have noticed that some of the equipment around the court seems quite old. You know… we might be able to provide you with some better facilities."

"Really?" Korin asked excitedly, and the priest nodded. "That wouldn't be an act of overindulgence?"

"No, of course not. We're all meant to have a little fun here and there. All we'll require of you is that you continue to utterly devote yourself to the faith and maybe attend a few more temple assemblies."

"Yeah, of course," Korin acknowledged without a second thought. "I'll come tonight."

"That would be great." The priest grinned.

Contrasting the brightness of Korin's trance, the dark reality of the night seized him. However, Korin's concentration and energy waned as his microsleeps increased in number and lengthened in duration. Rather than periodically arriving at the front doorstep of his consciousness, the blackness of his microsleeps crept through the back without him knowing. Korin knew he couldn't continue much further without totally blacking out, and so he made every effort to reach as far away from any danger as possible. Insects unmindfully splashed upon his face, while thick, messy webs smothered him. Before long, Korin's strength faded. He halted, standing in one spot, swaying from side to side. Just before closing his eyes, he noticed two people approaching him, vibrantly chatting with each other. There was also an orb drone floating in circles, brightly lighting the area with its surrounding mystical-appearing field – an aesthetic that certain *types* of people applied to their drones…

"Oh, look what we have here," one of the men said blithely.

"He doesn't appear too well," the other, skinnier one added as he approached Korin.

Although Korin could barely keep his eyes open, he knew mages typically used orb drones, especially with mystical aesthetics. "Keep away, mages!" Korin uttered boldly, though wearily. "I know about your manipulative ways."

Chuckling, the slightly chubbier one said, "Yes, of course, we're evil, and we're going to do bad things to you, like, uh… eat you. Yeah."

"Hey, don't frighten him," the other lectured, slapping his mate. "He's in terrible shape."

"There's no harm in a little bit of… oh, come on! We seldom appear threatening, so we should take the opportunity now."

"Well, he's probably not even really scared of us. He's probably far more concerned about those mutant wolves. You clearly –"

"Who are you, and what are you doing?" Korin demanded as he was about to raise his hand, clutching one of his wounds instead before grunting.

"He's asking *us*?" the chubbier one asked incredulously. "I think we should be asking *you* that."

"Well, he has a point," the other refuted.

"Really? You think he has a point? Maybe you're right – both sides here seem a bit strange."

Korin took one last glance at the mages before falling unconscious.

"Hmm," one of the men expressed seriously, standing over Korin. "We best bring him in now before he gets worse."

Chapter Two

Revelations and a New Life

A squawking voice saliently emerged from the throbbing haze of sounds, zipping back and forth. Korin's actions were mostly automated responses to surrounding stimuli, as he was still only somewhat conscious. His heavy eyelids hoisted from their crusty shelves, only in their rustiness to come crashing down again. After wobbling his head for a moment, Korin stretched his neck in a fully conscious effort, completely opening his senses to reality.

"Thank Benkhlar's Crystal! He's up!" an old woman cried out. "How are you feeling, young man?" She softly held Korin's head.

Korin moaned and coughed, slightly sore all over. "Where am I?" he asked, not remembering recent events.

"You were out cold for almost a week!" The lady patted his arm. "What the flaming potion were you doing out there in the forest? Bloodied and bruised all over, you were."

Korin didn't respond.

The nurse then turned around to continue working as Korin's memories began returning. Slowly, Korin awakened to the full extent of the pain in his muscles. Although bearable, the discomfort was enough to keep him from wanting to move much. When he scanned the room, he noticed certain squiggly symbols finely branded on stained equipment. He recognized their source, and a shiver ran down his spine. Before overtly reacting to the mage environment, he continued studying each object. Inside warped glass on the table off the far wall, fresh potions were effervescing, greatly contrasting the ones beside them that were fermented – one was frothing over, gradually dripping into a puddle feeding the ants. The flower-wilting substance, fortunately, didn't reach Korin's nose.

Confused and worried, Korin finally asked, "You… you're a mage, right?"

"Yes, indeed I am. And we've got some news for you!" She chuckled, almost cackling.

"Please, what happened?" he asked intently before clearing his throat.

"A couple of local mages brought you in, and we've taken care of you ever since. If they weren't there, you surely would've died. Not just from your wounds, but from many types of poison." She waved a vial of purple liquid.

Right, the poisonous branch, he thought. "Oh, man… thank you." He groaned, trying to sit up.

"No problem at all," she said, lightly grabbing his cheek. "Rest up. Someone will see you shortly."

Before the nurse left, she cleaned the mess on the table and floor before it attracted any more unwanted attention. While waiting, Korin unconsciously jolted in anticipation every so often, sporadically opening his eyes to see if anything dangerous – conscious or not – approached from any angle. Once he relaxed into his setting, he felt like reaching for the dipping vaults above, but his arms refused to comply with his desires. He closed his eyes and snugly pushed his head back into the pillow, registering he needed more recovery time.

"Oh, you're here! Good timing," the nurse said to another mage just outside the room.

In the first second of opening his blurry eyes, Korin swore he saw waves of energy pulsating from the middle-aged mage who entered. Light glistened off her bright blue eyes as she stared directly at Korin; she was nevertheless quite peripherally aware of her surroundings. Dirt covered her hole-ridden cloak, making it seem as if she had survived a wild storm; but underneath was a clean, black overcoat, buttoned together with gold trimming, covering a regal, green dress. She was also well over a head taller than the nurse of average height.

"Thank you. May I have a moment alone with him, please?" the red-haired mage asked the nurse, who okayed her request. "So," she said, surveying Korin acutely as she sat next to him on the bed, "it appears you've been through quite an extraordinary experience. Please, tell me your name."

After a few seconds, he responded, "I'm Korin." And, hesitant to reveal more information, he then asked, "What do you mages want with me?"

"Quite blunt, I see." She smiled. "Well, Korin, I would like to ask some questions, if you don't mind. I can then inform you about something rather interesting."

He slowly replied, "Sure. Go on."

"Great. So… it seems a little strange for one to merely wander into a forest filled with fearsome creatures. Kind of dangerous when you think about it. I'm curious: what *were* you doing?"

Korin delayed his answer as he pondered the evil that *was* his religion. Even with the total rejection of his beliefs, Korin felt as if he needed to scrub off the remnants which still clutched him. He wished to discuss his background, but Korin also realized he had no-one he could trust. Given such deceptions occurring throughout his life, he wasn't going to simply and naively trust anyone now. Still, Korin knew he had little choice, sighing and deciding to indulge her slightly.

"Something happened. There was a girl." Korin looked down as the tall mage raised her eyebrows. "She's… she's trapped in a cave. We have to go and find her!"

"I see," she calmly responded. "Please elaborate on the situation."

"Look, we have to go and find her." Korin tried to lift himself up, but the mage held her hand out.

"I can understand your frustration, Korin, but we need answers before rushing off into the forest on a potential wild bird chase."

Korin sighed again. "Fine. It-it's complicated." He held his head.

"Please, take your time, Korin," she said tenderly, staring at him attentively.

"Could… could you tell me who you are first?"

"Sure. You may divulge what happened later; you'll be interested in what I have to say." She stood up with a self-possessed posture. "I'm Helena Valen, Chancellor of Teloston University." She paced to the other side of the bed, looking out the window. "I'm currently out here on… personal business and was earlier informed about you and your situation."

"Wh-why would you stop in for me?"

"Well, when the doctor was determining what poisons were in your body, he discovered something rather different about you. An unexpected twist in your fate, it seems. You see, Korin," she said, turning around with another smile, "you have the ability to wield magic. You're one of us."

A mage? Korin thought, heartbeat racing. *Did… did she mean what I thought she meant?*

The picture was obvious. He deep down knew exactly what she meant. His breathing quickened. Korin's life had hitherto been turned upside down, but his head spun even more with this revelation. Over the course of a few seconds, his face turned from appearing confused to that of being drugged, hanging low with his mouth agape, eyes now unevenly squinched.

"Wh-what?" He blinked rapidly as incredulousness crept into his mind. "There has to be a mistake. I'm no mage," he stated hesitantly.

"You are, without question, a mage, Korin. Only the blood of a mage would react the way it did to this particular poison, and the tests came through positive regarding your blood type. And you needed a blood transfusion. Mage blood. I know this may come as a shock to you, so I'll give you a moment to process it."

When Helena stepped outside, Korin wondered if the priests knew about his mage blood all along. He believed they may have, as the clergymen had acted rather peculiarly around Korin within the last couple of months. But then again, they were going to sacrifice him. That alone would elicit strange behaviours. Plus, Korin's interest in serving the religion also increased at that time, so that was possibly another reason. Still confounded on their reasons for wanting to kill him, Korin wouldn't have been surprised either way.

Helena finally re-entered with her commanding presence, asking, "It's virtually unheard of for parents not to inform their children of their latent abilities, but I assume your case is exceptionally unique?"

Staggered with the information he had received, Korin felt that the doors to his secrets had been blasted open, so he had no qualms telling Helena more now. He slowly and sadly answered, "I was adopted by Temple followers when I was young. Five, it was. I can't really remember much about my parents before that."

"Temple?" She folded an arm, one hand holding her lips. "What religion do you belong to?"

"Did," he replied swiftly. "It feels strange saying that." He almost chuckled. "I followed Sacrenderism. I'm not sure if you know about it, but –"

"Oh, I'm definitely aware of it." Her tone changed grave. "Please, continue."

"Well, I live… or lived in Orchopolis. It had numerous Temple followers and communities, but the last temple I went to was on the city's outskirts, near the Kirelory Forest. It was –" He stopped, having too many thoughts jumping around. "Do you know anything about my parents?"

"No, I'm sorry; I barely know a thing about you, and there are far too many mages on Juntas to know personally. Anyway, I've organized for someone to arrive and aid you with integration. He'll be able to help you find your parents. Plus, the police and other bureaucrats will be here shortly to register details, ask many personal questions, and then release you."

"Wait! As I said, there was a girl. Evelyn… I think was her name. We have to find her."

"I will request for the police to form a search party, but you won't be able to go, unfortunately."

"What?" Korin shouted angrily, clenching his bedsheets. "How come?"

"First of all, you need to rest," she told him firmly. "Second, as a mage that's about to reach maturity -- we could tell from your blood -- you will be required, as by the decision of the CGM, to attend a mage university before full citizenship rights are granted. There are, of course, detention facilities, special-needs centres, and a few other particular places available, but you're clearly no idiot, nor are you handicapped."

Korin didn't persist, fully comprehending the weight of the political system and law. He remained silent with an angry face, thinking about Evelyn for a moment longer.

Helena had to quickly take a call on her watch, leaving Korin again. There was now nothing left for Korin to lose. A whole new reality was about to open up for him, and the prospect of magical studies excited him, even though he hardly showed it while staying still.

Helena finished her call on a serious note, returning to the room to tell Korin that, "All students born in your year will be able to harness their full magical abilities when the New Year begins. A very good student counsellor will be here shortly to walk you through the formalities. Your timing is impeccable. Your university life begins tomorrow, even though technically classes won't start until a week's time."

Great! Korin thought. "So, will I go to Teloston University with you?"

"Although nearby via the transportals, Teloston isn't the closest university, but you'll be inducted there since the enrolment process would be otherwise delayed. Don't worry, even though the CGM both regulates and funds practically all mage universities, Teloston is an outstanding university." She paused before seriously asking, "Please tell me that you're aware of the basics of how the Caelverse Government of Magi operates."

"Oh, yes. I wasn't living under a rock," Korin replied, feeling the need to be clear of certain stereotypes.

"Good. Many non mages do not bother educating themselves on certain matters outside of their autonomous zones."

"Yeah, I know. And I'm also aware of a few other things about you mages."

"*Us* mages now."

"Sorry, of course. I was also taught – or indoctrinated, I should say – about how evil mages are; or rather, their practices. If mages were to convert and stop their magic, we thought that they would be morally fine."

"Yes, I'm aware of such *teachings*. It's stupefying that our own home world is filled with those who hate us. Fear not, you'll be treated well, and I'm sure you'll fit right in."

Another mage knocked on the door, but instead of waiting for an answer, he walked straight in. Instantly, Korin thought the man looked like a friendly version of Visten, just with hair, which happened to be whisking from the breeze coming through the window. His jumper appeared as if it was something a family member had knitted for him, one to be worn around a cosy fireplace; his yellowy-brown eyes were even like lit timber.

"Helena! Good to see you!" the man expressed brightly.

"Yes, I heard the university sent you. Thank you for coming, Rolan."

"No problem at all. Good to move about. They were pretty brief with the details. What brings you out here, by the way?"

"Oh, I have my reasons," she responded standoffishly.

"Not going to tell?" Rolan smiled coyly.

"No." She smirked. "Just personal business."

"Yes, I assume you're quite busy and all. There's word that you'll enter politics."

"It's a possibility. You never know." She was about to turn around, but Rolan continued grabbing her attention.

"Perhaps you'll end up being the archmage!" Rolan chuckled. "You were never really the academic type, anyway. Always on the go, venturing about."

"Well, I was never a professor. I was granted my position due to my previous work in other fields."

"Like being a peacekeeper High Commander."

"Amongst others. Now, let's not forget why you're here, Rolan." She turned around. "Korin, this is Rolan Sastrel. He'll be taking you to Teloston University."

"Nice to meet you, Korin." Rolan shook Korin's hand warmly. "Sorry, what was your surname?"

"Tarkelt. I was able to remember my last name before being adopted."

Helena interjected, "The nurse only just mentioned that he may need another day in bed. My apologies. I didn't realize. Still, you'll need to be here for the police when they arrive."

"All good," Rolan responded, waving his hand. "So, how are you feeling now, Korin?"

"I…" Korin tried lifting himself up, failing. "Yeah, I may need another day."

"Sure, I'll be back tomorrow. And, I'll bring you some decent clothes when I do."

"Plain clothing, Rolan," Helena added. "Anyway, I'll still be in the area, so I'll pop in tomorrow, too."

Soon after Helena left, the police and a few other authorities arrived, but Korin decided to keep the information he told them vague and minimal. They were understanding of his situation and funnily enough didn't press too much on him. Of course, it helped that Rolan was there to brush off any persistence on their part. In a couple of hours, he was given permission to leave; and after everyone had left, Korin laid back down to finally get some decent rest again. If it weren't for the fatigue, he would never have gone back to sleep with his over-excited thoughts.

***

Korin's muscles still ached a little the following day, but his energy was through the roof. After stretching and jumping out of bed, his legs wobbled and tingled, but they were nonetheless able to continue supporting him. He noticed a few dry blood stains on his patient robe, and he was unsure how much longer he'd be wearing it. Right on the bedside table, however, were a fresh set of long pants, a t-shirt, socks, and everyday shoes. The unusually-warm winter – due mainly to the extra fire moons – was coming to a close, so such garments were suitable. Even when he followed Sacrenderism, Korin fancied various mage aesthetics, but the clothing he was provided with was actually very simple and virtually identical to modern, normal non-mage human attire. When he removed his robe, Korin stared at some of his cuts, lightly touching them to see how they felt. He knew he'd heal soon, anyway, so he finished getting dressed without overthinking the matter.

Once clothed, Korin walked out of the room, spotting Rolan talking to Helena. The counsellor's clothes were slightly more professional that morning, while Helena still retained her dirty cloak.

"Excellent! You're up!" Rolan cheered. "Looks like you're ready for your first day."

"Yeah, I'm feeling great, actually," Korin replied, continuing his stretches. "Some of the wounds are a bit sore to touch, but I bet I could run a marathon now."

"Your attitude is healthy, Korin," Helena said, "but do try to keep yourself from further injuries."

"Oh, come on, Helena," Rolan countered. "Where would *you* be if you never pushed yourself?"

Helena delayed her response. "Fair point, Rolan. Come, this way."

Before leaving, Korin thanked the nurse and doctor, saying his goodbyes. The nurse grabbed his cheek again before giving him a big wet kiss, wishing him all the best. Korin didn't mind the attention, but he certainly wasn't going to kiss her back. Most of the ten buildings outside were log cabins, seemingly isolated from the rest of the world. Indeed, it was a developmentally-restrained, intermediate *zone* between mage and non-mage autonomous territories; although, only mages conducted operations there in what was termed an 'E zone'.

In a clearing in the distance sat a dragon, whose expression seemed more like a dog waiting for its master to take it for a walk – placid, though, set for any action. Its lack of scars or any damage signified a comfortable, peaceful life, while its scales appeared more velvety than coarse. The claws, too, looked polished and rather small. It blissfully rocked its head back and forth before breathing onto the dirt, playing with the whirling soil. The dragon's eyes were bright blue with circular pupils, and its horns were smoothed and slicked back. Despite its demeanour, it was still capable of killing most creatures.

Rolan turned to Korin, saying, "Although there's a fence around this zone, we'll have to be careful, as mutated khastwolves have been spotted in a nearby area."

"I know. I encountered them before." Korin looked at his almost-healed wounds.

"Ooh." Rolan gave a squeamish and shocked expression. "How'd you survive?"

"Again, these are from falling over in the forest multiple times."

"Ah, okay. Still, you didn't tell the police about the khastwolves; and Helena didn't mention them to me before, either."

"Well," Helena responded, "Korin still has to tell us his full story. We'll definitely have time to discuss *that* later." She inclined her head. "Now, I look forward to seeing you again, and I hope everything goes well for you. Alas, I need to take my leave. Goodbye for now."

Helena marched over to the dragon, who greeted her warmly with a happy shrill and nod. It lowered its head and wings, allowing her to saddle up; and once the powerful creature lifted off, the ground shook while dirt whipped through the air and all over the settlement. As Helena soared high into the sky, the dragon gave a carefree screech that blared over the green expanse, ringing continuously.

"We can't take a dragon, too?" Korin asked, hopeful.

"Oh, no." Rolan chuckled. "Minoris dragons are restricted to those with licenses."

"Same goes for common dragons, I take it?"

"No, common dragons – morkol dragons – are locked away in high-security zoos and sanctuaries. For a reason! But I don't really know what they do with the other varieties of dragons on other worlds, so if you move off world, perhaps then you could ride them."

"Will we be riding any creature, though?"

"Well, I think it *would* be fun to ride one of these korlorns back," Rolan said, motioning to a couple of majestic, wild horse relatives, "but with your condition and the mutated khastwolves out, I think we best leave the same way I arrived – by hoverbike."

Unlike the steel-framed hoverbikes Korin normally saw in non-mage autonomous zones, the bike before him was mostly formed from a spongey and ultra-lightweight material. Korin knew about mage tech and how such technologies had a special kind of crystal integrated into them. This crystal, called unichite, was itself composed of four primary crystals called neurachite, aerochite, holochite, and charchite. It was the neurachite that had a synthetic brain that mages could psychically tap into, but Rolan simply used the holochite's holographic interface with his hands for starting up the bike.

"Don't you mages use your minds to activate stuff?" Korin asked.

"Sometimes we do," Rolan replied, hopping on the front seat, "but this isn't my bike, and so it's a bit harder to connect with things that you're unfamiliar with. Keep in mind that connecting with neurachite isn't magic. Anyway, hop on the back, and we'll get going."

As Korin approached, the neurachite's dendrites became clearer through the translucent, light-blue aerochite frame. He got on the bike, and without any notification, Rolan speedily took off, leaving Korin frantically gripping the side railing. Rolan was naturally using the bike's manual riding mode instead of the autonomous one, enjoying the freedom of movement. Undulations pervaded the dirt road, causing the electromagnetically-lifted ride to be very bumpy; but after two minutes, Korin was able to ease into it – though he still expected Rolan to try something irresponsible. Rolan's vibrant chatting, however, numbed such thoughts, and Korin didn't bother enquiring about helmets.

One muscular korlorn galloped nearby, almost as if racing against the vehicle. Behind its massive curly horns, gold streaked down the animal's thick mane, whipping out in a seemingly unruly manner. Fractally rippling out from the centre across its back, its tiny glowing marks added finishing touches to its majesty. The animal soon dashed away in another direction, but the essence of the wild remained riding alongside Korin.

Before long, the two mages entered a mage-exclusive zone with a city nearby. An underground tunnel appeared in view, and Rolan soon pulled over before returning the vehicle. Noises boomed from behind the walls, making Korin feel like he was about to encounter something of epic proportions. The counsellor then proceeded behind thick, crisscrossed walls to where the *subroute* station lay. Original, meticulously-crafted paintings adorned the walls behind glass; and contrasting the beauty of the art's deep stories, rich colours, and exaggerated themes, the station's columns held numerous advertising posters – some via holographic screens and others with various types of paper. Symphonic orchestral music also lightly played, its cheerful and pleasant movements characterized by pastoral themes.

Many younger mages sat or leaned up against walls, listening to their own music or vlogs with their personal holographic interactive displays – or *phids*, as they were simply known. Emerging from various devices like watches or eyewear, the phids surrounded their bodies or just their visual field; and most of the people were practically glued to the visuals as if the world outside their immediate surroundings was a barren wasteland. Several mages were rushing about, squirming and slipping past dense crowds. A few people looked as lost as Korin as they stared at glowing overhead boards detailing times of arriving and departing capsules. Unattended magnetic trolleys carried excessive luggage, and one of the bags near Korin was leaking a cloud of unidentifiable dust – which he wondered if it was enchanted or not. A tattoo-covered mage had just exited a service tunnel, accidentally brushing his grimy overalls up against two mages draped in golden robes, their uppity noses scrunching as a result; no action was taken, though it was clear the high-profilers wished to unleash their magic.

Numerous tunnels and platforms were receiving tube-shaped transport capsules capable of carrying hundreds of people at a time. Hovering in coiling tunnels of luminescent energy, the capsules used powerful crystals to charge, while their launching systems opened and clutched the transport like spiders and their prey, shooting each off at blurring speeds.

With so many mages in an enclosed area, Korin's lungs took in vastly more oxygen as his stance turned rigid and guarded. After a short, though restless moment, he told himself to relax, knowing it was just ingrained, religious reactions. He nevertheless needed a couple of minutes to process the situation, remaining quiet the whole time.

Korin's capsule arrived shortly, and the plush seating inside relieved his sore body as he slumped into a groove; and once the doors shut and the barrier closed, the crowd's racket muffled.

After travelling at roughly three times the speed of sound, Korin soon reached the central station of the province's capital that featured both mage-exclusive and multispecieal zones – the latter being filled with a plethora of different kinds of species. When outside the subroute station, Korin felt as though he had finally passed the gorge of no return. He had visited the capital before, but today was very different, and the mesmerizing panorama around him seemed to teem with more vibrancy than he had ever seen.

The massive intersecting complex connected with the city's closest mage university in one direction, the central business district in the other, and the transportal hall directly in front. In the sky were a few airships and planes, but these were mostly drowned out by the thousands of mage and non-mage drones at any one moment – each with their own advantages and disadvantages – most delivering small goods, and a few on watchful patrol, beaming lasers over the population.

On the ground, thousands of different beings engaged in their various schedules. Of these beings, about one fifth was non-human – some alien, others local to Juntas, but all were sapient, except for the pets, such as the dogs. Most were still mammalian, but there were others like reptilians, arthropoids, and lithoids; and each passed each other without heated conflict, forming an unusual, eclectic sea. While some focused on their phids, others, however, gave or exchanged stares and glances at non-related beings ranging from curiosity, cordiality, awe, respect, confusion, disgust, distrust, hatred, and apathy. Some of the fairies zipped between and around a few of the aliens, never having seen such unfamiliar bodies before, while a few of the imps, specifically, pulled silly expressions at those who they thought were amusing. About half of the human population were non-mages – most *basic humans*; and if it weren't for some of the typical mage clothing and accessories – along with the skin colour of some of the basic human non-mages – they would've been indistinguishable from one another. Humanoid walking robots, on the other hand, were limited – in both type and number by law – but a couple were still present.

"Filthy mages! Your time will come!" a scraggly, destitute man shouted, continuing the verbal abuse until two mage law enforcers approached him. A heated debate ensued until the non-mage threw his full can of paint at the mages.

"That's it! You were warned!" the less-painted mage told the angry man, swiftly arresting him.

A few in the vicinity cheered and booed both sides; Rolan, on the other hand, called Korin's attention away, explaining a little history of the area. At the top of the stairs, Korin bent his head back to fully view the colossal stone hall. Gigantic, elaborately-detailed carvings of glory were engraved in the massive walls, flaunting the creativity and power the mages wielded. An enormous, doorless opening allowed for easy, mostly free-flowing access to those using the transportal. Everyone, including mages, had to pay a fee to use the system; but mages passed through a separate sensor frame. Suddenly, an alarm rang.

"Oh, come on! I'm a mage!" the man who triggered the alarm complained as security approached him for questioning.

The province's planetary ley lines intersected precisely in the centre of the hall. Technically, the lines never met; instead, they formed a node, where a gargantuan dimensional ring formed, hovering above the ground. The planar ring itself had two vertical facings or windows – an inner portal and an outer portal – but not all parts of the ring were active. Still, the visible inactive parts were nonetheless part of the overall ring. Depending on the position people walked through in the ring, they could access different transportals many kilometres away. It was even possible to see the destination before entering the ring; though, the visuals were somewhat distorted due to the intense energy in the area. The transportal in front of Korin only led to other places on Juntas, but the general effects were the same for any other transportal ring. Large stone stairs led up to two, separate circular walkways around and inside the ring, and there were dividers indicating which section of the transportal to take for particular destinations.

When Rolan began leading the Korin through the detectors, the young man worried if he had been wrongly classified as a mage, thinking the alarm would trigger. He then wondered if the frames would detect something peculiar, such as a defect in his blood; for all he knew, Korin could have potentially been a threat to the system. Fortunately, no alarm rang, and his heart relaxed. Korin and Rolan finally approached the ring, stopping just before the window. A deep hum accompanied a steady beat, physically waving the extra-tiny hairs on Korin's ears, which he could feel.

"You first, Korin." Rolan nodded.

"It's been a while since I've travelled through one of these," Korin said. "I used the non-mage entry before this. The system mustn't determine whether non-mages are mages, then. Anyway, how come you can't just teleport me to Teloston?"

"Oh, I can only proxport; you know, teleport within very short distance. I *have* managed to teleport longer distances a few times, but I need to train a lot to keep up such magical feats. Think of magic like fitness. If you don't use it, you lose it. Most mages can't do long-distance teleporting, anyway. On top of that, the majority can't use dimensional magic without doing many things first, like rituals, so it's very limited."

Hoping one day he'd be able to teleport anywhere at will, Korin then briskly walked towards the ring, vibrating greatly all over. He then wondered about the mage posing a priest and the portals that appeared, but the issue confused him, so he focused back on the transportal. When Korin passed through, he had to take a few seconds to gather his senses before asking Rolan, "How did the mages create the transportals?"

"We didn't. They were here all along. We just built the halls and established the parameters of use," Rolan said, dodging an alien's antennae. "Anyway, welcome to Crysten!" He held his arms out wide before both the province *and* state capital. "It's an exceptionally cultured city, but unfortunately, you won't be seeing much of it while at uni. Maybe during the holidays."

The transportal hall was similar to the last one – except grander in scope – while the outside complex was also similar, filled with many beings flurrying about their day. Advertisements and assorted information boards holographically waved and flowered, shooting overhead with bright colours – a couple passing right through Korin. The markets brimmed in the distance with goods and services of sundry types; and above the ranked, whipping stall cloths were many hallways of glass featuring patterns circling around like kaleidoscopes.

In their careless scurry, several people dumped rubbish on the ground or failingly threw their junk at the bins without much care. Although the drones didn't notice, at least cleaners – both robotic and biological – were present to clean up the mess. The roads in the distance admitted both wheeled and hover vehicle types – although, mainly the ones with greater amounts of mass needed wheels. Air-based vehicles and transport were highly-restricted, with anti-jetpack signs placed in so many places.

Even though Teloston was relatively close by, Korin and Rolan still took a short trip on the locally-bound subroute capsule to reach the edge of the enormous grounds, where a twelve-metre thick, black stone wall protected it; and, while as tough as steel and as hard as diamond, the stone wall was also fortified with electric currents on top. The university had also just switched on its transparent forcefield as part of its weekly inspection, domed high over the grounds, shimmering occasionally. With the forcefield's transparent nature, a flock of persistent, silly birds wouldn't stop bumping into it. The level of security was also enough to induce the feeling of assuredness and soundness without it being like a prison. Still, the outside atmosphere wasn't exactly *hospitable*, as it was, instead, *grandiose* – the commanding astrological and mythical artwork carved into the black stone reinforced this effect. Twelve equally-distanced, giant stone hands reached from the top of the wall as well in assorted passion, each holding, clutching, or almost throwing large 'everlasting' candles or torches lit with literal fire on top.

At the gates, Rolan activated a spherical phid from his watch that showed his personal ID, which he presented to the guards. Korin, meanwhile, had to show his papers. Rolan then proceeded through a series of reinforced sensor frames, and before Korin followed on, the young mage glanced back at the horizon with a mix of emotions, knowing a part of his former life had finally come to an end.

Chapter Three

Introductions

Massive trees thickly canopied the university's entry road; their branches, so meticulously tended, weaved into a multitude of designs, establishing an atmosphere fit for royalty. Assorted geometric patterns embellished the granite paths, a few even creating the illusion of three-dimensionality; but most impressive, however, were the giant statues, their feet alone as tall as the average person. Mist even blew up from jets at their feet, giving the exaggerated feeling as if the statues had descended from the heavens. Containing fantastic fluids, the nearby fountains synced with the harmonies of the ambient music in the air, forming amazingly-creative shapes and figures.

Most of the new students who entered kept to themselves, either reading paper pamphlets that flew out of information boxes, playing or fiddling with their own phids, or simply gazing around at the beauty of the university's entry road. Korin didn't feel the need to introduce himself to any of the other students yet, as he already had Rolan's company for the time being, who was talking non-stop about anything that sprung to mind.

After taking the university's subroute, Korin soon arrived at the Central Hub, the university's piazza, which could easily hold over 150,000 standing people at once on the ground level. It also held with the university's focal structural conglomerate: The Teloplex. Composed of multiple sets of edifices, the Teloplex contained most of the university's principal administrative body, as well as other amenities and sites. In the centre was the colossal and aptly-named Chalice of Virtue. Featuring friezes of various fables carved into its platinum stone, the Chalice even had large slotted gems of sapphire, emerald, and ruby to enhance the glory. Tall windows decorated the cup's circumference, with two appearing as if portals with their glow. Fittingly, the Chalice also had handles; curved with elegance, they still expressed strength and seriousness with their solid but sharp tips and protrusions. The university's fitting motto was also strikingly engraved on the building: *Apotheosis. Through. Virtue.*

Three towers called the Pillars of Elevation encircled the Chalice, each with thick fluting of traditional stone column fashion – just with radiating windows in the grooves. The towers widened near the top, where they held up a giant ring, the Aegis Halo. Connecting the towers, the Aegis Halo was etched with transparent markings that would glow during the night, and the Halo's resilient glass exterior encased a field of thousands of polyhedral crystals that drifted around as if an asteroid field – the further away a person was, the dustier they looked; the rooms inside the field accordingly had no windows to the outside world. Next to concealed defences and landing pads for certain vehicles, enchanted statues fortified the Halo's walkable roof, their diverse gazes upon the ground making them seem as if literal petrified gods. The towers wrapped up and over the Halo to merge and form a central tower, the Sky Tower, which narrowed as it ascended. Finally, the top was the crystal-formed Telos Spire, which established the pinnacle of the complex, emerging a vertical beam of light visible even during the day.

A few peoples' belongings were stuck in odd places here and there across the Teloplex, and even though the university hired janitors and used cleaning drones, bird droppings were numerous. At least, at times, the Central Hub would be clear of certain excreta, as the surrounding structure, the Provision Wreath – which, too, was still part of the Central Hub – sometimes would produce a glass dome from its roof, reaching over the ground. Shaped as a swirled, twelve-sided star, the Provision Wreath catered to the students with a food hall on the first floor, then a hospital and a childcare centre; it also had supplementary info and admin service spaces, as well as the security headquarters and some storage areas for the university itself.

A glass-covered moat filled with crystal-clear water brimming with fantastic aquatic creatures bordered the Provision Wreath, both inside the Central Hub and outside of it. Along the Wreath's rocky, undulating walls, moss, fungi, and flora grew around waterfalls flowing from the top of the four-storey structure. Arranged between the rock facings, stone columns or large statues functioned as jambs for the wide openings on the ground floor and the crystalized glass on the upper floors. Depending on the position one was in the Central Hub, either an edifice or nature itself enclosed the whole area; from the centre, it was a fusion of both.

Rolan decided to take Korin on a tour before doing anything else, showing him the magic and non-magic academic and training districts that surrounded the Provision Wreath. Filled with assorted connected and unconnected buildings, the academic rings were where most of the magical and non-magical education and research took place. Three districts were evenly established around the education districts, with the first featuring mainly private mansions, houses, apartments, lodgings, and, of course, fraternity, sorority, and order houses. The second district mostly possessed sports facilities and stadiums, while the third district was the entertainment and market one, featuring most of the shops and clubs, along with various halls, like the exhibition centre and the Performing Arts Centre – and, top of all that, it had an amusement park, too. Despite normally being in, or suited for, the 'auxiliary districts', some temporary small stalls and exhibits were allowed to exist in the Central Hub, and there were also various eateries in all of the said districts. A slim botanic perimeter separated the Provision Wreath from the academic districts, and then another for each of the auxiliary districts; and then another botanic perimeter separated those districts from the surrounding dormitory district, which spanned over eight kilometres in its circumference.

With security guarding it against the outside world, the university's subroute system was one of the primary ways of traversing the enormous campus, connecting to each dorm, as there weren't many parking spaces for individual vehicles on the campus, other than loading zones. An open sky-lift system surrounded the central sections, marked with floating crystals, glowing brightly, despite the sunlight. Circling the dorms was the Nature Reserve, which featured a zoo, a large lake, recreational sporting grounds, a shooting range, and enough environment for various nature-based activities. Protected ancient ruins were also scattered across the university. In total, the university was itself a small city, accommodating *up to* 120,000 thousand undergraduate students at once – not to mention the varying postgraduates, who may or may not have lived on the campus – along with some faculty that permanently lived on the campus, too.

The tour took Korin to the main areas of the university, except for those out of bounds; many were even prohibited for staff such as Rolan; and, that wasn't even including the private property on campus. Korin was told to watch out for specific areas, as a number of terrible things had happened to students who'd been foolish enough to explore without knowing how to defend themselves. He learned that many universities – like Teloston – were not only ancient but were also built on top of multiple, *deep* underground ruins, facilities, and assorted remnants. No-one in the modern age had fully explored the systems below ground. There were many ways for abyssal creatures to enter into such underground systems and later mutate to become monsters. Moreover, there were even accounts of epic monsters being permanently sealed away in order to starve them to death instead of having to risk lives by battling them. The thought of university study may have given Korin anxiety, but the knowledge of such monsters amazed him. As Rolan continued talking about other matters, Korin couldn't help but imagine what lurked below. He believed there would be a way to magically defend himself should anything happen, so he wasn't worried.

Before returning to the Central Hub, Rolan mentioned that the university paid for everyone's class materials. Because of Korin's situation, he would most likely receive a small stipend as an added bonus. Korin also had the opportunity of finding a job on campus, but Rolan recommended settling in first before looking for one.

***

"Right, let's get the formalities out of the way, shall we?" Rolan asked Korin as they approached one of the towers in the Central Hub.

The black granite floor inside the tower's lobby brightly reflected several flares of natural and artificial lighting, in addition to enduring numerous hard-soled shoes, which were maddingly clopping around. Most of the staff didn't even have a spare second to look at Korin as they endlessly pressed holographic buttons affixed around their bodies while occasionally grabbing geometrically-folded holochite paper flying and floating around. Golden plaques, professional headshot photos, and glassed certificates adorned the walls; and while Korin tried to absorb as much of the history while swiftly passing through, he was keen on leisurely scanning the pictures later on.

Rolan showed Korin to his office on the third level of the tower, gesturing for him to take a seat. Piles of paperwork scattered the shelves and desks, with one mountain ready to avalanche. Rolan, however, was able to quickly find a large, paper-bound document in the mess, dumping it on the table.

"I know what you're thinking; I'm not looking forward to it either," Rolan said, grinning at Korin's expression of dismay. "These… are the rules. Constantly. Being. Updated. The rule-makers need something to do, I guess." He tilted his head, smirking. "There are so many rules, most of them probably contradict each other. Anyway, you're meant to read through this and do a test… but," he said slowly, "since we have little time – and since I can sense that you seem the okay sort – I'll go through it with you." He roguishly smiled. "So, let's condense this a little. Um… don't go casting spells on others, shooting others, planting traps, etcetera, etcetera. Essentially, don't be a pestchul on rokesh. You get the picture," he said, but Korin didn't quite understand the rokesh part. "Oh, and you can't leave the university without permission, and… uh, what else? What else?" He tapped his pen on the table. "I think that'll do for now. First, sign this to acknowledge that you've read the rules, and then I'll go through the test and give a psychological assessment of you in the process."

Korin's eyes grew as he reached for the pen, its sharp laser activated. The holochite-formed paper's smooth texture and overall strong yet light and pliable nature was fortunately capable of resisting Rolan's puddle of coffee. When Korin signed the document, the ink glowed ethereally – his acknowledgement and signature were officially recorded in a database elsewhere. Rolan then placed the paper near a glowing crystal, which electrically charged it, in turn causing the paper to geometrically fold into an odd shape before floating away through a chute nearby.

Korin stayed silent, trying to keep his breathing patterns in check. *I'm not a bad person*, he thought, tapping his fingers on his leg. *I'm mentally fine. I'll pass.* The arch-priest then came to mind. *Oh, man… I even killed a person. I… think he's dead.*

Prickles harassed Korin's neck. He told himself that the arch-priest was pure evil, but he wondered if Rolan would discover his past actions, thinking perhaps Korin was a serial killer of sorts. He then rightly doubted that Rolan would ask if he had ever murdered anyone, but Korin still remained a bit nervous.

Rolan then summoned a phid around him via his watch, pressing a few buttons before continuing, "Yes, despite our technology, we mages have to back up all legal documents with paper; but I still also need a handprint signature, please." A holographic hand sign popped up in the air in front of them, and Korin pressed his hand against it in order to finish the process. "So, now for the test. Let's see… question, uh… forty-four: You somehow chance upon a mysterious potion set in a hidden cache somewhere in the university. What do you do? One: do nothing; two: inform the university administration; three: take and sell it; four: simultaneously fuse all the potions together and then run all the way to a non-expert, high-ranking faculty member – who also happens to be surrounded by sensitive political delegates – and berserkly shout like a terrorist while demanding what to do as it's frenziedly bubbling just before it's about to explode, potentially wounding or killing yourself and many others?" Rolan looked up critically, stalling. "Yes, something like that really did happen." He rolled his eyes, although it was obvious that he found it *somewhat* amusing. "Or five: gather your friends and transfigure the potions before consuming them all in one serving as a competition, soon having your bodies permanently transform into huge, mucous-filled sacs, not realizing in the first place that they were actually *philtres*, not *potions* designed for biotic transfiguration?" He looked up again with an unimpressed countenance. "Yes, that one also happened. Long story." He shook his hand, anticipating Korin's question. "So, which one?"

Korin held back a grin, having found the examples oddly humorous in a way. Finally, he said, "Inform someone, I guess."

"Yes, good answer. I have a feeling you're not going to be like some of the students we get. Despite filtering out criminals before enrolment, every year, there's always at least one extremist, among *many* trouble-makers." He lifted one eyebrow, analysing Korin shrewdly.

Korin tried not to laugh. "You can trust me." *Oh, shit… my reply wasn't serious enough.*

"Ah-ha," Rolan responded slowly. "We'll see. Okay, I'll just tick everything else." He finished the form, reaching for another set of papers. The information in the paper also linked up with Rolan's phid before he said, "So, except for the last semester, there are at least six subjects: four magic, and two to four non-magic. Fortunately, you can choose your non-magical subjects. And yes, I understand that it may be a bit hard to choose with so little time to decide, but we can go down later to the archetype determiner to confirm whatever decision you make now. Still, I'm unsure if things will change for you next year, as the university is likely rearranging how course work is applied."

There were many subjects in the list ranging from Business Studies to Engineering, and Linguistics to Sociology. The prospect of business was too foreign for Korin to even contemplate, while the medical subjects had no appeal to him whatsoever. Regrettably, he never got around to practicing musical instruments for long enough to consider music an option; Korin noted that there were performance requirements for entry, anyway. Indeed, most subjects had prerequisites of various kinds, so having a narrowed list made his decision easier. Rolan soon told him that he'd find a way to waive any requirements for lighter subjects, as Korin had no available schooling records. There were even Theology and Religious Studies, but he quickly scanned over them, slightly shaking his head.

Not even going there, Korin thought.

But Korin did like knowing about the world around him, always taking a more profound perspective on matters. He wasn't sure if that was ingrained in him through his religious upbringing or if it was an inherent trait. Either way, a few subjects of similar nature appealed to him. Vocational classes featured on a few other pages for those who didn't do well in school – or for students who had other interests and aspirations. Flipping through the pages a few times, Korin eventually turned back to the first.

"I'll go with Arts," Korin slowly said, wondering if he had made the right decision. "History and… Political Science sounds interesting. I'm not sure how I'd fare with some of the other subjects."

"Great. I did Arts, too."

Korin's non-magic classes were all introductory, so he had no choice in their subdisciplines. His first-semester timetable basically stated:

> *• Moonday: 9:00 a.m. – 12:00 p.m.: General Theory, Knowledge, and Psychicism (GTKP). 1:30 p.m. – 4:30 p.m.: Alchemy.*
> *• Earthday: 9:00 a.m. – 12:00 p.m.: Phasarchement. 1:30 p.m. – 4:30 p.m.: Conjuration.*
> *• Waterday: 9:00 a.m. – 12:00 p.m.: History. 1:30 p.m. – 4:30 p.m.: Political Science.*
> *• Airday and Fireday: Spare.*
> *• Starday and Sunday: Weekend.*

Rolan added, "Orientation is tomorrow, and the three-day camp is after that."

Korin eagerly took the paperwork, thoughts now focused on the camp.

"I hope I've covered everything," Rolan muttered, looking around. "Oh, your degree lasts three years, but I advise that you do well on your magic subjects, even if they may be unrelated to any future jobs; some prospective employers may unfavourably look at those who don't have good grades, as just one example. But don't worry too much; most graduates end up getting a C average for their magic. After your under-graduate degree, you're free to leave the uni and travel anywhere you like; though, many continue for a master's degree, as it's a general requirement if you wish to work for the CGM."

Korin hadn't even thought of a master's degree – the idea of just attending a mage university and possessing magic abilities was enough to twist his mind around.

"Okay, let's head down to the archetype determiners," Rolan said.

***

Before determining Korin's natural archetypes, Rolan still had to finish the matter of Korin's photo and identification, only taking a few minutes. Quite a few of Korin's personal details were left blank, and Rolan was surprised at how quickly the process went; he assumed he'd run up against an annoyingly-rigid bureaucracy... Well, the bureaucracy's weight still existed; the young staff that morning, however, were too high on some drug to care about formalities. The procedure also involved taking a blood sample and an etheric print – a capture of his spiritual auric energy via an auric scanner – to be stored away in a high-security vault. Since Korin had a recent blood transfusion, he would have to update his blood sample at a later date. He was also a little worried about the security of his samples...

After taking care of the matter, Rolan then led Korin down to a chamber in the basement level via the Chalice of Virtue, where crystals completely covered the interior surfaces, formed not just like twinkling stars but also as one giant formation – a toroid – so the chamber possessed no square walls. Each of the crystal particles were themselves in geometric patterns, twirling and spinning in their place. An external energy source powered the crystals, and their multicoloured glow smoothly pulsated in assorted arrangements, synchronously matching the deep and hypnotic noise they produced. One hundred and twenty-eight circular stone platforms decked the floor, all carved with fractal patterns and complex symbols, each connected to a network of crystals underneath.

"These are our archetype determiners," Rolan said, pointing to the platforms. "They're useful in a few ways, but I'll set it to career mode, so only a particular set of archetypes will be listed. Just stand on one, and it'll show you what you're suited for."

"Do I have to use magic?" Korin asked.

"No, no. The pads will analyse your etheric energy and then group that data into archetypes. It's not accurate, so it's more of a *hint* at which direction you're likely better off taking. Oh, I also forgot to mention before: your elemental type determines what school of magic you'll be able to excel in, so fire types excel in alchemy; earth types are good with conjuration; air types, like me," he said contentedly, holding his chest, "can easily store charms; and then water types are great at mysticism magic. Regardless of your type, you'll still study all the schools of magic. A few centuries ago, all the different types of students were separated, but now everyone is part of the same campus."

Korin hopped onto the closest circle, and a few seconds later, a light whirlwind of energy formed, engaging with every fibre of his being. A holographic shape formed around Korin, in turn forming numerous geometries inside, each with rocky textures. Eventually, an abstract image of a person leading others appeared across the crystals.

"I see," Rolan said, nodding. "I initially guessed a fire type, but you do indeed seem the cardinal earth type."

"So, what does this mean?"

"You got the leader archetype. You're more suited for leading. However, that doesn't mean you're suited for all sorts of leadership roles, and there are different kinds of leaders, like visionaries, organizers, etcetera. Maybe you're a bit of a fiery leader. Wouldn't want to get on the wrong side of you." He chuckled. "It also means that you'll do well with conjuration magic. In addition, it means it's possible that your astrological sun sign is in Determas. I think that means you chose a good set of subjects."

"Great!" Korin responded happily. "As I said, my given birthday was in that month, anyway."

"In case you're interested, some frat houses have restrictions on their elemental type in order to join them."

Joining a fraternity wasn't on Korin's mind at the moment, so the idea quickly brushed past him as he lightly shrugged.

All of a sudden, the determiner's windy energy unsteadily whipped around Korin, holographically expanding the rocky geometric shapes around him.

"Hey, what's going on?" Korin asked, feeling a strange electrical sensation all over.

"Uh… I'm not sure." Rolan grimaced. "It should settle down soon."

However, it didn't. The energy expanded and jolted like lightning, bursting around the room. Korin flinched and dodged every few seconds while frantically looking around, trying to see if he could mentally stop the power. Rolan, meanwhile, felt pressured to step back from the power gusting him.

The noise dramatically and discordantly rose, and the circles began to crack and crumble with small chunks rising into an emerging tornado; the surrounding crystals started fracturing and shattering as well, joining the lively action. Feeling culpable, Korin took the right course of action and leapt off, grabbing Rolan on the way. Debris ubiquitously flew as the miniature tornado discharged erratically shortly before the entire room fulminated. Rolan was too much in shock to contemplate using his magic for defence; and while only metres away from the entrance, both mages shielded themselves with their bare hands as massive shards fortuitously bypassed their trembling beings by centimetres. A few smaller shards scratched their hands, but both guys luckily avoided major damage.

In his stupefaction, Rolan stood stationary, finally glancing over at Korin, who paralleled him. He noticed Korin was fine, and he then stared back at the smoky ruins. "Oh, crap!" Rolan coughed out. "Oh, crap! Oh, crap, oh, crap… oh… crap."

"Wh-what did I do? I swear I did nothing." Korin responded, trying to move his fearfully stiff fingers.

"I don't know, but in our entire history, that has *never* happened before. Ah… oh, crap. Ah, let's get out of here before anyone sees this." Rolan grabbed Korin and fled. In their favour, no-one was in the vicinity when they reached the ground level. Remarkably, the cameras were also offline due to maintenance. Rolan then quickly turned to Korin, gravely saying, "Let's never speak of this again."

"Sure. Definitely. But won't someone find out eventually?"

"If anyone does, I'll cover for you; but just keep quiet. Now, let's hope nobody needs to determine an archetype for a while!"

The thick floor hadn't collapsed, and there was nothing visual in the room to signify that an explosion had occurred. Not a single person rushed in either, so their escape from the room with the stairs was swift and easy.

***

"Okay, I'll go and organize your stationery needs and other odds and ends," Rolan said while at the entrance, still looking a bit worried. "In the meantime, I suggest getting a unichite-powered wearable, like a watch." He then reached into his pocket and pulled out a coin of unichite before activating his phid. He typed some information in and then held the coin against the phid. Within a short moment, two slivers of the coin broke off before thickening a little. "Here, take these cheques to buy a cheap watch and anything else to keep yourself organized. Now, if you realize you need anything, I'll probably be in my office later. And," Rolan said, placing his hand on his thinning hair, "what else? Ah, yes, if you need any support – you know, because you've been through a rough period – speak to me or one of the psychologists in the Provision Wreath – but preferably me."

"So, that's it? I'm free to go now?" Korin asked, surprised at the easygoingness, anxious and excited at the same time.

"Keen to get out there, I see." He chuckled. "Yes, you're free to go. You should be fine. I'll see you later. Oh, and," he said, jumping in before Korin could speak, "we'll search the database for your parents and see if anything comes up. The police will sort that one out. Check in on them from time to time. Oh, oh," he yelped, raising his finger, "the welcoming assembly is at five o'clock. Head to the Central Hub and follow the rest of the students, and you should be fine. More will be explained then. *Until then*, you have free time to explore."

Before replying, Korin took a deep breath, taking in everything he had learned. At last, he said, "Thanks for all your help, Rolan. I really appreciate it."

"Aww, any time." He flopped his hand. "It's my job, after all."

Korin waved goodbye before heading out, stopping when spotting a meat-headed first-year student pushing around a regally-dressed goblin, gaining great pleasure out of doing so with his big grin. The four-foot goblin was trying to escape, but he kept falling to the ground as his coin-shaped cheques scattered. Despite the goblin's sharp teeth and claws, he didn't fight back.

"Hey!" Korin swiftly called out. "What do you think you're doing?" He approached the chubby lad, taking a forceful stance.

"What?" the first-year asked angrily. "Get your own fucking goblin."

"I suggest you apologize to him." Korin stared sternly without blinking. "Now," he added after a moment.

Another student suddenly approached Korin and stood right beside him, antagonistically looking at the bully. Patches of her white skin showed through her torn, mud-stained cargo pants, and when she wrapped her rough jacket around her waist, Korin noticed the tone in her muscles, triceps distinguishable from her biceps.

"You heard him," the girl said adamantly with a firm voice, massaging her ready fist. "Do it. Apologize."

"Another dantha-fucker?" the bully asked, crossing his arms, taking one step back. "Piss off. I was just having some fun."

"That's a load of khorshit," Korin replied. "Pick him up or leave."

After a moment of glaring with contempt, the bully reached over and roughly picked the goblin up, apologizing pathetically. The bully shot another glare at Korin before leaving without a word, although there were a few grumbles along the way. The goblin glanced at Korin, fake smiling before moving on to finish his task in the room. In return, Korin merely gave a perplexed look.

"Hey, nice work there," the girl said to Korin, smiling with a face speckled with very light freckles.

"Yeah, thanks for joining," Korin replied. "I would have taken him myself, though."

"I can fight, just so you know." She folded her arms. "I would've jumped him, too."

"Hey, I don't doubt you. Just saying."

"Fair enough." She shrugged, relaxing her stance.

"Anyway, when I actually think about it, a punch-up's probably not the best thing on our first day."

"True." She simpered. "So, I'm Terala." She held her hand out to eagerly shake Korin's hand.

"Nice to meet you. I'm Korin. As you may have picked up about me… I'm, well, kind of new to all of this."

Terala winced her feisty green eyes. "So? We're all new."

"Oh, um…" He scratched the back of his neck, deciding whether or not to say anything regarding his background. "Well, I… I only found out yesterday that… that I'm a mage."

"What?" Terala burst out loudly, almost laughing. "Get out of here! Serious?"

"No joke. I had no idea," Korin said, questioning his own words for a second.

"Man, that's intense. No, really?" She frowned incredulously.

"Yeah, yeah, I, uh…" He glanced down, and Terala noticed the almost-healed bruises and cuts on his hands.

"I can see why you're not afraid of a good fight." She looked impressed. "You're probably a fire type like me, right?" She grabbed the back of her hair, readjusting her sporty, auburn ponytail.

"No, earth, actually. For the most part, probably. You're the second person to think that."

"Huh. You'd think I'd be able to tell; fire seems to run through my family."

"You have siblings here at Teloston?"

"No, I'm… the oldest," she said guardedly as if her fire had diminished. "There are way more to come here, though. Ten more."

"Oh, wow. Will the rest of your family see you much now that you're here?"

"Probably not. At least in person. Uni rules and all. But I'll still be seeing plenty of them today."

"At least you get to see them off," he said, demeanour swiftly turning sad. "I wish I had my family here."

Terala was about to comment, but she glanced at the doorway, mumbling. "Just watch yourself when we head out," she finally said. "My family can be a little wild."

"Sure, but you're probably overexaggerating." Korin grinned. "No need to be embarrassed."

"Embarrassed? No, I'm just giving you a heads-up. So, where's *your* family?" Terala enquired as they began making their way outside.

"I don't know," Korin answered slowly. "But I've been told I'll find out soon enough." He brightened slightly.

Just before leaving, they saw the previously-bullied goblin shove one of his associates to the ground, snickering.

Frowning, Terala blurted, "What a cunt!"

The wealthy goblin then snatched a few mage supplies, running off with haste. The university security happened to be nearby, and they started chasing him.

"Wow." Korin looked flabbergasted. "I can't believe that guy."

"Yeah. They better get him," Terala added.

On exiting the building, Terala's family mostly kicked and screamed or played roughly. The only parent present was the mother, who happened to be chasing a set of rascally five-year-old twins.

"That's... one family you have there." Korin was taken aback in amazement.

Terala rolled her eyes. "I might have to catch up with you later."

"Sure. I'll see you later, then." Korin waved, but Terala had already begun bickering with her family. For a good minute, Korin continued observing all the lively family members as he carefully walked backwards. He wanted to see Terala again, thinking over their brief conversation shortly before losing focus to his attention-grabbing surroundings.

Unsure where to go, Korin found a map on a stand prior to making his way to the Market District on foot. Near one of the Provision Wreath thoroughfares, however, Korin saw vociferous protestors chanting, bearing signs, and handing out pamphlets from stalls. There was one group, in particular, that caught Korin's eye. Huddled together for strength – or considerably, instead, out of cowardice – the group appeared especially suspicious with how they moved and checked their surroundings. Dressed in pure black, their faces were masked with balaclavas, while most wore sunglasses to conceal their eyes. A few carried flags, championing their militant cause; and although intimidating compared to the other protestors, Korin nevertheless approached, not seeing any due cause for them to attack in broad daylight.

At once, a couple swiftly approached Korin, crossing their arms with aggression while blocking his path.

Korin stopped moving, holding his hands out. "Hey, just curious as to what's happening."

"Nothing's happening," one of the thugs aggressively said. "Now beat it."

Given that Teloston was his home now, Korin *had* to inquire. "Can you at least tell me what this is all about? Who are you guys?"

"You don't know who we are?" one asked doubtfully.

"No, I'm new here."

"He's probably just agitating us," the other guy said.

His comrade then replied, "Maybe. But it *is* the first day for newbies."

"Fine. Look, we're AMSA – Anti Mage Supremacy Alliance. Or Activists. Whichever. We're keeping the peace around here."

Korin found it a little hard to believe that they were keeping the peace with such an aggressive, suspicious attitude and stance, but he had no desire to provoke them, opting to ask neutral questions. "Okay, but what do you do?"

"We stop mage supremacists from rising again. Actually, the system is still run by mage supremacists, but we keep things from getting worse. Ultimately, we want revolution – to end the CGM and bring about true equality for all species."

Intrigued, though dubious, Korin asked, "Are there many of you? How do you join?"

"You don't *join* AMSA. Anyone can be AMSA. If you're looking to get active with others, then find some people who agree with the ideals. Otherwise, we're not a centralized organization."

The other AMSA member butted in, "Hey, we need this area now, so *get* lost. If you want to see us truly in action, we'll be on the streets next Waterday. Big fucking rally happening."

"Yeah, now get the fuck out of here."

Irritated at their attitude, Korin felt like replying, but he knew it was wise just to remain silent for the time being. He had no idea how violent they would turn, and he had to settle into the university before taking any drastic action.

Backing away with a glare, Korin's attention soon focused on two people ranting and raving, especially on the older student with his mechanical arms.

The mature student continued, "You puritanical luddites don't see the beauty in the coming singularity!"

"You're bloody insane!" the younger student countered. "You'll have us all turn into robots!"

"Don't make me use my rocket launchers on you!" he pointed his steel arms at the other person.

"Oi!" one of the security guards yelled, magically creating a ball of green energy in her hand while aiming it at the mechanically-limbed man. "Put your arms down!"

"It was a joke! Relax! I'm putting them down. They're not even linked up to my central nervous system. *Yet.*"

The student actually did comply, but the security guard remained suspicious of him, keeping watch. Korin kept out of the way, though he was surprised that the security wasn't dealing with the AMSA thugs. Turning around, Korin continued to watch various people loudly debating. Instead of focusing on any discourse, he decided to keep moving, as there was too much information to consume in one session.

***

While in the Market District, Korin searched for a shop that sold unichite watches, eventually finding one with a sign saying that it was closed for the day. Korin chose to walk around the corner, into the alley, and peek through the window to see if anyone was actually inside. It was unoccupied. As Korin backed away from the window, he turned around and smacked right into someone who had been running.

"Shit, sorry," the new student apologized, holding his head. "Ah, man, that hurt."

The youthful-looking first-year wiped his perspiring white skin under his blond hair that reached his eyebrows. His blue eyes were incredibly agitated, though they were filled with a small amount of fading, impish amusement. There was also a cartoony meme on his shirt, but Korin didn't understand it.

"You alright?" the blond student asked, looking apologetic as he helped Korin off the ground.

"I'm fine." Korin brushed the dirt off his clothes. "Why were you running?"

"I was –" He flinched before grabbing Korin, hiding behind the dumpster.

"What's happening?" Korin whispered worriedly.

"Shh. Wait," he whispered back as a large group of older, enraged students rushed past, covered in a multicoloured slime.

When the angry mob vanished, Korin asked, "What happened? Did you do that?"

"No," he replied guiltily. "Well, yes, but not really."

Korin stared in disbelief.

"It was actually an accident." The prankster began giggling. "I planned on using some stink bombs, but I used some other bombs I had by accident, and, well…" He laughed louder. "Well, you saw what happened. Again, it was an accident!" He raised his hands defensively as Korin continued staring without a word. "Hey, come on, you have to understand the situation."

Korin tilted his head to the side, thinking, *Okay…* "They looked pretty angry. Did they see your face?"

"Nah, I don't think so. Just my back." His presence now seemed a bit calmer.

"Quick, this way." Korin grabbed him by the shirt as he glimpsed the angry mob returning.

Both young men ran to the end of the alley; and, in their panicked haste, they clumsily climbed the splinter-inducing fence and landed awkwardly on the other side, scrambling to stand up before darting behind one of the next buildings without looking back. Korin couldn't believe he was already involved in so much drama this early on, but he knew he couldn't sit back and watch.

Stopping after a few blocks, the blond lad panted and said, "Phew, that was close! Thanks for that. I'm Sylas. Sylas Amicen." He happily held his hand out.

"And I'm Korin." He reached his hand out, swiftly withdrawing it as he noticed an object in Sylas's hand.

"Oh, sorry." Sylas slid the item back up his long-sleeved shirt that was under his short meme shirt. "Yeah, that's something I sometimes greet people with." He held his bare hand out again.

"Seriously, no pranks this time." Korin looked askance.

"No pranks. It's not like I intentionally try to cause trouble. Just enough for laughs." He chuckled brazenly before shaking Korin's hand. "Yeah, yeah, my parents warned me not to cause any trouble, otherwise they'd be up here, and, well, I don't want them coming up."

"It's funny you say that; I just met a girl who didn't really want her family bothering her as well."

"She'd understand how good it is to break free. Finally, I'm free!" Sylas stretched widely. "Do you feel the same, too?"

"Well," Korin said, pausing briefly, "I feel pretty free, actually." He stared into his own world as he momentarily contemplated. "I'm actually free. Free," he told himself aloud in amazement.

"I know, right? It's so unreal." Sylas smiled brightly.

"Yeah, it feels unreal, alright. I just overcame something… big and unreal. And now… now I'm free." Korin, at last, broke his stare. "It's a bit overwhelming, but I think I'll get used to this pretty quickly."

"Same, except I'm not looking forward to the assignments and exams."

"Well, I was pretty good with my school assignments, so hopefully it'll be easy. I think it'll be the magic classes that I'll struggle with."

"It might be the same for me. Who knows? Eh, meilek sona."

"Sorry, what was that?" Korin asked, utterly confused.

"You haven't seen *Lord of the Narvaks*?" Sylas asked, and Korin shrugged. He then stretched his wording while heightening his pitch as he asked, "What? It's from a show. Don't worry. So…" Sylas said, gazing around, "what were you doing before I bumped into you?"

"I need to get one of those unichite watches – or anything with unichite – and so I was about to buy one, but that store was closed."

"You don't have *any* unichite items?" Sylas asked with shock.

"No. Never had any."

"Well, I just bought this one yesterday," he said, holding up his wrist to show the watch's design of a steampunk wolf, "so I'll give you my old one. Perfect condition and great quality."

"Really? For free?"

"Yeah, man. I won't ever be using it again."

"Oh… thank you." Korin then considered the offering a potential joke. *Wait, he's not a thief, is he?* "You… didn't steal it?"

"Oh, no." He laughed somewhat cockily. "I have no need to steal things. I'm not like *that*. Anyway, I have to get going. I'll catch you later." He backhand-tapped Korin on the chest.

"Yeah, you, too." Korin smiled as Sylas departed.

Hmm… I feel like I owe him something now, Korin thought. *But what?*

Korin *was* in the Market District, but he considered paying him back another time; besides, Korin still hadn't received the watch. His lingering, warm interaction with Sylas, however, overshadowed the burden. Since Korin was also unsure what goods to purchase for himself, he was reluctant to spend any money for the time being; he thought about asking Sylas later for information, anyway, so he pressed on with sightseeing.

***

While strolling through one of the botanic strips between two districts, Korin noticed someone examining the flora in a rather peculiar way. Korin didn't say anything at first as he stared at the girl hopping around with a strange, handheld device. Her long, dark brown hair whimsically swayed back and forth, while her cute bangs almost reached her dreamy blue eyes. The sun brightly reflected off her soft, pale white skin; her springy legs, meanwhile, were covered in swirly-decorated leggings underneath a 'playful' skirt. The girl's shoes were pointy and slightly curled at the ends; and she was also wearing lots of crystals and mystically-symbolled jewellery.

"Can I ask what you're doing?" Korin questioned her with his arms crossed, confused.

"Me?" she asked with a spacey and dazed expression.

"Well, it's not like there's anyone else here." Korin smirked. "Sorry, I didn't mean to sound rude," he swiftly said.

"Oh, that's fine," she said in a lovely voice. "A few creatures raced through here and uprooted some of the plants. I'm just examining the area."

Korin noticed a bag with a few of the uprooted flowers inside. "So, you're a bit of a thief, eh?"

"What?" she asked with great alarm, opening her eyes wide as her neck stiffened. "No."

"I can see the flowers in your bag." Korin pointed as the girl quickly closed the top. "Relax, I don't care about a few flowers."

"Oh, okay, then." She breathed a great sigh of relief. "But some mischievous creatures really did pass through here."

"Yes, I'm sure they did." Korin smirked again.

"Honestly, I'm not a thief. The flowers will go to waste, and they're so incredibly beautiful. It's amazing how their delicate stems manage to hold up such heavy petals." She held the flowers close to her face, breathing deeply. "Here, smell," she offered without warning.

"They smell nice," Korin replied, though he only took a quick sniff. "You seem very interested in plants."

"I like lots of things!" she said perkily. "But I tend to use these flowers in particular in my recipes. My mother taught me how to make cookies with them, as they add a nice chewy texture when done right. I plan on making some myself. I can give you a few, if you'd like."

"That… that sounds great." Korin nodded, delighted by her geniality. "Are your parents here?" he asked as they began walking through the garden towards the Central Hub.

"Yeah, they're back at the main complex. I decided to go for a walk, and then I saw those creatures tear the place up. The security eventually caught them."

"That would've been an interesting sight." He snickered. "So… I know this might seem like an odd thing to ask, but… all mages have full mage ancestry or magery -- if that's even a word -- right?"

"I guess it's a word now." She smiled playfully. "Well, if you can use magic, then yes. Otherwise, you could have one non-mage human parent. Why do you ask?" She packed another flower away.

Korin thought for a moment, realizing that while he hadn't cast any magic yet, he had other factors, like his blood, pointing to full mage-hood. He then replied, "That means both my parents were mages." He paused, feeling easier about opening up to her about his past, having done so before with Terala. "Anyway, I'm not sure who my parents were, if you're wondering what I'm on about."

"Oh, I'm sorry to hear that," she responded, voice full of empathy.

"It's alright. There are people investigating the matter. And I only learned about my mage abilities yesterday, so I feel a little out of place here."

"Wow." She halted as if something had stung her. "Sometimes *I* feel a little out of place, so I understand how you're feeling. I've also met both mages and non-mages who've lost their families." She held his shoulder with another empathetic face. "I'm sure they'll find your parents soon enough."

"Thanks." Korin smiled at her. "I'm Korin, by the way. And you are?" He held his hand out.

"Celine. Sinova." She warmly shook his hand. "Although, I'm also called The Lost Princess of Maveria."

"You're… you're a princess?" Korin asked with amazement.

"Oh, yes! I have a secret mirror that I use to travel between hidden realms. Maveria is a veiled planet that no-one else in the Caelverse knows about."

"Wow! That's so cool." He beamed.

"I think so, too." She suddenly paused, looking a little embarrassed. "Oh… sorry, I didn't clarify that it's just a story I'm working on."

"Ahhh… right, I see. A story that you're writing for a book?"

"Yes, but it's just for me, so I put myself in it. I want to live among the alovexen fox people as an undercover spy. And… hey, look, my parents are over there." Celine pointed to a fit and healthy man, who was holding a newspaper, and a woman who looked like an older version of Celine. The mother was also carrying a baby girl in a sling, and a five-year-old boy was nearby, playing with a toy.

"Oh, so you've made a new friend already," Celine's father said when the two first-years approached, glancing cordially at Korin.

"Yes!" Celine replied instantly before Korin responded. "Korin, this is my mum and dad," she said, turning to her parents. "He doesn't know what happened to his parents, and he didn't know that he was a mage until recently, so he needs someone to show him a few things."

"I see." Celine's father shook Korin's hand. "Interesting. Well, if you need a place to stay when outside the uni, you're welcome to stay with us. Students are usually allowed out for a few weeks during the end-of-year holidays."

"Thanks, but I think I should be okay. I don't want to be a burden," Korin replied, feeling slightly overwhelmed by the generosity.

"Nonsense!" Celine's mother interjected. "We're always willing to help. Everyone feels nervous when they first attend university, so we understand if you feel the need for reservations."

"That's right," Celine's father added. "It's important to help out when appropriate. Now, Celine, do you want to come with us before we leave?"

"Of course. Hey," Celine said, turning to Korin to warmly wave, "I'll see you later."

Korin waved back, remaining put as he thought to himself.

Chapter Four

Settling in with Unsettling News

First-year students began pouring into the Chalice of Virtue when it was time for the welcoming assembly. In the centre of the building's cavernous lobby was a gigantic platform with many aeropad launchers; and when groups of people stood on the aeropads, the aerochite in the unichite expanded to form shells that encased the groups before shooting everyone off inside aerochannels. Numerous aerochannels were forking off in multiple directions at once, all leading to the circular hallway surrounding the Formal Hall – a theatre-styled auditorium – in the upper, main area of the building. The neurachite brains inside the aeropads were also able to detect abuse of the system, prohibiting particular students who cost the university needless energy.

Korin had never used an aeropad launcher before, but because there were so many people using them without much thought, he easily hopped on an available pad, which shortly began forming its walls. His feet slightly dipped into the spongey, translucent floor as the walls encased him and the rest of the students with a sound mixed between an electric buzz, sprinkling particles, and that of oily hands being rubbed around the ears. The aeropad then shot Korin up so quickly that he didn't even have enough time to properly process it. The walls then opened up, allowing the group to exit; and just after Korin stepped out, the aero-channel rapidly shrunk back down again. Korin was tempted to try it again, but he decided to continue to the main hall.

The hallway's giant windows allowed substantial light to shine through, the brightness greatly highlighing the assorted trophies, statues, and memorabilia along the walls. The Formal Hall, on the other hand, had its own lighting, but it was still very bright. Arching across the hall's ceiling, an epic mural illustrated momentous historical events and note-worthy traditions, seamlessly linking one milestone to another, detailing thousands of stories in single pockets. The characters felt alive, ready to move, shake, and jump with great emotion at their achievements. While it had only been recently crafted, the matte and grainy aesthetic created the impression that the mural was ancient.

Amongst a backdrop of insignias and assorted allegorical depictions, there was an ancient warrior who struck Korin's attention. The man stared with a stoic, though intense expression, magically charging a ball of red energy in one hand. The painting's obvious intended effect was to portray that the warrior knew full well that he alone was responsible for his actions, and that his descendants he trained — and bequeathed accumulated traditions to — were to be stronger than himself. Korin finally finished staring at the warrior, returning to the whizzing reality around him. Although Korin didn't see Terala and Celine, he did chance upon Sylas.

"It seemed you were in a rush when you left," Korin remarked.

"Well, to be honest, I had to fix something else. I think I better slow down on the pranks for a while." Sylas looked up for a second. "Until I'm settled in." He giggled.

Korin smiled. "No trouble from those mages?"

"Nah, they never found me." He suddenly frowned. "Why did you say, 'those mages'? It almost sounds as if you're not one yourself."

Korin gestured uncertainly. "I keep forgetting —"

"Forgetting that you're a mage?" Sylas looked puzzled before laughing.

"It's… a long story. I know this may sound weird, but… I only found out yesterday that I'm a mage."

Sylas stared for a few seconds. "You're telling the truth, aren't you?" he asked almost disbelievingly, and Korin nodded slowly. "If what you're saying is true, then there's so much for you to know. How are you going to —"

"I can explain later," Korin said as they were ushered down an aisle.

With the hall's forty thousand fixed seats – in addition to some extra unfixed seats for the larger students – all present uni faculty, and any other students from the other year groups who willingly attended, had to stand. Most students were chatting and hollering with either newly-formed acquaintances or friends they already knew from their respective high schools. Korin was glad he bumped into Sylas, otherwise he would've kept to himself, feeling awkwardly out of place.

It was the first time Korin was seated with all his mage peers, and although he spent most of the waiting time chatting with Sylas, he tried to absorb as much of his surroundings as possible. Various objects were thrown around, either flying and catching the attention of many with their fluorescent, glittering trails, or bursting and scattering debris over angered people. Sylas wanted to add to the mix of air displays… but he was all out of playful items.

There was a last-minute cancellation to the theatrical welcoming show, but the assembly continued on with Chancellor Helena Valen self-assuredly marching onto the stage, which featured a holographic screen in the air amplifying her image. "Thank you. Thank you, everyone," Helena's voice boomed throughout the hall. "Thank you," she repeated with a more assertive tone until the noise reduced to a minor hum. "Greetings. As some of you may know, I am Helena Valen, chancellor of Teloston University. Now, as newcomers to our university, I would like to first give you my warmest welcome," she said as the hall roared for a good minute, "and wish the very best for your duration here. Every one of you will graduate into a rapidly-changing world. Beta-four-twenty-three is coming to an end, and we draw closer to the dawn of a new era," she announced as zeal radiated from her eyes. "Whilst foundationally paved by the older generations, the era is to be – and will be – determined by the youngest, and then embellished by its posterity. We live in a very interesting period in history. A… Very. Interesting. Period," she delivered sharply, pausing as the hall turned deathly silent. "Your time at university will be met with challenges, pains, joys, and wonders. Throughout every moment, strive for excellence; for afterwards, there will be… many trials and tribulations," Helena said as a dark heaviness burdened her voice. "And good times, of course," she added quickly.

Helena carried on about the students' future, giving examples of recent postgraduates and their outstanding successes. She maintained that it was imperative to uphold the torch of mage teachings wherever alumni may be in the Caelverse. A few of the older, uncaring students were sniggering when they passed Korin in the aisle, having heard similar messages in the past. Korin wondered why they even bothered turning up to the welcoming assembly at all.

Although Korin was listening to Helena, he couldn't help but scan the seated students, noticing more and more losing their attention spans, notwithstanding Helena's spirited deliverance. The Chancellor's speech prompted Korin to think a little more about his future, but he couldn't imagine a single scenario in his head, being lost to his newly-found situation.

Once Helena finished, Korin thought she might have sought him out, but she merely exited the same way she entered. More university faculty took to the stage, drilling the university rules, procedures, and more; they also stated that the food hall wasn't open that night due to a complication. Many students moaned as a result, while both Korin's and Sylas's stomachs rumbled instead.

***

As Korin was exiting the Chalice of Virtue after the welcoming assembly had finished, an information drone appeared, quickly generating a holographic video with a recorded message from the Student Services.

The drone played, "Korin Tarkelt, your allocated room is located at Gamma-M-One-Hundred-And-Twenty-Four, Room Three-Oh-Twelve. For further assistance, please ask any of the assistance drones near the dormitories. Have a nice evening, and welcome to Teloston University."

"Hey, that's next to mine!" Sylas said excitedly.

"What?" Korin asked. "How'd that happen?"

"No idea, but that's cool with me."

To reach the dorms, most students took the subroute, but they were still within walking distance. Arced over two kilometres as part of the gamma sections of dorms, the first-years were essentially split into male and female areas, with many blocks for each group. Transgender, intersex, and non-binary people had to use separate gender-inclusive unisex blocks – and had priority placing for those blocks over any other students who wished to use them, too. The system had positive and negative discourse on both sides of the ideological fence, where protests existed before and after its implementation. Naturally, some of the students preferred having their own blocks – which allowed them to have their own safe spaces away from cisgender people – while others viewed it as degrading segregation. While groups of students like otherkin didn't have their own spaces, unsurprisingly, many decided to live in the aforesaid blocks if there were spaces left, should they not have already identified as transgender, intersex, or non-binary in the first place.

After using the subroute nearby, Korin and Sylas exited the station and arrived at the local dorm emergency, utility, and supply sheds, in addition to a security centre for drones and faculty. There were no roads, so the whole area felt as if part of one giant community.

Wafting past the cobbled walkways, the fresh smell of cut grass pleasantly fused with the sweet aroma of nectar saturating the air. Heart-shaped lockets lined the fence railings inside and outside the dorm block, glowing a variety of bright colours as they drew flashing fireflies partnering up with one another. Formed in a circle, their dorm block consisted of four stone buildings appearing as if one segmented structure, each three storeys high with balconies flush with thick columns engraved with elegant weaving patterns symbolic of the forest. Stone creature faces lined the balcony overheads, expressed in a multitude of ways – some leering, others laughing, and a few even looking as confused as a number of first-years. The edifices homed a courtyard, where a giant, mature tree grew from the centre, shading all the buildings, while a pebble-lined swimming pool circled it. The gazebos around the pool featured roofs pointy and bent like a fairy hats, with their guttering curved over the edges, curling daintily. Various colours speckled the construction, the spots either protruding in luminescent bumps or depressing in glistening pockets. Numerous mushrooms and assorted funguses grew everywhere, most filled with so much energy that a few looked like they would explode, vibrating and pulsing detonating reds. Others appeared like actual light-bulbs, while some piggybacked multi-classed families. Above the buildings in the shade of the giant tree were thin plants that were formed like spider webs, and the wind blowing their strings created soft vibrations in the air, the sound calming on the senses. While the all the buildings in the dorm district were homogenous, they were nonetheless decorated with just enough variances.

Now possessing a place of his own, a sense of security filled Korin; he could have been left homeless about a week ago, so the detailed charms and surrounding conveniences – along with the security guards patrolling in groups – were doubly assuring. Korin's bedroom was on the third floor, with the stairs right beside his room. A physical key was provided, but students could add other securities later. Contrasting the beauty outside, their rooms were basic and bland, containing a single bed, desk, chair, cupboards, and plain, white-painted walls. Students were allowed to decorate of their own accord. There was also a sliding door that opened up to a private shower room as well. Students also had the common rooms in the basement level, and decorating that was more of a democratic, limited process.

There wasn't much for Korin to do in his room, so he stayed in Sylas's, unpacking lots of odds and ends, which had been delivered to the bedroom door earlier. "Hey, what's this?" Korin smirked, picking up a holochite paper comic book with a naked nymph on the front.

"Uh, that's private." Sylas snatched it abashedly.

"I'm not judging." Korin almost laughed, raising his hands in defence. "At least it wasn't some kind of troll; maybe *then* I would think differently." He chuckled as Sylas returned with an odd countenance. "You… don't have comics of trolls having sex, do you?"

"No way! I'm not into *that* stuff."

"So, wait, troll porn exists?" Korin frowned, looking surprised.

"Yeah, I know someone who actually… eehh." Sylas shuddered. "Let's not talk about him. If you want something to read, check these out." He pulled out three paper comic books squared neatly away in a box, titled: *The Amazing Steambot*, *Battlelord Xendor*, and *The Catacomb Portals*. "I have a wide variety. A couple of ultra-rare ones, too. I like their collectible, physical nature over looking at holographic displays. Just be careful with them, please."

"Sure. I understand. I know wouldn't want someone's clumsy hands on my things," Korin said, thinking about his old personal belongings before being surprised that he was even able to finally relax with all the drama he had recently experienced. Although comic books weren't what Korin normally read, reading anything light-hearted felt relieving.

As Korin read, silence settled in while Sylas tried re-piecing one of his cartoon decorative possessions. After a while, Sylas grinned and then asked, "So… did you check out some of the girls?"

Korin pondered for a second before saying, "I thought you didn't want me looking through those comics."

"No, I meant the students here. In real life. Especially the ones that were next to us on the subroute."

From the door, a good-humouredly voice boomed, "You'll totally pick chicks up with those comics of yours." The lad's unkempt hair almost touched the doorframe, while his beefy arms looked like they could have ripped the timber away with his every movement. Cuts and bruises covered his dirtied white arms from previous antics, and his new clothes were already soiled with stains.

Sylas looked up, assuredly responding, "We'll see about that."

Chuckling, the tall guy said, "Sure thing. I'm Jaimas, by the way." He entered, holding his burly hand out to both guys, shaking strongly while receiving their names. "It seems we're neighbours now. I'm right next door to you, Sylas. If you need anything – and if the door's wide open – feel free to walk right in and let me know."

"Okay. Cool." Sylas nodded. "What are you up to now?"

"Actually, I came in to tell you guys that there's a piss-up tonight with a shit load of jinzhao."

"You're getting drunk on your first night?" Korin asked Jaimas.

"Yeah, man!" Jaimas laughed. "It's not like we have assignments due tomorrow. Coming?"

There was no way Korin was going to get drunk, but he wasn't sure how rejecting the offer would affect his future social standing. *Great, what do I say?* he thought before replying, "Um, no, I'm fine. Thanks for asking."

"You're missing out on some real fun. Why not?"

"I… don't drink. Probably has to do with my upbringing." Korin felt awkward, wishing to say no more.

"What? Get out of here! We'll have to do something about that! You'll help him out, though, right?" He turned to Sylas.

"Uh, maybe on the weekend." Sylas shrugged.

Jaimas shook his head. "Well, I'll definitely get you guys to come on New Year's, then. Anyway, I hear a bunch of guys calling for me. I'll see you later." He grinned.

When Jaimas left, Korin said, "For a second, I thought you knew him."

"Nah," Sylas replied. "I think he's just the social-butterfly type."

"Yeah, he seems pretty friendly," Korin said, thinking to himself for a few seconds. "So, do you know anyone here from school?"

"I never went to school; my parents hired professional tutors to teach me while I stayed at home. I did socialize with other people my age, but I mainly kept to myself. I know some of my acquaintances came to Teloston, but I haven't spoken to them in a few months."

"Being school-free would've been easy-going, I take it?"

"Yeah, you'd think, but my parents breathed down my neck about slacking off with work. I hated it. And although the tutors were pretty good at what they did, they felt… confining. I tried to skip as many lessons as I could." He giggled. "So many stories. Anyway, I guess I'm in a similar boat to you regarding social connections. I still could've joined a fraternity, but I think that they would have been too socially restrictive, as you have to do everything together, and I like my freedom."

Sylas's comments felt reassuring to Korin, as the latter's understanding of mage-related topics was limited, so simply going outside and meeting others was a slightly discomforting idea. Korin's continued conversation with Sylas helped him understand more about mages, giving him more peace of mind. He then considered that perhaps mages were a little more similar to many non-mage humans than he originally thought. There were already numerous cultural overlaps, and he was able to relate to Sylas in quite a few ways. And, it helped that his accent wasn't too different either; mages had exerted their influence into the different zones across the Caelverse over the years, after all. Korin also finally told Sylas about his background with the Temple. Sylas was shocked, but not that shocked – he knew that evil lurked everywhere in the Caelverse. There was so much that Sylas wished to ask, but Korin kept it brief, choosing to drip information later.

***

When Korin woke up the following morning, he shooed the usual, no-longer-there stray cat out of habit, and the unexpectedness of his surr-oundings made him pinch himself to establish the veracity of his situation. He looked around his room a few times, breathing deeply before smiling. Students were bustling and grunting outside, carelessly bumping against walls, speedily thudding on floors, eagerly banging on doors, joyfully screaming into the wind, and impatiently throwing a variety of clanging objects around. Although Korin desired to exit his room to see the lively activity, he needed a moment to absorb and process the newness; he then stretched to the furthest corners of his bed before embracing the openness, finally sitting up before wondering what to do until Sylas knocked on his door.

"Hey, I forgot to give you this last night," Sylas said, handing Korin a black watch. "I had that watch for two years, but I wanted a cooler design. Pretty cool, huh?" He showed the steampunk wolf again.

"Yeah, and thanks again. But I don't know how to use it."

"Oh, so it might take a while for you to utilize all of its functions, which means I'll have to show you how to use some things later. Did you have any of that non-mage digital electronic computer stuff where you grew up – especially the augmented reality tech?"

"The boarding school I went to was a bit strict on those things, so our exposure was limited, and I personally didn't own a communications device. It's not like Sacrenderists aren't allowed to use computers, but the Temple does preach a certain level of austerity. So, I guess I've missed out on quite a bit."

"Man, that would be too much for me. Alright, I'll set it up for you."

Using his mind, Sylas activated the watch, and holographic nodes instantly surrounded him before he reset his imprint on the neurachite brain, turning it over to Korin. The nodes then orbited Korin, enabling him to press the phid's basic key functions; although, Korin wasn't accustomed to using his mind to control it, and, instead, he had to use hand gestures, phid buttons, and voice commands. Sylas didn't show Korin much, other than how to make calls. Even other mages never used their minds for most commands, as it was impossible for certain tasks and functions.

After the short tutorial, both guys exited the room and reached the edge of the balcony, where sunlight flickered through the main tree's branches above. Both used one of the building's slides next to the stairs, almost, on the way down, bumping into a grouchy wongahwongah – a dumpy, translucent sapient amphibinoid that moved about on stumpy tentacle-like legs. Its flat nose was barely noticeable, as was its exceptionally-thin lips.

"Ergh!" the wongahwongah grumbled.

"I didn't know wongahwongahs had such a vast vocabulary," one passing student commented, snickering.

Thinking the wongahwongah was an animal for a moment, Korin bent over to pat it, but he desisted when the unusual being leered at him. "Are they all like that?" Korin asked Sylas.

"Nah, most are pretty friendly; but they have every reason to be in a shitty mood. Along with some robots and mages, they apparently clean this place for a living."

"Well, I won't make much mess," Korin told the wongahwongah, smiling. The wongahwongah, however, didn't reciprocate. It continued on, traversing the wall vertically with its suction abilities.

The morning light allowed Korin to see the dorm block in more detail. He noticed a couple of patches of graffiti and engravings, though none were largescale; most were merely small messages from bored or romantically-charged students. Korin observed another wongahwongah cutting the lockets off the railings around the dorm block, which had been left there by previous students. It gazed at each item with a glint of water emerging from its eyes, imagining and wondering; another wongahwongah, in contrast, blandly removed them without a second thought, tired of the experience.

"I wonder how much the uni pays them," Korin said.

Sylas shrugged. "Good question. I doubt it would be much. I think it'd be more interesting to know what they'd actually do with the money. Regardless, from a business standpoint, it doesn't seem like a good idea hiring them, as they aren't that skilled, from what I've heard. I think they're only here due to some government program to help them."

Korin didn't know what else to think on the matter. He then examined the courtyard again before approaching the main tree, impressed by its stature. All of a sudden, the tree rumbled before producing a face, its details of the same texture as the bark. Korin had seen plant-like beings called phytoids before, but never a pure tree that had a humanoid face of bark.

"Greetings!" the tree face said jovially in a deep voice. "Perform a certain action for me, new one, and I'll provide you with lots of secrets!"

Certain action? Korin thought before turning to Sylas. "Do you know anything about this?"

"Nope. I wouldn't trust it, though. It's probably just a charm. That or a holographic projection." Sylas glanced around to see if there was any technology nearby – and, after finding nothing indicative, he then squinted hard at the tree. "Yeah, charm magic, it is."

"I've never encountered a charm before. Or at least I don't think I have. Why not trust it?"

"Who knows who created it? Could be a trap for a practical joke." Sylas giggled. "*I* would definitely set it up for first-years." His giggling intensified. "Come on, let's go. I'm starving."

Korin curiously stared at the tree as he walked back, finally squinting to see if it was actually a charm illusion, but he was unable to see if it was one or not until the face disappeared. Even then, he wasn't able to determine what actually caused the face to emerge.

***

Numerous subroute capsules were active, transporting thousands of people to the Central Hub for breakfast. The enormous food hall was capable of catering to all the undergraduate students at once, while its numerous entrances enabled hundreds to enter simultaneously – in addition to flooding the hall with much sunlight. Moreover, capacity indicators brightly displayed above the entrances to indicate how full sections were inside the Wreath.

The interior themes varied in the building, but for the most part, emblem-fashioned fabrics draped tables, arches, and stands made of ornate timbers. Thoroughly unique in size and shape, pebbles constituted the dark cobblestone half-walls between certain groups of tables, the effect creating a cosier interior design compared to some of the massive, open layouts in other areas of the hall – all the while leaving enough openness to unite the surrounding visible sections as one, united place. Large floral timber beds hung from the creamy ceilings, smoothing out the intensity of the lights behind.

Mouth-watering smells of various delights filled the air, causing stomachs to rumble amidst the background of incessant rumbling and screeching of seats being drawn and tucked. Seeping through the cracks in the wall of chatter, tranquil music accompanied the smell. Students lined up in one of the many queues for their meals, and since there were many mage, robot, and non-human cooks preparing and serving the food, the wait time was short. In addition, students had a choice of food, so Korin and Sylas took the opportunity to heap their plates with nearly every option available. The staff were friendly, smiling and telling the students to dig in. Due to his high metabolism, Korin's tastebuds had adapted to eat nearly anything.

While walking back from the serving line, Korin witnessed many interesting events, such as the staff scolding a bunch of delivery people for not only their reckless transfer of dodgy crates – which were breaking apart – but also lateness, triggering a few surrounding heads to turn. There was also a heated quarrel between two first-years, who began fighting each other, ceasing when a muscular third-year ripped them apart and slapped them across the heads, warning them to 'get over it' a few times. Then, nearby, a bumbling student brushed past multiple people as he attempted to catch a small pet that he accidentally let loose, just as another person tried to enter the hall with a massive, hair-shedding creature – which wouldn't stop drooling – only to be turned back. A few first-years were also playing with some novelty balls, throwing them at each other, creating small, illusory explosions; one landed near Korin, who stood shocked for a second. The student who threw the ball apologized, but Korin could only read his lips due to the noise. Inevitably, one nervous, sickly student spewed up nearby because of food sensitivities; and, since numerous small fruits had previously dropped on the black-tiled floor before being torn and pressed into inexplicable flecks of browned grime, the mess detracted from the otherwise attention-grabbing vomit, causing a few oblivious people to slide over in the puddle. A number of those surrounding the scene laughed to varying degrees.

With all the liveliness around him, Korin's thoughts about his recent religious experiences were yet again placed off to the side as he soaked everything in. While he tried to find a table, though, a piece of paper flew into his face. It was an ad… of 'genderless breast implants'! Korin, of course, quickly grabbed it off his face, throwing it back into the air.

Sylas glimpsed the ad, saying, "Hey, they suit you! You should totally get them!"

"I'm right, thanks," Korin replied coolly. *God, that ad makes no sense.*

"You can't use ad-blockers on paper, so get used to seeing that shit often." He chuckled.

Korin noted what he said, observing people either looking through their phids, stationed holographic displays, or reading various paper flyers being given out, some of which floated about.

Just when Korin found a table, he happened to come across Terala.

"Hey, Korin, how's it going?" she greeted Korin enthusiastically.

"Excellent," Korin replied happily. "I think I'm really going to get used to this. Besides, I've eaten in food halls most of my life; but this one's nicer. A lot nicer. And busier. Oh, this is Sylas. Have you met?"

"No. Nice to meet you." Terala shook Sylas's hand. "So, did you guys see or hear what happened last night?"

"No. What happened?" Korin asked as he took a seat next to Sylas, opposite Terala.

"A bunch of guys got drunk last night and destroyed one of the main statues outside. Hundreds of jinzhao bottles were smashed everywhere."

Sylas looked at Korin with a smirk, saying, "Jaimas."

"Probably." Korin tittered. "We'll soon find out."

Terala continued, "And many were hospitalized with severe injuries."

"Well, we made the right decision not to go," Korin said, stretching his arms out with contentment. "Completely silly."

"What's up, ladies?" Jaimas asked as he suddenly waltzed up to the group, grinning.

"Don't call me lady," Terala answered, glaring at Jaimas, who continued walking as if no-one had said anything.

"Good Sarcof, he's fine," Korin said, puzzled.

"Who or what?" Terala asked with her head askew.

"Oh, it's… just a saying. I guess I have to stop using it now."

"Right," she said slowly. "So, you two know each other well?"

"We only met yesterday," Korin said as he noticed Celine walking by.

The dreamy-eyed girl stopped and gazed around oddly before sitting down next to Terala without any invitation. "I'll sit with you guys," Celine said merrily.

An awkward pause followed.

"Is that a smiley face?" Sylas nodded to Celine's rearranged food; the plate also had glowing, plastic nymph wings attached to the side.

Celine then responded with a coy smile and shrug before Sylas lightly kicked Korin's leg.

"She's fine," Korin muttered. "Hey, Celine, how are you?"

"Very well, thank you. I managed to nearly finish decorating my bedroom before coming here. But I think I might paint the walls later; maybe a korlorn in a purple and aqua forest with lots of crystals. I hope you're settling in?"

"Yeah, I think so. No *major* complaints so far. Anyway, this is Terala and Sylas."

"You look like someone I photo'd the other day," Celine told Terala.

"O-kay." Terala nodded, looking to her side.

"Actually, I captured the image through a surreal-lens filter, so it probably looks a little different. Here." Celine brushed her watch that was decorated with peachy 'flowers', and a concentrated holographic display activated, its default background picture of two illustrated moons smiling and hugging each other with arms. After opening a few files, Celine then showed the group a picture of a deranged-looking girl, who appeared to be bending into multiple dimensions with kaleidoscopic colours all around.

"It looks just like you!" Sylas told Terala, chortling.

"Yeah, thanks," Terala retorted. "Why does it look like *that*?"

"Well, I switched the surreal-lens filter to subjective mode," Celine explained, "so the images distort only when I look through the lens; basically, they automatically change according to my mental perspective."

"What the fuck? Were you on drugs when you took that, then?" Terala asked with a bemused appearance, about to laugh.

"Of course she wasn't," Sylas interjected. "It's the *world* that's drugged, right?" He giggled.

Celine quickly deactivated the screen while staring at the table, her face attempting to remain phlegmatic in front of her hurt feelings.

"Hey, I think it looks pretty cool and arty," Korin said. "Do you take pictures as a hobby or something?"

"Yes!" Celine replied, appearance lifting again. "I have a studio at home for pictures. And I'm also doing a Fine Arts program with a focus on photography."

"Huh. Maybe I should have chosen that. Get outdoors and see things."

"Oh, yes. And I love any place with a great atmosphere, even though I am pretty good at making dull stuff look good. I haven't fully read the course outlines, though, but I can't wait to get started."

"You know what I can't wait for?" Terala asked, deciding to change the subject, not really interested in what Celine was saying.

"Mind-bending drugs?" Sylas quickly answered.

"Yes… Mind-bending drugs. Exactly." Terala rolled her eyes. "Really, though, I can't wait to try out for hillseck."

"Do you think you've got a chance?" Sylas asked her seriously.

"Fuck, yeah! I'll outdo all the guys, too!" She stuffed half a bread roll in her mouth as if victory was already assured.

"What's hillseck?" Korin asked, causing Terala to choke.

After chaotically spitting her food out, Terala shouted, "Hillseck? It's only the best sport in the Caelverse! Where have you been? Living in a totally blackened cave? Oh… yeah… sorry," she mumbled, remembering Korin's background. "It's basically the most popular 'control the hill' game mages play. UHR, or Ultimate Hillseck Rules, to be precise. You should give it a go," she said in a softer tone. "The tryouts for competitive play are next week after our classes. I'm going. Come, see if it's up your alley."

"I think I might do that." Korin nodded his head with excitement.

"What about you?" Terala asked Sylas. "You game? No?"

"I could probably take you on," he challenged her breezily. "But I'll be, you know, busy… and all."

"Sure," she said slowly, grinning. "I get it."

"Hey, we still have to see *you* in the tryouts," Sylas niggled her light-heartedly.

Terala and Sylas's niggling continued as Korin's attention focused on a flyer that fell to the floor; the student carrying the bag of flyers had rushed off before Korin could say anything. Bolded, capitalized, and in large font, '**MISSING STUDENTS**' immediately grabbed Korin's eyes. He stared for a moment before picking it up and reading the text underneath explaining how students had recently been disappearing, and if anyone knew anything about it, they were to report to the university security or police as soon as possible. The faces of the recently missing were also on the flyer. Celine was successfully reading the text upside down, and her eyes enlarged. Terala stopped bantering with Sylas and began staring at Korin; meanwhile, Sylas continued without realizing that Terala had finished. Eventually, he turned to Korin as well.

"What's that?" Sylas asked Korin.

"Here, have a read," Korin said. "Is this typical?"

"I don't think so," Terala replied. "At least not like this."

"It's been happening for a few months now," Korin said. "We better be careful. I remember the priests –"

"Priests? What priests?"

It just occurred to Korin that he hadn't *properly* explained his situation to anyone but Sylas. He wasn't sure where to begin – nor how much to divulge – but after collecting his thoughts for a moment, Korin briefly explained the main aspects of his upbringing, relieved that he unburdened his chest. At the same time, it brought up a lot of negative emotions, though he remained relatively composed.

"That's pretty messed up," Terala stated gravely. "Will this Evelyn chick be okay?"

"Helena said she'd make sure a search party would be organized to look for her," Korin replied.

"How do you feel about abandoning your religion?" Celine asked.

There's… too much to say, Korin thought before answering, "I'll… explain more to you guys later."

"What?" Terala asked. "Come on! Tell us! This shit's big."

"No, I… really don't feel like talking anymore about it. I need some breathing space. I just… I've been through a lot; please understand that. I *will* explain more later. I promise. But anyway, besides what I've experienced, I have a feeling I'm going to be thinking over this whole missing-students thing for a while."

***

After breakfast, the first-years gathered in the Central Hub, where they were broken into groups of roughly forty. Student counsellors and other university staff then accompanied the groups to various spots around the campus. Korin was with Sylas, Terala, and Celine, having stepped out of the food hall together. Rolan happened to be close by, and so when Korin saw the counsellor, he joined up with him. After leading the group through one the thoroughfares in the Provision Wreath to a large tree in the surrounding botanic strip, Rolan merrily discussed what to expect over the course of the semester and how to deal with certain academic and social problems.

"Hey, Rolan," Korin began, "do you know much about the news of missing students?"

"Yes, it does seem quite troubling; but many students 'disappear' all the time, usually because they wag classes and find spots to hide or break out of the university. In saying that now, I hope I'm not giving anyone any ideas here." Rolan chuckled.

"I think you've given Sylas ideas." Korin giggled.

"Then I better keep an eye on you," Rolan replied jocularly.

"What?" Sylas reacted with alarm. "You don't have to worry about me. I'll be in the classes. Probably asleep, but I'll be there!" He laughed. "What about you, Rolan? Did you skip classes when you were younger?"

"Well…" Rolan replied uneasily, "I at least managed to finish uni with good grades." He waved his finger while grinning.

Most in the group laughed, but all were glad they didn't have to deal with an overbearing authority on their first, full day.

When everybody was dismissed just before lunchtime, Rolan approached Korin before heading off. "I see you've made some new acquaintances."

"Yeah, they've been fun to hang out with so far," Korin replied.

"Well, I can make some last-minute changes and place them and yourself in my group for the camp tomorrow."

Korin raised his eyebrows. "Sure. Great. That'll make things a lot more enjoyable."

"No problem. I'll see you after lunch."

With just over half an hour to spare, Korin and Sylas began making their way back to their dormitory. On the way, Korin observed that most students didn't use personal transport like cars – unless they were small devices like hoverboards – as there was very little need, except for when in the auxiliary districts. There were also flying restrictions, so nobody was liberally using magic to jump around the place; it wouldn't have mattered too much, anyway, as there were benefits to using transport over magic, such as being able to relax during the journey. Plus, unbeknownst to Korin, propulsion magic required great amounts of energy, which most mages couldn't sustain for long durations.

When Korin and Sylas surfaced from the subroute at their dorm neighbourhood, both saw a massive crowd gathering and cheering around two people. One was hand-standing on a floating, translucent jelly bubble, while another stood to the side, wearing metallic, spiky apparel. From what Korin overheard, the boys were waiting all night for the large bubble to emerge for their act. The spiky performer told everyone that he would dive through the other side so quickly, the bubble would remain intact, while the other performer would endure on top. The former darted back to a springboard, aligned himself up, then shot right through the bubble, landing into the railing across the other side, mangling his body and shouting in excruciating pain. The bubble burst, like most believed it would, and the hand-standing guy crashed on the ground, almost snapping his neck.

"Ooh!" cried many in the crowd at once. A few couldn't help but laugh at the cringe.

"Are they alright?" Korin asked Sylas in bewilderment.

"Probably not. Let's hope they can walk after that," Sylas said just before entering their dorm block. "Anyway, as I was about to say, what do you think of Celine and Terala? They're both pretty good-looking, hey?"

"Yeah… they seem pretty." Korin grappled with what to say next. "But I'm not looking to ask them out or anything."

"Oh, me either. Celine seems weird, and I think Terala would try and bash me up over the slightest of problems." Sylas laughed.

When Korin reached his room, he left the door open. While sitting on his bed, he saw unidentifiable objects being thrown and skidded back and forth on the balcony. He bobbed his head out the door, seeing a few guys playing around; they looked at Korin, realizing that they needed to take their games elsewhere. At that point, Korin's head started to spin as his eyes rolled around, struggling to stay open. The world around him shrunk as his senses began diminishing. His body still needed a little extra time to recover, having been living on adrenaline for the last day-and-a-bit. Korin told Sylas he'd miss the next activity, going to bed instead. He knew Rolan would understand.

It wasn't just the next activity he missed; Korin didn't wake for the rest of the day, except for a short period after sunset when Rolan checked up on him. Korin was fine; he just needed more rest.

Chapter Five

The Camp – Part One

Early in the next morning, Korin awoke to knocking on his door. At first, he merely opened his eyes, staring at the unlit ceiling without a conscious thought in his head. He shortly fell back to sleep, but the knocking continued, and so he reflexively jolted out of bed.

"I'm coming," Korin called out, stumbling before reaching the door.

"Hey, you ready, man?" a spirited Sylas asked.

"Oh, man, the camp. I haven't even packed." He clumsily rubbed his face, trying to hold his head.

"Don't worry. Rolan gave me this bag with camping supplies to give to you."

"Oh, of course. I forgot I had nothing *to* pack." Korin tried to laugh, grabbing the bag with relief. "Thanks."

"Luckily we were still with Rolan after lunch. Come on, the food hall is open earlier today."

Before heading out, Korin opened the bag and saw a shaving kit. He decided to quickly remove the facial hair he had been unintentionally growing; and after shaving it off, he stared at the fortnight's growth of stubble on his head, wondering what to do with it. He had recently shaved his head in preparation for a religious order he had considered joining; but now free of his religion, Korin felt a little silly having shaved his hair off, so he decided to let it grow again for the time being, brushing his hand against it a few times.

***

After breakfast, a rich orange bloomed over the horizon. Students had been designated their groups the previous night, so everyone knew where to gather for the day.

"Hey, Jaimas is here, too," Sylas noted, seeing the massive lad chatting up two girls. "Did you ask Rolan to place him in our group as well?"

"Nah," Korin replied. "That's a coincidence. I only told Rolan about you three."

"This way, guys." Rolan rounded up his group of forty campers – with a couple of them frowning at his use of the terminology 'guys'. "Remember, when we leave the uni walls, we're still subject to the rules, but the objective is to have fun and learn to work together as a team."

Three plain-looking administration clerks accompanied Rolan – two women and another man.

"Aww, that's a bummer," one student complained. "Some of the other groups get some really cool professors."

Rolan's still great, Korin thought, saying nothing verbally.

"Meh," another student uttered. "I don't intend on listening to anyone, anyway."

Rolan's admin clerks checked each camper to see if they were ready; it turned out one person hadn't even packed. Bickering ensued, and the group was stalled until suitable equipment was found for the student.

"What do you mean we're meant to *carry* our bags?" one bratty student shouted, stamping her feet at the massive amount of luggage around her.

"It's your first test, you stupid first-years!" a second-year student called out as he walked by, laughing.

Another second-year snickered before adding, "Yeah, and you'll be forced to march with all that up gravity-warped mountains."

A nearby first-year then commented, "Maybe you shouldn't have brought an entire shopping mall's worth of clothes with you."

The spoiled girl in question wasn't the only one complaining, however. It took a while, but two of the clerks managed to convince the girls why they didn't need *all* that equipment.

Terala sported green camouflage pants rife with pockets, in addition to a black, athletic tank top; her rough jacket wrapped tightly around her waist, despite the morning's coolness. The pouches on her small, faded backpack contained assorted survival equipment – there was no place for trivialities. Celine's bag also featured numerous compartments, filled, however, with unconventional equipment. Nevertheless, she was appropriately dressed in hiking boots, long khaki shorts, and a buttoned camping shirt. Sylas was also suitably dressed; underneath his professional camping jacket, of course, was another meme shirt. Rolan had provided Korin with plain clothing; having worn similar garments in the past, each piece felt normal to him. No-one had any technology that could connect to social media or the synopool at large, nor any other electronic equipment – be it neurachite or digital – as they weren't permitted on camp.

Celine was reading a physical book off to the side as Terala and Sylas were gathered around Korin.

"Can you believe some of these people?" Terala asked, staring at two meek boys holding large pillows decorated with cartoon girls straight out of an adolescent show. "I have no words. I really don't."

"There's nothing wrong with anime," Sylas countered.

Terala burningly stared at Sylas before replying, "That's not the point. I seriously don't know how they're going to survive without their mothers. *You* don't have one of those pillows, do you?"

"N-no. Of… of course not," Sylas answered awkwardly. "But I don't see the issue."

"How can you… just… I mean, look at them!"

"Okay, I see, but try not to associate *all* bad things with anime."

"Fine." Terala rolled her eyes. "You better not have anime underwear, though. Then you're in for a punching."

"I didn't know you mages had anime," Korin said.

"Yeah, non-mages were the first to create anime," Sylas said, "but then we adopted it and started making our own. Like crazy! I used to watch a lot of it when I was younger, but I don't watch much now."

Terala sighed with frustration. "Anyway, as I was going to explain before: you missed it, Korin. Yesterday, just before finishing orientation,

Rolan took us up on the sky-lift, and we had to guess which building was what; but then two massive freaky-looking birds suddenly started fighting mid-air right underneath us. They kept hitting the lift and almost threw us off, but luckily Celine acted quickly and threw Sylas's sandwiches off, and both birds flew after them. We would've died, otherwise."

"Mm, I'm still a little annoyed," Sylas added glumly. "Not at Celine, but they *were* some *good* sandwiches."

"But they smelled so bad," Terala responded. "That's probably why they went after them." She chuckled.

"What happened then?" Korin asked keenly.

"The zookeepers from the city caught them shortly after that, and we got down as soon as possible. I couldn't stop praising Celine."

"Wow. Any other crazy stuff happen? You had the whole day."

"Nothing crazy. A few fun things happened, but you didn't miss anything that important. I think you should be fine wrestling uni from here."

"Wrestling, eh?" Jaimas joined in. "I hope to see plenty of moaning and groaning in that slippery mud out there today." He nudged Terala before chuckling. "Not with Sylas, though."

Without tiring of the expression, Terala glared at Jaimas. "There are plenty of other girls you can gawk out."

"That's a shame. You look the type that'd do well mud wrestling." He grinned, eyeing her breasts. "I'll have to get some other girls to participate, then."

"Hey, Jaimas," Korin interrupted, "what happened to you the other night?"

"Oh, man, that was one night to remember! I'm totally out of jinzhao; but don't worry, I brought some... *marshmallows.*" He opened a suspicious pouch full of marshmallow-looking snacks. "There's enough to go around. Well, I'm actually going to make some deals now, so I'll *try* to save one for each of you." Jaimas patted Korin on the shoulder, taking off.

"Is he always that obnoxious?" Terala asked Korin and Sylas.

"We only met the other day," Sylas answered, "so who knows?" He then rapidly tapped his wrist. "Damn, I keep forgetting that I'm not wearing my watch. I hope I don't go nuts out there."

"Well, we'll tie you up if you do," Terala said, turning around to see Jaimas grinning. She then turned around again, not even bothering to dignify his dirty thoughts.

***

The first-years split up across parts of the province. On the way to his destination, Korin finally explained his background to Rolan, whose responses were very supportive and helpful. However, the counsellor didn't have too much time to attend to Korin, as he had other duties to focus on. Their subroute capsule soon reached an enormous camping ground in a cool forest, very similar to the one near Orchopolis. There were very few non-unichite-powered vehicles parked outside the area, and every group that arrived had to walk to their allotted locations, separating down different dirt trails.

"Here's a timetable of all the activities we'll be doing this long weekend," Rolan said as the admin clerks handed out flyers, which also contained camping and emergency information. "Let's keep things on track so we don't miss out on anything." He noticed a few students already tiring of their backpacks. "The cabins shouldn't be too far away from here."

"Is this forest clear of dangerous creatures?" Korin asked Rolan, thinking back to the mutated khastwolves that chased him.

"Yes, this is a designated camping area, so it's protected. No need to worry. This way, folks."

"So, do you normally work through weekends like this?" Korin asked as both he and Rolan led the way.

"Sometimes I do, but then I might have days off during the week. It depends. Regardless, I love working."

Being a counsellor wasn't the type of job Korin would ever envisage doing. He again tried to imagine what he'd do after university, realizing he still couldn't make a proper judgement, given his lack of knowledge on mage careers. "Do you have any kids at Teloston?" Korin asked, brushing past an overhanging branch.

"Uh… no… no, I don't," Rolan answered uncomfortably.

Intuiting something unusual with Rolan's reply, Korin slowly asked, "Are they too young or old, or is this a private matter?"

"It's –" Rolan sighed. "My family passed away a couple of years ago."

"Oh, I'm sorry to hear that." Korin regretted pursuing him.

"I'm okay now." He waved his hand in appreciation.

After a moment of uncomfortable silence, Korin was compelled to ask, "If you don't mind me asking, what happened?"

"They passed away in an accident. I prefer not talking about details, if you understand what I mean."

"Sure. Was this your wife and kids or other family, too?"

"Wife and kids. Two daughters and a son. I met my wife through an adventure course in a place similar to this, actually. Some of the best moments of my life. Anyway, students are like family now, so I treat everyone with the best possible care."

I think I get where he's coming from now, Korin thought, avoiding a massive ant nest on the way.

"I know it's hard for you because you don't remember your parents."

"Well, I have fleeting memories. I remember being on a large swing, and I fell over and hurt myself. My father came around and picked me up and gave me something. I can't remember what. And there are a couple of other memories, but that's it. Usually, there was a semi-interesting event."

"At least you had those very important first years with your parents; otherwise, you might have turned out drastically different."

"Are you saying I could've been bad or deranged in some way?"

"The young are incredibly malleable to whatever environments they're raised in."

"I see." Korin thought about his religious upbringing, resurfacing a suppressed anger. The whizz and thrill of his new mage environs had mostly drowned out the terrible experience he had the other week, along with his religious memories. He was about to turn intensely introspective on the matter, but too much was happening around him to concentrate.

On arrival, Rolan addressed administration and logistics before the students unloaded their gear in two of the three matching cabins. Wooden panels corked the windows, while a few slowly squeaked back and forth in the breeze. Weeds managed to squeeze through the floorboards – a few boards even sounded as though alive, groaning from having to yet again accommodate students without the prospect of retirement. The bunkbeds' stick-thin frames blended into the walls around them; as a welcomed feature amongst the ruggedness, they at least contained fresh mattresses.

All the boys dumped their gear on the beds, heading outside soon after. In the central area was a barbeque pit with a burnt animal on the spit, too far gone for even the crows and ants to bother with consuming. On the hill about fifty metres away were the outhouses, and although it wasn't scary looking at the site during the day, some of the students knew venturing out at night would be daunting. Most of the girls were still in their cabin, many moaning and complaining about their accomm- odation; some of the other first-years, they heard, were in luxurious locations. Thinking it would be funny, one of the boys picked up the dead animal and threw it on the girls' steps. As the ladies exited, a few screamed, while the boys laughed.

"It was the old cabin ghost," one guy claimed, laughing.

"That's not funny!" a girl shouted, scowling.

One of the female clerks told the troublemaker to clean the mess up before the students dispersed around the campsite, chatting in smaller groups.

On the way to the outhouse, Korin espied a girl in the near distance by herself. He studied her for a moment before caving in to his curiosity, unhurriedly walking over. Facing at his ten o'clock underneath a shading tree, the girl was drawing in a decent-sized sketchbook, thoroughly abs- orbed in her work; but as Korin approached, she immediately stopped and closed it. Stark black attire covered a slim physique, coupled with long black boots that were capable of subduing any man in seconds. The girl's dark hair reached below her shoulders, contrasting greatly with her pale white skin.

She turned her head slightly, critically saying, "You stepped into my circle."

"Sorry, what?" Korin asked, looking around, seeing a line drawn in the dirt around him, fortified with small rocks.

"It's rather obvious, isn't it?" she asked sharply, remaining in the same spot, though Korin didn't reply, speculating why she had drawn a circle. "Well? Are you going to leave now? Don't just stand there."

"Uh, o-kay," Korin said, slowly stepping out of the ring. "I didn't mean to –"

"I understand. You're careless. You're *all* careless," she said with a razor tongue. "And stupid."

Korin felt a wave of hatred hit him before he awkwardly responded, "Right, well, I'll… leave you to it."

He was about to back away when she turned to properly see him. Her face was amazingly pretty, perfect with delicate features, but her eyes stood out the most; blue and silver as if reflecting a wintery, mystical landscape, they pierced right into Korin – *right* into him.

"Wait!" she said, pausing as she continued staring into his soul. "You're different from the others. Aren't you?" She broke into a smile.

Korin's response was stalled as he wasn't sure what to say again.

"I take it back," she said, smile enduring. "What's your name?"

Sensing an odd presence emanating from the girl, he carefully said, "Korin. Korin Tarkelt." He smiled slightly.

"Well, I'm Priscilla Maycraft, and… I have a feeling we'll be spending quite a bit of time together on camp." Her smile turned mischievous.

Feeling as if her comment was peculiarly intimate, Korin asked, "Does this mean I can step into your circle now?"

"Mmm…" She looked up cheekily. "No, stay where you are for now," she said with an easy-going tone.

Korin tried thinking of something else to say, but he felt her presence warping his energy. He nodded, wondering what the flaming potion was going through her mind. Her flip in attitude threw Korin off, so he wanted to know a bit more about her in order to find out why she was so aloof and strange. He eyed her sketchbook, finally asking, "Do you like to draw?"

"Absolutely. Here, have a look," Priscilla said, opening her pad to reveal a fantastically-drawn and coloured picture.

Her own fantasy creature was in the centre, seemingly of the forest around it. Its head was purely skeletal, while its tree-branch arms contained many thorns and poisonous-looking flowers. The creature, however, was fuelled by a black, whirling energy underneath, appearing as if opening up to an evil dimension. Around the being were humans creepily hanging from ropes with their blood dripping on the ground, feeding the tiny critters emerging from the energy.

"Do you like it?" Priscilla asked, looking rather proud of her work.

"It's…" Korin held his neck, thinking it was a little too dark for his tastes. "It's well done, I guess."

"Why, thank you! It's better than that A.I. trash so many people 'make'. Maybe… maybe I should summon the creature." Her eyebrows elevated with excitement. "Now, wouldn't *that* be the delight to see?"

Her comments disturbed Korin immensely, creating dread across his face.

"Only joking. I don't have the power to summon anything of the like." She giggled. "Anyway, I plan on drawing what happens at camp." She grinned. "Maybe you'll be in it."

What? God, I hope nothing bad happens, Korin thought, about to shake his head. "Um, well, I do have to go…" He pointed to the outhouse.

"Of course. We can talk later." Priscilla waved, leaving Korin to stiffly turn around and awkwardly walk away.

Korin was unsure what to make of Priscilla, but as he was departing, he could *feel* Priscilla staring at him.

***

The first activity required a unique lake that was covered in a special thin sheathe of crystals, enabling people to literally jump on it without falling into the water. The adjoining mountains snugly and humbly wrapped the area without obscuring the skyline, allowing the early light to shoot over and shimmer brightly off the lake's glowing surface.

Rolan had his shoes off, moving the dirt between his toes as he announced, "The first activity involves a unified team effort in order to complete." He then gave a short lecture on teamwork, making sure everyone understood. "While you likely won't break the lake's surface, in the event that you do, don't worry, the lake is so salty that you will float, anyway. So, we're going to tie you all together, and you'll have to make it across the lake through the hoops. We'll try different combinations in the next rounds. Gather in, everyone."

"Um, how close are we getting to each other?" one student asked.

"Yeah, some people here smell," another person added while others snickered.

"People, people!" Rolan called out. "You'll have to put all that aside while you work together. Let's see if we can break a record." He looked into the distance, noticing something. "We'll see you on the other side."

The admin clerks began tying everybody together, first by encircling the group as a whole, then by weaving between people, restricting their mobility within the whole. Priscilla quickly moved next to Korin, grabbing his arm and placing it next to hers so they could be tied to each other. She shiftily smiled at him before staring back at the lake. Too confused about her agenda, Korin didn't react. It was too late to move, anyway, as he and Priscilla were interlocked with the surrounding campers. Everyone on the outside of the collective faced outwards, while the people on the inside were unevenly faced, tightly squished together. Rolan had already left, with two of the clerks only just departing as well.

"You like it tight, don't you, Jaimas?" a camper joked.

"Fuck, yeah! I love the ropes!" Jaimas responded, grinning.

"Great, you've got him aroused now," another person also jested.

"Not as much as Sylas," Jaimas added.

"In your fantasies," Sylas retorted.

Korin was about to comment, but the rope around his left arm suddenly tightened. "Ow! What are you doing?" he asked Priscilla as she twisted her arm.

Priscilla quickly let go before quietly saying, "I'm just having a little fun. You seemed bored." She shrugged nonchalantly.

Korin squinted at Priscilla as he tried to peer into her mind, worrying if matters would escalate into something terribly adverse. Just as Priscilla was about to say more, an obese student enormously farted, and a great commotion commenced.

"Come on, guys, we have to beat the record!" Terala cut in. "Are you timing this?" she asked the remaining admin clerk.

"Eh, I can restart the timer," the young clerk responded unenthusiastically. "Just tell me when you're ready or I'll start whenever you leave."

"Good," Terala said. "How come you're the only one coming with us right now?"

"Rolan only just realized that he needed to set something up," he explained blandly. "They'll be able to watch, though."

The continuing commotion fractured Korin's concern over Priscilla, enabling him to focus on the task. "We need to come up with a plan first," he called out.

"We don't need a plan. Let's just go already!" one large student cried out, pulling the collective with him.

"Whoa, hang on! We need to think this through!" Korin shouted as the group fell over.

Crashing and bouncing on the gelatinous sheathe, the group created waves that rippled out and back. They mangled their bodies into a mess as half the people lay on top of someone else. Korin happened to be off to the side, so he avoided being in both of those awkward positions. Still, Priscilla was rammed up close to him. Complaining noisily for a few minutes, many tried to explain their solution without success.

Korin, however, convinced most to give him their attention before loudly saying, "The people on top need to fling themselves together on three, while the ones underneath need to push at the same time. One," Korin said shakily, wondering if they were even listening. "Two," he said slowly, anticipating failure. "Three," he called out, and everyone successfully regrouped upright. Korin then continued explaining what they needed to carry out.

"What about the hoops?" Sylas asked.

"We'll figure that out when we get to them," Korin replied, mind filled with several strategies and potential fiascos.

Listening to Korin, the campers all synchronized, progressing rather well. The sheathe continued to hold without breaking anywhere, but trace amounts of rubbery splodges did splash on the students' bodies. Their footwear even made some imprints in the sheath. Ripples across the surface erratically reflected the sunlight, periodically blinding the students, just as the lake's crystals wafted up a peculiar, salty smell. Heads knocked into each other, and feet were trampled on; and although painful, it comparatively wasn't as awful as the experience of having one's face consistently rub up against a sweaty, smelly armpit! As the campers complained, Korin masked his discomfort, biting his tongue at times.

When it came time for the oval hoops, it was a different story altogether. As Korin climbed through the first hoop, the waves crashed against him, making him fall; the other people around him not only fell as well, but they twisted themselves up in the ropes and each other – one even hit his head on the steel hoop. In a disjointed throng, the campers were divided within the ring. The second half of the group struggled to climb through, but the waves created a counterbalancing effect.

Celine's body began sinking into a fat student's body, her face almost drinking from his man-boobs. She managed to grasp an unseeable, separate rope, escaping to find herself upside down. Terala writhed, thinking she could lead the way, though she only made her state of affairs worse as the ropes knotted around her, leaving her with contused wrists. Sylas couldn't help but poke fun at the situation, tricking a few people about what was happening.

After a strenuous effort, the young mages managed to figure out a solution, making it through the hoop; and with the same technique, they hopped through a few more hoops, reaching the centre of the lake.

"Hey, we're doing pretty well," Terala commented just before waves emerged nearby.

"Um, what's that under the water?" Celine nervously asked those aligned with her vision.

"What's what?" one of the students asked, jerking fitfully.

"Is it an object or a creature?" another asked in a panic.

"I think it's alive," Celine said, scaring them again.

No-one moved.

Apprehensively, everyone critically scanned the waving water, with one camper finally shrieking, "Oh, crap, I see it, too! It's coming for us!"

Within moments, most of the campers hysterically tossed around as they managed to spot the moving blur underneath as well. A brownish-green tentacle swiftly moved around the group, rapidly piercing through the lake's sheathe and rising high into the air. Magnetizing assorted barnacles, the tentacle whooshed around, dispensing large blobs of crystals that splattered hard onto the remaining unpierced sheathe.

"Fuck, fuck, get the ropes off me!" one person cried out, failing to untie the complex knots.

"They're too hard to get off!" another complained.

"Help us!" one cried for the admin clerk.

"Oh! I've never fought a monster before!" the clerk replied pathetically, shaking with fear. "Um… um… um…"

"Why don't you fucking shoot it?" Terala demanded.

"Oh, yes… um… okay." The clerk began to focus. "I need time to connect my aura up."

"Then hurry it up!" Terala continued.

"Please be patient!" The clerk shook, almost losing his wits. "Wait here. I'll get Rolan while I power my lumarchetrix."

The clerk fumblingly ran towards where Rolan was meant to be, but no-one was there. While everyone's attention was concentrated on the aerial tentacle, another sneaky limb surfaced and slowly slid around a couple of unsuspecting students, startling them with its smooth, though shell-covered skin.

"Don't scream. Don't scream," one of the boys told the girl next to him.

The lass, however, reacted immediately, almost deafening him as he stood locked right next to her mouth. The screaming wasn't enough to alarm the tentacle, but the curious appendage continued inspecting various people, feeling their skins for strengths and weaknesses. Another girl started kicking the tentacle, managing to inflict a fair amount of damage; enough, in fact, to make it shudder and submerge.

"Great!" one person shouted. "Only one more left."

"Who knows how many there are?" another rhetorically asked.

"There's no time to stall!" Korin shouted. "We need to get moving now. On three, everyone."

The gaggle of campers became a somewhat cohesive bunch, but it wasn't long until more limbs fiercely rose. Priscilla didn't say anything in her distress, remaining as close to Korin as possible. Jaimas repeatedly shouted, believing that he was drawing attention to himself, when he clearly wasn't. Meanwhile, Sylas and Celine hopelessly looked around, unable to do a thing to help out. Aggravated and annoyed, the underwater beast testingly lunged one of its tentacles at the edge of the group.

"Jump!" Korin shouted as everyone tried to bounce out of the way.

Their collective jump alone wouldn't have saved them, so the group also needed the waving sheathe to bounce them even further. Barely missing the attack, their efforts in dodging the tentacle came at the price of tangling themselves. Twisted and convoluted as they squirmed, some of the campers were upside down, legs and feet on top of faces.

Two people managed to break free before attempting to untie the others. Terala also managed to finally grab her pocketknife, but just as she was about to free herself, she slashed one of the tentacles that whipped across horizontally. It jerked upwards before fully ascending back again, bleeding profusely. Blood splashed on Terala, but she merely wiped it away, ready to continue slashing. The next tentacle was about to strike right down the centre of the group; and when it seemed like the campers were done for, a bright blue, fist-sized energy blast of magic energy, from the distance, shot it back with a repulsive force.

Rolan and the other admin clerks rapidly fired blast ball after blast ball from their hands, warding off the tentacle until it retracted back into the water. When the faculty arrived at the horde of students, they began hastily cutting the ropes, with many campers reaching out for their hands to be freed first. But just as it appeared like hope had been achieved, there was an intensely-loud rumble, and the water vibrated as if something was about to shoot through the entire group.

At once, everyone stalled for a moment in petrifying silence before hurriedly continuing on. One by one, the untied lot clumsily fled, many stumbling on the way. Korin was one of the last to take off, having to help a hopeless person who could barely move. With the guy's arms around his shoulders, Korin swore he was going to sink under, especially when he faltered a couple of times; it didn't help when the rumbles strengthened as the water shook evermore. Korin stared -- frowned -- straight ahead, concentrating on the edge of the lake. The tentacles at last re-emerged, but by then, most of the people had fled to the other side of the lake. While still on the lake next to Korin, Rolan turned around, blasting the multiple, furiously-shaking tentacles with more magic. Terala ran back into the lake, quickly helping Korin with the mentally-paralysed student, moaning along the way. The mysterious beast, however, didn't move toward the mages, who all soon reached land; its underwater form was too big for the shallowing water, and it accordingly remained in the lake, shortly submerging totally out of sight.

"Why would you put us through that?" someone indignantly asked Rolan before anyone could even begin to relax.

"And where were you the whole time?" another raged.

Rolan diplomatically responded, "We were watching you while setting up a device, but an issue arose that needed resolving, so we momentarily moved out of sight. There wasn't meant to be anything in the lake."

"Well, there was!" An angry student flipped his arms about.

"I want to go back now," another added, crying.

"Yeah, back through the lake!" Terala enthused at a disapproving and shocked group. "I'll do that again!"

As the clerks started head-counting, Rolan said, "Students have been using that lake for years. Nothing has ever attacked anyone. We're truly sorry for what happened."

"That's not good enough!" an infantile student shouted. "We need a safer space! A safe space! Take us back!" She brought out a wristband stating, 'You Deserve a Safe Space!'. "Now!" She screeched, shaking her fist at Rolan. "Now! Now!"

Terala responded, "Oh, come on! We're safe now."

The screeching student continued until three others joined her, each with pursed fish-lips. Without any clever or humorous intent, their clothing, too, appeared suited for children. Collectively, they shouted, "Now!"

Rolan and the female admin clerks were unsure how to respond, while the male clerk looked too nervous about doing anything.

The four students then formed a slowly moving circle, huddling together as they blubbered. "It's okay," one of the crying students croaked. "If we can't go back to our safe space, we'll create one here."

"What on Juntas are they going to try and do?" Terala asked quietly.

Another four students approached the circle, comforting the criers as they leered at Rolan and the clerks. The crying grew louder before the weak-minded students collapsed onto the ground, shouting as if in utter pain. One began choking before vomiting, her sickly saliva dripping endlessly. Red faces produced throbbing veins, half-covered in messy hair, which was tugged at madly.

Despite the anger held toward the supervisors, quite a few of the campers were also taken aback at the level of sensitivity on display, remaining mute. It was completely understandable to be upset and shocked over the terrifying incident, but the blubbering campers were taking it to another level. In fact, given their troubled, deep-seated emotions – and any excusable and sympathy-needing PTSD they may have had – they would've cried, anyway, even if the situation was much, much lighter. Whether contextual or in general, a safe space itself, moreover, was indeed desirable and justified, but a strong element of immaturity was imbued with their actions, and that nuance became more and more evident to many in the surrounding crowd, who placed their distress way off to the corner so they didn't act like the criers.

All of a sudden, Terala started laughing her head off, having to curl up on the ground as she lost control. A few other people caught the bug half a minute later, joining Terala to a lesser extent. The safe-spacers turned around and began screaming their lungs out, sharply cutting through and ending the laughter.

"Everyone!" Rolan shouted, quickly stepping into the middle. "Everyone needs to calm down now! We'll let you have your space," he told the criers, "and the rest of us will also take a break back at the cabins. Now!"

"Does this mean we'll miss the next activity?" Sylas asked.

"Yes, but it's mainly because it also requires the lake. Regardless, what's important is that we all work together."

Many people moaned. Terala, meanwhile, quickly changed her attitude, punching a tree. One clerk remained with the weak-minded students as the two groups separately made their way back to the campsite.

***

"Great," Terala muttered, kicking a stone. "I can't believe we're missing out on activities thanks to a bunch of cry-babies."

"That was unbelievably crazy," Korin said. "Is that normal behaviour? Common, I mean."

"I hope not. I remember cry-babies in school, but I never associated with them. At least it wasn't everybody here."

"I remember seeing events like that in school," Celine said. "But I was only in school for two years. Still, I do like safe spaces… but I would never want to be in their safe spaces. They don't feel right, and they wouldn't be safe for me."

Around the barbeque pit, the four students that had comforted the safe-spacers were heckling Rolan.

"Hey, guys," Korin butted in, "give Rolan a break. He's already justified himself. This was a rare incident."

"Even *if* it wasn't his fault, he still didn't accommodate for their feelings!" one heckler rebutted.

"Oh, give *me* a break!" Terala joined in. "Your sorry asses are screwed with *that* kind of attitude. How the fuck will you ever fend for yourselves in the face of danger?"

"Korin's only trying to make things fair," Celine added, and when the attention turned to her, she turned slightly red.

"Yeah, what they said," Sylas chimed in, snacking on a few nuts.

Korin was thankful that Celine, Sylas, and Terala helped, but he was too flabbergasted to add anything else.

"Thank you," Rolan responded. "I'll still take full responsibility, but I hope this hasn't ruined our weekend. Can we press on?" he asked the surrounding campers, who mostly mumbled with acceptance. "Fantastic. You did quite well on the last challenge, anyway, from what I heard. We'll carry on with the third activity soon."

When the students dispersed, Korin walked off by himself, needing his own safe space from all the ludicrousness. With his hands on his hips, Korin stared into the expanse ahead, lost in thought. After a few minutes of calmness, Celine neared, taking pictures of a flower with a basic, non-neurachite camera that she managed to sneak into camp.

She continued taking shot after shot, not *so* much to obtain the perfect image but, instead, to acquire multiple unique perspectives.

When Celine stood up, she approached Korin, fiddling with a few settings. "Hey, how are you feeling?" she asked softly.

"Okay," Korin answered coolly, his stare unmoving. "Just a bit disturbed by a few things."

"Maybe this will take your mind off things." She showed Korin a weird piece of graffiti she had taken. "Disturbing, right?" she asked perkily as Korin frowned. "Sorry."

"You're fine. I'm just concerned about –" He glanced over at Priscilla, who was continuing her drawing. "Never mind. Enjoying yourself?"

"Yes. I'm a little shaken up about the monster, but I should be fine."

"How did you manage out there? I couldn't see you."

"I don't think anyone could have seen me." She shuddered. "Not really the most pleasant of experiences, let's just say."

"And yet you're quite understanding of Rolan's situation. It's nice to know you're not retarded like some of the people here."

Celine awkwardly nodded. "Thanks. Let me know what's troubling you later."

Korin stood where he was as Celine took off, taking pictures along the way.

***

The third-scheduled activity was deep in the forest, involving a gargantuan tree with leaves so dense, most of the sunlight only shone through the gaps in the neighbouring canopy. Assorted fungi of nearly all manner of shapes and colours sheathed the massively-thick trunk; and high above, each mossy branch extended out erratically as if an entity possessed it. The tree and surrounding area weren't entirely natural; certain types of species tended to particular areas in the world, mystically grooming and guiding matter on an etheric level so it would develop in a particular way. Many of such beings were fairies.

"We'll use this tree for two of our activities," Rolan addressed the campers before everyone had to place protective equipment on, like helmets and padded suits. "The ground here is incredibly soft." He stomped his feet, partially sinking into the dirt. "So, if you fall, you'll barely get hurt. And the spores in the air will slow your fall, too. We'll let you try multiple times, and we'll play different games. Use the mushrooms to climb; but be warned, a couple of them will try to smack you if you get aggressive with them. You'll need to also watch for sap bubbles, which may momentarily ensnare you; but they won't hurt you. Rest assured, everything is fine. You're safe here. Remember, this will require a team effort. Are there questions?" he asked, and a couple of silly questions were fired his way. After answering the last of them – and also after attempting, yet failing, to convince the four main weak-minded students to participate – Rolan said, "Okay, your time starts... now!"

"Remember, guys," Korin announced to everyone, "we worked well when we had a plan instead of rushing through."

"Nah, fuck that!" one student yelled, running up to the trunk.

"Yeah, who died and made you the boss?" another asked, laughing at Korin.

Most of the students followed on, running up to the closest mushroom group. The girl who laughed at Korin also tripped over before even reaching the tree. With his frustration building, Korin was the last to take off, forgoing teamwork.

The first set of mushrooms was able to hold approximately five people before it caved in, rutting the surplus. Those who got stuck in the mushrooms tried climbing out, but their hands merely slid down the smooth surfaces. Students on the subsequent mushrooms reached down to those who were trapped; but as they did, other people began climbing up to *their* mushrooms, ruining those as well. When both sets of fungi had caved in, the campers scattered, running around the trunk to find their own approach points. In so doing, the first lot of students managed to resolve their situation.

Korin found his own starting point, climbing up to where a rainbow set diagonally grew above him. Its ridged texture allowed him to grip on and find his footing, but some of the colour transferred to his gloves.

He worried if it would spread, but it didn't, and so he relaxed after a moment of waiting. The next set of mushrooms was flat, so he easily reached for it; and, when he climbed on, the centre made a gulping nose before expanding like a giant boil, causing Korin to slide off. He lightly hit his helmet back on the rainbow set before 'falling' to the ground — or more like he quickly sank through the thickened atmosphere of translucent, yellowy-white spores that electrostatically charged up via Korin's increased but accordingly slower-than-normal velocity.

"Great," Korin moaned, readjusting his helmet.

He scanned the trunk for Sylas, Terala, and Celine, but he couldn't see them, guessing they were on the opposite side. Instead of trying the same path, Korin climbed up a new set of mushrooms, eventually situating between two unusual groups of fungi. The first was a sphere that bubbled out like chewing gum, shaking intensely as it reached its maximum size. To his left, the flat mushrooms fanned up and down; and since Korin didn't have much choice, he decided to reach for the latter. However, the first mushroom simply limped, leaving him hanging where a student from above abruptly came crashing down, hitting Korin on the way, who also fell to the ground again, missing the camper by centimetres.

His frustration grew.

Korin looked up, seeing other people falling through mushrooms that had opened up holes in their centres — in addition to soft fungi that acted like giant mallets, whacking the young mages who aggressively abused them. Korin finally spotted Sylas, who was quite a fair way up; but Sylas shortly fell, landing in a fluorescent-yellow 'octopus' mushroom that entangled him unintentionally. Sylas tried to twist, jump, and rip his way out, but he stopped, cursing at the mushroom. Terala was nearby, and she was about to leap to Sylas's aid, but the mushroom she was on was extremely sticky. She attempted to move her feet, but she couldn't budge. Wanting to help, Korin didn't wait to see what would happen, finding another set of ground mushrooms to climb up.

After ascending a few sets, Korin saw Celine in the distance by herself, off in her own world as she played with a fuzzy bulb reacting funnily to her movements. Although fine, she was virtually inaccessible, puzzling Korin as to how she could've reached her location. Another student above Korin fell, but this time, Korin was prepared, dodging in the nick of time.

As Korin continued climbing, he noticed holes in the tree, and a body-sized sap bubble emerged from one. Korin immediately knew he had to flee, so he leapt to the next set of mushrooms, almost losing grip. While it wasn't aggressive, the bubble intimidatingly followed in eerie silence as Korin trembled and squirmed, frantically kicking his legs back into the air to gain enough momentum to pull himself up.

Jaimas neared Korin, and the sap bubble turned and latched onto the former, bubbling and whisking the big lad down to the ground without any further drama, bursting on impact. Relieved and a little surprised, Korin then reviewed his options, realizing the closest set was a bit too high to reach. Priscilla, however, was on top, smiling as she looked down.

"Here," she said, holding her hand out.

Korin reached his hand up, but Priscilla quickly removed hers, giggling as she moved on.

I can't believe her, Korin thought. *What's her problem?* He shook his head irately before trying to scurry up the trunk to reach the mushroom above. He slid back.

Priscilla then popped her head out, reaching her hand down again. "Okay, I'm sorry." She grinned. "I'll help you this time."

Korin didn't reach for it, staring at her coldly instead.

Priscilla shrugged. "Your loss. I really wanted to help you this time."

"Fine," Korin said, reaching out his hand with a grave look.

Priscilla actually let Korin grab on, but she let go when a large group of pixies unexpectedly surrounded the tree. Compared to city-dwelling pixies, the present ones exhibited dreadlocks and other folky hairstyles, while their apparels were simple cloths decorated with the charms of the forest, like dried leaves. Leaving a faint trail of twinkling dust behind them, the pixies spun and zipped around for a moment.

"Hi," one of the pixies peeped, waving at Korin warmly. "Don't mind us." She, along with the other pixies, entered the tree's tiny holes, zooming in and out as they filled their pouches with small seeds. "Sorry, but we have to go," the pixie told Korin. "You mages should be able to defend yourselves when they come." She waved as she flew away.

Not liking the sound of 'they', Korin soon heard another buzzing noise in the distance before seeing the actual hoard of bugs. A metre in diameter, the tartulemoes – who were not native to Juntas – were vein-bulging bags of pus, with numerous antennas on top, working as their major sensory organs. Beyond that, they really only had wings, a gnashing mouth, and a drooping anus; most were drooling at both ends. Funnily enough, they weren't actually mutants.

"Get ready!" Korin pointed. "They're about to attack us!"

Rolan and the clerks had to again take a moment to connect to the supreme cosmic field of energy that permeated everything in existence before they could use their magic; but this time, they were able to do so in advance before the bugs arrived. Once tuned into the cosmic field of energy, they began magically shooting green blast balls of energy, while the students either hid in or around their mushrooms. A few jumped off the tree, finding cover elsewhere.

If only I could use magic right now, Korin thought.

Standing his ground, Korin fretfully grappled an incoming bug by the antennae, surprised he actually was able to grab them at all. The bug's gnashing mouth sent his mind haywire, and although the antennae were disgusting to touch with their twitching and fluttering responses, he didn't let go until he swung the bug heavily into the trunk, causing it to deflate slightly as it fell. A gas lingered behind – one so rotten, it made Korin gag. He wasn't sure if he'd have enough oxygen to handle the next bug, thinking perhaps diving his face into a mushroom and breathing its spores up close would have been a better option than continual gagging. As Korin was still catching his breath, the oncoming bug was shot down unconscious. He glanced around, noticing that it was Rolan who took care of the matter. Wanting to shout out his gratitude, Korin ended up saying nothing so as not to distract the counsellor.

Numerous sap bubbles popped out of the tree, bubbling the bugs and overwhelming them with their cleanliness. Even the funguses participated in the action, walloping the bugs. There happened to be a tartulemoe right above Korin, fighting with a mushroom; but it soon got a good thumping, crashing down to the fungus Korin was on. The bug was still conscious, but it could barely move, and Korin nudged it over with his foot.

Before any harm could be done to anyone, the still-conscious buzzing pus-bags learned who their superiors were, reverting to the literal shit-hole they emerged from earlier. A few remained, though they were unconscious on the ground, gradually emitting their putrid gas. Most of the campers cheered, but a few nevertheless cried hopelessly. Another couple growled with anger.

"This is the second time something bad has happened!" a girl shouted to Rolan.

Terala asked, "Have you been living in your mum's baby sling your whole life? Shit like this happens all the time in the wild. Deal with it!"

"Yeah, be grateful Rolan was here!" Korin added. "You guys are a bunch of bloody babies."

"Oh, shut the fuck up, Korin!" one of the students yelled.

Korin scowled as all desire to continue climbing the tree blew away. Prior to coming to the camp, Korin didn't expect such interactions with his peers. He had unconsciously built a mental wall around himself after the religious ritual, preparing for anything potentially bad, both on a life-and-death *and* socially-integrative level. But the vexatious and childish egos at present were of a different variety; they were just too unbelievable for the mental wall to even grasp, slipping through the cracks and over-riding his tolerance levels. His frustration reached its tipping point, and he jumped down, storming off without looking back, despite hearing several voices calling for him. One of the clerks followed.

***

It was lunchtime back at the campsite, and Korin was sitting by himself on a log seat, staring depressingly at nothing. Not even the numerous bright candy wrappers fossilized in the hardened mud gained his attention.

"Hey, you okay, man?" Sylas asked, sitting down next to Korin.

Korin slowly sighed. "Yeah, I'll be fine. I just needed a moment." While he wanted to focus on another topic, a pause followed. "Did you guys end up climbing to the top?"

"Well, Rolan had to call for security to properly clear the area first, but when we continued, some of us managed to reach the top. There were a few who didn't want to continue as well, so you might have seen them come back here earlier. *I* got to the top a couple of times, but at one point, I got tangled up in some weird mushroom."

"I saw. I was going to help, but then all sorts of shit happened."

Sylas chuckled. "Yeah, same with Terala. That didn't work out for her. The mushroom flipped her upside down, and she dangled by her feet for about ten minutes."

Korin couldn't help but crack a slight smile.

Jaimas then approached, holding a couple of food boxes. "Eat up, bitches," he said, handing the food to Korin and Sylas. "Korin, man, you need to relax. Those cunts got a blasting, and we all had fun in the end."

"Yeah, well…" Korin mumbled, jabbing a stick into the ground.

"Well, what?" Jaimas frowned. "Maybe you need to chill out with some of my marshmallows. Mellow you the fuck out. Later, though." He grinned, waltzing off to another group of people.

Terala sat next to Korin, legs sitting wide apart as if one of the boys. "Hey, I totally agree with you about the whiny babies, but you did miss out on some fun. Don't let them get to you." She grabbed a sloppy piece of sauced potato with her hand and shoved it into her mouth, licking her fingers.

"I'll try." Korin closed his lid.

"Hey, are you going to eat that?" Sylas asked Korin.

"No, he's saving it for me," Terala interjected, grinning.

"Piss off." Sylas light-heartedly shoved Korin's shoulder so the force bumped Terala off the seat.

As she picked herself off the ground, Sylas laughed as Korin lightly chuckled. Terala was about to shove back, but Rolan abruptly came over.

"I appreciate your concerns, Korin," Rolan said, "but you should be more concerned about enjoying yourself. Don't worry about me."

After a short moment of consideration, Korin nodded his head, smiling in return. Rolan then smiled back before carrying on with his duties.

"Hey, about your relig–" Terala said before stalling. "Uh, never mind."

Korin knew what she was about to ask, but he didn't answer. He then saw Celine sitting by herself. Now having picked himself out of an emotional rut, Korin wanted to move about. "Hey, we'll go sit over with Celine," he said, standing up as the others followed.

Celine was holding an unusual mushroom, inspecting it until looking up at Korin. "Hey, look at what I found. I think it's a little more conscious than most mushrooms. I wonder if I should name it."

"What, like a pet?" Terala asked, holding her hips.

"I don't know. Maybe. It seems to be aware of us."

"That seems creepy. The mushroom, that is. And maybe the naming."

All of a sudden, the mushroom growled sinisterly.

"Oh!" Celine said frightfully, juggling it haphazardly before chucking the fungus away into the forest.

"Good thing we came along," Terala said. "That mushroom was probably putting spores into your head."

Sylas then added, "Yeah, it would've convinced you to make us all take one home, too." He laughed.

"You're probably right. Thanks," Celine said, sighing before picking her book up again.

"So, what's the book about?" Korin asked.

"It's about an evil cult," Celine said, but before she could continue, their conversation was cut short when all the campers were called in for a safety talk the campsite security was conducting.

Chapter Six

The Camp – Part Two

An unusual cave was central to the next camp activity, and its peculiarity fundamentally came down to two factors; the first being that not a single person could detect even the slightest undulation of rock across its utterly black walls. In addition, the entrances oddly seemed two-dimensional, as if a cartoonist had simply drawn a cheap backdrop to a scene. Naturally, a few people looked confused and nervous.

"This exercise is a little different," Rolan addressed the campers. "The first objective will be to split up down these tunnels and then regroup with each other in the centre. It may sound easy, but there are a few complications. First, the branite in the walls absorbs nearly all visible light. Since you aren't able to use magic yet, you'll be using IR goggles to see." He grabbed one of the lightweight devices from a box at his feet, giving a short tutorial on usage. "The branite will also create optical illusions – even at the infrared level. There are also sections in the cave where your echoes will throw you off greatly. Listen carefully. And then you have various physical obstacles that you'll have to climb on, over, and around. Then when everyone meets up, we'll complete the activity in the centre. Look for a giant crystal ball. *We'll* enter the middle tunnel," he said, motioning to himself and the clerks, "while the rest of you will form equal groups and begin down separate paths."

Since there were forty students, ten lined for each path. Unsurprisingly, Priscilla eagerly jumped into Korin's group, keeping to herself for the time being. Korin shook his head as he picked up one of the goggles, hoping she wouldn't bother him. At least his group had no 'cry-babies', he considered.

The device functioned like non-mage night vision goggles, except that it was additionally equipped with a lens for detecting etheric anomalies, such as charm magic. More specifically, it detected fields of energy that *potentially* contained charms and did not absolutely determine if charms were present. He turned his IR illuminator on, seeing the tunnel ahead in a bright green. There was also a communications device and a tracker inside the goggles, but talking to the other groups was only allowed in case of an emergency.

Sylas, Terala, and Celine were with Korin, while Jaimas had already headed down one of the passages with another group. Considering what happened in the last two activities, Korin believed it was highly probable that more creatures – or even monsters – dwelled within as he led the way. The branite contained swirly patterns, which simulated optical illusions, alternating at different angles. Everyone consequently thought that they were either much closer or further away from the rocks… until it was too late. Korin stumbled over, creating a chain reaction with those close behind him. His goggles came off, having hit the rocks. Worried that he broke them, Korin floundered in the dark until someone stepped on his hand.

"Oops, sorry," one student responded to Korin's yelp.

Korin soon found his goggles, placing them on before almost jumping in shock at the illusion of a rock about to poke him in the eyes. Once he stood up, he backed into another student. Priscilla. When he saw who it was, he remained quiet, warily moving on as he again felt her stare on his back…

The illusions entertained Celine as she poked her head back and forth while waving her hands around. Most of the other campers were also mesmerized, wandering around until reaching rocks obstructing half the pathway. With a now more-cautious attitude, everyone delib-erately reached their hands out to feel for the actual location of grooves and protrusions.

Terala climbed up first. Her leg slipped on a surface, but she luckily managed to keep one hand gripped firmly in a groove. When she safely reached the other side, Terala helped the next camper over, but he slipped as well, splitting his legs apart before hitting his groin on a sharp lump. It looked more painful than it was, as the rock appeared to actually go through his body. Most oohed loudly, cringing and flinching. In a tight voice, the guy announced that he was fine, but a few didn't believe him, anxious about making it over.

"You boys are so weak with your man-junk," Terala said. "Come on."

"You first, Korin," Sylas said, grinning while tapping Korin's shoulder.

"Oh, how thoughtful of you," Korin responded.

"Hey, I don't want to ruin those rocks for you." Sylas chuckled.

The remaining girls climbed over before the guys, as a result challenging their dignity. Korin rolled his eyes before crossing with ease, and the other guys reluctantly followed, making it over without an issue.

Deeper into the expanding tunnel, Korin called out, "Hello!" His voice echoed continuously into an incomprehensible blur of reverberations, mirroring chaotically as if multiple Korins were competing with one another. The arresting moment gave him a slight chill as he imagined being trapped, indefinitely calling out for help.

Listening intently to the remarkable echoes their footsteps merely created, the ten campers remained relatively hushed until reaching an intersection.

"It's pretty obvious we have to go down the left path, towards the centre," Sylas said, despite hearing voices echoing from the other paths.

"But we have to follow the voices," one person rebutted.

"Not necessarily," Celine interjected. "Rolan mentioned that the echoes could trick us."

"So where do we go?" another camper asked.

Korin responded, "I'd take a safe bet and traverse down the centre path, just in case we can to go in either direction, if need be. We need to go down one, anyway, so let's just try." He took off immediately.

A fair way down, the tunnel expanded into a large cavern, copiously filled with spiralling hardened water and mineral deposits called speleothems. Their collective form looked like giant razor teeth, as if the cave had ended and a monster had begun. Water dripped every few seconds, echoing the cavern's pristine nature. The group spread out inside while some seized their breaths at the beauty, even though they couldn't see its rich colours. Terala couldn't help herself and *had* to climb up one of the ground-based speleothems, keeping herself amused. Celine, on the other hand, kneeled next to one to survey it.

"I think we should –" Korin stopped when he turned around, noticing Priscilla was no longer with the group. "Wait, where's Priscilla?" he asked the others as they turned around with bafflement, most shrugging. "She was just here a minute ago. Great. Priscilla!" he and everyone else shouted, hearing nothing in return. "It looks like we'll have to split up to find her. We can find each other back here, as this is a big, recognizable place."

Everybody parted ways, and Korin hastily made his way down one of the branching tunnels by himself, calling out for Priscilla, wanting to return to the task as quickly as he could. He was also irritated that his group probably wouldn't be the first to arrive as a result. Nevertheless, he affirmed to himself that he would *at least* beat the 'cry-baby team'.

"Priscilla!" Korin yelled in frustration, questioning why he even bothered. "Pris –" He froze in his tracks as he saw Priscilla in the passage to his left.

The gothic girl grimly stared at Korin as if she was literally frozen. Korin stared back, nearly freaked out by her weird, eerie presence.

"Wh-what are you doing down here?" Korin asked hesitantly.

"Nothing." Priscilla shrugged, smirking. What's it to you?"

Okay. You are starting to creep me out. Really creep me out, Korin thought. Before he said anything, she slowly stepped backwards into the darkness with another nefarious smirk. "What on…" He shook his head angrily. "Can you stop playing games, please?" he called out, questioning why he added the politeness.

He shortly realized that splitting up individually was a bad decision. While Korin carefully trod down the path, crying out the ridiculousness of the situation, he suddenly felt a presence behind him. Immediately, he turned around and saw that his senses were right; Priscilla was standing dreadfully close to him, looking rather smug. The shock then jolted him to move back a couple of metres.

"What's wrong?" she asked shrilly as Korin just *knew* that her eyes widened with excitement.

"What the…" he muttered. "Why are you doing this?" He took a defensive stance.

"Why aren't you with the others?" Priscilla tilted her head, attempting to mentally pry into his mind. "Don't they trust you? Don't you trust them?" she asked with great thrill, slightly shaking her head as if it was about to explode from over-exhilaration.

Korin tried swallowing his rapidly-building saliva, but he couldn't make his tongue move even a few millimetres.

"Relax. I'm not going to *kill* you," she added, though her comment didn't comfort Korin much. "So, you really want to know why I'm down here?"

Korin wasn't sure if relaxing was optional, believing she was about to say something diabolical. *Not kill me, but psychotically assault me*, he thought before responding, "Tell the truth."

Priscilla happily moved in very close to a fearfully-unmoving Korin, nonchalantly saying, "Exploring."

It certainly wasn't the answer Korin was expecting, nor the manner. Turning from creepy to innocently playful, her personality confused him greatly.

"What, did you think I was going to try and kill someone?" She snickered, moving her head in a way that indicated to Korin that she rolled her eyes.

Korin stiffly shrugged and seriously asked, "I… who knows?"

"Oh, please. Anyway, the crowd can feel a little burdensome, don't you think? It's nice taking a break from their moronic behaviour. I know how you're feeling, Korin. They're frustrating, aren't they?" She moved in even closer. "Morons. Superficial cretins. Not to mention the pathetic. We're in the same boat, you and I. Perhaps we should find the centre for ourselves. Come on, let's forget them."

Unsure of her motivations, Korin croakily said, "I'm not abandoning everyone. And I actually like a few people there. It'll still be easier with the group, anyway."

Priscilla sighed in disheartenment before replying, "Fine. We'll have it *your* way."

She took off immediately to head back to the group, leaving Korin standing still for a few moments, immobile with befuddlement. But just as he was about to move again, he heard whispers coming from the other direction.

"Dude, I'm not going there," a loud whisper echoed. "They're cultists."

Another unidentifiable person responded, "Look, I understand why you think that, but it's legit. Trust me."

"Sure, some of the ideas seem cool, but it just seems way too off for me," the first replied. "Like, why do they have to *revere* it?"

"Just… just come with me and test it out, alright?"

"Ugh… Fine. But I better be able to get out of it if they get too culty."

The voices shortly disappeared into the distance, and Korin momentarily forgot about Priscilla, speculating about the so-called cult. His thoughts on the matter fizzled out, as he realized being alone wasn't a good idea, so Korin quickly headed back as fast as he could, despite the passing adrenaline making his legs shaky. By then, the other nine students had returned, with Priscilla standing off in the corner.

"Hey, I think there are some guys down this tunnel." Korin motioned before leading the way, soon hearing voices bouncing off the walls, which grew stronger until the group finally reached the central complex featuring a giant crystal ball in the centre.

"Well done." Rolan clapped his hands. "Just two groups left."

Jaimas's group had won. Korin was a little disappointed that he didn't come in first, but the discontent faded swiftly. Most of the students then raised their voices to call for the last two groups that arrived soon after.

"This used to be an outpost during many ancient wars that occurred underground," Rolan explained. "Military officers would run up and down here, giving various directives to their chain of command. The crystal still works, but can anyone show us how to activate it?" Rolan patiently waited as most blankly stared. "Okay, take your goggles off," he said, waiting again before manually activating a couple of contraptions.

The crystal ball lit up with a swarm of energy, tossing and turning in all directions, lighting the branite-less room around them. In front of the purple walls were assorted steam technologies, analogue contraptions, and primitive mechanical computers. Rolan explained the history of the cave and technology, noting how much of it was based on secret knowledge kept away from not only the non-mages but the majority of mages, too; there were still believed to be *many* undiscovered – and more fascinating – innovations elsewhere in the underground layers across Juntas and the other planets in the Caelverse.

The group then played around with a few of the contraptions, in turn activating and manoeuvring large constructions in a massive room nearby, which they viewed from behind a glass panel. A few people wanted to go inside and play around on the equipment, but there was a hazard sign above, so Rolan decided not to allow it after some lengthy consideration. He was already under enough pressure.

***

Just after stepping outside the cave, Korin witnessed Celine placing a stone in a small bag. "Stealing again?" Korin perked an eyebrow as he folded his arms.

"Oh! Umm… it's… really tiny, though," Celine replied, scrunching her face guiltily.

"Yeah, yeah." Korin smirked. "The place was loaded with branite, so I guess a small amount wouldn't hurt."

"I'm not really a thief. It is… part of nature, right?" She shrugged uneasily with a few jerks. "The branite *is* fascinating, though. I might use it in my photography. I don't know how it'll affect it, but I'm sure I'll get interesting results."

"Probably," Korin said, glancing over his shoulder. "Hey, did Priscilla say anything when she returned?"

"Not much. Why? Is she bothering you?"

"Mm, she just seems… off the altar. I can't quite say what it is, but I don't trust her. For a moment, I thought she was going to stab me or something. Just watch yourself around her."

"It's alright. I have a pretty good sense of people." Celine chanced a glance at Priscilla. "So, is this the problem you had before?"

"Yeah. And there are other ones, but I guess she was one of the major issues."

"I wouldn't worry. The camp will be over soon enough, and when we get back to the uni, you'll have your own space."

Korin smiled back. "Good point."

Another camping group approached the cave, informing Rolan on the way that one of the activity stands was out of service. Rolan then told his group that they would have to skip the next exercise, hearing grumbles and complaints again.

To their bizarre misfortune, the other scheduled activities and their respective areas had also been rendered either unsafe, inoperative, occupied, or altered in some other way. Their remaining afternoon was an enormous letdown, consisting of basic backup exercises such as scavenger hunts, ball games, and orienteering. Nevertheless, most people had fun in the heat of their games.

On the way back from an activity, Korin happened to be alone with Priscilla. She had redeemed a part of her overall character in Korin's eyes after successfully working with him during one of the tasks, being rather nice to him. Their walk was in silence for the first minute as Korin looked up at the darkening sky, hoping to soon return to the campsite.

"So, I couldn't help but overhear about your recent discovery," Priscilla said. "Of being a mage. Is that true?"

"Yeah. Yeah, it is," Korin said, eyes still at the sky.

Priscilla's expression lit up. "You'd be feeling right out of place, then. Am I right?"

Korin stalled his response while squinting, thinking to himself about all of his conversations he had with Priscilla. He finally and firmly asked, "What's your angle here?"

Priscilla stopped walking with a stomp. "Like the others say, you need to relax. I'm not your enemy."

"Mm. Alright. But you need to tell me why you're acting like this."

"I'm not *acting*," she reacted defensively. "I'm different. Like you," she said softly. "There's nothing wrong with that."

Korin mumbled. "Fine. Is there anything you wish to add to the topic? I don't feel like talking much about my past."

"Well, if it's any consolation, I, too, lost my parents at the age of five," she said earnestly.

Korin's emotions instantly and crazily jumped all over his insides, but he externally kept himself under control. He was curious, though, as to why she lost her parents at the same age as him – and also if 'lost' meant dying or vanishing. "How much did you hear?" Korin frowned.

"Only what you mentioned to the others." She shrugged.

"Well… I'm… I'm sorry to hear that." Korin scratched his chest. "About your parents."

"It's alright. Thank you. And I extend my condolences to yours, too." She moved in front of him. "So," she said, smiling, "are you going to tell me more or have you had enough?"

"No. No more about my past for now. Let's just keep moving." He motioned.

Near the campsite, Korin and Priscilla heard a few noises behind a tree, soon spotting two students making out. The passionate display heated up, stirring a mixture of emotions in Korin. The students in question stopped, looking embarrassed before promptly walking off. Korin glanced at Priscilla, who stared back with a mix between a smirk and a simper. He chose not to say anything, continuing on to the campsite.

Dinnertime arrived, and everybody gathered around the campfire. If it weren't for the burning wood, the cloudy sky would've rendered the area almost pitch-black. The young mages were taking turns in telling ghost stories – quite a few revolving around missing students, due mainly to the news around Teloston – and Priscilla was next in line.

"Go on, Priscilla, tell us one," one person called out.

"Okay. I have a story." Priscilla beamed. "Someone began playing around with demons one day. Once empowered, the demons swarmed around *everyone*. And with their infinite numbers, they attacked all who weren't prepared. The end," she said merrily.

"What kind of a ghost story was that?" a camper asked, frowning.

"A fucking crappy one," another student responded. "Next, please."

"Did anyone at least survive?" a girl asked, receiving a shrug in return.

Korin kept his eyes fixed on the fire. *What the hell was that meant to mean?* he thought, freaking out a little.

A few ghost stories later, it was Korin's turn. But just as he was about to open his mouth, Jaimas walked over, craftily opening his pouch.

"Here, cook this," Jaimas offered quietly. "It'll expand your mind to new levels so you'll tell the most imaginative stories."

"No, I'm right, thanks." Korin waved his hand.

"Oh, come on, Korin," Jaimas emphasized slowly.

One grinning person asked, "Hey, what's this?" before grabbing the unstrapped pouch.

In his attempt to run away, the thief tripped, and the pouch flew into the air before landing in the fire, booming the flames up high with multiple sparkles flying in numerous directions. Rolan stood up, glaring at both Jaimas and the thief, though he had no proof as to what was inside. Jaimas then turned his attention to the idiot, arguing with him in private. With the 'marshmallows' destroyed, the only existing ones were the couple Jaimas had given out beforehand to a few students… and it was clear who they were, as they began ambling oddly around the camp, beginning to trip out. Rolan, of course, assumed they were either merely heading to the outhouse or grabbing more to eat.

Korin still had to tell his ghost story. "Well," he said, thinking hard, "it was a dark and stormy nigh–"

Piercing thunder clapped, its effect booming and rumbling like the ravaged stomach of the most fearsome beast. A few seconds later, thinly-spread droplets of rain almost unnoticeably splashed on their faces; but then, without any gradual transition, it began bucketing down. Tanking down, rather. The seated campers then jumped up, trying to cover their heads with assorted objects.

"Do you have a spell to cover us?" one student asked Rolan.

"No," Rolan replied as he picked up his supplies, covering them quickly.

The fire battled against the unabating water, whipping to the side before losing intensity and space, flickering as it was driven closer and closer to its source of sustenance. It diminished to an infantile state with mere embers glowing underneath sodden lumber. Rapidly, the light died, and darkness reigned for a frightening moment.

"Inside the cabins, everyone!" Rolan cried out before turning on a few lanterns that he had forgotten to switch on earlier.

The clerks activated their phids for extra light, leading the campers to the cabins as the thunder grew and rain thickened. Except, the marshmallow-effected campers didn't follow on, instead embracing the rain, gazing up as if receiving blessings from divine beings. With frustration, the clerks had to run back and forcefully move the drugged ones along, but the mindless students tripped over, hugging the thick mud. One even began making love with the ground, licking it like a frenzied animal, barely lifting her face off.

"No!" the camper screamed as she was picked up. "You can't break us apart! We're soulmates!" She tussled while being taken, screeching with a face lathered in so much mud the heavy rain didn't wash it all off.

The clerks managed to secure all but one camper; the last stripped off, making a run for it while chanting fanatically, spurring the other high students to chant as well while dancing around crazily. Rolan did something he wasn't meant to: he discharged a ball of bright red energy at the bolting student in the back, temporarily 'freezing' him with a slowing magic. It was fortunate that Rolan did, as the student was almost out of sight and would've been nearly impossible to find unless still making loud noises. Rolan fired a few more times, and the naked camper was taken in when the short-term slowing effect ceased, and the chanters grudgingly stopped, glaring at the uni staff. Confusing Korin, the 'marshmallows' were supposedly meant to 'mellow' one out, but he knew that people had various types of reactions to drugs.

Jaimas then received a short interrogation, but in the end, he managed to talk his way out of the situation. The clerks made sure everyone made it to their cabins safely, staying with the students for a few minutes until Rolan gave further orders. The night activity was cancelled until further notice, causing even more complaints; although, at least the most vocal were more understanding this time. Once the students were settled and all the 'everlasting candles' were lit, Rolan and the clerks returned to their own cabin, somewhat grateful that they could retire early for the night.

Left to their own devices, the males were able to entertain themselves with activities ranging from cards to general chitchat to light, playful fights. A couple unsuccessfully tried to enter the female cabin. Korin kept to himself, thinking over events, especially of Priscilla. The lively scene around him then blurred into the storm as he drifted to sleep.

***

Lightning struck terrifyingly close to the cabin, waking Korin up as it violently rumbled splinters out of the ceiling. The wind howled as if alive, feasting on whatever bits of nature it could toss around. There was also the rain's wall of monotonous beating, sounding as though it would destroy the roof at any moment. Despite the weather, Korin felt better than the previous night, looking back with regret at his morose attitude. Still, it was partly understandable, given the various problems he faced.

Although cosy enough inside, Korin wished to rise and move about; and upon opening the door, the wind pushed against him, drenching him in seconds, so he swiftly closed it so the rain wouldn't continue entering the cabin. While observing the tempestuous sky, he recalled a camp when he was younger, where none of the boys his age were following the rules the elders had set. Irritated, Korin yelled at his peers multiple times until they tired of his stance. He realized now that while having certain convictions on important matters was good, the morose corresponding attitude and means of achievement needed changing. A deep puddle of water lay at the base of the cabin, attracting his attention; and while gazing at it, Korin's imagination generated a moving image of a couple priests next to a few horned spirit frames. It jerked his mind to think of the ritual's potential outcomes, but he had too much on his mind as it was to continue mulling over it, so he quickly returned to his bed and drifted back to sleep…

"Korin, get up! Get up!" Sylas shouted, shaking Korin's body. "We have to bug out!"

Korin jumped up and dazedly asked, "What's happening?"

"It's flooding!" Sylas finished packing his last item. "We'll be underwater soon if we don't move out."

Korin glanced out the open door, noticing that the water had risen to the cabin's base, passing the stairs. Half the students were already outside, while the slower ones were still inside, doltishly fiddling with their belongings. One of the clerks hurried them up, shouting and throwing bags outside as she physically ushered a few people out. Some equipment *had* to be left behind. Korin speedily packed his gear, catching up with the rest of the campers trudging through the almost-knee-deep water, wailing in fear and distress. Korin's fatigue slowed his senses down, making the transpiring scene far more rapid and chaotic.

"Form a chain and stick together, everyone!" Rolan tried to shout over the torrential rain. "There's high ground a few hundred metres away!"

The campers had no other choice but to slog through the water, which was gushing by at an incredible speed, rising ever so quickly. Korin tried to reach Terala and Celine when the human chain was forming, but the clamour and commotion of the gaggle of students blocked his path. Blinding in itself, the rainfall thickly brewed with the gusting leaves, twigs, and insects, scratching and whipping across everyone's stinging faces. As the extraordinarily-turbulent lightning flashed, everybody's vision of their environment greatly enhanced for a mere second or two before drastically diminishing in the darkness. But before the campers could properly adjust back to the dark morning sky, lightning struck evermore rapidly, nauseatingly blinding them yet again.

One person after another slid, crying as their heads bobbed up and under the muddy water. Soon, no-one could stand, and they were whisked away, tumbling around in the water. Some equipment was instantly lost, including a body-sized anime pillow that slipped away from its owner, triggering him to cry…

Rolan and two clerks used their magic and attempted water walking; but this was effectively pointless due to already being in the water, which was also too chaotic; it was especially useless when they attempted to grab the students and help them from drowning. Depleted quickly of energy, their efforts were short-termed as well, and the staff were fully back in the water.

Down the stream, the campers attempted making their way to the heightened bank, but lightning struck a large tree nearby, causing it to fall. Jaimas happened to be underneath right as it collided with the water, and enormous fizzy waves then upsurged high into the air. He didn't resurface as the waves came crashing down, brutally thrusting everyone else's heads underwater.

Korin, followed by Sylas, Terala, and Celine, surged to the left side of the tree, while the remaining fretting and fluttering crowd were swept around the right side. After separating, the main group managed to climb up on the bank, but Korin's party had no accessible land as they were washed downstream. While struggling himself, Korin felt horrible he couldn't help anybody. Terala, at least, was able to find support… on the passing anime pillow. A special substance inside allowed the pillow to float as she lay on her stomach. She glowered, about to punch it, soon realizing such a decision wasn't so good. The savage water, nevertheless, upturned the pillow, ripping it out of her desperate grasp. Its escape enraged Terala, not just because it was her lifeline, but because she wished to personally destroy it later.

Sylas's bag had a flotation device, enough to sustain him alone. Holding on with both hands, he was in no position to assist anyone while holding on for dear life, as a simple mistake could have swept it away as well. Celine hadn't surfaced her head in a little while, though her arms were flipping around in the air. Korin managed to reach Celine, helping her up momentarily, only to have a lodged tree branch strongly jab him in his side, puncturing his skin.

"Ugh!" Korin yelled. *Not another branch!* He tried to utter.

The reactionary jerk led him to roughly faceplant into a floating pile of muck and small stones, which then stuck to his face. Fearing they would become embedded in his eye sockets if he opened his eyes, Korin tried to wash them off in the water, but clumps of dirt filled his mouth, along with a centipede, struggling for its life. After gagging and spitting the panicky centipede out, Korin glimpsed a log coming their way.

"Grab on!" Korin called out a few times.

When Korin grabbed the log, his hand sank through the bark; and when he hoisted himself on, his body instantly disintegrated it, leaving a smoky hole with thousands of scattering bugs. Korin fell back into the water as the blusterous wind grew stronger, blowing natural debris in their direction. Having to duck to avoid the more painful debris, Korin's lungs tightened while clutching for oxygen as he trembled before lifting himself up, taking in as much air as possible. A dead tartulemoe then floated by, its sack as gross as ever.

I am not grabbing on to that! Korin thought, wondering if he was being too picky.

It didn't matter, anyway, as an unidentifiable creature surfaced its large mouth, biting the bug and dragging it underwater. The huge creature didn't resurface, and there was nothing Korin could do except to swear and continuously kick his legs.

The constant change in sounds from the storm, to the underwater current, to the storm again, disorientated and confused everyone. Being tossed and shoved around like a ragdoll, Korin lost his sense of bearing, not knowing what was up and down. Memories of his life flickered through his mind as he wondered if he'd ever make it out alive.

Fortunately, the intensity eventually decreased as the group approached another bank, and the young mages immediately climbed out of the water in relief, uncaring about the sludge covering their clothes.

"Is everyone alright?" Korin coughed as the others nodded and panted, hardly looking at him.

"I… I can't believe Jaimas…" Sylas flopped his head down. "Did anyone see him come up?"

Having just caught his breath, Korin replied, "No, I could barely keep my head up as it was."

"Damn it!" Sylas spat some mud out, marching away.

"Sylas, we can mourn Jaimas later, but we need to get out of here as fast as possible. We don't know how long it'll take for this place to be flooded."

"Fine," Sylas replied dismally, returning. "Where do we go from here?"

Looking around for a few seconds, Korin said, "Back up the stream but along high ground. It looks like this trail here might be fine."

As they marched along the forest trail, the rain eased down considerably. Everyone's bodies had been pushed so hard that they still felt the river's movement, as their brains played tricks on them. Their squelchy boots and shoes began to harshly rub against their feet as the partially-hardening mud weighed down everybody's clothes. No-one had any desire to talk, their minds as grey as the sky's twilight. Branches snapped in the distance, but the group pressed on, believing it was only wildlife.

Celine scanned the area warily, intuiting something was off. "Korin, watch out!" She dived into him, pushing him out of the way as a large rock attached to a rope swung off a thick branch above. Both crashed to the ground, fretfully looking around as the rock continued swinging.

"Whoa! Nice work, Celine," Korin said, picking himself and a shaky Celine up.

All four then very carefully trekked along, keeping their focus on the branches above. With their attention up high, however, Korin, Terala, and Sylas stepped on a soft patch of grass that caved in, trapping all three in a hole. Their fall, at least, wasn't too harsh, as the grass braced the impact.

"Celine!" Korin called out. "Help, we're stuck!"

"Hang on!" Celine replied. "I have a rope in my bag."

"Agh!" a maniacal voice bellowed from behind Celine.

Immediately, Celine turned around, seeing an oblong-headed human holding a rifle, struggling to aim properly. Pus oozed and popped from its demented face, which snarled with crumpled, browned and greening teeth, appearing ready to eat anything. Although patchy on top, its wet hair grew thick around its back and neck. Its patchwork clothes, meanwhile, were covered in oil and bloodstains, ripped in places that exposed knife wounds.

Celine scurried for cover behind a tree, just missing the gunfire. Unable to properly think, she began virtually hyperventilating as the being closed in on her with grisly breaths.

"Throw something at it!" Terala shouted. "You can do it!"

Terala's shouting prompted Celine to grab the closest rock, but Celine's nerves halted her from turning around. Squeezing her eyes closed while trying to suppress the fear, she heard the breathing growing louder… and louder, intensifying to the point where it pushed the rain into the background. In a sudden daring decision, she jumped around the corner and threw the rock with all the might she had. For a moment, Celine wasn't sure what had happened, merely shaking as she stood in front of the unconscious attacker lying on the ground.

"Celine?" Korin called out after fifteen seconds of silence. "Celine? Are you alright?"

"I… I think so," Celine replied timorously, having just opened her eyes to see what had happened.

"Great. That's great, Celine. Could you help us out now?"

"Sure," she replied, not realizing that she was too shocked to move.

"Well, what are you waiting for?" Terala shouted.

"Oh, sorry. Um, I'm coming," Celine responded before unpacking the rope, helping everyone out.

Once the group was free, they approached the still-breathing attacker, noticing a mouse tail stuck between its canines.

"What *is* that?" Korin asked, so revolted, he couldn't help but stare.

"It looks like some type of non-mage hillbilly," Sylas answered, "but… weird."

Terala added, "It looks more fucked up than normal ones."

"He's probably a mutant," Celine said. "But I have a feeling something very bad happened to him. It's probably not a natural mutation."

"How do you know it's not a mage?" Korin asked Sylas.

"I'm just assuming because he's using a gun and not magic."

"Right…" Korin scanned the area. "Let's get out of here before any more show up."

The hike back was no longer depressing. It was nerve-racking. With their backs together at times, everyone vigilantly examined entire surroundings before pressing on. The trail eventually led to high ground overlooking the cabins, which were almost under water.

Near the campsite's hub, not far away, hundreds of students were either huddling or entering the subroute to leave. Rolan was present, speaking to a couple of emergency workers, who were on top of two stern and regal griffins, about to soar off. Even though the creatures were soaked, their beige plumages were still plumply thick, covering already-meaty chests. Their eagle claws heavily encumbered and ruptured the mud, looking as deadly as their once-mutant lion feet. Terala was no longer even thinking about her woes; instead, she approached the griffins and rescue workers with an approving face, feeling inspired as she stared into one of the creature's penetrating eyes.

"Thank goodness you're alright!" Rolan raised his arms. "I was about to have these rescue workers search for you. I couldn't do anything myself, as we saw you gush by at an alarming rate."

"We understand," Korin replied. "We're just glad to make it back — and that you're fine."

"Yes, I'm glad, too. I would've had so much paperwork to do!" He laughed. "Seriously, are you all fine?"

"We ran into a deranged hillbilly mutant thing that tried to kill us. In that direction. And I have a bad wound here." Korin showed the ripped skin around his abdomen, restraining himself from crying, even though the pain was getting worse.

"Ooh. Don't worry, we'll have you patched up soon."

"What about Jaimas?" Sylas asked anxiously.

"Jaimas is fine. He dived in time and missed the full blow of the tree, but his shoulder was injured."

Korin and Sylas exchanged big smiles, with the former asking, "What about everyone else?"

Rolan gave a thumbs-up to the rescue workers before answering, "They're fine, too. We had no idea any of this would happen. I'm shocked at how understaffed and unprepared the campsite was; that wasn't my fault. The rest of the camp has been cancelled, and I'm truly sorry for how it turned out. Normally, it's a great experience. Come on, let's leave."

***

Once back at Teloston University, Korin received attention for the wound on his side, being told to rest over the next few days. He didn't really mind not doing too much, as he also mentally needed rest. He was given non-magic medical treatment initially for a quick remedy, then later magic treatment. Despite the mysticism magic used on him, he was advised to rest, anyway, as the spell had only healed about three-quarters of the wound; and in general, repeated or additional healing spells on the same wound in a consecutive period were not encouraged due to potentially leading to various problems.

The last two of the following three days were the lunapex public holidays, the time of the month when one of the elemental moons fully transitioned behind the ecliptic crystal moon. Korin's still felt a lot of pain on the first lunapex day, but Sylas fortunately offered to bring him food while in bed. The lunapex transition began at eight o'clock at night rather than the Lunapex Mean Time of midnight due to Teloston's location on

Juntas. The perceivably-larger crystal moon transfigured the aligning water moon into yet another fire moon, totalling the number of fire moons orbiting Juntas to six, the effect causing likely increases in the temperature for the start of spring. The crystal moon itself produced special energy, its aura pulsating and glowing stronger than before; it also discharged some of its matter that orbited in geometric patterns.

Festivities were held across the university, and the noise managed to blare through Korin's room. He was at least able to watch the air displays from the balcony, keeping his spirits high. Most of the fireworks were short and explosive, but others perennially lingered, shifting and expanding over the sky, creating assorted images or optical illusions. Many drones were also used in the show, utilized in assorted ways, such as producing holograms of many things and beings – all the while giving the semblance of having certain textures. Jaimas didn't show up to the dorm, as he was still receiving medical attention, but Korin assumed he would've seen the show from where he was located.

As soon as the lunapex began, Korin felt a slight amount of energy coursing through his body. It was brief, but he knew it related to his magic abilities. He was actually expecting something extraordinary to happen, even if it might have been bad. For the rest of the night, he wondered what magic he was capable of using.

Korin continued recovering during the last lunapex day, but he was feeling considerably better, staying awake for most of the time. He mostly spent it reading about mage culture and university life, making sure he was fully prepared for his classes. Terala and Celine also visited, checking to see if Korin was feeling okay. There wasn't a lot they could do, but Korin very much appreciated their company. At the end of the lunapex, Korin reflected greatly on the camp, glad he was able to spend time with who he now considered friends.

Chapter Seven

Lessons Begin...

Despite the numerous lows, the camp had done its job; it broke the ice around Korin, strengthening the bonds with those he knew, and it also allowed him to feel as if he had achieved something within his short time at university. Korin's wound mostly recovered over the lunapex, so he was ready and fit enough for almost any physical and mental activity.

His classes also started that day, and he was still gobsmacked that he was about to learn magic. Korin had only read basic information on each class, hoping it was enough to keep pace. Unexpectedly, due to an issue with the majority of General Theory lecturers, the subject had been moved a few days ahead, with Conjuration moved to the forefront. Korin and his new friends were fortunately placed in nearly all the same classrooms for their magical subjects, except for the General Theory tutorial; Korin guessed Rolan had a role to play in that.

The buildings in the Magic Academic District were older than most of the others around the university. Most were made with an aging stone, but due to many restorations, the crumbling sections were few. There were two distinct styles from different ages, typically either the buildings had grand columned porticos leading to edifices with expansive rotundas, or they were a little more gothic, featuring ribbed vaults, charming flying buttresses, and detailed sculptural adornments; both styles, nevertheless, meshed together well, even as the buildings were rather close together, given that the streets were more like walkways than roads for vehicles.

Korin and his friends split off from many other students as they entered one of the many lecture halls. On the way in, there were cameras to determine if individual students had attended or not. Like the Formal Hall, the lecture theatre for Korin's Conjuration subject featured a mural expansive in its tale, focusing on the history and diligent dedication of researchers and their discoveries.

Before taking a seat, Korin's nerves inflamed, distorting the mural's inspiring vibes as he considered how little he knew. He even perceived the stupid-looking students as appearing more knowledgeable. Korin stopped walking, briefly standing by himself, engulfed in a waxing expanse of forlornness as the mass of individual students momentarily blurred into one, connected sea of unfamiliar magic. He closed his eyes, realizing that whatever challenges he faced, he would take them head on. It also helped that Sylas gave Korin a playful tug on the arm, grounding him back to reality. What Korin didn't take into consideration was that the university education was *forced* on nearly all mages, and so there actually were numerous idiots, in addition to those who had no intention of passing. Seeing as Korin was an earth type, conjuration was also meant to be the school of general magic he could be adept at, so Korin planned on putting in full effort.

Random shapes floated inside the holographic field on the stage, moving around the professor, whose grey, balding hair flared out at the sides. Dithering about the stage with various paper notes, the professor adjusted his thick spectacles -- an uncommon sight to be seen -- multiple times, which enlarged his frenetic eyes. Finally, he switched off the three-dimensional images in order to display class information on a concentrated, flatter screen.

"Welcome, everyone!" the professor addressed the students in an enthusiastic voice. "I'm Professor Nitsin!" He pointed his finger upwards. "To those who are unaware, the university is phasing out lectures, so this will be my final semester lecturing. Worry not, as I will still deliver fresh information to those who wish to watch on their devices in their free time – which I expect quite a few to do, seeing how Conjuration is the most exciting subject of all! Don't let other professors tell you otherwise! Conjuration requires a large amount of study, but the gems of your labour are indeed worth it!"

Sylas quietly commented, "He's so fidgety, he'd probably shake out enough gems for us."

Korin tittered, pen ready to take notes. He wasn't sure how to use all of the pen's functions -- the contextual touchpad confused him -- but it was able to write, and so that's all he cared about for the time being.

After addressing admin and logistics, Nitsin began with some historical and contemporary academic context, saying, "Although we have a brilliant grasp of spell geometries, researchers are still conflicted as to *why* such forms exist at the etheric level as they do. Professors across the board will teach contrasting ideas, espousing their views as doctrine, but dogmatism should always be carefully avoided. So, who believes what? Well, classical scholars deem that conjuration geometries are based on a consciously-created, universal language or code, while others state that these forms are purely emergent properties. It's still too hard to be absolutely certain at this point," he claimed, shaking his hand vigorously. "But while there *was* a major trend in the last couple of centuries promoting the latter, there, in recent years, has been a movement towards a middle ground."

As the professor carried on, he began to puzzle many of the students by throwing around all sorts of big and obscure words, terms, and information. A few in the audience mimicked the lecturer's energy, fidgeting pens and assorted objects. Korin, however, wasn't aware that the other students were perplexed as well. Fearing he would rapidly fall behind everyone, Korin sat forward, trying to pay attention, but nervous thoughts and internal chatter clouded his concentration.

"Classical theorists," Nitsin continued, pacing in a zigzagged manner, "maintain that geometric forms used for spells can be both a priori and a posteriori me–"

"When do we get to casting the bloody spells?" one student hollered, standing up.

"Yeah," moaned many other students at once.

"Look, look!" Nitsin raised his hands high in the air. "We have to cover many ideas and issues first before progressing. Simply jumping into the core of subject matter will leave you floundering like a troll in a nectar swamp."

His analogy instantly triggered a few of the politically correct, and gasps filled the hall. "Excuse me, but that's offensive!" one person called out.

"Trolls are sapient beings, too!" another called out.

The professor then apologized repeatedly, trying to ease the building tension.

While other students continued pestering Nitsin, Korin asked Sylas, "Are you getting this?"

"Yeah, totally. Geometries are, uh, a language… you know." Sylas slumped into his seat ashamedly.

Korin smiled, knowing at least he wasn't alone in not fully understanding.

"So, about the school… which one was I on?" Nitsin muttered to himself after the politically-correct students had mostly cooled off. "Well, as for the naturalist camp – which is greatly divided, too, by the way – they believe… some believe spell geometries merely possess the illusion of a language, and that, fundamentally, all workings are purely complex reactions within the context of self-organizing systems."

Nitsin started twitching his mouth while his hands indecisively moved from one place to another until finally inserting a neurachite data chip into a large neurachite analogue computer – or NAC, for short – and its information displayed illuminated notes on the screen. One explanation stated that mages tapped into the fabric of reality called the *Aether*. At its deepest core, this cosmic *zero-point energy field* that connected to absolutely everything in existence transcended both the vibrating physical and spiritual realms. Virtually all schools of thought agreed on that point. Two images then projected over the students' heads, one showing a spherical cymatic pattern that appeared as though a watery snowflake, and the other image had thousands of geometric forms, collectively looking like a fluorescent web.

"Is there math involved?" one student called out impatiently.

"Can we bypass this?" another student butted in.

"Yeah, when can we blow shit up?" another yelled out in frustration.

Nitsin jumped in, saying, "Again, please save questions for the tutorials; but yes, math is involved, but only for those making discoveries at the postgraduate and doctoral levels; and yes, you will be blowing sh—ah, stuff up, but not in the way you may be hoping. That will come through failure, not success; but more about that later."

Many in the crowd grumbled downheartedly.

"I bet you weren't expecting linguistics and math," Sylas said, turning to Korin as the pestering continued.

"No. I was hoping I'd be casting epic spells while riding dragons instead," Korin replied drearily, his nervousness now seeping away while being replaced with glumness.

"Well, if you want to ride a dragon, you can always try one of the otherkin here." He giggled.

"What?" Korin asked, confused. "Are they similar to dragons?"

Sylas giggled again. "Sure, why not?"

There was a pause before Korin said, "I don't know what otherkins are, but I have this feeling that you're alluding to something sexual."

"Well, it can be." He continued giggling. "A lot like to be ridden."

Korin shook his head while suppressing a chuckle. "There… there better be a way to magically erase the mental image that you helped to generate for me." Korin now felt somewhat relieved from the burden of the lecture. "Anyway, did your parents show you how to make spells?"

"Nah, they were too busy. They hardly used their magic, anyway. Always working."

"What about siblings or anyone else you knew?"

"Don't have any siblings. And my tutors never directly covered the subject. It's not like most of us mages grow up being able to do some of the epically cool things you probably have in mind. Sorry to burst your bubble."

Nitsin outlined a few basics that the students would learn in the following semesters, explaining how the lack or addition of particular geometries – along with their locations and positionings – could alter or distort a spell in a number of ways. "But here is the part where you all need to pay attention." Nitsin examined the room critically, waiting for everyone to give him their full awareness. "A badly-created spell can lead to a dodgy conjuration that may potentially explode in your face, either wounding or killing you."

Amidst many worried mugs were multiple hands raised for yet more interrogating. Meanwhile, Sylas turned to Korin, looking as cheery as ever. "How'd you live without magic, anyway?"

"Ah…" Korin was still trying to adjust to the idea of a spell potentially blowing up in his face, half-focused on what Sylas asked. "The same way you would have: without it."

"Oh, yeah!" Sylas smacked his own head. "Okay, but what about mage tech and all the other cool shit we have? I'd die from boredom without them."

"Well, non-mages have heaps of technologies, too, but it seems like you guys have it better."

"Yeah, I've seen some pretty cool non-mage tech, I guess. Hey, could you guys live without mage tech?" Sylas asked Terala and Celine.

"Sure," Terala answered. "I'd just go off into the woods and do other shit."

"I wouldn't get bored, either," Celine responded. "I already have heaps of hobbies that don't require complex things." She turned to Korin. "But I'm sure that you'll love what we have, and you probably won't miss much of your old life."

"I think you're right," Korin said. "Except this lecture is a bit much."

"I wonder if Jaimas is here," Sylas thought aloud.

"I wouldn't be surprised if he's wagging."

"Probably. *I*, for one, won't wag classes; but I don't intend on studying." Sylas chuckled.

After answering, evading, and dismissing a bunch of trivial and silly questions, the professor explained how the students' progress would be monitored and that they'd use safe rooms to test their spells. Of course, while first-years were only required to create holographic conjurations, not physical ones, it was still best to err on the side of caution. Moreover, they also only needed to establish one conjuration spell by the end of the semester; although, non-earth mages would be marked easier for casting the spell and only marginally easier for creating them.

Abruptly, a commotion started near the centre front of the hall. One of the students was shaking, appearing to have a fit. The paling, blood-shot girl then began coughing and gagging in a strange, guttural way, as if a creature was trying to escape through her throat.

The neighbouring students weren't sure how to help her, except one yelled, "Tap her back! I think she's choking!"

But before anyone could help the girl, she thrashed her arms around, rejecting all attempts of assistance. Screaming and growling with the rage of several angry people combined, she managed to twist and knot their stomachs in dread. The girl also grabbed her head, scratching it until drawing blood; she then spread the blood all over her face, gluing messily into her hair. While cursing incomprehensibly, she skewed her psychotically-shivering head to the side as she turned to the person next to her with chasmically-blackened eyes…

Suddenly, her body blurred for a split moment. A shift occurred. A shapeshift. Black tentacles a foot long then replaced her head's hair, whipping around furiously. Her hands were now clawed – as were her feet, which had ripped through her shoes – each with powerful limbs far outcompeting that of a lion's. The next second, her razor-sharp-toothed mouth dropped *wide* open, and she voraciously lunged at the frightened student, pinning him in a mangled position over the now-broken armrest, attempting to sink her teeth into him while he hopelessly fought her off. The young man's throat stretched as far back as it could, almost suffocating him, so he slightly tilted up for a moment to inhale a fraction of a breath. Merely peripherally seeing the girl, his head jerkily dodged the attacks as he tried kicking her body, only to leave her unscathed.

"She's possessed by a demon!" one of the tutors shouted.

"Someone get an exorcist!" Nitsin yelled to the tutors seated at the back of the hall before beginning his conscious connection to the Aether in order to charge his magic.

Most of the people that were remotely close by didn't wait to see what would happen, fleeing instead. In their frenzied clamour, the students jumped over seats, tripping, stumbling, and planting their faces into armrests, bruising and bloodying themselves. A few students landed on one another, squishing and pushing each other in their escape. Others near the aisles managed to have a clear run to the exits, screaming loud enough for those in the adjacent halls to hear. The students further away either started rushing out as well or were too excited and eager to observe what would transpire. One guy had his mouth agape as he gripped the seat in front, utterly thrilled at the action. His friend tried to haul him out, but the guy's eagerness was resolute, fighting back with one hand in order to stay his ground. Korin was situated at the back of the hall, so he stayed to watch the whole episode.

Luckily, one of the tutors at the front of the hall had already begun connecting to the Aether when he heard the girl cursing. It wasn't long before he charged his energy pool, and he raised his hand, pointing it at the possessed girl. The demon noticed what was happening and instantly stopped, glancing at the bright green ball of energy in the tutor's hand about the fire off. She then howled and jumped up, by default freeing the mangled student. As she fretfully scanned her surroundings, the first green blast shot her way, but it missed her by a couple of centimetres. Quickly, she grabbed the guy that was about to scurry away, using him as a meat shield.

By this time, Nitsin had charged his aether pool of energy and was able to fire a couple of blast balls at the demon when she was facing the tutor. The green energy, however, didn't instantly knock her unconscious as it would a normal person, and she growled when hit. In her fury, the possessed girl rampaged towards Nitsin, but multiple blasts from a few different people managed to subdue her in the end, knocking her unconscious.

"Everyone's dismissed!" Nitsin instructed the remaining students tensely. "Tutorials will still be on at the normal time, so please try to remain focused on your work!"

Some of the tutors at the back of the hall forced the students to leave. Korin tried to remain as long as possible to watch any further occurrences, though nothing of note materialized. He also didn't get to see whether the possessed girl shapeshifted back to normal or not.

Many of the other concurrent lectures were also cancelled due to the commotion; and with just over an hour left until the tutorials commenced, the majority of students at Teloston talked almost ceaselessly about the demon attack. Moreover, although the air was filled with a giant cloud of fuzzy, hysterical chatter, the one word which clearly stood out was 'demon', virtually sounding like every second word used.

"So, it *is* true," Korin said to his friends. "You guys also get demon attacks."

"Yep," Sylas responded. "In fact, mages are generally more susceptible to possession."

"But possessions aren't that common," Celine countered. "Especially the kind of possession we just saw."

"Yeah, true. I think it depends on the circumstances and your abilities."

"And transformations like that haven't been a wide-scale issue in at least recent history. How often did you see demonic possession?" she asked Korin.

"I've only seen a couple in my lifetime," Korin said, "but I've heard of more. They were pretty disturbing." He grimaced. "Still, nothing like that. Sacrenderists informed me about mages getting possessed, too, but I figured it could've been all lies when I stopped following it."

"What normally causes non-mages to get possessed?" Terala asked.

"I think it happens when people mess with the spirits. That, or they… huh, I was about to say 'those who no longer follow our religion'," he said, chuckling. "But it actually *was* the case that when people left our religion, demonic possession occurred. Unusual." He paused to think deeply. "I think that was one of the reasons why I believed in the teachings of Sacrenderism. At least no-one got possessed. Well, most of the time. There was this one time I –"

"Y-you're not… possessed, are you?" Sylas asked, face disturbed.

"No, trust me, I'm fine. I'd be raging by now if I was possessed."

"Oh, shit! He's possessed by a demon!" Sylas yelled loudly, pointing to Korin as the surrounding students either froze with fear or fled the area.

"What? I'm not possessed!" Korin responded as Sylas laughed loudly. "Ah, come off it." He lightly pushed Sylas, who continued laughing hysterically.

"I think something's possessing Sylas." Terala frowned. "You right there? It wasn't *that* funny."

"Yeah, it was." Sylas began to settle down.

"Great," Korin said, rolling his eyes. "Now everyone's going to think I'm possessed."

"Nah, you'll be fine." Sylas patted Korin's back assuredly. "There are so many people at Teloston, most would forget your face, anyway."

"Let's hope. Keep in mind that some people have good memories."

Celine broke in, saying, "You said that you stayed with your religion because of other attacks."

Taking his time to contemplate his past, Korin eventually said, "Now that I think about it, demons affected all people, regardless of their religious beliefs. Perhaps I was just brainwashed by propaganda. Regardless though, it wasn't all that common – kind of like with you guys. Sacrenderists would spread the word to try and convince everyone that they were safer with our religion. I… I can't believe I believed it all. They…" He was reluctant to give more details, sighing. "Let's just say I'm glad I no longer follow it."

***

Having to fill in name badges when they entered the tutorial room, the class of thirty students met with a middle-aged tutor, whose plain, black clothes didn't really do a good job at hiding her plumpness. No assistant tutors were present with her due to other obligations.

"It's great to finally meet you all. I'm Renola," the ruby-haired tutor delivered vibrantly. "I was in the lecture, too; and yes, I understand that you're all eager to know what transpired. What we *can* say is that the situation is being dealt with, and you are all very safe. It's not like it's contagious."

The 'contagious' part immediately made most of the students glance at one another with uncertainty.

"Anyhow, let's begin," she said before giving a big smile. "In the tutorials, we'll focus on the practical side of things, where we'll dive first into meditation practice; and then, in the coming weeks, we'll cover memory exercises, as you'll need to memorize the universal constants of basic patterns, along with how to best string together the most appropriate cymatic nodes during meditation, imagining forms from scratch."

Remembering the holographic images he saw in the lecture, Korin was flabbergasted, thinking, *We have to memorize all of that in our heads?*

"Meditation comes naturally to every mage," Renola continued. "There are different types of meditation, but today we'll focus on entering the mind before seeing astral energies. Although some of you may be able to see astral constructs during meditation, it's not a requirement for today. Yes, you'll pick this up rather quickly – no need to fret." She then picked up a folder, flicking through it.

"Too late. I'm fretting already," Sylas whispered to Korin.

"I hear you," Korin whispered back.

"You know those nightmares, where you're in an exam, and you've forgotten something important or you're naked?" he asked, and Korin slowly nodded. "Well, what if we enter our minds and have one of those about not meditating properly?"

Korin delayed his response before light-heartedly saying, "You're very good at creating the most awkward thoughts."

"Just helping you out." He grinned.

The class was told that when they could meditate, the next step was controlling their vision, mastering how to manipulate thought patterns and other imaginations to shape environments.

"Depending on the state of your mind," Renola carried on, "your surroundings can range from utopic to nightmarish. Just remember to intentionally focus on good things. When this process is mastered, your mental space can be shaped to your own will. For those who have certain traumas, the prospect of entering your mind may seem intimidating; but know that if anything terribly bad *does* begin to happen, the shock itself will normally eject you out of your mind instantly. In the *very* rare chance that meditation itself becomes problematic, there are counsellors here that can help."

Renola covered a few more basics before the class commenced breathing exercises on the mats. Eventually, they moved on to meditating. It seemed hard for the students at first, but after a while, the meditation felt natural and instinctual. Renola's tips were also useful in helping Korin delve deep within his being. His senses didn't so much diminish, as they, instead, refocused like a dial switching a focusing lens. The rustling sounds around him began to 'fade' away as a different type of noise emerged, vibrating throughout his ears, soon transcending his physical senses and enveloping his whole being.

It wasn't long before he successfully entered his own mind; but, so surprised by his success, Korin jumped back to reality, having to try again. Just like the tutor explained, for most people, there was nothing much to see at first in the blurry, dull void; but Korin then started randomly seeing a dirt path forming in front of him, and the clarity was so intense, he was able to focus on the complete details of every grain of soil. Korin realized that *he* was the one creating his environments, rather than experiencing a pre-existing reality. Moreover, Korin naturally felt that if he thought bad thoughts, they could easily manifest, so he focused hard on not creating anything dreadful; but the burden – whilst experiencing the heightened sensitivities of the mind – frightened him, and he exited his head, gasping.

At roughly that point, a couple of other students had also returned to waking reality. Utterly amazed, Korin was compelled to re-enter, but this time, instead of focusing on avoiding the creation of negative environments, he'd focus his intentions on positive thoughts, eventually creating a beach environment. As he walked, Korin marvelled at how he created nuanced cavities and ripples in the sand without even consciously doing so; his subconscious was actually faster than his conscious mind.

When he turned around, Korin noticed that his beachfront was fading away, where he had begun, and he had to focus on restoring and maintaining the visualization. Nothing there was permanent, except for that which was stored away in the subconscious – which, he was told earlier, was deeper than all the Caelverse's oceans combined. While it was the etheric where created patterns were stored for later use and spell finalization, the subconscious could store patterns, too, in turn affecting the etheric.

Knowing it was technically possible to see mentally-constructed spiritual energies of the astral planes during his first meditation, Korin – from what he had learned – attempted projecting his consciousness out of his mind while still meditating. Nothing happened for quite a few minutes until suddenly, for a brief moment, he floated forth beyond his internal world, glimpsing a couple of unusual energies around his body. These were his etheric energies, and just moments later, Korin managed to see his imaginations in a different context; they happened to be in his astral body, surrounding his etheric energy. That is, he had two layers to his spiritual energies. Of course, since it all occurred in such a short amount of time, everything seemed like a blur. After returning to his mind, he attempted seeing such energies again, failing. Korin's focus eventually waned, and he returned to the physical world just when the class was about to finish.

"Bravo, everyone," Renola said before Korin mentioned anything to his friends. "Well, that about does it for today. If you have any further questions, feel free to see me later."

***

It was lunchtime, and although there were no additional demon attacks, there *were* a few obviously fake rumours, such as the possessed girl giving birth to thousands of demon spawn, killing the entire medical staff in seconds. Most students didn't believe them. *Most.*

Korin was in the middle of explaining to his friends what he saw in his vision, but as they walked towards the Provision Wreath's food hall, Korin stopped when he spotted three people bullying an obese student, whose clothes had just partially ripped. Despite dark rings under his eyes, the alpha bully was a super attractive male, exuding a ladies' man vibe, having a male siren-like effect on the two girls rubbing his chest. Their long nails lustily dug into the alpha's chest, and he relished it with a bite of his own lip.

The scoundrel of a monarch meanly laughed. "He can no longer fit into his fifty-times extra-large-sized clothes."

"Look at it struggling to breathe." The brunette girl laughed cruelly as well, her eyes cold and dark. "It looks like it's about to die."

"Hey, fugly." The alpha bully poked the fat student's body.

"Ooh, watch out! Your hand may get sucked in, Sereck," the tall blonde girl said, chuckling.

"You're right. Maybe I should try something else instead." Sereck, their master, grabbed a large rod that happened to be nearby. "Here, poke him," he ordered, objection unwaveringly out of the question.

Grinning wickedly, the chosen girl grabbed the rod and was about to take action right when the other harpy quickly grabbed it, wanting to prove her worth with a psychotic, snarled face.

"Ladies, you'll both get your turn," Sereck said, voice so full of assurance. "You first."

The brunette sneered at her 'friend' before vexingly prodding the fat student harder and harder.

"Hey!" Korin spoke out. "Casually teasing is one thing, but you're taking this too far. Leave him alone."

"What? Are you two bum buddies?" the blonde girl asked mockingly before laughing.

"I don't know who he is," Korin firmly replied, "but there isn't any excuse for what you guys are doing. You've crossed the line getting physical here."

"Yes, and he crossed the line by a metre with his stomach." Sereck laughed again. "Why didn't you stop him from violently attacking all that food?"

Korin's blood started to boil as he clenched both fists at his sides, wide apart from his body. The alpha bully took note, ceasing his laughter.

"It looks like he's possessed," the brunette said, glaring.

"I know," Sereck responded, rolling his eyes.

"Listen, fuckfaces," Terala stepped in. "If you don't leave now, we'll shove your heads up the dantha's ass you came from."

"Oooh! Threats!" Sereck's face enkindled. "I'm turned on."

The blonde girl abruptly asked, "Why are we even bothering with them?"

"Yes, you may have a point," Sereck responded. "They're wasting our valuable time. Bye-bye, now." Sereck grinned, taking off, spanking both girls on the asses as he chuckled.

"Man, I hope they're taught a lesson soon," Terala said, grabbing the pole beside her tightly.

"Yeah, and I hope to be the one who makes sure of it," Korin added, turning to the obese student. "Hey, are you okay now?"

"I'm... I'm fine. I might need to go to the bathroom now," the lad said without much eye contact.

"Oh, right... well, I'm Korin, by the way." Korin held his hand out.

The large guy, however, merely muttered, "Oh, okay," before indifferently plodding off without even thanking Korin and his friends. At least Korin spotted the name badge still on him, reading, 'Hepteon'.

"Well, that guy seems friendly," Sylas commented sarcastically.

"The fat fuck didn't even say thank you," Terala added angrily.

"Hey, he's been bullied," Korin responded. "Maybe he needs time to recover." he shrugged.

"Yeah, I guess, but…" Terala said before trailing off with an incomprehensible mumble as they made their way inside the food hall.

After heaping his plate with food, Korin spotted Hepteon sitting down, chatting with a group of dorky-looking friends, thin and large. *I thought he went to the toilet*, Korin thought. Wondering about Hepteon's state of mind, Korin approached the table by himself. "So, how are you feeling now?" Korin asked Hepteon.

"I'm fine," he responded blandly.

"Yeah, look, this table is taken," one of the dorky guys stated disdainfully, placing a tray over a spare slot.

Hepteon said nothing as the rest of his friends gave Korin dirty looks.

Frowning with puzzlement, Korin said, "Um, okay. I'll… head off now." He then dismissively snickered, leaving immediately to sit with his friends, lost in his thoughts.

"Hey, so what did you see in your head?" Sylas asked Terala.

"Nothing," she replied concernedly. "I don't get it."

"You couldn't even imagine seeing your own hands?" Celine asked incredulously.

"No, just greyness." She shrugged. "I hope it doesn't mean sickness."

"Maybe you should see the tutor," Celine said. "I heard that –"

"I'll ask the tutor later. I better be fine. So, what about you guys?"

"My mind made a really nice forest," Celine answered. "I was feeding a korlorn, but then an angry-looking ogre stomped by in the distance, so I panicked and immediately stopped meditating."

"I would've stayed and fought it. Anyway," Terala said, turning to Sylas, "I bet you saw ogres, too. Naked ogres of your greatest fantasies." She laughed.

"You wish." Sylas swiftly grinned. "Actually, I did. And they were mud wrestling with you." He laughed as Terala's expression sharply turned sour. "With Jaimas, too!" He continued laughing. "No, but really, I just saw my room. Don't know why."

"It's probably a reflection of your inner state of mind," Celine said.

"My inner mind? My inner mind is my bedroom? There's more to me than my bedroom, you know. That doesn't make any sense."

"Our subconscious is gigantic, so I don't doubt that. It could be symbolic. Was it your old bedroom or your new one?"

"New." Sylas juggled two oranges high in the air. "What's your point?" He continued catching both without looking.

"Maybe you feel differently in that room. A radical change, perhaps."

"Mm, I don't know. Maybe you're looking too much into it. I've set my room up like how I did at home. At least now my parents won't ever go through my stuff again. I had to try new things all the time to hide some of my belongings from them. And the housekeepers."

"You mean, like, *those* comics?" Korin smirked as his focus finally entered the discussion.

"W…y… well, yeah. Obviously," Sylas said, rubbing his jaw.

"What comics are these?" Terala shot him a brow of suspicion.

"Oh, just comics with lots of, uh… action," Sylas promptly answered before Korin could even answer. Sylas then stared at him with a 'don't-go-there' expression. "So, what class do we have next?" he asked, purposely changing the topic.

"We have Alchemy," Celine replied. "I wonder if I could mix one of those with my recipe," she muttered to herself.

"Say what now?" Sylas asked, squinting at Celine.

"Oh, never mind." She smiled. "But then I *have* read that if I add one of those leaves," she trailed off again as Sylas looked at the others with bemusement.

Korin then asked Celine, "Do you think you can use the ingredients in Alchemy classes for your personal cooking?"

"I don't see why not. I'll get creative with whatever's left over."

"That seems like stealing."

"Oh…" Celine stared into the distance with musing eyes. "Well, I'll ask, then. I don't want to do anything bad."

Before responding, Korin stretched his arms out, and one bumped into a small drone floating by.

"My apologies," the drone said while simultaneously gesturing apologetically with an iconic face holographically projected out. "Do you wish to hear the latest rumour?"

"It's a rumour drone," Sylas said. "This will be interesting. Go ahead."

The drone's light swiftly turned green before it projected a rumour icon and declared, "The demon attack in one of the Conjuration lectures here on campus was a result of mage supremacists. The possessed student happened to be affiliated with a group of mage supremacists, who also became possessed as a result of their dark practices of sacrificing non-mages." The light then turned back to blue. "Do you wish for me to continue spreading this rumour, or do you have another rumour for me to spread?"

"Oh, I have a rumour!" Sylas grinned. "So, tell people that: The reason for the earlier demon attack is because of an outbreak of a new virus that attracts demons. The only way to protect yourself from the virus is to spray yourself with troll sweat. In fact, bathing in it will ensure better protection. Tell people that."

"Thank you for the information. I will spread this new rumour. Have a nice day."

"Sylas!" Terala almost shouted, trying to keep a grin from forming. "Did you make that one up on the spot?"

"Yeah." Sylas laughed. "Let's see if it works!"

Chapter Eight

Vice, Vengeance, and Visions

The Alchemy lecture hall doors were locked. There was no proper explanation as to why the lecture was cancelled, other than a notice merely stating that the workshops would be extended instead. Korin's workshop tutor, though, was nowhere in sight when he and the other students arrived at the lab… which was also closed, so only the basement lab was available. Still, no tutor was present.

Scarcely seeping through the rusting bars across the tiny, frosted skylights, light scantly glinted off the disordered mounds of sullied glass equipment. Even the lamps barely radiated beyond their concrete sconces sculpted with winged gargoyles clawing out of the nether planes. It didn't help that a dingy green haze permeated in spots of various thicknesses, which, nevertheless, camouflaged the mould festering on the stone-vaulted ceiling – as well as the layer upon layer of fossilized grime tenaciously etched across various utilities.

The history of thousands of concoctions had also permanently burned into the air, creating a mixed, faint scent of toxic smells and alluring aromas. But even the smells had to compete with a fading and cracked portrait of a traditionally-dressed professor leering from above, its irradiating aura swallowing the freshness emanating from the few virgin objects scattered around.

Curiously, tattered expanded holochite books were shoved into abnormal places; one choked a dusty air vent, another stupefyingly balanced potions with scribbles-for-labels, and a few were built as a fort for a couple of happy bugs. The books, moreover, were so dirty that they even appeared as if made of paper derived from trees. Many cabinets, additionally, were either unlocked or unhinged, most containing exotic ingredients and mysterious potions.

Despite the room's decrepit vibe, it had its own quaint charm – depending on one's point of view – and the darkness created a certain type of cosiness, restraining the limelight from one and all.

A couple of students arrived late, Jaimas naturally being one. "So, where's the teacher?" Jaimas asked, drumming the hefty desks as he waltzed around.

"Don't know," Sylas replied. "There's no note or anything."

"I think we should inform someone," a neatly-groomed girl called Sophia responded – her name badge *clear* as day, despite the lighting.

"Fuck that! It's our first day!" Jaimas chortled before examining equipment inside the cabinets.

During their wait, the students did as they pleased, most sitting and chatting or playing with their phids. Celine wandered around, inspecting ingredients, while Sylas joined Jaimas. Soon, Sereck – the bully Korin met before lunch – and his harpies arrived; all three glared at Korin, muttering profanities under their breaths.

Korin whispered to Terala, "I can't believe of *all* the people in our year group, those three are in this class. There are thousands! What are the chances?"

"Jhar, I know," Terala responded, swearing with an iconic name, which Korin had heard before. "It's like the Caelverse is out to get us."

"I think it should've imagined something else. I can't see how this all-too-coincidental arrangement benefits the Caelverse."

"I'm ready for a fight whenever you say."

It was virtually inevitable. Sereck threw a few things at a hooded-and-cloaked student sitting in the front row. At first, Korin waited to see if the hooded girl would do anything, but she didn't, and their laughter continued, making his body temperature rise. Korin then turned around, heatedly asking Sereck, "What's your problem?"

"My arm's too strong," Sereck answered casually. "I was trying to get you, but it hit her." He snickered.

"Stop it," Korin demanded firmly just before Sereck's wenches literally hissed.

"Sure, whatever you say," he replied in a derisive tone, kissing the air.

Korin turned back, waiting for something to happen, but nothing occurred, and the lone girl remained hunched over, writing in her notebook with a pen. "Do you know who she is?" Korin asked Terala.

Celine quickly bobbed her head above the desk, shocking Korin unintentionally. "You'll have to approach her up close," she answered quietly. "I couldn't see her face."

Korin grabbed his chest. "What were you doing down there?" He regained control of his heartbeat, his nerves still on edge from all that he had recently experienced.

"I found this!" Celine excitedly held up an odd instrument. "I'm going to see what it does." She gaily walked off.

Korin then stood up and made his way to the front to inquire into the girl's wellbeing. When he approached, however, he saw Priscilla smiling at him. His breathing quickened.

"Hi, Korin," Priscilla said, removing her hood. "Come to join me?"

"Uh… no… I… I didn't throw those things at you."

"I know. You're so sweet," she said, voice overwhelmingly syrupy. "You'd never do anything like that to me."

"Right… um…" He scratched his head. "Look, I'm going to go sit back down again."

"You'll come back for me, though?"

Korin stalled. Priscilla then motioned her hand for him to approach rather closely, but Korin remained still, imagining her stabbing him. He shortly felt as though he was probably exaggerating her character, but he was nevertheless cautious. She tilted her head as if he was being silly and that there was nothing to be worried about. Even then, Korin didn't comply, prompting Priscilla to slightly roll her eyes and raise her eyebrows, indicating she wasn't a threat. Cautiously, Korin advanced.

"Let's teach Sereck and those bitches a lesson," Priscilla whispered, waiting for a response that never occurred. "Well? They're only going to get worse. Better now than later."

Korin awkwardly sighed. "Maybe." He then needed a moment to think over their interactions during the camp. "Why do you want to work with me?"

Priscilla shiftily grinned. "Meet me in that closet over there." She took off quickly.

Puzzled, Korin waited a minute before trying to unnoticeably enter the decently-sized closet at the back wall, which was fortuitously situated in a groove surrounded by clutter. Once inside, he closed the door, and Priscilla immediately pressed her body against his, wrapping her arms around his head as she began kissing with a zealous intensity. Her lips, however, felt like they were drawing him into a deep chasm, being oddly pleasurable, as if he was falling without care. In her excitement as the making out intensified, she lightly bit his lips, tugging playfully. Almost losing himself in her embrace, Korin finally snapped out of it, grabbing her shoulders and keeping her at bay.

"Okay… Enough!" Korin coughed, regaining his breath as he continued holding her at arm's length.

"Come on," Priscilla responded, giggling while rubbing her hand over his chest, trying to move in closer.

Part of Korin wanted more. A lot more. And she knew it. Despite her dark nature, she was exceptionally pretty, and Korin needed to focus a great deal of energy on restraining himself. His uncertainty of her, in the end, helped his self-control. "What was that about?" he asked.

"I like you." She settled down.

"Okay, I… realize that. But why now?"

"Because we're away from prying eyes." She dipped her head in a way that indicated his question was silly. "It feels nice in here, too. Don't you just love the rich timbers? So many stories. There's so much character here. And the dark. Mmm." She squirmed with pleasure. "It makes me feel secure. Like, I can be me. Like, we can be who we truly are." Her body eagerly thrust towards him. "No pretence. No superficiality. No visage of any kind! Unmasked and raw." She breathed out sensually. "A world where true sensitivity can be experienced. A realm in which our subconscious is unrestrained to create from its infinite potential!" Her widened, mystical eyes grabbed Korin, glowing a powerful fervour. She then rubbed Korin's chest again, wriggling her fingers around. "Do you see what I mean?"

"Um, I've… n-never thought of it like that before," Korin said, unsure what else to add.

"Well… good." She smiled. "So, are you still in for teaching Sereck a lesson?"

"Do you know him?" Korin asked, but she shrugged in a way that was too hard to tell if she was lying or not. "What do you have in mind, anyway?"

"Let's have a look." Priscilla scanned the shelves containing assorted, liquid-filled vials. "Ah… this!" She grinned. "This will do perfectly," she said diabolically.

"You're not going to kill them, are you?" A sharp pain swiftly shot inside Korin's chest.

"No, of course not. Where's the fun in that?"

Korin stuttered before assertively responding, "You need to tell me your plan."

"I'm… *we're* going to simply make them sick. Just a little. That's all. Relax, Korin."

"How… how do I know you're telling the truth? I have no idea what that actually is."

Priscilla stared at Korin before unhappily replying, "Fine. Don't help. I don't need you."

Just as she was about to leave, Korin said, "Wait! I'll… I'll help."

Priscilla's face enlivened. "Thank you. I knew I could count on you, Korin. So, I need you to distract them while I place this on that pizza Sereck brought in."

As Korin left, he didn't feel excited nor happy about taking care of Sereck, but he pressed on. He was able to gain the attention of Sereck and his crotch-stroking girls, drawing them away from the pizza as an impish Priscilla administered the concoction. When the deed was finished, Korin sat back down next to Terala, with his eyes focused on the chair ahead, unsure of his actions.

He started panicking. *Fuck, what have I done?* Korin thought. *Maybe I should grab that pizza.*

Moments later, Sereck began uncontrollably heaving, accidentally throwing up over one of his girls before continuing on the floor. Everyone's attention focused on the drama, though Korin only watched to avoid looking suspicious. Korin didn't laugh, feeling as unclean as the vomit. Priscilla, however, was giggling quietly, glancing over at Korin who didn't notice. Sereck didn't stop, rushing out of the classroom as his girls worriedly followed, screeching as they did. Korin had wanted to teach Sereck and those girls a lesson only just over an hour ago but in his own, morally-justified way. In fact, he now felt compelled to make it up to Sereck before justly cracking down on him.

After a few minutes when the room settled down, Korin approached Priscilla. "He better stop spewing soon," he said assertively with a belly full of anxiety.

"Of course he will," Priscilla replied confidently. "But next time, we'll have to *openly* teach him and those *sluts* a lesson, so they know not to mess with us."

Us? Korin thought. *We'll have to see about that.*

"I'll look out for you, and you'll look out for me," she said contently, and then Korin nodded slowly before returning to his seat.

Terala turned to a sitting Korin, asking, "You okay?"

"Yeah. I'll be fine. I just need something to clear my mind. Anything."

"C'mon, Sylas, you can do it!" Jaimas cried, clapping his hands.

"Hey, guys, check this out!" Sylas called the whole class over, grabbing a few vials filled with red liquid. "I have no idea what's in these." He began juggling.

"What are you doing? They're dissolvent aquemicals!" Sophia yelled. "They can eat through your skin!"

Jaimas quickly responded, "As if they'd have skin-eating potions in a classroom."

"Read the labels, you idiot!"

"Wait!" Sylas yelled. "Skin eating?" Too staggered to properly focus, he dropped the vials on the floor. "Oh, crap!"

Suspended with shock at first, Sylas finally thought of a solution to the bubbling mess, promptly running over to fetch a bucket, momentarily fiddling with its lid. Sylas's panicky hands also made him drop the bucket a few times as he rushed over to the basin filled with diminishing silt marks reaching a mass of crusted sludge at the bottom. The water didn't pour out at first; instead, the pipes shuddered thunderously until a brown substance briefly oozed out. The rest of the class merely watched, backing away from the widening area of effect. After filling the bucket, Sylas splashed the water over the acid burning through the floor.

"What's water going to do?" Terala asked Sylas.

"It'll dilute it, I think." Sylas hurried to collect more water.

"But you're spreading it!" Sophia gasped.

"But, uh… get a mop! Get a mop!"

Terala hastily found a mop and prevented the substance from spreading, but the acid began deteriorating it as well.

"This should do it!" Sophia poured an appropriate, un-transfigured philtre over the mess, making the floor bubble furiously before smoking the entire room.

"What have you done?" Sylas started choking.

"Saved the room, dumbass!" Sophia barked back.

"I hope this goes away soon." He continued coughing.

Sophia opened the door and fanned as much of the smoke out as possible, but all the commotion unexpectedly caused the tutor to pop out of the supplementary room at the front of the lab. In his mid-twenties, the teacher had semi-long, bleach-blond hair and a nice tan on his somewhat fit body. His bloodshot eyes, however, were, at that moment, the most striking aspect to him. Everyone but Sylas, Sophia, and Terala had returned to their desks.

"What the fuck is going on here?" the tutor dazedly asked, frowning with confusion at the class.

One student answered, "They were juggling –"

"Yeah, juggling," Jaimas jumped in swiftly and very loudly, "uh, juggling with places to study after class." He then gave the other student a threatening countenance.

"Righto," the tutor responded casually, too zoned out to pay attention to the fading smoke. "You lot are early."

"Actually, *you're* late," Sophia informed him scornfully. "You've put us back thirty minutes."

"Alright, alright." The tutor held his head, clenching his eyes closed. "Settle down, girl." He flopped onto his chair. "So, this is your first class, right?" He tried to examine their faces, failing miserably.

"Ah, yeah, we're first-years," Terala answered, firing a dirty look.

"Good. I don't have to do much today." He rubbed his eyes roughly. "Open your books, and we'll start." A long pause then followed as the class waited for him to continue. "Well? Read! You're adults now. You do the bloody work!"

Many students glanced at one another, some smirking, others gaping.

Everyone's textbooks were uploaded to the synopool, able to be read holographically via their phids. Of course, a couple of people preferred using hard holochite textbooks, which nevertheless could still connect to the synopool; in addition, they were able to be compressed and expanded in size, with both states being incredibly lightweight. While Korin had a physical textbook, Sylas showed him how to access non-physical textbook through his watch; and when the holographic book was displayed, Korin 'laid' it down on the desk as if a hard book. The textbook and its first chapter respectively read: *Introduction to Alchemy*, 'The Fundamentals Part 1'. As the class read through the basics — concepts and facts which most pretty much already knew — the tutor sluggishly disappeared behind his desk.

All of a sudden, before anyone could do anything, the tutor popped his head out. "I'm just doing some alchemy down here." He giggled. "Some intense alchemy shit. Don't you be disturbing me now." He popped down again.

A puff of smoke then rose from the desk.

Instead of walking around to see, Jaimas thought of another idea. He ripped out a couple of pieces of paper from his notebook and then scanned them with his pen, its laser, in turn, causing the particles in the paper to form a particular way. Jaimas then placed the paper near a charchite, and the paper charged, quickly folding and forming into the shape of a penis. He then tossed it over the tutor's desk, hitting him on the first shot. Nothing happened. Jaimas grabbed more paper, this time dunking it into an odd-smelling substance found in a broken vial nearby before throwing again. On landing, the dildo generated a small cloud of gas, triggering the tutor to flare up with the nearby moths fanatically giving him all their attention.

"Oi, what the fuck?" the tutor yelled, flailing around as he fought off the moths. "What fugly dantha did that?" He stopped moving, scanning the class, arm up about to peg the penis at someone.

No-one responded – not even the 'good' students. Despite the act's juvenility, Korin found it amusing; he finally forgot about the ordeal with Sereck.

Rubbing his eyes relentlessly, the tutor dopily muttered, "Yeah, I fucking see how it fucking is. Fucking cunts… fucking… un-fucking-believable… I fucking can't fucking…" The tutor trailed off in a mumble before finally gathering himself. "No more messing around. I'll let you guys off this time. I'm pretty easy going like that." He chuckled. "Just… just keep reading, alright?"

Everyone was confused about the tutor's fluent switch in disposition. Jaimas decided not to aggravate him anymore, as the lesson had thus far been pretty chilled. A few minutes later, the students began quietly chatting amongst themselves. Meanwhile, Sylas noticed a peculiar piece of paper shoved in one of the desk's crevices, pulling it out after some effort.

"Hey, Korin, check this out." Sylas pointed to a comical, cartoony picture of a shifty-looking person holding a potion; the caption read: 'THE *INVESERI* POTION: See Through Most Fabrics! Have Fun And Be Responsible!' The below information described how to make and apply the potion to deviously see through people's clothing.

"Oh, and what do you intend on doing with that?" Terala asked from behind their backs, smirking.

"Uh… not peer through your clothes," Sylas answered abashedly.

"Sure. Give it here." She motioned.

"As if. Clearly, you wish to see through *my* clothes."

"Whatever you think, Sylas." She snickered.

For a few seconds, Terala didn't do anything until suddenly, she lunged at the page and grabbed it, cutting it into pieces with scissors before flushing them down the drain.

"Why the fuck did you do that?" Sylas complained.

"I wouldn't worry, Sylas," Celine chimed in. "You're bound to find the information elsewhere. Perhaps one of the libraries might accidentally have the information."

"Why'd you have to tell him that?" Terala crossly asked.

"Thanks, Celine." Sylas smiled mischievously. "I know I can trust you to have *my* back," he said before turning to Terala, grinning.

"I'll just destroy whatever you find, too," Terala brushed his remark off coolly.

"Unlikely. Good luck, though." He chuckled.

"You know, he's probably going to look through *your* clothes now," Terala told Celine, who returned to reading without commenting as her cheeks blushed.

"This is ridiculous!" Sophia called out. "We're not being taught anything!" She got up and marched around the table to see the tutor spaced out, gaping at the wall. "If you don't get up and teach us something, I'm going to get someone from the office!"

The tutor surveyed her groggily before unhurriedly standing up. It was a surprise he even moved.

"Thank you," she coldly said, returning to her seat.

"Look, I'll go, um… get some notes from out back, and, uh, we'll go through some things together, alright. Yeah? Good," the tutor finished saying before anyone could answer. He then ambled back into the supplementary room behind him and slammed the door closed. After a while, it didn't seem as if he'd reappear.

"Is he still alive?" Sylas joked.

"I've had enough!" Sophia complained. "I'm reporting this!"

When Sophia stormed off, the door to the supplementary room repeatedly banged, calling attention to moans and unusual noises increasing in volume.

Jaimas jumped out of his seat and dashed over to put his ear to the door. "He's rooting someone in there!" he whispered excitedly.

Most of the class quietly and giddily rushed over to the door to listen as the action grew louder. Feeling immature, Korin couldn't help but join in. Priscilla came to mind, but the scene soon engulfed such thoughts.

"Try and open it," Sylas whispered to Jaimas.

A few students searched for the key, but the noises stopped, and the doorknob rattled. Hurriedly, everyone made it back to their desks as the tutor moseyed out with his shirt unbuttoned.

"You, uh, doing your work?" The tutor unfocusedly glanced above everyone's heads.

Suddenly, a fluoro-red-haired woman with lots of tattoos and piercings popped her head out of the door, asking, "Hey, are you coming back in?"

One classmate cheekily asked the tutor, "What were you doing in there with her?"

"None of your fucking business!" the tutor answered. "She's my, uh, my assistant."

Another head then popped out the door. Instead of seeing another mage, the class saw a purple, vaguely-humanoid mammalian alien called a gosock; she featured four arms with as many breasts bulging from her tight-leather underwear, and finger-sized dorsal fins that looked like chunky feelers were also waving all up and down her head and back.

The purple woman then asked in a sensual voice, "Coming back to straddle the mantle?" She grinned.

"Oh, and who's she?" another student asked.

"Um, she's my… other assistant. Y-yeah," the tutor said, just as an obscure sex toy rolled out on the floor beside his foot. A fluorescent liquid drooled from it. And it mooed.

"Fuck off!" another student called out, grinning. "You three were rooting in there."

Gesturing with assurance as the mooing grew louder, the tutor responded, "Nah, nah, you're way off, mate. Way, way out of line."

"Out of line?" Terala asked. "What's that you've got there?" She pointed to the multifaceted apparatus attached to his clothes.

"Nothing you kids could handle." The tutor chuckled as he hopelessly tried to conceal it.

"You don't seem to be handling whatever that is too well."

"What?" The tutor asked offendedly, wincing and flinching back. "You think you could handle a puff of this? This is rokesh bud. You couldn't last a minute."

"Rokesh?" Sylas whispered. "No wonder he's so weirdly bipolar."

"I bet *I* could," Jaimas asserted, standing up eagerly.

"You? You think you can handle this?" the tutor asked irately as the horny mooing turned a little more aggressive. "Mate, you have no idea. No fucking clue, mate."

"Alright, give me a puff, and we'll see." Jaimas folded his arms, tilting his head boastfully.

"Ha! Righto. Here." He grinned, handing Jaimas the odd pipe.

"Ah, Jaimas, that might not be a good idea," Sylas warned as the mooing began gurgling – and it wasn't because it was malfunctioning.

"Chill, Sylas," Jaimas said casually, puffing a few times. "See, I'm –" His eyes whirled as his head spun right before his body keeled over.

"Shit! Victar's Robe!" the tutor yelled, trembling. "That was grade three bud. What was I thinking? Ah…" His focus returned. "Quick," he said, turning to his girlfriend – the redhead, "get some morelin weed."

The mooing, at that point, turned into an orgy, filled with an assortment of sounds. When his girlfriend handed him the morelin weed juice, the tutor poured it down Jaimas's throat while telling both lovers to find a particular tonic. Meanwhile, Jaimas made various groaning sounds as froth foamed from his mouth. As soon as the tutor received the tonic, he poured it into the frothing mouth, and it wasn't long before Jaimas stopped foaming. He nevertheless lost consciousness.

Sophia abruptly returned with their Alchemy professor, both looking horrified. With the look the professor gave, it wouldn't have been *that* surprising if her permed, greying hair transformed into aggravated snakes.

"Baran? What have you done?" the professor screeched at the sobering tutor.

"Taliah? Ah, he, uh…" The tutor blinked nonstop. "I-I can explain."

"Get out of here and head straight to my office! *Outside* my office. You two as well." The professor glared at both the guilty-faced girlfriend and the non-mage, with the latter appearing extremely concerned.

"I, uh…" Baran couldn't find any fitting words before awkwardly exiting the lab. As he did, the mooing sex toy gave an excited, approving noise!

Taliah then promptly called for someone to take Jaimas to the emergency ward as the class stared aghast. It wasn't long before a couple of people arrived, and after Jaimas left on a stretcher, the professor, now free, finally picked up the unusual sex toy with a pair of thick gloves and then threw it away, repeatedly smashing it while it was in the bin.

"My apologies for the trouble caused today," Taliah addressed everyone, catching her breath. "Again, Jaimas will survive. It may, however, take a while for him to recover – perhaps a week, at the very least. So, I can take over for the remaining time and cover the basics everyone should have learned by now. I –"

"What will happen to the tutor?" Korin asked Taliah.

"Never mind what will happen to *him*. As I was saying, most of you have probably gathered that numerous substances have devastating effects on the body. It's very easy to acquire an addiction, *even* after many years of training."

Sophia held her head back, saying, "Okay, okay, drugs are bad. We get it. Can we get on with the lesson, please? We're running out of time." She tapped a large clock that she had expanded through her phid.

"Wow! I can't believe how rude they're becoming," Taliah said aloud.

"No, we're simply keener to learn. That's what you want, is it not?"

The professor was stunned. Taking a moment to respire, she then faux-grinned. "Fine," she finally said. "But I want to explain a few points before we begin. In –"

"How come you didn't conduct the lecture?" a girl asked.

"Unfortunately, something came up last minute. The university has been slightly disorganized this week. The admin would've tried contacting Baran, but I assume they didn't get through. Anyway, the magic of alchemy encompasses the arts of enchanting and transfiguration; and, as a subject, we focus more so on biotic enchanting over non-biotic enchanting; that is, we enchant our own bodies, along with ingredients for potions to help us reach higher potential states. For the first semester, we won't be enchanting or transfiguring anything, nor will we be learning how to make potions. Instead, despite ever-changing pedagogical standards imposed on us, we will cover theory, equipment usage, math, item priming, and tuning into and choosing potential states."

Sophia abruptly enlarged a holographic clock again, rudely tapping it.

"Do you want me to teach or not?" Taliah snapped at Sophia.

"Yeah, I do. So continue." She smirked.

Taliah blankly stared. "Okay," she slowly said, stretching her hands out while breathing deeply. She then suddenly noticed the unlocked cabinets filled with dangerous substances, and her eyes grew with fear. "Nobody touch anything!" Taliah ordered as her hands quivered. "It looks like the winter-school researchers didn't clean up after themselves. I have no idea why they were even in this room. It needs a major renovation." She paused with an angrily-clued-on face. "Huh… I know why."

After locking the cabinets, the professor continued explaining the fundamentals of alchemy. As the students would later properly learn in General Theory, magic was a product of consciousness. Therefore, all enchanting was done via a mage's consciousness, universally in a meditative state, and generally with apparatuses. Confusing a few students at first, *quantum* and *etheric potential states* were said to be accessed during the process. As it was only the first lesson, Taliah didn't dive too deep into the quantum mechanics – just enough to explain the basic etheric, subatomic, and chemical phenomena.

"I hope I've covered enough of the basics." Taliah smiled.

"You couldn't get any more basic," Sophia monotonously added as some of the students sniggered.

"Well," Taliah replied, smirking, "there's no need for you to partake in the exercise today."

While seething, Sophia packed her equipment and stormed off yet again, though no-one really cared.

After reading through some of the theory, the class's exercise involved *priming* the etheric field of a set of leaves. Although the exercise would not extend beyond this, the main role, they were informed, was to manipulate the quantum properties of an item as a whole, allowing for much easier changes – and accessibility within – the item's etheric field. In other words, it would help the enchanter to access greater potential states. Objects and people had overall etheric fields – fields that were more than the sum of their quantum properties – and this overall field possessed a standard *quantum base state* while simultaneously holding many surrounding states of possibilities that were its etheric dormant potential. These possibilities had their limits relative to the item and the mage's ability to access them, too. When accessed and enchanted, base states could transfigure into *quantum trans states*, in turn biochemically transforming an object or person.

Their first-year equipment included bendy wires, chargers, magnifiers, and retainers – all made of varying crystals and rare metals. The geometrically-formed wires called *aligners* helped reorientate the flow of both the mage's consciousness *and* the energies of the charger crystal, a charchite, enabling the main effect to take place. The magnifiers strengthened this process, while the retainers kept the energy within as the changes stabilized. There were many types of techniques involved with altering the etheric energy, but once the etheric restructuring had taken place, it was normally a requirement for enchanters to finish the enchantment process quickly or else they would have to prime the item again.

Since there was still a lot of information to process, some people remained a little confused. Nevertheless, after Taliah gave a few demonstrations and explanations, the entire class commenced the exercise. Unlike the start of his Conjuration lecture, Korin detected that a few of his peers were a tad confused as well, and so by being in the same situation, he knew what level of understanding that was expected of him.

Every person individually worked on the exercise, but they somewhat ended up working in groups to help one another. Sylas started bending his wires to match the pattern in the book, jumbling and knotting them.

Terala noticed and leaned over. "How on Juntas did you mess that up so badly?"

"It's… My hands are stuck," Sylas said hopelessly. "Can you help?"

"What? Dude, they're just a bunch of knots. Ugh, fine, give me your hands." In a short time, *her* hands became stuck as well. "How the fuck did this happen? Sylas, this is your fault. Korin, can you help us, please?"

"How…" Korin frowned, perplexed. "Okay, just hold still." As he touched the wires, a static shock zapped him. "Ow! Shit!"

"Quick! They're warming up, too!" Sylas added.

"Okay… okay… if I just… The ends are locked in the middle!" Korin stated with astonishment. "Sylas, did you do this on purpose? Just to finally tie the knot with Terala?"

"Oh, please! Get me out of this!" Sylas yanked, but the wires tightened.

Korin attempted to place his hands in again, getting zapped once more. Celine had just returned from her toilet break and was stunned at what she saw. Without inquiring, she placed her hand in and attempted unknotting the wires, but she, too, got tangled.

"You were meant to help us!" Terala cried.

"I am helping!" Celine responded, but her dangling bracelets made matters worse.

What's more, her jewellery contained a source of energy that reacted to the wires, causing the latter to glow and eventually begin melting. All three panicked, thinking they would be burned, but the melting only turned the wires into a gluey substance, which then rapidly expanded into a puffy ball that looked like fairy floss. Although tight, it was peculiarly cushiony.

The professor then approached, crossing her arms. "Either dodgy wires or dodgy behaviour. Hmm." She icily examined their red faces, almost cooling them off. "Don't move. I have something for it."

Everyone felt calmer knowing at least Taliah knew what she was doing.

"I wonder if we can eat our way out," Sylas said.

"Too bad Jaimas isn't here." Korin chuckled. "He'd try it."

"Touch it. It feels weird," Sylas said, shaking the ball, which dragged the girls' arms up and down.

"Not so fast!" Celine reacted, appearing very helpless.

Korin hesitantly, though curiously, touched it, sticking his finger in before finding himself trapped as well. He rolled his eyes, not surprised by the outcome, whereas Sylas laughed, feeling great having eventually trapped Korin, too. The professor soon returned with a substance that fully melted the foam, releasing the relieved group. They were able to return to their task, though Sylas could only watch. Even then, he couldn't help but touch items here and there. Korin didn't mind, but he made sure Sylas didn't go overboard.

Once Korin adequately created the pattern with his wires, he positioned his crystals in the instructed order and proceeded to focus his intent on the leaves. The calmness he experienced during his meditation in Conjuration returned, and he felt his own etheric energy – and the crystal's – moving around. It wasn't so much the leaves themselves that glowed, as it was the charchite's energy that formed an aura. He tried 'spinning' the etheric energy per the instructions, but time passed very quickly, and the class stopped mid-task.

***

While seated in the food hall for dinner that night, Korin asked Sylas, "So, are you still going to look into making that potion?"

"Of course!" Sylas enthusiastically replied before looking sullen. "But I don't know where. I mean, I haven't actually *tried* to find it on the synopool yet." He activated his phid. "The trouble is, information is pretty tightly controlled. The government has an effective system in place, and they're able to block and censor a lot."

"Why would they block a simple recipe like that?" Korin asked, watching Sylas's concentrated screen angled between Sylas and himself.

"You'd be surprised how many ultra-nannies are out there pushing for this shit. They literally spend most of their waking hours finding new things to ban. There are ways to get around it, but it's tricky. You can also buy black-market NDCs – neurachite data chips, so you know – with heaps of stuff on them, but they're hard to come by."

"Celine mentioned libraries. Would libraries regulate books in a similar way as well?"

"It… depends. Newer books would have updated information, so they'd most likely have the same limited info like the sites found on the pool. As for older books… they're a possibility, but libraries have tech that can scan for 'problematic' content'." Sylas sighed, continuing his search for a little longer. "Nope. Nothing. I think there might be some specialty bookstores I could try, though."

"In any case, you wouldn't be able to use it without learning transfiguration."

Sighing again, Sylas said, "I guess you're right."

"You're still thinking about that recipe?" Terala griped, taking a seat. "I bet there are other potions out there that'd do more for your lust, anyway."

"Don't give him any ideas." Korin laughed. "It's probably too late now."

Sylas chuckled. "Yeah, you're right. Thanks, Terala."

Terala rolled her eyes, asking Sylas, "Wouldn't it be best to -- I don't know -- improve yourself, so you can easily pick women up, instead of resorting to voyeuristic schemes?"

"Yeah, but I aim to be a professional at my craft. Women love professionalism."

"Professionalism, my ass." She rolled her eyes again.

Before Sylas retorted, Jaimas walked by as if nothing had happened to him.

"Nothing seems to stop that guy," Korin noted in bewilderment.

"Yeah," Sylas responded, "and apparently, a lot of the other guys that he got wasted with took a few days to recover."

Terala sent Sylas a curious look. "I'm shocked you didn't drink with him."

"Well, I don't drink," Sylas replied before drinking a glass of juice in one swig. "Of alcohol, I mean."

"Really?" Terala asked in surprise. "How come? I would've assumed you drank a lot."

"Well, I never saw much alcohol growing up. Like, I was never around drunk high-schoolers."

"Oh, that's right," she said slowly. "You mentioned that your parents were strict, hey?"

"In some ways, yes; in some ways, no. They always wanted me to grow up respectable, so I could take over their business one day, but I have no intention of doing so. It's too mind-fuckingly-numbing. Funnily enough, I agreed that I'd do Business, majoring in Finance and Man-agement. I don't know if I should change, but I didn't know what else to do. I wonder if History and Political Science are laidback." He looked at Korin.

"My choices were pretty limited when I picked them," Korin said. "Plus, I have yet to start them."

"Yeah, maybe those would be a borefest, too. What about you, Terala? What other subjects are you doing?"

"Um, I... opted for a vocational subject," she said in a quiet voice without making eye contact.

"Vocational subjects are fine," Celine said nicely, detecting her insecurity. "I even thought about doing some. A few looked pretty fun. And perhaps my Fine Arts program is questionably vocational."

Terala wasn't expecting Celine's response, shortly saying, "Thanks. In my last year of high school, I didn't study that much, let's just say. I bet I could've gotten good grades if I did. I'm not an idiot. Anyway, I'm doing Emergency Services. I want to get out and explore the Caelverse and save people."

"That sounds like a lot of fun. Maybe I could take some emotionally-moving pictures of you saving people."

"Heh. Yeah, that would look cool." Terala warmly smiled at Celine.

"Well, hang on," Sylas said with a cheeky face, "if you're a bit of a rescuer, where were you during the flood?"

"Occupied trying to save people from anime pillows," Terala managed to deliver with a stern face.

"Wha'?" Sylas slumped in his seat. "There's… there's nothing wrong with anime."

Terala grinned, knowing she had touched a nerve.

As they continued debating the topic of anime, Celine tilted her head while gazing at Sylas's expensive rings and necklace for a while, finally pointing and asking, "Did your parents buy you those?"

"My rings? No way would I let my parents buy me stuff like this."

Celine stood up and walked to the other side of the table, placing her hand next to Sylas's to physically compare, poke, and pull his jewellery that happened to be straight out of a fantasy series he liked. Sylas simply let her, wondering where it would lead. She then said, "Maybe you should open a jewellery shop with those Business studies of yours."

"Mm," Sylas responded uneasily. "No, I'd be bored with that, too."

Before Celine responded, Jaimas unexpectedly sauntered up to the table. "Hey, did you hear what happened?" He rested his arms on the table, almost knocking two plates over.

"No," Korin said. "What happened to you? Are you alright?"

"Huh? Me? What are you talking about?" Jaimas grabbed a piece of Korin's food and ate it.

Wincing his face in confusion, Korin slowly replied, "You were knocked unconscious."

"Oh, yeah, *I'm* totally fine," Jaimas replied breezily. "I meant what happened to some other guys?" he asked, and the group gestured in the negative. "Well, there was another demon attack. One girl died. Apparently, a pen was driven right into her neck, and blood pissed out everywhere."

"Who's neck?" Korin checked his shoulder. "Is everything under control now?"

"Don't know. You never know who's going to get possessed." Jaimas stared at the group quite peculiarly, causing an uncomfortable silence. The stare then turned rather grim. His head started trembling as he began gagging, and in no time, his body convulsed. Hitting and scratching his face, Jaimas made all sorts of bizarre, demonic noises as a few of the surrounding people watched fearfully. Jaimas fell to one knee, clutching the table as he heaved, glaring menacingly as he grabbed his reddening throat with his other hand.

"Not you as well!" Sylas stood up.

"Nah, I'm just kidding!" Jaimas guffawed before informing those nearby. He then swiftly turned serious, severely leering at Korin's group, saying, "Let's hope none of us get attacked," before oddly walking off without concern.

"He had me worried," Celine said distraughtly. "I know that generally we're safe from demonic possession, but what if there's something unusual happening that's increasing the odds of possession? Perhaps we could use incantations to protect ourselves."

"I don't think that's necessary," Korin said. "I mulled over demon possession in general, and I think the people who got possessed were probably dealing with demons, anyway."

"Two in a short time is odd, though," Terala said.

"Those two people could've been friends or associates. Anyway, I don't feel like doing any rituals, if that's what you have in mind."

"Why's that?" Sylas asked. "Do you think they'll be too hard to do?"

"No, it's because… it's because I just don't want to. I…" Korin sighed. "I-I don't want to do anything remotely associated with my old religion. We performed many rituals. Ceremonial rituals."

"We don't have to do any rituals," Celine said. "I don't really know much about incantations, anyway. Maybe we could use special pendants instead. I'll look into it for you guys."

"Well, alright. But just remember that I now think that, at the very least, demonic possession mainly occurs through messing around with demons in the first place."

"So, are you ready to talk more about your old religion?" Terala asked.

"No! For the last time –" Korin stood up, angrily exhaling. "You just wouldn't understand."

"Well, try us. We're listening. And we're not going to think of you negatively."

Korin looked around at all the people busily eating and chatting; none had knowledge of his background or of the occulted religious issues outside of their safe space. The more he thought about his experiences, the angrier he became. His heart fluttered, conflicted between rage and a rising sea of various sad emotions. He felt hurt – hurt that he couldn't fully connect with those around him, especially his friends.

"Hey, Korin," Sylas said gently. "We'll try and help with anything you're dealing with, but you need to tell us what you're thinking."

Words tried to leave Korin's mouth, but quivering breaths were needed to keep his emotions intact, maintaining the visage of stability. Finally, he managed to utter, "You… you… wouldn't understand." Korin had suppressed his thoughts for a week in order to mentally cope with his new environment – and he had hitherto successfully done so – but the mental dam had at long last burst, and he realized he needed to evacuate immediately.

"We can go somewhere else if you need," Celine said softly, almost whispering.

Korin couldn't reply. He staggered before making his way out of the seating area, rapidly walking outside. As he was still in public light, he kept himself together. Just outside, though, Korin noticed a large **'MISSING STUDENTS'** poster looming above a few sobbing undergraduates who were saying how they would do anything to get their friends back. Although feeling sorry for the group, Korin wasn't in the mood to think about the dilemma. Still, the instant thought of others suffering took attention away from Korin's self-woes and ironically kept him from crying for the time being.

***

That night, Korin decided he needed solitude for numerous reasons. A lot had happened in his life in such a short period of time. His world had been twisted upside down, and even though slivers of the day randomly rushed through his mind, basically all he could think about was his religious background and how it fitted into his new mage habitat. It wasn't a simple matter of Korin suppressing his memories; there was still the fresh, energetic residue of recent events subtly sitting around his actual etheric being, building up like that of moisture around tiring legs during a morning run through a dewy forest. He lay on his bed, staring at the ceiling, blocking out the loud noises outside.

A more collected memory came to mind featuring a fifteen-year-old Korin standing in front of a large crowd of people at a ceremony, where he was being awarded a medal for bravely saving someone's life. Although he didn't actually fight the monster, Korin managed to survive the encounter.

"Do you know why you were able to succeed?" a priest asked Korin.

"I knew I had to do it. He would've died," Korin said firmly.

"Yes, that's technically right, but with my very own eyes, I saw Draghar watching over you. He helped you by providing additional courage and strength. He sees great potential in you – as do we. Hopefully now you can see that with Draghar's power, you can do a lot of good."

"Why me? Doesn't he have others to watch over?"

"You're special, Korin. What you did was spectacular. Most couldn't hope to survive against a monster of such power. It's unfortunate that we didn't get to raise you in a more… special way when you were younger. It's too late now, but you can still serve us in fantastic ways. I think it's best to pray tonight and thank Draghar for his aid."

Korin curiously asked, "In what *other* way would I have been raised?"

"Oh…" The priest chuckled. "I can't really say. I think you would have been an interesting case. You have remarkable talent, so we have…

other plans for you. Don't worry. You'll serve Sacrenderism well and prove your worth to Draghar." He patted Korin.

Once the memory passed, another was immediately recalled. Korin was praying in a small stone temple in the countryside during a beautiful morning, and he remembered opening his eyes and seeing a wispy sphere of light-blue energy floating in front of him. Korin knew it was a wisp, though he wasn't sure if it was a sentient physical wisp or a ghost wisp. He was nonetheless certain that it wasn't a non-sentient gas wisp or a drone wisp, though. The radiating being struggled to enter the temple, as if an invisible wall blocked it off; and just as Korin was about to inquisitively greet it, the wisp disappeared. Sitting back down, Korin felt a cold presence beside him, which grew stronger before slowly vanishing.

The memory passed, and one more initiated.

Another teenaged Korin was sparring with others his age. He was quite adept with the wooden staff, easily defeating his peers, who were envious of his skills. Eventually, they decided to gang up on Korin, striking him until he was on the ground in great pain. When they left, Korin angrily limped to the nearby temple, seeking the clergy's aid.

"You don't need them," a monk told Korin. "Draghar will provide all the company you'll ever need; and he'll never be envious of your fighting abilities as they are."

The short recollections ended, and Korin slumped over on his side in frustration for being lied to for so long. The thought of so many hours, days, and years wasted serving an evil religion played on his mind. Despite what he said at dinner, Korin wished he could go outside and talk to his friends about his experiences, but he continued to speculate that no other mage had remotely faced what he had gone through.

I need to move on from this. I'm a mage now, Korin thought. *But I can't just forget and let go of what they did. Of what they not only did to me but to everyone else. And Visten. I can't believe Visten was one of them. How many of the priests knew? Like, why were they... I... I can't believe I was lied to like that. This whole time. This whole time!* He shook his head in amazement. *While everyone else had a normal upbringing, I... was taught garbage. To serve evil. I cannot believe it. This whole time. I just... this whole time. I was serving evil. I cannot believe it! I- I- this... wow, I...*

Korin started crying softly, curling up while holding his blankets tightly. His thoughts collapsed into disarray, angrily, irrationally, and primitively jumping from one point of blame regarding his suffering and upbringing to another. Tears and nose-runs began to soak the pillow, spreading over half of Korin's scrunched face. He felt like his whole being would naturally and eternally curl up on itself, one without an ending to the misery.

Chapter Nine

Training Day: Forging a New Path

Korin's mind was burnt. In one way, it was beneficial. His ever-growing, prickly mental weeds needed decimating, along with the livid monsters thriving in that environment. There were no more tears to be shed, and tranquillity settled in.

Sitting up against the wall with his pillow, Korin felt as though he was now free to start anew, rebuilding from the night before. At first, he affirmed to himself that he would be more guarded against the effects of indoctrination and conditioning in the future – by anyone, religious or not. The momentum in thought allowed him to march on; instead of focusing on his religious past, Korin ruminated on the positive experiences of the last week as he fixedly stared at the opposing wall, knowing there were more interesting events ahead. Phasarchement – colloquially named *lucent* magic – seemed like both a fascinating magic and subject from the information he gathered, so Korin's excitement and energy began delicately flowering again.

About two hours of little movement and steady recovery passed; and when Korin heard his neighbours rising, he readily left his bedroom. As students poured into the food hall, Korin halted for a few seconds, realizing that even if no-one had a background like he had, they still had their own unique upbringings, and some may have had terrible experiences. Feeling a little too self-absorbed, he moreover considered the fact that his peers came from different social classes, all holding numerous stories. Regardless of everyone's circumstances, most were adjusting… to a fair enough extent; there were always some who *immaturely* whinged over everything.

"Hey… were you… crying last night?" Sylas quietly asked Korin as they lined up for food.

Korin hesitated for a moment before saying, "Yeah. Yeah, I was." His growing joy slightly diminished. "It's… this whole thing is really different and…"

"You don't like it here? Wait, I don't smell, do I?" Sylas checked his armpits and chuckled, trying to lighten the mood.

"No, I do like it here. Think… think of it like this: How would you feel if you were in a relationship with someone, and it turned out that they not only never loved you, but hated you, and used you for their own evil goals… your whole life?"

"Is this hypothetical person hot? No, sorry." He laughed briefly before turning serious. "I think I'd be pissed off."

Korin stared coolly at Sylas, again thinking that nobody would ever comprehend his experiences.

"I'm sorry," Sylas repeated. "I know there's a lot more for me to understand. Just trying to cheer you up."

"I know. Thanks. Anyway, that's just a glimpse of what I felt last night." He took a few seconds to absorb his bright scenery. "I feel a lot better now, and I want to put those memories behind me."

"Great. Well, if you need to talk, just let me know." He patted Korin.

When Korin spotted Terala and Celine, he didn't want to burden them with any more depressing thoughts, so he greeted them normally as if nothing had happened. Korin could tell they wanted to ask questions, but he maintained that he wouldn't unload his burdens.

"So," Korin said to Terala as they sat at a table, "did you find out why you only saw grey during your meditation? I noticed that you bumped into Renola right before dinner last night."

"She said that it was nothing. I hadn't gone deep enough or something like that. Renola then went on about another thing, but I didn't know what she was talking about."

"Maybe a demon was trying to get inside your mind," Sylas said before his face swiftly turned aghast. "Oh, shit, she's tur–"

Terala playfully pushed him. "Don't even think about it, Sylas. No demon will ever possess me."

Sylas laughed as if his joke would never *not* be funny. "Just looking out for everyone."

"Hey," Korin said to Celine, "didn't you say you'd research into special pendants for us in order to prevent demonic possession?"

"Yes, but I found too much conflicting information, so I wasn't sure what we could really use."

"What are *those* pendants you're wearing?"

"Most are astrological. This one's a Dreamas pendant – a dominant zodiac sign of mine. My birthday was about a month ago. And as for incantations, I couldn't see anything that seemed useful to our situation; but then again… I kind of got a bit distracted looking at honeycore designs. I saw some really nice flower stamps that I can use for some of my containers."

"I see. Okay, look, I think we'll be fine. Demonic possession in all likelihood occurs when you mess with the spirits. Doesn't matter if you follow a religion or not. All we'll have to do is just watch out for other people who may be possessed."

***

Most of the first-years had their Phasarchement classes outdoors; Korin's had his class in a small field of grass right next to the biggest forest in the Nature Reserve. Leaves and flowers of several kinds were blossoming, thickening the already-dense treetops as light managed to shine through, invigorating small creatures crawling into the sunny gaps. Birds chirped cheerfully, insects virtually hummed tunes, and barely any drones flew overhead.

The man in charge wore casual attire of camo-pants and a plain singlet – a style Terala highly approved. As he crossed his arms, critically scanning the area, the veins on his large biceps almost popped out. His high and tight haircut matched his assertive and strict stance, while his footing alone sent a wave of forceful energy through the soil. No part of the forest was a threat to him.

"Good morning, everyone," the fit man addressed the class. "I'm Cartras, your instructor for this semester," he enthused, clapping his hands hard. "As you'll come to see, I conduct my business differently than a lot my contemporaries. My *official* job is to make sure each one of you reaches a minimum standard set by the university. Three hours a week of training, however, is a pitiful amount in my books. If you want to reach your maximum potential, you'll have to put in more hours than that. For anyone interested, I run further training sessions. My *personal* goal is to see you guys exceed expectations. By the end of your degree, the university sets that you only need to attain average power levels in order to pass. However, I believe its possible for nearly every student to reach *elite* power levels if they put in the effort. So, before we begin, I want you to mindfully look at the most widespread version of the Noble Magehood Virtues."

Cartras pointed to a vertical flag divided by the *arch-elements*. Columned, traditionally-styled calligraphy was displayed in each section, appearing as if someone had taken their painstaking time making it. It read:

FIRE: Fortitude; Ambitiousness; Spiritedness — Honour.
EARTH: Temperance; Patience; Diligence — Responsibility.
WATER: Prudence; Profoundness; Receptiveness — Compassion.
AIR: Impartialness; Inventiveness; Adaptiveness — Justness.

Meticulously-designed symbols featured behind each caption, and all the virtues were equally encouraged. Only a few people, however, bothered to actually look at the flag with eagerness and conscientiousness.

One student with a contemptuous face said, "You can't impose your morals on us. It's against the rules."

Cartras remained stoically silent before replying, "I know. But I can impose educational standards on you, and the virtues are an extension of those requirements, so deal with it. And with that, respect falls under honour and justness. Dick with me or your classmates, and you'll feel it later on."

Quite a number of people glanced around anxiously.

"Feeling your what now?" Sylas whispered to Korin. Both giggled quietly.

"To clarify: I want you to put in a hundred and eleven percent, no matter what. I don't want anyone giving me any whining khorshit. You bloody well do your assigned task. Understand?" Cartras asked firmly.

Most of the class murmured back unsurely and timidly.

"Come on, people! Wake up!" Cartras screamed at the top of his lungs, more so in the vein of vitalizing the class than out of anger. "I asked: do you understand?"

Immediately, a large portion of the class shouted back, although some students shrieked merely out of fear.

"Who does this guy think he is?" one of the students asked another, sniggering. "He's not compassionate in the slightest."

"Ugh, I know. Such a brute," another commented in a puny manner, turning his head away in disgust.

Cartras resolutely marched over to the first student and stared him straight in the eyes. Their noses practically touched. "Whatever you want me to be, buddy." Cartras breathed heavily on the student's face.

Just as it seemed like the kid would talk or yell back, he actually burst into tears, curling up on the ground.

Another student suddenly approached. The girl's hair was bright red, half shaved off the side and crookedly cut around the edges, as if beauty and grace were somehow oppressive and vulgar. She angrily threw her jacket on the ground, revealing a t-shirt stating: 'End. Mage. Supremacy.'. Although, a few of the crudely-designed letters were crumpled under her bulging rolls. Another two students of the same nature joined her, both crossing their arms, scowling at Cartras with hatred.

"How *dare* you oppress us like this!" the social justice warrior shouted.

"Oppress you?" Cartras asked, dumbfounded. "Perhaps you need to flee the university, then." He chuckled.

"No! *You* need to leave! We're not going to tolerate your abuse and cruelty! No-one should be forced to cry. You're here to make us feel welcome and comfortable! If you don't stop this and apologize, we'll report on you and make sure you're not only fired but never get another job again!"

Cartras leered menacingly, cracking his knuckles before robustly replying, "Listen here, you degenerate. You can tell all the fucking people in the Caelverse you want, but I will still fail you if you choose not to comply. But obviously, you want a safe space. I get that. So, feel free to roam around and graze on the meadow over there. It suits you three. We won't disturb you. Go on."

His remarks mortified the three girls; and without another screech, each slowly backed away before waddling over to their safe space. A few people joined them out of their hatred of Cartras. Terala turned to Korin, shaking her head before rolling her eyes. Korin agreed with a smirk.

Cartras didn't pursue those who left, turning to address the class. "I will never ask of you what I wouldn't do myself. Listen to what I say, and do everything better than what you think you can. Got it?"

Everyone understood, with most replying back vigorously or at minimum giving the impression of enthusiasm. Korin found Cartras a little over the top – his methods were excessive, although understandable, given the faults of the education system – but there was a part of him he liked; he also not only preferred the vigour, but Korin appreciated the idea and practice of instilling virtues.

"In Phasarchement," Cartras said, "you'll still find some similarities to other magics. Essentially, you'll still focus on four main aptitudes. The first regards your connection to the Aether; the second involves holding energy in your lumarchetrix; the third is the actual channelling of your lumarchetrix energy itself; and the fourth is the area of conscious effect around you. Once you grow in power in all four aspects, we'll move on to more advanced techniques and practices to help continue building your power levels. An important thing to understand is that many variables affect one's consciousness, and one of the biggest is your own physical body. This means that you'll be exercising." He grinned for a moment, letting the implications settle in their minds. "The assorted physical activities we'll run through will require a focused and even meditative mind, which in turn will help develop your connection, holding, channelling, and area of effect abilities. Any questions so far?" he asked, but no-one said anything. "Good. To wake everyone up, we're going for a run." Before the run commenced, Cartras demonstrated a few warmup exercises, with the class following his lead.

Sylas whispered to Korin, "How are some of these people going to survive this?"

"It doesn't look good," Korin replied, finishing his last stretch. "At least Sereck isn't here to cause trouble." *And Priscilla*, he was tempted to say aloud.

"Are you guys up for a race?" Terala asked keenly.

"Of course," Korin said just before Cartras shouted for everyone to start the run.

The class began racing through the dirt path in the forest, and Cartras followed up the rear while shouting profusely, ensuring even the slowest was putting in full effort.

"Oh, Jhar, that doesn't sound good." Terala laughed, panting at the same time.

The track winded upwards along the considerably large hillside, and the distances between the students stretched. Korin and Terala were in the lead with a couple of others, but Celine and then Sylas trailed behind. Eventually, Terala and those nearby fell behind as well, resulting in Korin taking the lead by himself. Cartras seemed less and less influential as the gap widened, while Korin felt more and more confident the further he ran. The path branched off in two directions, and Korin's self-determination waned while questioning which one to take, so he waited for the class, panting heavily.

From nowhere visible, an azure ball of bright light emerged, weaving in and out of the trees down near the left pathway. Korin instantly recognized that it was some kind of wisp – one similar from his not-too-distant past. He remembered the cold presence he felt afterwards, but Korin considered that it had something to do with his former religion rather than the wisp itself. The current wisp silently beckoned Korin to travel off the pathway as it floated back; and without the slightest hesitation, Korin chased it with equal speed.

Shrubs, small logs, and other forest quirks were no problem for the wisp, while Korin's resilience enabled him to greatly hop, staggeringly zigzag, swiftly dodge, and sharply brush through as he sustained the distance. Moving steadily through the thickening flora, the alluring wisp seemed to make no noise. Rocks of enlarging size began to suffocate Korin's choice of direction, but he soon heard water gushing in the background, eventually reaching the edge of a small waterfall.

At the end of the flow, white froth dissipated quickly, mellowing as ordinary water into the relatively-clear pool, gleaming shifting shards of sunlight. The endless repetition of the splintering, crashing water calmed Korin as his breathing slowed. When he briefly closed his eyes, the wafting, freshly-moistened dirt smelled even stronger. Massive mossy rocks enclosed the area, cosily cribbing its undisclosed mystique with pockets of darkness in between. Soaking in the beauty for a minute, Korin turned to the wisp, which signalled for him to descend.

"Are you serious?" Korin asked the wisp, but it didn't respond.

Reluctantly, Korin took his clothes off and decided to take a leap of faith, diving into the clean and cool water. Korin then rose to the top and saw the wisp float towards the rocky wall through the waterfall, wondering if he was being led into a trap. When behind the waterfall, Korin observed the wisp moving in an out of the top of the wall, as if the rock was permeable. Confusing him at first, Korin soon detected that the 'rock' was an illusion – and in fact, translucent – so he began climbing the real rock to reach the gap. Once on top, he noticed that the top rock was creating an illusion when viewed at particular angles. Still, he wondered if there was anything else fuelling the illusion…

Shivering all over, Korin saw the tiny cave on the other side, so he hurried down and made his way to a rickety table with a small box on top; he also noticed a very old fleshless skeleton wearing ripped and worn clothes lying next to the cave wall. It didn't even produce an odour, but the cave itself did smell dank. While the outside light did enter the cave, the wisp helped provide a lot of light as well as it stayed still, waiting for Korin to proceed. After opening the box, Korin found a mouldy tree-paper journal with tattered sides and holes; only one, naturally sepia-toned page remained. At the top, the date read: 'Moonday 3rd of Dudesis, 7970' – about 2,500 years old. The entry read:

Forsooth, this will be my last entry. All the other pages afore today were ripped out. I have erewhile managed to keep low, hearkening for a mere moment of apricity, but the cultists are verily adroit at detecting energies. Petrei capitulated eftsoons cracking up, and they captured Drevele in an ambuscade, whilst Froden died from a lack of apothecary physics. The Gathering has doubtless slain the remaining members. Our order is obliterated. Grand Sorceress Backlevy has managed to unfurl her cult's constituents throughout the university administration, and the mass of students simply will not rise and shine, maugre their worsening conditions. And this is maugre witnessing one of their demonically possessed experiments in public! Ifsoever anyone perchance reads this, I, Narvell Jern, am doubtless dead. Prithee seize the pendant I am wearing, for it embodies a piece of an important whole, which, hark my words, aught to be [illegible and damaged handwriting].

The other side of the page featured three symbols. The first symbol contained a black moon with two adjoining crescent moons on its sides, while inside the centre moon was an inverted hendecagram – an eleven-pointed star – with a vertically-slit eye. Another large, 'translucent' moon lay in front, its centre instead containing a phlegmatic mask. Appearing even more menacing than the first symbol, the next drawing was roughly the same as the one that Korin saw when he encountered the mage who disguised himself as a priest back in Orchopolis. The last image also featured an eye, though it looked more neutral in its expression, and it was inside a twelve-sided star sitting right between two vertical and inverted triangles with arrows pointing up and down.

There was also a note at the bottom, reading: 'The black moon is Backlevy's, but the matter grows ever more wildering with the other two. I have briefly intelligenced the last one, but its connection to the first wilders me. The middle one is even more enigmatic, yet I have withal beheld the symbol on a couple of Backlevy's personal belongings, which she keeps hidden – even from her cult.'

Korin suddenly remembered the second image – he couldn't forget those creepy branches emerging from the black cloud and sinister eye in the centre. He also recalled teleporting to what he believed to be the fake priest's base of operations. Theories began flooding Korin's head. Then there was the rest of the journal, sparking more curious thoughts as to who and what were Grand Sorceress Backlevy and The Gathering.

Before pondering any further, Korin glanced around, spotting the wisp near the skeleton. On closer inspection of the bones, Korin noticed the mentioned pendant around the dead mage's neck. It was shaped as a dodecahedron with unusual slits and grooves, while a small crystal crowned the top. The jewellery was cold to touch, and instead of wearing it, Korin simply gripped the pendant before scanning the rest of the cave. There was nothing more to do, and the wisp flew outside without a goodbye.

When Korin reached the edge of the cave, he wondered how he would return with the journal intact. Since it was made of tree paper, it wasn't resistant to water damage, and he couldn't compact it to the size of a coin like holochite books. Still, he realized that he could swim with one hand holding the journal above the water, so when Korin slipped in, he managed to avoid the waterfall's flow and keep the journal unblemished as he swam to the pool's edge before quickly climbing out. Once dressed, Korin assumed his classmates had probably finished. He rushed back as fast as he could; and on return, Cartras – along with the slower students – had just finished the run, so Korin made his entry discreet.

"Where'd you go, man?" Sylas asked.

"I'll explain later," Korin replied, panting while slipping the journal and pendant into his bag. "How'd you go?"

"Terala keeps pointing out that she won, but at least I wasn't chased like a dantha."

"I hope everyone is feeling more alive now," Cartras delivered firmly. "Next time, though, I'll expect better results. Now, it *is* our first lesson, so we'll have a little fun." His watch abruptly buzzed. "Great." He looked a tad disappointed while flicking through a message. "The mind field is now closed for the week. Doesn't matter. We can use these stumps for a bit longer." He nodded at a grid of small tree stumps. "Right, our next exercise combines the physical and mental. One of your tasks will be to observe your thoughts and stay in the present moment. You'll need to overcome your distractions."

Sylas then jocularly added, "I'll carefully observe my thoughts as they wander off."

Terala light-heartedly said, "Fantastic. We can't even trust you to guard your own thoughts."

"But at least I'll watch them. Better than trying to thrash at them like you would."

"Nah, I'll do what Korin's doing now: keeping focused."

"Actually, my thoughts are all over the place," Korin said. "I have a lot to tell you guys."

"Like?" Sylas perkily asked, but Korin remained silent. "Come on, tell us."

"I will. Just relax." Korin smirked.

After speaking about keeping oneself present, Cartras continued, "Everyone, hop on a stump, and we'll begin. Practice standing still. If you get an itch, ignore it."

Many people, nevertheless, became restless, with their attention fixated on multiple bodily itches. Korin thought the initial part of the exercise was easy, not realizing he wasn't actually keeping present with the numerous thoughts raging in his mind.

"Good. It seems everyone's settling in," Cartras said. "Now for the tricky part."

Cartras powered up an aerofan, and its tentacle-like channels reached throughout the grid of students. Each channel then created a torrent of wind from their ends, blowing dirt, leaves, and bits of rubbish around. Korin's mind, at least, stopped rambling, now focused on the task. Due to its power, some people relaxedly leaned towards the wind to stay upright. Cartras's hands gestured to the internal neurachite where the limbs would move, and he loudly told everyone to pay close attention to subtle changes in the wind; his students were to focus and develop their intuitive senses. Korin wondered what Cartras meant, having learned too late when one of the tentacles nearby spun around and sent an unexpected current at him, smacking Korin from his side and pushing him to the ground. Many others fell as well, quickly hopping back on their stumps, only to find another current whoosh them over again. Cartras sped up his movements, and the airstreams warped in many directions. Korin couldn't properly watch his peers, but most people's bodies were shaking in anticipation of the next current, wrongfully moving into the wind. Two opposing airstreams actually caused a couple of students to lightly collide with each other as they fell, and complaining instantly began. Cartras took the wisest course of action and stopped the exercise, checking for any injuries, only to find that there was very little pain inflicted.

Grumbling, Cartras said, "There'll be plenty more of those exercises to come. Now, let's get to connecting with the Aether."

Cartras began explaining the basics of the Aether and how mages were able to connect with the infinite pool of energy at the zero-point energy field of all that existed. Being in a vigorous bodily state was essential for the initial connection, and so the exercise definitely helped charge their bodies. Mentally, they also needed stability and the ability to focus, so the class had to first relax for a moment before they began a deep meditation exercise. Normally, mages didn't have to meditate to tune into the Aether – except for their very first attempt. Different levels of skill and power altered connection times, so it usually took about forty-five seconds for novices and students, whereas masters could connect in about five seconds. Once tuned in, the Aether would fill a pool of energy around the mage's body in the etheric realm as a matrix of potential. For most schools of magic, this was the *general aether pool*; but for phasarchement magic, it was called the *lumarchetrix* – or colloquially *lumatrix* for short – which was a separate pool of energy.

Similar to his Conjuration class, the meditation felt instinctual for Korin. With the help of Cartras's decent instructions, Korin was able to sense an utterly powerful field of energy that had nothing beyond itself. Merely skimming the Aether's 'surface', Korin's body vibrated intensely as his brain tingled strangely; he furthermore could tell he wasn't able to fully merge with such a field; but even if he could, he intuited doing so would be an absolutely mind-blowing event. Eventually, Korin began drawing energy from the Aether, sensing it pouring around him as if it was being funnelled towards him. The energy basically all came at once, so his lumarchetrix instantly filled up, and he knew drawing any additional energy would just pointlessly scatter around his etheric body without coming into his personal lumarchetrix. Resultingly, he felt more alive; yet, it wasn't really a physical phenomenon, so he couldn't quite understand the feeling. Because the meditation wasn't a visual one, he couldn't see the energy either.

Korin then finished the meditation, feeling ready for the next practice. Some people couldn't yet connect, while others simply took longer. Within a few more minutes, Korin's friends were also able to tune into the Aether and fill their lumarchetrixes. Despite being able to draw from the Aether, everyone's etheric pools had different sizes, but most mages were able to intuitively tell how much energy they had left in their lumarchetrixes. Maintaining a permanent connection to the Aether was not possible, and attempting to do so would lead to *lumarchetrix energy exhaustion* – or just *exhaustion* – which was a different matter from simply *depleting* one's energy. Whether *depleted* or not, mages would automatically recharge their lumarchetrix. For the average graduate mage, it would take about two minutes to fully recharge their lumarchetrixes from depletion.

Two assistant tutors finally arrived at the class after dealing with problematic administration, and they were able to help the remaining people struggling to connect to the Aether, granting Cartras the ability to continue with the lesson. Cartras introduced and explained quite a few terms, which began to overwhelm some of the students; but certain terms were used repeatedly, which helped to sink into their heads. One such term was *default power level* or DPL, which was an easy term to understand. Every mage had a default power level, even though all DPLs varied per mage. The class also learned that most mages had similar power levels, so it wasn't as if some mages had god-like powers like that found in fiction. Still, one could increase or decrease their DPL to a *higher power level* or *lower power level* – also knowns as HPLs and LPLs.

Before moving on to actually channelling lumarchetrix energy, Cartras further explained that phasarchement magic produced a special type of matter called *ultrachite*. This matter would also form into various *ultra-state types* or USTs, which themselves had four *phasarchement archetypal classes* or PACs. So, in order of their listed types, ultrachite would produce either fully-body *shields* for various forms of protection; *discharges* for direct offence and subjugation; *vortices* for creating a vortex of gas particles that was used for supplementary methods of attacking; *soaker bombs* and *swarm clouds* for yet more supplementary attacks with various liquids; *propulsors* for propelling through the air; or *dimensional fields* for reorientating dimensions to pull off feats like teleportation. Most USTs would surround a mage in a full-body aura, but they could also be concentrated into particular forms – most notably for discharges.

The PACs, in contrast, determined the nature of these USTs. Coloured blue, *alpha* class was based on attraction and repulsion, while the green class, called *beta*, induced synchronization or desynchronization. With its yellow forms, *gamma* class could either entangle or separate matter, whereas *delta* class dealt with motion and motionlessness in a red aura. Each of these classes also had *positive* and *negative charges*, changing the nature of their *class-based effects*.

"The more often you use the terms, the greater the chance that you'll remember them," Cartras said. "Traditionally, we start off making shields, but today we'll focus on shooting discharges over there in the shooting range."

"Wait!" a weirdly-bearded hipster interrupted, holding his waist slightly bent to the side. "We're not *actually* going to be using phasarchement magic, are we? That's dangerous, you know."

"Yeah!" another student said. "We should only use simulators; not the real thing!"

"What the fuck are you people on about?" Terala had to butt in before Cartras even made a sound. "Holy fucking shit! Go wear a fucking diaper, you fucking babies!"

The two guys who complained briefly swore at Terala before storming off to the meadow where the other students were still grazing.

"Yeah, we're using the real thing," Cartras said, shaking his head. "Because we're real mages. Anyway, UST Two ultrachite – which we usually call 'blast balls' when formed – is a mage's primary mode of offence. Generally, discharges don't kill people, but you still need to take caution when training because if you knock someone unconscious, they could fall on the ground and hit their head on something hard like concrete, in turn haemorrhaging them. Of course, when in real combat against actual enemies – be it mages or non-mages – don't be afraid to unleash all that you have to attain victory. Sometimes, it's a matter of you having to kill or be killed."

"What?" someone whispered. "I don't like the sound of that."

"Sounds like something a mage supremacist would say," another person whispered.

"I knew he was a mage supremacist," the first student whispered back, spurring a few other whispers.

Everyone still part of the class then eagerly lined up at the shooting range featuring targets on swingable flaps.

Cartras heard some whispering, but he didn't hear the details, and he continued with saying, "I only want you to aim at the targeting range when you're ready to fire. Otherwise, keep your hands down. Technically, the discharge energy will first surround you in an unconcentrated form before you have to concentrate it into a ball, which you'll find it naturally and easily forming near the hands. You'll initially get very excited when you create your first blast ball, so try and keep focused on aiming at the targets without moving around."

After Cartras explained how to tune into particular UST and PAC energies found in the lumarchetrix, it made it easier for everyone to understand how to access and form the discharge UST. Pointing their hands at the targets in the range, everyone had to concentrate on channelling the lumarchetrix energy first into what was called *photomission energy* – the physically-manifested energy of the former in its pure form that powered the ultrachite. Subtle, particular hand gestures also helped in this process.

Korin utilized all the instructions that were given to him, and within a moment, a fist-sized ball of colourless ultrachite materialized a centimetre away from his palm. He could physically feel the energy pulsating back at him, but funnily enough, it was actually a psychological reason as to why his arm suddenly jolted back. As his arm moved, the blast ball haphazardly let off, flying high into the air at over a hundred kilometres an hour without hitting a single target.

Another student near Korin held his hand near his face as he fired,

and the recoil unexpectedly hit him in the nose, causing him to cry —
despite there being no blood or bruising. Korin now didn't feel as bad.
Several people giggled and sniggered.

Numerous blast balls suddenly pulsed in multiple directions as one
guy couldn't stop firing, hitting the ground and space between frightened
students. As many ducked and pointlessly shielded their faces without
actual shields, Cartras phlegmatically and swiftly blasted the unstopping
shooter with a red discharge before anyone was actually shot, freezing
him momentarily. The class sighed in relief, and Cartras took care of
the student, who soon returned to normal.

Unlike most of the students, Sylas was accurately hitting every target.
It caused Korin to speculate if he had prior experience. Korin then
enquired, learning that Sylas had played many simulators in the past.
After shortly accustoming to the discharges, Korin managed to hit target
after target at a rate of three per second; although, he couldn't tell where
on the swings he was striking, as the fist-sized blasts left no marks.
Cartras forgot to mention that a blast ball's trajectory, before it was fired
off, was dependant on both the positioning of the energy — relative to
where it was in the hands — *and* the consciousness of the firer; except,
some ultrachite classes added additional effects, such as delta-positive's
motion and heat seeking abilities for particular matter.

After a while of practice, it was time to move on to utilizing PACs.
The same principle applied when creating a UST; that is, the students
had to tune into the PAC and then channel it to alter the UST. While
the *state-based effects* of UST discharges themselves could, for example,
overload electrical systems, forcefields, and other ultrachite shields, the
class-based effects, conversely, added certain effects, like magnetism or
flashes of blinding light, typically affecting the whole quantum field of a
target that would collectively meet a certain *holistically-related threshold* —
that is, if a person were hit, the magnetic class-based effect would affect
the person as a whole — a *holistically-related form* — not in part. However, a
discharge's class-based effects against ultrachite shields were generally
weak at first until more successive consecutive hits could be made against
the shield; this was due to shields having certain inhibitors — which some
non-ultrachite properties also had.

Everyone was told to generate alpha-negative charges, and in only a couple of minutes, most were able to change their colourless discharges into bright blue, luminescent balls. Aiming back at the range, Korin shot the targets, causing them to push back due to the nature of the alpha-negative charge's repulsive pushing effect.

"Good, good," Cartras said firmly but happily. "Alpha-negative charges are great for pushing enemies over; or, in other cases, pushing their covers away. Once you reach average DPLs, you'll be able to exert over one thousand newtons of force – assuming the target weighs around one hundred kilos; so, with less weight, less force will apply, funnily enough. It's also effective at mentally making your opponents cower away, and they may even totally attempt to flee the battlefield."

Angry muttering abruptly appeared out of nowhere, and when Terala aimed at a flap, a drunken, scruffy administration officer stumbled into the line of sight, rambling in his sphere of thought.

It was too late. Terala had already fired a blast ball, striking the man. "Fuck!" Terala yelled. "I didn't mean to hit him."

Terala was about to run forward, but the range was still in use. Cartras quickly called the firing off, giving everyone a break as they figured out what to do with the old man. Even though Terala knew that the blast had only pushed him over, the novelty of firing at someone alarmed her briefly. She approached the old man afterwards, but Cartras said he'd handle it. In the meantime, the class continued practicing at the range.

Cartras eventually came back to the lesson, but he told everyone that some uni staff would come soon to sort the issue out. "I'll have a bit of paper work to do after this," he said, looking annoyed. "Okay, so, we're a bit short on time, so we'll quickly go over crystallized discharge mines and discharge melee attacks. Both are made from the discharge aura, but with mines, you can place them anywhere, and they're normally used as traps." Cartras then created an example of a mine, showing its spherical floating form that was absent of the chaotic energy of normal discharges. "It has the same power as normal discharges, but it can override an ultrachite shield's inhibitors, so it will have full class-based effects. Just note that they won't last forever; in fact, usually mines will only last about ninety seconds for those with average power levels.

Anyway, for discharge melee attacks, I'll get everyone to line up along those dummies over there."

As everyone lined up at the rank of dummies, Cartras pressed a switch, and each dummy began moving around, jabbing with spongey melee weapons. The class was then told that they had to crystallize the discharge energy around their hands, basically having to use a punching movement in order to move the energy through the air. The DMA, as it was abbreviated, would overload an ultrachite shield of the same power level in one hit, whereas normal discharges of relative power levels would require about twelve shots to overload the shield. DMAs, however, lacked class-based effects. Cartras then explained some tactics and movements for what to do in close quarters, giving some demonstrations before the class began.

When Korin approached the dummy, he began dodging the sponge weapon as if in a real fight. As with his training in the past with monks, Korin knew how to dodge attacks, and his movements caught the eye of Cartras. The instructor stopped to watch Korin, who finally managed to crystallize the energy before delivering a mighty punch to the dummy. Since the movement required a bit of strength, it felt extremely satisfying for Korin.

"Impressive movements," Cartras said, nodding. "While DMAs are only useful in certain contexts, if you have skills like that, you can make it work in more cases. I think you're going to do well this semester."

Korin simply smiled before returning to punching the dummy again, but Cartras called the class over to watch Korin. Although thrilled, Korin tried to keep himself from being too cocky, restraining a couple of his movements. He also correctly felt that some people thought he was a show-off.

There wasn't much time left in the lesson after that, so Cartras essentially just recapped what the class was taught. Still, with a few minutes left, most of the people were super eager to at least begin forming ultrachite shields on their first day, too. Cartras decided to quickly throw in a short lesson, though he'd go over it again in the next class. Forming shields was a similar process to creating discharges, and all it took was tuning into the shield archetype in the lumarchetrix. While shields could be concentrated into discs, for example, they naturally covered the user's entire body with about a three-centimetre gap. When Korin created his shield, it flashed a nice bright blue before shortly turning fully transparent. The shield was almost as light as air, and Korin could easily move around with it surrounding him, but technically, it was a strange 'solid'. The class was told that shields could totally block ultrachite discharges and fast-moving non-ultrachite matter like bullets – but this was only up until the shields reached their *overloading threshold* or when they were simply overpowered by something much stronger. This also meant that generally knives in normal knife attacks could penetrate the shields due to their slower nature than bullets.

Just before leaving, Cartras informed everyone about how that while some shields had automatic class-based effects – such as enhancing one's hormones and neurotransmitters – some of the effects needed *ultrachite phase charging*, with the charge normally only lasting for a short period. The phenomenon did not cost any extra energy, and some of the effects ranged from increasing the amount of attacks the shield could endure to creating mirages and even to a form of limited invisibility – which, however, effectively blinded the users.

***

It came to light that the old admin officer had been living in the forest for a few weeks, having set up a primitive camp nearby. His disgrace was mostly due to alcohol, but the man had fallen into depression due to being fired over an inconsequential matter. Cartras was ticked off after hearing the story. For many reasons.

After the class finished, Korin and Celine left together. "You were really good the whole lesson," Celine said. "Especially at the end with the dummies. But it looked like you were a bit reserved."

Korin thought that he might have actually seemed too cocky. *Are you able to read minds?* he thought. "Yeah, I just made sure that I did it right. Didn't want to show off."

"Well, just remember that it's okay to be excellent at something. And unique." She smiled. "Try not to let others bring you down; otherwise, you'll always feel frustrated and angry."

"I… appreciate your positive comments, Celine. Do you sometimes feel the same way, too?"

"I find being myself is more comfortable than being someone I'm not."

"Hmm… a part of me likes the idea of just being yourself, but it seems a bit silly. What if you're a terrible person?"

Puckering her lips, Celine suspended her answer as she fully considered what Korin said. "Well, I guess that means changing would be a good thing. Perhaps we should always aim to be better people, but I think it would also be best to take our own paths to do so. What do you think? Do you agree?"

"Yeah," Korin said slowly, nodding. "Yeah, I do." He couldn't find any flaw with the idea. "You're a great friend to have, Celine."

"Aww, thanks. But sometimes, we all have to fit ourselves in boxes in order to get by. Kind of like how we have to obey the university rules, even though some of them make no sense. But naturally, I think it's best to avoid boxes where possible. Actually, there was this one time I put myself in a tiny box…" Celine's face rosed as she glanced away. "Or perhaps we should just paint our boxes differently."

"Maybe. But before, I meant, like, do you have any skills you have to hide? Or end up hiding, anyway?"

"Um, well… sometimes my creative abilities. Like, there was this one time I created lunapex cards for everyone last year in school, and another person copied me. I think she always saw me as competition. She did a number of mean things, like telling everyone that I used blood as paint and that I was a literal nutjob out of an asylum. She tried to actually frame me with false evidence."

"That's sick. You didn't let anyone – especially that girl – get to you?"

"Mm, a little." Her skin slightly moistened under her eyes. "It would've been nice if they didn't destroy the cards. If people are mean, I'd rather go somewhere else than conform."

"I think I agree with you there. Anyway, I bet *I* would've kept your card," Korin said warmly.

Before Celine could reply, Sylas and Terala approached.

"So, are you going to tell us what happened when you disappeared?" Sylas asked.

Korin delayed his response, and Sylas's anticipation began rising incredibly high as he repeatedly tapped his thighs. "I saw a wisp," Korin finally said.

"A wisp?" Sylas asked, slightly surprised. "What kind of wisp?"

"Not sure." Korin shrugged.

"Well, sentient wisps are rare around cities, so that seems strange."

"I know what I saw. I wasn't half asleep."

"It could've been an hallucination," Terala said. "Perhaps your mind was playing tricks on you as an aftereffect from breathing in that acid potion-thing yesterday." She nudged Sylas.

"Oh, come on." Sylas rolled his eyes. "We all breathed that in, and we're fine."

"I don't know. You seemed pretty slow out there today." Terala laughed.

Celine then said, "Well, it's not like we're in the CBD."

"True," Sylas said. "I've heard that living wisps usually play tricks on people for shits and giggles; but so do ghost ones, too. They sound pretty based."

"It depends on what it did," Celine said.

Korin contemplated the occurrence before saying, "I think it was well-meaning. The wisp led me to a cave behind a waterfall. And I found this." He showed everyone the journal, rereading it with a surprised and intrigued group. "I have no idea who Backlevy is, nor what the symbols mean, but I remember seeing this one in that place where the crystal blew up."

"Man, I wasn't expecting this," Sylas said. "I thought you were going to say you stumbled upon some crazy orgy out there. And… Oh, crap. I just remembered I have to rush off for an appointment. I'll talk later. See you."

"Since the journal is old," Celine said, "you should check one of the libraries. Perhaps talk to someone there."

Terala interjected, "I was hoping we'd be able to train for the upcoming hillseck tryouts, though."

"Yeah, that's a good idea," Korin said. "Still, the journal…"

"Look, I understand this journal thing is probably important, but can you do something about it just a *little* later? This shit's ancient."

"Well, I'm busy this afternoon with a couple of things, too, like seeing a psychologist. I got a letter delivered in person to me saying that it was a requirement – not because I personally need to see one. But… I guess we *could* train, though I really do want to talk to someone about this journal."

"Perhaps it would be better having a good think about it before asking somebody, so you know what to ask."

"Hmm… yeah, I guess you may have a point. *One* day may not hurt. As you pointed out, the journal is ancient, after all."

***

On arrival at the Central Hub, Korin chanced upon Rolan, who was merrily walking by.

"Oh, I was about to contact you," Rolan said. "I met with the Bank of Crysten in order to deposit a grant for you. I suggest that you finish setting up an account with them, as I've done half the paperwork, and they're easy on students. You can find their branch in the Market District. And, you'll have two thousand posels in there when you're established. That should be enough for this semester. Don't go crazy with it. Now, if you'll excuse me, I'm relatively busy, so I'll see you later."

"Thanks, Rolan," Korin said. "I'll check it out."

"How the fuck did you get two thousand fucking posels?" Terala asked.

"Some sort of handout because of my situation. Do you want to come with me to the Market District? We have some spare time before lunch will be over."

Terala decided to come, while Celine had other plans in mind. Establishing the bank account only took a short while, and Korin now felt more secure than ever. While in the bank, Korin learned that he could still produce physical cheques for other people from his own bank balance, as the creation and usage of all neurachite-laced cheques were able to be universally tracked on a public ledger via the synopool. Still, a reason was required to be input on the ledger when executing such an action.

While exiting the bank, Terala asked Korin, "So, this religious community you were in, was it a monastery?"

"No. I lived in a boarding school. You have to understand that the Temple, as in the greater religion, is complex, and it's not all monastic. Most people don't live in monasteries, and the monasteries are quite selective. The Temple, though, welcomed everyone – lured might be a better word – so long as they adhered to the teachings. Even though the Temple preaches about sacrifices, there are still many rich people who follow the faith, despite it being a bit contradictory. Then again, there are different types of sacrifices, so rich people can sacrifice time, for example."

"I could actually see you in a monastery. You have that vibe. I don't mean that in a bad way. You're just very serious. I take it the priests personally raised you?"

"Yes, and no. When I was five, a couple of Sacrenderists took me in, but they died soon after. Car accident. They had lots of savings, so I was able to go to a boarding school instead of an orphanage – which the Temple still targets, by the way, for indoctrination. Not everyone who went to the school followed the faith, but it was strongly encouraged. *Strongly*. Anyway, the priests paid extra attention to me when I got older, but I was never raised into their little secret, which I have a feeling one or two of my peers were. And as for the monastery thing… well, I actually considered joining one, but I had several options after finishing school, so I wasn't sure what to do. The monastic order I thought of joining was quite austere, and they trained the monks how to fight. That is, there was a big emphasis on defence training – and learning history… so it's quite funny how I'm kind of doing that here. I actually went there many times, even when I was young, and I learned how to fight; but you can only join as an adult, and that's only after a couple of years of going through a period of following temporary vows before undertaking permanent vows."

"Wow. So… were all the priests bad?"

"From what I know, no, only a small number were. In fact, some of the priests at the ritual weren't even from the main community I grew up in. I recognized them from other temples in Orchopolis."

"But you've interacted with mages before. Did you avert your eyes when you looked at us?" Terala smirked before laughing. "Sorry!" Her face scrunched. "I'm so sorry. I didn't mean –"

"It's fine," Korin responded stoically. "You're fine. I think *I* should be more understanding of where you guys are coming from. Relax. I don't intend on being a drain."

"You're not a drain," Terala said with a gentle tone.

"I... I value your concern. Anyway, I was never really like that, but who knows how it would have turned out? I guess because my interactions were limited, I didn't do anything ridiculous. Actually..." Korin chuckled, looking down with humiliation. "One day, some sort of mage-created liquid spilled on me. Probably a potion. I then spent a week scrubbing my body and praying for hours every day that it didn't affect me spiritually. And that's not including the ridiculous rituals I did. It... it was worse than it sounds."

Terala tried to restrain laughing *at* Korin, but her giggling burst out eventually. "I wish I was there. You seem so different now."

"Yeah, I know." He folded his arms. "I think deep down inside we're all normal, and when that religious indoctrination goes, normality retakes control. Any indoctrination, I think. Actually, there were other stupid things I did, too." He shook his head, anger puffing out of him. "I'm so glad I don't follow that fucking evil religion anymore."

"And I'm glad, too. So, do you miss anyone?"

"Not really. Some of the priests had positioned me as some up-and-coming star in their ranks when I was older, and that added to the jealousy the guys around my age had of me. It still seems strange how the priests would raise me as such, only to murder me. If they saw me as being useful, you'd think they would've murdered some idiot instead. And no, it definitely wasn't because of all that religious nonsense Visten said."

"Maybe they had only recently found out you were a mage."

There was a pause before Korin responded, "Perhaps you're right. They acted noticeably weird around me a couple of weeks before the ritual. Anyway, outside of school hours, the priests had me doing various things by myself, so I always felt kind of isolated. Even now, it's…" He sighed, creasing his face. "I feel… not *isolated*, but… I don't know how to put it."

"Well, you're not alone now. You realize that?"

"Yeah, it's just that it's hard to talk about these things when no-one here has experienced anything like it. I feel like my guts have been ripped out, and I'm still alive because of some magic that I don't fully understand."

"You do know that there are mages who follow religions?"

"What? Really? I thought religion was a non-mage thing." Korin suddenly felt a little less special while simultaneously more relieved.

"Yeah, but not many do. Maybe ten percent. I'm not sure. The rest of us just have general beliefs without following any organized set or doctrine of rules."

"Oh…" Korin murmured, then a short break in the conversation followed.

"Wasn't it magic that saved you?" Terala asked, halting as a couple of hoverbikes whizzed by, with one stopping to have the rider cockily wink at Terala. He powered on, grinning.

Korin glanced at Terala, but she shrugged. He then said, "I think they might've used a magic potion or two and something else. Not sure. But… it's probably because I'm also strong-willed. Not trying to sound boastful, but that may have helped. Perhaps because I had all that faith instilled in me, I have this strong sense of hope. It's as if it's ingrained in my blood."

"So, there was a positive side to it all. It's better than being put down your whole life, only to turn out miserable."

"Well, in a *certain* way, you *may* be right, but I don't want to think of my religious upbringing as being good and necessary." Korin stopped talking, feeling like he had said enough about himself for the time being. "What about you? Do you feel better being here?"

"Besides putting up with some of the whingy people here, fuck yeah, I'm glad to be at uni. Although I only left home a week ago, it feels like I'm finally able to develop myself. I was always looking out for the younger ones at home. We still had heaps of fun, though, generally getting into trouble." She grinned mischievously. "I would always take the blame, of course."

"Being the oldest, you would've had a lot of responsibility."

Terala tried to respond, but she looked into nothingness with sadness. Her pacing even slowed, dragged down by her unearthing emotions.

"You… are the oldest, right?" Korin asked, his tone careful.

"N-not a couple of years ago. My two older brothers – Jerad and Maven – they… they died." She crossed her arms as if a cold wind bit into her. "Including my father."

"Oh." Korin momentarily thought about Rolan. "I can sense they meant a lot to you."

"Yeah. We did so much together. My dad and my brothers taught me how to do a tonne of things for myself like camping, and fighting, and riding creatures, and fixing shit. If you don't mind, I'd… like to talk about them some other time, actually." Her eyes carried a heavy weight when she glanced at Korin.

"Sure." He nodded. "I understand. Any time you're ready. So, if it's not a sensitive topic, what kind of trouble did you find yourselves in when you were left to lead the pack?"

Terala took a moment to gather herself. "I'd usually take them outdoors into forests and do all sorts of crazy shit with anything we got our hands on. That…" She lightened up, laughing a little. "That also included explosives."

Korin gaped. "Hopefully no-one died… I mean… sorry."

"No, no… it's fine. No-one died, but there'd always be at least one injury when we returned." Terala then proudly showed Korin a massive scar on her thigh through a large rip in her pants. "No, not from explosives. That was from jumping around on a crazy trampoline thing."

"What were you thinking?" Korin looked stunned.

"I'm not sure if we were." She chuckled. "I guess we just wanted to push the limit. I didn't tell my mum what we did when it was just her left, but word got around to her as to what we were doing. Our parents chose not to mollycoddle us, but at the same time, it wasn't as if they were all 'anything goes', if that makes sense."

"I think I know what you mean." Korin squinted, ruminating on what she said. "Still, did any of your neighbours say anything?"

"Well, again, most of our activities were way outdoors, and it's not like I was highly irresponsible or anything," she said, though Korin gave her a look of incredulousness. "Seriously! What we did *most* of the time was within reason. Well… yeah… Anyway, we also didn't sit around on our asses all day watching crap. That would've driven us mad."

"No anime, then?" Korin grinned as Terala stared without comment. "I've barely watched any myself – only what was snuck into the school. Sylas has naturally commented with what you could imagine."

"Yes, I know what he'd likely say. Although, we did watch certain hillseck matches."

Korin suddenly noticed a few people preparing for a protest nearby, and despite it appearing rather interesting, he decided to walk to the other side of the street to avoid them, as he was enjoying his conversation with Terala. "So, do you have any friends from high school here? Teloston has thousands of students."

"Uh, yeah… I don't know." Terala held her neck.

"Don't know if they're here or…?" He detected Terala's discomfiture rise.

"So, do you know where Celine went?"

"No." He thought for a moment before turning back to Terala. "So, you were saying?" He waited for an answer, only receiving an uncomfortable pause. "It's okay." Korin guessed what was going through her mind. "I didn't have any real friends back in Orchopolis. It's not anything to be embarrassed about. Is… that why you were reluctant to answer?"

"Sort of." She smiled uneasily, averting her eyes. "But you had a different upbringing. You had an excuse."

"No excuses needed. I understand if you don't want to hang around the people you grew up with. I sure don't. Look, forget about your past. I'm learning to." He chuckled. "And, hey, you and I think alike, so I'm pretty sure we'll continue to get along fairly well."

"Thanks, man. I have to admit that it's kind of hard for me to make friends." She sighed, making eye contact before glancing away again. "I guess that's just me."

"Well, I can't blame you with all these whiny people around. It seems you really hate them."

Adding no remark, Terala laughed with Korin. Her eyes watered slightly, but she didn't cry. Korin's friends had substantially supported him to this point, and he felt great being able to reciprocate the care.

"Also, people change friends all the time," he continued. "Then you have Celine. She doesn't really seem to have many – if any – friends outside of us, either. So, I think you'd find many others in the same place."

"Yeah, I noticed. Perhaps I should give Celine more of my time."

"And I'm also glad that I at least have others to talk to, as I had no idea what I would get into coming here. For all I knew, most mages could've been like Sereck. Now that would've been horrible!"

Terala coughed as she laughed, virtually as if her embarrassment was fleeing her body. A moment of quietness followed – one of growing mutual understanding and connection between the two friends.

Chapter Ten

Of Ancient and Modern Troubles

Knowing that his non-magic classes were about to begin, Korin finally felt moderately grounded in something conventional. Those feelings still remained when he approached the School of Social Sciences building located in the Non-Magic Academic District. Decorated with spiral volutes on top, as if magic petrified and sealed away the noblest and cardinal of political scrolls, the entrance's stone columns were positioned distinctly separate from one another, impressing upon those beneath it a feeling of authority with its steadfast ranks, towering over everyone while exemplifying sculpted figures featuring every other column, each stoically staring ahead as if wisely viewing the various dimensions of their political landscape – and, with their shrewd comprehension, taking upon the burden themselves to uphold and preserve the weight of social order illustrated in the frieze above, where the forces of order and chaos were balanced between the inherent political nature of people characterized by the detailed beasts birthing from wombs, lurching from the shadows, slithering around publics, raining from the heavens, and escaping from cages.

Korin was unsure of the creative origins of such architecture, but he had seen similar – though, less extravagant – works in non-mage zones. Still, he considered that it could've been influenced by the mages. When Korin looked at the surrounding buildings, on the other hand, he felt as if they were mightily out of place; one was a cobbled castle, and another could straightforwardly be described as a plain steel box, as if the greatness of modernity's innovation had taken a strange turn, reaching an ultimately-dire conclusion devoid of any nuanced substance, unlike what the Social Sciences building in front presented.

Once inside, Korin sat by himself in his own world. Compared to his first lecture the other day, the atmosphere was rather composed, with an element of seriousness. The students weren't forced to be there; they chose the subject out of interest. Such choice was reflected in their behaviour; they weren't engaging in any wild antics or shouting or rapidly moving around. At most, they merely messaged or played games on their phids while they waited. Initially, Korin's mind was mellow, but the weight of the situation dawned on him; he now had to compete against those who were serious about their studies. He nevertheless retained his confidence, learning from his experiences to focus on the positive, redirecting any doubtful thoughts into determination.

The History lecture itself continued to wash a sense of normality over Korin as it covered general ideas, methodologies, tasks, and topics he was going to study. A basic overview of the historical epochs of civilization was also mentioned. He learned that the First Epoch – of theorized sapient history – possessed a few different ages, each next to a total mystery, as only fragments of knowledge had been discovered. After a Caelverse-wide regress to primitive tribal societies, the Second Epoch followed; but it was during the Third Epoch that various written languages, mathematics, the modern calendar, and great feats of engineering emerged. The mages then established a mighty empire that spanned all of Juntas, which later led to the golden Fourth Epoch, where they conquered the Caelverse, enslaving many non-mages. Mages additionally spread their dominant and evolving language, Synvoric, reaching obscure aliens. Still, pockets of life continued to remain a mystery, in part due to their distances from the transportals. Abolitionist movements eventually gained more influence before securing non-mage freedom with the Grand Liberal Charter.

During the lecture's break, Korin exited into the hallway, surveying historical artefacts inside glass cabinets lining the walls. Not one item was of non-mage origin – at least within the vicinity. Korin knew that non-mages had a rich history of their own, especially when the Fifth

Epoch began, but despite all the bad things mages did in the past, he acknowledged civilization wouldn't be where it was if it weren't for the mages. He was intrigued at how certain items – seemingly small – had large-scale effects on society.

A scruffy geek approached, munching away on some overly-processed chips. He dipped his face down to survey the same cabinet Korin was examining, crumbs raining from his mouth, decorating the glass with the wonders of modernity. "I make this shit all the time," he said with great confidence, stuffing his face once more.

Korin was impressed, though a little amazed; he would have guessed the student barely lifted himself off the couch in his spare time.

"Just smelt the metal with some dragon glass in the fires of Mount Vorka," the geek said.

"Oh, right. Cool," Korin said, nodding. "I've never been there before."

"Yeah, you have to be at least level eighty-five to reach there."

Korin frowned, wondering what on Juntas he was on about, shortly realizing the geek was referring to a game. "Ah, I see. Well, all the best with that," he said before entering the hall again.

The last part of the lecture finished off explaining how that owing to corruption and instability, the Caelverse Magocratic Empire collapsed two centuries after the Grand Liberal Charter was formed, and power scattered, leading to the Fifth Epoch and the Crestfallen Age. Over seven hundred years later of despondence and little progress, the enigmatic Great Blackout occurred – a month when black, stormy clouds completely covered Juntas. Non-mages then rose in strength and population, but their power stagnated as they waged war after war against each other. In the meantime, mages gradually rebuilt under their newly-found Union of Organized States government that covered several systems in the Caelverse. Pagan and polytheistic religions diminished among the non-mages in favour of monotheistic religions; mages, in contrast, generally adopted non-religious spiritual ideas. Still, centuries later, the number of religious adherents decreased when the Illumination Age started. Religion nevertheless remained significant – more so for non-mages – and the humanistic ideologies which formed in the Illumination Age instigated more methodological philosophies; science and technology ably flourished, greatly uplifting the non-mages. Mages also tremendously increased their technological, economic, and political power, giving them enough leverage – coupled with their magic – to sustain hegemony over all planets with the creation of the Caelverse Government of Magi, which ushered in the current Sixth Epoch…

***

After the History tutorial ended, Korin proceeded to the professor's office with a few questions in mind. For so long, Korin's inquisitive nature had been suppressed under his mind-numbing religion, and he was glad he was now free to take the initiative for further historical inquiry. Inside the professor's room, expanded holochite books were scattered in disarray while the breeze whisked paperwork up into the air, a few appearing rather whimsical in their blithe flight. Dust flowed endlessly through the sunlight, which also gleamed strongly off the yellowed wall sprinkled with pinup notes sloppily piled on top of one another. While stroking his long, pointy-grey beard, the professor was at his table, jotting notes. He didn't notice Korin, as his beady eyes were fixed on a notebook, reading behind sophisticated glasses.

"Professor Finch," Korin said, knocking on the door.

"Come in, come in," the professor responded, motioning without looking at Korin.

As Korin walked inside, he spotted an expanded book jutting out of a shelf with a seemingly star-shaped image on the front. Unable to keep his hands to himself, Korin pulled the book out, revealing a twelve-pointed star between two inverted triangles with an eye in the centre. Korin couldn't believe it. He had only planned to ask some basic historical questions, yet there was the dodecagram symbol from the journal. Overwhelmed with so many theories, Korin felt that he needed an expert's opinion on the matter before researching further; and now, his hopes were high that the professor knew enough about the topic.

"Do you have an interest in the Sendrallic Order?" the professor asked, looking up.

Korin almost jumped in surprise before replying, "Sorry, what?"

"The Sendrallic Order of the Conjugational Age. Or have you just picked that off the floor?"

"Oh, just from the shelf here. Is that an organization of sorts?"

"Indeed. Well, it *was* an organization."

"Right, I see." A few things instantly made sense to Korin. "Did they write this?"

"No, that book was written *about* the Order."

"What do you know about them?" Korin asked, his excitement for the truth physically masked behind his stern face.

Instead of replying immediately, Professor Finch stared.

Korin stumblingly said, "Sorry, I –"

"I have time to explain. Please, sit down." Finch closed his notebook. "So, your interest in the Sendrallic Order is an objective, historical inquiry?" he asked, and Korin nodded genuinely. "I thought so. So, where do I begin? Hmm, do you remember my last slide on the end of the Fourth Epoch? Well, the empire's collapse led to a great deal of resentment and frustration. There were many failed plots to recreate the old empire, and mage supremacists, for example, were pushed into underground status. Note that prior to the collapse, cults generally had accepted social status, and the empire itself culturally maintained the fabric of these cults within and to a particular nature. However, more and more cults grew fanatical and dangerous; and after the collapse, the term cult became a pejorative, with many types of cults having underground status. While there was major dissatisfaction everywhere, most cults – whether radical or not – didn't even have any focus on politics per se, nor did they have any grand influence on most matters. But there was one cult, in particular, that was exceptionally interesting. And that was the Sendrallic Order."

With many questions rushing through his mind, Korin asked, "Were they mage supremacists?"

"No. The idea wasn't even on their minds. The Order didn't even think about non-mages; their studies focused on mage and magic-centric discourse and taboos. But it's possible that some individuals privately held such views. In point of fact, they emerged shortly before the formation of the Union of Organized States, so mages were in the midst of regaining powerful governmental structures by that time. The Order even formed about fifteen years before the Great Blackout, and some argue that it was a proper order at first before descending into a cult, while others argue the Order was a cult from the beginning."

"Do you think the Order caused the Great Blackout?"

"Ah, that's where it gets interesting! It would *seem* highly unlikely that a group of people could produce such an unnatural, terrible, and phenomenal darkness for a whole month, but a few anomalies have given rise to theories suggesting that the cause of the Blackout had its roots in the Order."

For a moment in silence, Korin imagined what such a blackout would've looked like, envisioning an epic cyclone ripping matter away from land and sea, feeding a beastly blanket of death above. Wondering how he'd survive in such a situation, a shiver of exhilaration ran down him. Korin then eagerly asked, "What are *your* thoughts?"

"Well…" Finch stroked his beard, rumpling his face with unease. "It's hard to say, but it's possible they played *some* role. I can't really say for certain either way. But as I was saying, the Order began with a gifted man named Xalinor Traven. He was… probably the smartest mage of all time, and he basically succeeded at anything he put his mind to. However, most of the authorities hated him, and due to his unconventionality, his ideas were ridiculed time after time as he constantly tried to prove the unbelievable. Most cults didn't draw in much academic fire, but since Xalinor was in broad academic light, he certainly received a lot of attention. Despite his critics then, his works were mostly valued posthumously. Nevertheless, without Xalinor's discoveries, we mages wouldn't be where we are today. He also achieved numerous accomplishments – both in and out of academia – but his push for the truth caused him to delve into dark and strange theories. I believe that Xalinor wasn't evil; he just wanted to explore and know everything."

Korin speculated if such a man would've been ridiculed in contemporary academia if alive. The potential perceptions of current students also popped into mind. *He'd probably be yelled at for not creating a safe-enough space,* Korin thought, laughing in his mind. "So, what were those achievements responsible for our development?"

"Well, he made many contributions in a number of academic fields. But, very importantly, he laid the foundations for modern science, in addition to giving us a profounder understanding of magical theory that we still, in many ways, teach to this very day. And, we can thank him for helping to greatly advance mage technology. Nevertheless, it took centuries to build on his theories due to several social and political problems. There are some that argue that Xalinor's works – listed in that book, by the way – were useful, but not necessary, as the non-mages increased their knowledge and would've inspired us, anyway."

Korin opened the book, reading Xalinor's bibliography, seeing such titles as, 'Understanding Infra-Geometric Forms: Vibrational Root Determinants and Their Interlacing and Emergent Stratums'. Naturally, Korin was clueless about their meanings. "Do you believe that?"

"No. Anyone who claims that doesn't understand the complexities of science and magic, nor our technologies, and is seeing matters through a social science lens. I may be an historian, but I'm not one to reject objective reality. Although there are some valid criticisms of Xalinor, he was nonetheless a genius. A true polymath. Anyway, in order to accomplish his goals, Xalinor formed the Sendrallic Order of the Conjugational Age; and while he purported to have made many discoveries – many of which remained undisclosed – one of the partially-disclosed discoveries happened to involve necrourgy. Now, of course, as you may know, necrourgy isn't a school of magic itself but a practice that falls *under* the various schools of magic. So, when asked to publicly perform this dark discovery, Xalinor declined, and so he was dismissed as a liar and a charlatan; some believed he was a lunatic. Others, nevertheless, defended him, noting that many necrourgic practices were – and continue to be – outlawed, so publicly performing it would have been foolish."

Korin had learned a little about necrourgy before – understanding that it was the art of working with the dead – but he had never thought too much of it other than generally thinking that it was evil. He again imagined the Blackout, but this time with an eccentric-looking man using magic to raise worm-filled zombie hands from the ground in the thousands, as if ready for an epic battle. Korin wasn't sure if he was over imagining things, and he suddenly speculated if the priests knew of such power.

Finch continued, "Over time, Xalinor actually did lose his mind. No-one knows for certain why. When he could no longer lead the Order, one of his disciples, Démont Salkesh, assumed leadership. She was an intensely loyal and even rabid disciple, and although Xalinor wasn't evil, she definitely was. But," he said, squinting gravely as his tone changed, "her true colours didn't emerge until later. Xalinor died soon after, and the Sendrallic Order was ripped apart by infighting, which took about two years. Each ensuing faction withdrew mostly from public sight – although, they hadn't fully disappeared at that point – and then the Great Blackout happened about three years later. During that month, the now-without-question cult – or cults – kidnapped and experimented on many people, performing some of the darkest practices possible. Stories of unusual and powerful forms of necrourgy emerged, but those were unconfirmed rumours, and there has been no evidence of any such magic existing in our history."

"So... were the experiments rumours or confirmed fact?"

"Oh, yes, that part is accepted by all scholars, but only the fringe and non-academic believe in the *types* of necrourgy said to have been performed."

Korin curiously examined the book cover. "Then, what's with the twelve-pointed star?"

"Unfortunately, there's no recorded writing on the matter, so no-one knows. Xalinor travelled extensively, so his symbols are etched in many places; but oddly, not a single trace of the reason has been discovered. Interestingly, he did conduct a little research at Teloston for a year, so you may see the symbol here and there. Anyway, like all forms, the dodecagram creates and symbolizes particular energy, but Xalinor's *application* of such known base energy is still a mystery.

"Right. And the cult's name?"

"There... there are conflicting theories on that. Again, no useful writings were found. Xalinor either wished to literally join two or more things together – I cannot say what – or it was a cryptic metaphor for something different."

Korin hummed before asking, "If anyone bore this symbol today, do you think that they'd be part of the Order?"

Finch shook his head. "No. I believe the Order is long dead and gone. It splintered off into different factions, too, as I said."

"Hmm… Okay, but what were these factions, and what were their symbols?"

"The most renown of these factions was or were the necroshapers – who are very popular among conspiracy theorists today. But no evidence exists of there ever being such an organization after its dissolution shortly after the Blackout. Their symbol consisted of an eye inside a hendecagram surrounded by branches and a web. Like this." He then showed an image on his phid that matched the symbol Korin saw after talking to the phoney priest in Orchopolis.

Korin snappily perked up, thinking, *That's it!* He then stopped asking questions, taking time to think to himself. In the meantime, the professor continued jotting the notes. The journal Korin found behind the waterfall came back to mind, and he contemplated the potential links between the symbols – especially the one Korin saw while escaping the priests, which happened to be the same as the so-called necroshapers. Even though Draghar's men were obviously evil, the phoney priest was also evil, yet the latter was seemingly working against the religion. But then another idea came to Korin: perhaps, he thought, the 'priest' wasn't against the religion but, instead, operating within its bounds for his own agenda, whatever that may have been.

Having only witnessed what he believed to be phasarchement magic, Korin wondered, *If he was a necroshaper, why didn't he use some crazy kind of magic on me and end my life? Well… he was probably savouring my death. But… couldn't he have used some sort of evil version of phasarchement magic?*

Continuing to contemplate exactly why the fake priest was at his ritual, Korin believed it was a little too coincidental that there just happened to be a necroshaper symbol in the background, and yet there seemed to be a conspiracy of sorts brewing – a grand conspiracy, Korin conjectured. He hummed before asking, "Well, what if someone were to possess a *necroshaper* symbol today?

Finch breathed out heavily. "Look, you have to understand that the ownership itself of such symbols does not mean that one is part of a literal necroshaper cult or any similar discipleship. And besides, numerous people join mock cults all the time or wear cultish accessories as fashion statements, having no real understanding of the history of such things. And then you have to acknowledge how enormous the Caelverse is, so there may be – indeed are – similar, if not near-identical symbols used elsewhere. Sometimes these symbols also get aesthetically revamped in different ways."

Finch's answer burst quite a few bubbles floating around Korin's head, and the latter considered if he was seeing and connecting too many unrelated dots. *But… there is some sort of conspiracy happening,* Korin rebutted one thought, feeling confused.

He theorized the fake priest *may* not have been associated with the Sendrallic Order, nor the necroshapers, but the usage or even mere possession of such a symbol was suspicious nonetheless – especially given the context. Korin had another conflicting theory suggesting that the evil mage he encountered could have been a collector of historical items and simply liked it as decoration. But it was all too coincidental, he kept thinking. Considering that there was a massive, unresolved conspiracy involving sanctioned priests and his religion, at least, Korin then believed it wasn't crazy to assume another – if not partially connected – conspiracy was also transpiring.

Korin promptly remembered more of the ancient journal entry he had read. "What do you know about Backlevy?"

"I assume you mean Minesta Backlevy and not Mirella Backlevy?" Finch smiled.

"Ah, yeah… the first, I guess. There's another?" Korin asked with confusion.

"Well, Grand Sorceress *Minesta* Backlevy used to be a professor here at Teloston around two and a half thousand years ago; and right now, we have a professor named Backlevy in our department. The irony is that not only is the surname rare, but they also look virtually identical." He chuckled.

"She isn't the same one, is she?" he asked fearfully.

"What?" Finch yelped slightly. "Don't be ridiculous! Minesta Backlevy died over two thousand years ago. Please don't think they're the same."

"No, no, I…" Korin turned slightly red, fearing an intellectual schism emerging. "I was just saying."

"Well… okay. I didn't think you were serious. So, regarding *Minesta Backlevy*… the… the Sendrallic Order – all of its factions, rather – disappeared very shortly after the Blackout, and there was absolutely no recorded activity of their existences thereafter. It's safe to assume that there are no secret necroshapers hiding somewhere today. However, one disciple, Minesta Backlevy, broke off before the Blackout and formed her own cult here at Teloston, taking a large quantity of the Order's knowledge with her. Like many of the other factions, she even dropped the Order's dodecagram in favour of an inverted hendecagram with another symbol entirely. Her symbol specifically possessed a few different moons with a mask at the front. Underneath her respected public image, though, Minesta's activities and her cult remained largely a secret. The Gathering of the Black Moon, as it was called – or simply, The Gathering – remained active for many years after the Blackout, although most of their deeds weren't revealed until much later."

"And are they, too, no longer in existence?"

"So… going back to Xalinor for a second, while he didn't discover the black moon, he did figure out a method to consciously connect with it in a particular way. For the people who were already aware of the black moon at the time, they were either individual venerators or they had their own cults; and of course, they became incredibly intrigued by the news of connecting with it, so they joined Xalinor's cult. Backlevy had a few pools of people to draw from, and she centred *her* cult around tapping into the black moon's energy as well, but her methods were… extreme. Are you aware of shadowist cults?"

"No, never heard of them." Korin leaned in.

"I see… Well, unlike necroshapers, shadowists are real; their cults remain hidden from public view due to their extreme beliefs and practices. These cults *derive* their origins from Backlevy's cult, having practically the same ideology; but they are not direct continuations of The Gathering."

"So, wait, what *is* the black moon?"

"You don't know? I find that surprising, as I assumed younger people would've had a greater awareness of it. Alright, I won't go into too much detail, but the black moon is basically a non-physical entity that is the collective embodiment of everyone's shadow selves – the archetypal aspect of ourselves that rests deep within our unconscious. The moon is also more than this, so it's also an entity unto itself. Anyone – normally mages – can tap into this source for various benefits, like psychological sensations and advanced psychic abilities. There are also practices involving activating current archetypal etheric energy in order to increase one's magic power levels. Not all methods of tapping into the black moon are equal, and so there are black moon practitioners who can access the black moon without undertaking any evil. Accordingly, it is still, for now, a legal practice. However, it is no easy practice, and most mages avoid it, as it can drive a person crazy or leave one vulnerable to demonic possession."

Demonic possession? Korin was about to blurt out before asking, "Do you know anything about the recent demon attacks?"

"I've heard a few rumours – something to do with mage supremacists. It's possible. But it could easily be the result of shoddy moderate black moon practice or even the work of shadowists. But sometimes possessions occur due to other factors, too. I would suggest that you avoid trying to tap into the black moon, as you clearly know very little about it."

"Oh, I don't have any intention of accessing the black moon." Remembering what he had read in the journal, Korin then asked, "But what about Backlevy? Were there possessions back then?"

"Yes, indeed. Not only did their rituals lead to demonic possessions, but Backlevy's circle also conducted experiments on people, which led to further possessions. A few of the cult members even became possessed, but the cult discovered ways to protect themselves."

Hmm... I guess demonic possession can occur even without messing with the spirits. I think. He then asked, "How bad were the possessions? Were there any transformations?"

"Some, indeed, transformed into horrific beings, but many were basic possessions without any shapeshifting."

"Right... So... what was their ultimate goal?"

"Their telos? I think The Gathering wished to physically manifest the black moon – as do most shadowists today. Otherwise, simply power."

Korin murmured as he thought. "Would there be a shadowist cult here at Teloston?"

"There have been cases of shadowists lurking in hideouts on campus. Naturally, people with extreme personality types are attracted to such organizations."

"Then, how would you find such a group? Again, I have no intention of joining."

Finch squinted before replying, "Hmm… usually secret fraternities and cults recruit in a few ways. Sometimes they may spot particular individuals who may be useful or suited to the cult. They may then ask candidates to perform certain tasks before moving on to the next stage of recruitment. If they don't yet share the same worldview, then there is a process of grooming and conditioning before initiation can begin. I've heard of sexual conditioning being one tool."

"Okay… but to back up a bit: are you *sure* there would be no necroshapers at all? Like, how would you be able to determine that they don't at all exist if you can't see them?"

"I understand your epistemological position, so, yes, it's technically possible for anyone to resurrect the ancient Sendrallic Order or one of its factions; and, accordingly, there *could* be necroshapers in existence; but it's clear what the reality is. Don't misunderstand me, I do believe troublesome students have probed into dark practices, and shadowists are a dangerous reality."

Korin suddenly remembered hearing a few people whispering about joining a cult during the camp. He couldn't recall the conversation exactly, but it sounded as if they were merely rebellious juveniles, who wanted to try something devious instead of being part of a grand conspiracy. Part of Korin wanted to believe that there actually was such grandiosity at play, but he considered perhaps the more mundane perspective of his professor had at least some validity. His mind then thrashed about, rejecting such so-called rationalities, realizing that dark forces really were at work. He even felt a little angry at Finch, seeing him as intellectually stubborn, yet Korin wasn't knowledgeable and confident enough to challenge him.

Korin slowly nodded. "Is there any further information I can find in the physical or synopool libraries?"

"It depends on what you're seeking. While there is a rich history stored in our physical libraries, you'd also stand to gain by visiting private physical libraries for additional information. There is always the synopool, but outside of academic journals and the top-tier media giants, there happens to also be a lot of unverified, unacademic rubbish on there. Too many crazy conspiracy theories. Be careful. Oh, and another thing: book burning was common for a few years after the Great Blackout, so certain information has been unfortunately lost forever."

Having processed enough information on the topic for the time being, Korin said, "Alright, thanks for that. I'll have a think about everything you said."

"It was good chatting, Korin."

When Korin left the room, he couldn't help but search for a door with Backlevy's name. Down a few hallways, he eventually found Mirella Backlevy's door with a sign explaining that she was on an expedition and wouldn't be back until the following year. Contact details were also provided. Korin decided to take a peek under the door, nervously looking over his shoulders a couple of times before looking. When he dropped down, he saw nothing of note.

Suddenly, a blackened figure smashed against the floor, moving erratically and causing Korin to literally jump up and crash against the opposing wall. He was about to flee, but the door remained unmoving. Expecting the door to fly off its hinges, Korin stood still, plastered against the wall for a good minute until finally taking another look, finding a beetle scurrying around on its back. Korin gripped his chest, laughing his tingles away.

***

Political Science was Korin's next subject, and the lecture hall was packed with a more diverse crowd than the History lessons, ranging from future sharks -- lawyers -- to hippies covered in dirt, beads, and more dirt. The overall chattering was louder, even though half of it didn't revolve around politics; of that which was, both the layman and erudite dialogue enthusiastically warmed up, drawing in those who were naturally quiet and aloof. Korin, too, leaned in, listening intently and silently to multiple debates. Political names and terms were flung around as if merely identifying family members and everyday utensils and practices, partially concerning Korin as he wondered if he had picked the right subject.

A young man then filled the seat beside Korin. Appearing as if he had been sleeping in the street, the guy's unkempt hair greasily reached over his ears, seemingly like it was dampening his hearing of the horrible music irradiating the vicinity from his unnoticeable phid. He kicked his shabby thongs off, bringing out the foldable writing table to rest his elbows on before planting his wasted face in his hands, remaining deadly still. Unsure if the student was awake, Korin refocused on the debates, but the music interfered with his concentration, annoying him. Sighing in frustration, Korin nudged the student, hoping to 'wake' him. After Korin delivered a light kick to the foot, the guy breathed in heavily with shock, looking foggily around the room. Finally, his eyes met Korin's.

"'Sup?" the student sluggishly asked, squinting to see Korin as he switched his music off.

"Hey," Korin replied. "You awake now?"

The guy snorted, shaking his head. "I have no idea what I'm doing."

Confidence flooded Korin. "You *are* here for Political Science?" he asked, taking short breaths to avoid deep concentrations of body odour.

"What is politics, anyway? I think most people need to chill the fuck out. This system, man. Too many… too many… I don't know. I'll be asleep if you need me."

Speechless, Korin merely nodded. A packet of what Korin assumed to be drugs then fell out of the guy's pocket, landing right next to Korin's foot. In unison, the university security entered the hall, beginning their search for something. Unsure if they were searching for drugs, Korin knew he couldn't let it sit there. He wasn't going to find himself in trouble. Nobody was looking at Korin yet, but he checked his surroundings, anyway, before making a move. Subtly, he grabbed the packet and shakily tried placing it back in the guy's pocket, but his nerves got the better of him, and the packet dropped multiple times in his attempts. Meanwhile, the security agents were nearing. The packet finally entered, but it soon fell out again. This time, Korin shoved a piece of rubbish in the pocket as well to keep the packet from falling out. That, too, fell out. Suddenly, the drug user's phid buzzed with an incredibly irritating sound, continuing without being answered. It drew attention.

That's it, I'm moving! Korin thought, about to stand up, realizing it would look suspicious.

All of a sudden, a small critter scurried past a few legs, causing a few squeals. When it dashed into the aisle, the security began chasing it, soon following it out of the hall. Relieved that the security had left, Korin nevertheless took the opportunity to move, anyway.

But just before the lecture began, a drone entered the room. "Korin Tarkelt?" it asked, scanning the room.

Feeling as if fate was trying to convict him, Korin slowly placed both his hands up.

"I have a message: Chancellor Helena Valen wishes to see you in her office after you finish your dinner. That is all."

Relieved again that he dodged what he perceived as another potential close call, he still wondered whether he was in trouble or that Helena simply wished to see him.

When the lecture began, Korin relaxed again. It helped that it was simple, covering basics, outlines, and course administration, so no strenuous focus was required. Interestingly, even though multiple conflicting political theories were objectively described, despite how crazy some were, the only one delivered with a bias – a negative bias – was that of conspiracy theories. The professor sniggered at such cases, with the student body following suit. Except, there was one student who raised his hand, stating that he believed in conspiracy theories, but he soon got an ear full of ridicule and laughter in return.

When the lecturer mentioned political factions, it jolted Korin's memory back to his first day at Teloston when he bumped into a few AMSA thugs. It was only a day a way before they were going to try something immense…

***

After Korin finished dinner, he immediately set off for Helena's office, only to find her discussing matters with one of the pro-vice-chancellors. The news was playing on the holochite screen near a wall, and a representative from the CGM's Consummit was addressing a group of reporters and officials. Two members of the Movement of the Machine were standing behind him, smiling.

"If we are to progress rapidly in the upcoming age," the Consummitman said, "we *must* augment our research into transbody technologies. The Movement of the Machine has done much to improve academic progress in this area – especially at Domitrian University, which leads in numerous academic rankings – and with our cooperation, we will –"

Helena remotely turned the screen off, gravely staring at the wall.

"They'll continue to push more of this on us," the pro-vice-chancellor said as he began pacing back and forth with heavy breathing.

"Yes, I know." Helena shook her head. "I can't believe they actually passed the bill."

"This ethos will rot away and destroy the core of who we are."

There was a pause before Helena said, "Our options are limited now, but don't worry, we'll… *welcome* them with open arms."

"What?" the pro-vice-chancellor shrieked. "We need to pour as much effort into stopping this as possible! Don't tell me *you've* lost the plot, too!"

"We can't proceed in the way you're thinking, Liam. The government won't allow it. But… I have a plan."

"This better be good. We can't sit idly by."

"Relax," Helena replied composedly. "I'll explain later. But for now, I have company." She glanced over at Korin.

"Fine. I know you have good judgement." He rushed out heatedly, leaving Korin stiffly standing.

"Hello, Korin. How are you?" Helena asked affably.

Seeing Helena alone again reignited the emotions Korin had the first time he awakened to his mage abilities. Her piercing presence shot and walled around him, and he felt a mix of joy and anger, gain and loss, revelation and confusion. Korin finally replied, "Good. I've… been a bit busy, though." He took one step forwards.

"Yes, I understand. Most new students have the propensity to feel as such."

"Can… i-if you don't mind me asking, what was that all about?"

Helena gazed at him, her demeanor as stoic as ever.

"I didn't mean to intrude," he said.

"No need to apologize. My door was open, and you need to know certain things. Do you know much about the Movement of the Machine?"

"A few things, yes, but not a great deal. What's happening?"

"They're spreading like wildfire. The Movement of the Machine believes that we – both mages and non-mages – are at a primitive stage of development and that we must *transcend* our nature with the aid of technology. Mechanists also espouse an anti-freewill worldview – that we are nothing but cogs in a deterministic system; choice… freewill… all supposedly an illusion. They aren't against magic per se but, instead, view it as inferior to that which is found in their utopic vision."

Having come to embrace magic, Korin definitely disliked such ideas. As for the issue of freewill, he had been told most of his life that while fate and destiny existed, he had the freedom to choose his path in life; but, the revelation of all the religious lies made him question such an idea. Still, given that Helena seemed to believe in freewill, Korin didn't dismiss the idea, either.

"They technically emerged in the middle of the Illumination Age. I heard you're studying History?" she asked, and he nodded. "Then you may learn more about the Movement. They're responsible for breeding genius inventors, scientists, and other academics that have extensively advanced particular technological trends, especially for the non-mages. The Movement, of course, is part of a broader set of people that embrace the trans-species ideology, some of whom are radically against the Mechanists. The troubling fact is that the Movement also has a powerful influence across the Caelverse, and their true goals, I believe, are of a sinister nature. Many cybernetic implants have negative effects on the magic gland, and the majority disrupt our etheric fields, in turn distorting our magic and our ability to cast magic. Ultimately, cybernetics weakens *us* and strengthens *them*. Understand that while it has been heretofore illegal in most cases for mages to modify their bodies cybernetically, this trend is rapidly changing. So, I *strongly* suggest avoiding any bodily 'augmentations' that connect with the central nervous system that they may offer and encourage."

"Don't worry. I have no desire to change my body like that."

"Good," she delivered swiftly, the one word holding great clout.

There was a moment of partial déjà vu for Korin. Learning more about the Movement of the Machine was just as interesting to him as learning about the Sendrallic Order from Professor Finch. Although he considered that the present-day Mechanist influences were potentially troublesome, the issues revolving around his religion and the other broader political and spiritual troubles seemed more concerning.

Confused, Korin asked, "So, why open your arms to them?"

"Well," she said, smirking, "sometimes opponents are easier to defeat when you move with them. Sometimes. But enough about the Movement. I called you in because I want to know more about your past. Please." She motioned for Korin to take a seat as she finally sat down herself, staring right into his soul.

Just as Korin was about to sit down, he glanced around Helena's room. Sculptures of muscular warriors were heroically posing; one held a trophy of war high in the air while his iron boot cracked the rock it was positioned on. Her romanticized paintings even contained historical events of mighty mages prevailing against difficult plights. The oil techniques emphasized strong emotions and a yearning for both individual and collective glory in a sea of chaos, generally filled with overly-stormy, reddish clouds blanketing legions of people projected into the world instead of towards the audience. No trivial trinkets adorned the furniture, and neither were there piles of paperwork or loose rubbish present like in Rolan's office. Her chairs even looked like thrones – overarching, spiked, and authoritative; their plain and undecorated nature gave emphasis to the overall form. The room allowed Korin a glimpse into Helena's inner realm, and naturally, he found the décor fascinating.

"You don't consider me an enemy, do you?" Korin asked hesitantly.

"Oh, no." She laughed. "No, no, no. Korin, please consider me your friend." She smiled warmly. "Why do you ask?" Her face turned critical as Korin breathed sharply.

Feeling like he had no choice but to properly answer, Korin said, "I mean no offence, but… you basically implied that you like to keep your enemies close by. And as you know, I also followed a religion that detests magic."

"I never said I keep my enemies close by. I mentioned a strategy that I *may* be using to my advantage. You're safe here, Korin. I don't want my enemies flooding these grounds." She lightly sighed. "I wish to share so much with you, Korin. There's… something… very different about you. Perhaps your past may enlighten me."

Korin considered her assurances for a moment, but he still had a level of uncertainty. Taking a deep breath, he finally decided to explain his upbringing. Thinking he wouldn't be able to articulate himself without becoming too emotional, words actually flowed out of him with ease.

"Thank you for telling me, Korin. It's much appreciated." She smiled again. "You've done a great service for all mages. This information will help with my investigations. Although I'm not in a position of judicial authority, I have contacts, and I will see to it that those priests are investigated."

With an unfocused gaze at nothing in particular, Korin was stunned that he hadn't told Helena sooner. It wasn't so much a matter of informing somebody like Helena about his situation, as it was the fact, instead, that he hadn't told a mage with authority to actually take measures against the priests. He speculated for a minute why he didn't consider the idea before, theorizing that he hadn't the time, energy, mental space, and knowledge of mages and their trustworthiness. But then it occurred to Korin that he also viewed the clergy and the religion *as* the authorities. It was imbedded in him that he had no-one to turn to, despite running into the mages. Indeed, Korin *escaped* from the authorities. The very act destabilized the potential emergence of such thoughts on having them arrested. Furthermore, he, *himself*, needed to take action and find a way to stop the priests when he would finish university. But the prospect of someone else simply taking charge and dealing with his problems – especially people who had never experienced *his* religious indoctrination – felt all too easy, as if his freewill was left redundant… as if he wasn't taking control of his fate.

Korin suddenly regretted telling Helena, but he then realized other people were suffering at the hands of the clergy. And that he couldn't allow. Someone else needed to seek justice, Korin believed, even though he strongly wished to be part of that process. "Thank you," Korin finally replied after a long pause. "But what are you able to do about it? Can the priests really be caught and arrested?"

"I can't guarantee anything. Again, I'm in no position to do anything personally. There are also, understandably, numerous laws protecting non-mages, so it may be hard at first, but we will catch those who committed such deeds."

"Good," Korin said firmly. "But what about the girl I saved? Evelyn?"

"One of the search parties found a ripped piece of clothing on a thorny shrub near the area. Was she wearing a white dress?"

"Yeah, she was. It looked pretty formal. I guess they dressed her up."

"Yes, the clothing looked rather odd, given the environment. Unfortunately, they found nothing else, so we're assuming she either escaped or was captured."

"I see. I hope she's fine." Korin took a moment to process what Helena said, and then he stood up with a mix of emotions. "Thanks again. It means a lot to me."

"You're welcome, Korin. We'll talk another time. Oh, before you go, there's one final thing: I want you to train your abilities as hard as possible. Consider this as one of the first of many steps in your *just* pursuits. It's all you can do for the time being before taking further action."

Taking to heart what she said, Korin nodded and silently left.

***

Later that evening, Korin was relaxing in Sylas's room with his back against the bedside. Sylas was also on the ground, despite a comfy chair next to him.

Talking about how bored he was in his Business studies, Sylas said, "Yeah, besides Jaimas in Alchemy, a lot of the other people are either too dreary or crazily sensitive, like those social justice warriors." He then tried activating a gadget, failing. "Then there are all those meatheads. On top of that, there are jerks like Sereck."

Korin extended one leg out. "I wonder what his problem is."

"I'm guessing either abused when young or born that way. And then you have people who are just stuck up. My parents had to interact with lots of bigwigs all the time; and their children – who were my age – were snooty as fuck. It's like they think they're better than everyone else because they have more or have it all." He shook the rattling gadget, chucking it on a junk pile in defeat.

"But having more doesn't mean you're snooty or a jerk. You're an example of the opposite. I guess that's why I get along well with you." Korin smiled, and Sylas returned the expression. "Speaking of stuck-up people, you remember that guy Sereck was bullying? Hepteon? Well, he and his friends were up themselves, too, despite not being the type of people who... well, let's just say they don't 'have it all', as you say."

"So, it wasn't just me?" Sylas asked with surprise as Korin looked confused. "Oh, well, I saw them sitting down with some of the comic books I normally read, and so I went up to them, and they just brushed me off like a piece of scum on the ass of some... troll or something."

"Really?" Korin couldn't help but laugh. "That's so weird."

"Yeah, exactly. I thought because we had something in common, I'd be able to at least talk to them. But nope. It's not like I was trying to be friends; it was just friendly social interaction. What's up with them?"

"I have no idea. Maybe it doesn't matter what they're into; some people are just cliquey."

"Yeah... so weird. And then you have people like Jaimas again, who are pretty cool with most people. Do you think they'll ever change? Like, are they doing that because they're shy or somewhat afraid?"

"Hmm, I don't think so. I was pretty nervous coming here, but I never acted like those guys. Then again, maybe *we're* cliquey as well without realizing it. Honestly, I probably wouldn't want to be friends with some of the people here, even if they wanted friendship."

Sylas mulled over what Korin said, saying, "True."

"Of course, I wouldn't be mean to them."

Celine unexpectedly walked past the room for a second before coming back, knocking on the open door.

"Come in." Korin motioned, glad to see Celine stop by.

"Hi," Celine said to both guys. "Hey, do you draw?" She pointed to a framed drawing on the wall.

"Ah, yeah, sometimes," Sylas replied enthusiastically, having anticipated a weird question. "It's from a show I watch."

"Oh, cool. I draw, too."

That's another person who draws well, Korin thought.

"Sometimes I'll muck around with A.I. art for fun, but given all the comics I read that are done by people, it inspires me to draw for real."

"So, why didn't you do a Fine Arts program?" she asked.

"Never crossed my mind." Sylas shrugged. "You may be on to something."

"Perhaps mix the business in with some art. In any case, I think it looks very good. You have great precision and attention to detail. Is it a particular art style or is that how it really looks?"

"That's based on what the character actually looks like. I'm probably better at copying things that I see than interpreting from an arty perspective. Is that what you're into?"

"Mm, from my own perspective, yes, from schools of art, no, not really. Not schools. I simply like drawing for the sake of drawing."

"Cool. You should watch it some time. It's called *Firewing Zero*."

"I might have a look, but I don't really have the time to watch anything." There was a moment of silence as she played with her handbag before opening it up. "Oh, Korin, here's a book I got for you. You may want to read it." She handed him an expanded holochite book, titled: *A Guide for Living in a Mage Environment*. "I thought it would come in handy, but you're probably rather busy, so you mightn't have time to read it."

Korin happily stood up to grab the book. "Thanks. I seem to be picking things up pretty quickly, though. I'll flip through it, anyway."

"I knew about that book because there was this one time I helped a haperchite find his way to Crysten. Well, with the help of my parents."

"Are haperchites those beings that look like they're mostly made of rock?" Korin asked, sitting down.

"Yes, a lithoid. He came from underground before stumbling onto our property, so that's how we met him. It was fun helping him, but he kind of wrecked some of our stuff by accident. Once we got to Crysten, we gave him that book to read." Celine began inattentively staring at some of Sylas's equipment with curiosity.

"Take a seat." Sylas gestured keenly.

"We were talking about Hepteon and his mates." Korin made room.

"Oh, I haven't talked to any of them, as they didn't really seem welcoming," Celine replied, sitting on the ground with her legs tucked underneath.

"There we go," Korin said. "That's all the confirmation we need."

"I also have another thing for you." Celine brought out a dried herb. "Your hillseck tryout is on in a couple of days, so you should try and get some decent sleep, especially the night before. Put this under your pillow, and it'll help."

Korin reached over and sniffed it. "Alright, I'll give it a try. Where'd you get it?"

"Alchemy lab…" She averted her eyes, knowing what Korin was thinking. "I read the label, and it was going to expire soon."

"Well, okay." Korin tittered. "Hopefully it hasn't lost its effectiveness."

"It should work. I also, unfortunately, won't be able to come and see you for the tryout, as I'm a little busy."

"That's fine. I appreciate your thoughts, anyway."

Chapter Eleven

The Explicit Kidnapping and the Deflowering

The General Theory academic and administration staff managed to resolve their issues, and it was finally time for the first lecture that Airday. Beforehand, Korin skimmed through his course outline and textbook, reading how the first semester covered various topics like 'origin theories' and 'magic ontology'. He learned that the mages had no consensus, nor any evidence, on not only how the Caelverse emerged, but the genesis of mages as a people themselves – in addition to all biological sentience and sapience. Their conflicting theories were also tied into their universally undecided-upon metaphysical beliefs; no religion was commonly embraced, but there was a general view that at least some supreme transcendent force existed. The origin theories, he understood, were essential to study, as the biological and spiritual makeup of mages fundamentally shaped their use of magic.

The lecture hall was similar to the one for Conjuration, having a studious vibe thanks mainly to the mural above. Korin took a seat next to Celine, noticing the bald lecturer fiddling with items inside a case, appearing rather uncomfortable in his tight clothing. One of his buttons even blew off under the pressure of his belly… When the hour struck, the anxious-faced lecturer glanced up, telling everyone he wouldn't be too much longer. He then rushed out to acquire something. The disorganization and lateness bothered a couple of students, but most didn't care, talking to one another in the meantime.

"So, how'd the psychologist appointment go?" Celine asked Korin.

"She said I was fine for the most part, but I'll have to see her again. She was kind of vague on why."

As Korin continued talking, Celine began drawing on her hand before gently grabbing Korin's hand to doodle on it. A space nebulae-looking substance filled her bright pen, its top fancily curled.

"How were your non-magic classes?" Korin asked.

"Nothing much happened. The Photography tutor was a little creepy, though. He licked his lips a lot. I wouldn't be surprised if he took weird and perverted pictures."

"I thought *you* took weird photos?" Terala butted in.

"N-no. They may seem odd to people, but they aren't weird in a perverted sense." Celine soon finished her drawing of Korin riding a dragon. "Do you like it?"

Korin warmly smiled. "Yeah, it's well done. I'm also glad you didn't draw me riding something like a butterfly."

"I was thinking of doing that, but I had a feeling you wouldn't like it." She giggled, touching a few of her pen's settings on a holographic interface, triggering a laser to emerge and scan the picture. "I've uploaded it to my cache." She then held her pen at the picture, and every bit of the ink jiggled off Korin's skin before floating in the air in its virtually-two-dimensional form. "Maybe I should've animated it."

"No matter. A still image is cool enough."

The picture gradually evaporated into the air, and the lecturer finally returned, placing one last item in his case just as Celine had to leave for the toilet. Korin only just noticed that there were suitcases next to the lectern, causing him to wonder if the lecturer was about to go on a holiday or had just returned.

"Time to begin!" the lecturer announced, clapping his hands. "So… uh… let's have some volunteers. No, actually, I'll choose. You, you, you, and… you. Oh, and you two over there." He rubbed his hands together rather gleefully, grunting with pleasure. The people he picked were some of the finest-looking in the crowd, and each lined up on the stage at the front of the hall as the lecturer assessed their bodies. "Good. Very good looking. You'll all do perfectly," the lecturer said, obtaining a few vials from his case before handing them to the ranked students.

"For the, uh… demonstration today, we'll have to first put you to sleep. Don't worry, the tonics only last a couple of minutes, so drink up, and we'll begin."

The subjects glanced at each other with unease, hoping the lecturer knew what he was doing. Soon after they drank their vials, each person dropped to the ground, knocking their heads hard on the stage floor. Shocked at the seeming carelessness, a few people in the audience stood up. The lecturer then rushed to pile the subjects on top of one another, shocking the audience even more. Grinning, the lecturer activated a large device, and a full-barrier forcefield emerged, barricading the stage from the class. Two of the tutors shot up from their seats at the front, uneasy about what was going to happen.

"And now… for the final part of the demonstration!" the lecturer cried, his voice transmitting through the speakers all over the hall. "I will initiate each volunteer here into the marvellous ideology of mage supremacy!"

All of a sudden, two men with balaclavas emerged from the closet, both holding a gagged pixie each, almost crushing their tiny wrists. Laughing menacingly, the henchmen – bearing a mage supremacist symbol of a skull-and-cross-bone stamped elixir in front of a lightning bolt – moved over to the pile of students and dangled the de-winged pixies above them. One of the tutors immediately rushed out to inform the authorities soon before another two started blasting the forcefield with their lucent discharges, only slowly beginning to overheat and drain the forcefield's energy.

The lecturer continued, "The blood of these filthy non-mages will condition the bodies and minds of our brethren towards the enlightened virtues of mage supremacy! I hereby call upon the demon lord, Merntra, to possess these newcomers. Here is your non-mage blood, My Lord! Now for the culling! Mage power!" he called, and the two henchmen repeated the chant with great fervour. Withdrawing a big dagger, the lecturer then rapidly stabbed one of the pixies in the throat, wrenching down and ripping her body almost in half, leaving a bloody mess with organs flapping out. "Spread it! Spread it now!"

The henchman holding the mutilated pixie then rubbed the dead body all over the sleeping students, causing students in the class to gag, shriek, or turn away in absolute horror. A couple of people ran to the forcefield, banging it with their fists as hard as they could, despite understanding the futility. The students then realized that they, too, could fire ultrachite discharges at the forcefield to weaken it.

"Now for you!" the lecturer told the remaining pixie, who was shedding all the water she had left in her body from her eyes.

Nobody was able to help the last pixie as the dagger plunged into her. The horrific process repeated, and many in the audience were now on the ground, hysterically in tears.

The lecturer then grabbed his suitcases and left an open letter on the lectern before priming an ultrachite dimensional aura. "This is it!" he shouted, looking very proud of his work. "Let it be known that not only I, Professor Marenov Khastanian, am an evil mage supremacist, but I am also behind all the student kidnappings! Yes! Indeed! I will take my new initiates away from this place to another planet – to indoctrinate them!" He evilly laughed. "You'll never find us! I may even return to kidnap more of you during the night!"

There happened to be a teleportation allowance device present, and the dimensional aura switched from its priming state to one with a flat circular portal window inside the space the device affected from itself. It then took just over a second to charge before the other destination was visible, and the yellow ring dropped over the sleeping victims, hitting the floor before shrinking and teleporting the students away. One of the henchmen had also magically created a portal for himself and his fellows with the help of a device, and all three quickly left as well. The forcefield generator stayed where it was, but it soon overheated, leaving the stage open once again. Most of those who had been crying on the floor stood up, but it was too late to take any action. Only a creepy, spine-chilling void remained.

After a brief moment of near-silence, one person shouted, "He could teleport *us* away at any moment, too! Let's get the fuck out of here!"

Believing it was safer to exit the area just in case a portal emerged, the students began pouring outside, shouting aloud their concerns. Mouth agape, Terala remained stunned; Sylas, on the other hand, was capturing the remaining moment from his watch. Filled with a dutiful sense of direction, Korin rushed to the front, telling one of the tutors about the open letter on the lectern before reading it with her.

Dear Teloston University,

I, Professor Marenov Khastanian, am an evil mage supremacist! I am also the true kidnapper! I enjoyed stealing every one of your precious students and plan to turn them into mage supremacists with the help of some demons! Oh, the non-mage blood we'll bathe in! Mmm, nice and fresh, too! If I feel as though they have no further use, I may wipe their memories and toss a few back. Or maybe I should turn them into sex slaves! Anyhow, I am on another planet, and you'll never find me! The Caelverse is too big! Enjoy your hunt!

Before Korin could discuss the letter, the tutor told him and his friends to exit. At first, Korin quarrelled, but he eventually left after Terala convinced him to leave. Students from adjacent halls popped their heads out, wondering what was happening.

"What did you see?" Sylas asked Korin.

Just before Korin explained, a bell suddenly rang. The PA system scrambled for a second before everyone inside the building – and the rest of the university – was ordered to assemble at the evacuation point in the Central Hub, causing massive unrest. Luckily, Korin and his mates had a head start, so they avoided most of the clamour on the way.

"He looked at me!" Sylas said, shaking. "Right in the eyes, then looked away. Jhar's mother, I can't believe how close that was."

"He said he may return," Terala noted. "You better be careful, as he may actively look to recruit you. Or turn you into a sex slave."

"Oh, great. Demons and now this guy!"

"Demonically-possessed people you can fight. The professor, on the other hand, seems to have been successful this whole time."

"Shit, I hope Celine's fine," Korin said, only just realizing Celine wasn't present. "I'll give her a call."

Thousands of students and staff from all over the campus flooded the Central Hub, clumping tightly together with frenzied babble. The demon attacks the other day didn't even cause such commotion. In fact, many thought a far more terrible demon attack had just occurred. However, the situation was different, as the kidnapper was still on the loose; and, when a high-ranking university officer appeared on the large screens across the Central Hub, the students learned that the purpose of the gathering was to inform everyone that matters were being handled and that they'd be safe in the meantime. Mages needed to perform certain actions in order to create any dimensional ultrachite, so its casting was not something that could be done every day – normally, it would only be cast over a day or two within a month; and, long-distance teleportation, specifically, was a hard feat to achieve. Since a device was used to help with the teleportation – and that the device was taken through the portal – the lecturer and henchmen could not teleport back to the General Theory lecture hall. Still, the hall would now be monitored at all hours of the day; and security increased around the university's perimeter, anyway.

For the remaining hour, students didn't return to their lectures, enabling them time to relieve their elevated nerves. The commotion didn't die down – it repeatedly shifted perspective. From bewilderment to apprehension and to anger at mage supremacists, many people caged themselves into tightly-knit groups, as if they were subconsciously shielding themselves from potential kidnappings; other people, meanwhile, were moving about at various paces, acquiring and spreading as much gossip as possible. Jaimas was very active in the last regard, bumping into Korin to provide news that wasn't verified in the slightest. Celine caught up with Korin, informing him that she was fine, though a little nervous and shocked. Korin believed it was probably better that she didn't see the event, anyway.

As soon as the screens activated again, heads in the Central Hub instantly turned their attention, as if by magical force. The university declared Marenov Khastanian the reason for the student disappearances, and Korin, funnily enough, felt an increased sense of security at least knowing the problem's source. But then… a few of Korin's theories he had running through his mind the other day popped up again.

Perhaps there's still a larger conspiracy happening, Korin thought before approaching one of the higher-ranking police officers standing nearby. Korin hinted at the possibility that there was more to the story, using the word 'conspiracy' before mentioning ancient cults and other seemingly 'crazy' topics. The officer sniggered at Korin, telling him that he needed to stop watching so many movies.

***

The tutorials were cancelled, and while most people remained inside their dorms for the remainder of the day, there were still numerous gatherings outside, each increasing in strength as rage over the incident boiled. Korin was deeply angry over the pixie deaths, but his rage was tempered by his shift in mental focus; he still believed that there was likely far more to the situation that people had to also consider.

There happened to be some guest speakers arriving at Teloston University that night to deliver speeches covering a few political topics. When hearing about this, Korin remembered the AMSA thugs on his first day mentioning that a massive rally would occur, so he figured the two were connected. With the tensions stronger than ever before on the issue of mage supremacy, more people were interested in the event about to take place. Korin was, needless to say, keen on finding out more, seeing as he was studying Political Science.

Around dinner time, Korin only grabbed two sandwiches from the food hall before heading outside to see the gathering crowds. As he was walking by the inner wall of the Provision Wreath, he happened to pass Priscilla, who was next to the wall in the dark, scrolling through a low-light phid screen. Her classy, gothic dress was tight around her waist — and a little frilly and lacy at the skirt — but she made sure it was nonetheless accompanied by her long, heavy boots.

"Hi, Korin," Priscilla chirped, her proximity immediately sucking away Korin's thoughts over events.

"What do you want?" Korin asked coolly, causing Priscilla to frown.

"What kind of a response was that?" She switched her phid off.

"A question, I suppose." Korin shrugged indifferently.

Priscilla gave an unimpressed look before sharply saying, "Sure, I have something to say." She cautiously and sharply scanned her surroundings. "I think that we should probably keep an eye out for each other – given what's happened."

"I should be fine. I know how to handle myself." He crossed his arms.

"Agh!" She lightly stamped her foot on the ground. "Stop being so hard, Korin. We're in the midst of a dangerous state of affairs."

"Mm." Korin uncrossed his arms, scratching his neck. "I guess you're right there."

Priscilla sighed before suspiciously saying, "I have a feeling… a *strong* feeling… that the student disappearances are part of a much bigger conspiracy."

Korin agreed with her, but he ended up saying, "It was just our Gen Theory lecturer. I managed to read his letter."

"What a dumb narrative. Do you honestly believe that? From the video I saw, the whole event looked like it came from a poorly-written comedy horror."

Korin felt rather silly with his response, replacing it with saying, "Look… of course I think there's more to the story. I was just saying."

"Hm. Right." She turned her head away.

Thinking of changing the subject, Korin recalled Priscilla's comments on camp. "Hey, I have something I've been meaning to ask you."

"Kiss me first," she demanded, standing her ground this time, waiting for Korin to take action.

Although they were in public view, Korin's friends weren't around, so he didn't have to deal with them asking multiple questions as to what was going on between him and Priscilla. Even *he* was unsure what was happening. Whilst Korin did enjoy making out with Priscilla last time, he was still uneasy about her. He wanted that information, and Korin knew she'd angrily walk away if he didn't embrace her. He leaned in and lightly kissed her on the mouth before taking two steps back. Her lips were still open for more, and despite another frown, he didn't let her have any.

"You said your parents died when you were five," Korin said firmly. "Were you religiously raised?"

"No," she said, and a few of his theories instantly disintegrated. "My aunt raised me afterwards. I assume that you were religiously raised, then?"

"Yes, but I'm not talking about it now."

She sighed. "*Fine.* Well, as for me, you could say that I… revere the moon. A special kind of moon."

There was only one moon that came to mind, given his thoughts of late. "What, like a black moon?" He chuckled.

Surprised, she said, "Yes! What do you know of it?"

"Wait, you revere the black moon? *The* black moon?" Korin was shocked for a second, then he quickly considered it made perfect sense for someone like Priscilla.

"Yes!" She approached him up close. "You should join me in my practices, Korin. Join me," she whispered, her voice feeling hypnotic, circling pleasurably into his ears, leaving Korin in a daze.

After a few seconds, Korin snapped back to his senses and firmly stated, "What the hell? I have no desire to join your weird religion."

"Religion?" she asked before chuckling, her manner oh-so haughty. "Please, I'm above religion. And so is the black moon."

"Yeah, but why do you worship it? Are you a shadowist?"

"I don't *worship* it, and I'm not a shadowist, either. You obviously understand very little about the black moon. Maybe you need to join me in a ritual to find out more."

"What? No!" Korin lightly shouted, prompting Priscilla to look with alarm. "This sounds like a religion. I've already told my friends about this. No rituals. Just, no."

"Our university coursework covers rituals later on, so you know. One way or another, you'll have to practice some kind of ritual. Besides, these are different kinds of rituals. Ones that *I* only know about." She smirked.

Korin leered at her with suspicion; there was something very odd with how she expressed herself – even more so than usual. *So, you somehow know more than the whole of mage academia on the matter*, Korin thought. "Sure you do," he said sarcastically.

"I do. Perhaps… perhaps instead of a ritual, we should do something… mischievous." She ran her fingers up Korin's chest. "Something a little… wicked!" She giggled, reaching for a kiss.

"Wait, what?" Korin stopped her. "Wicked? Listen, this black moon thing sounds too dark to me."

"Oh, come on." Priscilla rolled her eyes. "Figuratively. I'm not a bad person." She smirked again, brushing Korin.

Yeah, I don't know about that… "Look… I need to go now."

"Ugh. Fine. I understand if you're hesitant, but you should still *consider* my proposal."

"You haven't convinced me of anything. Anyway, I need to meet up with my friends. There's going to be some political stuff happening tonight. Good… goodbye." He took off.

"Wait!" she shouted, causing Korin to turn around. "You *will* join me, Korin. I know you will."

I doubt it, Korin thought, turning around to head off.

***

Terala quickly crossed her arms when Korin approached. "You can't go to this political thing," she firmly said. "We have the hillseck tryouts tomorrow. We need proper rest."

"I'll be fine," Korin said. "I won't be doing anything – just observing."

"Okay, but after we make the team – well, at least *I'll* make it – we're going to be practicing like crazy. Keep that in mind."

"I will. I'll see you tomorrow." He tapped her arm with assurance.

Giving a quiet humph, Terala disapprovingly left, leaving just Korin, Sylas, and Celine.

"Okay, guys," Korin said. "Thanks for coming. I can already hear the roaring from here."

"So, what exactly is happening?" Sylas asked, still playing a game, eyes fixed on the concentrated phid screen.

"From what I've been able to gather, there are some guest speakers coming to the university to give some speeches on the topic of mage hegemony in the convention centre."

"Don't you need tickets for it?" Celine asked.

"Yeah, but I think there's enough stuff happening outside to watch. Come on, let's go."

As they made their way to the protests, Sylas finished playing his game, happily saying, "Hey, check this out." His screen displayed the second-best ranked score amongst all mages. "Pretty good, eh?"

Korin lightly smiled. "Sure, but I suggest keeping focused tonight; who knows what will happen."

"Yeah, I'm focused. Don't worry." He finally switched his phid off.

Protestors of sundry sorts filled the streets, many marching with signs while shouting and chanting. Others were camped out for the night with pickets, tents, tables, and grills, blocking any potential traffic. Even though the police were numerous that night, they didn't remove the sitting protestors, as there were too many, and too much drama would've resulted. As Korin neared the convention centre, he noticed more and more AMSA thugs weaving in and out of the crowds, congregating in suspicious bands, dealing assorted rioting paraphernalia between each other. Different types of lights blared from multiple directions, bringing attention to concentrated areas while darkening others via contrast. From the bassy party music to the clanging of metals in furious demonstration, sounds blared so powerfully, Korin had to speak up close and repeat himself often to his friends.

In one area, a strong chant repeated, "Hey, hey! Ho, ho! The sexist beast has got to go!" Claps of sanctimony also coupled it.

The sexist beast? Korin thought. Curious to find out more, he was about to ask someone, but then one of the protestors handed him a pamphlet, reading, 'Revolt against the sexist! Challenge the beast!'

"What's it say?" Sylas asked.

"I'm reading it now. Basically, it's a warning against the speakers' rhetoric and the effects of indoctrination. While I think these protestors seem a bit off the altar, after my upbringing, I'm now pretty wary of any person or idea."

"If it makes you feel any better, lots of mages get indoctrinated all the time. You're not the only person. You have to watch out for these crazy fanatics. They'll appeal to your base levels. Sometimes *sexually*." Sylas snickered.

Noticing many of the dishevelled protestors nearby, Korin said, "I couldn't imagine some of the people here doing that."

"Perhaps *everyone's* indoctrinated." Sylas chuckled. "Including us!"

"I'm thinking the same thing," Korin replied with a smirk before noticing Celine calmly gazing around, finding the event fascinating. He then tapped her shoulder. "Do you know much about all these groups?"

"No, not much," Celine said. "I was never into politics. But I think I might take some pictures while I'm here." Instead of using either her watch or the nodes in a phid, she pulled out a device dedicated to taking photos. She then aimed the camera at a group of AMSA; but as she did, one of the masked thugs heatedly approached.

"Oi, get that fucking camera out of our faces!" the thug yelled.

Celine naturally flinched.

"Hey, watch it!" Korin quickly reacted, stepping in front. "She means no harm."

"Then get the fuck away from us! Now!"

Korin's temper began rising, but there were too many people around to fight back, so he glared at him shortly before ushering Celine away.

"Sorry about that," Korin said, looking behind him to see if any of them followed. "You okay?"

"I think so," she said, glancing around erratically. "Let's try not to stick around any of those guys for too long."

"Alright. Let's keep moving."

Nearby, a hobo-of-a-protestor hopped up on a dumpster, his eyes filled with rage.

"Oh, this guy," one person beside Korin said. "In the last protest I saw, he had maggot-filled garbage thrown at him."

"Hey, I can still see some of it in his beard," Sylas said, giggling.

"We must let that flower know we will *not* tolerate his propaganda!" the protestor shouted. "It's because of the likes of him that we have mage supremacists in our midst! Even *if* we assume the lie that he isn't a mage supremacist, he is still a gateway to mage supremacy, and we must shut him down!"

The poorly-dressed students around him cheered, beating the street dumpster like a drum, as if part of a tribal ensemble. Some of the protestors even began dancing tribally, and the air around Korin literally increased in temperature, as if they were summoning a fire.

"We mages need to check out privilege!" he continued. "We own the means and modes of production and strangle the poor non-mages daily with our brutality! Together, we can unite with our non-mage folk and form a utopia of pure equality! For the revolution!"

As the crowd continued cheering, the protestors near the fence to the convention centre rallied and began collectively shoving it. A couple of ranks of police officers and other security were behind the fence, and it wasn't long before they switched their ultrachite shields on; after the shields turned transparent, there were still a few noticeable glistening touches here and there on their surfaces. Zooming above the police in that one section were about eighty drones loaded with tear gas, rubber bullets, and energy for short electrical pulses. Using most phasarchement magic in many public areas was prohibited, and so the minute a protestor used a single ultrachite discharge, arrests with magic suppressor technology would be made. And they knew it.

Inevitably, the fence gave way and collapsed to the ground, the sound inducing a rush of exhilaration to all who heard, inciting a call-to-action effect. A large percentage of protestors in the first wave activated their ultrachite shields and charged forth in their fury, firing lucent discharges collectively in the hundreds. The police and security fought back as the scene appeared as if an impressive pyrotechnic show of luminescent blue, green, yellow, and red – each coloured ultrachite class with their own unique effects, from magnetism, to mental afflictions, to strange quantum entanglement, and even to a type of slow-motion effect. The police drones, meanwhile, launched tear gas to drive the less rabid protestors away from the vicinity, making the job easier. While the police were outnumbered, they held the advantage with greater power levels, punishing the students' shields far quicker than what the police and security overall endured. Due also to poor, reckless tactics, most of the protestors quickly experienced shield overloading; and while instantly left vulnerable to mere single attacks that could knock them unconscious, the protestors dropped like gassed flies as green discharges laid their final blows. Not a single officer fell.

Now more furious than ever, the second wave of protestors charged forth. This time, more AMSA adherents filled the ranks, so more discharges were naturally fired; those in AMSA were clearly not unwilling to face the consequences of being arrested for their cause. Coupled with the overall greater numbers of protestors, their tactics were slightly different. The police officers' shields were also strained from before, so they were closer to reaching their overloading point. However, their shields were also now charged with temporary class-based effects, becoming stronger in some ways. But with a few yellow discharges fired at the police, some of their shields instantly overloaded as a result of the entangled energies. While the police wore body armour, this mainly protected them against melee attacks, like from knives; so, while the armour could also block discharges from *directly* affecting their bodies, this was generally maybe for one or two attacks, and the striking discharge energy quickly managed to quantumly tunnel through the armour, hitting the bodies of those wearing the armour and knocking them unconscious.

Many AMSA members ran behind other protestors as if they were meat shields before supercharging their discharge auras. Once near the police, the AMSA protestors came out and threw their supercharged punches and instantly overloaded a number of officer shields. A few other AMSA members also attempted to *augment* their discharges, causing the class-based effects to fully work against shields despite their natural inhibitors; still, this was a chance-based phenomenon, and only two discharges happened to deliver full blows, knocking two officers back into the glass behind them, bloodying them. A few protestors even crystallized their discharges into mines, but their applications didn't suit the context of the battle.

The police began slowly dropping in strength, but overall, they managed to keep their ranks together. The drones were also still mostly present, as the anger was held more towards the police, so they were unsurprisingly the first targets. The police then set up a few last-minute barricades to help them, as phasarchement combat was better suited being behind cover. Naturally, the AMSA thugs came prepared, also lugging out some barricades before a more tactical fight began. Some of the protestors charged their yellow shields for mild invisibility. However, this effectively blinded them, preventing sight outside of their shields; and with the numerous discharges being fired everywhere, some inevitably hit their shields, ending the camouflage.

"This shit's getting intense," Sylas said, taking a video just as Celine was, too.

"I know," Korin replied. Not all the AMSA thugs were at the front line, and Korin noticed that many of them were spread out, plotting other schemes. "Hey, follow me," he said before leading the way through the crowds to an alley on the other side of the road.

Celine almost lost sight of Korin as she repeatedly turned around to take final snapshots of the event. When they reached the alley, Korin's suspicions were confirmed; a group of AMSA was plotting an event with a suspicious-looking bag.

"This should make a big enough explosion," one of the AMSA guys said to another.

"What should we do?" Sylas whispered to Korin as they hid behind a few crates.

"Wait a minute to see where they go," Korin answered.

But just before the AMSA group left, another group of students entered the vicinity, each bearing the same mage supremacist symbol from the kidnapping. Immediately, a fire fight began between the two groups, lucent discharges flying everywhere as shields lit up.

"What do we do?" Sylas asked.

"Don't open fire just yet," Korin said. "Wait till both their numbers dwindle first, then we attack whoever's left."

Much of the ultrachite initially thrown around was either red or yellow, the brightness contrasting greatly against the alley's dankness – especially so when some of the red discharges created flashbang effects on impact. The flashbangs mostly affected their victims due to how the magic worked, so it didn't negatively affect Korin and his friends. Although everyone had shields, each took caution to keep around corners, often blindfiring. One of the blue blast balls hit a sharp bin lid, which then rapidly spun in the air before passing through an ultrachite shield due to its slower-than-bullet-speed; as it did, it hit one of the mage supremacists in the head, knocking him out instantly. A couple of yellow shots hit the alley's dim light, and with the overloading nature of the yellow energy, the light began malfunctioning. Swear words filled the flickering darkness, each side of the fight sounding as if both ultimately and strangely on the same side – or one and the same. Those who had better cover behind objects avoided most of the discharges. However, one person began using alpha-positive discharges, magnetically drawing his opponent out from cover and into the main line of fire. Within a few seconds, the exposed guy's shield overloaded, and he was knocked unconscious with a green blast.

The shootout after that didn't last much longer, and both groups retreated after having lost a few of their members to the unconsciousness-inducing nature of beta-negative's energy. The bag of potential explosives, however, remained on the ground.

"Quick, let's get that bag," Korin said, racing forth.

Just as Korin snatched the straps, a couple of the AMSA thugs returned. Swiftly, Korin dived for cover while managing to fire two yellow blasts at the thugs each. The entanglement-inducing power of the gamma attack *fortunately* made a successful chance check against one of the shields on the first hit, overloading it instantly... but it also backfired and overloaded Korin's shield. Now without a shield, Korin didn't risk poking his head out to finish the job, nor did he want to call out to his friends that his shield was down, as the thugs could've seized the opportunity. Celine nevertheless noticed what happened, quickly helping Korin by providing cover fire. Free from being attacked, Sylas was then able to quickly launch a green discharge that instantly sent the vulnerable AMSA guy unconscious. The last remaining AMSA thug made a break for it very quickly, and no mage supremacists returned afterwards, so the coast was clear.

Staggered at his success of overloading his opponent's shield, Korin's hands still shook a little.

"Hey!" Sylas called out, breaking Korin's stupefaction while they were still in cover. "That the first time you shot someone with your magic?"

"Yeah. Yeah, it was," Korin said with thrill, almost about to laugh.

"Same here," Sylas said happily. "And you?" he asked Celine, who simply nodded back very quickly.

"Did Cartras mention how long the unconsciousness lasts for?" Korin asked.

"I can't remember if he did, but I know that generally for average power levels, one beta shot will knock someone out for about ten minutes; two shots an hour; and I think that three shots is eight hours. Since we're newbies, we best shoot them twice as much."

"What happens with more discharges?"

"Eh, I think it diminishes after that. We better shoot them a couple more times to be safe." Sylas then eagerly took care of the business, shooting the surrounding thugs already on the ground. Korin and Celine also helped out.

"Alright, let's get this bag to the police," Korin said.

"What about those mage supremacists?" Celine asked.

"We'll tell the police about them as well," Korin replied before leading the way again until he found some police officers. He approached with vigilance, saying, "We found this on those AMSA guys in the alley over there. Apparently, they were going to make it explode. And we also found some mage supremacists there, too."

The police eyed Korin and his friends with suspicion, but the head officer said, "Alright, we'll have a drone scan it. Keep out of trouble."

"Well, that was easy," Sylas said. "I thought they'd make us stay for questions. So, what now?"

Celine swiftly asked, "Is there any way for us to see the speakers now?"

"I just had a look on the pool," Sylas said, showing his friends some information on his phid, "but it's too late to buy tickets. Sold out."

Korin considered his options for a minute before a line of security officers passed by while escorting a group of students who had bought tickets but were yet to enter the building. Each was relentlessly heckled for even wanting to enter. "Tag along them. Maybe we can try this way."

Korin, followed by Sylas and Celine, slinked into the back of the group when one of the security officers turned away for a moment, barging some protestors. Once the officer turned around again, he noticed more people in the group, but he didn't say anything, as Korin and his friends didn't look or sound like the protestors. The surrounding chaos then grew, almost like the security would be overwhelmed at any minute as they were pushed closer and closer to Korin and his friends.

The walk – or march – through the scene seemed endless, but they finally arrived at the convention centre's doors – each gloriously high in their fashion, reflecting nearly nothing but the area's all-pervading spotlights. Everyone had to present either a physical tag or one on their phids.

"Crap, bad idea, Korin," Sylas whispered. "We've got nothing."

"I'll think of something," Korin whispered back.

The security stopped the final three, asking for proof of tickets; and just as Korin was about to say that a bunch of AMSA thugs had stolen them, the scene outside became even more chaotic, with objects flying in their direction.

"Quick, get inside!" the large security officer shouted.

There was no hesitation. Korin leapt inside, grabbing Sylas and Celine, who were nearly hit with a giant spoon. The glass doors held the attacks, and the security focused on keeping the doors secure instead of checking for tickets.

"Are… are we in?" Sylas quietly asked.

"Yeah, we're in," Korin said, swiftly moving away from the doors. "We'll have to keep a low profile, though." Just as it seemed that Korin had made it, there was another set of doors to pass through with more security. Approaching with hesitation, Korin managed to firmly say, "AMSA ripped our tags away. It's crazy out there."

"Yeah, and they hacked into our accounts," Sylas added.

"Hmm… names, please?" the security officer asked.

All three gave their names, hoping that another excuse would fall into their laps. As the security officer searched for their names, the introductory speaker had just finished, so it was time for one of the main guests: Magnolia Yasexybeast. Receiving an enthusiastic roar louder than what the crowd outside produced, he was also met with thunderous stamping of feet, which, alone, drowned out the exterior noises. Naturally, a few hecklers had bought tickets simply to boo him. Coupled with flashing coloured spotlights, loud dubstep music suddenly played from the surrounding speakers, and a few of his devotees followed him up to the edge of the stage, bowing repeatedly. Legally his last name, Yasexybeast was enough to rile up a few activists and social justice warriors on both sides of the political spectrum. The infamous man was draped in dazzling, glittering attire that quite literally came off a recent runway model show designed for him. His makeup and hairspray made his face and hair look exactly like plastic and his overall being: a doll – one, however, who had his own opinions. Strong opinions.

Just as Magnolia finished prancing to the podium, having meandered on the way, there were a few synchronized explosions, and various protestors barged into the convention centre from different openings.

The music stopped.

Even though each group of protestors had different political leanings, they had a common goal: to stop the speaker. AMSA was, of course, present, having made the explosions; but one group, in particular, seemed the most raving of the lot. The group was all female, topless with titties ranging from small and large, flat and sagging. Most had hairy and dyed armpits, completely exposed as they waved their arms about and fist-pumped the air. Their thin and flabby bodies possessed temporary tattoos consisting of various slogans and statements written in dripping blood; a few were fully-rendered animations of Magnolia being murdered in despicable ways, repeating again and again.

The security at the inner doors immediately left to handle the AMSA guys at the front of the convention centre, leaving the hall open for Korin to rush into and avoid the outside conflict. As AMSA was being dealt with, a few from the other protesting groups managed to slip into the inner hall. Many in the audience were annoyed, though a few found the scene either amusing or stimulating, nudging each other at the nudity. Sylas *had* to record the event; Celine, meanwhile… wasn't so inclined; that was until she put a filter on her camera. Korin wanted to hear what the speaker had to say, but he simultaneously wanted to see how the protests would turn out.

Unlike some of the other protestors, who stayed at the back of the hall while clanging metallic objects, the all-female group of protestors immediately ran up on the stage and surrounded the speaker, shouting and screaming in his covered ears – the horrid noises even surrounded all in the hall through the speakers. A couple of the girls carried a full barrier forcefield generator on the stage, activating it to trap them and Yasexybeast within. As soon as that happened, the admin officers in the crowd – along with the inner security – began shooting discharges at the forcefield, weakening its strength with every shot. Many students also began to help – despite not being allowed to use their discharges in such a place. Déjà vu, in a sense, hit Korin again.

"Do we fire as well?" Sylas asked Korin.

"No, keep a low profile. The forcefield will break shortly, anyway."

The girls on the stage channelled a deep-seated misery from their inner cores, expressing it in a fiery way that began to burn creases across their creaturized faces. Arms were thrust to the side in the same manner a bratty child would demand goods from their parents. At worst, it looked as if demons were about to charge through their throats, which were veiny and propelled forward. Short sentences devolved to rambling words, and words into incompressible shouts of fury.

Their acts appeared as if a ritual, where they took turns moving in and out of circles. One girl after another pulled their pants down, literally defecating with exhilaration around Magnolia's shoes as the others sadistically pinned him in his spot. A few barrels of a special philtre were then poured over the mess, in turn causing their waste to greatly enlarge and 'duplicate' while frothing and bubbling up, as if erupting. Pieces of corn and other unprocessed foodstuffs shot up and flung across the forcefield, splattering and drooling down while leaving skid marks. Several of the seated attendees flinched or shielded themselves in disgust, but the protestors didn't seem to care about being covered themselves. The girls then quickly forced a tonic down Yasexybeast's mouth, causing him to spasm and fall into the faeces. In their hatred, the degenerates could barely laugh, kicking the infamous man senseless with sharp shoes coated in a substance that caused purple boils to emerge.

All this took place in a very short amount of time; everything was clearly planned and executed thoroughly. The admin officers and security finally overheated the forcefield, and multiple types of ultrachite discharges were shot at the girls, who nevertheless had ultrachite shields activated as a backup. When negative-red discharges fired toward the stage, it caused *some* of the disgusting matter to slow to a near-halt, as if the properties on the stage were part of a movie in the midst of a slow-motion-effect scene. A few of the larger, solid foodstuffs which had been hurled up were now identifiable, spiralling slowly in the air as if gravitationally-bound in a planet's upper atmosphere. The rest of the security finally entered after finishing the AMSA thugs off, and they immediately began shooting blast balls at the raving girls, sending a few of them landing hard on the floor.

Most of the girls had stopped torturing Magnolia to deal with the threats. Two girls on the left of the stage turned to the nearby security, charging at full speed before being blasted, their saggy arms now twitching in their unconscious state. In their madness, a few of the girls started haphazardly shooting at audience members. A few of their blast balls shot the unshielded audience members unconscious, while some blue discharges began shooting toward the back of the hall. Korin grabbed Sylas and Celine, ducking behind the first line of seats in time to see a few blast balls flying above their heads.

"We need to shoot back!" Sylas shouted.

Korin replied, "Alright, but be careful if the security gets suspicious."

The overhead blasts nonetheless stopped, and Korin glanced over the seat, noticing the shooter had been knocked unconscious. Another protestor was nearby, wrestling with an audience member, kicking and screaming; she, too, was smacked to the ground. One protestor activated a small, non-magic proxportal disc set; and when she accidentally slid over and hit the ground, the side with the portal-entrance facing stayed where she was positioned – right next to her where the foaming and still-expanding analogue faeces was located. Meanwhile, the side with the exit facing had a drone attached to it, but it began malfunctioning, chaotically moving through the air. Since the two sides of the portal were naturally linked together, the foaming faeces shot through the exit and drenched audience members in the front in seconds. Screams of revulsion radiated through the hall. As the proxportal continued crazily spinning, it rained down on more people as the nearby students bolted out of the way, a few accidentally sliding over in the mess already on the floor.

"Oh, shit!" Korin cried, clutching the seat in front.

"Literally!" Sylas added, about to flee.

"This is the grossest thing I have ever seen!" Celine cried, keeping her eyes closed.

The portal then aimed at the hall's exits, spraying them for a good minute. With the doorways now dripping with shit, fleeing was off-putting. Korin stood his ground, anyway. While the drone stopped wildly moving around, the wormholing of shit still continued. Sylas popped his head up, and while he covered his mouth in disgust in case he gaged, he was utterly devoted to watching every bit of detail – along with the rest of the unflowering scene.

"Is it over?" Celine asked.

"Yes! Quick, look!" Sylas said, shaking Celine's shoulder.

Celine peeped over the seat, seeing not only the mess but also the outpouring of shit. "Ew, gross! You lied!"

Sylas laughed his head off. "Ah, now *that* was funny!"

"Sylas!" Korin lightly punched his friend. "It's almost over, Celine. I'll let you know."

"Thanks, Korin." Celine remained nestled on the floor.

Shortly after the proxportal had run out of energy, all the demonstrators were soon either knocked unconscious or directly arrested and taken away, leaving behind trails of slimy brown on the floor. Magnolia was picked up and carried outside for medical assistance, and the less extreme protestors lowered their banners, complying with the security as they were ushered out without any spectacle. Having no idea who Yasexybeast was, Korin was even more curious as to what he may have said to trigger such crazies. The event at that point was cancelled, but an unofficial meetup with audience members was organized elsewhere.

Korin turned to his friends, "Alright, that's definitely enough for one night. I think bed is in order."

"You sure?" Sylas asked. "I think they're handing out some special deserts outside the food hall right now."

"You're thinking of food?" Celine asked incredulously.

"Yeah, I'm starved!"

"Yes, I'm sure," Korin said. "I also need rest for tomorrow. Let's go."

Chapter Twelve

Hillseck: Sports Enhanced

About nine hundred contestants mustered inside Teloston's hillseck stadium, a modern structure externally formed with massive steel triangular slabs laced with fluorescent lights in long beams and twinkling sprinkles. In between the breaches, grassy flora sprouted like thick blankets, while the taller vegetation's branches curled up, crowning the stadium. Inside, the morning light shot through the pure glass roof and around the various Teloston-ensigned flags, each gloriously bold.

Sylas tagged along to watch as Korin and Terala were on the ground level, confident that they were going to thoroughly thrash at least half the entrants. There were still many fit people, a few showing off their bravado, flexing ostentatiously in daring poses. Whenever anyone walked past Terala, she made sure her posture was firm and self-assured.

Not everyone present had played Ultimate Hillseck Rules before, as many underage mages had difficulty controlling the neurachite in the equipment. Moreover, UHR required expensive equipment to either hire, purchase, run, and maintain, so unless they played it formally in school, they may not have had access to play it. Basic Hillseck Rules were the cheapest and simplest way to play, but there were lots of other varieties as well, such as Magic Hillseck Rules, which, obviously, required magic to play, but was more limited, so it wasn't as popular – even amongst adult and even more powerful mages.

The first-years outnumbered the second and third-year students – one reason being naivety. Males also outnumbered the females. While women were allowed in the main team, it was commonly understood that females typically were rarely – if at all – picked. This was simply because women were generally weaker than men, but there was still some skill involved with hillseck, such as accuracy, riding finesse, and dexterity, that could allow some talented women the chance to play with the guys. There was also, nonetheless, an all-female team that Terala could try for, but she wanted to play in the main team, for several reasons.

"That sounds like some crazy shit," Terala said to Korin after he told her what had occurred the previous night.

"Yeah, I swear, a lot of the people here are…" Korin said, depression building, "they're… they're not quite right."

"I totally agree. Fuck those crazy cunts. Still, it sounded like you had fun – in a way. Anyway, come on. We have a trial to smash."

"You're right. At least I have something positive to focus on – it's what I need; otherwise, I'd probably go crazy, too." He chuckled lightly.

"Morning, guys. I'm Coach Virkorska," a tall man greeted everyone enthusiastically with a voice loud enough for the participants in the back to hear.

The coach's icy-blue hair flared up as if he had been electrocuted, while grey hairs stiffly hung from his nostrils, their position unyielding despite his strong exhales. His grin was naturally wide as it exuded energy, whereas the deep scars on his face held many stories. A grey powder covered his burly hands, almost rendering his exceptionally-short fingernails invisible. Similar to Cartras, the coach wore a singlet exposing his large biceps; though, his were dotted with age spots, unusually-shaped moles, and even more scars.

"Me and my colleagues will be picking the best for the undergrad team. Most of you," he said with a pronounced and gruff 'ya' sound, "are now being given a number to come back later today, as there are too many of you." His elisions on 'ing' ending words were also quite distinct. "Damn equality rules. Bloody uni, ruining the whole assessment process. Nothing makes sense anymore," he almost muttered. "Anyway, as for those right in front of me now, c'mon inside, and I'll quickly explain what the deal is." He eagerly motioned with a large swing of his arm.

A transparent, domed energy barrier was activated over the field, and Korin stepped through its entry, transitorily feeling a sensation of being drenched with water. He ran his hands over his hair, expecting to wipe water out, and in confusion, he quickly repeated the action a few times. From the inside, the barrier was darkly translucent, preventing distraction during the game; at the same time, tiny staggered nodes across its surface generated light for the field. Korin remembered Terala telling him that the floor would open up for the game with a thin layer of crystal that would shatter when people fell onto it. Underneath the 'ice' layer, as it was called – despite not being actual ice or even cold – was a space where moving proxportal catchers would appear to teleport people back to their team bases.

The coach was wearing a set of sandecks – hillseck-approved hover skates, which hovered around fifteen centimetres off the ground. The hover skates, moreover, had suspension technology that allowed users to jump very high. Purely for aesthetics and team identification, sandecks produced a particular-coloured glow in the space between the skates and the surface they hovered from. Creating a faint voltaic noise, the glow itself featured thousands of tiny crystal shards erratically and electrifyingly swarming inside a cloudy blanket that occasionally wisped beyond its area.

"Normally there's a couple of people that enter the tryouts that have never skated before, the coach said. "If you're one of them, good luck to you today. You'll need it. Of course, some of you may have also only practiced on simulators before. Unless you're poor, you should stop with the simulators and get out into the real world. Bunch of wimps. The real thing is tougher." His bluntness caused Terala to giggle quietly. "Unlike most personal transporter devices like the majority of hoverboards, sandecks require effort, and they move based on basic force and momentum, not a motor. Too many pathetic people wanting a free ride. Well, it ain't happening here."

Terala had informed Korin earlier that hillseck required hover skates, and fortunately, he used to play various individualistic and team-based sports in the winter on frozen lakes with ice skates. The ice-skating sports weren't his forte, but he was still pretty good at them. He figured that hover skates wouldn't have been too different, but he was nevertheless a bit anxious. Terala, though, told him that hover skates were easy to use, so there was nothing to be worried about.

The coach set off to grab a handheld device, and on returning to the group of contestants, one of the students thought it would be funny to stick out a random pole he had brought in and trip Virkorska; the alert and agile coach, however, grabbed the pole while skating and swung the idiot through the field. When the coach let go, he pulled out the handheld device, pushing a few holographic tabs, which consequently made two proxportals appear – one on the floor and another floating above via an orb drone. The disrespectful and disrespectable lad immediately fell through the bottom portal, only to find himself falling through the top portal, recycling indefinitely. Nearly everyone laughed at him as he screamed helplessly.

"Hey, that portal trap looks kind of fun," Korin whispered to Terala.

"I was thinking the same thing," Terala replied. "We should provoke the coach, too." She chuckled.

"Agh, now, where was I?" Virkorska scratched his head as the falling first-year shut up from exhaustion. "Ah, yes, now for the aim of the game." He loudly cracked his knuckles, then his neck – both creating odd noises that everyone heard. "Since we play UHR here, you'll be using sentars. For those who haven't used them, we'll let you have a moment to get used to them before the testing starts."

Korin was a bit worried about the neurachite issue, but he had learned to use some neurachite technologies by now, so he didn't feel absolute dread at the challenge. Everyone was given a pair of gloves based on their size. The sentars, as they were called, were thin yet strong; both had nodes and focal point dotted in particular places, and it was from these nodes that various weapons and other combat equipment would emerge, which were either solid or non-solid. For UHR, only physical weapons were used, but these were soft and light, and it was really the stunning effect that stopped opponents. In fact, the blades that would emerge would only stun a player's *suit*, not their *body*, freezing them temporarily. The lightness, moreover, happened to make it easier for women to swing the weapons, and all a player had to do was make their blade merely touch another player's suit, so skill was a big factor in winning. Still, strength did play a role, too.

Using their minds, the contestants began to command the sentars; the second and third-year students had no problem, and it took a couple of minutes for a lot of the first-years to make them work. After focusing hard for a while, Korin eventually formed a weapon, which happened to be a staff. Terala, meanwhile, had two 'fore blades' – that is, blades from her lower fingers on her back hands. Each weapon was made of aerochite, and they could either be remained attached to the sentars, or they could detach and electrostatically levitate while in range. A magnetic force would pull the aerochite back should it ever move too far away from the sentars.

"Remember, staffs and blades," the coach said. "Nothing else. Now, as you should know, after you strike your enemies with your blades, you'll either push them to the ground or can just let them fall off. Strategies for what you'll do will vary based on the context. I'll be making sure you know what's the best thing to do." One of his eyes suddenly twitched rather madly. "The ground is your enemy!" he snapped, startling everyone.

"What the fuck?" Terala slowly whispered, and Korin expressed his shrug through a confused smirk.

"Fall off," Virkorska continued on like normal, "and you'll fall through the ice, where a proxportal will respawn you at your base. Doesn't hurt in the slightest. Unless you're a wimp. Ultimately, it doesn't matter how much you get hit, so long as you *destroy* the opposition by garrisoning the hill the longest." He pointed to a circle of floating light – about five metres in diameter – radiating upwards. "You're given an hour in UHR, and the score can be seen at your base." He pointed to one of the screens.

Terala had already told Korin the basic rules before, but the coach refreshed essential points for everyone with his own opinions. Eleven players comprised a team, consisting of one keeper, three defenders, two weavers, four chargers, and one roamer. Each role restricted the type of *orb* that could be grabbed, but all players could stop what they were doing and attack other players.

Chargers collected a *charger orb* to charge the *casark* – the hill – to unlock and prime it. Chargers more specifically had to deliver the charger orb through a series of ring-shaped *charger nodes* around the field – normally, this was done while holding the charger orb in one's hand as a charger skated through the node, but technically, the charger orb could be thrown through a node. After one charger node was activated, the chargers then had a limited amount of time to bring the charger orb to the next node. If the other team managed to grab the charger orb and deliver it through a node, then the charge for the original team would be lost. Once all the nodes were activated, the hill would unlock, whereupon the hill would throw out three charger orbs for the chargers to collect and throw through the perforations called *charger holes* on the now-spinning hill's forcefield to continue keeping the hill charged. When a charger orb was thrown through a charger hole, the hill would spit the charger orb back into the field again.

The keeper safeguarded a *keeper orb* floating around their body, while the defenders – or guardians, as they could be called – generally protected the keeper; both roles would also attempt to snatch the opposing team's keeper orb. When the hill was primed, only the keeper would enter, if they retained their own orb. Chargers did not score points; instead, it was the keepers who scored points by entering and staying inside the charged hill. Once inside the hill, keepers scored points every second – double points if two keeper orbs were possessed – but the hill remained open for the opposing team to enter and knock the keeper out. The defenders, at that point, would have to attack all rival team members *outside* the hill. If chargers failed to keep the hill charged, then the keeper would have to leave the hill, and the chargers would have to start charing the nodes again. The hill itself was not elevated, so it was a figurative label for the prime circular and central area to capture.

Augmenters raced against their opposing augmenters for the two floating *augmenter orbs* before skating geometric circles around the field with their orb. Once an augmenter had completed one circuit of the field, then, depending on which augmenter orb they grabbed, they could provide a benefit to their team – but only if the augmenter continued their circuit without any major interruption. The positive augmenter orb would increase the time limit chargers had for priming and keeping the hill charged. The negative augmenter orb allowed various types of orbs to emerge, which the roamers could grab. These orbs consisted of: *attack orbs*, which were used to throw and stun people's suits, like sentar weapons; *stonewaller orbs,* employed to trap and delay; *illusion orbs*, which induced illusions to 'blind' or distract opponents; and *cymatic orbs*, which were used to undulate the ice with various cymatic patterns, causing difficulty in skating. All of these orbs only provided temporary effects. If a specific orb was used, it would not reappear until the augmenter had completed another circuit. The roamers also could roam from one scene to another at their will, able to collect any orb they wished.

Rough physical contact was allowed in hillseck, except for a few actions, such as punches to the head. Regardless of circumstances, fallen contestants always reappeared at their home base, waiting out a detention time before entering the field again. There were also many rules to consider, and although the game's items were tuned to detect unauthorized or foul play, a referee was always present.

Virkorska at last released the portal-trapped idiot, turning to the group to say, "We're looking for raw talent, so we won't actually be playing the game. I know, it makes no sense. Bloody bureaucracy, telling us how to run things." Everyone expected the now-freed student to be instantly kicked out of the dome, but the coach approached him closely and sternly said, "No fucking around again. Got it?"

The student silently nodded before slinking back into the crowd as many of the contenders smirked.

The entrants were also told that they were being filmed from multiple angles so the assessment could be done more efficiently. Small drones were already whizzing around, and one zoomed just under someone's crotch. The coach then opened a couple of boxes full of sandecks for the first group of one hundred people, while another staff member obtained student names and information. Korin, funnily enough, only just learned of Terala's last name: Merandar.

The undergrads were given a couple of minutes to see if they had the right fit and feel. There were no trainer skates, so a couple of people quickly lost balance before falling. A few other newbies managed to continue skating, but it looked as though a mere dantha fart would've sent them to the ground. While the feel was similar to ice skates, it was still slightly different, but Korin managed to quickly adjust as he began skating. Depending on the force, the hover skates also bobbed a little, which was one of the major differences between them and ice skates. As Korin was successfully skating, a couple of other students annoyingly crashed in front of him. Repeatedly. Terala, on the other hand, was zooming around Korin in circles.

While staying still, Korin told Terala, "I thought you said you've only skated a couple of times."

Terala animatedly stopped right in front of Korin. "I guess I forgot to mention that I used to skate *a lot*." She grinned. "I'm a shoo-in for sure."

Terala continued showing off, surging between clumsy and fallen participants before jumping over them – by a couple of metres! Korin tried jumping on the spot, managing to reach roughly the same height as Terala's jumps. However, the landing was a different matter, and Korin artfully crouched down in time to prevent himself from falling. He then gained balance. Slowly. Worrying, Korin knew he wasn't ready for jumping – especially with some of the manoeuvres the other participants were pulling off.

Markers were set up on the field, and it was time for the first test. Multiple students at a time had to manoeuvre through and around the markers in a planned course, most failing when they had to quickly turn sharp corners. A few still couldn't manage to pass the starting line.

Thank God, Korin thought, trying to hold back a grin.

Terala dashed through the course, skimming past each marker with finesse and maximum speed as if her body were a finely-tuned instrument, plucked and strummed at the most appropriate timings. Her expression was serious, but Korin could tell she was enjoying every moment. The last part of the course featured a few different kinds of jumps, which Terala successfully executed. After performing an unnecessary but tricky manoeuvre for a finale, she returned to a mix of impressed and jealous faces.

When Korin began, he decided to keep himself steady, as he didn't quite know his limits with hover skates. He went slower than the better contestants when making the turns, but he was nonetheless successful. Even though numerous eyes were watching him, Korin managed to keep all distractions at bay. In itself, his performance was good, but not fantastic; but at a minimum, he didn't botch anything up, and he was thus better than over three-quarters of the students. For the jumps, however, he had to be even more cautious in order to sustain his balance. Although he succeeded at most of the jumps, they were still mediocre, and Korin instantly knew they wouldn't have been impressive enough to make him qualify – given that there were many others who outperformed him. Korin then returned to the crowd, where Terala patted him on the back, smiling. He barely looked at her. Luckily, there were more trials.

The participants were then lined up in two ranks facing one another, where they were to engage in sentar staff and sword combat, rotating quickly to the next person after a whistle blow. While their sentar weapons could stun suits, no-one was wearing any suits, so the test was based on who could strike the other person's body first; that, or if the other person fell over first. Korin decided to recreate a staff; he detached it from the sentar and then firmly gripped it, feeling that he had more control over it than before. This was *his* realm now.

Korin's first opponent was a dopey-looking loser who clumsily moved in, attacking without forethought. Easily dodging the attack, Korin simply let the kid fall on his own. His next twenty opponents were a mixed bag of the hopeless and the efficient; Korin knocked each out with barely a struggle. Terala was his next challenger.

"You know I can't go easy on you," Korin said, smiling awkwardly, still hoping all the best for her.

"As if I'd want you to," Terala replied, her hubris through the dome.

Korin allowed Terala to zoom in, knowing she was better at skating. In her cockiness, she darted behind Korin and lunged at him. At the same time, she left herself open too much, allowing Korin to strike her. Terala moaned with frustration, moving to her next opponent without comment. Korin felt a little horrible for diminishing her chances, but he soon considered she would succeed, as her combat skills were also proficient – compared to mostly everyone else.

When the two ranks had cycled halfway through, the coach app-roached each person, testing them in combat, most lasting mere seconds as if they were puny test dummies. Like an unstoppable beast in his charge, Virkorska shortly stopped in front of Korin with a heavy presence. His leer was one of curiosity and desire for challenge. The imposing muscle mass charged towards Korin, who rapidly blocked the blitz, frenetically bashing the coach's staff multiple times in succession before ducking and then weaving away from an attack. A gap opened, and Korin thrust his weapon at the coach's stomach. Nearly everyone who watched was speechless. It was the first time the coach lost that morning. Virkorska simply grinned at Korin before moving on to the next student. Korin's heart was still racing, even though he knew he did well; his nerves also momentarily prevented him from moving his arms back to their natural position as he watched the next participants fail. It wasn't just a matter of Korin succeeding that made him happy; it was also the fact that he matched an older mage's skills; it made him feel as though he could not only succeed in his new world but also add to its strength.

The following task involved throwing charger orbs at an enormous flat panel with numerous targets; since there were too many entrants – coupled with the 'annoying regulations' – they didn't bother testing on the forcefield around the casark. The game's magnetic tentacles, known as *mag-limbs*, weren't activated either; each of these mag-limbs would activate after the charger nodes were activated and magnetically bind to the hover skates so players could ride on one at any degree of rotation.

A couple hundred charger orbs suddenly zoomed onto the field, electrifyingly floating in the air, almost like an army of angry wisps ready to zap everyone into another frequency of energy. A whistle blew, and everyone reached for the closest charger orb before throwing them at the targets. When Korin placed his hand around an orb, it produced a fuzzy current, making his hand buzz, despite wearing sentars; his fingers were also easily able to sink in like grabbing a sponge.

Korin took aim, throwing with all his might, hitting a target on the first strike. Since he was there to compete, he rapidly grabbed one orb after another, successfully hitting every target – but not only any target, he hit the highest ones, as did Terala, with her athletically-strong arm, both standing out amongst their peers. The more orbs thrown, the greater the determination – and eventually, aggression – Korin channelled. His grunts grew louder each time. The aggression, though, wasn't needed, as the orbs were super light; it was a test for accuracy, but Korin and Terala managed to succeed in this, anyway. It helped that no wind was present, given that they were indoors.

Another whistle blew, and time was up.

Still shaking from his own highly-intense energy that he had heaps left to dispose of, Korin compulsively reached for more orbs, which had all vanished.

"Great work," Terala said, high-fiving a now very-confident Korin.

Even though the charger orbs had disappeared, a stray keeper orb floated by, naturally getting pulled into an orbit around Korin, non-physically massaging his body. He felt compelled to capture it, as if a feline playing with a buzzing insect; but a staff member abruptly yanked it away, storing it in a special container.

The coach then signalled everyone to gather in the centre for a quick debrief, finishing off by saying, "We have a lot of people to get through, so we'll let you know later if you made it. Now, out you get."

"Do you think we made it?" Korin asked Terala as they left the dome.

"Fuck, yeah! The others sucked."

***

Two days passed, with Korin waiting for *some* kind of response from the coach. And despite the intense happenings of the last two weeks at Teloston, there was nothing Korin found to take his mind off the wait. Without his subjective bias, it was partially true; for one, he couldn't really begin any assignments, as no specifications were issued, so at times, he was literally twiddling his thumbs.

That evening, Terala was hanging outside Korin's room, groaning about the wait. "Why haven't they informed us?" she repeated for the eighth time, banging her fist on the balcony's balustrade.

"It's because they like torturing people," Sylas retorted, exiting his room. "Didn't you pay attention to that coach's face? I don't think those scars are from hillseck."

"I know we made it. We just had to. Wait… how did he say he'd contact us?"

Korin delayed his response, saying, "Shit, I can't remember."

"Perhaps through a formal h-mail instead of a simple text message," Sylas said. "Have you checked?"

"Yeah, I checked my h-mail."

A mail drone suddenly flew by, quickly delivering two geometrically-folded paper letters, which floated towards Korin's mail slot.

"Do you think…" Terala almost whispered.

Korin quickly grabbed the letters, finding that both had Terala's name on them. "Oh… they're for you," he said somewhat dispiritedly while mostly confused.

"That's weird," Terala said. "Alright, here." She reached for them, quickly reading one, causing her stumped face to melt away. "I… I made it!" Terala screeched, madly jumping up and down on the spot like a little kid as she repeated herself.

"Hey, well done!" Sylas said. "Just don't fall off the balcony there."

"Congratulations," Korin said. "I knew you'd be fine."

"Oh, man." Terala finally stopped jumping, laying on the floor with her hands on her head. "Oh, what a relief!"

"Please don't tell me you pissed yourself," Sylas said.

"Not yet." She chuckled.

"Hopefully I'll make it, too," Korin said. "I *did* beat you in combat."

"Yeah, of course you'll make it!" Terala responded. "Come on. Cheer up." She hopped up. "Hey, you reckon the coach put my name on this one by accident?"

"I wouldn't put it past him. It's odd that they came to my mailbox, too. In that case, if you don't mind, may I look?"

"Sure. I doubt it's for me, anyway."

"Why would he send letters and not a text message?" Sylas asked.

"He actually mentions it in the letter. 'Bloody h-mail. I ain't using that shit,' he says. He then briefly criticises A.I. Literally. Look." Terala showed Sylas the letter. "Anyway, you going to read the letter?" She turned to Korin.

Korin slowly opened the letter, reading the message from Virkorska, stating: 'Korin, I need a word with you. My office.' His details and signature followed at the bottom of the letter. Korin stalled without changing his expression. He wasn't sure what the message implied, guessing he may have had the opportunity for another tryout. The idea instilled hope, though it caused Korin's anxiety to rise even higher.

"Well?" Terala asked. "Tell us already, damn it!"

Korin lightly shrugged, and then Terala snatched the letter from him.

"What's *that* meant to mean?" She frowned.

"Don't know, but I'm going to find out right now," Korin answered, dashing off without a second thought, leaving both Sylas and Terala behind.

***

Korin was almost out of breath by the time he approached the coach's office, having raced as fast as he could, annoyed at the various delays on the way. There was no way he was going to wait another day for the result; his nerves, otherwise, would've finished wrecking his body.

"Ah, there you are!" Virkorska shouted, exiting his office. "I need a word with you," he uttered deeply, expression grave.

"Uh, sure. What do you need?" Korin asked, gulping, still catching his breath.

"Where'd you learn to fight like that?" Virkorska closed in on Korin, almost like he was about to bash his head in.

"Professional monks trained me since youth." Korin stood with a cautious guard, one leg behind the other.

"I see." He scratched his nostrils, green particles flaking out. "You can fight with the best of them, but you still need more training. Usually, the best hillseck players are those who gained their skills outside the sport."

"Really? In what, exactly?" He fully caught his breath.

"I, for one, fought in in a deathmatch ring. See this scar here?" The coach pointed to the biggest gash on his face. "Got this from a volictun;

last guy I fought before I escaped that place. Touch it," he grunted with a crazy-eyed look.

"Oh, uh… yeah, I believe you." Korin grimaced, keeping his hands securely to himself.

"C'mon! Touch it," he persisted with his face close to Korin's.

"Ah, okay." Korin slowly poked the rough and peculiarly-textured scar, hoping his finger wouldn't catch a disease. "That's… pretty cool. I guess."

The coach seemed rather happy that Korin thought as much. Korin even felt like Virkorska would've handed down the scar if he could, as if an aesthetically-pleasing trophy to be paraded around respecting warriors. However, Korin knew nobody in his classes would ever think such things, and he definitely didn't find scars pleasing on the eyes – especially the odd one he touched.

"Yeah," the coach grunted. "You got to watch those bloody volictuns. They'll slash you good, you hear?"

"Y-yeah, absolutely. Uh, definitely don't want to mess with them." Korin was unsure what else to say, scratching the back of his head. He intuitively sensed that the coach wanted to explain all about his adventures; and although curious, Korin wasn't sure what tangent – or voyage, rather – the coach would go off on.

"Oh, I forgot to say," the coach said. "You made the team."

Korin's outward reaction was restrained compared to the fermenting feelings inside him. He wanted to race back and inform his friends, but he stayed put with a smile on his face, breathing out every last particle of oxygen from his lungs.

The coach continued, "I had to test a few people again, but I decided you didn't need any more. *However*," he said, firmly shaking his finger, "you need to seriously train on your skating and jumping skills. And I definitely want to make a good warrior out of you."

Korin looked perplexed, wondering what the coach had in mind.

"I used to be in the commandos. Elite bastards. More than just being in the army. Toughened me up, too. Well, I had already toughened up by that point. Too many wimpy, whiny students nowadays; you seeing me?" The coach gazed firmly into Korin's eyes.

Still rapt he made the team, Korin had to think hard about a response. He realized the coach was technically right, despite any craziness on his behalf. The students, or cry-babies, as Korin regarded, whined non-stop over the most ridiculous and petty of problems – some weren't even problems. Although a foible on his part, Korin found it too hard not to get *so* worked up about it. Sensitivities themselves weren't the problem; he recognized, for example, that Celine was a very sensitive person, but her actions were wildly different from the social justice warriors everywhere. Korin finally agreed with a nod, though more so with the general sentiment, hoping Virkorska wouldn't go overboard with any extreme ideas.

"Good," the coach responded, pausing to reflect. "You're not like that. You don't need some silly master's degree, either. I could mentor you if you want. A whole year with me!" He brutally pounded his chest, creating a loud thud.

"Oh, I haven't even really thought of the master's. It's probably something to consider later."

"Yeah, right. I didn't do a master's. Still don't have one. The system fortunately still allows me to work here. After uni, I had a mentor for a whole year. From the Temple of Frost. Not some religious cult or anything. Except for my first two weeks. Some lady had me picking berries and shit like that. Got out of that situation real quick! You're not some berry-picking, cookie-making girl, are you?"

"No, no… I do like cookies, though." Korin couldn't help but smile, lips puckered.

"Nah! What you want is meat! Lots of meat!" He clutched his hands as if about to murder something, shaking barbarically. "It's the food nowadays, turning young men into wimps!"

Korin was uncertain about the meat question, but he wondered if there were other causes for the childish behaviour amongst the students. He worried for a second, hoping he wouldn't be affected, but then he considered that many mages seemed quite reasonable. He also recalled that there were both excellent and pathetic non-mages, too.

"Too many artsy-fartsy types around, nuzzle-wuzzling all day. We need change!" Virkorska hammered his fist. "We need a revolution!"

He triggered Korin to think about politics and all the students shouting about revolution. "We need all the students fighting and training again. Like the good old days. You with me?" he asked, fire almost breathing out of him.

Given that politics was now a subject of great interest to Korin, he learned that reality was actually nuanced and complicated, so he wasn't sure how to reply. "We'll… have to see how events play out, I guess," Korin answered, feeling as though the conversation's end was overdue. "Anyway, I think I need to get back to…"

"Studying? Yeah, your teachers can be bitching sometimes." The coach shook his head. "I know what it's like. Well, I won't keep you. Off you go." Virkorska waved, grumbling to himself as he left.

Despite having to end the conversation, Korin nevertheless found it interesting, chuckling to himself on the way out.

***

As soon as Korin exited the building, he noticed Terala up against a wall with her arms crossed.

"Well? What did the coach want?" Terala asked, uncrossing her arms. "Did you make it?"

Korin answered with a smile, causing Terala to rush up and joyfully hug him like a teammate winning a sporting match. She squealed, too. It was something Korin hadn't heard before. That is, there was a moment of girliness that shone through Terala. Her eyes also beamed with the same child-like joy and excitement she experienced after reading her letter.

"So, what did he talk to you about?" Terala asked, walking and skipping backwards in the lead as they began leaving.

"He just wanted to talk," Korin replied, still over the moons. "The coach seems like a pretty cool and interesting guy, but he did seem a bit off the altar."

"Off the what?" She winced, almost closing one eye.

"Oh, that's just a phrase we had. What I mean is –"

"You mean off the sigil?" She started walking normally again.

"Probably. I'll try to use that one from now on."

"You realize we'll have to start practicing tomorrow? And after that, as much as possible?"

"Of course. But keep in mind that I have heaps of other things to do as well."

"Hey, why don't we go to the stadium now? I want to get into the playing mode immediately."

"We can check it out now, but we'll practice tomorrow."

"Alright. Good enough."

After Korin and Terala reached the hillseck stadium located in the Sports District, two second-year students approached them, smirking and nudging one another before puffing their chests out. Korin and Terala glanced at each other, both believing trouble was coming their way. One had a couple of scars across his buzz-cut hair; with the physique of a boxer, he indeed looked like he had been in a few decent fights in his life. The other male was *the* archetype most girls gushed over – perfect facial features, perfect build, perfect complexion, perfect... everything.

"Oi, what the fuck are you two doing?" the tougher-looking one asked, grinning.

"Yeah, this is our turf," the handsome one added. "Get the fuck out of here."

"Oh, great," Korin whispered. "What do you guys want?" he asked assertively.

"We're not going to be pushed around," Terala interjected.

"The cheek of these first-years." The tough one shook his head.

"The disrespect is astounding," the handsome one responded, holding back a smirk. "I think we should teach them a lesson."

"Yeah." The tough guy cracked his knuckles with an antagonistic countenance. "Especially since we have to work with them."

"Alright, we'll personally have to train you. Provide a few pointers."

Korin swiftly detected that the boys were purely messing around and had no ill intentions. "You're both on the hillseck team, aren't you?" he asked, nudging Terala.

The tough one laughed. "That's right. I'm Bendel." He reached his hand out to shake Korin's hand and then Terala's. "And this here's my bitch, Titus." He chuckled.

"Fuck off, cunt," Titus replied light-heartedly, giving Bendel a shove to the arm. "He only says that as he has no missus at the moment. Hasn't had action in a little while."

"Yes, well, it's hard to ignore you, Titus, as you do have a *tight ass*." Bendel vigorously slapped his mate's ass, his face grinning aggressively with amusement.

Titus gave a blithe glare before saying, "So, as he mentioned, I'm Titus." He exchanged greetings with Korin and Terala.

"Nice to meet you both," Korin replied, smiling. "How'd you know we made it?"

"We saw your pictures. They were up on a screen. Well done. Not an easy feat."

"Cool. Thanks. Terala and I were going to check out the stadium. You coming in, too?"

"Can't. The stadium's closed for maintenance. You can come back tomorrow."

"Ugh!" Terala flung her head back. "Why now?"

"Hey, patience," Korin said. "We'll make more room later. So," he said to the two boys, "what are you up to now?"

Titus glanced at Bendel, smirking before saying to Korin, "Training. Have to train, you know." He chuckled suspiciously.

"Training, indeed." Bendel tittered, moving something in his pocket.

"We'll all be training together soon, anyway," Titus said. "Don't worry yourselves."

"The coach will make us," Bendel added. "He'll breathe down your necks if you don't train on official training days."

"Quite literally." Titus chuckled again. "So… you're the only first-years who made the team. Most of the others are third-years."

"Wow," Terala uttered, looking at Korin happily. "There you go."

"And you're the only girl on the team," Titus added.

"And yet, I'll still show everyone up." She held her chin up high.

"Whoa, hold up, Miss I-Can-Do-Anything," Titus ribbed. "We still have to see you in action."

"Oh, you will!" She stepped forwards, approaching the boys closely. "I'll be the centre of attention."

"Ha! Okay. Whatever you say. I like your attitude. Anyway, we'll catch you guys later. We'll be… throwing a few orbs, you could say." He giggled.

"Yeah," Bendel said, smirking again. "Opening a few… portals." A giggle burst out. "And seeing a few… illusion charms. See you later." He nodded, and then both lads moved on, quietly saying other cryptic somethings.

"What are you thinking?" Korin asked Terala, who was leering at the boys with suspicion.

"Eeehh…" She shook her hand, indicating her uncertainty. "So long as they're good on the field, I'll be cool with them."

Retiring from the stadium, Korin and Terala continued chatting about hillseck as they made their way back to the subroute. Terala talked a lot about a famous hillseck player called Lecindy, who she looked up to; and as she was describing some of the stunts Lecindy pulled in her time, the two students heard an animal making strange noises nearby.

"What the hell was that?" Korin asked.

"Sounds weird," Terala said. "Maybe we should check it out."

Both decided to investigate, shortly entering a botanic strip before coming across a pit with a few large rocks in it. About ten metres away from the hole was a soil-coated feral animal chewing on what they perceived to be a human hand. The feral animal wasn't threatening, so their attention focused on the pit. Immediately knowing what was inside, Korin shivered, swiftly glancing around to see if they were in any danger. A few trees rustled in the wind, but nothing emerged, and there were no signs of suspicious movements or noises. Still, he began tuning into the Aether, just in case. Terala didn't even bother checking for danger; she slowly stepped forwards, peeping into the pit, turning away in disgust when she saw a mutilated corpse stuck between two rocks covered with a few leaves and some dirt.

"It's a dead body, isn't it?" Korin asked.

"Yes, but you *seriously* need to see it." She pointed with a puzzled and extra-alarmed expression. "It's… just take a look, and you'll see."

Korin stared confusedly at her before checking the body, seeing a rotting, though still-perceivable Professor Marenov Khastanian. "What?"

Korin asked with utter shock. "How… who? We need to quickly tell someone about this."

"We won't get the blame for this, will we?" she asked fretfully.

"The body looks like it's been there for a while. We should be fine. Come on. Let's go."

Just as they were about to leave, moonlight flashed off a piece of metal at the base of a shrub, catching Korin's attention. He stopped, slowly bending over to rummage through the foliage and discover a necklace with a sinister moon symbol.

"Hey! This is The Gathering's symbol," Korin said, riveted by the jewellery's very existence. "Backlevy's ancient cult."

"So, what, ancient cultists killed the professor?" Terala asked with bewilderment.

"No, it would most likely be shadowists – the modern-day version."

"Oh, yeah, I've heard of them; I was going to mention them the other day when you showed the journal, but I got sidetracked. So… they killed him?"

"It's pretty obvious. Who else would it be? Things around the university aren't right -- we have demon attacks and missing students -- and I just *know* there's a bigger conspiracy happening. I'm not going crazy."

"Well, if you believe it, I believe it. Still, it's only a necklace."

"Yeah, but if you think about it hard, you'd come to the same conclusion."

"Alright, so what's the big picture? Are you going to tell the police?"

After mulling for a few seconds, he said, "Not about the cult part. They might not believe me if I tell them. In fact, they'd probably view the idea with suspicion; like, I'm making up stories for attention or probably covering up some other evidence."

"Are you sure? As you mentioned, the body's been here for a while. It's not like two first-years like us would have any due cause, anyway."

"Trust me. The authorities don't seem to like so-called crazy conspiracy theories, and this may seem off the… off the sigil. And there are heaps of students here that I wouldn't trust with my life, so we'd be lumped in with untrustworthy people. And on top of that, I'm seeing a psychologist. Forced to see one. They'll definitely think I'm crazy or have an agenda, given my background. And you're associated with me, so you're no good, either."

"Great. Okay, fair enough. But then who the flying fuck was that in the Gen Theory lecture? It was only a few days ago. There's no way a body rots like that in such a short amount of time."

Korin suspended his answer to think over multiple theories, finally saying, "An imposter, I think. Someone in the cult. It's the only logical answer."

"Hang on," Terala said, pausing to collect her thoughts. "So, if cultists killed the professor, and then impersonated him, then –"

"The student kidnappings and demon attacks were blamed on him and mage supremacists."

"Right," Terala responded, mind blown. "But… you guys *did* see mage supremacists fighting AMSA the other night."

"Yeah, but mage supremacists have been around for a while. I think they're an established problem everyone already knows about. They're an easy scapegoat."

"True. In any case, all this means that we're still in danger."

"Well, not completely. It's not like *everyone's* disappearing. If we keep safe, at least for now, we won't be kidnapped."

"This is all assuming that the necklace isn't his, though."

Korin stuttered with frustration before firmly saying, "No. No way is this his. It's the cult's. I just know it."

"Hey, I agree with you. I was just saying. So, what's your plan?"

"I don't know." Korin shook his head, holding the necklace tightly. "And even if it was his, it's still a sign that there's criminal activity targeting people with these symbols. Either way, it's bad. There are just too many coincidences. Anyway, I think we should first tell the authorities about the body – and only the body – and then think things over. We'll most likely look into matters ourselves."

"Agreed. We better get moving before someone sees us."

Chapter Thirteen

The Cultural Imprisonment

In less than a day after the discovery of Professor Marenov Khastanian's body, rumours had already rapidly spread before the official news was announced. Korin overheard one rumour that Khastanian had killed himself in a ritual, releasing his energy and possessing every student on campus… And that wasn't the most ridiculous rumour.

A few weeks passed, and Korin's personal investigation into both Khastanian and cult activity was unfruitful. The students at Teloston eventually did learn, however, that Khastanian held some views at least sympathetic to mage supremacy; and so, even though most people acknowledged his death, there was a dominant, lingering view that the problems around campus, such as the kidnappings, were still solely because of mage supremacists. Korin wondered if Khastanian was targeted for that reason as an easy scapegoat… He also learned that there were assorted types of mage supremacists, each with different factions therein. The mage supremacists with the symbol of a skull-and-cross-bone stamped elixir in front of a lightning bolt were of the 'exterminator' variety, who wished to exterminate all non-mages from the Caelverse; then there were those that believed in ruling over the non-mages with slavery – which consisted of classical mage supremacists; and then there were the mage supremacists who just wished to have full separation from the non-mages.

Korin also did meet some individuals who openly and brazenly wore the cult symbol; and when Korin pressed them on the issue, they usually replied by mordantly saying that they 'totally want to kill everyone'. It turned out that they weren't actual shadowists and were, instead, merely silly larpers like Finch mentioned, so Korin dropped pursuing them. Korin also asked Rolan for all the names of the people who went on the camp, and he managed to track down two people who had similar voices to the ones whispering about a cult. Korin inquired into their personal hobbies, and it turned out that the two guys were part of a 'cult' fan club of a movie series. The fans did give off a strange vibe, but Korin considered that such 'cult' followers were probably just strange, anyway, so he dropped pursuing them as well.

Korin also discovered that the shadowist symbol was different to the moderate black moon practitioner symbol, which appeared very similar, except that it had a less scary eye inside a heptagram, which wasn't inverted. Moreover, there were two masks on the front moon – one happy and the other unhappy. Some moderate practitioners openly wore their symbol, but such practitioners as a whole weren't considered a menace to society; although, they weren't typically the types of people who held to general social conventions, and they weren't collectively organized as a single movement either.

In the meantime, Korin was settling into his classes and university life very well, enjoying himself despite the increasing work pressures and the threat of demon attacks; *and* also despite a few people teasing him about his non-mage past, laughing about his lack of knowledge of certain things. Brushing off such remarks, he nevertheless made more acquaintances, finding that not everyone was a 'stupid, wimpy cry-baby' – as Terala would also say – and many had cool personalities, interests, and histories; but his small circle of friends remained as it was, strengthening in closeness.

Terala still hadn't explained what happened to her brothers or father, but Korin had purposely deferred pursuing the topic; however, he did grow a greater understanding of her impetuses whenever she acted in a particular way to anything linked to them. Unsurprisingly, she talked about hillseck a lot, including the famous player called Lecindy, who, with her team, won many championships. Sylas, on the other hand, had a wealth of witty remarks to dish out whenever something bad happened;

but at the same time, Korin detected more to Sylas's charm, as if there was a lot he was hiding… Nothing immoral or foul on his part, though. Celine's imagination and wonder never ceased as she created all sorts of artwork, happily showing Korin during meals. Her company was the most pleasant of any person he had ever met. As for Jaimas, well… Jaimas was Jaimas as usual.

Then there was the oddly-behaved Priscilla, who continued with her moderately-mischievous plots, in addition to being… nicer and nicer to Korin. He found her increasingly suspicious and strange, though simultaneously, he happened to find himself agreeing, working with, and laughing alongside her at times. As soon as he would warm up to her, Korin would suddenly distance himself again when she would say or do something a little too off the sigil. It frustrated Priscilla to an extent, but she persisted. She also managed to assert herself over troublemakers like Sereck in the open, but craftily enough not to draw fire from them in the future. Priscilla would also make cryptic references to certain occult things and philosophies, and Korin assumed it related to the black moon. When he would inquire – both personally and as part of his investigation – she teased him with further cryptic messages. His curiosity climbed evermore, and when he asked again whether she was a shadowist, she denied it.

There were so many events and points of interest and concern that Korin's focus didn't stay merely on one matter. Regarding hillseck, for example, his skills increased during each training session, impressing the demanding coach. Virkorska didn't mention volictuns again, but Korin could tell it was on his mind, especially when the coach oddly gazed at him on the field. Korin could basically sense that the coach wished to train him to be prepared for a heap of volictuns. Titus and Bendel turned out to be fun to hang out with, even though some of their antics were beyond what Korin and Terala were willing to participate in. Most of the hillseck team were also companionable, though the aforementioned boys remained the closest to Korin and Terala.

No longer mandatorily needing to see the psychologist, Korin felt as though he was free from any debilitating effects his religion imposed on him. He even felt better that much of his own blood had regenerated in his body. Rolan was happy to hear the news, shouting Korin out for lunch at a nice restaurant. Helena, in contrast, was busier than ever, so there was minimal contact between the two.

Korin searched for information on Narvell Jern – the person who wrote the centuries-old journal entry on Grand Sorceress Backlevy – but there were no records with his name, nor the obliterated organization he was in. Korin assumed Narvell was either a nobody in the grand scheme of things and or that many records simply had been lost.

Over the weeks, Korin and his friends faced a few dangerous ordeals. One instance involved being trapped inside a building after a chemical explosion – which wasn't their fault; the roof was about to collapse, but they managed to figure a way out. Together with the other dangers around him – and with Cartras effectively encouraging him – Korin trained hard so that his phasarchement magic powers would increase beyond novice levels. He was doing well in his training, but there was still much progress to be made, though. Since phasarchement was very combat-focused and didn't require as much theoretical study compared to the other schools of magic – at least in order to *practice* the magic – it was his favourite type of magic and subject. The combat itself was another skill besides the very casting of the magic, and Korin was taught that mages would normally work in teams to overcome their adversaries. In some cases, depending on power levels, a group of mages could over-load a shield if everyone struck it at the same time. He was also advised that if greatly outnumbered, it was generally the case that withdrawal from a fight was the best option, but the context would not always be clear cut, and there were many factors to consider.

Korin continued to let more of his hair grow, opting for it to stay as a crew cut for the time being. Even though it was basically the same haircut he had before shaving it, the sight of it felt like a whole rebirth.

While learning more about history and politics, Korin was still unsure what to think of many issues, though he certainly developed an intolerance for blatant stupidity and arrogance. There weren't any other *major* polit-ically-charged nights, like the one with Magnolia Yasexybeast, and some of the students who protested that night were still serving detention.

***

Having exhausted all ideas on how to locate the present-day shadowist cult, Korin needed a break. It was a Fireday night, almost a week following the last lunapex, and Korin was chilling out with Sylas in his dorm courtyard. By then, Korin had learned that the phytoid face that emerged from the dorm tree was indeed a charm — so he was told — but he still intuitively felt that the charm actually did possess some interesting information and potentially profound secrets...

The wongahwongahs had recently cleaned off the numerous bottles and other garbage left at the table from previous students — of which Korin wasn't happy about. He had done his best thus far to clean up after himself, only leaving muddy footprints on the walkways once in a while. Sylas had been explaining how he came to be proficient at juggling; he developed his skills out of boredom when he was forced to study at home. There were no other distractions available at the time, as all his entertainment, such as gaming devices and assorted neurachite-based computers, had been confiscated. Since Sylas was ambidextrous, he had no problems with either hand.

A few mixed-gendered hipsters approached the tables, sitting down to chat amongst themselves. Signalling their so-called rebellious stance, their hair was asymmetrically-shaved, platted, twisted, dyed, and flopped over-and-around. Virtually all had piercings of some kind, along with an assortment of either oddly-shaped, designed, and or fitting clothes. Despite their nonconformist, nonverbal declarations, they kind of looked as if in uniform. Korin noticed that two happened to be in his Phasarchement class, though he had never talked to them. He had no problem with odd hair, clothing, or any such abnormal collections; moreover, there were other hipsters he had met who were fine, but the overall vibe of those present annoyed him, and the evening's settling atmosphere was spoiled, causing Korin and Sylas to cease talking.

One of the hipsters soon turned to Korin, asking in a drugged voice, "Hey, you're that guy that didn't know he was a mage, right?"

Korin sighed, wondering if he would have a repeat of some of the annoying conversations he had recently. *Yep. That's me. Totally know nothing*, he thought before plainly saying, "Yes."

"Wow, that's so amazing," the crooked-haired girl said as if she had heard something incredibly deep and insightful from the grandest of philosophers. "You must be really cultured. I feel so sorry that you had to come here."

Korin glanced at Sylas, frowning with bemusement. "Why do you think that?" he asked the girl, feeling a little more open to discussion, only for the sake of hearing something unbelievably silly.

"Mages have no culture," she said with disgust. "We, like, appropriate everything from non-mages."

Musing over her statement, Korin finally replied, "I don't think that's right. You have some pretty interesting architecture, as one example."

"That was probably stolen from... fairies. We exploited everyone in the past. And still do. I bet you must have hated mages growing up."

Korin felt uncomfortable blurting out his past to strangers, but he didn't want people having and spreading the wrong impression. It was hard enough gelling with a lot of his peers, and any more misinformation would've made such endeavours harder. "I didn't really hate mages; I simply opposed the magic and what they stood for," Korin said firmly.

"That sounds pretty cool, I guess," the same girl said. "I hope you still hold to such thoughts."

"No," he said slowly. "No. Not now. Definitely not. It's actually quite the reverse."

With a sharper and more aggressive tone, she asked, "You do realize that mages enslaved non-mages – and still do – right?"

Korin's slumped back instantly straightened up as he sat forwards, his interest in the conversation spiking in unison with his blood pressure. "Yes, I understand that," Korin said strongly. "I'm studying History. But that was in the past. And in any case, non-mages had slaves, too. In fact, I think there are parts of the Caelverse, like deep in unexplored jungles and other classes of worlds, where slavery still exists. Those slave trades are controlled by non-mages."

"That's a pretty hateful thing to say," she said vehemently. "You need to understand the wider context here. If you weren't a mage, I'd say that you were suffering from internalized misnescieny."

"What?" Korin asked as if he had sneezed out a ball of confusion, throwing his head forward.

"You know, hatred towards your own – non-mages. But you're a mage now, and you should check your mage privilege, as you're now part of the overall systemic oppression of non-mages. *All* mages are responsible for those recent pixie deaths."

"Look, I… I grew up with non-mages," Korin said, having to pause to gather his scattering senses. "We didn't experience any oppression – *as such*. Well, at least not where I came from. The other parts of the Caelverse might be a different situation. I've heard different things, and I don't know the full story. I'm still learning. But I do understand there are a lot of factors to consider, and there are, undeniably, corrupt and bad mages; but you have to understand that mages aren't out there, like, mass murdering non-mages. I only thought mages were evil due to their magical *practices* and how they could manipulate people that way. It was fundamentally because of a religious perspective."

"Well, you should read *The Semiotics of Cultural Imperialism* by Derilla Jaconda," she stated snobbishly.

"Um… alright. I'll read it. Have you read it?"

The girl instantly choked on her words, looking embarrassed and dumbfounded before scoffing with a nasty countenance, as if Korin were a moron. She then turned her chair back to the table, shaking her head as all her friends agreed with the same gesture. Sylas almost silently giggled, having nothing to say about the stupidity. A couple of the hipsters then threw their garbage on the ground, infuriating Korin.

"You talk about all this mage supremacy," Korin said, still having his chair facing the group, "yet you're just adding to the garbage the wongahwongahs have to clean up."

"Yeah, well," one of the garbage-throwers replied, "they need the jobs, anyway. We mages have wrecked their economy and society, so it's the least we can do." He turned around again. "Retard," he whispered.

Korin wasn't offended by the derogatory term in and of itself, but rather, he hated how the hipster wouldn't genuinely address the issue. Not only did Korin obviously feel such sentiments were horrible, but he also instinctively knew they were fallacious. Still, he wasn't sure how to articulate his intuitions.

Deciding to inculcate his point, Korin said, "I've only been here for just over a month, but mages, on the whole, seem like a force for good."

All the hipsters looked at one another with repugnance at Korin's statement, with one saying, "Force? You know, you sound like a mage supremacist."

Another friend added, "He gets along well with that Cartras fuck I've talked about. He's probably in league with him somehow."

"What are you talking about?" Korin asked loudly. "Sure, I like Cartras – and I admit, he does have an ego issue and goes overboard at times – but that doesn't mean that I'm 'in league' with him, as you say."

"Maybe not," the first social justice warrior said. "But you probably soon will." He turned to his group. "I could just imagine Cartras murdering hundreds – maybe thousands – of non-mages, and then, later on, the police find, like, this mass grave with all these bones in his backyard. I wouldn't be surprised if he eats people. Truly a monster."

"Why the hell would you think that?" Korin asked, about to jump up.

One scrawny guy said, "He just looks like a mage supremacist. I mean, look at his muscles. Why would you have such big muscles, anyway? What's the point?"

Korin was at a loss on how to reply. He placed his hands across his temples, wondering how the flaming potion their minds could have become so warped in the first place. Sylas stayed quiet, and Korin had forgotten he was even present.

"We're trying to get him fired," one social justice warrior added, triggering the whole group to snigger.

"You're a bunch of cunts!" Korin stood up, slamming his chair into the table. "Come on, let's go," he said to Sylas. Korin knew he was going to be sitting alone in his room, left to his angry thoughts. He quickly understood that wasn't the healthiest plan, and he stopped marching, thinking of what else he could do. "Hey, I might just go for a walk," he told Sylas. "Alone."

"No problem," Sylas said. "Just don't punch anyone on the way."

"I'll try not to," Korin said, taking off.

***

Keeping out of a confined space was the best strategy for Korin, as it did help him vent a fair amount of his anger. His meandering course eventually led him to the central plaza in the Market District, filled with nightclubs brimming with hooting, banter, and laughter. In full swing, the plaza was mostly packed with partygoers, a portion of which were hipsters.

Damn it, there's no escape! Korin thought.

Not all the hipsters present were terrible, but they certainly weren't the greatest eyecatchers, nor were they socially dominant. Most of the partygoers were actually far too apathetic to ever be social justice warriors, and that, funnily enough, wasn't a good thing, either. Some of the dominant attendees – male, female, and otherwise – appeared like dolls out of a toyshop; their makeup, lacking cultural depth, fashioned a superficial veneer, while their facial expressions appeared universally prefabricated to fit the scene, changing to two or three moulds like at the mere press of a button by the surrounding flashes of light and stimuli. The clubbing attire was glamorous, tight, and flashy; and although not necessarily bad, there was nonetheless an air of pretentious uniformity. The older, doctoral students present happened to be part of this demographic as well. Most of the people were taking selfies at least once every two minutes. A few were literally nonstop taking them for minutes on end, with one being knocked to the ground in her unmindful walk, continuing to take picture after picture as if nothing had happened. Really.

Unadorned steel scaffolding senselessly threaded around the convoluted walkways, while grey, standardized slabs of concrete uniformly jutted out of the buildings, almost like they were mechanically materializing, about to extend for infinity without purpose. Blocky metallic railings, doorframes, and furniture vividly reflected their surroundings, none mirroring anything of substance other than the coldness of modernity and its so-called sophistication. Large, abstract art gazed upon uninterested people; the soulless paintings of cubic, colourless eyes sucked Korin's energy away, while the artworks with mere, criss-crossing lines confused and dulled him. Practically the same across all the clubs, a repetitious drum beat blasted around him, slowly numbing his senses, almost naturally attuning to him like his own heartbeat. The rhythm itself was okay, but barely a creative melody arose on top of the beat. And unlike the gourmet smells of the Provision Wreath's food hall that, alone, could seemingly feed the hungry, all Korin smelled were obnoxious perfumes and fragrances trying to overpower one another, battling inside his nose as he coughed and sneezed.

Korin was surprised that mages embraced such culture – or lack thereof – believing it was only the non-mages who engaged in such recreations and environments. His mind paused after reality smacked him in the face. With resistance, he wondered if the social justice warriors were actually correct. *Oh, God, I don't believe it*, he thought, depression sinking in. *Please, they can't be right.*

In his religious past, Korin imagined the mages as mysteriously-cloaked beings, circling around in esoteric and ritualistic form near smoky torches, wielding masterfully-forged weapons of the rarest alloys engraved and tinted with cryptic symbols and unworldly necrodusts, embracing the blood of their victims in their zealous quest for the power to conquer the seemingly, never-ending entropic decay of life, all high up in grandiose, yet foreboding recherché-stone towers that would have taken centuries to build – built, of course, not only on the works of initiates of the highest and strangest occult knowledge, but also on the backs of magnificent extinct creatures of dreams long past – lurching over horizons of treacherous swamps and impassable pales of their own wickedly-creative making, extending well above heavy, deathly, and unnatural mists slowly absorbing the evaporated soul essences of hundreds of epic tales, all the while exuding torsional, cyclonic, and dimensionally-warping auras surpassing even that of the most spectacular auroras. But... nope. A part of him, however, wished to see that due to the sheer superficiality, triviality, and degeneracy around him. A *part* of him... he'd never *actually* want such evil.

He noted that the Noble Magehood Virtues were, for the most part, lacking. Sure, this was downtime, but it was an archetypal energy that permeated their every other action, anyway, only surfacing to its full actuality in the scene before him. And the muralled warrior in the Chalice of Virtue's central hall flashed before him, as if a physical manifestation.

Korin couldn't put his finger on it, but the drastically-different modern culture juxtaposed the traditions a little too differently…

Sighing, Korin was unsure how to revolt against what he was witnessing; but the desire to revolt nonetheless *was* strong. Very strong. Taking one more look at the soulless eyes on the nearby wall, he aboutfaced and was hit with another set of eyes – ones that quickly dug into his soul. They were also accompanied with a cheeky smirk.

Priscilla's trademark, unmoving deathly stance made her stand out, and her gothic apparel, too, heightened this effect, as if blackness oddly was a form of light. Korin couldn't understand why she was in such a place, believing she may have been shopping rather than clubbing; then it quickly dawned on him: she was there because of him.

"What are you doing here?" Korin asked.

"What am *I* doing here?" Priscilla responded, tapping her chest. "The better question regards you."

Korin considered explaining his frustrations, opting instead to merely say, "I was taking a walk. I needed fresh air."

She tittered, gesturing at the area. "You think this place has fresh air? Come on, I saw the way you marched out of the dorms. Why here?"

"I honestly don't know why *here* exactly. I just went somewhere. I… needed space."

"Then look around. Tell me what you see."

Korin didn't even glance around, squinting at Priscilla instead. *I know what you're thinking.* "Yeah, I hate it here as well."

Priscilla haughtily cackled, drawing a few heads. "Don't you like getting hammered? Surely, it's a lot of fun!" She then approached him closely. "So… it looks like I didn't even need to wake you up to your *empty* surroundings. Well done. It's one of the reasons why I like you. You want more. Don't you? I know you do. Admit it."

She was right. Needing purpose, Korin loathed the scene around him, but his suspicions of Priscilla's aims grew.

Continuing, she said, "I can feel it – the surrounding shallowness clutching your essence – your passionate, brutal essence – dragging you into the nadirs of stagnant, meaninglessness waters. You want a *truly* worthwhile pursuit."

Focusing solely on Priscilla, the clubs withered away from Korin's peripheral vision. He would sometimes dismiss her ambiguous observations, but this time he was hooked. "What do you mean by 'worthwhile pursuit'? What, political?"

"This transcends politics, Korin; but in a way, yes, I guess you could say it has *some* political relevance. Did you march away because of something to do with politics?"

Exhaling, he said, "Sure. You could say that."

"Well, then you'll want to hear what I have to say. Change is coming, Korin. Can you feel it?" she loudly whispered, though Korin didn't respond. "Can you feel the moon? Her calling?"

He looked up. "Um… no, not really."

"Hmph. Maybe you're not ready, after all. Perhaps another time." She quickly turned around.

"Oh, come on." He eagerly grabbed her arm before she left – unbeknownst to the smirk on her face. "Try me. What are you on about? The black moon again?"

She leaned in, almost as if for a kiss, mouth to his ear. "I know ancient occult knowledge. And I can feel what you're capable of. You and I aren't like the others here. We're different. Feel it, Korin. Feel it. If we work together, we can achieve something amazing. Join me, and I'll show you," she said with a hypnotic voice as she sensually ran her hand over his body.

Korin blinked rapidly, as if falling asleep, relaxing into her energy, which crawled all over him. It took a moment before he comprehended the hypnotic hold she had over him, triggering him to mentally shake her off. He then grabbed her shoulders, keeping a safe distance while asking, "Are you trying to hypnotize me?"

Priscilla smirked. "Of course I am!" she said perkily. "And you *love* it!"

"What? Why?" He scowled. "What are you trying to do to me?"

"Relax, Korin." She chuckled. "I'm teasing. I mean well." She then took her hood off, slowly reaching in for a kiss.

Heartbeat racing, Korin was no longer drowning in 'meaningless waters'… but he was, indeed, drowning – in his own anxiousness and confusion. He knew she was craftily drawing him into a tenebrous tunnel full of deviousness of great magnitude, but he felt compelled to follow, even if blindly. Her energy relentlessly drew him in. The pleasure took hold. Giving in, he embraced her, but it wasn't long until the kissing ended, and she took his hand.

"Follow me." Priscilla led the way.

Korin was about to ask where they were heading, but he knew he'd only receive either a cryptic or witty answer. The club scene no longer bothered Korin; he was about to do something interesting, albeit potentially dangerous. In fact, the idea of doing something esoteric while everyone else engaged in the mundane with its superficial flashiness actually stimulated him – it was no surprise to him now as to why Priscilla liked elevating herself via the mysterious. A clandestine 'worthwhile pursuit' awaited him… It sure as hell beat not having a purpose – a sense of purpose lost after his religious abandonment – though it was a shock to Korin that it took Priscilla to give him one. Simply the thought of the coming pursuit with Priscilla made everyone around Korin feel increasingly ignorant and mediocre.

Chapter Fourteen

The Black Moon Initiation

The party music ceased thumping away as Korin and Priscilla made their way from the Market District to the Private District. While they marched without a word towards the lofty, higher ideals of the esoteric, a small mansion with the aesthetics of a cobbled castle came into view, the stone burnt grey and half covered in dark mosses. The conical turrets featured moon symbols, but the moderate black moon sign – different to the shadowist one – was most prominent on the mansion's entrance. Instead of entering through the front, Priscilla led Korin around the side into the courtyard, where a couple of other people were preparing for a ritual. Both wore black robes in sacred fashion, adorned with symbolic regalia.

The more senior of the two people glanced at Priscilla before approaching. "I haven't seen him here before," the priestessly woman said, curiously scanning Korin up and down.

"I plan on initiating him," Priscilla said. "Alone."

"Hmm…" She hummed disapprovingly. "Do what you want, but it's recommended having another one or two people for the ritual. But if that's what you two wish, go ahead and use one of the initiation areas, as the courtyard is mostly vacant tonight. Meriel, Drake, and I will be initiating two others soon, so we'll be busy. If, for any reason, you do require assistance, you'll find a couple of people inside."

"We'll be perfectly fine."

Priscilla led Korin behind a thick hedge to where a stone alcove sat.

Before the structure on the ground lay two circles linked together, both formed with patterned lines of silver and dark purple crystals. As soon as Korin saw the circles, he recoiled out of habit before telling himself that it was okay to perform rituals – he was going to perform them for his university coursework eventually, as Priscilla told him earlier. Still, despite being eager, hesitancy grabbed the back of his mind.

Priscilla's serious demeanour changed as she playfully skipped towards the circles, turning around to grin at Korin. "Finally!" Priscilla clapped her hands. "I've been waiting weeks for this moment. I knew you'd come in the end."

"Congrats," he breathed out. "You got me here. Now what?"

"The first step towards enlightenment!"

Korin thought it was best for his displeasures to be challenged, so he said, "You know I don't like rituals."

"Yes, I'm aware of that. But this isn't your childhood. I'm not one of those corrupted priests. Surely you can foresee the fun you'll have with me instead?"

"Mm… we'll see. So, what is this place, and what are we going to do, exactly?"

"This is a temple for black moon practitioners. Think of this place like you would a gym, except that you don't need to pay fees to enter, and you can receive free support and resources when available. You can also work by yourself, if you wish. As a solitary practitioner myself, this is my personal preference. Still, even *I* decided to have assistance with my initiation when I came to Teloston. I would have done so with my aunt before coming, but it's not practical until one's magic is activated. To be clear, the initiation isn't into a group, but rather, it's an initial phase of a journey involving the black moon. An undefined path. And since I wish to work with you, I'm not limiting myself to solitary work; but naturally, I will require my own space when we aren't working on major endeavours. Anyway, for what we do now, well, I will initiate you via a ritual."

The emotions of excitement and uncertainty conflicted so greatly with one another inside Korin that he had to put up yet another barrier before proceeding, asking, "You're definitely not a shadowist?"

Giving Korin a snide look, she said, "Do I look like an evil cultist to you?"

Taking another glance at her gothic attire, Korin's mind wasn't swayed. "Well, you could be. *Are* you a shadowist?"

Priscilla frowned. "I told you, I'm not in that cult. But so what? What if I *were* in their cult?" She shiftily smiled. "Would it be such a bad thing?"

About to flip his arms and hands in the air, he replied, "Yes, because they're evil!"

"Oh, and what do they do that's so 'evil'?" she condescendingly asked with her nose held high.

"Well, um… they're… up to no good."

"Brilliant answer!" She slowly clapped. "You don't even know, do you? Perhaps you should investigate more into such matters before revealing a foolish level of ignorance." Priscilla shortly shifted back to her chirpy demeanour, excitedly saying, "Perhaps… perhaps we should join them."

Korin coughed, almost choking. "No! Are you kidding? I'm not joining the shadowists. You're sick!"

"I'm just jesting." She placed her hands on her hips. "But seriously, if I were to join, I'd expect you to have an open mind and at least hear what they would have to say."

Korin crossed his arms, his openness totally closed off.

"Don't worry, silly, I'm not in their cult." She smirked again. "Now, may we continue, please?"

Delaying his response, Korin finally said, "If you're not in the shadowist cult, then what makes you different from those cultists? This whole place seems very culty, and those people back there looked like cultists."

"As I said, think of this like a gym; you're free to enter and leave any time you want as an individual. Look, do you want to embrace a path of greater meaning, power, and understanding, or do you want to go back to the clubs with those morons jumping around and getting drunk?"

Korin glanced over his shoulder, despite being unable to see the clubs behind him. There was no way he was going back to that scene, though he still wasn't blindly accepting what Priscilla had to offer – at least not the full story. Keeping deadly still, Korin's stare was even more intense than Priscilla's. He knew, though, that in order to at least advance in his search for what was happening around the campus, he had to continue forth, regardless of the potential shadiness and sinisterness. Korin acquiesced to the situation fate dealt him, taking a step forward. But then he stopped. He had to think. At least for another minute. Abetting thoughts outweighed the negative, and he managed to take another step forward. After stopping, the interval of thinking shrunk, and he took another step before another few, each one causing Priscilla to glow with glee. Soon, he stood beside her. "Fine. Let's get this underway."

"I'm happy. Truly happy. Thank you," Priscilla said genuinely. "I know you're suspicious of me, so whatever I say will never satiate your hunger for truth, but by undertaking the ritual, you will see the black moon for yourself. Now, the process involves two major parts; the first involves a transformation of your reality, so you can tap into the black moon; the second involves your first trial. We black moon practitioners seek to properly understand archetypal energies – more so for the ones that are taking place within a particular period of time. You will be presented with an archetypal energy for the second part. The objective is to understand how it relates to the context of the whole collective consciousness while also aligning your energy with it. This may seem simple, but it's a far more complex phenomenon that requires great study and practice. By doing this, your power can increase. Also note that while shadowists will do this, too," she said as Korin's eyes widened, "they also engage in *other* practices. We won't. Okay, wait here."

A shed was nearby, and Priscilla entered it to acquire a set of items. When she exited, she placed a small charchite into one of the circle's power slots, powering it. Priscilla then grabbed Korin's hand, indicating for him to sit in one of the circles. He silently took a seat, waiting a moment before Priscilla placed a pendant around his neck. Next, she withdrew a paintbrush, dipping it in a glowing paint before painting his hands, its drying effect feeling rather tingly. After painting his hands, she pulled a small blade out, alarming Korin. She told him everything was fine and that she only needed a small amount of blood. It didn't take long for him to follow through and let her lightly cut his palm before she gathered it in a vial. The following preliminary act involved drinking a substance from a bottle appearing centuries old. He was unsure if it was a potion or tonic or something else, but since he didn't see any transfiguration occur, Korin assumed it would've likely been a tonic.

"Drink," she said.

Korin didn't bother asking what it was, anxiously taking it before swigging it down.

"Now, relax." She grabbed his hands, holding them. "I will guide you through the whole process, so listen to what I say. All of this will occur in your mind, so close your eyes."

It took about ten minutes before Korin felt some kind of sensation. He was patient, and after a few more minutes, his senses started shifting. His body buzzed even more, and his head woozily rotated. Discomfort set in before Korin felt increasingly nervous about what was happening. Everything that surrounded him then rapidly blurred until it faded away and was no longer 'there' for him; he didn't move away from his reality, but rather, all tangible entities disappeared from his perception. Even Priscilla's hands 'disappeared', blurring into mere odd sensations touching his body – which itself was also no longer perceived as a 'body' but, instead, an unclear extension of his consciousness.

Oh, man, I've done it this time, Korin worriedly thought. *What the fuck is happening? Relax, relax, relax. I can't do anything now. Shit… just relax. It's just in my mind. It'll be over soon.*

In only a moment, he could barely string together articulated sentences in his mind. Now so 'removed' from reality, there was nothing for him to grasp on to – nothing familiar, nothing understandable, nothing natural. Mental clarity was fully destabilized. But then… something emerged. Light… dark… a silhouette… of a person… something to identify, despite being vague. The being floated towards Korin, its form a little more distinguishable. Ultimately, it remained fuzzy. It wore a robe… a ceremonial robe… and a skulled head… of an animal. A creature. Unknown to Korin. It shifted… left… right… up… down… as multiple beings and a collective, single entity. The shifting intensified, turning into… a dance… a rhythmic dance… feet stamped… to a beat… ritualistically dancing to a synced beat. Intricate forms were absent… there was only repetition. Simple repetition.

Esoteric symbols flashed and pulsed from everywhere, stamping his vision. Lights emerged… bombarding him before diminishing, rendering him in the dark. Then they returned. Repeating. Fractals emerged. The lights fractalized.

A voice finally emerged, its nature deep and distorted. "Deep. Go deep within yourself."

At first, Korin couldn't think. Confusion dominated his consciousness. The figure then repeated both the mantra and the dancing until the directive was inculcated into Korin's instinctual mind. He knew what to do now without even thinking about it. The hypnotic rhythm kept Korin from thinking, lulling the conscious mind away so he could begin exploring his inner self… or rather, another self… Blurred scenes from his recent happenings appeared, the most prominent being at the clubs in the Market District; emotions of disgust and anger arose, clouding the already-blurred visions into a state of misty colours and warped energies. The scenes visually faded away, and all that was left were deep-seated emotions… first as sensations, then visually as cloudy energies, as if a rainbow… a smorgasbord. All of these energies, however, remained 'disconnected'… until they began amalgamating. Another cloud then emerged… shadow is a more appropriate term, as light emerged from behind Korin. The cloud corporealized into a figure, male in energy. Although his mental state wasn't clear, Korin was able to instinctually guess what it was: it was him.

Able to approach the figure, Korin raised his hand, with the figure mirroring his actions. Although mirroring Korin, it certainly was no mirror, and its depth was too much for Korin to fathom consciously.

"Join it," the voice behind Korin instructed. "See from its perspective."

In one way, it was terrifying staring at the figure due to the deep energies it held, but there was also a comfortable sense of security that it emanated. Korin was no coward, and he decided to face the being, placing his hand *into* the being's hand before taking a couple of steps toward it, partly merging with it. A shockwave shot through his mind; it wasn't physical… it was purely mental. Too many subconscious thoughts and emotions were now a part of his conscious mind – so much so that they couldn't fully be part of his conscious mind. The heightened sense of awareness oddly enough caused more disorientation. He knew if he continued existing in such a state for much longer, he'd go mad.

The skulled person returned, this time pointing at a sphere of light above. Although hard to determine at first, it became clear that it was the crystal moon. But before long, it turned black, its texture changing to a liquid form, rippling concentrically before fuming tentacles past the thin silver lining of light. As fearsome as it was, it didn't attack, its being merely… existed. Suddenly, it withdrew into a field of infinite darkness. Just when Korin was about to turn around, a cloud appeared in front of him. Cold, moist, and amorphous, it simply floated. Korin wondered if something would emerge from it, but nothing did. The music softened as another form of confusion set in. After waiting a short while, Korin realized that he needed to do something, but he had no clue. He tried a few things, such as entering it and speaking to it, but nothing occurred.

Before any debilitating madness could be set in stone, though, the disorientating effect of the drug passed. Korin's senses returned, and the world of the familiar securely held his mind. His hands quickly reached for the ground, touching it repeatedly. With his earthy temperate, Korin innately relished the grounding nature of the return. He opened his eyes, expecting maybe a final symbol or two to flash out of nowhere, but only a tiny amount of blurriness momentarily remained.

"How are you?" Priscilla asked.

Korin took a moment before responding, "I… don't know what to think about it. It was probably the weirdest thing I've ever experienced. You said that there would be a trial at the end, but nothing happened."

"So, while I couldn't see what was in your mind, the circle helped me to partially see into it -- the voice was me, by the way -- and you seemed to pass certain thresholds. You *would* have seen the black moon, right?"

"Yeah… but then all I saw was some cold cloud. Is that what you're meant to see?"

"So, if you don't specifically tune into a particular archetype, then the black moon can manifest anything for you; it could be based on what's happening to you personally, or it could be what's happening in society at large — or anything else. Some trials can be quite puzzling, where you have to complete a series of puzzles."

"Well, if that was a puzzle, it had me completely stumped."

"Hmm… fair enough. Consider that a shadow version of something can actually be its literal and obvious opposite. So, if it was cold, perhaps the real archetype was heat."

"Right, so a fiery rock or something?"

"Maybe. Regardless, you passed the initiation part, and that's what matters for the time being."

"So, no increase in power, then?"

"No. And even if you 'pass the tests', there are still other integration procedures to consider – which require practice. Usually, a mentor is needed to help. For some, it may take years. For others – especially for those who are," she said, hemming, "*naturally* talented – it can be done in a much shorter period. But it also depends on what you do, too. That is, there are shortcuts, depending on what one is willing to do. It's also ideal to have a greater level of integration with your own shadow self first, so there is still groundwork to be done, along with other preliminaries, too – but this can tie into post-trial integration as well."

The information was a bit of an overload for Korin; he then only just remembered how attempting a connection with the black moon could result in demonic possession. "Wait… I'm not possessed?"

"No. I don't believe any demons came. When done correctly, initiation rituals don't draw in demons, unless the initiate has problems with demons in the first place. I know what I'm doing. Again, it was only an initiation ritual. Also remember: until you can truly realize the unconscious and integrate it into your conscious mind, you'll always be directly ruled by it. Therefore, we black moon practitioners seek self-empowerment, and with greater psychic powers, this, of course, would prevent issues like demonic possession."

"I see. So, do I need to take that potion or tonic again in order to connect?"

"No, and it's not safe to regularly take the tonic. It's more of a jump start. It wasn't a potion, either, as I didn't transfigure it. And even the equipment here, like this circle, are not needed. However, when attempting to tune into certain archetypes, using tonics and equipment – not necessarily the ones we used – is either a lot easier or sometimes even necessary. This is especially the case if you wish to avoid tapping distortions and bad connections which can cause incorrect perceptions. Usually, the best time to perform a deep ritual, where one fully goes into that space you experienced, is during a lunapex, so we practitioners take a whole month for both preparation and integration, along with doing simple rituals in the meantime. I can explain later how to perform deep rituals for the next lunapex."

Taking some time to review what transpired, Korin was glad to see that not only that nothing bad happened but that he was also now on what he felt was a meaningful path to self-empowerment. He nodded and lightly chuckled. "Alright, so what now?"

"I think that's enough for the night in regards to the black moon. However, the night is still young enough for you to help me with something. Are you feeling fine enough for some risky activity?"

"I still feel a little weird, but I think I can. What do you mean by risky?"

Priscilla grinned. "We need to *borrow* someone."

"I hope you don't mean kidnap."

"Kidnap is such a harsh term."

"So, *basically* kidnap? Hang on," he swiftly said, thinking about all the kidnappings around the campus and his theories about the cult. "No, this crosses the line. This… this is what the shadowists are doing. They're the ones behind the missing students. And you… you…"

"Oh, please. We're only going to hold her for one night. Then we'll chuck her back. She won't go missing for more than a couple of hours. Seems quite different than *missing*, can't you see? Plus, you have no proof that shadowists are actually behind the kidnappings."

"No, but I swear to God that I'm right."

"Sure, you could be right. I don't doubt you. But I only intend to… ask her a few questions. Nothing more. It's ethically sound and justified. Trust me. *Trust me.* Don't worry, no harm will come to her, and she won't remember anything."

Grunting with unease, Korin said, "If you only intend to ask a few questions, then… fine. But why?"

"I'll inform you of the details later. It's best we –" She stopped when one of the black moon practitioners glanced at her from afar. "Meriel!" Priscilla called out. "We need to complete *that* task. Now."

The girl's pale face oozed with irritation and alarm, but she nevertheless marched over, subtly placing away a notepad and pen; and when she grudgingly approached, she feigned a smile.

"Korin," Priscilla said, introducing the girl, "this is Meriel. She'll be helping us. Isn't that right?" she sharply asked with a glare behind the stare.

"Yes," Meriel struggled to say. "I… love helping you, Priscilla. Anything for *you*."

Korin winced, saying nothing about her bizarre response.

"You're so kind, Meriel. Where would I be without you?" Priscilla tried suppressing a giggle.

"What *must* I do first?" Meriel asked, folding her arms.

"You *must* address me as Mistress. You should know this by now."

"Yes… *Mistress*. How must we complete your task?"

"Did you acquire those tonics?

"Yes. They're inside. I can collect them if you wish."

"Excellent. I knew I could count on you," Priscilla said 'sweetly'.

Although wanting to ask about Meriel, Korin focused on the task, saying, "Please tell me these tonics are safe."

"Of course," Priscilla said. "Everything is perfectly accounted for. If those tonics fail, *someone* will be in a lot of trouble. Isn't that right?" She looked at Meriel.

Shakily breathing, Meriel replied, "Yes, I understand perfectly."

Looking askance, Korin chose to remain silent, fist pressed against his lips.

Priscilla continued, "The first part of the operation will consist of us locating the researcher, which should be easy, as I know her general whereabouts during these hours. Since she'll likely be in public sight, we'll have to drug her before we can lead her back here. Otherwise, if no-one is looking, we can shoot her unconscious with a beta discharge, drug her, and then when she wakes up, we can take her here before drugging her again for the interrogation. Are we all good?"

I don't believe this, Korin thought. *Maybe the researcher did something bad, so Priscilla has found a way to justify it. Another Sereck, maybe.* Sighing in his mind,

Korin finally 'approved' with a grudging hand gesture before saying, "Let's get this out of the way. Just don't cross any line out there, Priscilla."

"When do *I* ever cross any line, Korin? I always maintain myself within acceptable parameters."

Yeah, right ON the perimeter, he thought as he began departing the black moon temple with Priscilla and Meriel.

***

Fate ironically struck Korin again as he had to head back to the clubs that night, the dread of the hipsters and mindless partygoers sickening him. Priscilla, of course, scowled at all around, her line of sight almost like scorching headlights. The research scientist they were after would usually go clubbing on Fireday nights, and Priscilla showed an image of her face to Korin on her phid.

"Time to split up," Priscilla said. "If you find her, call, and we'll regroup. Don't go having fun out there now, Korin." She snickered.

"It's tempting," Korin struggled to jest, "given that you still haven't told me everything. Anyway, why are we doing this *right* now?"

"There's a reason. That's all I'll say. Are you ready?"

"Mm. Yeah. Alright, let's go." Korin then waited for Priscilla to leave before catching up to Meriel, who gave a clear 'help me' look. "Is everything fine?"

"Yes. Everything is fine," Meriel said, nervously looking over her shoulder.

"You look really edgy."

"Well, we are about to abduct someone. That's not a normal thing people do."

Yeah, she's right. Not normal, indeed. "Hm." Korin, too, glanced over his shoulder to see if Priscilla was present or not. He then charily asked, "You and Priscilla on good terms?"

"Of... of course," Meriel said, her pitch rather high. "Good terms. Good terms. Nothing bad." Her eyes remained wide and unblinking.

"You sure? Priscilla's not like most girls, and she's never mentioned having any friends. And you two seem quite odd together."

"No, I have no idea what you mean," she speedily answered. "We're on good terms. Can we please move on?"

"Alright. If you feel the need to say something, let me know." Korin stared before slowly departing an unmoving Meriel.

Shaking his head, Korin's mind focused more so on the strange relationship than the task at hand. Shortly later, however, while just outside a club entrance, Korin noticed an odd object stuck to a girl's pants; without being conscious of it, he gave a weird, curious expression as he stared. He was, moreover, very close behind her. The girl then abruptly turned around, seeing Korin staring at her backside.

"What are you doing?" she asked him, frowning in disgust.

"Ah…" Korin closed his eyes as his head shivered. "There was…"

"I know *exactly* what you were doing!" she remarked scathingly before marching off.

"Ooh, you've upset Bexy," one guy said, chuckling. "Wait until her friends arrive."

Korin flushed as most of the nearby people either glared or giggled. Deciding to leave the area, he eventually walked past a seemingly out-of-place sideshow with a performer balancing a glittering, jolting ball of goo on a peculiar rod. Eyes fixated on the show, Korin slowly walked with his head turned. Without seeing her, Korin bumped into Bexy; his brain consequently shook up, in turn causing him to accidentally touch multiple places on her body as he repeatedly apologized. Growling with fury, she turned redder than Korin.

"You're sick!" Bexy cried out. "Don't you *dare* come near me again! Or else!"

"But, but… it was…" Korin stumbled as she left.

Hearing numerous murmurs regarding him and his actions, Korin felt the need to vacate quickly, so he headed down a dark alleyway, seeing a naked woman standing by herself. Distraught and jittering, the young lady struggled to keep herself together. Her face wasn't immediately recognizable due to her hysterical appearance, but Korin soon realized who it was: the research scientist.

"Are you alright?" Korin reached his hand out, unsure if he should've looked away.

"I-I'm… I'm fine," the researcher stuttered before cackling bizarrely, as if partially choking.

"Are you sure?" he asked right before she pulled out a knife from her clothes on the ground, grinning at Korin.

Before Korin could connect to the Aether and activate his lumarchetrix to help him, the girl rapidly and sadistically stabbed herself in the gut, repeatedly jabbing while trying to pull her entrails out in the process.

"What the fuck?" Korin yelled, running over to her.

Relying purely on survival reflexes, he managed to clutch her arm, keeping the dagger away from both bodies as it remained in her grasp, juddering insanely fast. Her screeches reached his soul as Korin literally kept on his toes. Still alive with adrenaline pumping through her, she thrashed around and managed to pull Korin's trousers down while ripping his t-shirt. While in Korin's hands, the research scientist looked up at him, coughing and grinning menacingly as her blood rapidly poured out. She gave him the dagger, and her eyes changed from evil to innocent, looking at Korin hopelessly, saddened, and in pain.

"I-i-" the research fellow stuttered, "it… wasn't me." She coughed again, passing away quickly.

Before Korin could properly think, a few people saw him holding the dead woman and gasped. Bexy was one of the first to see him.

"He raped and murdered her!" Bexy shrieked at the top of her lungs. "He's a sex fiend!"

Korin was motionless, only stuttering after ten long, excruciating seconds. "Wa-wait, wait! I didn't do anything!" He was ready to cry, though the impact of the moment held back tears.

Other people poured into the alley, and a couple of security officers soon entered as well. "Put the knife down!" one of the officers ordered, possessing a green blast ball in his palm.

"I-I didn't do it," Korin responded, beginning to go dizzy from shock.

"Put. The knife. Down!" the officer ordered again, patting the air with his other hand.

Korin slowly placed the knife down as he carefully laid the body on the ground, finally putting his hands in the air. His eyes dilated, but heavy-duty lights soon beamed over his body, sending his diminishing senses down the drain. Then, one of the officers shot him.

***

Light blared through one of Korin's opening eyes, blinding him as he fully woke. After a moment of adjusting to the light, he sat his semi-numb body up and saw a sombre man staring at him expressionlessly. His stocky body filled Korin's immediate vision, whose peripheral view was still blurred.

"Are you ready to talk, Korin?" the balding man asked seriously.

"How… how do you know my name?" Korin rubbed his eyes, wondering where he was located… until he saw magic suppressor cuffs on his wrists, preventing him from using magic.

"I'm an investigator. I know things. Are you ready to talk?"

Korin quickly recalled everything that had occurred, registering that he had passed out – which was the first time he had ever passed out from an ultrachite discharge. "Yes, but I didn't do it."

"From the beginning. What happened?" he asked coldly.

"I… I was down the street… and… ah," he spoke nervously with a shaking hand, which went along with his explanation, "and I saw her just standing there, and then she stabbed herself. I ran up to her and…. and tried to stop her, but I believe a demon possessed her."

"A demon?" An eyebrow of his shot up, breaking free from the rest of his stone-sculptured face.

"Yeah, just before she died, her eyes changed."

"And you –"

An officer barged into the room. "I have news!" He motioned for the investigator, who got up. "We have another stabbing case," his words seeped into the room as Korin overheard. "This time, there were witnesses. The kid stabbed himself. Supposedly, a demon possessed him."

"Well, I think that explains a lot," the investigator remarked before entering the room again and sitting opposite Korin. "I believe… hmm, just wait here for a while, and we'll clear this up." He exited, closing the door.

Alone now, Korin clenched his fists and lightly tapped his forehead, worrying what verdict the police would deliver. He couldn't believe that his whole life – his new life – was about to come crumbling down. Looking around at the sterile surroundings, he dreaded being locked up for years to come, all because he wanted to rescue someone. Despite needing the now-dead woman for Priscilla's cause, the attempted rescue was itself an unconditional noble act on Korin's behalf. He heard no external noise, just the solitary silence of his potential prison. Korin desperately wanted to see his friends so they could reassure the university police he would never rape and murder anyone, but he realized that his non-mage past would potentially work against him, and that played on his mind for a good hour. He also wondered if the police were going to ask about his plans to abduct the research fellow. Knowing he couldn't blame Priscilla simply because he chanced upon a demon attack, he nonetheless began to regret taking up the task with her, as it could now backfire with the police. In effect, being inside the station turned all that 'greater meaning' he felt into goo before being thrown into the trashcan. Half the emotions he felt now were that of foolishness.

The investigator then entered the room again, sitting down with a phlegmatic appearance, saying nothing as he stared at Korin, who placed his hands over his face. Korin's feet also repeatedly shook, nerves about to spread onto the floor.

Oh, God, this is it. I'm fucked, aren't I? Korin thought.

"Okay, Korin," the investigator said, delaying his verdict for what seemed like a *long* moment, "you're free to go."

"What?" Korin opened his eyes, taking a short while to process what he heard. "Oh, man, thank you!" He jumped up with joy, shedding a few tears while shouting aloud his thankfulness. "I tried to save her," he said solemnly. "Really."

"I believe you did. We could tell because demons leave a temporary etheric imprint on the ex-possessed. Please try to avoid any further trouble. We scrubbed off most of the blood, but make sure to have a shower."

"Sure," Korin said, smiling, despite the blood on him. "I'll… phew!" he uttered, still shaking off his nerves. "I'll head off now. Thanks."

When Korin left the room, he collected his confiscated watch before having his magic suppressor cuffs removed. After exiting the station, Korin activated his phid, seeing that he had multiple missed calls, all from Priscilla. Thinking about what to say to Priscilla, he delayed calling her back for a few minutes. Finally, he called. "Hey."

"Hey?" Priscilla cried out. "Were you off getting shit-faced while grinding some slut?"

"No," he replied sternly, incapable of even bringing himself to quip. "There was a demon attack, and I was put in jail. I'm out now."

"Oh… Are you alright?"

"I'm fine. Look, I managed to find her. The thing is, *she* was the person who was possessed. And now she's dead, so your plans are over."

"Damn it! Ugh! Alright… fine. I'm glad you're okay, though. Can you meet with us now? We're at your dorm block – we checked to see if you were there."

"Okay, I'll be there shortly."

On the way to the dorm block, the demonically-possessed research scientist repeatedly flickered through his mind. Never had Korin been so close to such a killing – even the recent pixie deaths weren't that close. The feelings of gladness and relief of his release were quickly ripped from him in a sensation similar to how he imagined his guts would've been ripped from his bowels. Again and again. The woman's eyes lightly scorched his vision, and he had to shake the sight away. He checked his hands often, thinking there would be massive amounts of blood present; but only stains remained – though the sight was dreadful enough.

At the botanic strip separating the dorm blocks from the inner uni auxiliary districts, Korin noticed some unusual movements, so he opted to move in and investigate. Just as he entered, Korin saw a fully-cloaked figure carrying what looked like a body bag over his broad shoulder.

"Oi!" Korin yelled. "What are you doing?"

Instead of answering, the stranger immediately dropped the bag, fleeing over the thick bushes. Blindly eager to apprehend the kidnapper, Korin tried to tune into the Aether as he stumbled through plants that cut and stung him. This was it: Korin finally found what was potentially a shadowist in action. He believed there was no way anything would stop him in his tracks. The kidnapper then ran on to the road before darting behind a building, but Korin still kept pace. After around forty-five seconds, Korin finally charged his lumarchetrix, and then he tried aiming his hand in his bumpy run, shooting green discharges centimetres past the guy's head. More of his shots missed the man, and Korin would've made an accurate shot if it weren't for tripping on a rock.

"No!" Korin yelled, unable to believe anything stopped him.

Rapidly jumping up, Korin noticed that the kidnapper was out of sight. Searching around for another minute in a panic, Korin came to the understanding that he had two choices: either continue with what was a potentially futile chase or run back and secure the body just in case it was retaken. Although it was tempting to persist onwards, Korin just had a feeling he'd have the opportunity later to stop the kidnapper, so he decided to run back to the body bag, unzipping it to find an unconscious student inside.

A few people walked by through the botanic strip, and when they glanced through the bushes, they witnessed Korin crouched over the bagged student, so they called for the security, who happened to be nearby. Korin was about to flee, staying in the end, as he realized he had been proven innocent of the other event earlier. Still, he found the string of misfortune flabbergasting.

"It's not what it looks like!" Korin said as the security officer advanced.

"Don't move!" the officer ordered fiercely.

Korin slightly rolled his head, obeying the order before being knocked out again with a green discharge. Just as Korin was about to fall to the ground, the officer used a red discharge with the ideal power level to slow his fall to soften the landing. The officer then called for transport, placing Korin inside when it arrived. Again, Korin was transported to the police station in an isolated part of the Market District.

***

Once back in the same jail cell, the balding investigator who probed Korin earlier entered again – this time, with an icier stare.

"Look, I know what you're thinking," Korin said, holding his hands out in defence.

"Trouble seems to follow you, doesn't it?" the investigator asked. "Or perhaps you *are* the trouble. What's your excuse now?"

With more confidence than last time, Korin explained the incident, swiftly adding that he was innocent for emphasis. Without blinking – or even moving a centimetre – the investigator continued peering into Korin's being.

Finally, he asked Korin, "Do you have any information on the missing students we've placed on posters everywhere?"

"No. Why would *I* know?" Korin thoughtlessly said, thinking the question was crazy before realizing he actually did have some information on the matter, such as the cultist necklace he found near Khastanian's body, signifying potential shadowist activity. "If I did, I would've informed someone," he managed to lie rather well, despite also being involved with an abduction plot.

"Yes, I'm sure you would have," he replied sarcastically. "Anyway, you may be telling the truth about the bagged student. We're looking into how long he was unconscious for. Given that you were only out for ten or so minutes, we'll be able to deduce if you're innocent or not."

"Good. You'll find that I'm innocent," Korin stated robustly before the investigator exited.

Instead of feeling hopeless and inert, Korin gripped the bench underneath with his fingers, almost digging his nails into the timber. He didn't believe he'd be locked up, but it felt as though some unknown force was annoyingly working against him. Instead of creating pleading dialogue in his head, he imagined punching people. Bad people, of course. A few minutes later while Korin waited in unnerving silence, an officer informed the investigator about the results just outside the door.

The investigator re-entered, leaving the door open. "Yet again, the results are in your favour, Mr. Tarkelt. When you leave, I suggest that you return to your dormitory the quickest route possible. That way, you'll hopefully avoid trouble."

Korin didn't say much before he uncomfortably left the station once more. A few of the prior witnesses from the clubs saw him again, all yelling for the security and police. Korin irately explained that he was vindicated, even telling the witnesses to freely check with the police. The students, nevertheless, continued yelling before shortly being officially informed of Korin's innocence. He sensed that they wanted to keep yelling, anyway.

There were more missed calls on his watch, so Korin called Priscilla back, telling her what had happened and that he had had enough for the night. Priscilla understood.

While making his way back to his dorm, Korin kept his head down, not only to avoid contact with anyone that saw him earlier but to also avoid more trouble. However, Korin reconsidered his thoughts; he knew he couldn't ignore trouble if he saw it.

Chapter Fifteen

Lusty Drama in the Sanctuary

Demonically-possessed students frothed at the mouths as they rapidly jumped out of the alleyway windows, shattering glass over numerous corpses oozing organ tissue. The raging horde then fought their way toward a bruised and scarred Korin, who stumbled over, turning around to scream just as the ground began slowly verticalizing into a cliff wall. Korin gripped a hole in the cliff, but heavy rain weakened his hold, and he slipped, falling…

Falling until literally waking up.

Korin's heart thudded rapidly, granting him the energy to jump out of his bed and move around like a frenzied buzzing insect. As he began to realize where he was, his movements faltered until he finally relaxed, resting on the ground. He knew the possessed girl he tried to save was the cause of the nightmare. On a much deeper level, he was still very shaken up and disturbed about what he witnessed – what he closely experienced. But that wasn't the only issue.

There was still the matter of the rape allegation; and whilst he was cleared, Korin believed rumours would most likely linger on with other students, dispersing into senseless stories. And there was also the kidnapping he saw. The feeling of knowing people were being abducted was indeed agitating. The unfamiliar individuals in such cases seemed, in a way, like everyday news – people met with unwanted circumstances all the time; but the experience of the chase made the event all the more real, all the more fleshed out, as if the mere knowledge itself was an empty husk, waiting to be filled and transformed into something corporeal, which could only be understood at face value, like seeing the details of someone's features while up close, compared to the fuzziness of afar. It lingered. Stained in his mental vision.

Korin felt yet another burden upon him – that his experience *necessitated* his pursuit of those responsible, that the experience spiritually intertwined with him and bonded to his very investigative trajectory. His friends came to mind and the possibility that they, too, could be abducted. The thought made him even more empathetic toward those who had friends missing. This, alone, gave him a higher sense of meaning – one that helped partially fill the void that emerged after the jail cell incident the previous night, where the greater sense of meaning he had gained from the black moon was turned into goo and thrown away.

Korin's arm rested across his face as he lay in total wakefulness, numb to the playful noises outside. It was the weekend, so he allowed himself to rest a bit longer, having already slept in to eight o'clock. After a while, the troublesome thoughts in his head settled; his mind relatively mellowed. He opened the door for fresh air, returning to his bed before hearing footsteps on the balcony.

"Hi, Korin," a familiar voice said with a sultry and mischievous tone.

Frowning under his arm, Korin thought, *I need rest.*

Wishing he was just hearing things, he then swiftly glanced at the door, seeing Priscilla smiling precisely like the tone of her voice. Her dress was a little shorter than usual, and a little frillier and friskier, though as black as ever. It was the first time she had visited him in his bedroom – not just the dorm block.

What have you got planned? Korin thought, thinking of many possibilities. "Are you –"

Priscilla abruptly moved out of sight.

Korin quickly got to his feet, taking a peek outside the door. "Can I… help you?" he asked, placing his hand on his head.

"Well…" Priscilla said, continuing to smile as she rocked her body from side to side with her arms together behind her back. "I have a lot of spare time today, and I want to have a little more fun than normal."

"You want to do another ritual?"

"Yes, but not until later. I want to have some unrelated fun first."

Why do I have the feeling you're going to pull some really crazy shit today? Korin assumed, not only thinking back to the previous night but also to a recent prank, believing Priscilla was going to amp her game up. "Look, if by fun you mean something like humiliating Sereck again, then no, I have no intention of doing anything nasty."

"Oh, please. I wouldn't do *that* again." She giggled lightly. "I'm an imaginative type. Let's get creative this time."

"No. I'm not hurting anyone," he said firmly, crossing his arms.

Priscilla, too, crossed her arms. "Do you really think I sit around all day and think about harming others?"

"Well… maybe… yeah." He shrugged, uncrossing his arms.

"Well, okay, you're right. I do." She rolled her eyes, smirking. "But I would never do anything extreme. Then again, in all actuality," her tone changed serious, "I prefer doing more productive things with my time than concerning myself with imbeciles."

"Like? With all the payback, it seems you really *are* concerned with others."

"I'm not the nasty one, Korin. Other people are. They merely get their just deserts. That's the natural order of things. Pacifism is for the weak, but that doesn't mean I initiate arbitrarily. You know that. I simply teach people a few lessons. And, why not have fun in that process? May as well, as their retribution is inevitable in one way or another. There's no point in being depressed over it." She shrugged her arms, though she was fully self-assured.

"Your perspective is… I don't know." He shook his head.

"Well, Sereck seems to have had enough for now. I think he's learning. Anyway, what's your problem? You seem uptight and aggressive towards me now. You were okay last night – for the most part."

"I had a shitty time last night, okay? I mean, with the whole demon thing. Not the part with you, though."

"Fine, I understand. I think you need to take a break and have some… *fun.*" She walked her fingers up Korin's bare chest. "And I have something special planned tonight. It'll be a wicked experience. I want you to be there with me."

Am I the only one you'll be having fun with? he thought, exhaling heavily with restlessness. *What is it about me? I'm different, as you say?* Korin then considered he was being a bit too cold with Priscilla. He did enjoy her company when she wasn't doing anything too devious or overly strange. "Alright," he said, lightly smiling. "I wanted to rest today, but I guess we can do something together."

"Aww. I knew you'd come around. So, I want to play a game," she said, spinning around Korin and entering his room. "Oh, how dull! Your room needs a makeover." She turned around. "Well, it's a good thing I brought you a gift." She pulled out a gothic-styled clock featuring the phases of the crystal moon positioned where each number would normally be. "I got it from a neat little shop that nobody seems to know about."

"Uh… thank you," he said as Priscilla gleefully hopped onto his bed, sensually fondling his sheets. Korin's heart raced again, though not in a fearful way. The way she was hugging his pillow and biting her lip threw his senses haywire. He stood still, unsure what to do as heat built inside him.

Priscilla beamed and said, "I want to play hide and seek. But first, let's play some tag. You like tag, right?"

Korin wasn't sure if she meant literal tag outdoors or something metaphorical in his room. He glanced outside, viewing the beautiful sunny morning and intuiting that whatever would happen that day, he was going to be swept into Priscilla's unusual mind games. Indeed, his own mind kept going back and forth on the matter.

Priscilla continued, "Since you've been thinking a lot about cultists, I think we should rename the game. I'll call it, 'Escape the Cultist'."

"What?" Korin chuckled in surprise.

"Yes! You'll play as the shadowist, and I'll run away."

"I don't want to be the cultist." Korin folded his arms.

"Oh, I think you'll make a great shadowist." She grinned. "You were quite good last night. Anyway, you're it!" she cried, raising her hand to use an aerosol magic suppressor on Korin, the unscented liquid feeling like a thin spray of water.

"Hey, what the hell was that?" Korin wiped his face.

"You can't use magic or even connect to the Aether for about two minutes now." She then raised her hand again, this time with a red discharge ready to fire off. "Don't move or I'll shoot and freeze you." Priscilla stopped retaining a ready discharge in order to keep her aura from overloading, but she kept her hand pointed at Korin to show that she would still instantly shoot. She then approached him and lightly slapped a rub-on tattoo on his forehead before quickly acquiring a mirror to show Korin. "Now you're part of The Gathering. See, you bear its symbol now. Congratulations on getting initiated."

"What have you done to me?" Korin angrily replied when he saw the shadowist cult symbol stamped on his forehead, coloured in black.

"If you want the symbol off, you need to catch me first, as only I have the proper removal sticker. Now…" She placed her finger on her chin. "What should I do if I have to wait for a while? Hmm… Oh, I know! I still have your blood from last night." She pulled out the vial of Korin's blood. "I wonder what I should do with this?"

"What the fuck are you going to do with my blood?" Korin panicked.

"What was that? You want me to play with it? Okay!" Priscilla then shot Korin before dashing out of the room while teeheeing.

The red discharge basically immobilized Korin while sending him into a state of suspended animation. And while it only lasted a couple of seconds, it made Korin feel a little sluggish afterwards. Korin shook his head and was able to shortly regain his normal self. He looked again in the mirror, horrified at the symbol. He had to get if off. Immediately. And then he had to get his blood back, as he was unsure if Priscilla was just teasing or actually serious about doing something extremely devious with it.

Hurriedly placing a t-shirt, suitable pants, and some socks and runners on, Korin ran outside, spotting Priscilla exiting the courtyard. Taking the slide down, Korin raced to where the subroute entrance was located. He assumed Priscilla would've tried to access the subroute, but he noticed her running beyond the station and between other dorm blocks. It occurred to him that the capsule wouldn't be arriving then, so waiting in the subroute would've allowed Korin to catch up.

Priscilla ran through another dorm courtyard before exiting; and eventually, she entered the botanic strip separating the dorms from the inner districts. It also happened to be very close to where Korin had noticed the kidnapper the previous night. For a moment, Korin questioned if she was the culprit. Then he remembered it was a male with broad shoulders. The foliage was much clearer in the day, and he noticed the broken branches he made whilst chasing the mysterious figure.

Near the edge of the other side of the botanic strip, Priscilla had picked herself up after tripping, looking back to see Korin, who had caught up. Priscilla quickly sprayed Korin again, though his tolerance levels would reduce the timespan of the effect. Thinking quickly, Korin grabbed the bottle off Priscilla and sprayed her. She was about to dash away, but Korin swiftly grabbed Priscilla from behind, holding her arms tightly as he tried to stop her from taking any other course of action. Now up close, he noticed that her neck smelled of a mix between lavender, sandalwood, and some other exotic scents. She wrestled, pushing Korin with her back.

"Oh, yes!" Priscilla cried out with pleasure, panting. "You're more aggressive than I realized. Where have you been this whole time?"

Korin was stumped as to what to say back.

"Well, having fun, Korin?" She chuckled. "I sure am." She continued trying to wrestle out of Korin's lock. "Tighter, Korin, tighter!"

Her demands utterly confused him. Priscilla was obviously physically weaker than Korin, though she put up a decent bout. He couldn't see where the removal sticker and vial were, guessing she might have had hidden pockets. Moreover, even though he couldn't properly see her face, Korin *knew* that she was grinning. While still short of breath, she started moaning with pleasure. She flicked her head back, pressing it against Korin's cheek, repeatedly whispering for him to fully pin her down.

Suddenly, a couple of people passed along the footpath ahead.

"Help!" Priscilla yelled. "Rape! He's raping me! Help me!"

Korin dropped her as if holding hot irons, speedily placing his hands in the air. "I swear I wasn't raping her! She's lying!"

One of the students happened to have already been connected to the Aether; and, despite it being against the uni rules, he began shooting ultrachite discharges in Korin's direction. Priscilla quickly grabbed the magic suppressor before she and Korin scrammed; and although they began separating, Korin changed his course, continuing his pursuit of Priscilla, who was laughing along the way. The shooting soon stopped, and Korin guessed Priscilla's laughing signalled to the shooter that she wasn't serious.

Turning into a large storage shed, Priscilla disappeared; and when Korin entered, he caught his breath, surveying the spacious area, hoping she wouldn't finally turn on him and lunge with something deadly.

"Priscilla!" Korin shouted, voice echoing and pinging off hollow metal containers. "You went too far there! Rape is a serious accusation that can destroy people's lives!" He waited for a response, hearing nothing. "Well? Are you going to apologize? Are… are you even here?"

Another spray of liquid hit Korin, and Priscilla contently twirled right in front of him.

"Of course I'm sorry, Korin," Priscilla said cheekily. "If you're locked up in prison, I'll have no-one to truly have fun with. And that would be bad." She giggled. "Don't worry, I would've told them the truth. You know me, silly. Anyway, I'll be outside one of the Towers of Elevation." Knowing the magic suppressor would be weaker on him this time, she decided to quickly go, but not before stroking his arm and reaching for a short kiss on the lips. "Catch me, Korin!" she said with great ecstasy, eyes wide open. "Catch me!"

Priscilla shot a flummoxed Korin again with a delta-negative blast before bolting off. Despite finding Priscilla a little too strange, dark, and suspicious, Korin couldn't help being aroused at her personality quirks, feeling compelled to follow, as if she was magically pulling him in.

Once freed, he dashed out, taking the closest subroute capsule to the Central Hub. When he exited the station under one of the Provision Wreath's thoroughfares, he saw Priscilla at the base of one of the towers, waving tantalizingly. Korin raced on, whizzing past bystanders who seemed so normal, so orderly, so sane. He felt like he was losing himself in a crazy world, foolishly forgoing his new sense of self that took an immense struggle to build after its collapse following his religious ritual.

Why am I doing this? Korin thought, nearly forgetting about the mark on his head.

Contemplating what depths she would dive to for thrills, Korin briefly stopped in his tracks, hoping he was making the right decision going onwards; but he needed that mark off, regardless. Priscilla occupied one of the aeropads inside, having purposely delayed herself so Korin could see where to go. When he approached, the shell wall closed, and he considered that she was going straight to the top. The other aeropad soon became available; and after entering, he smashed the top holochite button repeatedly, pushing right past the haptic hologram. A sense of danger escalated as the aerochannel rose, slowly squashing down the other raging and erratic emotions Korin had.

He then had to follow Priscilla through to the Aegis Halo. Once nearing the roof of the halo, there were warning signs saying that the roof was closed for maintenance. Obviously, much of the tape was ripped apart when Priscilla made her way through previously. When Korin reached the roof, he saw that a large section of its railing had been previously ripped off for some reason. No-one else was present. Priscilla was about fifteen metres away, right at the edge of the roof. Korin worried that at *this* moment she could turn on him, perhaps wanting to push him off. He knew he was stronger, but anything was possible. Although propulsor phasarchement magic allowed mages to slowly fall, hover, or greatly jump, Korin wasn't advanced enough yet to use the magic as a backup. Even then, he summarizingly knew that propulsor ultrachite had its aerial limitations. He also assumed Priscilla couldn't use it either.

With the wind strongly blowing her hair, Priscilla faced Korin, gleefully saying, "You'll never catch me, Korin!" She laughed, turning around and slipping over the side before managing to just grab the edge. "Help!" Her legs swung greatly in the wind.

"Hang on!" Korin shouted, though a heavier gust of wind stopped him momentarily.

Crouching slightly, he moved with caution, hoping he wasn't too slow. The ground appeared very far down, and Korin imagined the halo giving way. Physically and mentally speaking, everyone seemed even further away from the crazy reality he was ensnared in – to the extent that she was the only person who was able to physically notice him. Her eyes were full of fear – an occurrence he had rarely seen before.

As she dangled, her alluring power over him, strangely enough, didn't diminish. It strengthened.

"I'm so sorry!" Priscilla exclaimed. "I would've pulled you up on that mushroom if I could," she referred to the tree activity on camp.

All of a sudden, two large creatures flew by, playing with each other rather aggressively, pulverizing each other. Both flew into the Aegis Halo, causing a part of the edge to shudder and in turn vibrate through Priscilla's hand, which lost grip. Priscilla screamed, though the creatures overpowered it with their screeches.

In the nick of time, Korin reached for her hand. "Priscilla!" he shouted, but the pulverizing continued, and his foothold lost traction. "I have you!" he called as he just managed to grab on to a small steel lump, struggling to keep his position, let alone get back up.

Priscilla was at a loss for words, looking back and forth at Korin and the ground. Before long, the creatures flew off, allowing Korin the opportunity to pull himself and Priscilla up. For a moment, Korin swore they weren't going to make it. Priscilla was about to comment, but she silently and securely held him as the wind gusted frenetically; and despite the wind's coolness, Korin felt a pleasant warmth around his stomach as she hugged him.

After thanking Korin, Priscilla softly said, "We should probably get down now."

"Yes. That would be a *very* good idea," Korin asserted. "No more games."

***

Their descent was one of silence, both still overcoming shock.

Once on the ground level outside in the Central Hub, Priscilla said, "Okay. Okay. You got me." Her smile resurrected from the grave. "But we're not done yet; let's see how good you are at hide and seek."

About to ask why she hadn't learned her lesson, Korin thought, *I don't get it. Why don't you just want something simple like flowers and shit?*

"Remember, you're the crazy cultist, so get even more aggressive!" She pushed his shoulders while biting her lips. "Come on, *drag* me into the cult. Discipline me. Indoctrinate... no, *fuck* with my mind and soul!"

Man, this is peak crazy now, he thought. "Can I at least have the removal sticker now?"

"I don't have it on me right now. You'll have to let me have a head start to hide, and then you can find me. And to do that, you'll have to figure out the following riddle: Looming over others, I tick away the ages. With my moving hands, I help schedule where the market engages. For each passing moment, I display the day's stages."

"What's that meant to mean?" Korin asked, dumbfounded.

"Fine, I'll give you a hint: it's an old building; and when you find it, I'm down a stairwell, around the side. Outside. You *should* be able to find me with *that* information. Bye, now."

Priscilla swiftly left Korin to speculate what she meant. As he began pacing, he realized he needed to cover his forehead with his hand to avoid more looks from the public. He then circled the Teloplex for a good ten minutes, where he considered quitting.

She just: Does. Not. Stop, Korin thought, reflecting more for a minute before sighing. *I'm going after her.*

Eventually, a place came to mind. There was an ancient clock tower in the Market District, so he decided to look, seeing no harm in doing so. Engrossed in his goal, Korin observed very little of his surroundings on the way. When he arrived at the clock tower, he spotted stairs leading below ground level to a gridded, rusty gate indented two metres in the wall. Sunlight couldn't reach it, and right on top was a decaying wooden sign reading, 'Prohibited Area'.

Of course, Korin thought. *What's she got planned for me?*

For the fact that the stairwell was basically out of sight, he didn't have to worry about being caught entering. The gate creaked heavily on opening, causing the water sitting in the moss on the stone-vaulted ceiling to drip. The ancient vibe brought Korin's mind back to his religious ritual, but he tossed away the sudden thought, pressing on. He soon reached a thick wooden door, abruptly seeing a rectangular peephole opening, with Priscilla peeking through.

"You have to work out the puzzle over there," Priscilla said. "It'll unlock the door."

Korin saw an elaborate contraption, wondering how long it would take to solve. He glanced back at Priscilla, noticing the skin under her eyes subtly shifting, indicating satisfaction on some level. Placing his hand on his neck, Korin stared at the contraption before fiddling with it, successfully unlocking the door within two minutes.

"What?" Priscilla yelped, her body now in full view. "How did you figure that out so quickly?" she asked, and Korin shrugged, smiling as he waltzed in. "Well, I intend to upgrade it."

About to reply, Korin stopped to scan the room, unsure if he was shocked or not. At last, he asked, "What… is this place?"

"It's my sanctuary." Priscilla motioned her arm with delight. "It's nice to have a place away from the drunken idiots out there."

Although he found it impressive and arresting, Korin was a tad disturbed by some of the aesthetics. Skulls from a few different creatures lined the antiquated shelves, lying next to other deathly ornaments. There were multiple framed paintings; one included a misty, thorny forest filled with red eyes staring from the shadows; another picture was of a nebulous, dark form reaching its tentacles around obscure objects; then there was a painting featuring hundreds of luminescent green ghosts with odd shadows surrounding an ancient stone tower, all under a black moon piercing through silver-lined clouds. One desk even had exquisitely-carved dragon claws bordering its sides. Priscilla had quite a few new, yet old-fashioned tree-paper books mixed in with deteriorating hardbacks that featured fading, elegant patterns, appearing as though they contained esoteric knowledge held well before mages even existed. Some of the titles included: *Advanced Sex Magic Rituals*, *The Complete Tales of Vornara*, *Ancient Orders and their Influence*, and *The True Fate of the Witches*.

Shattered timber boxes were in one corner, appearing as if a few creatures had broken free from a trafficking shipment. Mould even thrived around small grates on the thickly-bricked, stone walls. A couple of dusky-red crystal lamps pumped light into the room, combining well with the fine candles lit on the chalked, patterned circles on the ground. In the centre was a plump mattress with maroon and black silky blankets. Naturally, her pillows were frilly, too.

Priscilla softly said, "I haven't invited anyone in here before. It's a work in progress. I had to lug some stuff out, but a few items are still a little heavy. And I also need to find a way to stop the leak in that corner over there. Just imagine what the place will look like when it's finished. It already has that special castle-dungeon touch."

Unsure what to say, Korin ended up saying, "Yeah. It's… interesting." He paused. "The crystals are nice, but I'm not sure if I would call it home."

Priscilla didn't look too happy, and Korin felt a bit awful for hurting her feelings. She then dropped the frown. "Well, as I said, I need to make it into something special. There's still a lot of work to do."

"I see." He continued examining the room. "Well, now that I'm here, are you going to give me that sticker to remove this symbol?"

Priscilla reached for a sheet of paper on her desk. "Have you ever read *Makora's War*?"

About to ask his question again, Korin then replied, "No."

"That's a pity. Well, there's a scene I really love, and so I decided to write a poem about it. Here, listen." She cleared her throat. "The dance now finished and the ballroom clear; still did the agent wish to domineer. In his frenzied lust, he shredded my dress; half naked I stood, ready to transgress. His fine vestments, too, were torn away; only masquerade masks were to stay." Priscilla stopped reciting, glancing around her room. "Hm, there's a mistake in the following line. I wonder where my pen is."

Korin waited patiently as she searched for her pen, but she couldn't find it.

"It's a really good pen, too. You've seen it in class. Great for stabbing people." She giggled. "I write with people's blood."

Wincing, Korin said nothing. *She's probably just joking around*, he thought.

"Oh, I know where I left it. I'll grab it later, so I'll have to recite the poem another time." Priscilla sighed. "Anyway, if you want the sticker, you'll have to force me to give it to you. In a ritual." She smiled coyly before lightly shoving Korin. "Come on, Mr. Hillseck Player, let's see how strong you are."

"What?" he asked with bewilderment. "I'm not going to force you like *that*."

Priscilla groaned, throwing her head up before saying, "Come on, Korin. You know I'm not going to give you the sticker. Make me, like you're some fanatic shadowist forcing me into an initiation ritual."

"Look," Korin said, exhaling, "can you just give me the sticker? We can do some other ritual if you want."

"Nope. You have to make me." She placed the sticker behind her back before stepping backwards, unwaveringly staring into Korin's eyes, with her mouth slightly agape. "I'll start us off. So… Fine, I'll comply," she said in a softer voice. "What will you have me do for the initiation ceremony?"

By simply not moving, Korin virtually shrugged.

Priscilla rolled her eyes before marching over to him to kick him. "Play along! Come on!" Her aggressive voice returned.

"Ow! Alright." *I'm going to have to play along here*, Korin thought. *But this seems so ridiculous!* "Um… you have to go… into that circle over there."

Priscilla glanced at the circle but chose not to move.

"Well? Are you going or not?" Korin asked.

"No." She crossed her arms. "Actually, let's say that we're both already in the cult, and you have to discipline me because I've been out of line."

Irritated, Korin finally 'ordered' her by saying, "Okay, go over to… the table there and write an essay on your bad behaviour." *God, that sounded lame*, he thought, about to physically cringe.

Smirking, Priscilla strolled over to her bed instead. "No. I don't want to write an essay," she said cheekily. "I prefer doing my own things instead of obeying your orders. I think I'm going to jump on the grand sorceress's bed instead; and if she returns and sees me doing it, she'll discipline *you*." She smirked. "You better stop me." She then hopped on her bed, jumping up and down like a kid. While keeping her pace, she threw a pillow at Korin, who finally moved as a result. "I'll throw something harder in a minute!"

"That's it!" Korin yelled, running over to the bed before leaping towards Priscilla, who swiftly jumped off.

"You won't catch me!" Priscilla continued.

Korin was about to continue chasing her, but he momentarily stopped to assess his situation. He still had an untrusting inkling about Priscilla – the eerie chalked circles didn't help, either – though he could tell what she was actually wanting. Without having any control over it, lust grew inside Korin, making Priscilla's already-pretty face appear even prettier and more seductive than before, especially in the red light, which accentuated the lusty energies throbbing around.

Although he felt like he had stepped into her world at the Teloplex, the current moment seemed as though he was now completely disconnected from the reality outside. Roped into her energy, Korin took a couple of steps around the bed just as she took an equal number in the same direction. He followed on, entranced. As they circled the bed, Korin was caught up in the vortex. Priscilla then held the sticker out over the bed, and Korin finally dived for it, falling over to the other side, next to Priscilla. She was about to leap away, but Korin grabbed her leg, tripping her onto the bed. Turning around quickly, she found Korin hopping on her, grabbing the arm that held the sticker. Priscilla's panting increased, with a small amount of her breath blowing onto his face. With her free hand, she managed to grab the sticker from her ensnared hand, placing it down her breasts.

"Come on. Take it," she panted out while Korin was fully on top of her. "Pin my arms down!"

Korin wasn't sure who was pinning who down; he nevertheless clutched her arms by her side. As she lightly moaned, her legs wrapped around him, tightening and pulling his waist in. Having never been in such a position before, Korin hesitated; thoughts began to haphazardly spring forth from the well of his subconsious. He had grown up with assorted ideas crammed into his head, many being religious. Priscilla had also destabilized the already-shaky foundations of his new identity, the effect worsened by the fact that intense emotions submerged his rational mind. Like earlier, his mental vision was stained.

His frayed religious foundations made him ask, *Shit, what do I do? Is this okay? Now? What am I allowed to do? I don't know what to do!* Korin wished he had figured out such matters sooner. He then continually thought of why Priscilla was so keen on him, speculating if there were other motives.

"Come on! Ravage me!" Priscilla yelled excitedly, closing her eyes, waiting whilst Korin awkwardly thought. "Well, what are you waiting for?" she asked impatiently, opening her eyes after an emotionally-withering moment.

Korin was *still* hesitating in making a decision.

"Well?" she asked desperately, waiting even more as the excitement in her eyes dwindled and finally began dying in a wretched struggle.

Korin *still* did nothing.

"You…" Her panting both loudened and shortened in timing as she purposely tried to express her feelings. "Agh!" she groaned with great frustration. "You're so unbelievable! Get off me!" she yelled, scrunching her face bitterly.

"Look… I…" Korin muttered, unsure how to explain what was going through his mind, opting to mention something else instead. "You have to give that sticker to me."

"What?" she asked sharply. "You're thinking about the sticker? Now? Really? Just… agh!" she almost screamed. "Get off me!" She hit him, looking like she was about to cry.

Korin slowly complied, and then she hopped off the mattress as well, crossing her arms, appearing as if she'd rip out weapons from her sides. For a short while in silence, Korin tried to think of an appropriate choice of words, though he couldn't find one.

"Fine," Priscilla finally broke the silence. "You can have your stupid sticker. And that vial with your blood is on the table there."

Avoiding eye contact, Korin grabbed the sticker and the vial.

"I want you to leave. Now." Priscilla pointed to the door as she, too, avoided eye contact.

Without replying, Korin awkwardly took a few steps forward and stopped. He wanted to apologize, but he sensed that further words would've added fuel to the fire. Korin virtually felt the word 'NOW!' transuding from her furiously-closed lips and searing on the back of his neck. A few seconds after he stepped outside, the door slammed incredibly hard.

Chapter Sixteen

Infiltration: An Explosive Encounter

It was broad daylight during Korin's march of shame. The events with Priscilla rotated through his head again and again, becoming heavier with each turn, causing him to almost cry – even though the humiliation sent him into a trance every so often that made him appear like a zombie. He understood that he still had unresolved religious ideas lingering in his head and how they cluttered and hindered a proper and responsive course of action, but he was now too lost to know what he should've done. In his mentally-absorbed state, Korin barely noticed brushing past people; when he *did* notice, his responses were apathetic and sluggish.

Korin stopped plodding, finding a wall to slump next to and sit out his woes for a good half an hour. Visoring his face with his hands, Korin's presence blended into the gutters around him. At least, he considered, no-one else knew about the incident, but he anxiously hoped Priscilla wouldn't say a word about it. He concluded she wouldn't, as she was a very private person, but the thought of it being a possibility felt crushing on what little ego he had remaining. At that point, he no longer had *any* of the 'higher meaning' sentiments from the previous night left in him. Part of Korin wanted the intimate scene to have continued to its conclusion, but every time he thought about the thrilling possibilities, it depressed him even more. He had to stop thinking about it. He needed something to distract his mind. Korin glanced around, opening his senses to the world around him, hoping to see anything that could steal his focus. Assorted distractions inundated his vision, though none were strong enough to drown his sorrows.

Having missed breakfast, Korin's stomach rumbled, and the hunger didn't help his mood. When lunchtime arrived, he felt capable of 'walking' again; slowly, he made his way to the food hall, continuously thinking to himself how stupid he had been. For brief moments, he wasn't sure if he believed what had happened was real. The walk, in the end, did him enough good to make him functional within reality – sitting down would have caused him to coil in on himself.

Before entering, he finally noticed that he still had the cult symbol on his forehead, so he pulled the sticker out, placed it on, and was glad it worked immediately in ridding the tattoo. Korin tried not to think about it anymore, but he was surprised no-one had said anything about it; still, he considered that he didn't pay attention to any particular faces the people who passed him potentially made.

After grabbing some food inside, he happened to bump into his friends, so he created the visage of emotional stability – though, it was obvious that something wasn't right. *I should've just gone to bed*, Korin thought. *Damn it, it's too late. I'm here now.*

"Hey," Sylas said, nudging Korin as he sat down, "Jaimas said he saw you and Priscilla up on the halo above. That true?"

There was no point in lying. Both were exposed in the open sunlight. "Yeah… that's… correct," Korin replied embarrassedly with a hint of dreariness, thinking of a way to change the topic as he reached for a glass of water.

With a confounded expression, Sylas added, "Jaimas also said you and Priscilla were about to fall. Why on Juntas were you two up there?"

"We… just happened to be up there." Korin shrugged, taking another gulp of water, hoping almost anything would disrupt their conversation. "She was… playing around and then almost fell," he said sluggishly, dodging Sylas's unwavering vision burning through the thin veil Korin had erected.

"Wow! Well, try not to let her drag you into any more dangerous situations, man."

"Yeah, I'll definitely do that in the future. Believe me." He almost chuckled.

"You still think Priscilla's up to something bad?"

Please stop asking about her, Korin thought. "Maybe. Maybe she is. I don't know."

"Man, I wouldn't trust her. There's got to be something you can think of. Something really out of the blue. Like, this one suspicious thing that can help determine if she's actually going to fuck you over or something."

Korin curled his toes. Priscilla's passion alone for the black moon sure raised suspicions, but she wasn't 'fucking him over' – at least there was nothing he was aware of. "She's most likely up to something devious. I get it. But I don't feel like thinking it over now."

Sylas's concerned look was relentless. "It's probably best you try and think it over now before she does anything bad to you. Better safe now than sorry later."

Korin continued eating without a word, and Sylas eventually dropped the subject. Verbally. Soon, Korin felt a *little* more open about recent events. "What if... what if she has an interest in the black moon?"

"You mean, like a shadowist? The cultists we're looking for?"

"No, she's... just a general black moon practitioner."

"But does she worship it like a lunatic?"

Korin's neck stiffened. "She doesn't *worship* it... She just... *reveres* it."

Sylas was about to chuckle. "So, she worships it."

Korin couldn't look at Sylas, knowing how disconcerting it sounded. "Dude... she's a cultist."

"She's not a cultist, okay?" Korin was fatigued of the question in her defence, even though no-one had asked before.

"How do you know that? She's a perfect candidate for being in a shadowist cult. She's weird and creepy, and... and... she worships the fucking black moon!"

Moving with caution, someone abruptly approached from the table nearby. "Korin," she said, glancing around with a concerned face.

Barely able to look around with his stiffened neck, Korin glimpsed Meriel standing at the end of the table. "Meriel?"

"Yes, I need to talk to you about Priscilla."

Korin's blood felt like it had been injected with poison as he tensed up. Hoping Priscilla hadn't mentioned the earlier incident, Korin kept quiet, repeatedly saying in his mind for Meriel to leave.

"Do you know Priscilla?" Sylas asked.

"Yes. I do. About last night," she said, turning to Korin.

No, please don't go there, Korin thought.

"You said that if there was anything bothering me, I could speak to you. And yes, there is. But you need to keep this a secret. From everyone." She looked at Korin's friends.

"Hey, *we'll* keep it a secret," Terala said. "We're with Korin."

Korin then nodded, not saying anything else.

Meriel took a moment before saying, "Okay, well... it's... it's Priscilla. I'm very worried about her and what she'll do."

Terala leaned in with alarm, quietly asking, "Do you believe that she's a shadowist?"

Taking a moment to reply, Meriel said, "Yes. I... I even have proof. Shadowists usually recruit from general black moon practitioner circles. She tried to recruit me, but I refused to join."

Terala swiftly continued, "So, are these shadowists responsible for the missing students?"

"Y-yes, absolutely."

"And do they also have some part to play in all these demon attacks?"

"Oh, yes. They're definitely to blame."

"I knew it. We were right, Korin. Alright, show us the proof."

"I'll show you soon," Meriel said. "I can't talk about her plans here right now. She's... she's planning something. Something big. Tonight. Meet me at Fifty-eight Lokfer Street just before dinnertime. I need you to tell me everything you know about Priscilla. Everything. Um, this is really important, and... look, my life is in danger. She's going to kill me. But... but I have a plan."

"Alright, we will," Terala spoke for the group.

"Okay. Great. Thank you," Meriel said, leaving the food hall hastily.

"Wow. There you go, Korin," Terala said. "She's fucking messed in the head."

Korin couldn't reply. His shame transformed into disgust at how close he was to Priscilla – at how close he was to carnal intimacy! Blood rushed from his head, making him rather woozy. It was a good thing he was sitting, as he would've either fainted or at minimum taken a hard knee on the floor. He felt like every bit of Priscilla's residue left on him needed purging with extreme magic he couldn't even comprehend. Priscilla's desire for Korin made him feel even more confused than before. He also couldn't believe that he was suckered into tapping into the black moon, even though he knew it was what the shadowist cult worshiped. That part potentially sickened him the most. Still, at least his first and only ritual only *partially* connected with the black moon and whatever archetypal energy that was put forth – that much he was glad about. There was also no strong lingering sensation from the black moon other than that found in his memories, but he still felt unclean.

Korin soon curled his whole body, closing his eyes, thinking, *Yuck, yuck, yuck!*

"Hey, relax, Korin," Sylas said, patting his friend. "We'll find out what she's up to."

"I don't think it's just her, though," Terala said. "Remember, we're dealing with an entire cult here, so she'll have many cultist buddies. We'll need to be extremely careful tonight."

***

When Korin returned to his bedroom, he immediately hopped into the shower, unsure if he'd ever leave, as the water didn't wash away the endless thoughts he had of Priscilla. He imagined opening his eyes and seeing black water and slime around his feet, so he dared not open them. Korin repeatedly scrubbed his body with soap, and the bar eventually halved in size.

An hour passed.

For a brief moment, he felt a moment of psychological respite, as if some part of Priscilla was finally being purged from his system… in a certain regard. Carnally speaking, however, his task was far from over, as he still acknowledged her incredible physical attractiveness. Regardless, his thoughts over Priscilla and his growing disgust were at least turned into a passion for stopping her and any events and plans she was engaged in. Korin still feared being exposed for near-intimacy when he would confront Priscilla in front of everyone, but he believed he could either justify his actions or craftily divert the topic before his friends started asking too many questions. He hoped.

All the pieces of Priscilla's intent started forming together in Korin's mind. He smacked his head, unable to fathom how he didn't conclude that Priscilla *actually* was in The Gathering of the Black Moon – a name that he believed the modern shadowists kept due to Priscilla's use of the term. Korin definitely had his suspicions, but he kept brushing them off. He wondered why he did, and then an idea came to mind: he was under a spell or some form of hypnosis. That is, Korin already 'knew' the truth when dealing with her, but the hypnosis pushed the truth to the side. She even openly admitted to hypnotizing him; and when Korin challenged her, she told him she was merely joking. His mind, he considered, was also not in the most stable place after arriving at Teloston, and he had many other issues racing through his head, clouding his judgment. He was basically the prime candidate for recruitment into the cult.

Looking at the broader picture, he analysed Priscilla's other oddities, such as her unexplainable desire and perpetual insistence for him *and only* him; he was sure there was no-one else she chased for recruitment, as she never hung around other people. But then he realized how self-absorbed he was, only just remembering Meriel mentioning that Priscilla tried to recruit her. Nonetheless, there was no way he was ever going to join an evil cult – or any cult – especially not after his religious experiences, and Korin kept thinking hypnotically manipulating him and conditioning his desires gradually over time with potential occult magic would be the only successful way of recruiting him; it would've otherwise been futile through standard recruiting means. Priscilla even took a while to actually initiate him, and the initiation ritual itself barely answered Korin's many questions, leaving him in the dark before supposed full 'enlightenment'.

Nevertheless, Korin was angry at himself, as he considered that he should have been more aware of the subtleties of indoctrination and conditioning now that he was free from his religion. Indeed, he affirmed to himself in his first academic week that he would *never* let it happen again. He even remembered Sylas humorously saying how fanatics sometimes used sexual means to sway people to their cause. Furthermore, Korin recalled Professor Finch mentioning how some cults recruited: usually, a single member would reach a potential candidate and then either condition them or bait their true intents. Given that the shadowists were small in numbers – at least compared to the whole student population – recruiting would naturally have been done one-on-one, he supposed, and so it was not like she would've tried to recruit many people at any one time.

Korin felt like he was trapped in an endless cycle of indoctrination, escape, and more indoctrination – escaping from Priscilla being the latest. Interestingly, *he* was the one who had to roleplay the cultist Priscilla escaped from; he now recognized the purpose of such a 'game'. Even some of Priscilla's books detailed various manipulations, such as her hardback on sex magic. Korin also just learned from Sylas that Vornara was a mythical succubus devoted to chaos; he didn't find it surprising Priscilla had a book on such a being.

It all made sense to him now.

After another hour of virtually meditating in the shower, his earthy depression instantly converted into uplifting fumes, which fuelled his determination to stop Priscilla, shortly igniting and making him explode with energy. He went down to the common room underneath the dorm block, using the punching bag until he was ready to leave. Korin was ablaze, his inner fire blasting all over the room.

***

Fifty-eight Lokfer Street was located in the Private District. Construction tools and surveying equipment lay rusting on the barren lawn, while the modern house's interior featured unpainted concrete and plastered walls blemished with water stains. A great deal of rubbish was stuffed and clogged in cracks and holes, partnering appropriately with an assortment of lowbrow graffiti from the most juvenile of students.

Korin had convinced Celine to come, and the gang of four waited in the entrance hall, expecting Meriel to soon show up. After a few minutes, Korin decided to call out for Meriel, hearing nothing in return.

"This better not be a prank," Sylas said.

"There's no way this is a prank," Korin responded. "I just know it."

"Well, it's something *I* would do." Sylas giggled. "Sorry. I know. It's not the time for laughing."

"Let's check the place out," Terala said.

Everyone walked through the house, finally seeing Meriel's body hanging in multiple segments on hooks connected to a steel frame. Her insides were dangling out of her body, while fresh blood echoingly dripped on the floor. The jaw was sprawled over the ground, whereas Meriel's mutilated face remained open, as if a disfigured zombie, ready to attack. Korin, Terala, and Sylas gasped while Celine screamed, bursting into tears a few seconds later before dropping to the ground and curling up. Terala immediately started tuning into the Aether, deciding to scout the place for hostiles, while Korin stared at the body, paralysed with jamming emotions.

He thought back to Evelyn, knowing she could've looked just like Meriel. His stomach consequently whirled before he felt like erupting at any second, filling the room with the same dripping substance in front of him. Although, instead of blood, it was his warm, unprocessed lunch, spurting out as he dropped to one knee. Hard. Sylas puked as well, almost as if the vomiting was contagious, while Celine was too far outside reality to even notice. Terala returned, informing the group that no-one was in sight, although none of her friends paid any attention.

Korin's imagination got the better of him as he vividly and involuntarily visualized the priests hacking Evelyn's body to pieces. He opened his eyes and swiftly turned around, just in case a priest was right behind him. Hallucinatory temple walls emerged from the ground, as if resurrecting from ashen, detrital crypts, crumbling stone on the way and rising high into a reddened, stormy sky. The walls shifted and warped in dimensions, inflating as if possessing an ego of some sickly kind – its energy exerting and pressurizing all around him. Twisted religious symbols burnt into his mind as chaotic fires erupted, scorching the entirety of his surroundings in a possessed rage. Evelyn powerlessly and eerily floated in front, holding her hand out in terror as she begged Korin to help her. He shakily reached out for her, but she was instantly pulled away into the dark, infinite expanse as she screamed reverberatingly, causing the shiver which ran up Korin's spine to feel like the long cut of a cursed knife.

Korin was then left to sit in blackened despair when the hallucination ended, mentally alone with nothing but haunted feelings. He eventually managed to re-establish the fact that he was now at the university, away from the troubles he had escaped from.

"Are you alright?" Terala asked again as Korin slowly stood up.

"I'm fine." Korin bobbed his head, still shaking. "Just give me two seconds." He breathed deeply, fully regaining his state of mind before looking over at Celine.

When Korin bent down to aid Celine, she thrashed about, yelling, "Go away!" She then resumed crying, turning her head away and hiding under her flailing arms.

"Celine, we have to leave." Korin held her. "You don't want to be next to the body."

Celine opened her eyes and took another glimpse at the remains, bursting out once more. Facepalming himself for even mentioning the body, Korin then tried to persuade her to move, but she continued yelling. While unsure what to do, he kept his eyes averted from the body, lest he have visions again. After five minutes, Celine's senselessness dwindled through fatigue, allowing Korin to help her move outside. She eventually came to her senses.

"I've never seen anything like that before," Celine finally said. "I'm really sorry for yelling at you." She tried to smile, but salt-filled tears saturated her lips, making her wipe continuously.

"It's alright," Korin responded empathetically. "I was pretty shaken up, too. Look, we should get moving."

"Okay." Celine wiped away her remaining tears, standing up unsteadily with Korin's help. "Again, I'm s-so sorry." She cried again.

It seemed Celine was trapped in an infinite loop she couldn't escape. Korin had to be more assertive this time, telling her robustly that she would be all right. In a short time, Celine managed to stand again. In her unstable mental state, she repeatedly flattened the crumpled frills on her dress as a subconscious method of trying to find stability through repetition and distraction.

Terala returned after another scouting. "Hey, guys, I found a trail of blood. I think we need to follow this immediately."

"Good finding, Terala," Korin responded. "We'll definitely follow it. I also just realized something: Not only did Meriel say that something big was going to happen tonight, but I recall Priscilla," he said, gulping with abhorrence, "I recall Priscilla saying the same thing."

"Then we better take off as soon as possible."

"I'm not sure if I want to go," Celine said softly, sitting down again.

Korin understood Celine needed time, but the sunlight was waning rapidly. Celine's fragility – especially at that point – made Korin cautious about what he'd say to motivate her. Taking into consideration that she sobered up, Korin believed she would be fine, granting her another moment.

"Celine, are you ready to come with us now?" Korin at last asked when Celine stood up.

"I don't know," she replied faintly. "I think I need some time to myself."

"C'mon, Celine," Terala almost shouted. "We need to stop this psychotic bitch; and the rest of the cultists, too. *And* we're about to find out what's happened to the missing students. We need to do this."

"Yeah, we need your help," Sylas added. "Korin can't keep awake if he chucks up too much," he said jocularly.

"Yeah." Korin smiled, rolling his eyes. "They're right." He looked at Celine, holding her warmly while rubbing her shoulder. "Celine, it's okay. You don't *have* to come with us, but we sure *will* need your help. There are many people counting on us. I don't think you should be afraid. We're a team, and we've survived other ordeals. Remember the storm at camp? That was devastating, and yet we survived. Then there was the hillbilly. I not only would've died from that rock trap, but that... thing would have killed us and perhaps eaten us if it weren't for you. We couldn't have survived without you. We need you, Celine."

"Yeah," Sylas and Terala agreed simultaneously, moving closer to Celine.

Celine's eyes watered as she held back tears. The group comforted her for a few minutes, losing focus on the situation at hand. Celine cried uncontrollably, unable to stand without the full assistance of her friends. Warm tears spread to everybody's clothes.

After a while, Celine croaked, "Thank you for the support." She then paused. "Alright, I'll come." She nodded, wiping away her last tears. "I don't want anything bad to happen to anyone. Especially not you guys."

"Great." Korin smiled as the sun fully set. "Let's go and find these cultists."

Just before leaving, Korin espied a pen on the ground. He bent over to examine it, noticing that it looked just like Priscilla's – a grey stone pen with a gargoyle head, its tail curled round the pen's body. It had a bit of blood on it, and Korin considered that Priscilla would've stabbed Meriel once before using other bigger equipment to fully chop her up. He wiped the blood off with a nearby rag before clutching it hard with anger.

***

The trail of blood was more of an inconsistent dotted line that followed a footpath to another property in the Private District. The letterbox read, '36 Harcon St'. A concrete fence cloaked the garden, except for a few large trees crowding the view of the two-storey building. No-one was in sight as Korin and his party effortlessly entered the front gate – although, anyone could've seen them from within the building. Wild grass covered the edifice's foundations; many of its grotty, pale bricks were smashed in, chunks laying bare on the ground covered in foliage. Sneaking from one tree to another, the uncamouflaged four reached one of the windows stencilled with grime, jolting it open with a few shoves. Everybody was fully connected to the Aether in preparation; and while they had the opportunity to use gamma-positive shields that granted near invisibility, it wasn't suitable for the context, not only because of how it would make users blind to everything outside of their shields, but also because the camouflage would only last a few seconds at novice levels before needing to recharge.

The first room was dark, though a moody lamp lit the area ahead. Korin gave a few hand signals as the others cautiously moved toward the next room. As the group crept, Sylas accidentally stepped on a shard of glass, crumpling it shrilly under his foot. He carefully lifted his leg away from it, but there happened to be smaller shards still stuck to his sole, crinkling again when he placed his foot down. Sylas looked at his friends, who fearfully froze, waiting for him to mime 'sorry'.

As soon as Sylas did, a tinny material abruptly hit the ground in another room, instantly alerting the group that they weren't alone. At once, they each readied a different type of ultrachite shield and proceeded onwards, forming into a cluster with their backs together; Korin took the lead, Terala and Celine the sides, and Sylas the rear. Stepping out of the room, each attentively scanned the vicinity.

The moody light suddenly flicked off.

In their panic, everyone flinched, waiting for another incident. There was nothing. As all four tiptoed on, their clothes rubbed and shuffled, penetrating the surrounding silence. A scant amount of moonlight entered, though it wasn't enough to help the group distinguish anything beyond a mere metre. Another rattling noise triggered them to almost jump, but nobody could see any movement. Sylas soon, however, noticed an unusual glimmer, so he fired an alpha-negative blast ball at the location, sending what sounded like a human body to the wall. Abruptly, numerous blasts of bright and rapid ultrachite discharges fired right next to Korin before hitting the wall behind him. Immediately, he and his team ducked, finding cover behind a long desk with a back panel; alpha-negative discharges then thudded against the desk, pushing it back, but the movement swiftly eased down when the group's shields reduced the class-based effects with their inhibitors.

"Find the lights!" Korin shouted, only to notice moonlight shining off a knife about to strike him.

With nerves of steel, Korin swiftly dodged the attack before grabbing the attacker's leg and tripping him over. Grunting with a male voice, the cloaked assailant snagged the dropped knife, reaching over to jab at Korin, who grabbed the knife-wielder's arm, holding off the strike with his strength.

"Don't shoot this way!" Korin quickly shouted to his friends, as he and the attacker were frantically moving about, where Korin could have easily been hit instead. "Keep firing above the desk!"

Reluctantly, Korin's friends continued blindfiring over the desk at unidentifiable targets, providing enough cover for Korin, who managed to push the attacker up. Korin then slipped, *just* missing the next knife attack that naturally passed through his shield. As a result, Korin accidentally smashed into glass jars on the desk. Fortunately, no shards cut him. He used his free leg to kick the psycho, creating a painful-sounding moan, guessing he hit his groin. Korin wanted to shoot the guy, but he remembered learning that when it came to knife fights, multiple stabbings could occur way before a defender could even overload the other's shield. Nevertheless, now with a free opportunity, Korin was able to properly concentrate a supercharged melee attack and overload the opponent's shield in one punch. Subsequently, Korin simply used beta-negative blasts to knock him unconscious.

Korin then joined his friends in the firefight, registering for the first time that they didn't know exactly where they were firing. Since the blast balls were only luminescent light, they didn't radiate enough light to brighten the whole area, so it was still relatively dark in the room. The glass jars were now in the direct line of fire, and a few were shot, crashing to the ground around Korin.

"I swear we have to be hitting something!" Terala called out.

"You just hit a window!" Sylas responded.

"No, she didn't," Korin replied, shaking off glass. "Keep firing!"

"Do you know if I've hit anyone?" Celine asked Korin as she remained in cover.

"Don't know," he replied. "It doesn't matter. Just keep firing, and you'll hold them off."

"Ah, shit, I'm overloaded again!" Sylas shouted, staying fully in cover as he waited a good seven seconds for his discharge aura to cool down before firing again. Just when he recovered, Sylas activated his phid, *somewhat* lighting up the area.

"Turn it off!" Korin quickly reacted. "It's revealing too much of us."

"Fine," Sylas replied, "but I swear I'd otherwise be able to get some good shots in."

More and more discharges began to tunnel through the desk at the quantum level, hitting Terala's shield. They also happened to be alpha-positive this time instead of alpha-negative; and since the previous discharges had already overstimulated Terala's shield's inhibitors, the current ones fully pulled her into the desk's back panel.

"Shit, I can't get out!" Terala cried out.

Korin managed to pull Terala away from the back panel, and fortunately no more alpha-negative discharges hit it, so the desk wasn't pushed back as a result of Terala's absence of pushing against it. In her rage, however, Terala stood up to shoot, but more alpha-positive discharges hit her, depleting her of energy as well as magnetically lifting her in to the air towards the attackers. Terala, however, swiftly clutched on to the desk before she was fully pulled back.

"Quick, grab her!" Korin shouted as he and the others pulled Terala back behind the desk.

But just before an unshielded Terala returned to their cover, a yellow blast ball hit her. "Ah! I'm being zapped!" She flailed around in pain.

"Stop moving!" Sylas called out. "It's making it worse."

"Right, I forgot." Terala attempted to restrain her movements in order to keep the electric shocks to a minimum for the next few seconds. She struggled, grabbing herself tightly. While she stopped moving for the most part, the yellow attack was actually intended to overload Terala's shield; but funnily enough, her shield was gone due to her being depleted, so the attacker's discharge was mostly pointless.

"Should we do the same thing to them?" Celine asked.

"No, I have a plan," Korin said. "Celine, focus on shooting delta-positive to home in on them and keep them occupied so they don't move. Sylas, you focus on trying to pull their covers away from them — even if it means you only slightly move them. Terala, just wait until your energy recovers; I'll get your help shortly. Meanwhile, I'll sneak around and hit them with gamma to hopefully overload them."

Celine immediately began shooting; she didn't have to be accurate, as the homing effect caused the attackers to stop moving so much, and that's all that really mattered for Korin's plan. Sylas peeked around the side of the desk, seeing how a large chair was used as cover for one guy. Sylas managed to pull the chair away from his opponent to a degree, and when Korin snuck closer, he had a good line of fire, where he shot a few gamma-positive discharges, soon overloading the person's shield. Immediately, Korin switched to beta-negative and shot the guy a couple of times to knock him unconscious. Korin couldn't believe his luck with his gamma-positive blasts succeeding so quickly, hoping his streak would continue.

Korin then snuck back to the desk, asking "Terala, you should have enough energy now, right?"

"Yeah, I think I have enough now."

"Good. Provide me with cover fire while I get even closer. I think the others are a little further away. I need a better angle."

"Alright, got you."

Korin peeped around the side of the desk, seeing no-one in sight. He then crawled forwards, finding himself behind some other overturned furniture. As he glanced out again, a couple of shots were made his way, so he remained behind cover until Terala began firing to clear the path. Korin then snuck up slightly closer, noting that three more attackers remained. Sylas again managed to drag two covers away, causing two of the opponents to hastily move; this then allowed the homing discharges to hit them. With the opponents now with weakened shields, Terala finished off overloading one shield before shooting her opponent unconscious. Korin, meanwhile, was able to shoot a few gamma blasts in, overloading the other guy's shield as well with quick success again. However, it overloaded his shield as well, and Korin no longer had the opportunity to forthrightly knock him unconscious.

"Crap," Korin murmured, remaining in cover. "Quick, Terala, finish him off!"

Terala knew what to do, intuiting Korin wasn't able to move. She jumped up on to the desk, having a good view of the room. She then managed to shoot some beta-negative discharges at the second last person, instantly knocking them unconscious.

Korin then believed that one person remained, so he bolted forth before quickly charging a DMA. When he turned a corner, he punched the last person, overloading the shield instantly. Korin then shot the person unconscious.

At that point, Korin and his friends weren't sure whether they had actually defeated everyone, so they waited in cover for a bit longer to see or hear anything in particular. The wait seemed endless, and Terala's apprehensive hand let off a blast at nothing, triggering the whole group to fire as well.

"There's nothing there!" Korin shortly called out. "Relax. I think they're finished."

Sylas acknowledged the reality of the situation, but he let off another blast – just to be sure. Korin merely gave a 'why?' expression, which nobody could see.

"Well, you never know," Sylas intuitively replied to Korin's countenance.

After two minutes, everyone stood up. Celine hit the light switches, and they all saw their adversaries, including the mess around them. It was apparent that the attackers were students, due to their youthful appearance, though no-one knew their identities. The knife wielder was also wearing a shadowist necklace.

"Shadowists," Korin said gravely. "And I don't think they're larpers. We're definitely at the right place."

"But where's Priscilla?" Sylas asked, lifting a cultist's arm with his foot.

"Perhaps she's yet to arrive. Or maybe she left earlier. There's bound to be more of them."

"We haven't checked the whole place yet," Sylas said. "Could she be upstairs?"

"I doubt it. We made enough noise to alert anyone. Let's have a look around first, and then we'll wait, ambushing them when they come. Oh, and shoot the bodies a few more times to make sure they're completely out for at least eight hours."

After they shot the bodies, Korin said to simply leave them where they lay. In the next large room, everyone spread out, examining the ordinary utensils and decorations, dumbfounded they didn't notice anything incriminating or cultish. However, Korin shortly spotted a hidden door behind what looked to be a moved cabinet jutting out slightly from the wall.

"Hey, come over here, guys." Korin motioned. "I have a feeling I know where this goes."

"Missing students?" Terala asked, with Korin nodding back.

The thick, soundproof door opened to a stairwell with sound absorbers above. As if they were nourished by a source of energy below, the cracks in the walls swelled the deeper the stairs descended. Despite the murky haze, a bright light radiated from a giant toroidal crystal inside a machine at the bottom of the deep basement. Sure enough, there were also prison cells; only a tenth of the hundred was occupied, though. Shadowist symbols also decorated the walls, overlooking the room as if exercising a conscious energy. The stench of sweat and body odour intensified the further they walked down the stairs; the most overwhelming factor, however, was actually the despair in the air.

In his shock, Korin almost slipped when he saw the missing students. Two of the prisoners were shaking their heads repeatedly, muttering to themselves incomprehensively. Another two were picking fights with imaginary monsters, grappling the air; one even somersaulted. There was another person who kept walking into the cell walls, already looking like the dead with a face covered in bruises. Four students could barely move, malnourished to the point where they were basically skin and bones. The last student was curled up on his bed, rocking back and forth, attempting to block out the noises.

Korin let out a lamenting murmur, quietly saying, "This is worse than I imagined."

"We have to release them now," Terala said, aghast and angry.

"But most are crazy," Sylas rebutted apprehensively. "What if they attack us?"

"Yeah, we might have to leave them until we get the police to arrive," Korin replied before cautiously approaching the cells.

When he glanced back at the stairs, Korin saw Celine quivering with her eyes shut. Immediately, he returned to her, and she opened her eyes, giving him a 'get-me-out-of-here' look. Celine's shock and fear blocked her from crying, but Korin wasn't sure how long she'd manage to keep her emotions under control – and if she would even stay in the building.

"We'll only be a short while," Korin assured Celine. "Wait here, and don't look at anyone."

"I really want to help." Celine grimaced.

"Just keep watch and warn us if any more cultists come."

"Alright," she said, taking point at the top of the stairs.

Korin, Terala, and Sylas slowly examined one prisoner after another, with all the crazy ones approaching the bars.

"We'll come back for you when we get help," Korin stated firmly to the prisoners.

"Curse you!" one insane student yelled, banging his head against a bar until it bled. "I'll kill you when I get out!"

Korin winced, wondering if the bars would even hold. "Wow." He looked at his friends. "The thin ones probably won't be able to walk, so they'll have to wait as well."

"Just remember that something bad is about to happen tonight," Terala said. "We probably don't have long before other cultists arrive. Either we hurry and tell the police now, or we best bunker down and hold off whoever arrives."

"You're right. Shit." Korin took ten seconds to think. "We'll deal with the cultists. We don't want to risk losing these guys."

"Hey, there's someone way over there." Sylas pointed to the last missing student, who had just appeared at the bars.

At the end of one of the rows, the last student seemed normal enough, despite being utterly agitated. Korin knew they had little time left, but he wanted to acquire information before doing anything, just in case it could be of help.

"Who are you?" Korin asked warily.

"Please, don't let me out yet," the young male said tiredly, hunching over with crossed, shaking arms.

"What? Why not? Are you sick?" Korin took a step back.

"In a way, yes. Th-there's a demon attached to me."

Korin took two large steps back, glancing at Sylas and Terala, who followed suit.

"It's okay," the prisoner said. "You're safe while I'm in here. I'm… I'm Darsan, by the way."

"Alright, Darsan, how did you get possessed?" Korin asked. "Can we help you?"

"I hope you can. An-anyway, th-they did this to me. The ones who wear the moon symbols. They're called shadowists. I'm in control for the moment, but when the demon comes, it takes over."

Korin had too many questions, deciding to re-ask, "But how did you get possessed?"

"The shadowists captured me in the middle of the night. I was taken to their base. I… I don't know where it is."

"So, this isn't their base?" Terala asked, looking around with surprise, seeing lots of shadowist symbols and experimentation equipment.

"No, The Gathering –"

"Of the Black Moon," Korin rapidly said.

"Yes, well, that's wh-what I overheard them calling their cult." Darsan coughed. "I also remember overhearing them talk about someone called Backlevy. Grand Sorceress Backlevy. I vaguely remember reading some history on the topic here before being abducted."

"So, they even kept the name. I *knew* the cult had been resurrected all along." Korin clenched his fist. "I'm so glad that wisp showed me that journal," he said to Sylas and Terala before turning back to Darsan. "Please, go on, sorry."

"But that's just the name the shadowists call themselves here at Teloston Uni. Shadowists call themselves by different names elsewhere."

"What do you know about shadowists in other places?"

"Nothing much. I never overheard the cultists here making any contact with th-those outside of Teloston. While I'm unsure, it's still possible they contact one another."

"I see… Anyway, you mentioned something about their base."

"Yes, that's right; this isn't their base. The Gathering uses this basement for their experiments on us, with many powered by that machine with the huge crystal there. They haven't moved it, so they bring us here when they need to run certain experiments."

So how did you get possessed? Korin thought impatiently.

"They don't bring everyone here, of course; the majority of the missing students are used for other purposes. I don't know exactly what they're doing, but I know the shadowists conduct rituals during the lunapexes. They use the missing students in addition to freshly captured ones for one n-night only."

One night? Korin almost blurted out, remembering Priscilla wanting to capture the research scientist for one night before releasing her. *Oh, God… she was going to be one of these victims.*

Darsan coughed horribly, provoking a few grimaces. "As for me, well… the rituals are really dark, and it seems that demons are attracted to them. A few people get possessed, I think as a by-product of whatever The Gathering is doing."

"You say 'by-product'. Does the cult, in any way, mess with the spirits?" Korin asked.

"I don't know, but I don't think so. Possession isn't their intention. Instead, it's the techniques in the rituals – and the rituals themselves – that seem to greatly increase the chances of possession. It's pretty intense stuff. Not something most mages can normally do. Anyway, after finishing a ritual, the shadowists chuck most of the one-nighters back into the uni after wiping their memories."

Shivers shook through the uncaged three.

"Unluckily for me, they decided to keep me around for experiments. At least my memory wasn't wiped. Although, sometimes I wish it was."

"God, I wonder how many of the possessed are walking among us," Korin muttered before quickly wondering if the research scientist had been a victim for one night at an earlier point.

"Again, not many get possessed, but I think quite a lot of people are taken in for the lunapexes. Probably over a hundred each time. This…" Darsan coughed heavily, blood hitting the ground. "This… all of this, keep in mind, is only from what I overheard and glimpsed, so I'm not sure about the whole situation here."

With the persistent thought of catching a disease from breathing too much, Sylas asked, "So, how are you able to keep the demon at bay, then?"

"Demons latch on to people but can't control them twenty-four hours a day. They need to recharge – like how we need sleep."

"What about the cultists?" Korin asked. "Are they possessed?"

"No, they greatly protect themselves during the rituals, so they don't get possessed." Darsan scratched his hair, and a few flakes of weird grime floated to the ground, causing Sylas to rapidly cover his mouth while rumpling his face. "We even had a professor come in here for a bit. He was possessed, too."

"Wait, was this Professor Marenov Khastanian?" Terala asked.

"Yes, I think that was his name. Rather large guy?"

"Yeah, what happened to him?"

"They ran a few experiments on him, and then as they were transferring him out of here, he managed to escape, grabbing some stuff on the way. Not sure what ensued after that."

"We found him dead in a ditch," Terala said. "His body was completely fucked up."

"Hmm… that seems strange. The cult wouldn't leave a body lying around, as they make good use of all bodies. Maybe it was the demon."

"That would make sense if it was," Korin said, thinking that the cult wouldn't have easily ruined their scapegoat like that. He then wondered why Meriel's body was left in the open before returning his thoughts to Khastanian. "What stuff did he grab, by the way?"

"I think he just grabbed a handful of random things from the table; for evidence maybe – basically, whatever he could hold; but he dropped most of it on the way while escaping. I remember seeing a shadowist necklace and something else left in his hand when he was at the top of the stairs."

"Huh…" Korin paused. "Maybe that was the same necklace we saw near his body. Hmm…" He then began thinking of what happened to the research scientist before jumping to other topics. "So, even though you say you don't know exactly what the cult is doing, surely you've theorized what their motivations are?"

"I have, but it's too hard to really say. I think power, ultimately." Darsan paused. "Wait!" he shouted before coughing, as if choking and gargling acid, struggling to continue standing.

"Please, what else?" Korin's heart thudded rapidly.

With a croaky voice, Darsan replied, "They're planning a big ritual on the Midfire Lunapex. Something to do with the plasmanaries being aligned in a certain way. There'll be sacrifices involved. But again, I'm sorry, I don't know where their base is. However, I think I know what may help you. See the etheric data analyser there?" He pointed to a fist-sized device on the table, components scattered around it. "The cultists use the EDA to help with their experiments, and they even collect data on themselves. The last time they used it, they were talking about how – um, I think because of all the rituals or something similar… I'm not sure – they generally have a unique energy signature around them, which flares up during the lunapexes. When aimed at a target, the EDA will light up, indicating whatever energy codes are saved in it."

"So, we could basically identify the cultists and then follow them to their base," Korin noted. "Right?"

"Yes. The trouble is, it's broken, and it would most likely be locked, too. And it's not like it'll be totally accurate, either, as EDAs are never perfect."

"We'll find a way to fix and use it." Korin carefully picked the device up, being vigilant not to allow the shattered pieces inside to fall on the ground. "Anyway, have you seen someone called Priscilla come down here?" He grabbed the additional components.

Thinking hard, Darsan said, "I don't recall that name. Sorry. There are many cultists, and most don't even come here."

"She might be using a pseudonym, anyway." A few hypotheticals then popped into his mind. "Hmm, what about someone called –"

"Oh, no!" Darsan howled out. "I can feel its presence." He trembled, moaning with abnormal pain. "There's one… very… important… thing to know." He heaved, holding his head tightly as Korin anticipated the information like a dying man waiting for a drop of water to emerge from a near-empty bottle. "The reason…" He screamed in pain. "The reason…" His body violently started to shake. "The r-r-rea-son… er… agh!" He shook uncontrollably.

Darsan finally let out a demonic roar and dashed around the cell like a maniac, banging his body against the walls and bloodying himself in the process. The paling body shortly stopped moving, while his head creepily dangled, facing the ground. In the eerie silence, Korin and his friends braced themselves – despite Darsan not physically transforming.

Darsan's head then menacingly shot up, blackened eyes deathly staring at the group. "You cannot take him from me now," the demon spoke through Darsan's settled body.

"Oh, great," Terala whined. "Here we go. Let's get the fuck out of here."

"Hey, guys," Celine interrupted timidly. "The cultists are here."

"No, no, no," the demon replied in an impish manner. "You're all alone."

"Right." Sylas snorted. "Like we're going to listen to a demon."

"You'll regret ignoring me!" It rapidly banged against the bars, startling everyone.

"Let's go. C'mon." Terala motioned. "I've seen enough demons for a while."

"Wait!" Korin yelled. "We can learn a few things. You go upstairs, but I'm asking it a few questions."

Terala grabbed her head, frustrated at Korin's contextually-questionable inquisitiveness. After a disagreeable moment, Terala left the basement with Sylas and Celine, preparing for the cultists.

Korin turned back to the grinning demon. "What's *your* stake in this? Why are you possessing students?"

"No-one is possessing anyone." It tried to hold back laughter.

"Seriously, why are you doing this? If you don't tell me, I'll leave. That's right, no more fun for you."

"Hm." The demon pressed Darsan's face through the bars, glaring at Korin. "A signal emerged, and I raced for it. You physical creatures and your naughty rituals are a blessing," it hissed out with a slightly-skewed head. "I don't care who it is. A body is a body."

Korin squinted. "What force do you work for?"

"I don't work for any force. I'm just here to have fun. Don't you want to play?" It reached through the bars, trying to grab Korin.

Knowing he was unlikely to obtain any further information of note, Korin backed away with a glare before racing up the stairs. As Korin left, the demon screamed, wrecking Darsan's vocal cords.

A firefight had already begun with a new wave of cultists, and there was only one dim lamp in the background providing just enough light to see things; naturally, the ultrachite shooting by added its own light, but it was limited in range. Korin took aim from the basement door, while his friends were behind nearby furniture, firing at the cultists positioned at the room's entrances. He noticed that the cultists they had taken down earlier were still unconscious on the floor, so it certainly was a new wave of cultists. Having a greater advantage than last time, Korin fired one blast ball after another, causing his discharge aura to overload in a few seconds. The cultists even managed to shoot his shield a few times – but not enough to build enough effects to affect him greatly, nor overload his shield.

Suddenly, a visible, gaseous wave of energy exploded from one of the rooms, prompting everyone to stop shooting. All sorts of items blew in their direction, in addition to bits of the edifice's structure. Flames then emerged, eating the walls and ceiling in the adjacent room at an alarming rate. The conscious cultists fired a few more times, but once the flames entered the main room, they began fleeing, shouting on the way. With the area free from hostiles, Korin exited his safe spot, looking around to see if there was anything that could be done to stop the fire. Just behind him, the ceiling gave way, caving lumps of timber and debris, blocking the basement with a furious fire.

"We need to leave!" Terala yelled, shielding herself from a wave of fire.

Korin stared at the blockage, knowing he couldn't remove it and help the students underneath in time. He also understood that ultrachite soaker bombs – which he had barely practiced using – were made of a liquid that were not good at extinguishing fires; even delta-negative vortices, he believed, wouldn't help much against such a fire. His shields, too, would be incinerated super fast if they went through the fire. The surrounding furniture was now alight, smoking vast, horrible fumes, significantly diminishing their vision. Terala grabbed a motionless Korin, dragging him two metres before he knew he had to escape.

All the entrances were now blocked, except for one, which led to a seemingly dead-end room. Fortunately, windows were present, and the group rushed for their lives, clumsily diving out of one and onto the coarse grass. A piece of Korin's clothing had been singed from the heat, but no-one caught fire. Unbeknownst to them, there were numerous dangerous chemicals in the basement, staging the next explosion, which blew pieces of brick and timber through the air.

"Run!" Korin shouted as chunks of debris flew over their heads.

The noise was enough to alert most of the university. Bricks that had been shot high up were now falling down, ramming hard into the ground, some instantly digging in, a few bouncing and shattering along the way, and others tumbling and skimming like rocks over a pond. Everybody jumped and rolled away, nearly being nicked multiple times. Capable of entering his shield due to its relative speed, one brick landed a centimetre from Korin's groin.

"Oh, man!" Korin let out with relief. "Let's get out of here before anyone sees us."

Exiting the property was simple enough; the group kept to the shadows as they sprinted, crept, and ducked through the streets, avoiding detection. They had no intended destination other than somewhere non-suspicious; and once winding back to the Central Hub, everybody was safe from any suspicions, despite panting and looking overly worried. With their minds overwhelmed, no-one said anything for a couple of minutes until they caught their breaths.

Celine sniffled. "We… we left all those sick people back there, and… they're… dead now."

"I know, but there was nothing we could do," Korin remarked, irked at his lack of choice.

"Not to mention the cultists still on the ground," Sylas added.

"The cultists are the ones who did it all!" Terala stated earnestly. "Not our fault in the slightest."

"I'm not sure if the cultists were responsible for the fire, though," Sylas said. "They seemed surprised as well, with what they were shouting and all. It sounded like a gas explosion."

"Possibly," Korin said. "Maybe they left a stove on or something. I wonder… I wonder if Priscilla was in the second wave of cultists." With scattered emotions, he was unable to comment on her further. "Hey, are you alright, Celine?"

"I'll be fine," Celine answered, sadness engraved on her face.

"Should we inform anyone about this?" Sylas asked.

Korin considered his options for a moment, palming his head. "We're in the same situation as before – we don't have any proof. If we *do* report what we saw, then we'll screw ourselves over, as the blame could easily be placed on us for many reasons – especially now since the authorities are a bit suspicious of me. And…" He sighed. "I haven't even told you guys what happened to me last night. I'll… explain later. Anyway, even Meriel is a little problematic."

"Her body should still be there," Terala said.

"Right. Well, hopefully. Still, I think in order to avoid suspicion, we could just tip the police off anonymously. Does anyone have any ideas on how that could be done?"

"I think I can do something," Sylas replied. "Leave it to me."

"Great. Thanks, Sylas. At least there's one positive here: we now know more about the cult and the missing students." Korin abruptly stopped talking as multiple groups of people passed by – quite a few talking about the explosion.

"Well, there's no need to tip them off about the fire now," Terala said. "Just Meriel."

Korin said, "Yeah, but it looks like we'll have to discuss more elsewhere, as there are too many ears here."

Chapter Seventeen

The Aftermath and the Math

"At least we know what's happening now," Korin said to his friends as they all left the food hall. "Hey, had we recorded what we saw, would that have been sufficient proof?"

"Nope," Sylas answered. "Because people are able to produce fake content with perfect graphics, any recorded material only warrants investigations, not prosecutions."

"Right. I see. Alright, well, even though the EDA – if we can get it fixed – will only work during the lunapexes, our priority from here will still be to search for any signs of cultist activity."

"At any rate, we know Priscilla is involved," Sylas added.

"I know. I know. I'll –" Korin rubbed his face, as if he had just woken up. "I'll confront her personally."

"What? Why personally? Are you two secretly in a relationship?" Sylas chuckled.

"No." Korin's face began turning red; fortunately, Jaimas approached the group to interrupt.

"Hey, where were you, man?" Jaimas asked Sylas. "You were meant to come and see the performance. It was fucking epic!"

"Oh, crap. Sorry, I forgot about it," Sylas replied before glancing over at Korin, who slowly shook his head, prompting Sylas to remember that he had to keep their knowledge of the cult a secret – especially from Jaimas, considering that he was a *loud*mouth. "I, um… I was at a… debate. A… political debate," he lied, looking from side to side. "Yep, I love my… uh, politics."

There was silence – awkward silence.

"You didn't go to a political debate." Jaimas squinted. "You did something… something secretive. Probably a secret meeting with a secret group in a secret hideout, secretly telling all sorts of secrets to secretly secret your secrets. Hmm."

"Oh, no. It-it's not like that." Sylas tried to suppress a smile.

"Yeah, I'm on to you guys. Especially you, Sally." Jaimas nodded at Celine.

"It's… Celine," she corrected him softly.

"Oi, Jaimas, you dick!" a nearby mate of his called out. "You coming?"

"I'll catch you guys later," Jaimas said, giving Korin's group an 'I've-got-my-eyes-on-you' gesture before lumbering away.

"Great," Korin muttered, "now we have to deal with Jaimas potentially spying on us."

"He'll probably forget," Sylas said. "And don't worry about Jaimas forgetting your name, Celine. That's just Jaimas."

"It's okay," Celine said. "I'll probably send him something later with my name on it. He'll definitely remember, then."

"Hey, look, I'll see you guys later," Korin abruptly said, quickly taking off to see Priscilla.

Korin knew his friends wanted to ask him questions about Priscilla, but he wasn't going to stop, feeling as though they'd be able to determine what was going on. He considered confronting her was the best option, because telling the police would've been problematic on his end, potentially embroiling him in the case of Meriel's death. Moreover, if he tipped the police off anonymously, then all he would have really said was 'she did it', with no sufficient evidence. Even the pen wasn't evidence, as Korin could've simply stolen the pen and dipped it in Meriel's blood; he kind of regretted taking it, and it was too late to place it back at the scene. Besides, Korin knew he'd end up interacting with Priscilla, anyway, through his Alchemy class.

The closer he approached Priscilla's sanctuary, the more intense his memories and imaginations became. The pure cringe swamped him, in turn causing his every movement to slow.

Oh, God, what am I doing? Korin thought. *I should probably see her later.*

Half his mind was still thinking of Priscilla *before* he heard what Meriel had to say, while the other half saw Priscilla as an evil monster, serving a perverted cult. Despite what Korin was told, the former half existed because of the passionate emotions he felt around her, making him incapable of thinking straight. He had to keep telling himself that it was artificially induced – at least to a degree, as she was objectively beautiful, after all – and that she intended to lure him into a sexual ritual to recruit him into the cult.

When Korin arrived at the gate at the bottom of the clock tower, he noticed a padlock. He wasn't surprised. Staring at it a few feet away, deliberating what to do, the sunlight on his face vanished. He turned around, seeing Priscilla standing at the top of the stairs, scowling intensely, as if she had replaced the power of the sun with another force.

"Why are you here?" Priscilla asked sharply.

Korin was about to stutter a response, but he swallowed hard, overcoming his anxiousness, as he knew he had to be firm in order to uncover the truth. "Missing something?" He glared.

Priscilla winced as her eyes sharpened. "Did you steal something of mine?"

Without replying, Korin merely brought Priscilla's pen out.

Alarm wrapped her face. "Where… where did you find that?" Her respiration increased.

"On the ground. Somewhere." He jolted his eyebrows.

"Where?" she asked demandingly.

Stalling for a few seconds, Korin decided to push the topic, asking, "What were you doing yesterday afternoon *and* last night?"

"How dare you even ask me such a thing! Why are you asking me such questions? What, do you think I'm *up to* something?"

"Perhaps."

"Well, if you think I *did* something in particular yesterday, then… well… I have an alibi. Yes. An… an alibi. And anyway, I know what you *didn't* do!"

Korin knew what Priscilla was referring to, and her remark cut him deeply, cracking the foundations of his retort, which consequently never came. Both their breaths rapidly increased as their chests visibly moved.

"I have the higher ground, Korin," Priscilla added. "And I think you know it," she bitingly said. "Don't try and enter my sanctuary. You'll fail trying. Painfully," she said with pleasure.

"I wouldn't want back in there, anyway," he responded, trying to think of a witty reply. "It was a creepy dump." Korin broke his mould, slowly marching up the stairs. Priscilla held her ground, and both stood mere centimetres apart. "If you try anything," he said, pausing for effect, "know that I'm capable of stopping whatever you do. I've already proven that I can cut through your games."

"Oh, you've cut through nothing yet, Korin," Priscilla replied with a slightly raspy tone. "Don't come near me again."

Korin leered at Priscilla one last time before dumping the pen at her feet and then angrily marching off.

***

A week passed, and during that time, Korin attempted to spy on Priscilla by following her around the campus, finding nothing incriminating. Stalking her wasn't the most pleasant of tasks, and he was nearly caught a few times, having to justify his whereabouts. Priscilla, obviously, remained suspicious. In addition, his friends tried to find leads on cultists, with most of their investigation involving spying on general black moon practitioners, who attended the temple Korin went to with Priscilla in the Private District. However, they, too, also found nothing… incriminating, at least; but his friends did notice that virtually everyone who practiced at the temple were incredibly odd in character, having strange daily habits. One example included a practitioner who would growl at a blank wall for twenty minutes every evening before going to bed, as if she were possessed by a demon.

Everyone who died in the fire was identified via the DNA in their bones, as well as with a weak correlation with the dissipating etheric energy still lingering in the atmosphere; ten were acknowledged as some of the 'missing students'. Darsan was one of those recognized, and Korin and his friends attended his funeral. Celine brought the flowers. Since there were numerous explosions in the building, it wasn't absolutely clear to the police that there were prison cells; the debris, nevertheless, did raise strong suspicions.

The police also made a separate list for the cultists who died, as they weren't on the roll of 'missing students'. However, while the police were highly suspicious of them, they had no evidence to suggest that shadowists were captors nor that any cult was involved. When Korin investigated the dead cultists' backgrounds, he either found little to no associations – friends, places of interest, etcetera – or they led nowhere or note. In fact, none, he learned, had ever attended the moderate black moon temple. He ended up guessing the cult had somehow covered their tracks. Interestingly, Korin found barely any further information about Meriel as well, so he assumed that the cult – and more specifically, Priscilla, in this case – covered their tracks regarding their victims, too.

In the meantime, Korin took the EDA Darsan recommended using to an expert for repairing and unlocking. The specialist said that it would take a while to fix, and there was no guarantee that he'd be able to unlock it nor even find any way to extract the data from the neurachite brain. Still, because the expert wasn't presented with just the brain, the chances of using the EDA again were greater due to the brain being connected with the rest of the device – if it could be fixed. At least there were still just over two months until the Midfire Lunapex.

Later that day, Korin also learned that the scientist that Priscilla wished to capture for one night happened to be working on some prototype crystal. He wondered if the crystal was what Priscilla was going to 'interrogate' her about, thinking it was definitely possible, seeing no other motivation other than general cult experimentation. Still, the crystal's main potentials were to be used for more mundane industrial applications, so he wasn't sure what Priscilla would've done with it. Nevertheless, he did hear that it was capable of tuning into particular etheric energies, but these, too, seemed mundane.

Waiting for the lunapex was a last resort, so while brainstorming ideas for finding the cult's base, Korin *did* come up with an alternative plan to locate old buildings that The Gathering used over two millennia ago. However, most of the buildings that Backlevy personally used no longer existed now; and of the existing ones that had been renovated many times, there was nothing notable to find. Instead of giving up on the idea, Korin resolved to check out one of the buildings that existed on the same *location* that Backlevy used for her activities. The original structure Backlevy used was torn down over two millennia ago, and many different buildings on that spot were built and demolished over the centuries. A small, non-academic mansion now rested on the location, and it was said to not be associated with Backlevy at all. Moreover, it wasn't associated with any other current-day fraternity or sorority. Despite this information, Korin insisted on inspecting the small, unassuming mansion built with mainly red bricks and timber, appearing quite old with its aesthetics.

Known as the Veisan Mansion, the building wasn't open to the public, so Korin's gang snuck in, finding nothing related to the cult in any way. They even checked behind cabinets and bookshelves for hidden doors. After meticulously rechecking every room, Korin started the search again for the third time, but his friends thought enough was enough. Sylas ended up playing a game on his phid whenever Korin wasn't around, grinning with guilt when caught, whereas Terala kept banging her head lightly against a wall like a child. Celine, meanwhile, couldn't help but revert to the wonderful dreamland inside her head as she gazed at nothing in particular. At times, Korin secretly wished he could drop the task and join her. All four eventually resigned from their search, not knowing what else to do.

Even though everyone realized there was a looming threat, they weren't capable of devoting all of their time to investigating such matters, anyway. Their university workload was mounting, and the semester was flying by. Understanding he had to hit the books and temporarily place cultist investigations on the side bench, Korin began studying in his room that night, starting with Conjuration.

His holochite textbook provided both information on the mechanics of conjuration magic and a list of assorted geometric forms typically needed to create first-level conjurations: holograms. Beginners usually didn't create moving holograms or produce haptic feedback, and such feats were only requirements of the second semester. The first step involved taking an etheric snapshot of an item that one wished to replicate. With a few ideas in mind, Korin chose to create a hologram of himself standing still, as he figured that he could use it later in battles to dupe enemies.

Prior to meditating, Korin stared at himself in the mirror, ensuring that he had a good visual grasp of himself. He had the option of taking an etheric snapshot of his actual body, but he decided to take a snapshot of an astral imagination of himself, so he didn't have to stand up during meditation. Plus, having a combative pose would be more contextually realistic in combat than seeing a person meditatively standing with his eyes closed. There were other options he could've used to change this, but they merely added difficulty to his task.

When he did begin his meditation on creating an imagination of himself in the astral, he couldn't help but create all sorts of imaginations, all unrelated to his task at hand. The issue occurred for a couple of hours, and when slivers of his goal would shoot to mind, he'd focus, only to lose concentration yet again. With practice, he was able to place his distractions to the side, creating an image of himself after a few attempts. It took slightly longer to get the nuances right -- he wanted to make it look perfect -- and the figure before him finally stood nobly in a warrior pose, face aggressive and feet distanced, ready in attack formation.

Korin was ready for the next phase, which involved tuning into the energy of the imagination before inducing a cymatic field of the aggregate frequency in the etheric. Doing so was a two-fold challenge, but the first stage was a little easier. Once he tuned into it, Korin had to project the vibrational resonance of the imagination out; and after many attempts, he managed to notice a remarkable watery pattern that took a fluorescent and holographic appearance. Then came the matter of taking the snapshot of the etheric energy. Although it contained too many details for him to truly note, the snapshot would only be an outline of what he was seeing. This process was not what he thought the name suggested; that is, Korin spent quite a few hours trying to capture the outline of the vibrational resonance field. Still, he eventually succeeded; but once completed, he felt fatigued and needed rest.

For the next day, Korin eagerly began projecting the snapshot he took out into his own etheric aura. The process was similar to projecting the full etheric data of his imagination out before, so it didn't take long. On completion, the energy spherically surrounded him. He noted the types of different nodes in the cymatic field's interference patterns, and he exited his meditation to begin memorizing particular geometries in his textbook that would've been appropriate. These geometric forms, as he had already learned, were of a variety of shapes, sizes, dimensions, rotations, and positions. After a few hours of learning and memorizing as much information as possible, he fell asleep.

Korin's next task involved linking the nodes together with appropriate geometries. Reaching from one node to another, Korin began mentally establishing his first connections, their forms like straight beams of transparent and fluorescent energy as well. So mesmerized with what he saw, his mind wandered, and the shapes distorted, forcing him to scrap pieces multiple times and start over. Sometimes his visualizations didn't emerge as he anticipated. Korin yet again saw numerous creations of his own mind pop up from time to time, including both random and known objects and people. However, these were astral imaginations that he could simultaneously see while creating tangible etheric geometries. There were some nights when there were too many distractions, Korin felt as if he was losing his mind, especially when they grew weirder by the end of the exercise. One case was when a cube turned into a bunch of pens, which then grew weird legs and began fanatically dancing around a fire with fractal patterns that soon changed into a fluffy bed with giant teeth, gnashing away at trees – formally the pens – before sitting down on a cosmic rainbow with a cat's head at the end of it, each engaging in an intellectual conversation inside a teapot – its owner, a gargantuan ogre, watching from above – all before changing to a simple glass of water… Korin certainly finished up for the night after that episode!

He eventually learned not to even bother suppressing his internal chatter, as that created more dialogue to emerge. Instead, he kept observant of his thoughts until they diminishingly silenced, and his attention to his task was given full power; the same followed with most of his illusory distractions. The rhyming techniques he developed earlier also faded away, giving rise to pure instinct. The geometric shapes soon began to seem like a web, the effect flustering on his evolving concentration. Eventually, though, Korin managed to finish off the last geometric form, relieved that his job was done… so he believed. He still also had to connect to the Aether to substantiate the spell and see if it worked.

After returning to the normal world after his meditation, Korin was buzzing with thrill – and some apprehension. He then rushed off to the testing spaces to test his spell.

***

All the rooms were occupied, so Korin waited and watched spells through the ballistic-proof super glass, protecting everyone from deplorable spells. The student in front of Korin cast a spell, and although the conjured firearm was fine at first, it shortly turned green before blowing up. His friends laughed, telling him that he was lucky he didn't try the spell back in his room like originally intended.

Korin entered the now-free room and placed his slightly-shaking hands across the glass. Connecting with the fabric of the zero-point energy field around him involved the same process as when fuelling his lumarchetrix; except, for his conjuration magic, the Aether fuelled a separate pool of energy that powered the spell stored in his etheric aura. Still, actually *casting* conjuration spells was another challenge because it required meditative concentration to funnel the gathered aether energy into a particular spell. Then again, the meditative concentration wasn't radically different from phasarchement, in that he didn't need to be fully meditating.

Now ready, Korin managed to tune into the Aether…

"Hey, come on!" a student yelled at Korin. "Hurry up! We don't have all fucking day!"

Korin lost all concentration as he glared at the intolerable, pig-nosed student stuffing his face with an ice-cream-pizza-donut thing which dribbled past his demented grin and pudgy neck. The boy finally moseyed away, leaving Korin to regain his concentration.

Alright, it's fine. He's gone, Korin thought; but just at that perfect moment of attentiveness, the ugly student returned.

"Oi, you suck!" The first-year banged on the glass, depositing food marks. "Hurry the fuck up or else I'll shove my jackhammer spell up your ass!"

"Do you fucking mind?" Korin yelled.

The boy merely snorted and laughed like an idiot, parting again to annoy another person. Korin tried concentrating on his spell again, but the apprehension of being bothered once more caused his mind to repeatedly hit the brakes. For a few minutes, no disturbance followed. Thinking the annoyance had ended for good, Korin sighed in relief. He focused again.

"Hey, shithead, suck on this!" the piggish boy yelled before rubbing his naked, dirty ass on the glass as he laughed hysterically.

One of the older, bigger students approached, yelling, "Get the fuck out of here, you fucking dantha-fucker!" before pushing the brat out of the room.

"Finally!" Korin said aloud as he heard the commotion in the background disappear.

Knowing the problem had been dealt with, Korin relaxed and held his hand out again. At first, his eyes remained closed, but he opened them when he felt the energy in his aura change. Before him, fluorescent geometric forms emerged, all inside the same luminous cymatic field in his etheric aura – so, technically only Korin could see it. In Korin's excitement, though, he lost focus, and the cymatic field disappeared.

After dealing with the brat, the older student returned, saying, "Don't worry, you'll get used to it."

"Thanks," Korin replied. "Will he be back?"

"Oh, I don't think so. You won't have to worry about him again." He laughed.

"Again, thanks." Korin smiled. "Are you waiting for a room?"

"No, I'm only here because of my little sister. She succeeded the first time testing her spell. I'm sure you will, too." He toasted with his bottle.

With peace of mind restored, Korin carried on, recreating the cymatic field, which soon condensed, and a pure holographic image of Korin emerged in the room, its form without distortion – perfect as intended. He could feel the Aether's energy powering the spell like he was controlling another force rather than it merely coming from his body. Korin then tightly closed his fists and jumped into the air with satisfaction. In so doing, his conscious connection to the stored spell unintentionally cut off, and the spell ended.

"Wait!" the older student hollered. "You have to see if it remains stable without doing something crazy."

The joy immediately turned to nervousness as Korin recreated the spell and then waited for any problems. After a while, it was clear nothing detrimental was going to happen; and, while Korin wasn't using other magic, the hologram lasted nearly three minutes. He couldn't simply move it around, unlike in the phasing stage, so if he wanted to move it, he would have to turn it off and recreate the conjuration. He also knew a spell's central location couldn't move too far away from the caster, otherwise, the spell's connection would cut off and end. After Korin's aether pool depleted and the spell ended, a sense of elation flooded Korin for having made his first, major magic accomplishment. He stood amazed, grinning. He had just cast his first spell – a feat he would never have imagined a few months ago.

"Good work, bro." The older student high-fived Korin.

"Thanks, man," Korin said. "I better tell my friend to make the same spell, as he's pushing it for time."

"Yeah, that's what happens in your first year. And the second. And the third." He laughed.

***

When Korin arrived back at his dorm, he decided to inform Sylas, knocking very hard on his door.

"Hey, what's up?" Sylas asked, opening the door.

"I cast my first spell!" Korin quickly answered.

"Wicked. Let's see it."

Korin immediately focused again, and although he thought he'd succeed, nothing emerged. Frustrated and confused, he shook his hand as if it were broken, trying a few more times before saying, "I swear I did it before."

"It's alright, I believe you. You could be exhausted of energy for some reason. It happens."

"Right, okay," Korin said, happy that he wasn't defunct in some way. "Well, what about you?"

"I admit, I'm having trouble with mine." Sylas plopped on his bed, exhaling cheerlessly.

"So, you *have* started?" Korin was a little shocked.

"Yeah, sort of." He senselessly rubbed a toothbrush against his blanket, looking around uneasily.

Korin knew precisely what Sylas was thinking. "You've only looked at the pictures." He smirked.

"Yep." He tittered. "Well, if you say it's easy, I'll give it a shot."

"I didn't say it was easy, but I think you're capable of doing it. Anyway, if it weren't for all the time required for our other subjects, I'd love to create more conjuration spells."

"Crap. Don't remind me about studying the other ones." Sylas dumped some accessories on a large heap of belongings, his additional, never-opened textbooks right at the bottom.

"When are you going to start?" Korin asked as a strange device tumbled down to his foot, bouncing repeatedly.

"Probably the hour before exams." He lightly giggled. "Well, my Business program has me doing all sorts of little assignments. Some are group based."

"Just remember that having a spell or two – with some other training – will help us in the future. You know, against cultists."

Sylas grumbled. "Fine. I'll open my books."

"Good. But you'll need to clear off the dust if you're going to read those physical ones." Korin chuckled. "Why do you even have those books if you never use them?"

"Well, when I arrived at Teloston, I just ticked all the boxes in the catalogues, and so they were delivered to me. Meh, I had the money."

"Alright, well, we're meeting up for an Alchemy study session tomorrow. You may as well get into the mindset now."

When Korin returned to his room, the pride he felt in accomplishing his first spell shifted to an imagination involving a priest. Korin told the clergyman of his achievement, hoping to receive praise. The idea suddenly sickened him before Korin imagined the priest's response. On reflection, he believed that had the priest praised him, Korin would've gone about his day feeling a stronger connection to his religion through psychological reinforcement. But the reality was different. Had the priest *actually* known about his so-called evil, wicked, sinful, blasphemous magic, Korin would've been cast aside as deeply unholy and or reindoctrinated through special programs. The lack of praise in itself wasn't uplifting, but Korin quickly grew to recognize that such praise, while nice, was a crutch. It was far more pleasurable to view the practice of casting spells as an act of rebellion. And it was through this rebellion that he gained his new sense of direction, one of freedom – of internal navigation – as opposed to external direction, especially by those who *were* the true evil. Moreover, the thought of possessing the ability to create holograms at will was basically like creating new mental constructs, countering the old religious thoughts and archetypal constructs still lingering and festering in the depths of his subconscious.

And his first spell was just the beginning. He was in training mode now – training in a foreign land for a comeback. For retribution. But the foreign land of his, the realm of mages, was his real home now. There was no turning back, except in the case of unleashing justice on the evil that fostered him. His sadness grew to anger and purpose, coursing through him and providing an added energy.

Korin's thoughts then switched to his parents and what their reactions would've been like had he told them of his first spell. Since he didn't know their social background, he wondered what their beliefs, attitudes, and goals were; he wanted to believe that they weren't part of the religious conspiracy, and he ended up doubting it, as the religion was against magic. The actuality of his situation nevertheless doused his fiery energy, saddening him; although, he didn't cry as he continued lying on his bed. He still hadn't heard a word back from the police, but he trusted that they were working hard on the case. There was not one photo of his parents or anything but his brief memories, so he couldn't channel his emotions into something concrete. His mind was a cloudy mix of hope, fading anger, and depression, with nothing to adequately grapple. But in that grey mist was a distant light that glowed just enough to keep Korin focused and moving forward.

***

The next evening, Korin met up with his friends in a spare Alchemy lab, sitting around a table that unevenly rocked back and forth with the slightest of added pressure. The overhanging light flickered as it gently swung, giving the appearance that it could drop at any minute. While everybody borrowed the essential Alchemy supplies from the supply room, each brought some of their own equipment. Korin brought a few books for group work, while Celine's belongings were spread out in a circle with rays around the alchemy equipment, each contained in handcrafted boxes covered with her own artwork of honey aesthetics. Sylas brought out an anime figurine he had on him, placing it right next to Terala to lightly piss her off – the revealing clothing on the female nymph making it worse. Having dumped a sweaty rag on the table from a recent hillseck practice match, Terala was inclined to pick it up and drape it over the figurine, but she was too fatigued to even bother.

"Out of all the senses," Sylas said, "I still think eyesight spells are the best."

"Maybe," Korin responded, "but there are ways to block certain vision."

"I think all the senses are great in their own ways," Celine said. "It would be really nice to try honey in a different way.

"I guess you guys have some valid points," Sylas said. "Anyway, I have something to announce."

"He's joining a cult," Terala interjected jocularly.

"Already have, actually." Sylas chuckled. "I performed my first ritual the other day."

Korin quickly added, "I bet they welcomed you with free blood, right?"

"Yeah! And I received a pet demon, too."

"Of course." Korin snickered. "Those cute little things need their food. Can't let them starve."

Sylas chuckled again. "But seriously, my birthday's coming up."

"Oh, then we'll have to do something," Celine said brightly.

"Awesome. I haven't planned anything, so I'll see how it goes. It's actually two weeks from now."

"Two weeks?" Terala loudly asked. "We don't have enough time to prepare, so we can't celebrate it." She grinned, playfully chucking some paper at Sylas, who quickly pegged it back. "Hey!" She managed to grab it. "Mine's next month, just before the lunapex, so let's prepare for that one instead." She chuckled.

Korin grinned before saying, "We really only have the time and resources to focus on one birthday; and since Sylas's birthday is first, we choose Sylas. Sorry, but you'll be left in the cold."

"In the heat of summer?" Terala asked. "Hey, if you want to cool me off during summer, I'm down with that."

"All I want is for someone to do my tests," Sylas said.

"Or you could focus on studying now," Korin said, "and get a different gift later."

Sylas moaned. "Yeah, yeah. Let's get this started." He expanded his holochite textbook. "No!" He closed his eyes. "Please, no. It's unbearable already." He grimaced.

Celine then asked, "If you don't mind me asking, what are you finding difficult?"

"Nothing. Except the will to actually study."

Terala swiftly commented, "He's probably one of these people who doesn't study and yet passes everything, usually with flying colours."

"Actually, the funny thing is, that's how it normally turns out with my exams." Sylas smiled impishly. "Maybe I shouldn't worry at all!"

"I think you just need to find a good source of motivation," Celine said. "If you're interested in a subject, you'll learn faster."

"Yeah, but what would that source be?" Sylas asked, leaning in, more willing than normal to learn. "I can already learn quickly and don't mind the practical side of things. I just don't *feel* like *studying* the theory and all the math."

Celine drifted off into her own world for a minute before responding, "Do you watch any shows that have complex magic systems that even we don't possess?"

"Yeah, all the time. Why?"

"Well, aren't you interested in learning all the details in their lore?"

Korin interjected, "I see where this is going. She's got you there, Sylas. You wouldn't stop talking to me the other day about the weaponry in *Firewing Zero*."

"Okay, okay," Sylas said. "So, what you're saying is that if there's some overlap with what I like outside of class, perhaps, then, I might find it interesting to read, and therefore study?"

"No," Terala said, grinning. "What she's saying is that you should stop watching anime altogether, because she thinks it's shit, and that this quantum stuff is even better!"

Korin added, "You should draw some pictures while you study. Quantumwing Zero."

"Yeah, I can *totally* see that," Sylas said, rolling his eyes. "And *Firewing Zero* isn't anime, by the way."

"Okay, but why watch a bunch of silly cartoon fights when you can read all about the amazing world of calculating relatable potential states in Alchemy?" Terala's face reddened as she planted into her arms on the table, laughing nonstop.

"You're not making my case any easier!" Celine told Terala.

"Yeah, now you've *really* turned me off studying." Sylas folded his arms.

"No, don't do that!" Celine said. "Look, when you read about all the weaponry in that show, you're most likely researching into the minutiae of its systems, and so if you practice studying our own magic, you'll probably have an easier time understanding other complex systems for your own personal enjoyment."

Terala wanted to add more in her hysteria, but Korin kicked her.

"Do it. Kick her," Korin whispered to Celine, who smirked back and acted accordingly.

"Ow! Okay." Terala stopped. "Fine." She suppressed another eruption of laughter. "I'm just messing around."

"Yeah." Sylas squinted. "Alright, I'll study." He sighed. "Anyway, I wish you were in my Gen Theory class, Celine. For motivation. The tutor is horrible. He always pushes us to the last second. Literally. And he has a massive, weird clock on the wall." Sylas shuddered. "It… stares at us." He glanced behind his shoulders as if it could've been there. "Every second someone is late is a second which has to be paid back later. He's such a creepy, creepy grouch. And he constantly rubs his hands, too. They're also crusted with… I don't know what it is. He reminds me of some old guy from a show called *Veir's Mystery*."

"He sounds far worse than our former Alchemy tutor, Baran," Korin said. "I wonder where he is now. Probably smoking something wild, oblivious to what's happening around him."

Groaning lightly, Terala added, "I actually want him back. At least he wasn't boring like the tutor Taliah gave us. I wouldn't be surprised if he was in a literal competition with our new Gen Theory lecturer. I swear they have no personalities, whatsoever."

"Well, at least he lulls the troublemakers to sleep, like Sereck," Korin said. "Anyway, let's get this study out of the way."

Chapter Eighteen

Sticking Together

During one afternoon, Korin met up with seven of his hillseck teammates in one of their bedrooms. Since there were quite a few fire moons around Juntas, the summer heat practically blazed into spring prematurely. The worst part was, the room's air conditioner had just broken. Veins consequently emigrated to the surfaces of saturated skins, which sizzled humidity into the already-ridiculously stuffy air. All the guys endured the heat, crammed in various spots, chatting or playing with their phids as loud party music played in the carefree atmosphere. Using low-energy delta-negative vortices to cool the room would have been too annoying to use for the context, so no-one used them.

Bendel was adjacent to Korin, radiating so much heat that a mirage formed around him, making his tattoos move as if they were of the temporary animated variety. "So, Korin," Bendel said, "we'll have to go over that strategy again, as the practice didn't go that well."

"Yeah, I know," Korin said, making himself comfortable at the side of the bed. "I just couldn't get that flip right."

"It's alright. Most can't do it, especially on their first attempt. But relax. You're still great at hillseck. Far better than me when I started."

"That's because you played like a dying dantha," Titus chimed in. "And still do." He chuckled.

"Get out of here." Bendel lightly kicked Titus. "Clearly the illusions orbs have warped your perception.

"Sure they have." Titus grinned. "Nah, of course you're good; but

I'm the greatest player. In the Caelverse." Titus flexed his muscles, his smugness stronger than the heat.

"How about against Korin's fighting skills?"

"Hmm… You know, I have an idea. Although we battle in training," Titus said to Korin, "we should have a proper duelling match. Just sentar staffs with mild shocks."

"I'm up for that," Korin replied. "Unsure how it'll turn out, though."

"Ah, I think you've got a good shot, Korin." Bendel nudged Korin's shoulder. "Titus likes to boast a lot, but it's usually just show for the ladies."

"The ladies would come for me, anyway." Titus chuckled. "You know, Korin," Titus said, leaning in, "by being on the team, you'll find that the ladies will chase you. But sometimes you attract too many. Remember that one last year who wouldn't leave us alone?" he asked Bendel.

Bendel shook his head in amazement. "Yep. Crazy old Salarah. She stalked Titus at first, and then she attached herself to me."

"Latched is a better word," Titus added.

"Yeah, and it turned out Salarah made a stalker shrine of me. That was fucking messed up."

"Disturbingly messed up. She even had a large vial of your blood hooked up to a doll of herself."

"I still have no idea how she got that," Bendel said. "And then when I made it clear that I didn't want her following me, she turned *really* weird and nasty."

"Salarah literally spread khor shit *all* over his room."

"Wow, that's crazy," Korin said. "I hope that doesn't happen to me," he muttered.

"What? You have a crazy stalker already?" Titus asked keenly, slowly rubbing his hands.

"Um… no… I…" Korin said, his redness turning into prickles.

Both Titus and Bendel glanced at each other with funny looks.

Pacing his words, Titus said, "Hey, I think I remember hearing about you saving some crazy girl up on the Aegis Halo. Watch out, man."

"Yeah, she's definitely a crazy one," Bendel added, holding a small box, wagging it. "You have to watch out for them. Don't stick your staff in crazy. I'm serious. Don't worry. We'll have your back if you get into any trouble. They need to be kicked out of the uni. But again, I suggest you watch yourself. These crazy bitches may be madly into you now, but that madness will lead to hatred later on."

"Great." Korin grimaced, unsure what Priscilla had in store for him.

"I thought you were with Terala, though."

"No, she's more of a sister to me."

"Oh… Well, then, I'll have to chat with her later." Bendel grinned. "Work my magic."

"Terala isn't one to sleep around. You'd be up against a brick wall trying to get anywhere. If she can beat you at anything, then you're not worthy in her eyes. Plus, I wouldn't let you." Korin chuckled.

"Hmm… alright."

"So, what happened to that girl?"

"Salarah?" Titus asked. "She transferred to another uni when we proved her guilty of doing all that shit to us. Her friend moved, too. She was pretty hot, though, hey, Bendel?"

"Oh, fuck, yeah. I'd bend her over a balcony railing any day! Ravage her fucking senseless. Kind of like that redheaded nurse we saw in the food hall the other day. Man, the things I'd do to her. You know the one, right?" Bendel asked Korin.

Just as Korin was about to answer, Terala knocked on the door, immediately entering before sliding past a couple of the boys on the floor. "'Sup, guys?" Terala squeezed in next to Korin. "Talking about tactics?"

"Oh, yeah, absolutely. Weren't we, Korin?" Bendel smirked.

"Uh, yeah… tactics. Titus says he wants to challenge me in a duel."

"A duel?" Terala asked perkily, receiving casual nods. "Then let's get this duel going, guys!" She clapped her hands.

"In a moment. We're relaxing," Titus responded. "We'll head down to the common room and do it there. Hey, Korin, you should've signed up for official duelling comps. It's a little late now."

"I think I had too much on my plate at the time," Korin replied. "I still do. Hillseck is enough for now."

"True," Titus replied slowly, nodding his head leisurely.

"So, Terala, when are you going to bring us our sandwiches?" Bendel asked, suppressing a giggle.

"As soon as you grow balls out of that vagina of yours." Terala grinned. A few of the boys heard, laughing hysterically. Bendel hung his head.

"Ooh, burn," Titus chuckled out. "We'll be waiting forever, then."

Bendel finally retorted, "You know, that sounds like some intense internalized misogyny there, Terala."

"Oh, I wasn't paying out vaginas in general. Just your crusty one." Terala chuckled before giving a teasing expression. "You mad, bro?"

"Ha! No. You can't ever get me down. So," he said, grinning, "do you, like, even cook?"

"What, like how I'm roasting you now?" she asked, grinning back as a few of the guys laughed again. Bendel remained quiet. "But, yeah, of course I can cook. Before coming here, I'd go hunting all the time. Killed rabbits and cooked them over fires."

"Oh, that's right. You were feeding your family."

Terala crossed her arms, glaring before firmly saying, "That one wasn't funny."

"Sorry. I… I didn't mean anything by that," Bendel said solemnly.

"Hm." Terala held back from saying anything as she mulled. "Alright. So, yeah, I learned how to make some tasty meals, as we picked all sorts of wild herbs and spices."

"Cool," Bendel said nicely. "You seem to know your shit. It'd be fun camping with you."

"Well, I never considered my outings as camps. I was out too often. It was basically everyday life."

"Right. So, what's your craziest tale, then?"

"Craziest?" Terala asked herself aloud, looking up. "Well, it depends. One of them consisted of getting lost at night. We wound up at some crazy lady's cabin, and there were pictures of actual dead and tortured children all over her walls, among other weird shit. She arrived back at her house and then stared at us without saying anything. Shit got intense, and –"

"No, wait!" Titus interrupted. "Save it for night-time. Tell it slowly with details. We'll bring popcorn, too. And we'll also go into one of the forests. Off track."

"Yeah, good idea," Bendel said. "We also have some fucked up shit to tell."

Korin was about to chip in, but a dirty rag was thrown onto his head, and a few of the guys laughed.

"Sorry, Korin," one guy shouted. "I was aiming for Bendel."

Korin decided to throw it back onto the guy's face, chuckling; Bendel then grabbed a filthy rag from a pile, hurling it onto the same mate.

"Right, that's it!" the same guy hollered, standing up 'confrontationally'. "You're both going down!" he proclaimed, and a rag-throwing fest ensued before escalating into a sportive brawl.

Terala fought alongside Korin, mostly skirmishing from the sides because the wrestling involved pushing each other to the ground, smothering the opposition; it would've otherwise felt a little awkward for her to be in the centre of the action. When the boys piled on each other, Korin wound up in the middle, squished in a heavy sandwich. The back of his head had two hands pressing up against it, and even though he was pinned down, Korin managed to grapple two guys, one in a lock between his forearm and upper arm, and the other with his left hand. His ass got kneed, causing him to squirm. Titus managed to reign supreme for a while until half the guys ganged up on him. The sweat induced stickiness between them all, and although the brawl wasn't serious, Korin almost choked from a lack of air. When Korin barely managed to slip out of the pile, he had to gather as much air as possible, forgetting it was already hard to breathe in the room. A few items around the room broke, but no-one seemed to care as they playfully shouted and grunted.

The fight eventually mellowed before ending, and everyone resumed what they were previously doing. Shortly after, Bendel announced the duelling competition.

***

Down in the common room at the basement level, the boys moved the furniture to make room for the match. As the hillseck team surrounded Korin and Titus while vigorously chanting, they drew the attention and attendance of many others in the dorm block. The prestige of the symbol-decorated room disappeared, seeming now like an alley behind a dingy bar, filled with shirtless guys ready to make a quick posel on whoever would beat the other man into the fiery pits of Seckaphon. Their laughter and jokes, on the other hand, contrasted the visual display. Korin loved the atmosphere, flexing his neck while stretching his legs.

"Gentlemen and, uh… lady," Bendel announced, looking over at Terala, who held her hips, head bent to one side.

"I've told you: I'm not a lady," Terala stated firmly.

"Right. I forgot. Ladies and gentle-girl." He laughed as half the guys hooted.

Some of the team members playfully pushed Terala in jest before she shoved them back.

"Ah-ha. Gentle-girl. Terala's a gentle-girl," one guy teased Terala, nudging her repeatedly.

"Fuck off, Bendel!" one team member yelled. "There's only one lady here, and it's you!" he shouted good-humouredly as the others guffawed.

"Okay, okay." Bendel chuckled. "Everyone, we have a special fight for you today!" he aroused the audience with a theatrical voice. "As the challenger – a newcomer with a dark and troubled background – we have Korin Tarkelt!" He grabbed Korin's arm, enthusiastically raising it into the air. "On the other side, we have… a dantha ready to be thrashed!" he joked, causing the crowd to laugh.

"Oh, come on!" Titus held his hands out as he couldn't help but laugh a little, too. "Where's my support?" he asked as the mob cheered Korin.

"Alright, alright." Bendel settled down, signalling for everyone to lull the volume with his hands. "Titus Tristen, one of the indisputably best duellers, wishes to fight Korin. You know the rules. First to get hit loses!"

Bendel gestured for the fight to begin with a large swing, giving the impression he would've pulled a muscle. While wearing some borrowed sentars, Korin formed an aerochite staff before he cautiously moved towards Titus, who was grinning the whole time. Terala was at the front of the crowd with tightened fists, eyes fixated on the match.

"Alright, Korin, let's see what you've got," Titus said.

Titus was incredibly agile, swiftly moving around, as if his feet were on fire; he struck at Korin extraordinarily fast, but Korin dodged the attack and swung his staff, missing Titus. Although he tried to keep his cool, Korin's nerves cropped up, despite the frivolity of the match. Instead of trying to strike first, Korin waited for his opponent to let his guard down, but Titus's attacks were too fast to find holes; Korin could only counter them. Titus became fairly cocky and jumped around, thrusting his staff at Korin, who also jumped to the side, striking Titus's weapon so powerfully that it knocked it back, creating a good opportunity to strike. From there, Korin moved up for a final blow, but Titus managed to leap amazingly far, striking unexpectedly. Korin blocked the attack, and then both contenders opened their guards, hitting one another at virtually the same time, the shocks jolting them to the ground in light pain.

"Ooh, you're both gone!" Bendel called out, and the crowd moaned in frustration.

"Hey, I want to fight now!" Terala quickly said before the crowd dispersed.

Most of the guys were exceedingly keen to watch a girl fight, cheering vigorously again, with many starting to place bets. When Terala heard a few scoffs, her determination rose.

"C'mon, Terala!" one guy shouted. "Make sure you grab him by the fucking balls!" He gestured, tightly clasping the air before animalistically licking it. Terala rolled her eyes in return.

After Titus stood up, he said, "Sure, I'll take both you and Korin on. This time, you can use non-shocking shields. Oh, and that was a good match, by the way." Titus shook Korin's hand.

"Yeah, I've learned a lesson or two," Korin replied.

"Any strategy?" Terala quietly asked Korin.

"Hmm, he gets cocky, but he's pretty good all round. I think with the two of us, though, we'll beat him."

Titus created an aerochite shield with his left sentar, while his right hand wielded a lateral blade, with the form having emerged from the focal points on the side of his fist. Korin matched Titus, whereas Terala decided to wield two shorter fore blades that emerged out of the back of her fingers. Appearing more vicious in her stance than the guys, Terala moved in first, rapidly taking a shot at Titus, who instantly blocked her with his shield. Instead of waiting for another sensible moment to strike, she continuously belted the living shit out of Titus's shield. Korin simply stood still in respect of her savagery. Titus was then pushed to the ground as Terala's frenzy continued, but he also managed to secure a good launch position before shoving her into the air with his shield. She fell hard to the ground as her weapon retracted through shocked focus; and just as Titus was about to strike her with his sword, Korin dived in time to defend Terala. Titus then cunningly relinquished his shield for another blade, dropping to the ground to slice at Korin's unguarded area. With Korin out of the picture, it was only a matter of seconds before Titus struck Terala out as well.

A few in the crowd lost the bet, shouting angrily; many hoped to have seen Terala beat Titus in a few seconds flat. Even so, most cheered both sides for their impressive display; and when Korin and Terala stood up, they humbly acknowledged the victor.

"We'll have to do this another time," Titus said. "You guys were great."

"Of course," Korin said. "I'm glad we had the match."

Terala was naturally disappointed, though she somewhat learned her lesson as to be more cautious in the future.

***

Dark clouds and a massive temperature drop were welcome changes the following day, allowing everyone to walk outside with ease. Korin was out taking a stroll through one of the botanic strips with Celine; and just after they crossed a small wooden bridge set up over a beautiful stream, a chufet – a small, furry animal – suddenly ran past their legs, followed by another before zooming almost out of sight. Distorchite crystals were set up in a ring on the pathway, creating an impressionist depth-of-field effect for everything behind them, as if everything seen through the ring was part of a painting; as such, it was hard to see the chufets properly, but they were still visible.

"Come on, let's see where they go!" Celine grabbed Korin, chasing after the animals. Outpacing the two mages, the chufets eventually ran up a verdant oak tree, which shaded large parts of the nearby footpath and road. "Follow me." Celine climbed the tree first.

"You're pretty fast at climbing," Korin called out close behind. "You climb trees much?"

"I used to climb trees all the time when I lived at home. What about you?" she asked without looking down.

"Yeah, when I was younger. There wasn't much else to do at times."

"Hey, I found them!" she whispered loudly.

Korin caught up, reaching one of the highest branches, finding the chufets eating the nuts they had gathered.

"I wish I had one as a pet," Celine said, adoring their cuteness with enlarged eyes. "Too bad they don't allow pets in our rooms."

"Surely there's a way to bend the rules?" Korin asked.

"Maybe." She simpered. "I know they allow small animals like fish, but nothing like these. Hmm, actually, I probably wouldn't want to keep a chufet in my room; they need the outdoors. It would be kind of cruel." Celine activated her phid's basic camera mode, taking a few pictures until she was satisfied with the results. She then slowly reached over to pat one of the chufets, but they jumped away. "Oh…" She looked disheartened. "Let's see if they return."

During their wait, thunder lightly rumbled, and the white noise's soothing atmosphere filled the bumps in the trail of thought in Korin's mind, granting him a moment to effortlessly reflect on his time at Teloston. Celine, too, took a moment to reflect as she peacefully lay on a branch. The period of quietness between the two felt natural and not one born out of awkwardness; there was a knowing acceptance and trust in one another.

A twig abruptly landed on a Korin, who had been spacing out. Then another. He looked around, seeing nothing noticeable, except for Celine, who was holding back a smile. Korin stared until she properly looked at him; he then grinned, hopping up to begin chasing her. She excitedly squealed, immediately taking off to quickly grab one branch after another.

"I'll outpace you!" Celine called out. "I'm a nymph of the forest!"

"No longer an alovexen undercover spy?" Korin asked.

"I can change at will. We nymphs can do anything."

"Quite the power you have there," he said as he caught up.

"Well, you haven't seen *all* my powers," she said, smiling from behind a branch. "So, what are you?"

"Uh, a dragon, I guess," he said without thought, unsure if it was actually the creature he suited.

"At least you're not a tartulemoe." Celine giggled. "We don't want you stinking up the tree. You know, in all seriousness, I'd love to ride dragons one day. You'd come race with me?"

"Yeah, that's if I ever get to ride a dragon."

"My grandfather rode a morkol dragon once. He said it was the scariest and most thrilling thing he ever did."

How was that even possible? Korin thought.

A butterfly then landed on Celine's shoulder, and she deliberately managed to place her hand underneath, holding it out. "Or a giant butterfly. I think a giant butterfly might be better." She giggled again. Once the butterfly flew away, Celine took off once more, but the thin branch she was on snapped, giving way.

Luckily Korin was nearby. With a trembling arm, he immediately grabbed Celine, staring fearfully into her bright blue eyes filled with numerous imaginings of the worst outcomes. He shortly pulled her up to the branch he was on, asking, "You okay?"

"Yes! Thank you." Celine quickly hugged Korin, the tightness unremitting for a good minute. Her head also rested securely on his shoulder, almost as if she was part of him.

Korin patted her hair, comforting her state of mind back into its usual self. It took a while, but Korin also mentally shook away the fear of her dropping. "That was a little too close." He finally looked at her calmed eyes again. "Can't nymphs fly?"

"I guess I've yet to practice flying."

A large group of people were unhurriedly walking on the road nearby, spoiling the atmosphere with their loud and juvenile antics. Korin wanted to see where Celine's imaginations took her, but the moment fizzled out after waiting for the crowd to leave.

"Perhaps we should head down now," Korin said.

"Oh, but I'd like to see if the chufets return," she said downheartedly.

"Alright. We'll wait," he said, sitting back on a branch. "Hey, I know this is an odd time to ask, but it's been over a month since we saw Meriel. You withdrew quite a few times, and I'm wondering how you're feeling now."

"Better…" She smiled faintly, taking half a minute to process her thoughts. "Thanks for asking. I'm not used to facing demons and cultists."

"Yeah, I understand. I take it you've lived a very serene life?

"For the most part, I think. I grew up in a peaceful house surrounded by lots of trees." She tapped a large branch contently. "Our house was pretty far away from the suburbs, so there weren't many neighbours. And I rarely saw anyone else my age, so I guess I avoided a lot of drama that way, too. It actually gave me extra personal time, so I used that to focus on lots of hobbies."

Thinking of Terala, Korin cautiously asked Celine, "I haven't seen you bump into anyone you knew from school. Have you seen anyone?"

Celine looked off to the side when she answered, "Well, since I was home-schooled for most of my life, by the time I did the last two years of high school, most people had already formed tight relationships, and I guess I found it a little hard to fit in."

Korin was delighted at how she was so trusting of him to simply reveal her situation. "I see. That's not a bad thing on your half, though. Did you have special tutors like Sylas?"

"No, my mum taught me most of the coursework, but occasionally, the odd specialist or two was hired."

"At least you had a healthy environment. I swear some of the people here must've had some toxic schools to be as retarded as they are now."

"Oh, I agree," she said, surprising Korin slightly with her bluntness. "And even though I went to a pretty good school in comparison to most of the surrounding public ones, there were still many problems, so I kept to myself."

"Probably for the best." Korin chose not to probe any further on the issue. "Anyway, your house must have a lot of land, I take it?"

"Yes, a few acres." Celine's appearance gladdened. "We have many animals, and I learned to ride some of them. It was hard saying goodbye to them, and I do miss them. We had one funny korlorn called Alty." She chuckled. "He ended up going blind, but he could sense who was near him, and he was always protective of me when someone unfamiliar came on to the property. Although, I could sense Alty was disheartened when I rode on or spent time with the other animals." She glanced around to see if the chufets had returned.

Korin wondered what Celine would have thought about Terala's rabbit hunting, but it was another topic he didn't wish to bring up just in case it was too sensitive of a matter. "Yeah, I don't think they're coming back."

"You're probably right. Still, they left their nuts." Celine grabbed one, cleaning it before taking a bite. "Mmm, I love these. We should collect some. Try it." She handed Korin the half-eaten nut.

Approving the taste, he said, "Alright, let's go." After descending the tree, both started their picking of low-hanging nuts along the road, and when there was a respite in the conversation, Korin warmly stared at Celine, who self-consciously smiled. "You know... I really like spending time with you, Celine."

"And I really like spending time with you," Celine replied, nudging Korin.

After another moment of heartfelt silence, they approached a tree laden with berries. Celine picked a handful, passing a bunch to Korin; the fruit's skin was coated with a sticky juice, causing both hands to temporarily glue to one another. He didn't mention anything this time about her taking of substances from the university; it could hardly be construed as stealing in the most conservative of judgements.

"How do you know if they're free of poison?" Korin asked.

"You don't trust me?" Celine asked, looking a little hurt.

"Of course I trust you." He unexpectedly thought about Priscilla before quickly removing her from his mind. "I'm just curious."

"Oh. Well, I wouldn't hand you anything I wasn't sure about. I know my berries." She nudged him again.

"Okay," Korin said, and then Coach Virkorska came to mind. "I'm sure you and our hillseck coach would get along quite well." He tried not to giggle.

"Why's that?" Celine smiled while squinting.

"Let's say he has a love of berry picking. Talks about it all the time." Korin couldn't help himself laughing.

"I guess I won't be seeing him out here in the garden, then."

"No. No way. I don't know what he hates more, actually – the berries themselves or the berry picking."

"Well, maybe he just needs the berries cooked into something nice."

"I don't think that would work. Maybe if you slathered them in a giant meat roll, then it'd pass. Or maybe if there was some violent competition to gather the most berries."

"Perhaps it's best to keep my distance from him. Is he a bad coach? Or bad in general?"

"No, he's fine. He'll yell at us, but we all brush it off and laugh afterwards. He kind of loses his power in that regard." There was a louder rumble in the sky, and rain at last drizzled down. "That does it for now. Perhaps we should head back and figure out what to do for Sylas's birthday."

***

Sylas's birthday finally arrived, but he unfortunately fell sick, remaining in bed for quite a few days. He and his friends had to cancel their activities, but at least he received some nice gifts. Korin gave him a few pranking devices, and sure enough, Sylas received them with great appreciation.

After Sylas recovered, he and Korin agreed to take it easy one morning, heading to the Market District to browse the shops.

"Hey, if you have lots of money, why don't you eat here?" Korin asked Sylas.

"I prefer eating with you guys. Plus, the food hall is actually pretty good. Especially those special pies they sometimes give out. Mmm." He cheerfully held his fit stomach. "Every now and then, I might grab a bite from here, though."

Korin was so accustomed to his old boarding school providing him food that he didn't think much about eating at places *directly* charging a fee or anywhere else non-socialized, unless it was food he made, picked, or caught. Of course, he would still take food to his bedroom to eat, though. "It seems a lot of people other than students eat here, too."

"Yep, that's another reason; they'd probably start chastising us about breaking the rules or something if we sat nearby."

Drawing in a lot of attention, a fretful-looking student was making a call to someone on his phid, yelling, "What do you mean you're out of troll sweat? Another month? Do you understand the severity of the situation? There are demons everywhere! I'll pay twenty times the price to get my hands on some! Agh! I can't believe this!" The student abruptly finished the call, grabbing his head with anxiety. He then immediately made another call to his mate, this time saying, "Lucas, we need to bathe together. Yes, with that troll sweat you got."

Korin looked at Sylas, who mirrored his astonished face. "Is that…?"

Sylas slowly said, "I… think so," before giggling for a moment. His astonishment – along with a hint of revulsion and, yes, even guilt – kept him from fully laughing, however.

Korin giggled to an extent but mostly cringed, unable to fully believe what he had just heard. "Man, that can't be real. It has to be a joke."

"It sounded as though he was serious. I'm in just as much shock as you are. I definitely have to spread more rumours from now on!" He laughed harder this time – although, it was still reduced due to his shock. A part of him knew he'd be laughing much more later on.

"We'll have to tell the others about it." He shook his head. "Anyway, you wanted to try one of those toys out, right?"

"That's why I'm up. I brought a few of those tappers." Sylas grinned, holding a tiny device designed to be placed on a person's back.

"The package said it'd tap them every thirty seconds for ten minutes."

"Yeah," Sylas said, appearing as if he would grumble. "If I recall correctly now, I think there are ones available that last longer."

"That seems a little cruel at that point," Korin said, thinking back to his purchase, purposely choosing the ones with the shortest time span.

"Yeah, yeah. I guess you're right. Ten minutes is good enough."

"Alright, so who should we put it on?"

"Well, I've got quite a few here, and although they *are* my birthday present, I'll let you try one first. Just sneak up to anyone and lightly place it on their back."

Korin took a tapper and sought out the closest group sitting around a shaded table. He approached a seated girl, and, in a seemingly creepy manner, he stood close behind her, stalling. A few seconds later, the girl turned around, shooting up in horror and disgust.

"You!" the unfamiliar girl screamed. "I don't know *how* you're allowed outside, but *you* are a *disgusting* sex fiend!" She spat on the ground, storming off. Her friends swiftly followed, all glaring at Korin as they left.

"Wait, I didn't mean to…" Korin held his hand out, soon flopping it down, knowing that there wasn't anything he could do to change their minds. He plodded back to Sylas, embarrassed. "You can go." Depression soaked the atmosphere. "I think I'll just make things worse for myself."

"I knew I should've shown you how it's done," Sylas said, shaking his head before casually approaching a group to slyly place the tapper on a lad's back. The act came so naturally to him.

Sylas craftily returned to Korin right before the virtually-invisible tapper firmly tapped on the person's shoulder three times, hovering away for thirty seconds before repeating. Attempting to keep his laughter under control, Sylas giggled lightly. At first, the tapping appeared to create confusion, but after a few minutes, frustration built quickly as the student stood up, slamming his chair into the table, looking like a maniac as he waved his arms around. He stripped his shirt off, scouring every smidgen for anything bug-like before stomping on it as if the shirt was on fire. Thirty seconds passed, and the maddening tapping continued. This time, the guy started blaming his friends, shouting and causing quite the commotion.

All the while, Sylas's laughing increased, as did Korin's, drawing in almost as much attention as the uproar. Soon after the ten minutes finished, the victim and his group of friends spotted Sylas and Korin, glancing at each other with suspicion. At this point, the two pranksters had already stopped watching, too caught up in their own laughter as they dropped onto a bench with their eyes closed. Korin hadn't laughed so hard in a while, and he repeatedly brushed off the inner voice telling him how immature he was being.

His laughter died, however, when he opened his eyes and saw the group of large third-years right in front of him, crossing their arms with brutally-angry faces. He began nudging Sylas.

"I know. I know," Sylas responded, still laughing. "The dumbass kept going."

"Uh, no… Sylas, you need to open your eyes," Korin said, still on the bench.

"I don't think I can. Oh, man, that was funny. I wish I recorded that."

"No, seriously, Sylas, open your eyes," Korin stated adamantly.

"Okay, what is i–" Sylas stopped laughing – immediately. "Oh, crap."

"Dumbass, eh?" the group's leader asked. "You know, you look awfully familiar to me." He wagged his finger.

"I… don't think we've ever met," Sylas said, standing up with Korin.

"Oh, no. We definitely have met before." He smirked, glorious revenge glinting in his eyes. "I think I need to return the favour you gave us when you first arrived at the university," he said gleefully.

Instantly, both Korin and Sylas realized who they were… but it was too late to connect to the Aether and prepare for any confrontation.

"Well, here you go. Paid back tenfold," their leader said, throwing a ball right between Korin's and Sylas's legs.

The group of third-years rushed away as quickly as possible, leaving the explosion of multicoloured goo to froth up and clutch both guys in a sticky mess. After slipping over, they appeared as if one disfigured monster. The centre of the mess was the strongest, literally attaching Korin to Sylas in a near-unbreakable bond. Their limbs on the outside possessed some mobility, but when they tried standing up, both failed multiple times.

"Oh, great." Korin moaned. "I knew I shouldn't have done this."

"Well don't blame me!" Sylas reacted, trying to move his shoulder away from Korin. "You bought those damn tappers. I was in prank's anonymous before today."

"Sure you were. Look, we need to get out of here. For all we know, this could harden even more."

Sylas moaned back, his chin almost getting stuck.

"Okay, think of this like the lake at camp," Korin said. "On three."

Korin and Sylas were finally able to stand up, moving in step with one another so the slime wouldn't trip them over. Tiny patches stuck to the ground with every step, but most of it remained on their bodies.

Virtually everyone was either gawking or laughing at the two boys, but it wasn't *overly* embarrassing because the slime covered half their heads, partially concealing their identities from those who didn't witness them before the explosion. Part of the hardened slime soon warped in the centre, twisting Korin behind Sylas in file rather closely. During their awkward march, the two boys crossed paths with the group of angry girls who had stormed off previously.

Pointing with a very judging finger, one of the girls shouted, "And he has a slime fetish, too!"

"There's nothing wrong with that!" an odd-looking student rebutted. "He's parading his love! Can't you see that, you bigot!"

Naturally, an argument followed, embroiling numerous bystanders over the topic of slime-sexuals. Very funnily enough, there happened to be a slime-sexual in the crowd. Yes, really.

Heat was building up inside the slimy mound, and it appeared as if Korin and Sylas were in for some trouble; but luckily, a few other pranksters were nearby, grinning mischievously before stomping the slime, unintentionally breaking it up.

Once freed, Korin and Sylas cleaned themselves off, noticing that most of the attention was no longer on them. Still, they had enough for one day, leaving promptly as the social justice warriors and the other assorted and offended do-gooders began eating each other up with their squabble.

Chapter Nineteen

The Match and the Party

With only a few weeks in the semester remaining, the Midfire Lunapex dawned ever closer, setting a heavier and heavier burden upon Korin. Simultaneously, the pressures of his upcoming exams encumbered him, and the two issues entangled with one another. He would plan to investigate a particular matter, only to shortly place it off to the side as he fell behind in his university work. At least when the Study Week arrived, Korin was able to catch up with the lost ground.

Sylas, on the other hand, finally became concerned, cramming his study and shouting loud profanities from his room at most hours of the day. Terala didn't like studying as well, but she made sure she studied hard in the cram period because she actually needed to pass her magic classes, as her Emergency Services program required it, despite it being vocational. Celine was the most organized of the group, having completed most of her assignments before the Study Week; although, she admitted it was hard to concentrate at times – her efficiency resulted more so through interest than from actually being squarely organized. Korin and his friends were aware of the importance of their magic classes, anyway, as they needed to be magically proficient in order to defend themselves against future danger. Although Korin had the opportunity to practice USTs beyond shields and discharges, he chose to focus just on those, both as a means to help increase his channelling powers and also to increase his combat skills. Still, he would eventually have to practice the other USTs more in order to fully improve in phasarchement. Like practically everyone else in his year group, he was still at novice power levels – though, at the higher end.

On the morning of the first exams before breakfast, Korin needed time to himself to reflect on the semester. To effectively do so, he decided to return to the roof of the Aegis Halo, properly viewing the landscape this time without having to rescue anyone whilst foolishly approaching death.

His musings led him to consider the overall picture of his experiences – he was glad about what he had accomplished thus far, but Korin still deemed he had much room for personal development. His reflection turned meditative, awareness and energy now tuning into the environment. Although the brightening blue on the eastern side assisted his vision, it was still dark enough to allow the shadows to cloak the setting's various details, delicately balancing on that essential thin line between mystery and exposure. The flock of birds ahead continuously shifted their patterns; even the most individualistic conformed to the collective will in the end. A light shower had pattered the previous night, but the heat had already evaporated most of the water, rising with it the smells of the gritted stone beneath. The forests glowed with light auras, their mysterious inhabitants about to retire for the night, ready to hide from the mages. Drones buzzed to-and-fro like insects – apiece or together, their business seemed insignificant compared to the surrounding vastness. By the end of the session, Korin's energies were charged.

***

There was a great sense of relief in the air once the exams had finished, even though the students were yet to receive their results. Korin was nervous beforehand, thinking he hadn't studied enough; but afterwards, he felt confident that he did reasonably well, though Terala kept telling him that men overestimated their abilities. It would've been more nerve-racking if the first-years hadn't performed practice tests prior to their exams. Korin experienced no dramas, except for one test, where he sat next to a very smelly person; and, Korin also swore he saw dubious activity during a few of the tests. Still, he couldn't confirm his suspicions of cheating, as he had finished nearly every test at the last minute, whereas many of those who he was suspicious of finished earlier.

The students' magic classes were also graded differently to their non-magic classes; essentially, it was a matter of expectations and standards than a typical scoring guide. That is, the university was more so concerned with imposing standards to meet and then exceed than with grades – at least, until, the final semester in year three. Any student who failed a magic class would have to suffer a soft form of punishment later by trying to learn old content – voluntarily – in their own spare time in order to keep up, as classes essentially continued on from previous semesters. The final grades for magic classes weren't *that* important – as in, they weren't set in stone – as postgraduate mages could either develop further or degenerate after university; but in order to prove their powers to certain prospective employers at much later dates post graduation, postgraduate mages would still need to undergo testing and accreditation of some kind. Ultimately, until the final semester, the 'grades' were general indicators of progress, but each assignment and form of testing were set in stone as to what they were and when they were to be completed by.

The students were nearly ready to celebrate, but before any major parties began, almost everyone's attention focused on the hillseck games, with Contella University holding two matches that Starday for the County Cup. The other two single-elimination matches for the first round were held that day at another university in their county, Sirenvay. Korin was lucky enough to be in the first match, competing against Ritrae University.

The hillseck field was identical to Teloston's, and its stadium had a similar interior design as well, except the exterior had a bubbly aesthetic instead of a spiky one, as if the people there were somehow a 'soft bunch'… so Bendel considered. Korin had multiple nightmares about the game, ranging from lateness to injuries. Still, he was able to get *enough* sleep, remaining sufficiently fit for the day.

Korin's friends were able to see him before the match in the chambers underneath the field, outside the locker rooms. The hillseck uniforms were tightly-fitting and protective compression gear, as if between performance-designed gym wear and smooth, leathery dragon armour of the noblest order, padded at the shoulders for extra appeal. All the uniforms were officially approved, so stunning times were equal for all players. While complimenting Korin's ripped physique, Sylas thought it appeared uncomfortable, but Korin repeatedly affirmed that it was actually comfortable as he flexed his body.

"Yeah, they're fully protected," Korin referred to his genitals, confidently standing with his hands on his hips. "You can even kick them if you want."

"Oh, man, I'm going to enjoy this!" Sylas said, kicking Korin's balls with pleasure.

"Yep," Korin said, unfazed. "No box needed. It doesn't matter much, anyway, as sentar weapons are pretty soft; but it's cool, nonetheless."

Terala emerged from her changing room, and both guys couldn't help themselves but look at her backside, given that her everyday pants were generally looser. Sylas nudged Korin, who smirked back.

"I have cheeks up here, guys," Terala said, pointing to her face.

"You should wear that all the time." Sylas chuckled.

"I'll wear you in a moment," Terala muttered.

Celine approached Korin. "Here," she said, trying to place a shiny button on his hillseck outfit, although it wouldn't penetrate the material.

"What's that?" Korin asked.

"It's a good luck token."

"Those things are effective?" Sylas asked with surprise.

"I'd like to imagine they are." She shrugged with a modest smile.

"Aww, thanks, but we can't wear anything else out there," Korin said, hearing the coach calling for the team, his deep voice banging against the lockers. "I think I have to go now. I'll keep the button in spirit."

"Hey, where's *my* good luck token?" Terala asked, slightly hurt.

"You're with Korin, so you should be fine," Celine answered.

"Mm, alright," Terala mumbled, marching off.

Assuming the good luck token wouldn't actually work in all practicality and therefore wasn't an act of cheating having it in spirit, Korin waved goodbye to Sylas and Celine before entering the locker room, where the team was huddled. As the coach heavily clomped on the ground with his boots, his non-physical weight applied as well.

"Right, guys," the coach said, "this game's for real." He paused to squarely eye his soldiers. "Even though we could face a loser team in this round, you still got to keep a sharp game. Good thing we're not losers. Remember, we're winners!" He clenched his fists as the team roared their testosterone into the room. Terala included. "We're conquerors!" he enthused as the team erupted again, fists rising into the air. "We're annihilators!" he exclaimed aggressively as the team cheered a little less this time. "We're devourers!" the coach growled frenziedly as the cheering quieted down dramatically. "We'll rip through their skulls and –" The coach discontinued after growling and violently using his hands to explain, quickly discerning that he went too far as the team merely stared. "Er, but, uh… that doesn't mean that you can slacken off today, I mean. Treat this game like the final match. Now, as my old mentor once said: To crush –" He stopped, scratching his head with unease. "Uh, never mind. I believe in you guys. Now, go get them!"

A short moment of silence followed.

"Yeah, that's right!" Bendel shouted, triggering the team to cheer heartily again.

Uniformly dressed in black and blue, the eleven players then had their own motivational and tactical chat before moving on to the field. Titus had been thrust into the position of team captain a few weeks prior to the match, which he was ambivalent to, given that he liked his roguish autonomy. On the other hand, Titus did enjoy the glory, and he was undeniably the best on the team. The old team captain was still present, but he had to reduce his involvement in training sessions due to external, time-consuming factors. Both players led the chat, anyway. It was revealed that their opposition normally used tried-and-true tactics, which meant the Teloston team had a slight advantage in anticipating what they would likely enact.

"This is it," Korin said, gripping Terala's hand and arm. "I'm pretty excited about this. And a bit nervous, to be honest."

"Don't worry. You have me on the team." She smiled. "Let's go."

On the way out, the team picked up their officially-inspected sentars and sandecks. Korin completely missed the opening ceremony, but he didn't care, as he wouldn't have been able to properly focus and enjoy it with his anxiety. Though one of the best fighters, Korin was also one of the least efficient skaters. He was consequently placed as one of the most critical roles, the keeper, because little skating was required *when* inside the hill, and most of his job involved fighting. A lot of pressure was on him, but from all his training, he believed he was ready. Bendel and Terala were his guardians, and Titus, now the team captain, assumed the role of the roamer. Being a woman – and given her talent for skating – Terala was more suited to being a charger, but she nagged the coach for her position as a defender that game; she didn't get the role, but as part of their game tactic, the other two defenders were with the augmenters, so technically Terala was a temporary 'fourth defender' – one with limited rights – until the hill was secured.

As both teams entered the stadium, the vast audience gave a rousing cheer, standing up in droves as flags and other sporting paraphernalia waved and tossed back and forth. Soaking in the atmosphere as exhilaration and tension pumped through their bodies, the players waved back at the spectators. While some of the team members were in different fraternities, they were all playing for Teloston University, and this was clear by the audience's flags. Being hailed as a sporting competitor wasn't new to Korin, but it sure felt like it now, given his radically new setting. The externally-transparent and internally-translucent barrier shut out the audience's high energy, creating an isolating effect beyond just the noise level, granting players the environment to fully focus.

A keeper-orb suddenly approached Korin before rotating around his body, its presence, this time, feeling heavier than ever. He and his guardians were twitching, ready to shoot off as soon as the green light flashed. The rest of his teammates were also in their respective groups at their home base, waiting to charge into the centre of the field, cryptic winks, eyebrows, and nods relayed to one another. The opposing team stood out significantly in their red patterned uniforms, especially because blues saturated the field – most particularly the ice's light blue colour.

The other hillseck orbs emerged from the sides across the field, while the magnetically eye-catching hill called the casark was already situated in the centre of the field, radiating light like that of mystical riches shining out of a greatly sought-out treasure chest. A soft forcefield surrounded the hill; and it was turned on for testing once more before the game began, where it spun around while pulsating a hypnotic noise deep enough to make people tingle lightly. Connected to the marvellous centrepiece were the mag-limbs, which were also tested, moving about like an octopus's limbs, waving up and down so chargers could reach their charger orbs for when the second phase of the charging commenced. The mag-limbs looked like openings to outer space, unfathomably vast with their night-sky patterns of suns and stars of legion magnitudes. They then switched off, ready for the game. The charger rings then emerged, each at different locations around the field, where they stood stationary without turning off. Twenty-two proxportal catchers were also situated beneath the ice, ready to follow each designated player.

"We're so going to win this." Bendel chuckled cockily. "Ready, Korin?" He waved his staff before Korin nodded back, giving an affirmative movement with his own staff.

Finally, the starting flash signalled, and every player raced toward the centre at maximum speed. The first to reach their intended targets were the augmenters; both augmenter orbs were narrowly snatched up by Ritrae, and they promptly began zooming around the field, following the glittering, arranged geometric trail on the ground the augmenter orbs were producing in advance.

The opposing keeper locked in on Korin, who consequently chose to stay still. Terala zoomed a little in front, ready to take on the first opposing defender, whereas Bendel stood beside Korin as one of the Ritrae defenders attempted to flank them. Clumsily moving towards Terala, the other keeper and defender weren't prepared for Terala's fury and slick skating skills; she bobbed under their attacks before spinning around and slaying one of the defenders by stunning and pushing him to the ground. The ice instantly smashed and opened up, causing him to fall through to the proxportal catcher underneath, which teleported him back to his home base. The ice then swiftly reformed, allowing other players to skate over the area. Just as Terala was about to tackle the keeper, a third opposing defender literally charged out of the blue, shoving Terala to the ground without the slightest challenge, like a vehicle smacking a pedestrian. She vanished instantly.

The third opposing defender was using the double-edged bulldozer tactic – effective in one way but fallible on the other hand due to being able to easily crash. While holding both weapons in front of his tank-of-a-body, the bulldozer's uniform seemed as if it would rip at the seams and muscle protrusions. The bulldozer kept on charging towards Korin and Bendel, both of whom split up to dodge the wall. Now by himself having three opponents chasing him, Korin was about to head towards the centre of the field, but a teammate of his happened to sneakily knock the bulldozer to the ground, giving a thumbs-up to a very relieved Korin. With only two opponents chasing him now, Korin turned around to face them, zooming in and slaying the second defender with relative ease.

"Fuck!" The Ritrae keeper mimed.

Bendel eventually returned, ganging up with Korin against the keeper; but just as Korin was about to make his strike, a roamer's attack orb was thrown at him, stunning him and causing him to fall to the ground.

Korin smashed through the ice, and the teleportation felt like any other, except for the embarrassment and concern it brought. He was surprised that the opposing augmenter was able to succeed and produce the roamer orbs, despite the extra support the Teloston team provided for their augmenter. Korin also expected to meet Terala back in detention at their home base, but it turned out she had already left. Behind the base's entry line, Korin was beside a charger mate of his, waiting to be allowed back into the field after the thirty-second penalty. Once free after restlessly pacing along the line, Korin zoomed back into the field, attempting to reunite with Bendel and Terala, who were fighting off a skilled roamer. Korin's presence drew attention to the situation, so the Ritrae bulldozer headed their way.

Not again, Korin thought.

But just as it looked like trouble was approaching, Titus zipped across the bulldozer's path, hitting his legs and sending him to the ground. Titus couldn't join Korin at that moment, as he was now engaged with two angry chargers. With three against one, Korin and his defenders slashed right through the enemy roamer, quickly turning around to find the other keeper and defenders nearby. With no more obstacles, the three-on-three match came down to skill. Korin didn't let his mates seize all the action;

all three zoomed in rank, taking their opponents by storm, flurrying their staffs insanely fast, and knocking out each opponent at basically the same time. Before the keeper fell, Korin stretched out to risky levels of balance to grab the other keeper orb, pulling it into his own orbit.

"Yes!" Korin yelled before high-fiving his mates.

"Good work," Bendel said. "Now we play the waiting game."

"Should we help the chargers now or focus on something else?" Terala asked.

"Um…" Bendel scanned the area. "Shit, watch out!"

The opposing roamer not only was back on the field, but he threw an illusion orb at Korin, which managed to strike him. A cloud of tiny bits of interconnected holochite, distorchite, and neurachite then rapidly surrounded Korin, visually and subjectively smearing, smudging, and blowing all matter out of proportion. It was as though Korin had stepped into a fabled canvas filled with beclouded pastels and undetailed, amorphous forms, where ingredients drizzled and splashed seamlessly into one another. Although he had seen such illusions in training, the sight was still awe-inducing, causing Korin to stall. While the audience couldn't see what the illusion looked like from their angle – as the holograms were projected toward Korin – a small camera on Korin's uniform allowed vision of what he was experiencing to the audience via multiple screens across the stadium.

"Guys, keep close," Korin said. "I can't properly see anything."

Suddenly, a giant red blob rushed for Korin. He wasn't sure what it was, but Korin immediately and frantically started swinging his staff at the blob, hoping to hit its staff accurately. Appearing as part of some deranged person's mind, a blue cluster of warped figures kept close by, and it was a struggle for Korin not to bump into his mates. The bulldozer also appeared out of nowhere again and smacked Bendel and Terala to the ground, frustrating Korin immensely. When it seemed like the plan was lost, the opposing augmenter crashed into Korin, and both fell to the ground. The power of the illusion orb's cloud consequently stopped, and the resultant change in reality threw Korin's eyesight into disarray, compelling him to shut his eyelids and shake his head before readjusting to normality. Illusion orbs cycled through different types of illusions for each time they hit opponents, so it was not like Korin was going to get used to it that game – should the opposing roamer hit Korin again.

Because Korin fell, the opposing keeper's orb had been relinquished from Korin's orbit. Nevertheless, it was still floating in the field, ready to be picked up. Korin knew he had to rush to grab that orb, but the thirty-second penalty of returning to his home base prevented him from doing so…

Korin cringed with anxiety. *Oh, God, don't let anything happen.*

At least he didn't have to pick up his own keeper orb, as it naturally teleported back as well. He then sighed with relief after spotting Terala and Bendel protecting the other orb, belting the opponents who got close. Including the bulldozer. Finally.

Once back on the field again, Korin swooped up the opponent's keeper orb, meeting back with his defenders. Meanwhile, the Teloston chargers had almost activated the hill.

"Good work, Korin," Titus said, approaching. "Keep those orbs, and we'll win this."

The pressure on Korin mounted.

Titus added, "Stay near the hill and move in as soon as it activates."

"Got you," Korin said. "You want us to attack the chargers?"

"Only if they're in the vicinity. Otherwise, keep safe until then." Titus zoomed off, wiping out an enemy charger on the way.

"Come on, let's go." Terala nudged Korin.

After nearing the centre, the Teloston chargers had finally charged the hill, and the hill was unlocked, and the mag-limbs also activated. One of the mag-limb tentacles slid underneath Korin's hover skates, pulling him up. His sandecks automatically magnetized to it, bound to its sparkly substance. Staying upright was trickier than it looked, as, at any one point in time, players could rotate at any degree. Korin always found the mag-limbs the hardest in training, and it was no different that game; he accidentally revolved around, flipping upside down, his sense of bearing now weakened. The mag-limb, fortunately, had lifted and stayed up high, so Korin didn't hit the ground. The tentacle both curled and spun around the casark, and so Korin kept the same pace;

but there happened to be another player coming his way, unaware of him. Trying to swing himself upright, Korin managed to dodge crashing into the other guy by a few centimetres; his head, otherwise, would have been very sore indeed! Since his position was that of the keeper, he wasn't permitted to grab the charger orbs and prime the casark; he was nonetheless allowed to slay opposing chargers. Still, Korin had to get off the limb and enter the hill. With a pounding heart, Korin jumped off the mag-limb, grimacing while propelling himself forward, thinking he was done for, hands reaching out as if about to hit something hard. Just before hitting the ice, Korin jerked his legs down, fully flipping himself right-side-up. His training at long last paid off.

I can't believe it worked this time, Korin thought.

Without a single glance at his surroundings, Korin focused his attention on entering the hill, which was now a different colour. The atmosphere thickened the closer he approached, vibrating energies throughout his body. The forcefield only blocked charger orbs, and when he passed through, its fuzzy energy zapped him, causing his hair to slightly raise for a second. Once inside the hill, Korin felt as if he was truly in his domain. All of his teammates had to continue with their vital roles, as without them, Korin had no chance of even lasting a minute inside. Instantly, the casark whooped, indicating Teloston was scoring points by the second – double points, as Korin held two keeper orbs.

Terala was right outside the hill, giving Korin a firm nod before turning around to fight off as many combatants as possible. They soon overwhelmed her. The Ritrae team's main focus was now on stopping Korin. Since the hill was open for his opponents from three hundred and sixty degrees, Korin kept spinning around, paranoidly thinking that there was someone right behind him. For roughly half the time, there actually was a player ready to strike him down.

The bulldozer tried to enter, but special courtesy was given to him to prevent him from entering. Titus finally grabbed a now-available stonewaller orb, utilizing its bubble-shaped barrier to momentarily trap him and the bulldozer inside so the latter couldn't go anywhere – even the ground was blocked off, so he couldn't teleport back. Rage fumed from the bulldozer as he maniacally tried to ram a swift Titus repeatedly. The barrier literally fogged up to a degree as the humidity built.

Flinching and jerking with trepidation, Korin exhibited the characteristics of being on a speed potion as he slayed one player after another. Realizing their strategy was futile, the Ritrae team changed tactics, fully regrouping before heading together for the hill. Titus was free again, meeting up with Bendel and Terala; each shouted as they put up a good fight, but all three fell within a minute.

The other six Ritrae players circled Korin, grinning while zooming in. Korin braced himself, ducking when one player swung at him. In his lowered state, Korin spun his staff in a circle, hitting three opponents before jumping up to block an attack from behind him, holding his staff over his head as if posing for an epic photo. From there, Korin relinquished the staff, creating two weapons to backstab his opposition, literally kicking the player away. As for the final two attackers, Korin belted their oncoming weapons, hitting one before reaching over and warding off the other. A weakness in their tactics opened up, and Korin managed to exploit it, cutting through their defences to send both flying off balance. In the brief moment he had alone, Korin recharged his senses with some breathing exercises, not even bothering to waste a second looking at the timer.

Ritrae regrouped to try the same strategies again and again, but every time they attempted to stop Korin – in addition to the chargers – they failed. Korin was on fire.

The game then stopped for halftime, and the Teloston team spent most of it discussing further strategies in taking the hill again. When they re-entered the field, the Teloston team managed to retake the hill, where Korin succeeded in staying inside the whole time. Not once during the remaining game did the Ritrae team succeed in their goal; and when time ran out, Teloston University was the clear victor.

Coach Virkorska bolted into the deactivated field like another bulldozer, seemingly about to tackle Korin before hugging him. 'Hugging'.

"Okay. Please. Enough." Korin gasped for air.

"That was truly a murderous performance." Virkorska shook Korin's hand and shoulder in a manner that was too hard to determine if he wanted to kill Korin or that he was overwhelmingly happy. "Oh, and a great job from the rest of you guys as well. But, let's hear it for the champion of the match!" He bashed his hands together.

Most of the team didn't clap for Korin. Instead, they ran up to him, yelling, "Yes!" and, "Come on!" before demanding victory chest-bumps.

For obvious reasons, Terala didn't participate in the chest-bumping. She clapped instead.

"Again!" one teammate yelled, hitting Korin's chest even harder with a higher jump.

Korin was then lifted onto a couple of shoulders before being taken for a run around the field, which now had a floor covering the ice. In their frenzy, Korin almost fell off, laughing. The surrounding players raised their arms in the air, yelling out their excitement and enlivening the already-roaring audience even more. Rapid body waves channelled through the crowd while streamers shot into the air, spiralling and puffing out into themed explosions and insignias. Relishing in the glory, Korin attempted to spot people he knew in the audience, but there were too many people to sift through.

After the team settled down – to the point where they could process actual words, at least – both teams ended up shaking hands. Korin at last caught up with Terala, who was over the moons with her smile.

"I knew we'd win!" Terala shouted before strongly hugging Korin.

"I can't believe it!" Korin replied with a big grin. "I'm feeling on top of the world at the moment. You were fantastic out there, too."

"Thanks. I fell a few times, but I wasn't going to give up. I have a feeling, though, that the coach might put me back as a charger for the next match. At any rate, I now don't have any desire to punch anything for at least a day."

"That's good to hear." Korin chuckled.

"Again, great work, Korin!" Bendel remarked. "We'll definitely beat the other teams, for sure."

"We still have to watch them play."

"Yeah, but the next game isn't on for another three hours. We're celebrating now. Come." He motioned.

Titus then approached. "Hopefully we'll still be sober enough to watch the next game." He laughed.

"There are still major parties on later tonight, too," Bendel said.

"The first-years are having their own," Korin said.

"Yeah, I heard you guys booked the Dundil Mansion," Titus said. "We'll be heading to another party, though. If we make it."

***

Later that evening, the majority of people in Korin's year group headed over to the Dundil Mansion in the Private District, a mansion and property big enough to host a party the size of the first-year student body. Most people took advantage of the opportunity of it being open during the holidays, as parties in the dorm blocks were limited so as not to disturb people's sleep. Knowing he would be up late, Korin napped before turning up by himself to the party, which was already in full swing.

Electronic dance music blasted from speakers nearly everywhere, the vibration causing even the soil particles to dance. The gardens were impressively luxurious, with an assortment of tall, topiary plants from wild creature figures to the crazy abstract. There were also many stone statues, and it was fortunate that the guests didn't break them with their reckless behaviour. In effect, it almost seemed like the statues were consciously frowning at the scene in front of them. Gazebos and other small structures were nestled cosily next to beautiful rock pools, many filled with plump cushions-for-furniture and tropically-designed torches. As if a ceremony was about to take place, large spotlights lit the stately mansion, accentuating its golden walls of stone.

Soon after entering the mansion, Korin noticed Celine wandering around by herself, examining the ornaments in the huge lobby. Compared to the standard party dresses nearly all the other girls wore, Celine stood out with her quirky dress featuring physical pseudo roses inside a peachy, sheer fabric. By now, Korin learned that Celine didn't dress up for social approval, though she definitely liked compliments and warm regards. She was nevertheless aware of her oddity and the

attention she gained for it. But her dress actually looked very nice —
especially on her — and it wasn't *that* odd; she also wasn't receiving any
flak for it either.

"Hey, Celine," Korin said loudly so he could be heard over the noise
and music.

"Hey." Celine waved as her unexcited expression brightened. "Terala
said you'd probably arrive late. I wasn't sure if you were going to turn
up at all."

"Yeah, I was pretty tired," he said lethargically. "You just arrive?"

Before Celine responded, a silly student in his drunkenness tripped
over beside them, groaning and laughing. Celine didn't look too impressed, moving to the side before answering, "I've been here for a little
while. Anyway, I baked cakes for everyone. You can try one. They're in
the kitchen."

"Great. I'll try some later. I hope there's enough for everyone. There
are thousands here."

"Well, I couldn't cook *thousands*, unfortunately. Oh, congratulations
on the game, by the way." She smiled. "You were really good."

"Thanks. Thanks, Celine. I'm glad you saw it. My nerves are still a
bit twitchy. Look." He showed her a repetitious twitch in his arm. "I
didn't get to see you after the game because my teammates wanted to
party a bit. I don't think they'll be doing much for the next day or so."
He shook his head.

"Hey, Korin's here!" a voice boomed. "Hey, everyone! The man of
the match!" Jaimas stomped over and grabbed Korin's hand, lifting it
high in the air. "Whoo!" He prompted the crowd to cheer and clap.

"Okay, thank you, Jaimas," Korin responded, remaining modest,
not relishing in the glory this time.

"Since your next match isn't for another couple of days — and that
our exams have finished — you can finally get smashed tonight!"

"Yeah, fucking wasted!" a nearby student hollered, grabbing Korin
with exuberance.

"C'mon, let's smash our faces!" another yelled, storming into the next
room with his mates.

"We'll see." Korin rolled his eyes slightly.

"Come on. This way," Jaimas said, holding Korin's shoulders as they moved through the lobby.

Glancing back, Korin saw Celine still standing in the same spot, so he motioned for her to follow. Jaimas soon led Korin into a large room with a glass chamber in the centre. Terala was inside with someone else, both floating as they chugged down an alcoholic substance as part of a competition.

"Come on, Terala!" the crowd cried.

"I think this might be her fifth battle," Jaimas told Korin. "She's on a streak."

Yet again, Terala won the round, ceasing at the end, exiting. "Um, hi, Korin," Terala said, swaying like she was on a rocking ship, burping. "Er, I, er…" There was a delay before she chaotically vomited across the ground, tumbling over in it. Terala looked up with her head still spinning, face half covered in her own bile. "Oh, man, sorry about that," she said, looking like she would puke again.

While trying to avoid the vomit, Korin picked Terala up, asking, "Shit, are you okay?"

"Yeah. I'll be fine. I just need to sit down." She held her hands out, stumbling.

"You don't drink. Why'd you go that far, anyway?"

"I… I don't know," she answered, thoughts not quite together. "They… dared me, I think. I wasn't going to say no." She hopelessly held her head.

Korin frowned. "Yeah, but –" He sighed. "Fine. Just take it easy from now."

"Alright," she said, clumsily wiping her face with her clothes.

As he watched the mess that was Terala, Korin found the situation incredibly vulgar.

"Your turn, Korin." Jaimas nudged him.

"Maybe later," Korin lied, scrunching his face in disgust. "I have to help Terala."

"Alright, we'll compete with each other then."

Korin turned to Celine, saying, "Hopefully Terala will be fine."

Celine replied, "She –"

"Korin! Hi!" a sprightly, attractive girl said, squeezing herself between Korin and Celine. "I'm Jency. Nice to meet you." She fiddled with her half-filled glass, ignoring Celine as if she didn't exist.

The girl absorbed all of Korin's peripheral attention away from the surrounding scene, instantly captivating him. "Um, nice to meet you, too." Korin smiled back as Celine walked around so she wasn't blocked off.

"Would you like to dance?" Jency brushed Korin's shoulder sensually.

"Ah… yeah, sure," he replied dopily, inadvertently losing focus on helping Terala. "You don't mind?" He turned to Celine.

"No, that's fine. I'll keep Terala company," Celine responded tactfully.

"Okay, I'll talk soon," Korin said as he was slowly pulled away.

Jency began dancing straight away, dynamically moving with sheer confidence, drawing attention from those around her. Korin, however, had barely danced in his life; and of the dancing he did, it wasn't to party music – it was formal; so, to avoid embarrassment, he kept his movements rather simple and lowkey. The repetitive music soon numbed his minor concerns, and although the dancing was somewhat fun for him, Korin's awareness mainly centred on Jency, who became more and more alluring. It just dawned on him – he didn't know how she knew him.

"Nice work in the hill today," Jency remarked as she slowed her movements, moving closer to Korin. "I watched you the whole time." She giggled.

"Well, I couldn't have done it without my teammates." He shrugged self-effacingly.

"Oh, you, stop being modest." She hit him lightly, smiling coyly.

Korin smiled back, not knowing what to say. "I haven't seen you around before. What classes are you in?" he finally asked, not sure if it was the right question, given the context and mood.

"Oh, just the basic ones, along with Psychology and Sociology. I don't know *what* I'm doing." She giggled again. "Anyway, now that the semester's over, we have lots of time for fun." She pressed her body against Korin, whose body temperature rose.

"Yeah. Yeah, we do," Korin dumbly said, lost for words as his strong attraction to Jency made him lose nearly all sense of reason.

Jency smoothly placed her arms around Korin, staring right into his eyes. "Hey, let's go upstairs," she said discreetly, grinning.

Grabbing Korin's hand, Jency led him through the thick crowd of dancers. Despite the music, Korin's heart pumped so heavily that he still heard it. Every thought that tried to spring to mind was smothered by the throbbing, primal urges lurking in his core. He knew what was coming. Since his encounter with Priscilla, he had, indeed, thought more of the matter. Korin had fully dropped his religious dogma and all the close ideas associated with it, feeling no boundaries regarding sex now – apart from assault and a few other issues, of course. The sense of social freedom was almost as exhilarating as his anticipation of events. His confidence even improved, or at least he believed it did; he had yet to put his imaginations into practice. Reality was always a different story.

One of the rooms Jency checked was a bedroom. After furtively closing the door behind her, she immediately grabbed Korin, fervently pushing her lips against his, sloppily pashing him. Kissing while walking backwards, Korin fell to a comfy chair, and Jency hopped on top of him, giggling. Korin still lacked experience in taking the lead, and Jency's intense, assertive energy drove the power dynamic, leading and over-whelming Korin, who passively followed. He thought his newfound confidence would've made him more active, but there was still that elemental uncertainty of inexperience holding him back. Her crotch was sitting on his, slowly pushing against it. As she was somewhat drunk – and, in her feverishly-animalistic, careless ecstasy – some of her saliva gradually trickled down Korin's neck.

Jency then rapidly took her shirt off before continuing to kiss Korin, who was too caught up in the moment to remove his clothes. She also held her hands around his head and neck, gradually sliding one hand down his body, exciting him incredibly as he squirmed slightly; but just as Korin thought her hand was going to go down his pants, she started rubbing herself instead. He held her firm ass even tighter, but a loud bang on the door killed their heated moment. One second later, the door swung open, and the lights turned on.

"What the fuck is happening?" an older, muscular student yelled, scowling at a shocked couple. "Get the fuck off him now!" he ordered Jency, who promptly leapt off Korin, grabbing her shirt.

"Kieran! Uh… he… I…" Jency responded without a cogent thought.

Kieran didn't know who to begin shouting at as he stood stationary, giving the impression that he was about to explode.

"It's not what it looks like," Korin finally responded. "I had no idea you two were together."

"Shut it!" Kieran ordered with an assertive hand gesture. "You!" He pointed at Jency. "I'll deal with you later. And as for you," he said to Korin, his glare alone doing the pointing this time, "I'm going to fucking kill you!"

"Hey, look, I-I really had no idea. I'm not that type of person. I would never have –" Korin stopped as he saw Kieran charging up a spell.

It wasn't long before Kieren alchemically shapeshifted; his new body looked similar, except that he had much bigger muscles, each quivering rapidly in excitement. With veins popping out of his thick neck, he grunted with a far deeper voice as he glowered at Korin.

Korin had understood trouble was coming his way, so he had already began tuning into the Aether; still, he needed more time, so in order to stall Kieran just a bit longer, Korin asked, "What did you just do?"

"Transformed." Kieran flexed while roaring menacingly. "It was fortunate that I had transfigured earlier," he said, bringing out an empty vial, "so I didn't have to waste time on doing so now."

"Wait, what kind of potion and spell was that?"

"Why does it matter to you? You'll be dead in a moment after I literally shove your head up your fucking ass!"

As Kieran resolutely began approaching, Korin had just connected to the Aether. He immediately proceeded to fire a couple of beta-negative blasts, knocking Kieran unconscious immediately, causing the hulk to fall hard on the floor.

"What have you done to him?" Jency angrily yelled at Korin, alarmed at the large thud when Kieran hit the floor.

"What have *I* done?" Korin shouted. "He's still alive, and I doubt he's even hurt for that matter. And why the fuck would you try and sleep with me when you have a boyfriend?"

"You can't blame *me* for that!" She held her chest.

"How… I… I don't even know what to say now." Korin shook his head, unable to believe Jency's arrogance, thinking perhaps she'd also say that she was the 'victim'. "That's it, I'm out of here. I suggest calling security, as he might do something to you."

"Right," Jency replied, eyes averted.

Feeling as if he had lowered his integrity to a new low for even engaging with Jency in the first place, Korin took one last angry glance at her before storming out. He unapologetically bumped into numerous people along the way as his fury rose. Many of the first-years were taking drugs, some too spaced-out to even notice who nudged passed them, anyway. Needing to vent his anger, Korin wanted to pick and throw one of the ornaments he passed, but too many people were close by. When he approached a clear space, however, Korin grabbed a jar and threw it at the wall, smashing it and startling some of the partiers. A small amount of guilt arose, but Korin's anger squashed it down. He searched for a place to be alone with his thoughts, soon finding a small, isolated balcony free of people.

At first, his mulling revolved around Jency's dishonesty and unbelievable arrogance before what he wondered as possibly base behaviour on his own part, regardless of her cheating actions. He realized his intent probably wasn't in the right place to begin with, sensing as though it, like his awkward moment with Priscilla, wasn't well thought out. The flipside experience, at least, awarded him an epiphany. He remained on the balcony for a while as his intuitions and thoughts slowly gathered in his heated mind.

Although the recent encounter was, indeed, pleasurable on one level -- Korin didn't deny that -- he knew something wasn't right either. His newfound understanding led him to grasp the actual sensation he was experiencing: one of emptiness; like plain sugar, the lusty play was tasty yet unsatisfying. While there was far more to acknowledge, his mind expanded to that which surrounded him.

A disgust grew inside him for the party's atmosphere and the degenerate actions of his peers. The root cause, he intuitively cogitated, was an overtly obvious indifference and avoidance of virtue and the authenticity of one's reality; a pathetic numbness born of the cowardly avoidance of self-reflection – an entrenched norm that was insanely and savagely defended when brought to light as if corruption compelled such people to cover for the slimy beasts in the depths of their souls. Their actions massed – and could only survive – in a realm of murk and mire. At its highest levels. There was also the larger dimensional aspect involving motion and consequences – in this case, senseless and meaningless misdirection; although, Korin definitely felt a particular type of direction was present – a collective, unconscious, and nearly unspoken pressure to conform to the acts he saw.

Korin went back and forth on self-reflecting and critically analysing the party. He sensed that his short-lived experience with Jency was as hollow as the surrounding purposeless sea of mediocre nonsense passing as the height of fun. While apprehending his religious upbringing was pure garbage at best, he also felt as though the degeneracy he was swamped in was troublesome and unsettling in its own ways. His ruminations were primitively articulated, but the intuitions were on the mark; he certainly, now, wasn't going to engage in any more degeneracy.

The frustrations of social isolation he had months ago resurfaced, and his anger built. Korin didn't want to spend a second more in what he considered a cesspit, feeling like there was a bubble of gunk already around him. He began leaving.

On the way, he found a bathroom, where he washed his face – and neck – repeatedly. Coupled with his new outlook, he felt much cleaner. Rage, however, reigned inside him, beginning to consume his soul. The cleanliness he momentarily held fell as he imagined his energy literally scorching the bathroom, burning it into utter blackness. He was falling into yet another pit. When Korin looked into his eyes, he quickly realized his fury was heading down a negative path, and he was glad he registered the problem immediately, completely shaking off such extreme emotions. After climbing out of the second pit while exiting the bathroom, Korin spotted Sylas laughing with two girls.

"Hey, there you are!" Sylas called out for Korin. "Where have you been this whole time?"

Korin's frustrations were bubbling inside his throat. He physically felt it, and he was about to yell, but Sylas was his friend. He struggled to keep cool. "Somewhere," Korin grumbled. "Look, I'm going to leave now."

"What?" Sylas asked incredulously. "It's too early to *leave*. See those girls over there?" He pointed to two pretty girls who keenly waved back. "I was planning you'd –"

"I'm not doing anything else," Korin interrupted coldly.

Pausing for a couple of seconds, Sylas asked, "Are you okay, man? Those... those girls are looking for action. Are you in?"

"No, I'm *not* in," he emphasized greatly, leering; and despite his sharp tone, it was nothing compared to the well of anger underneath.

"But it's..." Sylas paused again, understanding Korin wasn't going to budge. "Okay, I understand. Something happened, and you need some space. But *at least* say hi to them."

Korin considered his proposal, only because it was Sylas. "Fine," Korin finally mumbled. "But then I'm leaving straight after." He respired greatly, walking up to greet them.

"Hey," Sylas said to the girls, "I bet you recognize Korin here."

"Hi, Korin," both girls enthusiastically said at once.

"Congratulations on the game earlier," one said flirtishly. "You were the best there."

Restlessly looking around, Korin responded, "Yeah... look, I've had a long day, so I need to go."

"Oh, that's too bad," one girl said. "Sylas told us a lot about you." She smiled seductively.

"Mm. Right, I'm off now," Korin said, taking his leave.

"Hey, Korin," Sylas called out, taking a moment to think of something convincing to say. "Try not to linger on whatever happened too long. You'll feel better sooner." He smiled with compassion, waving.

Korin acknowledged that his friend was right, but he was too ticked off to verbally agree. Just as Korin was about to exit, he noticed Celine wandering around by herself again. He felt horrible that he abruptly left with Jency, dumping the responsibility of Terala on Celine.

"Hey, Celine." Korin struggled to smile. "I'm heading off now. Are you staying?"

"Not sure." Celine shrugged. "I can come with you."

"Um... sure, if you want; but I'm not doing anything else tonight."

"That's alright," she replied cheerily as they started leaving. "I'm not doing too much, anyway."

Walking through the crowd with Celine had a calming effect on Korin. The way she moved was so serene and blithe, especially in comparison to the partygoers. Korin was about to ask if anyone liked the cakes, but near the exit, he glimpsed quite a few cake slices splattered up against the wall, drooling down before slumping on the ground next to trash littered everywhere. He guessed that they were Celine's, and he recalled her mentioning about how people in her past destroyed her creations, like her lunapex cards. Korin chose not to say anything, pointing away from the mess so she wouldn't be upset. Korin supposed that Celine put a fair amount of effort into her deserts, and yet, at least a certain number of people – perhaps most, he thought – couldn't have given a shit about her handiwork. He wasn't concerned about whether they liked the cakes or not; it was, instead, the immature despoiling and destructive nature of their actions that vexed him. Filtering through Celine's energy, his umbrage was soon watered down into mere unhappiness.

While a few metres outside the mansion, Jaimas was hollering over a random performance before he turned around and literally jumped over to Korin and Celine. "Hey, where are you two off to? Oh, *I* see." Jaimas grinned.

"No, Jaimas," Korin replied sternly. "We're about to leave. We've had enough for the night."

"What? Get out of here!" Jaimas was about to playfully push Korin's shoulder, but Korin deflected it. "Oh, you're serious. But there are so many cool things that are yet to happen. You've got to at least stay for the wartui field."

"What's… that?" Korin asked curiously.

Jaimas laughed loudly. "You sound like you've been living under a rock. Okay, so it's like an epic, collective drug, but without any aftereffects or addiction. And, I know what you're thinking; the thing is, it's totally not a drug. Trust me."

"Uh, I don't know," Korin mumbled, conflicted with wanting to leave while simultaneously being ensnared by Jaimas's energy. "Is it safe to use?"

"Yeah, of course! And as I said, it's totally not a drug; but damn me to Seckaphon is it fun!"

"It sounds like it could be fun." Celine simpered. "I wouldn't mind trying."

"Well…" Korin sighed, almost grunting. "If *you* want to try it, I'll… give it a go."

Korin felt better that he stepped out of his emotional rut while concurrently being angry for not giving in to eternal rage. Despite some of his antics, Jaimas was different from most of the people at the party – in his own Jaimas-y way – and Korin still liked him. Korin then believed that he was probably a little too critical of everyone around him; however, that didn't mean Korin softened to the degeneracy *itself* everywhere – just that he wasn't so deadly furious.

"Great, they're setting the field up out back," Jaimas said, carelessly throwing his cup on the ground.

Korin was about to angrily comment, but he asked, "Setting it up? So, what is this thing, exactly?"

"Spores. A bunch of plants release a field of spores, which surround you like crazy."

As he walked, Korin hoped the atmosphere wouldn't be filled with the same energy inside the mansion thriving under the shallow and seemingly-happy mask of 'fun'. The back of the estate contained a large swimming pool complex, more beautiful gardens, a big patio, a marble courtyard, along with other areas and utilities. In the courtyard, a mesh of fairy-lights hung overhead, flashing in accordance with the music's beat. When Korin entered, he noticed a few people establishing potted, red-bulbed plants.

Just as Korin was about to ask Jaimas a question, the big lad had already turned his attention to a random group to do something silly. The overall vibe in the courtyard wasn't as dank as inside, as most of the partiers were too busy dancing to really engage in anything *too* degenerate for long enough to drag their energies down. Being outside helped Korin increasingly relax, and when he looked over at Celine, who was quietly gazing around, a warmness grew inside him.

"Want to dance until they set this off?" Korin asked, shrugging.

"I'd love to," Celine replied enthusiastically. Unexpectedly, she took Korin's hands. Unlike the individualistic dancing around them, Celine's dancing was playful, pushing and stepping back and forth as she giggled. Korin lightened up almost instantly.

The bulbs blew off the plants, releasing a green fume, which permeated the area. A jelly-mesh texture smothered their bodies, but it was the electrically-charged field around the spores that produced most of the effects. Korin could sense the movements of many others in the courtyard, and when the closest people to him shifted in one direction, Korin was compelled to move in the same manner, as if being pulled or pushed lightly. In one way, it was similar to being on a crammed subroute capsule, just without the discomfort. His body seemed like it would bend and wave before he felt like he would eventually melt away into the field. However, the collective waves became stronger when there were large, sudden movements. At one point, two people dramatically fell over, in turn sending a diminishing ripple across half the courtyard and throwing Korin and Celine to the ground.

"Ooh, you alright?" Korin asked, laughing as he stood up.

"I think so; but I can't get back up." Celine laughed as well, holding her hand out.

Korin struggled a bit with picking her up, managing in the end. He embraced Celine closely with his arms securely holding her. Their breathing matched. Celine was his friend, but he found her wildly attractive, both physically and now on a deeper level. For a moment, Korin stared at Celine, not knowing what to do. Celine was different. She wasn't a random floozy, nor was she a plain or ugly flower. Unfortunately, Korin had also never been in a *proper* relationship before, and he panicked. He didn't want to spoil or ruin the friendship. Korin wasn't exactly sure what Celine felt, but her feminine, pleasant, and unique energy utterly allured him. Deciding to take what he considered worthy of a risk, Korin drew Celine in and kissed her. She closed her eyes as she keenly embraced him, entrusting Korin, who passionately ran his hand through her thick hair. Coupled with the effects of the field, time seemed to stand still.

Suddenly, Celine was ripped from his grasp, and the blissful moment was lost in a panic. She squealed, and Korin feared the worst. He jolted as he opened his eyes, seeing Celine on the ground again. His heart relaxed.

"I need help again," Celine said, smiling as she reached out.

Korin picked Celine up, both laughing at what had happened. The music itself acted as an agent in the field, and when the music slowed, it encouraged the two heartthrobs to dance slower and closer together. The more time spent in the field, the more significant the effect it had on the mind; their heads began to internally rotate around and around.

"This feels really weird." Korin laughed as he stopped dancing, swaying now in the one collective movement of the field. "Have you felt anything like this before?"

"No," Celine replied as she also stopped dancing, observing the atmosphere.

The lights above appeared blurry, with groovy trails behind them. Although blissful, the experience became taxing on their consciousness. But that wasn't the main problem; Korin and Celine didn't know it, but their fatigue was greatly affected by the lower energies of those nearby, exacerbated via the field as an indirect side effect.

"I think I've had enough," Korin said, attempting to leave, walking very slowly so they didn't disturb anyone else.

When they left, both dropped to the ground, noticing others lying in various spots, having also retired from the field; although, some people were simply passed out due to drugs. So exhausted after the field – and without even realizing it – Korin and Celine shortly passed out on the grass.

Chapter Twenty

The Descent – At Last

For the week following the first Dundil Mansion party, Korin was very busy. For starters, he had to deal with unusual post-class administration procedures because of his different background and circumstances, all in addition to the standard admin forms all students had to complete. And then, of course, once the hillseck team recovered from the first party, their coach forced them – physically – to practice before their final two matches. It was a good thing they did practice, as their competition was fiercer, but the Teloston team prevailed in the end, winning the County Cup, granting them access to the Province, State, and hopefully, World Cup games later in the year. Titus and Bendel wanted Korin to get a tattoo in honour of their victory, but he was a bit unsure of the idea, deciding he needed time to think it over. They were naturally a little disheartened.

Korin maddeningly wanted to spend time with Celine during the week, but he had little opportunity. Even when both found time to meet up, something would occur, calling their attention to more concerning matters. One such matter regarded the etheric data analyser they acquired earlier from one of the cult's basements. Korin received a call explaining that the mechanical side was fixed, but access to the neurachite brain's memory was still locked. The specialist said that he had done all he could to safely hack into the EDA, and there was potentially a way to bypass its safeguards, but that would entail a major risk of losing all the data therein, with supposedly a less than one-in-one-thousand chance of success in normal circumstances. Rituals and magic would only marginally increase the likelihood and could cause other problems. Korin didn't like the odds, so he decided not to risk it. However, the expert did say that the last-used application and settings were still active and were able to appear on the screen when powered up. In other words, Korin could still use the device but not alter its settings or explore any of the EDA's data. The expert also expounded on how EDAs worked in general, saying that they didn't show actual etheric energy but, instead, tuned into etheric energy, in turn displaying feedback results through the device. Virtually all results were never accurate, as etheric energy was 'broad', so to speak, in the sense that it possessed various probabilities. Thus, the EDA was generally effective at presenting correlative data, not concrete data. If Korin were to use it during the lunapexes, he was told, it was possible that his search could be distorted, as the EDA could pick up the energies of those who he wasn't searching for – that is, non-cultists; but such signals would be faint and could flicker on and off.

Understanding the limitations of the situation, Korin acknowledged that it was still his best, established hope in locating the shadowists, so he accepted the state of affairs, paying the specialist before taking the EDA. With a backup now in place, Korin was somewhat reassured; but he, and his friends, still frantically hunted for cultist leads with the little time they had with each other, worrying that the missing students would probably end up dying due to their unsuccessful efforts. At least the EDA was fixed *before* the major lunapex – the one Darsan said would involve sacrifices.

It was also Terala's birthday on the Starday before the lunapex; and even though Korin planned to celebrate after the upcoming ritual, Terala still managed to celebrate her birthday by thrashing the last team and gaining lots of glory afterwards. She didn't follow up on her drinking games from the first party, having regretted it the following couple of days. Korin was pleased with the news. As for her presents, Korin also left buying her something to the last minute, failing to find anything in time. Sylas, however, was actually organized – yes, organized – buying Terala a present, which only came in the mail later in the evening, so he waited for the next day to give it to her.

***

The last day of the month dawned, and since Crysten was four hours behind Lunapex Mean Time, their time zone always saw the start of the lunapex before the day ended. That morning, Korin and his friends were eating their second last meal in the food hall before it shut down for the lunapex festival during the night.

"Hey, I got you something," Sylas said to Terala, plonking a wrapped present on the table.

"You actually got me something?" Terala asked, somewhat amazed.

"How could I forget about you? You're the loudest one here!" Sylas chuckled.

"Very funny. Okay, let's see." Terala reached for the present, unwrapping it rapidly to see a frame containing an ultra-rare uniform from an old, famous hillseck player. "Is… this?" Terala's gaze was as tight as her grip.

"Yep, it's the actual uniform of that hillseck girl you kept talking about. You know, Lecindy. The one who was on that team that won all those championships."

"You… actually got… you actually got… her uniform?" Her eyes widened greatly.

"Yeah, the one she had for her retirement match."

"You… actually got…" Her staring continued; and although her face was still, her hands shook, in turn shaking the frame.

"Yep… I wouldn't open it, though. Well, *I* wouldn't open it. I like to preserve really rare stuff. But it's up to you." He shrugged.

Terala finally glanced at Sylas, slowly placing the frame down before leaping at him, causing Sylas to flinch, thinking that she was about to attack him; instead, she gave him a big hug. "Thank you."

"Oh… you're welcome." Sylas awkwardly hugged her back, unsure if she would change her demeanour at any second.

After hugging Sylas, she stared back at the frame, remaining quiet for the time being; it was obvious that she was going to talk about it nonstop after the shock wore off.

"I also have another present. Here." Sylas brought out another gift, grinning.

Terala was still too staggered to immediately grab it, so Sylas had to deliver it to her hands. Slowly, Terala opened the wrapping, only to find an anime character doll, scantily clad with cute, bubbly eyes. Terala's look of amazement turned to one of pure vexation, the frown turning into a scowl. Sylas unsurprisingly laughed, banging the table in amusement, while Korin and Celine giggled.

"Think of it like a mascot," Sylas said.

Terala would naturally have tossed the item, but she placed it on the table, her mixed emotions preventing her from killing Sylas. She sighed and then focused back on the frame.

When the mood settled, Celine cleared her throat and said, "I also have something to give." She then gave what Terala guessed was another frame, finding, indeed, that it was – except that it contained a collection of professional photography work of Terala in the heat of the hillseck games, a few of her striking opponents, and others performing an array of aerobatics. "I was up late last night getting the images just right," Celine said. "This one where you're jumping up and just missing the blade is my favourite. I hope you like it."

After a moment of examining her gift, Terala let out a soft, "Aww," before smiling and sniffling. A tear also emerged.

"Wait, are you crying?" Sylas asked.

"No! I never cry!" Terala exclaimed swiftly, hardening up before warmly turning to Celine. "Thank you, Celine. I really appreciate it."

"No problem. I enjoyed making it."

"You should've used your surreal-lens filter." Sylas chuckled.

"It was on my mind." Celine shiftily smirked.

"I'll keep this on my wall next to my bed. Again, thank you." Terala hugged Celine.

"Well, I'm glad you didn't have to sing happy birthday to yourself yesterday," Sylas cheekily said to Terala.

"Yeah, the hillseck team was a blast last night, but it's a pity I had to go to bed early. I hope this was worth it, Korin."

"We needed our rest," Korin claimed. "We don't know what we'll face tonight."

"But we still haven't found anything," Sylas said.

"I know, but we can't give up now. Many people are counting on us. Anyway, we still have the EDA as our last hope." Korin brought the device out, staring at it anxiously before everyone remained silent for a few minutes, worrying about upcoming events that night. Korin was then the one to break the silence, saying, "Hey, I received my grades this morning. How did everyone go?"

"I got straight A's for my photography courses," Celine said. "And then I got exceeding expectations for General Theory and Alchemy, and then an M plus for Conjuration and Phasarchement."

"What?" Sylas yelled irately. "Cartras gave me a straight meeting expectations mark. How did you beat me?"

Celine merely shrugged and smiled.

"Well, there was an essay," Korin said. "Did you get your results for that?"

"Oh, of course!" Sylas responded. "That explains everything."

"Or does it…" Korin squinted and then chuckled.

"It does. I handed Cartras only one sheet of paper with a few paragraphs on it. I also folded it into a fish and even doodled halfway through it. He wasn't impressed."

"Okay, but the essay didn't matter much. But it makes a little sense. Anyway," Korin said, turning to Celine, "that's fantastic. But I'm not surprised. You worked pretty hard."

Celine smiled graciously, though Sylas and Terala didn't pick up on her more-than-happy expression; they were yet to find out how Korin and Celine felt about each other. By chance, every time the couple displayed affection for one another during the little time they had together, Sylas and Terala weren't present.

"So, what else did you get?" Korin asked Sylas.

"Let me think. Conjuration: M plus; Alchemy: M; Gen Theory: M minus. Ugh, if only we had a lecturer who didn't send me to sleep. Um, Finance: C plus, and Management: B. I'm just happy I passed. I bet I could've done *way* better if I properly studied and put effort into my assignments."

"That's not bad. Considering. Then again, Conjuration was an easy mark after constructing a spell. What about you, Terala?"

"What about *you*, Korin?" Terala returned the question rapidly.

"Um, alright. I got an M plus for Conjuration, Alchemy, and Gen Theory, and then an E minus for Phasarchement," he said, grinning and nodding his head proudly, "and a B plus for History. Unfortunately, due to some annoying complication, I got a C plus for Political Science; but I did well on the exam. Come on, Terala, tell us. We'll try not to judge you. Much."

"Fine." Terala sighed. "M for Conjuration; M for Alchemy; M minus for Gen Theory; M plus for Phasarchement." She glowered at Korin as he smirked. "And a B for Emergency Services. It was all classroom work for this semester, so we'll get out-and-about for the next one. Maybe rescue a few people."

"That'll be cool if you do," Korin said. "Hey, it looks like you tied with Sylas."

"Yeah, but I was distracted this semester – especially with hillseck."

"Well, in any case, Celine won, so we should give her a prize later. Anyway, we need to get moving, guys." Korin stood up, and when all four moved outside to begin individually scouting the university again, Korin turned to Sylas before separating, scratching his head with discomfiture. "Hey, Sylas," he said with a regretful tone. "You're probably wondering about the party and –"

"Dude, don't even worry." Sylas flopped his hand. "I knew you just needed time to recover."

"Thanks. I apologize for being short with you."

Sylas tilted his head before saying, "I just hope that you're feeling better."

"Yeah. A lot. I won't say what happened, but… yeah…" He exhaled his pent-up emotions.

"Well, I still feel sorry for you, as you missed out on some *real* fun. Best. Night. Ever. Those two girls were –"

"I-I think I can imagine," Korin interrupted. "I'm fine. I… take it they aren't interested in you now?"

"Nah, they were only interested in that one night."

"Right." Korin nodded, deciding not to say anything more. "Alright, I'll see you later."

***

For most of the day, Korin searched for leads, exasperatingly finding not a single trace of anything other than his own misinterpretations of happenings. He also, yet again, tried entering Priscilla's sanctuary, seeing a thick cement wall blocking the path, so he guessed either the university permanently closed it off, or she was very adamant about nobody entering. Although the lunapex didn't begin until eight o'clock that night, the crystal moon felt about ready to transfigure the elemental moon, even though the former was yet to glow with its own energy.

Korin had dinner on a side bench in the Central Hub, barely paying attention to each bite of his large sandwich, thinking only of the important task of saving the missing students. This, of course, was despite music blasting throughout the air, in addition to the thousands of students, faculty, and other beings busily preparing for the lunapex celebration. Most people wore costumes and masks resembling the relevant crystal moon in accordance with the Centras zodiac's energies and its embodied characteristics. Other people, meanwhile, wore attires representing an elemental moon they hoped for or predicted would manifest. Since the lunapex wasn't just a static zodiac itself but rather a holistic event of celestial energies, many different types of animals in diverse forms and contexts were associated with certain themes and archetypes – many with overlaps with one another. The more culturally common a primordial beast was, the deeper it would be ingrained in the subconscious of those in society.

Live musicians marched through the streets, blowing and banging their wind and percussion instruments to up-tempo beats. Draped with warm curtains adorned with stylized icons, scaffolding had been placed along the footpaths and roads, forming high walkways featuring areas ready for varying performers. Dualistic artwork symbolically personified the masculine and feminine polarities of the sun and crystal moon, both abstractly gravitating around one another; virtually all celestial beings were caricatured with expressions. Drab utilities were also animalized and enlivened with either artwork or decorations; sewer grates had faces, and signposts wore hats. One could even see the smell of food sizzling in the air; the greasier the food, the yellower the steam. In a few spots, the mist drifted incessantly, feeling like concentrated sprays of liquid. From thick cotton tents to iron wall-sconce fixtures, incense burned far and wide, creating varyingly thick clouds.

Korin met up with his friends, learning that they had the same level of achievement. Sylas nevertheless lightened the mood, handing snacks to everyone. He was also wearing a meme shirt stating, 'The Rumour Drone Is Always Right'. In the centre, of course, was a picture of a rumour drone. When Korin saw the shirt, he instantly chuckled.

Sylas grinned. "It's true! It's *always* right."

"Indeed," Korin replied.

"No, really. Look." Sylas showed him a jar of troll sweat. "They're selling it at that stall over there."

Korin gaped at the sight before shaking his head and laughing. It caused him to feel a bit better. Sylas also had another laugh while the girls joined in, too.

When the laughter eased down, Korin noticed that Celine wore a red papier-mâché moon necklace instead of her regular jewellery. "Where did you get that?"

"One of the stalls. I didn't take long. I figured I wouldn't have found anything in that time."

"Yeah, I know," he said depressingly as if he hadn't laughed just a minute ago. "It looks nice, by the way." Korin inhaled a large amount of incense, which calmed his senses. "So, it seems like we won't be able to do anything until eight o'clock, which is… about five minutes away."

"Do you think it'll be too late by then?" Sylas asked.

"Well, you have to consider that the lunapex only just begins at eight, and the cult has two days, basically, to do their ritual, so they may not start straight away. Well, I'm hoping. I really am."

"Can I have another look at the EDA?"

"Sure," Korin answered, handing it over before taking a seat to rest his legs again.

Eight o'clock finally struck, and the crystal moon discharged a portion of its crystals like an explosion, birthing multiple energies while beaming with a vibrant glow as well as flaring out a reddish-orange hue with large swirls. The spotty brown and yellow gas elemental moon then began transfiguring. Like with general shapeshifting, there was a radical change in the etheric coding. In a split moment, the gas moon shifted realities, where a short blur occurred before the materialization of yet another fire moon, which shone around the crystal moon with its min-sun nature. For only a split moment, it *seemed* like the totality of summerness had practically blazed out of the heavens, as if the celestial bodies had been burnt to ashes, unable to guard and keep the summer god's wrath at bay. The night sky was still filled with stars brightly shining down, and the crystal moon's colour didn't detract from the night, nor was it too imposing and intense. It was as if it had reached a peak level of intensity, enough to stimulate wonder without being too selfishly glaring. A rush of energy wrapped around Korin, uplifting him from his wearying and worrying task of finding the missing students. Despite the intensity of the situation – and also despite the fact that Korin had seen such a lunapex many times before – he and everyone else momentarily stared at the wonder-inducing crystal moon. The fireworks and other air displays began, but Korin's attention immediately turned to Sylas.

"It's working!" Sylas shouted.

Korin tensely jumped up and ran over to check the device, noticing that the holographic, translucent screen showed a faint trail of energy behind two people, who were swiftly making their way through the crowd.

"They're the only people who are lit up," Sylas noted.

"Then they're probably cultists," Korin responded. "Quick, before they move out of sight." He darted off as he excitedly thought, *We found them. We finally fucking found them!*

Korin wanted to go on and on about how mentally draining it was trying to locate the cult over the course of the semester and how much joy he experienced in spotting even the most modicum of trails; but he stayed quiet as he channelled his heightened sense of enthusiasm into springy feet, following on. The energy trail was short as well, and the group had to keep the pace fairly close so they wouldn't lose the cultists. Sylas mentioned a few times that some other flickers emerged around other people, but Korin told him that they were most likely false positives and that they had to focus on the first two students they initially saw. Because there were so many people in the vicinity, keeping a low profile wasn't necessary, so their chase was easy enough for the time being…

However, a random group of first-years surrounded Korin, eagerly grabbing him to quickly take a few pictures of him with each other, congratulating him again on the last hillseck match. Korin tried to tell them that he was in the middle of something *drastically* important, but the surrounding noise and physical rambunctiousness drowned him out. It also didn't help that the students in question were in a frenzy, already half drunk. Sylas was still holding the EDA, but he, Terala, and Celine continued on immediately, otherwise, they risked losing their only chance at finding the cult's base. Without creating a commotion, Korin finally broke free and resumed the pursuit, infuriated that he had lost sight of his friends. He tried calling Sylas on his watch, but he didn't answer, and Korin assumed it might have been on silent. It was also the same with Celine's and Terala's.

A hooded Priscilla suddenly entered the vicinity, skulking through the thickening crowd. Utterly grateful for the sighting, Korin lightly pushed through one person after another trying to reach Priscilla, who managed to slip through at the same pace without a single shove. She continued beyond the Provision Wreath along one of the main roads, heading in the direction of the Private District. Just behind her, one of the marching bands came by, blocking the path; and by the time Korin raced around, he had lost sight of Priscilla.

He cursed loudly.

There was no way Korin was going to give up, so he continued running along the main road until reaching the Private District. He then ran down one of the streets, trying to hold on to hope, which was vanishing rapidly. He even smelled some troll sweat on a couple of people he passed… but there was no time to laugh or even think over such idiots. Needing a view of the area, Korin ran up the side of an apartment building, its steps seemingly about to collapse as they greatly rang. Korin reached the top safely, scanning the vicinity. Although he couldn't see Priscilla, he managed to spot his friends trailing the cultists. Korin bolted down, hopping over numerous objects that he considered were thrown at his feet by some unknown cosmic force in order to slow him down – or that he was magnetically drawing them in like that in a maddening dream. He nevertheless soon caught up with the others, who were standing outside the small Veisan Mansion they had previously scoped over two months ago, and the sight both shocked and partially confused Korin.

"What the fuck?" Terala almost shouted. "We checked that place, for Jhar's sake!"

"I know!" Korin responded, fully regrouping. "I guess I *was* right. The Gathering is still using this location after all these centuries."

Sylas then maintained the confusion by saying, "But there was nothing there when we checked."

"Yes, but we probably missed something. Come on," Korin said, motioning as he began sneaking on to the property.

When they approached the building, Sylas asked, "Should we go through the front entrance?"

"Pfft, no," Terala scoffed. "It'll be a window again, right?" she asked Korin, who firmly nodded.

The mansion's interior looked virtually the same as the last time they checked; old-fashioned, nonevil-looking cupboards lined the walls, filled with ordinary, everyday utensils. In one room, however, there was a moved bookcase in front of a stairway leading down.

"What?" Korin whispered in frustration. "God, we checked behind there!"

"How did we miss it?" Sylas asked, utterly flabbergasted.

"Hold on. To be safe, we best scout the area first before looking," Korin said, and the group split up momentarily.

After two minutes of finding no-one, Terala clapped her hands, enthusiastically saying, "Time to check this out."

Although there was, indeed, a door behind the bookcase, there *also* happened to be an opened wall-panel in front of the door with no perceivable handle, unlike the other hidden door they encountered at Harcon Street. The nuanced difference made everyone shake their heads.

"Lesson learnt," Sylas said. "There is *always* a hidden door."

"Yeah, we'll keep that in mind next time," Korin noted.

Sylas and Terala quickly made their way down the stairs before Korin turned to Celine; and although he had talked to her in private before, Korin wanted to recheck to see how she was feeling now that they were so very close to the cult's base.

"Are you still okay with this?" Korin asked Celine, firmly holding her arms.

"Yes, I'm definitely coming with you," Celine replied with a tense face. "I recovered last time, so I'll be okay. And I really want to save everyone."

A sense of thrill swirled inside Korin as he imagined being side by side with Celine in what he expected to be an epic fight. He gave her a kiss on her tender, stomach-melting lips, wanting to say more, but time was running against them.

While expecting the foulest when entering the deep-underground basement, Korin saw nothing unusual. A few engraved shadowist symbols adorned the walls, and right at the end of the long room was a large steel door that looked like it was capable of withstanding a very powerful blast. Creeping carefully through the open door, the first thing Korin saw was a spiralling staircase that could have given quite the workout for most of the students on campus. And that was merely regarding its descent. Nearby, however, was a shaft for an aerochannel, ready to be used.

Korin took one step into the room and already his footing echoed. Since he heard no other echoes, he considered that Priscilla and the unknown cultists they were following most likely had exited at the bottom, which was where Korin's gang assumed all the action would be held. The aerochannel wasn't connected to any source of power, but fortunately Sylas had a charchite on him to power it up. The shaft was dark, and the descent long – so long, that Korin wondered if there was actually a bottom level at all. There were even another two aero-channels that they had to take in order to get down to the bottom.

At last, though, they reached the end, and inside the sparsely-decorated room was a door leading to a massive lobby featuring numerous stone doors on all sides of the cult-symbolled, grey slabbed walls. With a deeply-engraved shadowist symbol, there was one imposing door larger than the rest. Its black stone was grainy and undulated, tinged with a cold blue that shimmered off protruding points, as if the evil contained in its structure had waxed over thin ice, making it part of the door itself. At their feet was a thick mist, and Korin hoped it wouldn't darken like the one at his religious ritual. Despite the lobby's antiquity, a modern floodlight was present, providing decent lighting for the whole area.

Sylas was fiddling with the EDA, thinking *he* could hack into it, just as Celine examined a nearby statue in her own world, only to place her papier-mâché necklace on it. Aware of the danger, they were all nonetheless connected to the Aether, ready to instantly use their phasarchement magic.

Here we are, Korin thought, staring gravely at the main door. "Hopefully it's still unlocked."

Korin decided to crystallize some discharges into mines for a surprise attack before opening the door, shortly forming three beta-negative mines, which orbited around his body. He then tried to open the door, but it didn't budge. His friends then helped, pushing as hard as they could before suddenly hearing voices and footsteps echoing from the preceding room. Everyone immediately created lucent shields. Korin manifested an alpha-positive shield; if phase-charged, it would allow for a short window to resist more discharge attacks to prevent shield overloading. Terala, meanwhile, featured a delta-positive shield to help enhance her speed and strength – it was a choice that Korin liked as well. Celine's beta-negative shield was able to automatically desynchronize from attacks and conscious attention, making her less of a target – which was ideal for her fighting style. And of course, the tricky Sylas chose to generate a gamma-negative shield, which was capable of temporarily scattering light to create mirages via a phase charge. All four were ready to change tactics in an instant, so it wasn't like they were locked into only one shield.

To keep their attacks evenly balanced as a group for the time being, everybody had different blast balls ready. Terala had the pushing nature of alpha-negative in one hand, while Celine generated a delta-negative discharge for slowing enemies. In order to overload enemy shields much faster, though, Sylas had a gamma-positive one. Since Korin still had beta-negative active, he was about to create a green discharge as he grabbed one of the mines with his spare hand.

Just as all four were ready to fight, Korin whispered, "Wait! We don't want to alert the whole cult."

"Then what should we do?" Celine asked.

After scanning the room, Korin pointed to a smaller door that was left ajar, saying, "Quick, through there." Korin was the last to enter, and when he closed the door, it locked automatically. *Oh, great,* he thought, wondering if anyone else heard the locking mechanism. With only his lucent mines partially lighting up the area, Korin didn't say anything as he waited for the cultists to pass by; and after two minutes, the noises ended. "It's locked," he whispered, activating his phid for some light, as his mines had disappeared by that point.

"There's got to be a way to open it," Terala said, activating her phid as well.

"There might be a key nearby," Celine whispered, prompting everyone to begin searching every nook and cranny for a key. Deciding to walk to the other side of the room, Celine spotted a door made of solid stone, situated next to a greened, porous wooden wheel, appearing as if it had recently surfaced from the bottom of an ocean after many centuries. "Maybe there's a way back through this door over here."

"Mm… perhaps," Korin responded, feeling hesitant at the skull and crossbones on top of the door featuring a phrase in an undecipherable language.

"Let me guess, 'Keep out or die', right?" Sylas asked cynically.

"It's probably no worse than the other door."

Korin and Sylas grabbed the wheel, heaving while turning the rigid setting. Creaking as the wheel turned, the door slowly opened, releasing a musty odour.

"I wish we had anti-smell tonics," Sylas said, voice muffled, having dived his nose into his sleeve. "Or at least have brought a fan to blow this away."

Terala facetiously remarked, "I don't know. I heard this musty scent makes you more attractive to danthas. Surely you don't want to miss out on *that* type of action?" She laughed.

"Yeah, not funny. You come closer and smell this." Sylas coughed.

"I can smell it from here. It doesn't matter – we need to keep going."

"Easy for you to say," Sylas continued to reply. "You're not turning this." When the door fully opened, the serious tension rose again. "Is it just me, or does it look like the cult hasn't been down here in a while? There are no lights or anything."

"I think you're right," Korin said, "but we don't have much choice. Hopefully it'll lead back to the lobby."

"Wait, why don't we try to blast a hole through the door back there with gamma-negative?" Sylas asked.

Korin looked at the door and thought for a moment. "We don't know how long it would take with the chance rates. It could – and likely would – take ages, so it's probably not worth it. Plus, a hole in the door would look suspicious and probably alert the cultists immediately."

"Okay, but let's keep it as a backup option, just in case this alternative route gets crazy."

The previously-settled dust flew into the air as everybody moved through the deathly corridors. Eventually, one of the paths led to an ancient prison block filled with bones so brittle, one disintegrated when a scruffy, boil-plagued rat fearfully scurried past. Unusual moths were fluttering by, with a few approaching the light now entering in the room. Indecipherable scribbles covered the cell walls, most lacking the imprinted, hopeless, and frustrated feelings they once contained.

"Wow," Terala uttered. "There's so much down here. I wish we had time to explore."

"We'll come back later for the tour," Korin responded.

"Whoa!" Sylas yelled, almost tripping. "Stupid skull." He kicked the unusual skeletal head onto the wall, smashing it into dust.

About ten metres away was a perforated sack attached right up the side of a wall, its crusty, hardened material appearing as if it would've been slimy and snot-like at one point. Looking a little thicker than a bull's, a horned skull stuck out of the top.

Suddenly, brutish, yellow eyes opened inside.

There was a cracking noise as the skull slowly moved, and then a heavy bellow followed. Jagged claws eagerly reached out of the sack, ripping it and allowing the creature to stumble out before shaking from its long slumber. Although it clearly seemed weak from its lack of food, the gaunt, lanky stature was actually its natural shape. The brown and scaly creature continued stretching its previously-cramped body, shakily opening its large jaw, revealing a long, forked tongue, somewhat matching its strong tail now swinging back and forth. Strange goo even started dripping from disgusting holes in its body. Its skull then skewed to the side as the creature realized it wasn't alone.

"Oh, shit, oh, shit!" Sylas cried out.

"What in Jhar's hole is that?" Terala asked.

"A jekorna," Celine answered, though no-one heard her as she basically mimed it out in fear.

"We'll find out later. Just shoot it!" Korin responded.

Korin delivered the first shot, hitting the skull with a beta-negative shot to simply send it unconscious. However, the skull merely jolted back slightly, and the creature then glowered before taking a more aggressive stance. Korin shot again, this time aiming for its body, guessing green discharges didn't affect the creature through *its* bones – or at least not easily. Nothing happened again. Terala then aimed her hand, shooting the same discharges as Korin, though to no avail.

"Why aren't they working?" Korin asked.

"I think it might have mutated into a monster," Sylas responded. "They can resist certain attacks."

Now enraged, the creature bowed its head before charging at the young mages, who all jumped to either side, missing the horned rampage by seconds. The beast subsequently hit the wall at full speed, crashing to the ground. Had it hit everyone, their shields would've done nothing to protect them.

"I suggest we run now!" Sylas cried.

"No, shoot now!" Korin shouted. "Try delta-negative." Korin and everyone else then began blasting the creature with red discharges, partially slowing the monster while also attempting to potentially send it into a state of suspended animation. The shooting occurred for a while, and when everyone stopped, the creature didn't move. It was a success. "Okay, now we run!" Korin stated, taking off immediately without another look at the monster.

The prison block was fully caved in at the end, leaving the group panicking as to where to go. "Could we go through there?" Sylas asked, pointing at a vent.

"It's worth a try," Korin said before opening the rusty grate. About to usher in the others first, Korin then said, "Wait, I'll go first. It could be dangerous."

At any rate, there was air inside. As the group moved through, their every movement against the metal walls created loud clanging noises, echoing far. Their phids were still the only sources of light, and it seemed like there was no end in sight. Finally, one came into view, providing a slight sense of relief. Before the group exited, however, a loud knock reverberated across the walls, causing all four to immediately stop in terror. Another bang made each flinch again.

Sylas and Celine were in the middle when the third strike occurred; but this time, a claw penetrated a weakened part in the steel, ferociously thrusting up to the vent ceiling as it nearly sliced them both, who together squealed…

Looking slightly different from the last jekorna's, the claw ripped back out, only to shoot up again in the same spot. Celine's dress tore a little at the end, and her legs squirmed right out of the way. The EDA Sylas had in his pocket fell out, tumbling through the hole in the vent. There was a loud smash, and it was clear that there was no hope of retrieving it. With the monster's presence, there was also no time to complain at length. As everybody flailed about in the tight vent, each banged their heads hard against the metal. But now that holes were available, Korin shot a few red blasts through each, hitting the monster.

The clawing stopped. Temporarily.

"We need to move!" Korin shouted. "Come on!"

Korin led the way to the end of the vent, where a concrete floor began. The left claw this time penetrated another section of the vent, and for a moment, the young mages stalled, all aiming their trembling hands out. They eventually understood waiting wasn't the greatest decision, so they pressed on through another vent, crawling on all fours for quite some time as they continued hearing the monster screech.

"Please tell me you see the exit!" Sylas called out.

"You'll know when I see it!" Korin responded, glancing back, not noticing the sudden steepness ahead of him, yelling as he fell down the slide. Korin soon hit a grate, relieved that he stopped without splattering. Suddenly, a familiar head popped in front of the grate. "Jaimas?" Korin asked with shock.

"Hey, you look a little stuck," Jaimas said. "Need a hand getting out?"

"Um… yeah, can you open this?"

"Hold on," Jaimas said before grabbing a nearby metal bar to rip the grate off.

"Hey, Korin, you alright?" Sylas called out.

"Yeah, I'm all good. I'll let you know when to slide down." When Korin got out of the vent, he called for the others to come down, too.

"Oh, man, I am so grateful to see you!" Sylas said to Jaimas, who grinned back.

To his delight, Korin noticed that they were back in the lobby with the large stone door engraved with the massive shadowist symbol. Korin then charily asked Jaimas, "Wait, so, what are *you* doing here?"

"Well, I knew you guys were up to something secret, being so secrety and all. So, I secretly overheard you secretly talking about a secret cult, and then I secretly followed you before I had to secretly hide from the cultists. Why should you guys have all the secret fun?"

"We're embarking on a dangerous endeavour here, Jaimas. You do realize that?" Korin asked condescendingly, crossing his arms.

"And what makes you guys more able than me? Shouldn't it be easier if more people help?"

"Well, yeah, but we have to be discreet about this. We can't just barge in there with a whole brigade, you know."

"Why not?" Jaimas asked before examining the large door.

"Because they could all scram, and we'll be back to square one. We took all semester trying to find this place. We can't just mess around and screw our only chance up. We also don't exactly know what we'll be facing. And there's just too much to say about it right now, anyway."

"Whatever." Jaimas shrugged nonchalantly. "I'm only one person, though. And now I know. So, I'm coming with you guys."

"Fine." Korin rolled his head. "Let's get on with this. So, we need to find a way through here." He soon spotted a rod-like object with a plain surface. He then considered it could be used as a wedge of sorts, but the metal bar Jaimas found seemed a better option.

"Hey, that could be the key," Jaimas said.

"I'm pretty sure they'd have a more elaborate design." Korin smirked. "It's probably for something else."

"Gimme that." Jaimas snatched the rod off Korin, finding a hole, where he inserted it. The rod then glowed as the door rumbled, opening to reveal a gloomy, candlelit hallway beyond. "There we go." Jaimas grinned. "What would you guys have done without me?"

"We would have missed the ritual," Celine answered. "We're very thankful, Jaimas."

"Yeah, thanks, Jaimas," Korin acknowledged him grudgingly.

"You're welcome, Korin." Jaimas grinned while he teasingly rubbed Korin's hair.

Korin then glared at Jaimas with a 'don't-do-that-again' look prior to staring down the hallway radiating evil. There was a moment of irrevocable silence before Korin said, "Alright, this is it, guys." He nodded slowly at everyone. "Let's go."

Chapter Twenty-One

The Ritual

Upon entering the hallway, a sinister energy enveloped everyone, sending prickly chills through their skins. Along the walls, antler-shaped sconces held long-lasting candles burning ghostly flames, their waxes creating a collective aura of cool, biting indigo. While the path was only around a hundred metres long before it splintered off, it seemed much more than that on the way down.

"Please don't tell me we have to split up," Sylas said, fists trembling.

"Let's stay together for now," Korin said. "We'll try this path first. Going around the side might be best, as we could potentially flank them."

After ascending the short path to their right, the candles along the wall ended. The next main route bent around and continued for a fair distance, its barren walls possessing no decorations. At first, it seemed as if they had taken the wrong path, but Korin was right: going through the base directly would've been problematic. Everyone stuck closely together as the foreboding intensified while penetrating further and further into the cult's base. With feet arched in footwear, everybody was ready to jolt at the split of a second. Flinches were pre-engaged. There was so much to say, though nobody uttered a word.

A cave aperture appeared at the end, opening up to a rocky window overlooking a vast, capacious cavern. Just as predicted, The Gathering of the Black Moon was performing the ritual, right in the centre.

"Lights off," Korin whispered as they reached the edge. "Keep low."

He lay on his stomach as the others followed. "Save your energy by keeping your shields off for now."

In the centre of the ritual was a large, spiky crystal floating in the air, emitting a green, spikily-bubbled aura of light and energy. A set of smaller, different crystals lay around the bottom of the platform, along with an electrical energy generator transmitting power to the main crystal. Engraved with fractals and shapes, assorted crystal-reflector walls encompassed the ritual in various places, retaining, reinforcing, and stimulating the energies within.

Close to the centrepiece were seven masked and dedicated cultists clutching an equal number of petrified hostages at knifepoint; each aligned with a heptagram-shaped trench trimmed with tiny crystals. Another seven masked cultists circled around the trench, holding and waving various items, their ritualistic form a dance in itself. Connected to the star-shaped trench was a larger outer channel of the same shape, evenly dipping towards the inner one. Forty-two students were divided up at its seven tips, huddled in confined cages. A few relentlessly banged on their prisons as battered and bruised faces pushed between bars, while most cried and wailed in despair. Some had scraggly hair so knotted that it appeared part of the bondage. A number sat in curled positions, utterly destroyed on the inside, merely murmuring incomprehensibly.

"The end is coming!" one prisoner muttered, shaking all over as he turned his head slowly to his side as if he had no neckbones. "The end is coming!"

"Shut up! Shut up!" the one beside him retorted, covering his ears.

Another jittering student began scraping and bleeding his flaking skin across a sharp piece of steel jutting out from the bars in order to avoid the impending horrors. All the prisoners had magic suppressors attached to them; and even if they hypothetically didn't, there was no way any of them could've used magic in their current states.

Caged hallways were above the outer trench, compartmentalized with khastwolves locked up inside – ones, of course, with monstrous mutations. Riled up with the prospect of fresh meat, the monsters grizzled with mega sharp teeth, eyeing the prisoners off. With the little space available, a few of the khastwolves paced back and forth, knocking their pincers against the cages, the friction almost causing sparks.

A few metres away from the head of the inner star was a massive stone shrine featuring a shadowist symbol sculpture on top, its form chiselled roughly. The cult leader was right in front, casting an incantation from a parchment on a lectern, her words loudened with speakers. Her voice was also distorted and deep, altered due to the sinister, slightly different and senior mask she wore featuring longer horns. She was also speaking in another language, although Korin managed to register a couple of words – one being 'Backlevy'.

The rest of the cult – roughly three hundred people – gathered around the centre of the ritual, though they were definitely still part of the overall act. Collectively, they were bending the etheric reality around them with their conscious intent and united will, aiding the process by chanting a heavy, dark melody; a few of their notes dragged on almost as if the gravity would increase, tearing the fabric of reality, opening up to a nightmarish dimension.

At once, the seven inner cultists raised their daggers before plunging them into their victim's throats, voraciously ripping them apart. As the blood gushed into the trench, the seven cultists began fanatically hacking away at the dead bodies, ravaging them senselessly and sickeningly loving every moment. In a frenzy, the cult leader thrust her arms high into the air, almost screaming as the chanting increased in volume.

"Oh, no!" Celine peeped.

"Shit, we're too late," Sylas whispered. "What do we do?"

"Oh, God." Korin was taken aback at the sight, struggling to gulp. "They… they outnumber us, but I think we have an advantage up here, so we may be able to shoot quite a few before they even notice."

"Are we right to strike now?" Terala eagerly asked, her anger-filled breathing loud enough for Korin to hear.

"Wait for my prompt." Korin readied his aim.

Just as Korin was about to speak, a discharge shot right into his back. Having experienced the sensation a couple of times before during training, Korin knew what it was right before he entered a brief state of suspended animation.

"Too late," an evil voice uttered behind Korin.

After four seconds when the suspended animation wore off, Korin turned sluggish. However, Korin managed to peripherally see a robed figure finish placing non-chained magic suppressors on his wrists. His friends were also in the same situation. One of the cultists then placed his boot on Korin's back, adding pressure every second. Korin couldn't wait to jump up and smack him in the face, but he knew that it would be futile attacking when he'd fully regain his senses.

"You'll all be coming with us," the same man said. "You are to place your hands on your heads and keep quiet."

Once everyone's senses had fully returned, the cultists forced the group to stand up before shoving them through one of the corridors downstairs. Korin and his friends were also outnumbered, so even if they didn't have magic suppressors on, attacking was going to require a very clever plan. Now up close, Korin could properly see the shadowist symbol featured on the masks' foreheads, a couple engraved in a design that appeared to bleed. All the masks were similar, though they were not the same; still, all were silver, phlegmatic, and had either a few horns at the top or a mane of horns. A couple of masks had no mouths.

"How did you know we were here?" Korin risked speaking.

"We saw lights flashing," one of the cultists replied. "How very careless of you," he said with a mocking tone.

"What do you plan on doing with us?" Jaimas asked.

"Silence!" another cultist ordered harshly.

Jaimas glared ahead, scrunching his lips. Celine, on the other hand, mostly kept her eyes closed, knowing that she couldn't do anything. Terala glowered back at her captor every few steps, elbowing him while receiving shoves in return, whereas Sylas scanned every cranny around him, hoping to find something to stop the cultists. After arriving in a locker room, Jaimas persisted with disdainful commentary.

"I said shut it!" the senior cultist shouted before a green discharge abruptly blasted him to the ground.

All of a sudden, a couple of green blast balls fired, swiftly knocking all the cultists – who were unshielded – unconscious, leaving Korin and his party standing in complete shock. More shots were then fired to completely keep the cultists unconscious for a longer period. A masked girl stood at the doorway with another charged blast that soon dissipated. Although wearing a cultist robe, her clothing underneath was partially visible; it was precisely the same apparel Korin last saw Priscilla wearing. Her stance was still antagonistic as she stared critically at Korin and only Korin.

"Pris-Priscilla?" Korin asked, remaining deadly still. "Wh-why did you shoot them?"

The girl didn't respond for a good ten seconds. Finally, she took her mask off, confirming her identity. "They would have killed you," Priscilla answered with a grave face. "You do realize that?" she asked as if Korin was a dullard.

The build-up of fear, speculation, and confusion over Priscilla throughout the semester reached its final tipping point, overstimulating his mind and numbing him into a dumbfounded state. Despite Priscilla's help, Korin couldn't simply accept that she had just saved them. He initially conjectured if she had an ulterior agenda before thinking it was potentially an illusion.

Have they already taken me into the ritual? Korin thought. At long last, he moved. Very slightly. "Ye-yeah, but… aren't you part of the cult?"

"I think you need to have your head checked out," Priscilla snapped. "You clearly understand little about me. In no way am I part of this shadowist cult. Why would you think that? Because of this mask I was wearing?"

Although still feeling numb in one sense, Korin's mental senses, at least, cracked through. He knew he wasn't hallucinating. It was real. Priscilla's answer shattered numerous glass houses Korin had manufactured in his mind, all of which were disjointed and poorly designed. Nevertheless, Korin's mind quickly tried to sweep and scrape up the pieces of his imaginations and projections of what Priscilla was and wasn't, pouring them back into another dodgy vessel. His old theories would not die.

"Well, because… you…" Korin paused, his astonishment irradiating the room. "We learned what you did over the semester. You were the one who murdered Meriel!"

"Me? Murdered Meriel? You're such an idiot. That was The Gathering. *They* murdered her."

"But… Meriel told us that you were in the cult. She claimed to have proof and that you were planning something big that night. She was concerned that you'd murder her or something, and –"

"That's not true in the slightest," Priscilla responded, gritting her teeth.

"Well, we even found your pen at the crime scene."

"She stole that from me! And Meriel was one of them, too. She tried to recruit me, and I refused to join. Meriel then threatened me, and so I managed to, let's say, put her in her place. She wasn't happy, and she no doubt sought to get out of the situation; so she naturally would've had plans on murdering *me*. What *did* she say to you, anyway?"

Korin shuddered at falling for such deception. *I… I was tricked. But… Priscilla! Priscilla's the evil one… right? No… wait…*

Korin was still in too much shock to immediately respond, so Terala said, "She wanted information about you."

"I was talking to Korin. Butt out of this," Priscilla retorted icily.

"Hey, we're all involved with this!" Terala responded fierily. "We saw some fucked up shit along the way."

"That's not surprising; but I only wish to speak with Korin, thank you very much."

"Oi, we're risking our lives being in this place," Jaimas added assertively. "We're going to ask you questions, whether you like it or not."

"And I'm going to ignore you, whether you like it or not." Priscilla sneered.

"Hey, guys," Korin said, glancing around. "It's alright. I'll speak. I just needed a minute."

"Fine, but don't let her fuck with your head." Terala crossed her arms.

"Oh, yes, of course!" Priscilla said, her sarcasm rather scornful. "I'm really just here to *fuck* with Korin's head. That's all I'm thinking of! Please." She flicked her head in a way that expressed her disdain.

Nobody responded.

Priscilla then continued, "Ugh, yes, Meriel would've tried to obtain information about me, but the shadowists killed her off because of her misdeeds."

Korin asked, "Then why did they leave her body in a public place like that? We heard that the cult doesn't do such things, and they usually use bodies when possible."

"Yes, that does seem strange. I don't know why, but I have a feeling that killing her right there was an act of blind rage. They probably would have planned on either taking the body later or destroying the building with her in it. But since that same night a few cultists died in that large fire, maybe the same ones who killed her were then unable to finish off their act. Either way, they aren't the nicest of people, as you may have gathered. Meriel was the only one who knew about me, and The Gathering continues to know nothing of my... investigations."

Korin squinted at her final, suspicious wording. "Do you have any proof of your innocence?"

"I told you: I had an alibi. In a way, it's also fortunate you picked that pen up. The police harassed me for a little while, but they concluded it wasn't me. There, I hope you're happy."

"Okay... Fair enough. But Meriel *did* say you were planning something big that night."

Priscilla didn't answer, glaring back with intense anger in her eyes, both reddened and moistened. Korin intuited he wasn't ever going to receive a reply to that question, but he also detected the issue was unrelated to Meriel, like the answer was already exuding from Priscilla. Korin then remembered that he was about to ask Darsan about Meriel, but after the demon interrupted them, Korin's mind-wandering and speculative hypotheticals about her dropped off. Moreover, a week after the event, Korin noticed very little of Meriel's connections; it raised suspicions, but those suspicions were focused in the wrong direction. Korin then realized that even if Priscilla did kill Meriel, it would've been an act most likely on behalf of the cult, anyway. That is, in both cases, the cult killed Meriel.

"But... you were slowly conditioning and hypnotizing me all along. And you..." Korin glanced at his friends, realizing that talking about sex wasn't the best idea. He turned back to Priscilla, expecting another angry face dismissing his remarks, but instead, he saw her smirking. "Wait... were you?"

"Maybe. But you liked it." She was about to giggle.

"What?" Terala asked, taking a step forward. "What the fuck were you doing to Korin?"

"Ugh, settle down," Priscilla told Terala. "Sure," she said to Korin, "I was conditioning you; if you wish to put it that way. Consider, though, that any form of training is a form of conditioning. And, you're subject to forms of hypnotism all the time, such as in advertisements. There's nothing wrong with what I did."

Man, her philosophy is so demented, Korin thought before asking, "So… that means you were conditioning me into doing rituals with the black moon, right?"

"Yes, of course. But I wasn't manipulating you into joining The Gathering. I don't like shadowists."

Great, so I was actually right about her all along with her black moon cult… thing… Kind of… Korin said to himself before thinking over what she did the night prior to Meriel's death. "Okay, but I remember a guy called Darsan talking about how the cult kidnaps people for one night before chucking them back on campus. You, too, planned on doing that with the research scientist."

"Needing her for one night was just coincidental. She was working on a crystal that I was curious about. That's all."

"Fine, but what about all the other stuff you've done?" he asked, feeling like bits of him were being chipped away.

"And what *stuff* would that be?" Priscilla asked as her animosity rose.

Korin desisted his questions for a moment, recognizing that there was not one piece of concrete evidence of her being in the shadowist cult – or of her doing anything evil. Her personal philosophy was indeed questionable, and there were a few instances he remembered where Priscilla happened to be suspiciously in certain places at certain times, but there was nothing absolute. It dawned on him that practically his every experience with Priscilla was either misinterpreted or distorted through a bad perception of some kind. Despite being critical of other students for jumping to conclusions about anything without taking into consideration multiple factors and nuanced points, Korin, too, fell for this fallacy, not grasping Priscilla's nuances. He truly felt ashamed and contrite for his thoughts and actions against her, feeling beneath dirt. Korin was about to cry, but he closed his eyes, sucking up his emotions to stay intact while in front of everyone.

"I'm… I'm so sorry for thinking that –"

"Don't even bother," Priscilla reacted sharply, nearly crushing Korin's devitalized soul. "Be glad that I haven't shot you already and left you for the cult to recapture."

Taking his time to reply, Korin believed that he really had to convey the message that he actually was guilt-ridden and apologetic. "I really am sorry," he said slowly as she seethed as if about to strike venom from her eyes.

"Hey, guys!" Terala interrupted. "What the fuck? The ritual is still taking place! We need to get moving."

"Terala's right," Korin said faintly. "We need your help, Priscilla. Please."

Priscilla mulled over the situation before angrily sighing and saying, "We can't just unlock the cages with everyone in sight. I also believe there are more people imprisoned elsewhere, but we should focus on the ones about to die tonight. If you're going to enter, then you'll need their masks and robes first."

Sylas and Jaimas noted what Priscilla said, quickly crouching down to unmask the cultists, revealing unfamiliar students. There was no time to bother tying them up, but Jaimas did grab the keys to unlock the magic suppressors around their wrists. There were also additional cultist bodies on the ground, all knocked out by Priscilla before Korin had arrived.

"Here," Sylas said, handing a robe and mask to Korin.

The mask was cold to touch, and placing it on felt darkly oppressive, though oddly protective. For the time being, Korin kept it off.

"So, what *is* the cult trying to do?" Jaimas asked Priscilla.

"The ritual is part of a major enchantment, and they're extracting certain etheric energy from the prisoners to help with the process."

With the powerful energies around in the cultist base, the black moon suddenly flashed in Korin's vision, its nature feeling darker than he had experienced before. A second later, he felt another energy flash, but he was unsure what it was, though it certainly was evil. "What…" Korin gathered his senses. "What role does the black moon play in all this?"

"Shadowists, in general, corrupt the black moon, and wish to see its physical manifestation. However, I believe that this ritual is different from their normal rituals, so I don't know what they're trying to achieve here. I will admit, the crystal I was after, the Yinora Crystal, is the same one that they are using to enchant. It's a prototype crystal, which was named after the researcher we were looking for that night. While Yinora and her team were developing the crystal, they inadvertently discovered that it could tap into certain etheric energies. The crystal wasn't designed for such a purpose, and the discovery itself isn't of interest to most people; but for those with knowledge on certain matters, it sparked some interest – namely, the cult. I then became interested in it after finding out what the cult was after. Still, I think the crystal's application in most contexts is limited, so it's not like I have any use for it… at least for now. The Yinora Crystal they have is actually infused with some other crystals, and I tampered with it, which –"

A thunderous noise boomed through the cult's base, sending a shudder through everyone.

"That… might be the crystal," Priscilla claimed, voice nervous.

"What did you do to it?" Korin asked worriedly.

Priscilla shot a glance at the doorway before saying, "Through there. Take the tunnel, and you'll see."

"Wait, aren't you coming with us?"

"Of course." She briefly surveyed the room. "I'll be with you soon."

Korin looked at Priscilla with a newfound suspicion, sensing her reply wasn't quite right. His friends headed for the tunnel, and Korin shortly followed on; but just as it seemed like he had fully left the room, Korin glanced back, seeing Priscilla raiding one of the lockers. She slipped a few items into her bag, shutting the locker door, only to see Korin staring at her. Priscilla stalled before moving to the doorway, approaching him with an icy expression.

"Well? You want to save everyone, right?" Priscilla asked. "This way, then."

Korin didn't bother asking what Priscilla grabbed; focusing on the task at hand, he placed his mask on.

After running through the tunnel, Korin and Priscilla arrived at the cavern with the others, noticing that the cultists had ceased chanting. The crystal was discharging powerful electrical energy, shooting up at the enormously-high ceiling. The cult leader had also stopped her incantation, frantically looking around as dirt and pebbles descended. She ordered an underling to switch the energy generator off, but an electric bolt zapped the cultist dead when he approached it. Annoyed, the cult leader took it upon herself to shoot some blast balls at the generator, disabling it. However, this didn't stop the crystal erratically discharging energy – energy which was mysteriously emerging from an unknown source, confusing the cultists. The cracking crystal also looked like it was going to explode, causing those in the inner circle to relocate.

Just as the cultists moved, the crystal created a shockwave, its angle mostly directed at the ground. A small fissure then emerged in the ground, derailing one of the arms on the star-shaped cage, concurrently breaking the circuit box connected to the khastwolves' collars. As the hallway turned on its side, the metal screeched and bent before the crystal struck a bolt of energy at it. A cage door was blasted open, and a khastwolf crawled out; the monster then ripped its collar off before stretching its arms out while howling with excitement. The caged students screamed for their lives, trying to keep as far away from the edges of their prisons as possible. Another fissure occurred, and the entire cage system twisted and turned, splitting apart. Coupled with the wild energy zapping by, the hallways essentially opened, and all the khastwolves either climbed out or managed to claw their way through the breaches. Even the cultists were petrified, slowly backing away as the khastwolves scanned the environment for the best prey to devour first.

The cult leader knew the creatures would leave the easier prey for last, as the imprisoned students couldn't move anywhere, so she opened the cages with a device, 'freeing' the captives. The khastwolves were about to attack the cultists first, but they reconsidered with their new, easily-escapable prey.

"What have you done?" Korin asked Priscilla.

"I didn't expect all this to happen," Priscilla replied. "Be careful. The khastwolves have been pumped with chemicals, so they'd likely be more resistant to beta attacks."

"Wait, aren't they already resistant to such attacks, being monsters?"

"Yes, but they would have even more resistance now."

"Great," Korin muttered.

"What do we do?" Terala asked Korin.

"Uh… we'll take cover behind those rocks and start shooting," Korin said before dashing over to one of the large rocks scattered around, digging his body tightly into the grooves for safety.

Once the shooting began, the cultists quickly responded by fleeing to the other side of the cavern, where there was an exit. Seeing the ultrachite discharges firing at them, the cultists had no idea who – and how many – they were up against. In any case, there was a looming catastrophe. As the crystal's fracturing power intensified, shards of energy shot at the roof, triggering a large fall-down of rocks, which smashed ground-shatteringly hard, smoking up a massive dust cloud. The collapse left a rocky slope facing the central area of the cavern, where the cages were, while the other side was of a vertical formation near where two-thirds of the cult happened to be located, exiting. Although unseeable from Korin's standpoint, a deep crack formed in the ground, making it too hard for the split-off cultists to reach the rock wall, except for those that could utilize enough propulsion phasarchement magic. Still, not one cultist jumped back over with such power.

When the dust settled, every conscious being broke from their panicked suspension, continuing with what they were doing. For one-third of the cult, their attempts at fleeing were stopped, with many realizing they couldn't jump over the now-formed gorge; and, for many reasons, running to the main entrance was off-putting; that is, it meant being exposed, in addition to potentially finding themselves later in a trap. However, a couple of older, more powerful cultists were able to use propulsion magic to jump over, cowardly leaving their comrades behind. The remaining cultists grudgingly turned around to face their situation, firing discharges.

All the previously-imprisoned students either started running away from their cages and the khastwolves, or they were too petrified to move, closing their cage doors, hoping the monsters wouldn't attack. The khastwolves jumped high into the air, landing, however, on the cultists first, shredding them with amusement. Guts and tattered robes flung like they had been chucked into a blender. Energy blasts fired everywhere as well, a large number missing the rapid monsters.

The cultists spread out, finding cover, with a few shortly spotting Korin and his companions, knowing that they weren't one of them, despite the masks and robes. A few cultists created basic gamma-positive shields to camouflage themselves, but the khastwolves detected the cultists through their powerful sense of smell and their agilely-sensitive eyes, noticing nuanced discrepancies in the atmosphere. Still, the cultists managed to avoid most of the *attention* – but this came at the cost of minimal participation in the action, as shooting discharges revealed their locations.

Terala shouted as she openly fired two discharges at once with both hands at those closest to her, not entirely thinking as she left her top body exposed. "Got another!" she would cry before looking over at her friends to see if she was winning. None, however, paid attention.

Celine was right next to Korin as she kept behind the rock most of the time, only peeping out every so often to attack those close by as well. She was shaking and flinching, but she managed to keep her nerves under control for the most part. Sylas was blindfiring, thinking his tactic was working perfectly, yet he only occasionally hit a cultist. At least his strategy was *somewhat* effective. Had he openly fired, he surely would've shot more people. Despite his talkative nature, Sylas remained mostly silent, only opening his mouth to grunt and curse.

Priscilla would scan the area first, duck to plan her attack, and then quickly aim over her rock, taking one cultist out at a time. Jaimas, on the other hand, acted like an unrealistic commando found in the movies, forsaking his rock to run circuits around the area, firing all in sight while war-screaming, attracting much-unwanted attention. Jaimas also literally ran into cultists, shoving and bashing every one to the ground before firing at their sorry asses. He kicked their bodies for good measure, too. His delta-positive shield eventually took such a beating that it finally overloaded, leaving him to strangely have every blast then miss him by centimetres as he undauntedly continued on with an energy that did not seem to diminish in the least. While recovering from an overloaded discharge aura, Jaimas merely used his body as a weapon.

In the first two minutes, the cultists dropped from ninety-eight to eighty-eight; they now turned extra careful, making it harder to hit them.

Korin's primary goal was to save the missing students, and he knew he had to take immediate action when he saw one being devoured alive. Turning to Celine, Korin firmly said, "Stay here and keep safe."

Celine removed her mask. "Shouldn't you wait until more of them are knocked out?"

"No, I need to go now," he said before taking his mask off to kiss Celine intensely.

Wishing he could stay, Korin let go of a clutching Celine. With a delta-positive shield, Korin's senses enhanced as if he was on performance-enhancing drugs or potions. Even though he mentally complained about running into obstacles prior to entering the Veisan Mansion, this time, he cherished their existence as he crouch-ran and rolled around obstacles to reach the closest cage. He approached a rock and grabbed on with one hand, lifting himself into the air, legs kicking back and forth while he accurately shot gamma-positive blasts at two cultists with his free hand, as if the blood flow to his head gave him increased competency and strength – in addition to making him feel like time had slowed for a brief moment as his eyes noticed assorted minutiae flinging to-and-fro – all before shortly regaining normality as his body flipped over to then land on a slippery pile of mud and skid right under a sharp metal pipe, only to then rapidly pick himself up and whisk past blast after blast shot at his direction.

"Over here!" Korin shouted, motioning for the unlocked students to move. "You can exit there!" He pointed to the entrance. "I'll cover your backs."

Korin fired at a nearby khastwolf to guard everyone, forcing it to back off, but the prisoners wouldn't flee until Korin approached them even closer. Eventually, the group of six bravely ran or limped out to Korin, folding their arms as if rocks or khastwolves would fall on them at any second. Since the students were the closest of the lot, their route back was minimal, managing, in the end, to reach the entrance without being killed.

"Run!" Korin yelled. "Just keep running until you see a giant door!

After that, take the aerochannel or the stairs in one of the rooms from the lobby. Go!"

None hesitated, fleeing immediately. Korin sprinted back into the action, but he found himself face-planting the ground as if a giant, blunt metal rake had hit his back. He turned around, seeing a khastwolf lurching over him with wigwagging pincers. The claws, fortunately, had only backhanded him, leaving no cuts. Scurrying on his back, Korin knew the khastwolf wasn't just hungry; the chemicals rushing through its body heightened its aggressive temperament. The pupils were immensely dilated, and its body quivered.

Just as it was about to slice Korin's face in half, Jaimas neared and laid several blasts into the beast's back, causing it to howl and leap into the air. Jaimas's discharge aura overloaded again, and before it seemed like the two guys were dinner, a few of the nearby cultists began frenziedly firing at the airborne khastwolf until it landed and collapsed. It continued squirming until a few more blasts rendered it unconscious. The group of nearby cultists were obviously suspicious of Korin and Jaimas, unsure if they were part of the cult or not; but they ended up focusing on one of the other khastwolves instead, with the two infiltrators being left alone. Jaimas kept running, just as Korin scrambled back to his feet, pressing on.

The second, larger group of freed prisoners was a collection of those who had fled their respective cages, having gathered in numbers for safety. While stalling in cover, the group knew what to do when Korin arrived, but they were too frightened to make it without his help. A few were still a little unsure of him since he was wearing a cultist mask.

Come on, Korin thought, impatience rising.

Korin then yelled as deeply as he could, ordering them to run to the exit. His throat turned coarse. The commanding order prompted the group to move, and they all scurried through the field of unconscious bodies and splattered blood, a couple squealing along the way. Korin had to join them, making sure the khastwolves backed off. One persistent beast would've been a problem, but Terala covered Korin in the nick of time. A few of the missing students stumbled and tripped on the way, with one too weak to even stand again. Korin knew he couldn't be the one to carry him back, ordering, instead, for a couple nearby to take action as he crouched and cover-fired. However, there was *another* mess-of-a-person, who continued tripping; one of the khastwolves grasped him in a deadly strike, jumping away with him before devouring his prey behind cover.

Crying out in anguish, Korin felt as if he had failed. He was about to blindly charge at the khastwolf to attempt killing it, but when he glanced back at the fleeing students, he refocused so they wouldn't die on him as well. They were close to the exit, anyway; and once the captives escaped, Korin sighed in relief. There were more to save, though.

The only remaining prisoners now were those still in the cages – except for two people, who had individually taken cover elsewhere. Korin checked if Celine was fine, seeing her in the same cosy position, avoiding all drama. Korin then dashed and dived towards the centre of the area, almost colliding into Priscilla, who had turned around from behind a rock.

"There's no time to stare at me!" Priscilla expressed caustically.

Korin, nevertheless, continued staring, with Priscilla giving an insolent countenance behind her mask before going back to sniping cultists.

Many of the present cultists were undergraduates with average power levels, so they couldn't simply use dimensional USTs without having already conducted particular rituals during lunapexes; and since the lunapex had only *just* began, this was out of the question. Still, a few of the elite cultists were able to use dimensional energy, having coincidentally been prepared. Many of the average-powered cultists nevertheless used assorted magic. One cultist cast a holographic conjuration, and its display of an entire movie provided an extremely distracting show of lights, enough to attract the khastwolves and disorient them. Another cultist conjured a rifle with loaded ammunition. However, when they fired it at the incoming khastwolf, little did they know that the khastwolf had rapid regenerative abilities, recovering from the bullets. Another two cultists nearby also conjured firearms, and with all three shooting the khastwolf, it was enough to kill it before it could recover. Other cultists were also conjuring very effective covers for protection.

There was one cultist who transfigured himself into a beast with sharp claws via an alchemical spell; he then charged at one of the khastwolves, laying his claws into the monster with just as much ferociousness as the khastwolf possessed. The khastwolf's organs were then exposed from the massive wound, and blood began gushing out. Looking like it would have died, the khastwolf, however, lunged back, ripping the transfigured cultist's head off. Instantly, the cultist phased back into his original body; and while the cultist's original head was intact, the cultist was in literal shock, where internal haemorrhaging occurred. Blood ran out of his nose, and even though the cultist *may* have survived, the khastwolf passed out, falling on the cultist, where it penetrated the cultist's body with its claws.

A few of the elite cultists were using dimensional magic to proxport, jumping from one place to the next before shooting a khastwolf in the back before quickly jumping to the front as the monster would turn around, in turn shooting its back again before repeating ad nauseam until victory. One of the cultists used alpha dimensional energy, utilizing its gravitational effect to telekinetically lift up a sharp, big shard of steel above a khastwolf before disengaging it to send the steel straight through the khastwolf's body, killing it basically instantly.

Korin had hitherto managed to keep out of the way of the more powerful cultists, but one finally neared him. This cultist was also using dimensional energy, except he was manipulating localized time around him in a red aura, moving way faster than anyone else. Instead of remaining in the same spot or the same line of fire, the cultist zigzagged. To keep up with the cultist's movements, Korin tried shooting *at* the cultist before attempting to shoot *where* the cultist would run towards. However, the cultist overloaded Korin's shield first; and when he reached Korin, instead of shooting with a beta-negative discharge, the cultist drew a knife, ready to plunge it into Korin's heart. Just as the blade was in the air, a khastwolf clawed the cultist's back, immediately killing him. In only a single moment later, though, the khastwolf collapsed on Korin from exhaustion of ultrachite attacks. The spiky chest just missed Korin, but the body's weight and its fall took a toll on Korin. Groaning as he climbed his way from the body, Korin knew he would've had bruises as a result of the fall. Still, Korin concentrated on where to move next, setting off when he was ready.

In order to reach the following group of prisoners, Korin had to tumble to avoid the crystal's discharges of energy. Every sequential blast sounded louder than the last, even though Korin felt like they were slowly diminishing his hearing. Scraps of metal extensively lay around, hindering Korin's task as he tripped on one, almost spraining his ankle. Cultist bodies were also mounting up, though many were unconscious. There was one body, which Korin almost stumbled on, that had its guts sprawled out over an eight-metre diameter, right next to a passed-out khastwolf, who seemed to have had a grin still on its face.

The cage closest to Korin had never properly opened, and the people inside were still trying to open it with their bare hands. Knowing he had nothing guarding his back, Korin took the opportunity to charge his conjuration spell. When it began phasing into reality, Korin could see cymatic field's luminescence; but since it was only of his etheric aura, it didn't illuminate the physical area around Korin. In the meantime, the cultists were rapidly dropping in numbers, while only five khastwolves remained. Meanwhile, Korin's mates were still behind their respective rocks – except for Jaimas – shooting when and where they could.

Due to the surrounding distractions, it took a little longer than the standard time for Korin to phase the conjuration into reality. Once finished, the spell formed an exact holographic replica of Korin. While still technically focused on the spell with his mind, Korin began multi-tasking as he attempted to open the cage. Telling Korin to hurry, the students cried nonstop, their voices increasingly drowning out under the noise around. Just as he was about to shush the prisoners so he wouldn't lose concentration, a khastwolf started clawing away at the hologram, prompting Korin to turn around.

"Whoa, that was close," Korin muttered as he cowered.

Unsure if he should've shot the khastwolf and alerted it or waited for someone to take care of it, Korin hesitated for a few seconds before choosing the former option – seeing how no-one else was attacking the monster. Shooting beta-negative discharges through the conjured hologram, the dumb khastwolf didn't realize that they came from the real Korin. Soon, it fainted from enough attacks, and Korin turned around to the prisoners again.

"Almost there!" Korin shouted as he relinquished his conjuration to help recharge his energy quicker, as he felt that his lumarchetrix was nearing depletion again.

The last bit of the cage was stuck, but since Korin had a delta-positive shield, he knew he was in a stronger state, so he grabbed the bars with his bare hands and pulled them as hard as he could, bending them just enough so that the prisoners could escape. It helped that they were already damaged.

Korin's lumarchetrix depleted again. With shaking hands, he then looked back at the khastwolf, sighing in relief and some disbelief. One of the students suddenly nudged Korin, thanking him while trying to redirect his attention. Due to being depleted, Korin had to wait a little while before utilizing alpha-positive discharges in order to siphon as much energy as he could. When he regained a bit of aether energy, Korin created an alpha-positive shield and immediately began phase-charging its attraction power. After it shortly activated, multiple blast balls within the affectable radius curved towards the shield, allowing Korin to absorb their energy into his lumarchetrix. Korin was also phase charging another power to be able to withstand far more discharges, but this was taking a long time, so with the added energy received, he prematurely began firing blue discharges back at the group of cultists; and when he hit one of the cultists, the discharge turned the guy into an attractive beacon for further discharges, making Korin's job easier while also helping to replenish even more of his energy. While the attraction was only temporary until more blasts hit the cultist – and that it was only valid within a certain angle of trajectory – Korin still found success for the most part.

Soon, the cultist switched targets, granting Korin the chance to then finally lead the prisoners to safety. The run back was almost trouble-free, but there was one khastwolf nearby, which Korin was oblivious to, and it almost killed him. The monster fortunately landed next to Korin unconscious, its arm brushing against Korin's leg. When Korin finally noticed the khastwolf, he scanned the area to see who shot it, seeing that it was Celine. Her now-unmasked face was full of terror as she stared at it, but there was a resolution in her eyes that Korin wasn't going to die. In that split moment, Celine appeared more combat-primed than any time beforehand, and the sight astonished Korin. While masked, Korin couldn't facially gesture his appreciation, and he was about to run over to thank her, but he abruptly noticed a few of the freed prisoners being attacked. Before Korin arrived to help, however, a khastwolf killed the assailing cultist.

At this point, nearly all the remaining cultists were either knocked unconscious or dead. Now with a securer environment, Korin saved the last couple of groups with comparatively great ease; but just after he had escorted the last person out, the crystal became too unstable, blasting the ceiling above the entry, causing another cave-in. Korin was close by, dodging the falling rocks just in time, his body wearying from all the rolling. When he stood up, he looked at the pileup with dread, believing that he and his friends would probably not escape. He fired at the rocks in frustration, soon turning around after insisting to himself on finishing the job. Only one cultist remained.

"Damn, this last guy keeps dodging our attacks!" Terala complained, almost shooting the cultist as he ducked.

Only one khastwolf endured as well, but this one was a little sneakier. Instead of jumping around in the air, it raced and squirmed around the fallen rocks, finally leaping onto the last cultist. While clawing away, the khastwolf exposed itself to Korin and his band of rescuers, eventually howling before rolling off unconscious, leaving the cultist a bloody mess.

The battle was over.

Death permeated the glowing cavern, and if it weren't for the raging crystal, a haunting feeling would've settled in immediately. The mission, therefore, didn't feel complete, though it at least didn't induce the need for insanely-sustained panic. Korin glimpsed the last cultist move his arm, so he headed over to him.

"Hey, Korin!" Sylas shouted, racing over to grab his shoulder. "We really need to leave now."

"I'll catch up with you in a second," Korin replied. "I think the only way out is to head over the large rock pile to the other side. Go!"

Sylas hesitated for a few seconds, in the end taking off with Terala; Priscilla shortly followed. Meanwhile, Celine stayed, but Korin adamantly told her to go as well. Multiple times. She soon took off, hoping that she had made the right decision listening to him. Jaimas, in contrast, simply ignored Korin's instruction, remaining to check out the nearby khastwolf, observing it breathe in its unconscious state.

Korin finally turned to the cultist, glaring with disgust. "First of all, why did you join the cult? And secondly, what was the cult trying to achieve tonight?" He refrained from helping.

"I…" the cultist replied, coughing blood. "I… I joined… first out of curiosity. I always had an interest in shadowists. It has its pros and cons. I… I guess I got caught up in it all." He sighed, struggling to rebreathe. "I do hold dear to the ideals of The Gathering – we all do – but today… I saw something." He groaned. "It made me question her… our leader. I was… humming and hawing today about it… and, maybe I'm wrong… but… I'm not sure if she can be trusted… But what does it matter? I'll be dead soon."

"No, please tell me!"

"Ugh… alright… she… I think it's possible she may have ulterior motives… like, she's working for… this may sound crazy, but… it's possible that… that she's a necroshaper."

Korin's eyes widened.

The cultist continued, "The concept of a necroshaper itself doesn't… doesn't seem bad to me. In fact, it… it seems kind of cool, you know… It's… it's just that… it seems like we're being controlled by another force. That's my issue. Like, what are we even doing?"

"What proof do you have?"

"No proof, but there's… some… evidence… in-indic-ating… that… that –" He reached his arm out, just touching Korin as he passed away.

The cultist confirmed Korin's deeper conspiracy theories, but just as he was about to cogitate on the issue, small rocks began to fall from the ceiling again, hitting Korin. Before moving on, Korin searched the cultist for anything informative, noticing nothing but his watch. He was about to take it when Jaimas made a loud comment. Korin then responded, "Be careful it doesn't wake up and claw you."

"Hey, don't worry, man. Just hurry up with what you're doing," Jaimas said, kicking the khastwolf before putting his face right up to its mouth. Intensely curious, Jaimas pried its saliva-filled mouth open, putting his head in while checking its yellow and bloodied teeth. "Hey, this is pretty cool," he said, voice echoing inside the reeking mouth.

"Jaimas!" Korin flinched. "What the fuck are you doing? I would *not* do that if I were you!"

"Relax, I'm fine," Jaimas responded casually. "It won't be waking any time soon."

"Seriously, Jaimas, I *really* suggest you get your head out of there now!"

"Why? It's not like I get the opportunity to do this every day."

Jaimas stuck his head in even deeper as Korin shuddered, unsure what else to say. All of a sudden, a loud snapping noise occurred when a large rock fell nearby, hitting a metal pole. Korin finally broke his stare and looked back at the cultist, taking the watch before unmasking yet another unfamiliar face. After he unsteadily stood up, Korin approached Jaimas, telling him to move out with him, relieved that Jaimas's head wasn't bitten off.

Both guys then made their way to the pile of fallen rocks, scaling it quickly, each rock feeling more insecure than the last. While almost at the top, Jaimas unfortunately slipped and tumbled over, smashing his body down the heap and onto the floor.

"No!" Korin cried out. "Jaimas!"

Dust showered over Jaimas, rendering him out of sight just before unliftable rocks rained from the ceiling and completely buried him. Korin dashed down again when all was clear, trying to move the rubble without success. Korin then tried shooting gamma-negative blasts to destroy the rocks, but this was futile, timewise, as well, due to the very low chance rates of successfully causing damage. For a moment, it felt as if a repeat of Evelyn. He even hammered the rocks, bruising himself. Only now, however, the khastwolves had been defeated. It wasn't a matter of him giving up last time with Evelyn – he had to flee; and now as more rocks came crashing down, many of which Korin had to keep dodging – along with the discharging energy almost hitting him as the crystal was about to explode – Korin grudgingly knew he had to press on this time as well, finishing his climb before seeing the vertical slope on the other side. Being dead wasn't going to help Jaimas. He noticed the giant crack in the floor, wondering if it had impeded the rest of the cult from crossing over. Luckily, a large rock had descended earlier on the crack, forming a one-way bridge of sorts. Korin spotted his friends near the exit, meeting up with a saddened face.

"Where's Jaimas?" Sylas asked worriedly.

"He didn't make it." Korin panted wretchedly. "I'm so sorry, but there's no time to explain; we need to move before we're buried, too." He waited for Sylas to respond. "Look, we have to go," he asserted, hoping Sylas understood how gutted he was as well.

After letting out a long cry of anger, Sylas gathered himself, apprehending both the danger he was in and for the fact that he couldn't return to the ritual scene.

"I suggest putting your masks back on," Korin said when Sylas was ready. "The cultists are still in there."

There were three pathways from the doorway, and the group decided to take the one on the right. It was clear that the tunnel was circling around the cavern, and Korin guessed it would lead back to the start. Five robed figures suddenly ran by a parallel tunnel, with the cult leader in the middle. Between the two tunnels was a lower floor, so running to the other side would've taken at minimum a minute; and while the cult leader was capable of easily using propulsion ultrachite to reach the other side, she remained where she was, for reasons unknown to Korin. Everybody in both groups tensely aimed their hands at their opposition without running down. It was an equal match in terms of numbers, yet no-one fired in their curiosity and suspense.

"You!" The cult leader pointed furiously, her voice still masked. "You're not one of us, are you?"

Wondering who she really was, Korin was about to reply when Sylas answered, "Of course we are."

"Liar!" the cult leader yelled. "You're the ones responsible for the calamity out there! How dare you! *How dare you!*" she repeated a little slower with greater emphasis. "The rest of us will be here shortly to outnumber and deal with you. There's no hope for you."

In contempt of the danger, Korin's built-up curiosity forced him to stay and ask her questions. "What are you trying to achieve with all this madness, anyway?" he asked assertively.

"Nothing you're capable of understanding. And that's all you'll ever know."

"Well, I know what shadowists do in general; and with all the information that I've gathered over the semester, I can draw certain conclusions. This cult of yours, The Gathering – The Gathering of the Black Moon – is a resurrection of an ancient sect here at Teloston, which was led by someone called Backlevy."

"Hmph. Nosy little shit. Yes, Grand Sorceress Backlevy was the leader of the ancient circle known as The Gathering. Congratulations on knowing basic history." Despite the mask, her sharp, sarcastic tone was still perceptible. "Although you're *aware* of us, you will never learn of what we *intend* to do."

"I have theories as to what it may be."

"Ha! How amusing. Of course you would. Now, run if you want, but know that you'll be caught."

"We need to leave now," Terala said, nudging Korin.

Korin understood, and his group slowly began backing away with hands still aimed at the cultists. Once clear of the corner, Korin's gang shut the door, barred it, and then ran for their lives, running nonstop as stitches grew to stabbing sensations. While using delta-positive shields for the added speed boost, everyone nevertheless kept pace with each other. Korin swore he heard footsteps from behind, but he was too focused on what was in front of him to look back. In fact, he was worried that he'd run into traps along the way, glancing up at the ceiling several times. His intuitions were correct, except instead of coming from the ceiling, the walls discharged a field of gas, causing the group to cough and gag before it induced wooziness; all five then concentrated as hard as they could to move forth.

Fortunately, everybody happened to be near the end of the gas field when it was activated, so they only breathed a partial amount of the toxins. They eventually reached the main door to the massive lobby, which was fortuitously still open with no cultists nearby. Sylas had enough charge on his charchite to operate the aerochannels again so they didn't have to climb the stairs, and the ascent was just as maddening as the first time they used the channels. The effects of the gas had infiltrated enough of their anatomies, and their visions warped. Too mentally exhausted, nobody properly registered why.

When they exited the last aerochannel, their footing became numb… then silent… and then seemingly non-existent, like they were in a dream. Lightness. Lightness was all they felt. From there, a weird twist in sensation to that of heaviness. After exiting the mansion and pulling their masks off, the group, one by one, crashed on a plump patch of long grass on the property next door, surrounded by thick trees and bushes.

Chapter Twenty-Two

Renown: A Reward or Burden?

Flickers of the morning light pierced through the leaves and struck Korin's face. He awoke, but it wasn't the sun that caused it. Instead, it was an unusual bird that began licking him, its tiny frame housing bulging eyes and a large tongue that it used for licking *everything*. Korin couldn't help but giggle, calling out for it to stop. He finally shooed the bird away, laying back down, not knowing where he was or what had transpired. Just as Korin was about to fall asleep, the bird returned and started licking his face again. This time, he fully woke up, stretching his sore body, remembering what had occurred when he noticed the cultist robe he was still wearing. Everyone else soon woke up, silently gazing around at each other, rubbing their unmasked faces.

"Was… was that real?" Sylas asked after a while.

"Yeah, I think so," Korin replied, examining his mask before glancing over at Celine, who dazedly stared at the ground. *Oh, good, she made it.*

Terala squinted as if she had too much to drink, slowly asking, "So, who was that leader with the weird voice?"

"I have absolutely no idea," Korin said, watching Priscilla, who was leaning up against a tree, looking like she was about to vomit. "Maybe Priscilla knows."

Priscilla heard Korin, but she didn't respond.

A nuisance in Korin's pocket called his attention, and he fiddled with it for a moment, pulling out the cultist's watch. *Hmm… I might get someone to hack into this later,* he thought.

Korin then unevenly picked himself up, surveying his environment. It suddenly dawned on the group that Jaimas wasn't with them, and Sylas transitioned from relative happiness to miserableness. Without shedding tears at first, Sylas closed his eyes and plonked hard on the ground, tumbling slightly. Jaimas was closer to Sylas than anyone else there, so Korin let him have his space. Celine turned away, lightly crying, whereas Terala sat down with a halo of depression, unable to believe what had taken place. Terala thought about throwing something; and when she picked up a pebble, she didn't even have enough motivation to throw it. Since Priscilla had barely interacted with Jaimas, she wasn't crying.

Feeling horrible he wasn't able to do anything when Jaimas fell, Korin recollected the event over and over as each pass became more crushing. Korin eventually approached Sylas, placing his hand on his friend's shoulder. "Hey, sorry about Jaimas."

"I can't believe he's gone," Sylas mumbled, wiping away a tear.

"He was a really great guy. I feel so stupid and bad for acting rude to him before," Korin said before sighing heavily and shakily.

Sylas didn't wish to talk any further, face planted dispiritedly on a knee. Korin was about to mention that he would make sure Jaimas received a good funeral service, but he abruptly realized that the group was still in potential danger.

"I'm surprised the cultists didn't come out and get us," Korin muttered. "Wait here." He intuited that Sylas didn't wish to move. "Hey, Terala, come with me, and we'll check the mansion out just to be sure there's no threat."

Terala hopped up immediately, and she and Korin jumped over the fence, noticing police tape lining the garden and mansion's front entrance. There was more tape inside, but they didn't see anyone. Korin and Terala scoped the place carefully before heading down to the basement, but all that was left inside the room beyond the heavy steel door was a smoky ruin of rubble, as if explosives had been used, completely filling the vicinity and making it impossible to enter.

Unsure if it was the cult's or the police's doing, Korin glanced at Terala, frowning with confusion. "At least we're not in any danger." Korin shrugged. "Let's head back."

When they exited, Celine was still a little teary, though she was comforting Sylas, who was still in the same miserable state. Priscilla was still present, washing her mouth out with a tap nearby after recently vomiting. While waiting for Sylas and Celine, Korin continued discussing recent matters with Terala before he eventually turned his attention to Priscilla, who had fully recovered. He wanted to approach her, but his stirring emotions made his head spin as if they had recreated the toxins he had breathed in the previous night. There was so much Korin wanted to ask, but he knew such answers were permanently sealed off — just like her sanctuary. But he still had a mission to complete. He had to speak with her.

"Hey, Priscilla," Korin said uneasily while approaching her. "How are you feeling?"

Priscilla glared for a second before changing her expression to a somewhat friendlier one. She approached Korin very closely, almost with her body against his. "Oh, so you're being nice to me now?" she asked 'nicely', though the strong bitterness was clearly present. "Only now, after all we've been through? It took a while."

"You know, I *am* sorry," Korin said firmly. "Please recognize the extraordinary context here."

"I *might* accept your apology. Maybe I need to think it over." Priscilla fluttered her eyes as she moved her face closer to Korin's, teasing a potential kiss.

All of a sudden, Celine approached Korin's side, instantly holding his hand as she frowned at Priscilla.

Korin glanced warmly at Celine before telling Priscilla, "You still have a lot to explain. Like, how much do you know about the cult, and how did you get such information? *And* what *else* were you doing down there?" He thought of the items she took from the locker room.

Priscilla backed off, glowering at Celine's hand holding Korin's, utterly offended and disgusted. She held her heart, breathing in tightly as her eyes watered. "Why would I ever tell you that?" Priscilla shouted in a raspy manner, scrunching her face with hatred before dashing off without a second look.

A part of Korin would've ripped away with Priscilla's leaving, but luckily Celine's energy kept him emotionally stable. Celine looked at Korin, frowning in a way that indicated the desire for an explanation, and Korin straightaway knew what she was thinking.

"It's a long story," Korin mumbled. "I'll explain later. But don't worry, we're not together."

Celine silently accepted what he said as the truth, though it was clear to him that she had many thoughts running through her head – thoughts that would surface later.

Sylas was already standing up at that point; he soon plodded over to Korin with confusion, his face dreary and stained with salt. "So…"

"Again, I'll explain everything later," Korin basically interrupted. "Let's just head to the Central Hub and find out what's happening first."

Before leaving, all four removed their robes, folding them up under their arms with the masks inside. There was no way they were going to discard potential disguises. They then decided to quickly place the disguises back at their respective dorms before going to the Central Hub.

***

Mages of all ages stumbled around the campus, drunk, hungover, and tired from the previous night. Some students kept walking into objects, unable to find their way around, while a few other people kept stumbling onto the ground after repeatedly struggling to their feet. There were many gargles and murmurs of regret, all horribly contrasting the sweet, morning bird tweets. The streets were replete with litter and random effects, while muddled, drooping streamers and arbitrarily-splashed paint covered walls and fences. Birds, ants, and numerous furry animals gathered in for the greasy feast of 'food' lying on the ground, tables, and even on clothing students had previously stripped off. A few workers were up and about, cleaning the mess and readying for the daily activities and shows.

Korin's stomach grumbled ferociously, as did Sylas's. The food hall wasn't open the previous night, but it was now, despite it being a public holiday. Needing sustenance badly after their energy-draining action, Korin convinced Sylas to grab at least something to eat before doing anything else. *However*, while still in the Central Hub right before entering the food hall, Korin gaped in total shock when he saw Jaimas casually walk by.

"J-Jaimas?" Korin said as Sylas stood paralysed with disbelief.

"Hey, Korin and Sylas!" Jaimas shouted before breezily stopping in front of the boys.

"You… you made it!" Korin exclaimed happily, about to laugh his sorrows away. "I can't believe you're alive!"

Jaimas then grabbed Korin and a paralysed Sylas by the shoulders, blithely saying, "Hey, and I'm glad you guys made it out, too. Fuck me, that was epic!"

Celine and Terala caught up with the guys, yelping before joyfully greeting Jaimas with just as much shock. Sylas, meanwhile, broke free from his paralysis, continuously commenting on how astounded and happy he was, hands tightly crossed behind his head.

The cave-in still confused Korin, and he spluttered, "Bu-but, h-h-how, I mean, you, just… how?"

"Whoa!" Jaimas looked taken aback. "Did you breathe in too much dust down there? You seem like you can hardly breathe. You right, mate?"

"Bu-but?" Korin stared at Jaimas, whose face remained casually expressed. "How on Juntas did you get out of there?"

"Oh, I found a tunnel and walked right out." He flopped his hand nonchalantly.

"Yeah, I figured *that* part, but those rocks smothered you. It would've been impossible to escape. How'd you get out?"

"Korin, Korin, Korin… I'm Jaimas." He grinned, proudly holding his chest. "Anyway, you guys look like you need something to eat. Oh, but first." He grabbed Korin's hand, raising it into the air. "Hey, everyone!" Jaimas bellowed, stopping numerous people from their chatter, the effect, in turn, rippling throughout the Central Hub. "Look who's here! It's Korin, Sylas, Terala, and, uh, Celine," he said as Celine shut her eyes, grateful that, at the very least, he didn't say another name.

Suddenly, practically everyone began exuberantly clapping and cheering, overpowering Korin, who was trying to ask Jaimas what was happening. The sounds of hundreds of pieces of cutlery in the food hall nearby could also be heard, each chiming against plates in a domino chain, blaring through the doors as attention was given to the spotlight that was Korin and his friends. Korin finally broke through to Jaimas.

"I told them what happened," Jaimas answered Korin. "We saved the missing students, and now we're being hailed. Lap it up."

Korin interjected with his finger. "Not all of them. Some died, and there are still more people missing; and we've yet to find out what's really happening."

"Well, close enough. Anyway, when I escaped, the festival was still on, and some of the missing people who escaped were on a podium explaining what had happened. When I saw them, I stood up as well, explaining about you guys and what happened."

"Okay, but are you going to explain how you survived?"

"Eh, maybe later. I'm going to crash somewhere. I didn't sleep at all. There's a big party later. See you." He patted Korin on the shoulder. Before leaving, he talked to several other people on the way, including Sylas, who followed.

As Korin stood stationary, numerous people approached to thank, congratulate, and ask him and his friends questions. There were a few that apologized for still thinking he was a 'sex fiend', too. The crowd mounted. If it weren't for the praise Korin had recently received for his hillseck winnings, the appreciative stimuli would've been too overwhelming, as he hadn't, otherwise, received anything of the like in a long time. It wasn't just a matter of gaining praise from nothing; he had endured a fair amount of negativity from his peers, so the spike in social appraisal was staggering. The past was now behind him, and he appreciated the gratitude for his efforts. Korin remained humble, and he made it clear that it would've been impossible without his friends.

When finally lined for food inside the Provision Wreath, Korin had to allow others to pass him as people still relentlessly approached him. From winning the hillseck County Cup to saving the missing students, virtually everyone – that was awake and sober within the last few hours – knew about Korin. He couldn't believe how he easily fit into the university at the beginning of the year *because* he was unknown and that nobody cared about him. It would seem, then, that an unsung reputation would continue to be suiting, but Korin found the flipside just as good. At least for the time being.

Eventually, Korin managed to grab a plate of food, and the seemingly endless line of people eased off after Korin loudly said he'd happily discuss more later. He needed his space. As did his friends. Engrossed in their thoughts at the table, Korin, Terala, and Celine didn't speak much, nor did they really eat. The gratitude's elating effects then violently clashed with their lingering cult encounter. Soon, the latter came to dominate their minds as if forming a powerful, harrowing collective over their heads, flooding them with strong mental images so they repeatedly experienced, in a sense, the scene again and again.

"That was some pretty dark shit we saw there," Terala murmured.

"I think I'll go hide in one of the gardens for a whole week to clear my head," Celine said cheerlessly. "Thank goodness we don't have classes for a while."

"I might join you," Korin responded. "After sleeping for a whole day or two, that is."

Sylas arrived at the table, sitting down with a big grin on his face. "So, what's the plan, guys?" He rubbed his hands.

Korin glanced at Sylas, taking his time before replying, "We'll see. I might speak to someone first before resting. Maybe."

If it weren't for Sylas, their depressed conversation would've meandered into the desert to die. Their spirits soon lifted again as they thought about the future and how they were definitely going to save the rest of the missing students and stop The Gathering the Black Moon.

When all four finished their meals, they headed out of the food hall, where they crossed paths with Chancellor Helena Valen, who looked as professional as ever in her summer-fitting dress. Korin also fully saw her bare arms for the first time. In spite of her age, they were toned. Seeing Helena made Korin's nerves twitch, even though she didn't pose a threat.

"Oh, there you are, Korin. May we talk, please?" Helena asked before glancing at his friends. "Alone?"

"Sure. I'll see you guys later." Korin waved his friends goodbye before giving Celine a small kiss. "Where do you want to go?"

"We'll just go for a walk." Helena motioned him to follow. "So, I received news that you and your friends were the ones responsible for saving the missing students. Is that true?"

Korin agitatedly scratched his head. "Yeah. We… saved a lot of them." He hardly believed that he had been raised to *basically* abhor mages, and now he had saved many of their lives. "There are more out there, though."

"So I've heard. There was also a dark ritual; is this correct?" She slanted her head, eyes fixed on Korin.

Dark is an understatement, Korin thought before saying, "Yeah, there was. The cult was about to sacrifice all of them, and… they had a powerful crystal in the centre. They were supposedly enchanting it, but I don't know what for."

"I see." Helena took a moment to think to herself. "I also heard there were khastwolves. Quite the accomplishment for just you and your friends. I take it you didn't tell anyone else about the ritual beforehand?"

"N-no. No-one else," he answered, a tad worried about how she'd react.

Helena halted, her energy instantly triggering Korin to stop as well. "Korin, although I thank and congratulate you on your efforts, you should've told someone about this. Not only are you not equipped to fight –"

"But we succeeded."

"Hm. Yes, you're right." She smiled with an unsatisfied twinge, wanting to continue making her point but realizing Korin was actually right.

"We had our reasons," Korin said, thinking of a way to appeal to her sense of rationality, "such as not having any proof for ages; and then when we did, it got destroyed, like in that large fire over two months ago. We also needed a great deal of discretion, as unwanted attention could've backfired on us and potentially gotten us killed."

Helena slowly nodded her head, finally saying, "I understand perfectly. However, you must realize that you're now publicly known. Perhaps in future your plans will have to adapt to your new state of affairs. And yes, it's clear you have plans."

Korin opened his mouth, but he wasn't sure what to say, remaining speechless.

"I think my intuitions about you were right from the start," Helena said, as if proud to have Korin by her side. The two began walking again. "You're both capable and willing to meet challenges, and to go to depths which most won't and can't. And you've proved it. Well done, Korin."

"I had the help of my friends, of course."

"Indeed. But I am of the impression that you were the one central to the efforts. Hereafter, however, I do advise that you inform the… authorities. Of course, that may not be so easy, so…"

Knowing the authorities, for one, would be sceptical of him and any ideas he may have – despite now being shown proof of cult activity – Korin hummed with hesitative thoughts. "Perhaps I can just personally tell *you* about important issues."

Helena's face lit up. "Well, that's probably all that's necessary. Perhaps, I think, we should keep it like that." She smiled as if winning a small victory. "Feel free to come to directly."

"Sure. But how come you can't just send the police or anyone else under the university and clean sweep the area for cultists?"

"We'll do what we can, but I'm not free to simply issue commands like that. The university administration is complex. You must also note that the university only owns half of the tunnels and systems underneath; and, please also consider that of those systems, many are permanently sealed away for our safety. Should any of those areas now be open, then we'll be forced to search inside and then close them again. Opening up unknown areas could lead to several types of outbreaks of who knows what, and I will not – and am not allowed to – risk such an action. But since the cultists have most likely been in operation for quite some time, it's clear that the particular areas they have accessed haven't posed too much of a threat to them. There are also other reasons for the limitations, and there may be other complications in this process, so I will inform you of the progress. Anyway, I have news on your old religion, Sacrenderism," she said as Korin's heart smacked speedily against his chest, feeling overworked and in need of a holiday. "Are you aware of what has happened?"

"No, please tell me," Korin said quickly.

"The Temple's prophet just passed away in his sleep. Ninety-five, he was. His funeral is being held on a planet called Gertras, where the Temple's capital is located."

Helena allowed Korin time to cogitate the update – his stunned face signified the need, anyway. Over the last month, Korin's former life had slowly drifted into the background as he found himself too caught up in the dilemmas at Teloston. Although Korin now identified as a mage, he still felt connected with Temple issues. Despite the prophet being on another world, the news made Korin want to see everyone he knew at Orchopolis again and find out how they were handling the prophet's passing. The train of thought then led Korin to imagine showing his peers how much he had changed, even though he never fully connected with anyone there.

"So, have they chosen another prophet?" Korin finally asked.

"Not yet. It may take a little longer than normal, actually. I also feel that this will be a significant turning point for not just Sacrenderism but for all those who don't follow the religion as well. Still, most of these changes will occur and unfold in the long run; your time at university will go quickly before anything major happens. Although I understand your background is giving you concerns – and that your interest in worldly events is great, in consideration of your studies in Political Science – your focus is best served inside the walls of the university."

"Sure, but I still want to know about these things. Also, do you have any news about the priests back in Orchopolis? Have you been able to prove all the evil things they're doing?"

"No, alas, the government hasn't. My contacts tried their best, but there was too much red tape. And, there were other problems, such as incompetence and potential corruption. Not of *my* contacts, of course."

"Hmm." Korin stopped walking, looking down with a demoralized face. "What about Evelyn? Any more news?"

"I'm sorry, but there has been no other news."

"That's alright. I still hope she made it."

"Yes, I hope so, too. Anyway, while I'm sure that I'll read a detailed report later tonight – as the police will ask you many questions – was there anything else in particular you learned of last night that you can mention before I take off?"

While there was so much to say, Korin initially couldn't think of anything. "No, not really. Well, actually… yes." Korin wondered what Helena thought about conspiracy theories, believing that she could have held views on any side of the fence. He then remembered his conversation with her a couple of months ago, and it seemed like she had her own conspiracy theories. When he addressed particular events that he believed were related to such grand conspiracies, she merely asked further questions without denial – which Korin answered to the best of his knowledge. After a moment of consideration, Korin said, "I know this might sound a little off the sigil, but… I believe what I'm about to say could be legitimate. I managed to speak to one of the cultists before he died, and he… mentioned that the cult leader is potentially a necroshaper – you know, the group of evil mages that emerged from Xalinor Traven's cult around two and a half thousand years ago."

"Mm, interesting. Is there any proof?"

"No, unfortunately there's not. But… but I just *know* it's the truth."

"Yes, I recognize that. It's possible that it might be true – your judgment has demonstrated to be heretofore correct – but it could likewise be false. For now, it's perhaps best not to get hung up on potentially-extraneous information. Your attention should be on matters that you can discover and handle. In the event of it being true, I doubt you could do much. At least for now. Anyway," she said, smiling greatly, "again, you've done well, Korin. I… think I may have a special task for you when the next semester starts. I can't say what it is yet, but I believe you're more than capable for the job. Are you in?"

"Sure," Korin replied keenly. "I'm up for anything."

Assorted Details

Caelverse Details

The Cosmology of the Caelverse

<u>Note:</u>

For this section, I have gathered the essential information of the *Caelverse* (pronounced sail-vurs) from a separate book I have published called *The Caelverse Compendium*. Essentially, the Caelverse is a different 'universe' that I have created. If you wish to have a proper understanding of how the Caelverse works, then you will need to read the compendium. The following information is also written from the perspective of someone living in the Caelverse.

<u>Structural and Astronomical Overview:</u>

The Caelverse is a massive horn-torus-shaped system that features what astronomers believe to be 589,824 *planets* divided equally in orbit around 32,768 *suns*. Each sun has its own respective *solar system*, so there are also 32,768 solar systems. Giant, planet-less *C-stars (constellated stars)* form 32,768 *sets* of twelve geometrically-positioned *constellations* around each solar system, all among a sea of nebulae, one parsec (roughly thirty trillion kilometres) away from their respective systems, ringed perpendicular (from their centres) in relation to the circular direction of travel the solar systems take through the Caelverse. The solar systems also are part of *solar clusters*, which are specific sets of vertically-walled solar systems, each with 256 suns that vary in distance and geometric location from one another;

therefore, there are 128 solar clusters. There are also unconstellated *L-stars* (*loose stars*) that situate between and around the solar clusters in far greater number than both the suns and C-stars.

Since the Caelverse is a horn torus, the centre has a point; however, the centre is shrouded, so while the geometry of the Caelverse is clear, it is still unknown what exactly is at the centre. Most theories suggest that the central point is a gateway to a space beyond the Caelverse. Not only has no-one ever reached the centre of the Caelverse (as space travel and teleportation is limited), there has not been any evidence of anything emerging from this possible gateway either. Although the origins of the Caelverse are unclear, it is generally theorized that it was at least the product (though not necessarily a conscious creation) of an external force – whether physical and/or spiritual. Since many shrouds block access to a person gaining such knowledge in the astral realm, it is also unclear whether the Caelverse directly or indirectly connects to any other physical system of similar or different structures. Most theories nonetheless suggest the Caelverse is part of a multiverse; regardless, other timelines do exist, which mages have verified from etheric observation.

Despite there being many competing cosmological theories, it is nonetheless clear that the Caelverse is in a constant state of change. At one 'end' of the Caelverse is also the gigantic *Great Black Wall* (GBW), a vertical field filled with many black holes and a strange gas that appears like a liquid. For some unknown reason, the black holes do not coalesce, nor do they consume the surrounding gas, so they are called *micro* black holes compared to the hypothetical large black holes that could exist. The majority of astronomers theorize that the GBW will consume every solar system in roughly 66,585,605 years' time – as of the year B-424. The GBW, more specifically, will supposedly take 524,288 years to gravitationally rip *each* solar cluster to shreds individually. The 'first' solar cluster (named: *SC1*) is already experiencing slow destruction, with wild cosmic rays causing massive environmental damage; even the planets' natural gravitational distortions are wildly distorted to further extremes. With an estimated 1,029 years left before complete annihilation, nearly all willing sapient lifeforms have permanently relocated to other solar clusters from worlds. Many black market and unlawful activities occur in SC1, despite strong government entry restrictions.

Given the geometrically 'perfect' number of suns and solar clusters already present in the Caelverse (respectively 32,768 and 128), it seems unlikely the GBW has consumed other solar clusters in the current cycle of history. Still, the GBW would have had a starting point, so it should take 69,730,304 years for the GBW to completely move through the Caelverse from its original starting point. Whatever the case, it is generally believed that the Caelverse will reform its solar clusters after the GBW has consumed everything. One reason for this is that advanced psychics have tuned into the celestial bodies of the Caelverse, discovering that their various (though vague) etheric energies exist in multiple different time periods of our current reality. This means that there would be different *cycles* of reformation for the *same timeline*. In other words, the energies exist in different time periods of our current timeline that extend beyond our *current* cycle of history; *but* this simultaneously does not mean *itself* that the energies *necessarily* exist in other timelines (although they still do).

Planets and Transportals:

Planets are sorted into *tiers* and *classes* (specifically, *planetary orbital tiers* – POTs – and *planetary structural classes* – PSCs), with every solar system having the same classifications. There are three POTs, with T1 (Tier One) planets being close to their sun, T2 planets being in the *prime habitable zone*, and T3 planets orbiting far away from their sun. T1 planets are so close to their sun that they experience scorching temperatures, where surface temperatures reach well beyond liveable standards. Some T1 planets have atmospheres while others do not; for those that do not have atmospheres, the temperatures reach extremely cold levels during the nights. T2 planets, on the other hand, contain most of the life in the Caelverse; but even then, there are many places on these planets that are uninhabitable for most beings. T3 planets are basically the opposite of T1 planets; that is, they are too cold for normal life – both during the day and night, regardless of whether a planet has an atmosphere or not.

It takes *exactly* 360 *Standard Days* for *all* T2 worlds to orbit a sun (making one *Standard Year*), whereas *all* T1 worlds complete an orbit in a mere thirty-three Standard Days exactly. Meanwhile, T3 planets take exactly twelve Standard Years and thirty Standard Days to fully orbit their sun. Spacecraft have nevertheless been able to reach and land on T1 and T3 planets. Initial exploration was with unmanned probes, but eventually manned spaceships were able to establish colonies on these planets. However, due to the extremely harsh conditions (not just the temperatures), only basic colonies (all living underground) have been able to survive up to this point. Psychic mages have also detected particular etheric activity from underground – the kind of etheric activity that lifeforms produce and possess. However, this is largely distorted, so it is unclear whether other life exists on these planets or not; but in all likelihood, at least some unknown alien life exists.

Each POT has a set of six PSCs that universally occur in an established order throughout the Caelverse. The first PSC are C1 (Class One) worlds, and it is from C1 planets that the Standard Day of twenty-four hours is set. Other classes may have their own days, but when dealing with interplanetary affairs, the Standard Day is used. T2-C1 planets are the most habitable and inhabited places in the Caelverse, exhibiting an array of lifeforms from bacteria to fully sapient beings. Their terrains are generally temperate, but they also feature deserts, tundra, mountainous regions, vast oceans, and of course, polar ice caps. Shaped as globes, each have a diameter of 50,968 km, while most have axial tilts establishing seasons.

From the crust to the end of the lower mantle, all C1 planets have a 'honeycomb' or 'cellular' structure; in a few places, it is more akin to a sponge. These natural structures form what is typically called the *grand caverns*, which are massive areas featuring an array of lifeforms (for T2 planets), oceans, cities (T2), and more. Given the amount of mass that C1 planets possess (as well as all other planets), it would seem as though the gravity would be too much for most inhabitants, but this is not the case due to each planet having specially-warped gravity.

In contrast to C1 planets, C2 worlds are ring shaped. The majority of C2 planets are toroids resembling doughnuts, but a decent number appear like the ornamental jewellery worn on fingers. Coupled with the shape and rotation types of the planets, this results in some areas being naturally much colder or warmer. For doughnut worlds, even the topography has greater extremities, where large mountainous regions have formed near the inner section far greater than that found on C1 worlds. Then there are regions that never truly see night due to light reflecting and refracting off the inner planetary walls. These factors add more problems to the weather, and so it is not just the high rotational speeds per se that create harsher and more unusual weather in comparison to C1 planets.

Harsh habitability issues also apply to C3 planets, which are worlds that are geometrically 'pinched' in assorted directions, causing the planets to resemble shapes like cubes, pyramids, hexagonal prisms, octahedrons, dodecahedrons, and more (but not cones or cylinders). Such worlds do not have straight edges; instead, the edges curve inwards towards the centre of the planet. Essentially, the planets are not actually cubes, for example, but, instead, *concave cuboids*. Substances like water will typically flow to the centre of a face, where most of the planet's atmosphere will be located, too. So, for said planets, there is basically just one giant ocean in the middle. This is followed by a ring of vegetation, and then the climates become increasingly arid the further away from the centre; it also becomes increasingly harder to breathe any oxygen (especially amongst the incredibly high mountains around the edges and corners).

C4 planets are more extreme, however, and they can appear in any kind of shape. Usually, though, these shapes are of bizarre, asymmetrical forms. There are also other topographical formations that essentially add to the overall shape, and these include examples like: hand-like super-mountains; continental-sized chunks of land that float in the air; chasms that extend to the mantle; and calderas and 'craters' the size of continents (with some walls stretching up to the inner radiation belt). In a few places, curled landmasses allow people to basically walk upside down, and this phenomenon can even apply to the aforementioned examples; so, super-mountains, for example, may seem easy to 'climb', being horizontal to the climber; or, the climber could *effectively* be subject to the planet's standard gravitational levels (based on the real gravity) when climbing. Some C4 worlds also have slowly morphing gravitational distortions, so these geographical features do not necessarily last, and new formations occur over time. Lifeforms on these planets are typically more fearsome, too.

The following PSC, C5 worlds, have *some* greater extremities, but overall are safer than C4 planets. Still, they are not easily colonizable for a variety of reasons. C5 worlds are considered the 'mimic' or 'microcosm' class due to the fact that some of their mass mimics their solar system's mass in *form*. So, the central form of a C5 world is akin to the sun – but only in form (shape), not its actual mass or properties. Orbiting the 'sun' are also the solar system's planets and other celestial bodies. Each body is able to stay in their 'orbit' within the whole C5 planetary area (without colliding into one another) due to the distinct gravitational distortions within the warped gravitational field. Most of the C5 mass is actually found in a geometric 'frame' around the mimic masses. Normally, this frame takes the shape of a cube, but it is not limited to this shape. A large gas cloud is also found inside the frame.

The final PSC, C6 planets, is the most extreme of all – in terms of habitability. Devoid of practically any native sentient life (including simple flora), C6 planets are wastelands, where they lack water and proper atmospheres. They also experience extreme exposure to cosmic radiation and electrical winds, and it does not help that they also feature the *great storms* in the centre of their forms. That is, C6 planets are formed as a double cone(-like) structure, where at the apexes, a gigantic and powerful electoral storm constantly persists. The base of each cone is roughly flat, and given their distances from the great storms, these locations are much easier to build on. Most settlements are mage government military outposts and (highly-regulated) civilian colonies, followed then by various private research stations and corporate operations. Like with other harsh worlds, some illegal activity exists on these planets as well.

All planets (of every POT and PSC) possess intense radiation belts that make travelling outside a planet incredibly dangerous and expensive. Thus, very few spaceships exist. All space travel occurs within the confines of a solar system, too, as travelling to different solar systems and solar clusters would take exceedingly too long – more than many lifetimes for the average being. Regardless, living too far outside of a planet has repeatedly been shown to alter one's consciousness and physical state, so permanent or long-term space living, for now, is not ideal. Accordingly, the only way to travel to other planets in another solar system or solar cluster is via teleportation (specifically, magic) or the *planetary transportal system* (PTS), which consists of the naturally-formed planetary portals found on the nodes of the crisscrossing *ley lines* of each planet, which are potent potential fields in the form of lines that geometrically form across a planet's surface. The ley lines do not actually *fully* crisscross, and, instead, they form observable energy nodes that circulate and then help to produce a single giant ring each, which people may walk through to reach other transportals.

The majority of transportals are *general transportals*, which lead to adjacent ley line nodes on the same planet. Since multiple ley lines intersect with one another, general transportals lead to multiple different transportals depending on the position a person walks through the transportal ring. So, if a person walks through the north part of a ring, then they will access the other transportal north of their location. Both parts of the ring, in this case, will be of the same size and shape as one another – which is a characteristic that all *window* portals possess. Accordingly, not all parts of a transportal ring will have *active* portals, but even the inactive parts of a transportal ring will still be visible. Most planets have between 700 and 750 general transportals, and some of these will be closer to one another than others (in their geometric formations).

There are then three types of *interplanetary transportals*; all three types, nevertheless, only lead to transportals of the same POT (so, T2 transportals can only lead to other T2 transportals). Therefore, as stated before, the only way to travel to other POTs is via magical teleportation or space travel. To access other PSCs within a solar system, one must travel to the north and south poles (or equivalents) of a planet. So, the *interclass transportals* found at C1 north poles lead to C2 worlds (at their north pole equivalents) in their respective solar systems – and vice versa. C2 south pole interclass transportals lead to C3 worlds (at their south poles) and vice versa, while C3 north poles lead to C4 worlds (at their north poles). This repeats to C5 and then to C6 worlds before C6 worlds lead back to the south poles of C1 worlds.

To travel to other solar systems within the same solar cluster, a person must find one of generally two to four *inter-solar transportals* located in various positions on a planet. Normally, these are found near the equators on C1 worlds and the equivalents on other PSCs; and each inter-solar transportal will generally lead to an inter-solar transportal in an adjacent solar system. *Inter-cluster transportals*, on the other hand, are the rarest type. Only one solar system (the central one) in a solar cluster will possess inter-cluster transportals. However, all planets in the solar system will feature two sets of these transportals, each leading to adjacent solar clusters with their respective PSC; the only exception to this is the very first and last solar clusters in the Caelverse (SC1 and SC128), which are each next to the GBW; and so, only one inter-cluster transportal from their respective adjacent solar clusters will lead to these fringe solar clusters. In other words, SC1 transportals do not lead to SC128 transportals and vice versa. Unlike the other interplanetary transportals, inter-cluster transportals differ completely in location on a planet for each solar cluster.

<u>Moons and Lunapexes:</u>

Every planet (of all POTs and PSCs) possesses one *crystal moon* (or *prime moon* or *transchite moon*), which is naturally made almost purely of an aggregate crystal called *transchite*. Crystal moons would be translucent if it were not for their immensely-thick bodies, having universally-standard diameters of 12,742 km when measured at *base form*. Most crystal moons tend to have homogenous, bright colours, but a few beautifully flaunt the rainbow, depending on the levels of different types of crystal found within the aggregate. They also feature different kinds of patterns across their surfaces, including geometric, fractal, and standard crystalline structures. Crystal moons also orbit at an average distance of about 407,744 km from their planets.

All planets in the Caelverse each also possess another twelve moons known as the *elemental moons* (or *archetypal moons* or *shapeshifting moons*), divided up into the *archetypal elements* of 'fire', 'water', 'air', and 'earth'. Elemental moons vary in size (though, generally, they are around 12,742 km in diameter), and their mass varies. Elemental moons also have a *circular orbit* of 611,616 km from their planets. This means that all the elemental moons have a fixed distance. They also orbit their planets approximately every 32.7273 Standard Days. Both crystal and elemental moons have *prograde* motion in respect to their planets – namely, C1 worlds; so, when viewed from a bird's-eye view from the north pole of a C1 world, the moons *orbit* in the same direction of the planet's *rotation*. For clarification, this is a moon's movement *around* the planet and not itself the moon's rotation (its spin) on its own axis. This means that all moons in the Caelverse perfectly synchronize with one another with any alignment relative to their planet.

Elemental moons consist primarily of one state of matter (not including the cores and parts of the mantles), so air moons are mostly made of gases, water moons, liquids, earth moons, solids, and for fire moons, a heated state based on properties of the first three that induces various states *and* processes like plasma and literal fire, respectively. Of the fire produced, most is charged with plasma, anyway. A water moon, for example, does not have to consist of H_2O, and it can, instead, be any standard liquid while also minimally possessing properties in other phases/states such as solid and gas. For example, ice (a solid) can form in clouds, which are a mixture of liquid and gas. Nevertheless, in order to turn a heavy metal into a liquid, for example, higher temperatures are needed, and so most water moons are mainly filled with H_2O.

An earth moon's surface may entirely be a desert of sand, and its crust may comprise of lots of metallic, solidified substances like iron, gold, or mercury. In addition, a fair few earth moons possess orbiting rings of dust and rock. Gas moons may have gaseous auras and/or large jets and streams of gas shooting out. Liquid, nonetheless, tends to form around the cores of gas moons as a result of their overall density. Fire moons range greatly, too, with some *appearing* as if mini suns, while others can be completely covered in molten, plasma-charged rock. Their brightness in the sky, though, is not too bad for most inhabitants on a planet.

All planets experience *lunapexes*, which occur every thirty Standard Days in relation to one crystal moon's orbit around a planet. Essentially, lunapexes are a time of significant observable and mysterious energetic changes, affecting the planets in a myriad of ways, both physically and etherically. With 360 Standard Days in a year, there are also twelve months per year; and the 28-day, four-week month features an additional two days for the lunapexes at the beginning, with each planet in the Caelverse (of all POTs and PSCs) experiencing the event simultaneously – despite whatever day length a planet experiences. Although throughout the year many celebrations are held, generally public holidays (for mages) are reserved only for the lunapexes, making twenty-four days in total. A month starts on the days and dates known as *L1* and *L2* (short for Lunapex One and Lunapex Two) before normal days begin, with Moonday starting on the 3rd, followed by Earthday, Waterday, Airday, Fireday, Starday, and Sunday before repeating to Moonday. The last day of the month is accordingly Sunday the 30th. For clarification, L1 and L2 will never be a standard day such as Moonday or Airday.

The lunapex process begins when the crystal moon first phases into the *lunar eclipse* (where a planet is directly positioned between the crystal moon and sun). Technically, the true moment of the eclipse is momentary, but the lunapex *effects* last two-and-a-half days, which is precisely the length of when the crystal moon passes (aligns) through (and with) one type of *zodiac sign* (which is a particular archetypal energy in the context of *astrology*). The calendar, however, only acknowledges two days; but this is a cultural issue, not one of astronomical alignment. Precisely, a lunapex itself – and all of its effects – occur only at and provisionally post eclipse; and so, even when a crystal moon is very close to the eclipse, there are still no lunapex effects prior to it fully eclipsing. In other words, the lunapex is a distinct birthing event and not one of *mere* proximity itself; it is just that the location that a crystal moon possesses during this period happens to be an important factor.

When an elemental moon aligns behind a crystal moon during a lunapex, the crystal moon will also channel physical and etheric energy toward the moon in question, *transfiguring* it (that is, crystal moons cause the elemental moons to shapeshift). The elemental moon may have been an air moon before the lunapex, but the crystal moon may transfigure it into a fire moon, for instance. The process is basically the same as how mages transfigure and shapeshift matter with alchemical magic – just without the spell crafting and magical activation. Crystal moons will contain a new etheric code for a new elemental moon, which it ties to the aligning elemental moon at the beginning of a lunapex. A crystal moon is able to derive these new etheric codes due not just to its powerful nature but also to its relationship with the elemental moons; essentially, the crystal moon will tap into a specific set of potential states that the elemental moons possess via the etheric, with one of these states being selected via differing probabilities and other influences (like, astrological). From this, the shapeshifting will result in the elemental moon changing its very structure, drawing from said etheric states.

The following zodiac, lunapex, and month names are:

Equamas: Cardinal air zodiac; **Dawnair Lunapex**; Month: **Primsis.**

Origas: Fixed air zodiac sign; **Midair Lunapex**; Month: **Secunsis.**

Agilas: Mutable air zodiac; **Duskair Lunapex**; Month: **Tersis.**

Automas: Cardinal fire zodiac; **Dawnfire Lunapex**; Month: **Quartsis.**

Centras: Fixed fire zodiac; **Midfire Lunapex**; Month: **Quintusis.**

Adventras: Mutable fire zodiac; **Duskfire Lunapex**; Month: **Sextusis.**

Determas: Cardinal earth zodiac; **Dawnearth Lunapex**; Month: **Septisis.**

<u>Stablas:</u> Fixed earth zodiac; **Midearth Lunapex**; Month: **Octasis**.

<u>Practas:</u> Mutable earth zodiac; **Duskearth Lunapex**; Month: **Nonusis**.

<u>Emotas:</u> Cardinal water zodiac; **Dawnwater Lunapex**; Month: **Decisis**.

<u>Privas:</u> Fixed water zodiac; **Midwater Lunapex**; Month: **Undesis**.

<u>Dreamas:</u> Mutable water zodiac; **Duskwater Lunapex**; Month: **Dudesis**.

<u>Additional Celestial Bodies:</u>

The Caelverse has many other celestial bodies and oddities. For example, beyond the planets in a slower orbit are the *plasmanaries*, which also contribute both direct physical and etheric (including astrological) effects upon other celestial bodies. These luminaries are gigantic spherical orbs, and they consist entirely of a special plasmatic energy that generates and constantly churns moving patterns and colours that have the appearance of, but are not limited to: lava lamp gloops; hundreds and thousands; spinning discs; fibre optic lights; crazy balls; looping strings; paint being mixed or even splashed in water; spirals; electricity; glitter; clouds (normal and stormy); froths; bubbles; oils; inks; spiky magnetic fluid; flames; flowering energy; fractals; waves; raindrops; reflectors; and more.

Varying greatly in nature as well are the *comets* and *asteroids*, with each solar system possessing comets and asteroids of completely different sizes, numbers, orbits, types, and more. Both, of course, exist outside of the solar systems as well. There are two main kinds of comets: *normal comets* and *frame comets*. Normal comets are large chunks of rock, dust, ice, and gas; and when they pass near the sun, they release gases and other particles, forming a surrounding atmosphere called a *coma* and then a *tail*. Frame comets, conversely, possess harder materials that form windowed shells or bubbles around gases that barely escape. The 'windows' are transparent glass, and the ionized gases within them glow strongly; these comets, accordingly, lack *visible* tails (but they still possess tails).

There are several mysteries in the Caelverse as well, most of which are outside of the solar systems. One of these mysteries includes the *leviathan clouds*. Formed mostly out of cosmic dust, leviathan clouds happen to resemble monstrous entities of gigantic proportions; that is, these leviathan-looking clouds average about three times the size of a sun, and each take a different form, so some are more dragon-like, while others have jellyfish type structures. Then there are the strange *asteroid fields* of varying sizes situate between the solar clusters, each mostly filled with what are likely standard minerals. Many parts of the asteroid fields also form into figure-eight patterns. *Torn dead planets* also exist amongst the asteroid fields; these are what look to be planets, but they are too shattered to be considered actual 'planets', and the etheric data gathered from them show absolutely no life.

Other anomalies have been spotted throughout the Caelverse, but they are so small that they could just be loose debris from the other celestial bodies. Most of these are attributed to matter from the asteroid fields; but naturally, there is always conflicting speculation. Still, some of this matter is ring-shaped, but since geometric shapes are part of the fabric of the Caelverse, this is not necessarily anything interesting. Some unsupported theories, nonetheless, suggest that these rings are broken gateways. Odd electrical 'elastic bands' also float in deep space, but there is little understanding of what these structures exactly are and what they are capable of doing. Except, however, they do sometimes produce frequencies akin to music. Then there are also a number of distorted black shrouds — besides the massive shroud in the centre of the Caelverse — called the *black mystery shrouds* of varying sizes throughout the Caelverse, and uncovering what lies hidden behind or inside them still remains completely a mystery…

Phasarchement Details

Condensed Phasarchement Information

<u>Note:</u>

For this section, I have provided a condensed version of the information found in a separate book called *The Caelverse Compendium*. This school of magic that I have invented (*phasarchement*) is extremely complex, so in order to have a full and even adequate understanding of how it works, you will need to read the compendium. Still, I decided to provide basic (though very limited) information so that you can have at least some reference point besides what is mentioned in the story.

The Fundamentals:

Phasarchement as a word derives from two words plus a suffix; namely, *phase*, *archetype*, and *ment*, altogether pronounced: fayz-är-ki-mu*h*nt (in other words: phase + arche from archetype + ment, like from state*ment*). Essentially, phasarchement (alternatively spelled *phasearchement*) magic is the art, action, result, and state of manifesting specific archetypal energies and masses of different but particular phases or phase states. For phasarchement magic, mages will draw upon the *Aether* (the zero-point energy field and medium permeating all of reality) to fuel a particular but major component in their etheric aura, which, in turn, can be channelled to physically manifest various phenomena. Similar to a mage's *general aether pool* (GAP), this auric *matrix* in the etheric realm is called the *lumarchetrix* (or colloquially the *lumatrix*, for short), which is derived from *luminescent*, *archetypal*, and *matrix*. Meanwhile, the tangible, physically-manifested *energy* inside or outside of any manifested mass from this matrix is called *photomission energy*, with the name existing to help distinguish it from energies originally found in the Caelverse, as the former will return to the Aether.

As with all other schools of magic, phasarchement is consciousness-based, so mages must be conscious enough to connect to a source of power that has such potential rather than manipulating any energy alone. Hence, the lumarchetrix is the necessary medium for this magic to materialize *and* structure the photomission energy in a way that allows it to form into particular matter. The lumarchetrix, for this reason, contains the archetypal potential of multiple *classes* (known explicitly as *phasarchement archetypal classes* or PACs) and their embodied *types* (more specifically, *ultra-state types* or USTs). Fundamentally based on the essential flow of energy in reality itself, PACs are archetypally broader and more universal in their inherent manifest constitution than USTs, which are more corporeally existential, exhibit in particularized occurring phenomena in the form of states of matter when collectively formed. The particles in a manifested UST form are collectively and simply called *ultrachite* for the sake of brevity. These PACs and USTs are inherent to the lumarchetrix, and, therefore, no spell crafting is involved with the magic.

All manifested UST forms appear within the user's *area of conscious effect* (ACE). For most mages, this is physical *auric* space is generally just over three metres in diameter around the user (with the central point being the centre of their bodies – so, around the sternum). When any ultrachite particles move outside of the aura, they will no longer be powered by the user, so they will shortly (but not immediately) disappear. With usage, the lumarchetrix will begin to *deplete* of energy, but mages automatically refill it with more aether energy while engaged with the phasarchement magic itself. The recharge rate is known as the *lumarchetrix recharge rate*, which is the same as when a mage recharges their GAP. For the average mage, it takes about 35 seconds to initially connect to the Aether to fill their lumarchetrix, and thereafter, it will take about two minutes to refill it from depletion (and only after a short time penalty for depleting). Mages cannot keep connected to the Aether forever (that is, they become *exhausted*), so they have to switch off their lumarchetrixes eventually. Every time a mage creates a new form, they are charged with *creation energy costs*, then after that, *maintenance energy costs*.

Mages can experience various problems, such as *lumarchetrix channel overcharging*, where their UST forms cost more energy than what they should normally cost. This can result from their lumarchetrixes being *desynchronized*. *Lumarchetrix channelling instabilities* can also occur, and this involves a chance of users being unable to even create any UST forms. Regardless, mages will always have a maximum channel rate, so they cannot channel all of their energy at once. In fact, mages will have a *default power level*, causing them to only channel energy at that default level. Nevertheless, mages can create *higher power level* and *lower power level* UST forms, but these require new creations.

Mages can also choose to change the *particularized effect phase* of their ultrachite via an *ultrachite phase charge* (UPC); but even without consciously doing so, ultrachite will change such phases either automatically or through external force, such as when a mage's ultrachite shield will inhibit incoming ultrachite particles from another mage, in turn lowering the UST form's *active particle level*. When such a phase change occurs, the ultrachite will behave in different ways, creating or limiting various *class-based effects*; so, with a lower active particle level, the UST form will be weaker. Some phase charges will also only last for a certain period, while others can last indefinitely until they UST form is switched off.

There are six UST forms and four PACs. The UST forms contain ultra versions of their standard solid, liquid, gas, plasma, superconductive, and spacetime crystal versions. These will also respectively form into shields (to protect the user), discharges (to attack opponents), vortices (for supp- lementary combat effects), soaker bombs (to throw at opponents and cause mild problems), propulsors (to propel oneself in assorted ways), and dimensional fields (to warp the fabric of space time for various benefits). Shields will not seem like a solid material, but they are super effective at protecting mages – except, generally, in the case of slow-moving sharp objects like knives – and they will fully cover a mage's body. Discharges can be shot out of the user's aura, and these will also *overload* a shield with enough hits – normally, this is 12 consecutive hits for average power levels, respectively. Even when an opponent is shielded, a discharge can still affect the shield (and technically the user) with class-based effects; but when the user is directly affected in this case, it is usually to a much weaker extent, and there are some class-based effects that do not practically affect the user. So, once the opponent is unshielded, mages can then impose certain class-based effects on the opponent directly, such as turning them unconscious.

Vortices are basically only useful against opponents while they are up close, though they have their contextual uses. Soaker bombs are like water bombs; they can be thrown and then they will splash on impact. When they do, most of the particles will cover an opponent, and a small percentage of the particles will form a 'swarm cloud' around the opponent, causing further irritation. Propulsors are expensive to create and maintain, so their uses are very limited. Dimensional fields are even more energy-expensive, and they can only be created after having performed certain actions, like doing rituals and drinking potions (but the extent of this depends on one's power levels).

The PACs, on the other hand, are labelled: alpha, beta, gamma, and delta. Each of these will have positive and negative charges (*positively-charged ultrachite* and *negatively-charged ultrachite*) known as *alignment charge types*. Alpha deals with attraction and repulsion, whereas beta focuses on synchronization and desynchronization. Gamma, on the other hand, is fundamentally based on entanglement and separation. Finally, delta manages motion and motionlessness. Each UST form of any PAC will also possess various *default-tuned powers* (DTP) that create the class-based effects, but these DTPs can be altered on a new creation as an *alternative-tuned power*. Particular DTPs can also be switched off or lowered in power via changing their effect phase, which may be helpful in certain contexts. In all, it may seem like these powers are extremely deadly, but there are many limitations, which the following index will not detail.

UST and PAC Index:

Alpha Class (Attraction & Repulsion):

UST One/Ultra-solid (Shields):

Positively-charged ultrachite DTPs:

1: Automatically absorb energy from various things that come into contact with the user's shield. This can help to replenish the user's lumarchetrix. Effectively, though, this DTP can mostly only absorb energy from other UST forms – notably other shields and discharges – and not really from other sources of energy.

2: Increase the capacity to absorb more energy via a UPC. This does not increase the ability to absorb more energy from different types of sources. This DTP, moreover, will only last a short while before deactivating again; and once it has ended, the shield will overload.

3: Attract incoming ultrachite discharges via an active UPC. Coupled with the second DTP, this makes the alpha-positive shield the 'tank class', where they can absorb more energy from opponents while also being the main target, keeping attacks away from allies.

4: Automatically affect the minds of those within the vicinity with a magnetic field modulated in a particular way, in turn causing attention to fall on the user.

5: Automatically grant the user the ability of magnetoreception, which allows them to visually see, and instinctively sense, magnetic energies.

Negatively-charged ultrachite DTPs:

1: *Repel* ultrachite and non-ultrachite matter, along with high-powered electromagnetic radiation (such as from laser attacks) – all when actively UPC'd.

2: Automatically affect the minds of those within the vicinity with a magnetic field *modulated* in a particular way, in turn warding off (most types of) sentient beings (and robots) from physically approaching up close.

3: Automatically grant the user the ability of magnetoreception, which allows them to visually see, and instinctively sense, magnetic energies.

UST Two/Ultra-plasma (Discharges):

Positively-charged ultrachite DTPs:

1: Magnetically attract (that is, pull) matter on impact by pulling the affected matter towards the user. The average mage can exert a force of up to around 1,200 newtons.

2: Cause affectable targets to become attractive beacons for close ultrachite discharges of all PACs (except for beta-negative, when applicable), along with other magnetically-affectable matter, such as bullets.

3: Absorb energy from sources of energy on impact, delivering the energy to the user's lumarchetrix. In the inefficient case of absorbing energy from non-UST forms, and if the user is near the affected matter with their shield, the energy can power their shield.

Negatively-charged ultrachite DTPs:

1: Magnetically repel (that is, push or knock over) matter on impact by pushing the affected matter away from the discharge's trajectory. The average mage can exert a force of up to around 1,200 newtons.

2: Repulse opponents with mind-affecting magnetic energies (that are modulated in a particular way) to ward them off with two distinct levels: *avoidance* and then *retreat*.

3: Repulse an opponent's etheric energies, with the DTP focusing on the lumarchetrix.

UST Three/Ultra-gas (Vorticies):

Positively-charged ultrachite DTPs:

1: Absorb (that is, redirect) and accordingly *demagnetize* ultrachite and non-ultrachite magnetic properties.

2: Electrostatically attract the surrounding air molecules (outside the vortex), causing a vacuum on the outside which then causes the neighbouring air molecules to fill the void by sticking to and inside the vortex.

3: Increase the availability and absorbability of a certain energies, with the default setting being lumarchetrix and photomission energies, respectively. ATPs can also focus on other etheric energies.

<u>Negatively-charged ultrachite DTPs:</u>

1: Create a repulsive gas that extremely disgusts most biological organisms.

2: Increase an opponent's vulnerability to mental repulsions by magnetically altering their receptibility to particular effects on the mind – namely, but not limited to, alpha-negative discharge repulsions.

3: Increase the vulnerability of an opponent mage's lumarchetrix to particular repulsions – namely, alpha-negative discharge repulsions.

UST Four/Ultra-liquid (Soaker bombs and Swarm Clouds):

<u>Positively-charged ultrachite DTPs:</u>

1: Soaker bombs: Possess *electrophilic agents*, which bind to and accept electron pairs from other compounds, in turn creating an effect found in pepper spray.

2: Swarm clouds: form a fog that absorbs light, rendering the victim left to attempt seeing through a partial veil of darkness. The statistics for the lighting vary greatly per context.

<u>Negatively-charged ultrachite DTPs:</u>

1: Soaker bombs: create a repulsive mucous, which not only feels like other kinds of mucous (which most beings normally find repulsive), but the particles will also affect the brain, causing further disgustingness.

2: Swarm clouds: form an encompassing mirror that partially reflects visuals back at the victim.

UST Five/Ultra-conductivity (Propulsors):

<u>Positively-charged propulsors:</u> generate a latent magnetic field on creation that can be UPC'd and then used like a grappling hook (or reverse tractor beam) to reach normally-unreachable locations and things.

<u>Negatively-charged propulsors:</u> repel users from particular properties that they contact. More specifically, the surrounding ultrachite will cause the user to bounce off solid (and sometimes some liquid) surfaces.

UST Six/Ultra-spacetime crystals (Dimensional Fields):

<u>Positively-charged ultrachite DTPs:</u>

1: Create a field of artificial *attractive* gravity, where the particles will concentrate mostly into a small 'singularity' in the centre. Since gravity is not technically a force, this can lift really heavy objects up.

2: Suck large amounts of non-user-created photomission energy from present ultrachite into the singularity's gravitational abyss, rapidly depleting opponents.

<u>Negatively-charged ultrachite DTPs:</u>

1: Create a field of artificial *repulsive* gravity, where the particles will concentrate mostly into a small 'singularity' in the centre. Since gravity is not technically a force, this can move really heavy objects.

2: Automatically affect (normally completely negate) non-user photomission or lumarchetrix (or any other etheric energy) absorption within basically any space of the area of effect at nearly all power levels — regardless of whether a mage is shielded or not.

Beta Class (Synchronization & Desynchronization):

UST One/Ultra-solid (Shields):

<u>Positively-charged ultrachite DTPs:</u>

1: Strengthen the user's level of synchronization with their lumarchetrix via a UPC. An ATP is also available for increasing the synchronization with one's GAP. This DTP can help: reduce overcharging costs; establish a stronger connection with the Aether; reduce instabilities; and decrease the desynchronizing effects of another mage's beta-negative energies.

2: Automatically keep the user's mind synchronized, which, in turn, decreases mental desynchronizations, whether from ultrachite or non-ultrachite attacks.

3: Grant the user a limited version of *synchro-reception* — a power found in mysticism magic and (generally advanced) psychicism. This ability allows a user to focus on a particular object, person, or phenomenon and synchronize with them, in turn allowing the user to (later) identify them with visual cues (like brighter or darker colours) and/or intuition via etheric overlays.

4: Allow the user to actively synchronize with other mutually-permitting mages (who are also using the same shield) to share and redistribute lumarchetrix (and other etheric) energies.

<u>Negatively-charged ultrachite DTPs:</u>

1: Automatically desynchronize particular properties; and, within the context of phasarchement magic, this specifically affects non-user UST Two and Three particles that come into contact with the shield, switching their effect phase from active to dormant, in turn neutralizing their class-based effects *as if* a 'boosted' inhibitor ability.

2: Automatically desynchronize from (and thus avoid) ultrachite discharges – and (many kinds of) non-ultrachite things – that either normally chain via synchronization, lock onto, or home in on energies, particularly ultrachite shields.

3: Automatically desynchronize ultrachite and non-ultrachite-based mental synchronizations that are inflicted on the user.

4: Automatically desynchronize from the conscious *focus* of those on a battlefield by emitting a conscious-altering, modulated magnetic field, thereby increasing threat-reduction levels for the user.

UST Two/Ultra-plasma (Discharges):

<u>Positively-charged ultrachite DTPs:</u>

1: Synchronize (that is, firstly home in on) with incoming, non-user ultrachite discharges in the air before hitting and synchronizing with them to nullify or at least weaken them before they reach their target.

2: Chain on impact to similar materials to the material that which the discharge initially hits, causing the power to split into a weaker *set* of DTP effects on the next hits.

3: Synchronize with an opponent's mind on impact, inducing varying degrees of *harmony* (that is, it can cause calmness and then pacification, and it can even make an opponent support the user).

4: Synchronize an opponent's current generated ultrachite with their lumarchetrix, locking the opponent out from changing or using other USTs, PACs, and alignment charge types they are currently using.

Negatively-charged ultrachite DTPs:

1: Desynchronize from certain forces (like magnetic forces – including potentials) that draw in discharges.

2: Desynchronize mental faculties, affecting a being's level of consciousness. This is a mage's main form of subduing opponents.

3: Desynchronize mental faculties (in a different way to the second DTP), affecting a being's sense of *time*.

4: Desynchronize an opponent mage's lumarchetrix channel (or other etheric energies – including their GAP – as an ATP) on impact.

UST Three/Ultra-gas (Vortices):

Positively-charged ultrachite DTPs:

1: Synchronize with an opponent's energy (any energy) and very physical being, causing the user to intuitively feel where and when the next attack may be coming from, in addition to feeling certain mental energies.

2: Synchronize the user with any opponents inside the vortex, allowing the user to influence an opponent's movements.

3: Increase an opponent's vulnerability to ultrachite and particular non-ultrachite synchronizations.

Negatively-charged ultrachite DTPs:

1: Desynchronize an opponent's mind from their environment, causing the victim to lose or lessen their ability to (properly) sense or detect certain (physical and etheric) energies, things, or properties.

2: Desynchronize the coherence quantum properties may possess, in turn causing various changes to wave functions and other assorted quantum phenomena.

3: Increase an opponent's vulnerability to particular kinds of desynchronizations (whether from ultrachite or non-ultrachite attacks), with the most evident effect affecting mental cognition (which includes effects such as tachypsychia, chronostasis, flash-lag, and unconsciousness).

4: Increase an opponent mage's vulnerability to lumarchetrix desynchronizations.

UST Four/Ultra-liquid (Soaker bombs and Swarm Clouds):

Positively-charged ultrachite DTPs:

1: Soaker bombs: create an adhesive effect, causing various things to stick to one another. For example, this can cause an opponent to be either partially or 'totally' stuck to the ground.

2: Synchronize with the user's aura, enabling the swarm to produce a faint holographic veil of the user's position around the victim.

Negatively-charged ultrachite DTPs:

1: Soaker bombs: create an adhesive effect, causing various things to move with little to no friction. As a result, opponents can slip on their feet extremely easily – even with grippy boots.

2: Swarm clouds: effectively desynchronize vision, creating a partial veil that visually and sonically delays what is happening outside the swarm.

UST Five/Ultra-conductivity (Propulsors):

Positively-charged ultrachite DTPs: synchronize with various types of matter, with the micro propulsions creating friction both mechanically and non-conventionally via fluctuating electrons between the propulsor and the interacted matter. This enables one to:

1: Synchronize specifically with the air by creating micro propulsions that generate conventional and non-conventional friction, in turn increasing air resistance and reducing fall speeds.

2: Synchronize specifically with liquids by creating micro propulsions that generate conventional and non-conventional friction, in turn granting the user the ability of water walking or running.

3: Synchronize specifically with solids by creating micro propulsions that generate conventional and non-conventional friction, in turn allowing users to 'stick' to and scale various surfaces like walls and ceilings.

Negatively-charged propulsors: create a field that propels against – and only against – gravitational geodesics, allowing one to jump higher.

UST Six/Ultra-spacetime crystals (Dimensional Fields):

Positively-charged dimensional fields: synchronize (or more specifically, phase lock) with the current, localized spacetime when actively charged, essentially 'marking' it for the user as a reference point for later return when they rewind time. Basically, the user (and anything else in the aura's space) physically flows subjectively backwards through time.

Negatively-charged dimensional fields: desynchronize the user from the physical spacetime they inhabit, in turn causing them to only exist in the etheric with their etheric body.

Gamma Class (Entanglement & Separation):

UST One/Ultra-solid (Shields):

Positively-charged ultrachite DTPs:
   1: Collectively entangle their particles at the quantum level via a UPC, in turn camouflaging the user. This effectively blinds the user, though.
   2: Entangle phonons inside phononic crystals (found throughout the shield), which help to soundproof the user.
   3: Quantumly entangle with the particles of other particular things (normally other gamma-positive shields), allowing for communication at any distance.

<u>Negatively-charged ultrachite DTPs:</u>

1: Scatter and diffuse built-up energy via a UPC, in turn allowing for feats like quicker overloading threshold recovery rates and phase inhibitor recover rates.

2: Automatically break apart particular ultrachite and non-ultrachite quantum entanglements through decoherence and entropy.

3: Scatter light via a UPC, causing an optical phenomenon akin to mirages, except that they can appear vertically and/or horizontally.

UST Two/Ultra-plasma (Discharges):

<u>Positively-charged ultrachite DTPs:</u>

1: Electrically shock opponents; and, as a byproduct, the majority of particles in the atmosphere around the opponent will entangle and induce further shocks.

2: Establish multipartite entangled states at the quantum level in particular ultrachite and non-ultrachite systems, which then enables for the delocalization of all their electrons, which, in turn, can help to *overload* various systems. This may help to overload ultrachite shields much faster.

3: Create a chance of physical entanglement with certain things in the vicinity when the active phase particles release on impact, in turn allowing for quantum energy teleportation.

<u>Negatively-charged ultrachite DTPs:</u>

1: Potentially separate matter via probabilities at the quantum level, specifically affecting the atomic lattices in various things. Basically, the DTP can *cut* a *chunk* of matter out of some overall matter. More precisely, if the discharge were to hit a concrete wall, it would cut out *one* chunk of the wall out, not multiple, no matter the power level, if, of course, it were successful at passing the aggregate chance check of an item.

2: Sever particular ultrachite and non-ultrachite quantum entanglements through decoherence and entropy.

3: Sever etheric energy from an something. This is very limited, and it practically does not work against opponents with ultrachite shields.

UST Three/Ultra-gas (Vortices):

Positively-charged ultrachite DTPs:

1: Cause particular things that enter the vortex (usually, projectiles) to gain potential nonlocal backfire issues – or increase the backfire problems of projectiles with such issues – via quantum entanglement.

2: Entangle particular things (apart from the user's) with non-related quantum and potential fields, changing the thresholds of what constitutes an item as a distinct item.

3: Entangle an opponent mage's lumarchetrix channel, creating a chance that they may accidentally use the wrong UST or PAC *on creation* (but not whether alternative-tuned powers are used instead of DTPs or vice versa).

Negatively-charged ultrachite DTPs:

1: Create rifts in ultrachite and non-ultrachite (energy) systems, in turn inducing or increasing their destabilization.

2: Prevent molecules from forming together. Against ultrachite shields, this basically diminishes their overloading and inhibitor recover rates.

3: Increase the vulnerability to – and speed of – decompositions. This DTP *itself* does not cause decompositions and, instead, acts as a *catalyst* in aiding decompositions.

UST Four/Ultra-liquid (Soaker bombs and Swarm Clouds):

Positively-charged ultrachite DTPs:

1: Soaker bombs: potentially cause various particles they hit – or are in the vicinity of – to quantumly entangle.

2: Swarm clouds: weave a web of transparent, ever-changing entangled patterns, which normally distracts most beings.

Negatively-charged ultrachite DTPs:

1: Soaker bombs: form an acid to dissolve particular substances. Unlike most non-ultrachite acids, the soaker particles do not (or at least barely) affect organic compounds, so this is mostly limited to non-organic matter.

2: create a partial veil of fractured angles of the surrounding area like broken glass, causing difficulty in seeing the surrounding area.

UST Five/Ultra-conductivity (Propulsors):

<u>Positively-charged propulsors:</u> quantumly entangle a field of affectable particles (specifically, gas particles) – via a UPC – at a concentrated part of the ACE (normally below the user's feet) while coupling them with added propulsor energy that causes the particles to propel *as* a collective field. The air particles will accordingly have increased hapticity, allowing the user to stand on them as if they were collectively a platform.

<u>Negatively-charged propulsors:</u> automatically hover against particular matter, lifting the user off the ground and keeping them separate from it.

UST Six/Ultra-spacetime crystals (Dimensional Fields):

<u>Positively-charged dimensional fields:</u> entangle different locations in the fabric of space, in turn causing portals to open to one another (after a UPC), allowing the user to teleport.

<u>Negatively-charged dimensional fields:</u> separate dimensions via a UPC. The user's UST Six aura will separate the user (and whatever is inside the whole aura's space) away from everything in the external world with effectively an impenetrable barrier.

Delta Class (Motion & Motionlessness):

UST One/Ultra-solid (Shields):

<u>Positively-charged ultrachite DTPs:</u>
1: Automatically affect the user's neurotransmitters and hormones via electrical stimulation, modulated magnetic energy, and a particular frequency of pulsating air molecules.

2: Automatically enhance the user's sense of kinetic energies. For the most part, this ability relates to sound and thermal energies, so users can either see sound waves and/or heat radiating from objects (*thermoreception*).

3: Automatically keep the user's temperature levels at optimal levels (up to the default power level) based on reflexive biofeedback.

4: Automatically decrease or stop the slowing effects of *quantum locking* (including *spatial quantum locking*) from delta-negative discharges and similar phenomena by means of particular quantum vibrations that specifically affect the fabric of their relative spacetime via a local field.

Negatively-charged ultrachite DTPs:

1: Increase inertia levels by means of a special form of spatial quantum locking, which involves anchoring to the fabric of their *relative* spacetime via a UPC.

2: Stop the movement of all gases from entering or exiting the shield via a UPC, which can help users in settings with toxic gases around.

3: Prevent most 'slow-moving' matter (in most standard contexts) from *tearing* through the shield via a UPC, like knives.

UST Two/Ultra-plasma (Discharges):

Positively-charged ultrachite DTPs:

1: Seek out motion and heat, homing in on particular targets. The discharge does not intentionally seek targets unless energetically triggered by things that possess a certain *level* of *both* heat and movement.

2: Create a flash of bright light, blinding opponents.

3: Create a loud bang at the initial impact location, with the sound being able to extend beyond the victim or other materials.

4: Induce *vertigo* in most biological organisms. There is also a chance that robots may experience this effect or something similar due to the nature of the charge.

Negatively-charged ultrachite DTPs:

1: 'Freeze' things on impact by surrounding them with a wall of increased inertia via spatial quantum locking.

2: Cause sentient and non-sentient beings to enter a state of flash-suspended animation. While not as powerful as beta-negative, this does have beneficial uses for certain applications; and after the suspended animation wears off, the victim will generally feel sluggish and confused.

UST Three/Ultra-gas (Vortices):

Positively-charged ultrachite DTPs:

1: Vibrate with a particular frequency, in turn causing motion sickness in organic beings, which is then followed with issues of neuropathy, disorientation, disequilibrium, and even rash-decision making.

2: Vibrate the non-ultrachite air molecules to such an extent that the vortex causes them to possess hapticity (so, basically, it will feel like the air molecules will have some sort of solidity); and normally, these particles will cause annoyance and distraction when they batter against opponents.

3: Fill the atmosphere with hot particles before gradually increasing the temperature by trapping heat energy, thereby potentially burning opponents who spend too long inside.

Negatively-charged ultrachite DTPs:

1: Impose speed limits on things. Specifically, a delta-negative vortex will automatically and rapidly increase the inertia of its particles (via a form of spatial quantum locking) when objects or opponents inside the vortex begin moving at or beyond a certain speed limit.

2: Fill the atmosphere with cold particles before gradually lowering the temperature even further by expelling heat energy, thereby potentially freezing opponents who spend too long inside.

UST Four/Ultra-liquid (Soaker bombs and Swarm Clouds):

Positively-charged ultrachite DTPs:

1: Soaker bombs: act as a chemical primer for certain phenomena, in turn allowing for different types of combos to occur.

2: Visually rotate the partially-visioned environment around the victim at any angle, potentially inducing motion sickness.

<u>Negatively-charged ultrachite DTPs:</u>

1: Soaker bombs: form into a foam around opponents, causing annoyance and difficulty with movement. While foam is a two-phase state (that is, there are gasses trapped in bubbles within the liquid structure), consider that the ultrachite-liquid is still a form of liquid.

2: Swarm clouds: create a partial veil that blurs the victim's surroundings through a sense of slow motion. The swarm can also contract the atmosphere to fashion shrinking non-peripheral visuals (so things appear further away).

UST Five/Ultra-conductivity (Propulsors):

<u>Positively-charged ultrachite DTPs:</u>

1: Detect various types of motion while possessing a natural and automatic avoidance response to certain types of things that approach. That is, the propulsor automatically propels itself (and, accordingly, the user) slightly out of the way from particular incoming ultrachite and non-ultrachite matter.

2: Automatically create micro propulsions that increase the user's speed (and anything else within the propulsor's field).

<u>Negatively-charged propulsors:</u> enable the user to hover in the air via a form of spatial quantum locking.

UST Five/Ultra-spacetime crystals (Dimensional Fields):

<u>Positively-charged dimensional fields:</u> accelerate time relative to the external reality outside the aura.

<u>Negatively-charged dimensional fields:</u> decelerate time relative to the external reality outside the aura.

Additional Hillseck Information

This is a typical UHR (Ultimate Hillseck Rules) field. The plain grey area is the field itself. The two rectangles on the sides are the team bases. The black circle in the middle is the hill (it is not black in the actual game). The flower-looking design around the hill is representative of the mag-limbs. The larger flower-looking design is an example of a trail that the augmenter orbs will produce when the augmenters grab their orb. The augmenters would have to follow the trail/pattern around the field. The small triangles are representative of the charger nodes. Normally, chargers have 15 seconds to charge the next node (by moving a charger orb through it) before the time resets. If a positive augmenter circles the field with their pattern, then the said time increases to 30 seconds. Once the chargers have charged the nodes, they then have to keep the hill charged, throwing charger orbs (15 cm in diameter) through holes on the outside of the hill about 50 cm in diameter. Three orbs appear at once now, and orbs are thrown back into the field again. A 15-second timer still applies for one charge. The mag-limbs can both help and hinder players.

Moonday 3rd of Dukeis, 1910

Forsooth, this will be my last entry. All the other pages afore today were ripped out. I have erewhile managed to keep low, hearkening for a mere moment of apricity, but the cultists are verily adroit at detecting energies. Petrei capitulated eftsoons cracking up, and they captured Drevele in an ambuscade, whilst Froden died from a lack of apothecary physics. The Gathering has doubtless slain the remaining members. Our order is obliterated. Grand Sorceress Backlevy has managed to unfurl her cult's constituents throughout the university administration, and the mass of students simply will not rise and shine, maugre their worsening conditions. And this is maugre witnessing one of their demonically possessed experiments in public! Ifsoever anyone perchance reads this, I, Narvell Jern, am doubtless dead. Prithee seize the pendant I am wearing, for it embodies a piece of an important whole, which, hark my words, aught to be

Dictionary

<u>A posteriori:</u> Knowledge based on what has been observed; from known facts ('from the later').

<u>A priori:</u> Knowledge and reasoning derived from deduction instead of dependently from past experience ('from the earlier').

<u>Abet:</u> To encourage or assist with something (usually wrongdoings).

<u>Abolitionist:</u> A person who advocates for the abolition of something (usually slavery).

<u>Ad nauseum:</u> Something repeated so often that it becomes annoying.

<u>Aesthetic:</u> A philosophy concerned with beauty and artistic taste.

<u>Aggregate:</u> The total or gross amount of something; formed as a whole unit from smaller elements.

<u>Alumni:</u> Former members of a group or institution, normally academic.

<u>Amorphous:</u> Having no clearly defined shape or form.

<u>Amphibinoid:</u> A being that is or resembles an amphibian – a being that can live on land but also thrive in water (like frogs).

<u>Apotheosis:</u> The highest point of being/existence (through the course of one's development); the absolute climax; the elevation to divinity.

<u>Aquemical:</u> A non-drinkable, non-enchanted liquid.

<u>Arbitrary:</u> Something existing at random, by chance, or without reason.

<u>Arch-elements:</u> *Archetypal elements*; fire, earth, air, and water are the primary archetypal elements – opposed to chemical elements (like iron).

<u>Archetype:</u> A fundamental characteristic, form, pattern, or model, which all things are based on, derive from, or can be sourced to.

<u>Archmage:</u> The executive position and leader of the CGM.

Arthropoid: A being that is or resembles an arthropod, with the most common ones looking like insects.

Askance: Mistrust, suspicion, or disapproval, usually facially expressed.

Askew: Not straight; at an angle; if someone looks askew, their head would likely be tilted; but it can be figurative for disapproval.

Astral: Of the second level of spiritual reality; a mentally-constructed dreamscape that many spirits can be found in.

Atrium: A large, central open space connected to other parts of a building.

Austere: Severe; stern; serious; strict; forbidding; without excess.

Aura: A distinctive atmosphere (sometimes with a measurable space) surrounding something; there are different types of auras, such as a distinct spiritual aura with spiritual energy around something/someone.

Auxiliary: Adjective: Supplementary; additional; reserve. Noun: supporter.

Azure: A bright blue colour, like a normal sky.

Balustrade: A railing braced by *balusters* (architectural upright support).

Based: Slang for the opposite of cringe; something that is cool; the word is otherwise used to mean: established as the foundation of something.

Beclouded: Something that is obscured, as if by a cloud.

Benkhlar's Crystal: A famous crystal that is believed by some people to have healed millions of people in the ancient world.

Bequeath: To leave or give something (beneficial) to someone (by will).

Bludgeoning: To heavily strike to something; sometimes repeatedly.

Blusterous: (Of wind) loud and aggressive; stormy.

Bug out: A term for leaving or retreating quickly.

Cache: A storage of some items, usually hidden.

Calligraphy: The art of decorative and beautiful handwriting.

Capacious: Containing lots of space/room.

Cardinal: Adjective: In astrology, it is of a sign that initiates and leads; as a noun, it is a leading rank in an institution, normally religious.

CBD: Central Business District; the main part of a city.

CGM: *Caelverse Government of Magi*; the supreme government of the Caelverse *controlled* only by mages (with *some* non-mage *involvement*).

Charily: Cautious; warily.

Chortle: Laugh in a loud, gleeful manner.

Cis-gender: Of a person who identifies with their assigned sex at birth (so not transgender).

Cogent: Something (like a thought) that is clear and logical.

Cogitate: To think, ponder, or meditate over something deeply.

Concentric: Of circles, one inside another with the same centre.

Consummit: The legislative branch of the CGM.

Contrite: Feeling sorrow or remorse over an action/thought.

Contuse: To injure without breaking the skin; to bruise.

Corporealize: To make something corporeal – to give form to.

Countenance: An appearance, one normally expressed with a face.

Culpable: Deserving blame.

Cymatic: An effect of sound and vibration, which forms visual patterns.

Dantha: …

Déjà vu: The sensation of having experienced something before.

Dendrite: A branched extension of a nerve cell.

Detrital: Of *detritus*: the debris of a material; organic waste from the dead.

Discordant: (Of sounds) harsh and jarring due to lacking harmony.

Disdainful: Expressing contempt or a lack of respect.

Dishevelled: (Of a person's clothing or appearance); messy; disordered.

Dodecahedron: A 3D shape with 12 plane (flat) faces.

Doltish: Stupid; slow-witted; dull.

Effervescing: Typically of a liquid, which gives off bubbles.

Elision: The omission of one or more sounds in speech.

Enkindle: To set on fire; to arouse and inspire.

Entropy: (Gradual decline into) the state of disorder or randomness.

Epistemology: The theory of knowledge.

Epoch: A division of history based on major existential shifts regarding sapient lifeforms themselves.

Erudite: Learned; having great knowledge.

Espied: To (suddenly) see/catch sight of something.

Ethereal: Light, airy, and/or delicate, having a ghostly trait; seemingly of the spiritual realms but is not. Not to be confused with *etheric*, which is of a spiritual realm and matter.

Etheric: Of the first spiritual layer or reality around the physical realm.

Ethos: The fundamental values and spirit of a person or society.

Exacerbate: To make something (already bad even) worse; aggravate.

Excreta: Waste matter from the body, typically of faeces and urine.

Extraneous: Not directly related to the subject of question; irrelevant.

Faux: An imitation of something; not real.

Fiasco: Something that goes completely wrong; a complete failure.

Firmament: The vault of the 'heavens'; the sky (and its curve).

Flaming potion: A common euphemism where 'flaming' replaces 'fucking'; the potion, here, is of a shocking potion, so the term of shock.

Flummoxed: Bewildered; confused; perplexed.

Fluting: Grooves across a structure's surface, creating a decorative form.

Flying buttress: An arch extending from an upper part of a wall to a pier.

Foible: A weak or flawed characteristic of someone.

Foreboding: Noun or adjective: a feeling (or an implication) that something bad will happen.

Forlornness: Alone and sad due to being forsaken or abandoned.

Forte: Something someone excels at; a strong ability.

Fractal: A complicated pattern; magnification reveals that it never ends.

Fraternity: Friendship; a group of people sharing interests, values, or a common profession; an exclusive organization of peers or students.

Frieze: A band of sculpted decoration usually found within and across an *entablature* (that is, the upper part of a building, usually the entrance).

Fugly: A portmanteau of 'fucking' and 'ugly'; really ugly.

Fulminate: To violently explode; otherwise, to vehemently protest.

Furtively: Doing something secretly to avoid attention (and dishonestly).

Gargantuan: Enormous; tremendous in size.

Genesis: The origin or beginning of something.

Gibbous: Displaying convexity (convex) at both sides; when the moon is more than half full.

Gobsmacked: Absolutely astonished; astounded.

Guffaw: A loud, heartily and boisterous laugh.

Haemorrhage: The loss of blood, normally a lot in a short time.

Haptic: Relating to the sense of touch (so *haptic holograms* can be touched).

Hegemony: The dominance of one entity over another, usually political.

Heptagram: A seven-pointed star with seven straight strokes.

Heretofore: Before this point in time; until now; hitherto.

Hipster: Someone who follows the latest trends yet are supposedly not of the mainstream culture.

Hitherto: Up until now.

Homogenous: Of the same or similar kind of nature – alike.

Hubris: Extreme pride, arrogance, or self-confidence.

Hum and haw: Hesitate while thinking over a decision.

Humanistic: Of *humanism*: various philosophical stances that focus on humans and their agency more so than non-humanistic (spiritual) forces.

Impetus: A driving force behind someone or thing; impulse; stimulus.

Impressionist: Of Impressionism – an art movement – focusing on loose brushstrokes, atmosphere, and mood.

Indefatigably: In an extremely persistent and tireless manner.

Irrevocable: Something that cannot be revoked; final; unalterable.

Jamb: A side-post or lining of a doorway or aperture.

Jhar: Jhar Matheor, a famous ancient man who supposedly did and accomplished so many different things that it would have been impossible to do so in a single lifetime. Given the breadth of his activities, he 'can' be invoked for and against assorted people and things; usually the name is now used in light profanity, such as 'Jhar's breath, that's silly!'

Jocular: In a joking and playful manner.

Juxtapose: To place things side by side for comparison.

Khaki: Dull greenish or brownish-yellowy colour, typically of a fabric.

Khor shit/khorshit: A profanity usually meaning something is nonsense, derived from a stupid animal with horrible-smelling faeces.

Larper: Someone who *larps* (Live Action Role Play – LARP).

Ley lines: Potent potential fields in the form of lines that geometrically form across a planet's surface as a result of a planet's unique frequencies.

Lithoid: A being that is or resembles a being made with silicon (in other words, they look rocky).

Luddite: A person opposed to new (or the advancement of) technology.

Macrocosm: The greater complex structure/reality of something.

Microcosm: A miniature version of a greater complex structure/reality.

Microsleep: A short period of sleep that lasts within seconds.

Modicum: A small quantity of something, normally desirable.

Mollycoddle: Verb: To treat someone in an overprotective way.

Monastic: Of or relating to a monasteries and monks (and their lifestyles).

Monotheism: The belief that there is a single god.

Mordant: Having a caustic, biting, or sarcastic attitude.

Morose: Sullen and ill-tempered.

Multispecieal: Multiple species; normally in reference to multiple species living or simply being in a particular geographical zone.

Nadir: The lowest point of something (whether physical or social).

Nebula: A cloud of gas and/or dust in outer space; if something is *nebulous*, then it is vague and mysterious, like how a cloud or a mist may obscure something.

Necrodust: Special dust infused with or of necrotic beings (undead).

Nefarious: Villainous; wicked.

Nether planes: Dark and mysterious (and evil) planes in the astral.

Nonchalant: In a manner that is or appears casual, calm, and relaxed.

Occult: Hidden from view; concealed; taboo; usually involves elements and activities from and with the spiritual planes.

Om-chanting: A continuous vocal sound with an 'om' ('aum') syllable.

Ontology: A specialised branch of philosophy dealing with the nature of being – basically, how things relate to one another.

Ostentatious: A pretentious show of display to impress others; showy.

Otherkin: A being who identifies as a member of a different species, so if a mage were to be an otherkin, they would identify as being non-human.

Pagan: Someone who practices a religion or spiritual practice that is not of the typical monotheistic religions that came to prominence.

Parable: A simple story to illustrate a particular lesson, usually religious.

Paraphernalia: Miscellaneous articles/equipment for a particular activity.

Pedagogical: Related to teaching and teaching methods.

Pejorative: A word or phrase expressing negative connotations.

Perennial: Lasting for a long time or forever; existing at all times.

Perforated: Pierced with (or simply has) a series of holes.

Phid/PHID: Short for: personal holographic interactive display.

Philtre: A non-drinkable enchanted liquid.

Phlegmatic: Having an unemotional, composed temperament.

Planar: Of or relating to a plane (geometry).

Plumage: A bird's feathers, collectively.

Polyhedral: Refers to a polyhedron: a 3D shape with flat polygonal faces, straight edges, and vertices, like cubes and tetrahedrons.

Polymath: A person whose knowledge widely spans different subjects.

Polytheism: The belief in many gods.

Portico: A covered porch leading to the entrance of a building.

Posel: A basic monetary unit from one of the currencies in the Caelverse.

Posterity: Future generations (of a people).

Posthumous: Occurring after one's death, like a publication or award.

Propensity: A natural inclination or tendency for something.

PTSD: Post-traumatic stress disorder.

Pyrotechnic: A firework or other similar display.

Quantum: A discreet quantity; usually used in physics (*quantum physics*).

Quantum entanglement: Where quantum particles are linked together and can affect one another – even at great distances.

Quantum tunnel: Where quantum (subatomic) particles move through various types of barriers (that is, other matter).

Rambunctiousness: Wildly boisterous; difficult to control; exuberant.

Recherché: Rare; exotic; arcane; obscrure.

Ribbed vaults: Structural ribs (on a ceiling) in the form of arches.

Rotunda: A round building (or part of one), usually with a domed roof.

Rut: A groove or furrow (in the ground); a situation where one is stuck; so, if someone were rutted, they would be stuck in a rut.

Sacrenderism: A major monotheistic religion in the Caelverse with a formal, centralized church, headed by a *prophet*. One of the religion's greatest principles is that of sacrifice.

Salient: The most noticeable or important point of something.

Sanctimony: An act as if morally superior to another being.

Sapient: Intelligent enough to be able to think; humans are sapient.

Sarcof: An ancient place of refuge, one told in Sacrenderist parables.

Schism: A split or division, whether physical or social.

Seckaphon: A hellish place in the astral realms, one with lots of fire.

Sentient: Capable of seeing or feeling things; debates ensue over what is sentient or not; conscious to a certain level.

Sepia-toned: Something with a reddish-brownish 'old' or antique tone.

Serrated: Having a jagged edge.

Shoo-in: Someone who is certain to win or get ahead in something.

Simper: To smile coyly, ingratiatingly (flatteringly), or in a silly manner.

Singularity: The state or quality of being singular. It can be applied to many contexts, such as physics, technology, or even on a social level.

Sporadically: Occasionally and at irregular intervals.

Squinched: Where the muscles (of the face) are tensed up; a squint.

Sorority: The female alternative of a fraternity.

Stoic: Possessing composed and austere emotions.

Sullied: Soiled; stained; polluted; tarnished.

Surreal: Bizarre; strange; something unusual out of a dream.

Suspended animation: A slowing or stoppage of bodily functions and consciousness, like with hibernating beings.

Synopool: A mage-created and operated technological interconnected system of information and communication that utilizes *neurachite analogue computers* as its base; similar to non-mage internets.

Tee-hee: A type of giggle, one with a derisive tone.

Telos: The ultimate goal, aim, or end.

Tempestuous: Turbulent; wild; violent; tumultuous; stormy.

Tenacious: Clinging or adhering to something closely.

Tenebrous: Dark; obscure; shadowy.

Tetrahedron: A triangular pyramid.

Thoroughfare: A passageway (like a road or path) between two places.

Timorously: A timid, nervous disposition.

Titter: A short, suppressed laugh; a type of giggle.

Topiary: (Of plants) trimmed and clipped artfully or beautifully.

Toroid: A figure of toroidal shape, resembling a torus – a circular shape with a hole in the centre (like a doughnut).

Transgender: Of a person who identities as a different gender to their assigned sex at birth.

Transhumanism: The belief that humans can and should develop beyond their current biological form, usually with technology and science. *Transbody technologies* have already been implemented in people's bodies.

Trans-speciesism: Like transhumanism but for any other species.

Ubiquitous: Found or existing everywhere at once.

Umbrage: Annoyance; offence; displeasure.

Unabating: Not becoming weaker and losing intensity.

Unbeknownst: Without knowing of something.

Undulated: A smooth, up-and-down motion or texture or outline.

Unremitting: Never slaking and continuing without stopping.

Unsung: Non sung about; not celebrated or praised.

Utopic: Of or resembling a utopia – the ideal, perfect place/society.

Vexatious: Causing vexation: to cause annoyance and trouble.

Vociferous: Expressing loud (vehement) opinions and/or sounds.

Voltaic: Of or relating to electricity generated by chemical action.

Volute: Something that is spiral or scroll-shaped, normally of stone.

Voyeuristic: Relating to a *voyeur* (one who watches others in sexual or private moments), normally deriving pleasure from it.

Wag: Truancy – intentionally being absent from an institution (that is, when one skips classes, etc.).

Waxing: In the context of moons, it is when the illumination is increasing (getting stronger), so this applies to both gibbous and crescent moons.

Wench: A young woman, typically a prostitute or of a similar manner.

Zodiac: A wheel of archetypes, normally used in the context of astrology (individually: a *zodiac sign*); it can also relate to the geometric region of the ecliptic plane around a celestial body like a planet.

About the Author

I was born in Brisbane, Australia on the 15th of May 1988, and I have mixed European ancestry. I hold a Bachelor of Communication from Griffith University, majoring in journalism and politics, and a Master of Arts in philosophy from The University of Queensland, specializing in politics, ethics, and economics.

~~During blood moons, my Illuminati buddies and I make sacrifices to Moloch.~~ I adhere to a set of spiritual maxims; three of these include living healthily, being the best version of yourself, and leaving the world a better place than what you inherited. In my free time, I like working on various creative pursuits, engaging in philosophical discussions, reading, playing video games, working out (lifting), discovering new music (I love metal, especially symphonic metal), and adding to my enormous meme collection…